ALSO BY JEFF VANDERMEER

FICTION

Annihilation

Authority

Acceptance

Dradin, in Love

The Book of Lost Places (stories)

Veniss Underground

City of Saints and Madmen

Secret Life (stories)

Shriek: An Afterword

The Situation

Finch

The Third Bear (stories)

NONFICTION

Why Should I Cut Your Throat?

Booklife: Strategies and Survival Tips for the 21st-Century Writer

Monstrous Creatures

The Steampunk Bible: An Illustrated Guide to the World of Imaginary Airships, Corsets and Goggles, Mad Scientists, and Strange Literature (with S. J. Chambers)

Wonderbook: The Illustrated Guide to Creating Imaginative Fiction

AREA X

AREA

HARPERCOLLINS  PUBLISHERS LTD

THE SOUTHERN REACH TRILOGY

JEFF VANDERMEER

HarperCollins Publishers Ltd
2 Bloor Street East, 20th Floor
Toronto, Ontario, Canada
M4W 1A8

www.harpercollins.ca

Library and Archives Canada Cataloguing in Publication information is available upon request.

ISBN 978-1-44342-845-3

Designed by Abby Kagan

Printed and bound in the United States of America
RRD 9 8 7

For Ann

CONTENTS

ANNIHILATION

01: INITIATION

The tower, which was not supposed to be there, plunges into the earth in a place just before the black pine forest begins to give way to swamp and then the reeds and wind-gnarled trees of the marsh flats. Beyond the marsh flats and the natural canals lies the ocean and, a little farther down the coast, a derelict lighthouse. All of this part of the country had been abandoned for decades, for reasons that are not easy to relate. Our expedition was the first to enter Area X for more than two years, and much of our predecessors' equipment had rusted, their tents and sheds little more than husks. Looking out over that untroubled landscape, I do not believe any of us could yet see the threat.

There were four of us: a biologist, an anthropologist, a surveyor, and a psychologist. I was the biologist. All of us were women this time, chosen as part of the complex set of variables that governed sending the expeditions. The psychologist, who was older than the rest of us, served as the expedition's leader. She had put us all under hypnosis to cross the border, to make sure we remained calm. It took four days of hard hiking after crossing the border to reach the coast.

Our mission was simple: to continue the government's investigation into the mysteries of Area X, slowly working our way out from base camp.

The expedition could last days, months, or even years, depending on various stimuli and conditions. We had supplies with us for six months, and another two years' worth of supplies had already been stored at the base camp. We had also been assured that it was safe to live off the land if necessary. All of our foodstuffs were smoked or canned or in packets. Our most outlandish equipment consisted of a measuring device that had been issued to each of us, which hung from a strap on our belts: a small rectangle of black metal with a glass-covered hole in the middle. If the hole glowed red, we had thirty minutes to remove ourselves to "a safe place." We were not told what the device measured or why we should be afraid should it glow red. After the first few hours, I had grown so used to it that I hadn't looked at it again. We had been forbidden watches and compasses.

When we reached the camp, we set about replacing obsolete or damaged equipment with what we had brought and putting up our own tents. We would rebuild the sheds later, once we were sure that Area X had not affected us. The members of the last expedition had eventually drifted off, one by one. Over time, they had returned to their families, so strictly speaking they did not vanish. They simply disappeared from Area X and, by unknown means, reappeared back in the world beyond the border. They could not relate the specifics of that journey. This *transference* had taken place across a period of eighteen months, and it was not something that had been experienced by prior expeditions. But other phenomena could also result in "premature dissolution of expeditions," as our superiors put it, so we needed to test our stamina for that place.

We also needed to acclimate ourselves to the environment. In the forest near base camp one might encounter black bears or coyotes. You might hear a sudden croak and watch a night heron startle from a tree branch and, distracted, step on a poisonous snake, of which there were at least six varieties. Bogs and streams hid huge aquatic reptiles, and so we were careful not to wade too deep to collect our water samples. Still, these aspects of the ecosystem did not really concern any of us. Other elements had the ability to unsettle, however. Long ago, towns had existed here, and we encountered eerie signs of human habitation: rotting cabins with sunken, red-tinged roofs, rusted wagon-wheel spokes half-buried in the dirt, and the barely seen outlines of what used to be enclosures for livestock, now mere ornament for layers of pine-needle loam.

Far worse, though, was a low, powerful moaning at dusk. The wind off the sea and the odd interior stillness dulled our ability to gauge direction, so that the sound seemed to infiltrate the black water that soaked the cypress trees. This water was so dark we could see our faces in it, and it never stirred, set like glass, reflecting the beards of gray moss that smothered the cypress trees. If you looked out through these areas, toward the ocean, all you saw was the black water, the gray of the cypress trunks, and the constant, motionless rain of moss flowing down. All you heard was the low moaning. The effect of this cannot be understood without being there. The beauty of it cannot be understood, either, and when you see beauty in desolation it changes something inside you. Desolation tries to colonize you.

As noted, we found the tower in a place just before the forest became waterlogged and then turned to salt marsh. This occurred on our fourth day after reaching base camp, by which time we had almost gotten our bearings. We did not expect to find anything there, based on both the maps that we brought with us and the water-stained, pine-dust-smeared documents our predecessors had left behind. But there it was, surrounded by a fringe of scrub grass, half-hidden by fallen moss off to the left of the trail: a circular block of some grayish stone seeming to mix cement and ground-up seashells. It measured roughly sixty feet in diameter, this circular block, and was raised from ground level by about eight inches. Nothing had been etched into or written on its surface that could in any way reveal its purpose or the identity of its makers. Starting at due north, a rectangular opening set into the surface of the block revealed stairs spiraling down into darkness. The entrance was obscured by the webs of banana spiders and debris from storms, but a cool draft came from below.

At first, only I saw it as a tower. I don't know why the word *tower* came to me, given that it tunneled into the ground. I could as easily have considered it a bunker or a submerged building. Yet as soon as I saw the staircase, I remembered the lighthouse on the coast and had a sudden vision of the last expedition drifting off, one by one, and sometime thereafter the ground shifting in a uniform and preplanned way to leave the lighthouse standing where it had always been but depositing this underground part of it inland. I saw this in vast and intricate detail as we all stood there, and, looking back, I mark it as the first irrational thought I had once we had reached our destination.

"This is impossible," said the surveyor, staring at her maps. The solid shade of late afternoon cast her in cool darkness and lent the words more urgency than they would have had otherwise. The sun was telling us that soon we'd have to use our flashlights to interrogate the impossible, although I'd have been perfectly happy doing it in the dark.

"And yet there it is," I said. "Unless we are having a mass hallucination."

"The architectural model is hard to identify," the anthropologist said. "The materials are ambiguous, indicating local origin but not necessarily local construction. Without going inside, we will not know if it is primitive or modern, or something in between. I'm not sure I would want to guess at how old it is, either."

We had no way to inform our superiors about this discovery. One rule for an expedition into Area X was that we were to attempt no outside contact, for fear of some irrevocable contamination. We also took little with us that matched our current level of technology. We had no cell or satellite phones, no computers, no camcorders, no complex measuring instruments except for those strange black boxes hanging from our belts. Our cameras required a makeshift darkroom. The absence of cell phones in particular made the real world seem very far away to the others, but I had always preferred to live without them. For weapons, we had knives, a locked container of antique handguns, and one assault rifle, this last a reluctant concession to current security standards.

It was expected simply that we would keep a record, like this one, in a journal, like this one: lightweight but nearly indestructible, with waterproof paper, a flexible black-and-white cover, and the blue horizontal lines for writing and the red line to the left to mark the margin. These journals would either return with us or be recovered by the next expedition. We had been cautioned to provide maximum context, so that anyone ignorant of Area X could understand our accounts. We had also been ordered not to share our journal entries with one another. Too much shared information could skew our observations, our superiors believed. But I knew from experience how hopeless this pursuit, this attempt to weed out bias, was. Nothing that lived and breathed was truly objective—even in a vacuum, even if all that possessed the brain was a self-immolating desire for the truth.

"I'm excited by this discovery," the psychologist interjected before we had discussed the tower much further. "Are you excited, too?" She had not asked us that particular question before. During training, she had tended to ask questions more like "How calm do you think you might be in an emergency?" Back then, I had felt as if she were a bad actor, playing a role. Now it seemed even more apparent, as if being our leader somehow made her nervous.

"It is definitely exciting . . . and unexpected," I said, trying not to mock her and failing, a little. I was surprised to feel a sense of growing unease, mostly because in my imagination, my dreams, this discovery would have been among the more banal. In my head, before we had crossed the border, I had seen so many things: vast cities, peculiar animals, and, once, during a period of illness, an enormous monster that rose from the waves to bear down on our camp.

The surveyor, meanwhile, just shrugged and would not answer the psychologist's question. The anthropologist nodded as if she agreed with me. The entrance to the tower leading down exerted a kind of presence, a blank surface that let us write so many things upon it. This presence manifested like a low-grade fever, pressing down on all of us.

I would tell you the names of the other three, if it mattered, but only the surveyor would last more than the next day or two. Besides, we were always strongly discouraged from using names: We were meant to be focused on our purpose, and "anything personal should be left behind." Names belonged to where we had come from, not to who we were while embedded in Area X.

Originally our expedition had numbered five and included a linguist. To reach the border, we each had to enter a separate bright white room with a door at the far end and a single metal chair in the corner. The chair had holes along the sides for straps; the implications of this raised a prickle of alarm, but by then I was set in my determination to reach Area X. The facility that housed these rooms was under the control of the Southern Reach, the clandestine government agency that dealt with all matters connected to Area X.

There we waited while innumerable readings were taken and various blasts of air, some cool, some hot, pressed down on us from vents in the ceiling. At some point, the psychologist visited each of us, although I do not remember what was said. Then we exited through the far door into a central staging area, with double doors at the end of a long hallway. The psychologist greeted us there, but the linguist never reappeared.

"She had second thoughts," the psychologist told us, meeting our questions with a firm gaze. "She decided to stay behind." This came as a small shock, but there was also relief that it had not been someone else. Of all of our skill sets, linguist seemed at the time most expendable.

After a moment, the psychologist said, "Now, clear your minds." This meant she would begin the process of hypnotizing us so we could cross the border. She would then put herself under a kind of self-hypnosis. It had been explained that we would need to cross the border with precautions to protect against our minds tricking us. Apparently hallucinations were common. At least, this was what they told us. I no longer can be sure it was the truth. The actual nature of the border had been withheld from us for security reasons; we knew only that it was invisible to the naked eye.

So when I "woke up" with the others, it was in full gear, including heavy hiking boots, with the weight of forty-pound backpacks and a multitude of additional supplies hanging from our belts. All three of us lurched, and the anthropologist fell to one knee, while the psychologist patiently waited for us to recover. "I'm sorry," she said. "That was the least startling reentry I could manage."

The surveyor cursed, and glared at her. She had a temper that must have been deemed an asset. The anthropologist, as was her way, got to her feet, uncomplaining. And I, as was my way, was too busy observing to take this rude awakening personally. For example, I noticed the cruelty of the almost imperceptible smile on the psychologist's lips as she watched us struggle to adjust, the anthropologist still floundering and apologizing for floundering. Later I realized I might have misread her expression; it might have been pained or self-pitying.

We were on a dirt trail strewn with pebbles, dead leaves, and pine needles damp to the touch. Velvet ants and tiny emerald beetles crawled over them. The tall pines, with their scaly ridges of bark, rose on both sides, and the shadows of flying birds conjured lines between them. The air was so fresh it buffeted the lungs and we strained to breathe for a few seconds, mostly from surprise. Then, after marking our location with a piece of red cloth tied to a tree, we began to walk forward, into the unknown. If the psychologist somehow became incapacitated and could not lead us across at the end of our mission, we had been told to return to await "extraction." No one ever explained what form "extraction" might take, but the implication was that our superiors could observe the extraction point from afar, even though it was inside the border.

We had been told not to look back upon arrival, but I snuck a glance anyway, while the psychologist's attention was elsewhere. I don't know quite what I saw. It was hazy, indistinct, and already far behind us—perhaps a gate, perhaps a trick of the eye. Just a sudden impression of a fizzing block of light, fast fading.

The reasons I had volunteered were very separate from my qualifications for the expedition. I believe I qualified because I specialized in transitional environments, and this particular location transitioned several times, meaning that it was home to a complexity of ecosystems. In few other places could you still find habitat where, within the space of walking only six or seven miles, you went from forest to swamp to salt marsh to beach. In Area X, I had been told, I would find marine life that had adjusted to the brackish freshwater and which at low tide swam far up the natural canals formed by the reeds, sharing the same environment with otters and deer. If you walked along the beach, riddled through with the holes of fiddler crabs, you would sometimes look out to see one of the giant reptiles, for they, too, had adapted to their habitat.

I understood why no one lived in Area X now, that it was pristine because of that reason, but I kept un-remembering it. I had decided instead to make believe that it was simply a protected wildlife refuge, and we were hikers who happened to be scientists. This made sense on another level: We did not know what had happened here, what was still happening here, and any preformed theories would affect my analysis of the evidence as we encountered it. Besides, for my part it hardly mattered what lies I told myself because my existence back in the world had become at least as empty as Area X. With nothing left to anchor me, I *needed* to be here. As for the others, I don't know what they told themselves, and I didn't want to know, but I believe they all at least pretended to some level of curiosity. Curiosity could be a powerful distraction.

That night we talked about the tower, although the other three insisted on calling it a tunnel. The responsibility for the thrust of our investigations resided with each individual, the psychologist's authority describing a wider circle around these decisions. Part of the current rationale for sending the expeditions lay in giving each member some autonomy to decide, which helped to increase "the possibility of significant variation."

This vague protocol existed in the context of our separate skill sets. For example, although we had all received basic weapons and survival training, the surveyor had far more medical and firearms experience than the rest of us. The anthropologist had once been an architect; indeed, she had years ago survived a fire in a building she had designed, the only really personal thing I had found out about her. As for the psychologist, we knew the least about her, but I think we all believed she came from some kind of management background.

The discussion of the tower was, in a way, our first opportunity to test the limits of disagreement and of compromise.

"I don't think we should focus on the tunnel," the anthropologist said. "We should explore farther first, and we should come back to it with whatever data we gather from our other investigations—including of the lighthouse."

How predictable, and yet perhaps prescient, for the anthropologist to try to substitute a safer, more comfortable option. Although the idea of mapping seemed perfunctory or repetitive to me, I could not deny the existence of the tower, of which there was no suggestion on any map.

Then the surveyor spoke. "In this case I feel that we should rule out the tunnel as something invasive or threatening. Before we explore farther. It's like an enemy at our backs otherwise, if we press forward." She had come to us from the military, and I could see already the value of that experience. I had thought a surveyor would always side with the idea of further exploration, so this opinion carried weight.

"I'm impatient to explore the habitats here," I said. "But in a sense, given that it is not noted on any map, the 'tunnel' . . . or tower . . . seems important. It is either a deliberate exclusion from our maps and thus known . . . and that is a message of sorts . . . or it is something new that wasn't here when the last expedition arrived."

The surveyor gave me a look of thanks for the support, but my position had nothing to do with helping her. Something about the idea of a tower that headed straight down played with a twinned sensation of vertigo and a fascination with structure. I could not tell which part I craved and which I feared, and I kept seeing the inside of nautilus shells and other naturally occurring patterns balanced against a sudden leap off a cliff into the unknown.

The psychologist nodded, appeared to consider these opinions, and asked, "Does anyone yet have even an inkling of a sensation of wanting to leave?" It was a legitimate question, but jarring nonetheless.

All three of us shook our heads.

"What about you?" the surveyor asked the psychologist. "What is your opinion?"

The psychologist grinned, which seemed odd. But she must have known any one of us might have been tasked with observing her own reactions to stimuli. Perhaps the idea that a surveyor, an expert in the surface of things, might have been chosen, rather than a biologist or anthropologist, amused her. "I must admit to feeling a great deal of unease at the moment. But I am unsure whether it is because of the effect of the overall environment or the presence of the tunnel. Personally, I would like to rule out the tunnel."

Tower.

"Three to one, then," the anthropologist said, clearly relieved that the decision had been made for her.

The surveyor just shrugged.

Perhaps I'd been wrong about curiosity. The surveyor didn't seem curious about anything.

"Bored?" I asked.

"Eager to get on with it," she said, to the group, as if I'd asked the question for all of us.

We were in the communal tent for our talk. It had become dark by then and there came soon after the strange mournful call in the night that we knew must have natural causes but created a little shiver regardless. As if that was the signal to disband, we went back to our own quarters to be alone with our thoughts. I lay awake in my tent for a while trying to turn the tower into a tunnel, or even a shaft, but with no success. Instead, my mind kept returning to a question: *What lies hidden at its base?*

During our hike from the border to the base camp near the coast, we had experienced almost nothing out of the ordinary. The birds sang as they should; the deer took flight, their white tails exclamation points against the green and brown of the underbrush; the raccoons, bowlegged, swayed about their business, ignoring us. As a group, we felt almost giddy, I think, to be free after so many confining months of training and preparation. While we were in that corridor, in that transitional space, nothing could touch us. We were neither what we had been nor what we would become once we reached our destination.

The day before we arrived at the camp, this mood was briefly shattered by the appearance of an enormous wild boar some distance ahead of us on the trail. It was so far from us that even with our binoculars we could barely identify it at first. But despite poor eyesight, wild pigs have prodigious powers of smell, and it began charging us from one hundred yards away. Thundering down the trail toward us . . . yet we still had time to think about what we might do, had drawn our long knives, and in the surveyor's case her assault rifle. Bullets would probably stop a seven-hundred-pound pig, or perhaps not. We did not feel confident taking our attention from the boar to untie the container of handguns from our gear and open its triple locks.

There was no time for the psychologist to prepare any hypnotic suggestion designed to keep us focused and in control; in fact, all she could offer was "Don't get close to it! Don't let it touch you!" while the boar continued to charge. The anthropologist was giggling a bit out of nervousness and the absurdity of experiencing an emergency situation that was taking so long to develop. Only the surveyor had taken direct action: She had dropped to one knee to get a better shot; our orders included the helpful directive to "kill only if you are under threat of being killed."

I was continuing to watch through the binoculars, and as the boar came closer, its face became stranger and stranger. Its features were somehow contorted, as if the beast was dealing with an extreme of inner torment. Nothing about its muzzle or broad, long face looked at all extraordinary, and yet I had the startling impression of some *presence* in the way its gaze seemed turned inward and its head willfully pulled to the left as if there were an invisible bridle. A kind of electricity sparked in its eyes that I could not credit as real. I thought instead it must be a by-product of my now slightly shaky hand on the binoculars.

Whatever was consuming the boar also soon consumed its desire to charge. It veered abruptly leftward, with what I can only describe as a great cry of anguish, into the underbrush. By the time we reached that spot, the boar was gone, leaving behind a thoroughly thrashed trail.

For several hours, my thoughts turned inward toward explanations for what I had seen: parasites and other hitchhikers of a neurological nature. I was searching for entirely rational biological theories. Then, after a time, the boar faded into the backdrop like all else that we had passed on our way from the border, and I was staring into the future again.

The morning after we discovered the tower we rose early, ate our breakfast, and doused our fire. There was a crisp chill to the air common for the season. The surveyor broke open the weapons stash and gave us each a handgun. She herself continued to hold on to the assault rifle; it had the added benefit of a flashlight under the barrel. We had not expected to have to open that particular container so soon, and although none of us protested, I felt a new tension between us. We knew that members of the second expedition to Area X had committed suicide by gunshot and members of the third had shot each other. Not until several subsequent expeditions had suffered zero casualties had our superiors issued firearms again. We were the twelfth expedition.

So we returned to the tower, all four of us. Sunlight came down dappled through the moss and leaves, created archipelagos of light on the flat surface of the entrance. It remained unremarkable, inert, in no way ominous . . . and yet it took an act of will to stand there, staring at the entry point. I noticed the anthropologist checking her black box, was relieved to see it did not display a glowing red light. If it had, we would have had to abort our exploration, move on to other things. I did not want that, despite the touch of fear.

"How deep do you think it goes down?" the anthropologist asked.

"Remember that we are to put our faith in your measurements," the psychologist answered, with a slight frown. "The measurements do not lie. This structure is 61.4 feet in diameter. It is raised 7.9 inches from the ground. The stairwell appears to have been positioned at or close to due north, which may tell us something about its creation, eventually. It is made of stone and coquina, not of metal or of bricks. These are facts. That it wasn't on the maps means only that a storm may have uncovered the entrance."

I found the psychologist's faith in measurements and her rationalization for the tower's absence from maps oddly . . . endearing? Perhaps she meant merely to reassure us, but I would like to believe she was trying to reassure herself. Her position, to lead and possibly to know more than us, must have been difficult and lonely.

"I hope it's only about six feet deep so we can continue mapping," the surveyor said, trying to be lighthearted, but then she, and we, all recognized the term "six feet under" ghosting through her syntax and a silence settled over us.

"I want you to know that I cannot stop thinking of it as a *tower*," I confessed. "I can't see it as a tunnel." It seemed important to make the distinction before our descent, even if it influenced their evaluation of my mental state. I saw a tower, plunging into the ground. The thought that we stood at its summit made me a little dizzy.

All three stared at me then, as if I were the strange cry at dusk, and after a moment the psychologist said, grudgingly, "If that helps make you more comfortable, then I don't see the harm."

A silence came over us again, there under the canopy of trees. A beetle spiraled up toward the branches, trailing dust motes. I think we all realized that only now had we truly entered Area X.

"I'll go first and see what's down there," the surveyor said, finally, and we were happy to defer to her.

The initial stairwell curved steeply downward and the steps were narrow, so the surveyor would have to back her way into the tower. We used sticks to clear the spiderwebs as she lowered herself into position on the stairwell. She teetered there, weapon slung across her back, looking up at us. She had tied her hair back and it made the lines of her face seem tight and drawn. Was this the moment when we were supposed to stop her? To come up with some other plan? If so, none of us had the nerve.

With a strange smirk, almost as if judging us, the surveyor descended until we could only see her face framed in the gloom below, and then not even that. She left an empty space that was shocking to me, as if the reverse had actually happened: as if a face had suddenly floated into view out of the darkness. I gasped, which drew a stare from the psychologist. The anthropologist was too busy staring down into the stairwell to notice any of it.

"Is everything okay?" the psychologist called out to the surveyor. Everything had been fine just a second before. Why would anything be different now?

The surveyor made a sharp grunt in answer, as if agreeing with me. For a few moments more, we could still hear the surveyor struggling on those short steps. Then came silence, and then another movement, at a different rhythm, which for a terrifying moment seemed like it might come from a second source.

But then the surveyor called up to us. "Clear to this level!" *This level.* Something within me thrilled to the fact that my vision of a *tower* was not yet disproven.

That was the signal for me to descend with the anthropologist, while the psychologist stood watch. "Time to go," the psychologist said, as perfunctorily as if we were in school and a class was letting out.

An emotion that I could not quite identify surged through me, and for a moment I saw dark spots in my field of vision. I followed the anthropologist so eagerly down through the remains of webs and the embalmed husks of insects into the cool brackishness of that place that I almost tripped her. My last view of the world above: the psychologist peering down at me with a slight frown, and behind her the trees, the blue of the sky almost blinding against the darkness of the sides of the stairwell.

Below, shadows spread across the walls. The temperature dropped and sound became muffled, the soft steps absorbing our tread. Approximately twenty feet beneath the surface, the structure opened out into a lower level. The ceiling was about eight feet high, which meant a good twelve feet of stone lay above us. The flashlight of the surveyor's assault rifle illuminated the space, but she was faced away from us, surveying the walls, which were an off-white and devoid of any adornment. A few cracks indicated either the passage of time or some sudden stressor. The level appeared to be the same circumference as the exposed top, which again supported the idea of a single solid structure buried in the earth.

"It goes farther," the surveyor said, and pointed with her rifle to the far corner, directly opposite the opening where we had come out onto that level. A rounded archway stood there, and a darkness that suggested downward steps. A tower, which made this level not so much a floor as a landing or part of the turret. She started to walk toward the archway while I was still engrossed in examining the walls with my flashlight. Their very blankness mesmerized me. I tried to imagine the builder of this place but could not.

I thought again of the silhouette of the lighthouse, as I had seen it during the late afternoon of our first day at base camp. We assumed that the structure in question was a lighthouse because the map showed a lighthouse at that location and because everyone immediately recognized what a lighthouse *should* look like. In fact, the surveyor and anthropologist had both expressed a kind of *relief* when they had seen the lighthouse. Its appearance on both the map and in reality reassured them, anchored them. Being familiar with its function further reassured them.

With the tower, we knew none of these things. We could not intuit its full outline. We had no sense of its purpose. And now that we had begun to descend into it, the tower *still* failed to reveal any hint of these things. The psychologist might recite the measurements of the "top" of the tower, but those numbers meant nothing, had no wider context. Without context, clinging to those numbers was a form of madness.

"There is a regularity to the circle, seen from the inside walls, that suggests precision in the creation of the building," the anthropologist said. *The building.* Already she had begun to abandon the idea of it being a tunnel.

All of my thoughts came spilling out of my mouth, some final discharge from the state that had overtaken me above. "But what is its *purpose*? And is it believable that it would not be on the maps? Could one of the prior expeditions have built it and hidden it?" I asked all of this and more, not expecting an answer. Even though no threat had revealed itself, it seemed important to eliminate any possible moment of silence. As if somehow the blankness of the walls fed off of silence, and that something might appear in the spaces between our words if we were not careful. Had I expressed this anxiety to the psychologist, she would have been worried, I know. But I was more attuned to solitude than any of us, and I would have characterized that place in that moment of our exploration as watchful.

A gasp from the surveyor cut me off in mid-question, no doubt much to the anthropologist's relief.

"Look!" the surveyor said, training her flashlight down into the archway. We hurried over and stared past her, adding our own illumination.

A stairway did indeed lead down, this time at a gentle curve with much broader steps, but still made of the same materials. At about shoulder height, perhaps five feet high, clinging to the inner wall of the tower, I saw what I first took to be dimly sparkling green vines progressing down into the darkness. I had a sudden absurd memory of the floral wallpaper treatment that had lined the bathroom of my house when I had shared it with my husband. Then, as I stared, the "vines" resolved further, and I saw that they were words, in cursive, the letters raised about six inches off the wall.

"Hold the light," I said, and pushed past them down the first few steps. Blood was rushing through my head again, a roaring confusion in my ears. It was an act of supreme control to walk those few paces. I couldn't tell you what impulse drove me, except that I was the biologist and this looked oddly organic. If the linguist had been there, perhaps I would have deferred to her.

"Don't touch it, whatever it is," the anthropologist warned.

I nodded, but I was too enthralled with the discovery. If I'd had the impulse to touch the words on the wall, I would not have been able to stop myself.

As I came close, did it surprise me that I could understand the language the words were written in? Yes. Did it fill me with a kind of elation and dread intertwined? Yes. I tried to suppress the thousand new questions rising up inside of me. In as calm a voice as I could manage, aware of the importance of that moment, I read from the beginning, aloud: "*Where lies the strangling fruit that came from the hand of the sinner I shall bring forth the seeds of the dead to share with the worms that . . .*"

Then the darkness took it.

"Words? Words?" the anthropologist said.

Yes, words.

"What are they made of?" the surveyor asked. Did they need to be made of anything?

The illumination cast on the continuing sentence quavered and shook. *Where lies the strangling fruit* became bathed in shadow and in light, as if a battle raged for its meaning.

"Give me a moment. I need to get closer." Did I? Yes, I needed to get closer. *What are they made of?*

I hadn't even thought of this, though I should have; I was still trying to parse the lingual meaning, had not transitioned to the idea of taking a physical sample. But what relief at the question! Because it helped me fight the compulsion to keep reading, to descend into the greater darkness and keep descending until I had read all there was to read. Already those initial phrases were infiltrating my mind in unexpected ways, finding fertile ground.

So I stepped closer, peered at *Where lies the strangling fruit*. I saw that the letters, connected by their cursive script, were made from what would have looked to the layperson like rich green fernlike moss but in fact was probably a type of fungi or other eukaryotic organism. The curling filaments were all packed very close together and rising out from the wall. A loamy smell came from the words along with an underlying hint of rotting honey. This miniature forest *swayed*, almost imperceptibly, like sea grass in a gentle ocean current.

Other things existed in this miniature ecosystem. Half-hidden by the green filaments, most of these creatures were translucent and shaped like tiny hands embedded by the base of the palm. Golden nodules capped the fingers on these "hands." I leaned in closer, like a fool, like someone who had not had months of survival training or ever studied biology. Someone tricked into thinking that words should be read.

I was unlucky—or was I lucky? Triggered by a disturbance in the flow of air, a nodule in the W chose that moment to burst open and a tiny spray of golden spores spewed out. I pulled back, but I thought I had felt something enter my nose, experienced a pinprick of escalation in the smell of rotting honey.

Unnerved, I stepped back even farther, borrowing some of the surveyor's best curses, but only in my head. My natural instinct was always for concealment. Already I was imagining the psychologist's reaction to my contamination, if revealed to the group.

"Some sort of fungi," I said finally, taking a deep breath so I could control my voice. "The letters are made from fruiting bodies." Who knew if it were actually true? It was just the closest thing to an answer.

My voice must have seemed calmer than my actual thoughts because there was no hesitation in their response. No hint in their tone of having seen the spores erupt into my face. I had been so close. The spores had been so tiny, so insignificant. *I shall bring forth the seeds of the dead*.

"Words? Made of fungi?" the surveyor said, stupidly echoing me.

"There is no recorded human language that uses this method of writing," the anthropologist said. "Is there any animal that communicates in this way?"

I had to laugh. "No, there is no animal that communicates in this way." Or, if there were, I could not recall its name, and never did later, either.

"Are you joking? This is a joke, right?" the surveyor said. She looked poised to come down and prove me wrong, but didn't move from her position.

"Fruiting bodies," I replied, almost as if in a trance. "Forming words."

A calm had settled over me. A competing sensation, as if I couldn't breathe, or didn't want to, was clearly psychological not physiological. I had noticed no physical changes, and on some level it didn't matter. I knew it was unlikely we had an antidote to something so unknown waiting back at the camp.

More than anything, the information I was trying to process immobilized me. The words were composed of symbiotic fruiting bodies from a species unknown to me. Second, the dusting of spores on the words meant that the farther down into the tower we explored, the more the air would be full of potential contaminants. Was there any reason to relay this information to the others when it would only alarm them? No, I decided, perhaps selfishly. It was more important to make sure they were not directly exposed until we could come back with the proper equipment. Any other evaluation depended on environmental and biological factors about which I was increasingly convinced I had inadequate data.

I came back up the stairs to the landing. The surveyor and the anthropologist looked expectant, as if I could tell them more. The anthropologist in particular was on edge; her gaze couldn't alight on any one thing but kept moving and moving. Perhaps I could have fabricated information that would have stopped that incessant search. But what could I tell them about the words on the wall except that they were either impossible or insane, or both? I would have preferred the words be written in an *unknown* language; this would have presented less of a mystery for us to solve, in a way.

"We should go back up," I said. It was not that I recommended this as the best course of action but because I wanted to limit their exposure to the spores until I could see what long-term effects they might have on me. I also knew if I stayed there much longer I might experience a compulsion to go back down the stairs to continue reading the words, and they would have to physically restrain me, and I did not know what I would do then.

There was no argument from the other two. But as we climbed back up, I had a moment of vertigo despite being in such an enclosed space, a kind of panic for a moment, in which the walls suddenly had a fleshy aspect to them, as if we traveled inside of the gullet of a beast.

When we told the psychologist what we had seen, when I recited some of the words, she seemed at first frozen in an oddly attentive way. Then she decided to descend to view the words. I struggled with whether I should warn her against this action. Finally I said, "Only observe from the top of the stairs. We don't know whether there are toxins. When we come back, we should wear breathing masks." These, at least, we had inherited from the last expedition, in a sealed container.

"*Paralysis is not a cogent analysis?*" she said to me with a pointed stare. I felt a kind of itchiness come over me, but I said nothing, did nothing. The others did not even seem to realize she had spoken. It was only later that I realized the psychologist had tried to bind me with a hypnotic suggestion meant for me and me alone.

My reaction apparently fell within the range of acceptable responses, for she descended while we waited anxiously above. What would we do if she did not return? A sense of ownership swept over me. I was agitated by the idea that she might experience the same need to read further and would act upon it. Even though I didn't know what the words meant, I wanted them to mean something so that I might more swiftly remove doubt, bring reason back into all of my equations. Such thoughts distracted me from thinking about the effects of the spores on my system.

Thankfully the other two had no desire to talk as we waited, and after just fifteen minutes the psychologist awkwardly pushed her way up out of the stairwell and into the light, blinking as her vision adjusted.

"Interesting," she said in a flat tone as she loomed over us, wiping the cobwebs from her clothing. "I have never seen anything like that before." She seemed as if she might continue, but then decided against it.

What she had already said verged on the moronic; apparently I was not alone in that assessment.

"Interesting?" the anthropologist said. "No one has ever seen anything like that in the entire history of the world. No one. *Ever.* And you call it *interesting?*" She seemed close to working herself into a bout of hysteria. While the surveyor just stared at both of them as if *they* were the alien organisms.

"Do you need me to calm you?" the psychologist asked. There was a steely tone to her words that made the anthropologist mumble something noncommittal and stare at the ground.

I stepped into the silence with my own suggestion: "We need time to think about this. We need time to decide what to do next." I meant, of course, that I needed time to see if the spores I had inhaled would affect me in a way significant enough to confess to what had happened.

"There may not be enough time in the world for that," the surveyor said. Of all of us, I think she had best grasped the implications of what we had seen: that we might now be living in a kind of nightmare. But the psychologist ignored her and sided with me. "We do need time. We should spend the rest of our day doing what we were sent here to do."

So we returned to camp for lunch and then focused on "ordinary things" while I kept monitoring my body for any changes. Did I feel too cold now, or too hot? Was that ache in my knee from an old injury suffered in the field, or something new? I even checked the black box monitor, but it remained inert. Nothing radical had yet changed in me, and as we took our samples and readings in the general vicinity of the camp—as if to stray too far would be to come under the tower's control—I gradually relaxed and told myself that the spores had had no effect . . . even though I knew that the incubation period for some species could be months or years. I suppose I thought merely that for the next few days at least I might be safe.

The surveyor concentrated on adding detail and nuance to the maps our superiors had given us. The anthropologist went off to examine the remains of some cabins a quarter mile away. The psychologist stayed in her tent, writing in her journal. Perhaps she was reporting on how she was surrounded by idiots, or just setting out every moment of our morning discoveries.

For my part, I spent an hour observing a tiny red-and-green tree frog on the back of a broad, thick leaf and another hour following the path of an iridescent black damselfly that should not have been found at sea level. The rest of the time, I spent up a pine tree, binoculars focused on the coast and the lighthouse. I liked climbing. I also liked the ocean, and I found staring at it had a calming effect. The air was so clean, so fresh, while the world back beyond the border was what it had always been during the modern era: dirty, tired, imperfect, winding down, at war with itself. Back there, I had always felt as if my work amounted to a futile attempt to save us from who we are.

The richness of Area X's biosphere was reflected in the wealth of birdlife, from warblers and flickers to cormorants and black ibis. I could also see a bit into the salt marshes, and my attention there was rewarded by a minute-long glimpse of a pair of otters. At one point, they glanced up and I had a strange sensation that they could see me watching them. It was a feeling I often had when out in the wilderness: that things were not quite what they seemed, and I had to fight against the sensation because it could overwhelm my scientific objectivity. There was also something else, moving ponderously through the reeds, but it was closer to the lighthouse and in deep cover. I could not tell what it was, and after a while its disturbance of the vegetation ceased and I lost track of it entirely. I imagined it might be another wild pig, as they could be good swimmers and were just as omnivorous in their choice of habitats as in their diets.

On the whole, by dusk this strategy of busying ourselves in our tasks had worked to calm our nerves. The tension lifted somewhat, and we even joked a little bit at dinner. "I wish I knew what you were thinking," the anthropologist confessed to me, and I replied, "No, you don't," which was met with a laughter that surprised me. I didn't want their voices in my head, their ideas of me, nor their own stories or problems. Why would they want mine?

But I did not mind that a sense of camaraderie had begun to take hold, even if it would prove short-lived. The psychologist allowed us each a couple of beers from the store of alcohol, which loosened us up to the point that I even clumsily expressed the idea that we might maintain some sort of contact once we had completed our mission. I had stopped checking myself for physiological or psychological reactions to the spores by then, and found that the surveyor and I got along better than I had expected. I still didn't like the anthropologist very much, but mostly in the context of the mission, not anything she had said to me. I felt that, once in the field, much as some athletes were good in practice and not during the game, she had exhibited a lack of mental toughness thus far. Although just volunteering for such a mission meant something.

When the nightly cry from the marshes came a little after nightfall, while we sat around our fire, we at first called back to it in a drunken show of bravado. The beast in the marshes now seemed like an old friend compared to the tower. We were confident that eventually we would photograph it, document its behavior, tag it, and assign it a place in the taxonomy of living things. It would become known in a way we feared the tower would not. But we stopped calling back when the intensity of its moans heightened in a way that suggested anger, as if it knew we were mocking it. Nervous laughter all around, then, and the psychologist took that as her cue to ready us for the next day.

"Tomorrow we will go back to the tunnel. We will go deeper, taking certain precautions—wearing breathing masks, as suggested. We will record the writing on the walls and get a sense of how old it is, I hope. Also, perhaps a sense of how deep the tunnel descends. In the afternoon, we'll return to our general investigations of the area. We'll repeat this schedule every day until we think we know enough about the tunnel and how it fits into Area X."

Tower, not tunnel. She could have been talking about investigating an abandoned shopping center, for all of the emphasis she put on it . . . and yet something about her tone seemed rehearsed.

Then she abruptly stood and said three words: *"Consolidation of authority."*

Immediately the surveyor and the anthropologist beside me went slack, their eyes unfocused. I was shocked, but I mimicked them, hoping that the psychologist had not noticed the lag. I felt no compulsion whatsoever, but clearly we had been preprogrammed to enter a hypnotic state in response to those words, uttered by the psychologist.

Her demeanor more assertive than just a moment before, the psychologist said, "You will retain a memory of having discussed several options with regard to the tunnel. You will find that you ultimately agreed with me about the best course of action, and that you felt quite confident about this course of action. You will experience a sensation of calm whenever you think about this decision, and you will remain calm once back inside the tunnel, although you will react to any stimuli as per your training. You will not take undue risks.

"You will continue to see a structure that is made of coquina and stone. You will trust your colleagues completely and feel a continued sense of fellowship with them. When you emerge from the structure, any time you see a bird in flight it will trigger a strong feeling that you are doing the *right thing*, that you are in the *right place*. When I snap my fingers, you will have no memory of this conversation, but will follow my directives. You will feel very tired and you will want to retire to your tents to get a good night's sleep before tomorrow's activities. You will not dream. You will not have nightmares."

I stared straight ahead as she said these words, and when she snapped her fingers I took my cue from the actions of the other two. I don't believe the psychologist suspected anything, and I retired to my tent just as the others retired to their tents.

Now I had new data to process, along with the tower. We knew that the psychologist's role was to provide balance and calm in a situation that might become stressful, and that part of this role included hypnotic suggestion. I could not blame her for performing that role. But to see it laid out so nakedly troubled me. It is one thing to think you might be receiving hypnotic suggestion and quite another to experience it as an observer. What level of control could she exert over us? What did she mean by saying that we would continue to think of the tower as made of coquina and stone?

Most important, however, I now could guess at one way in which the spores had affected me: They had made me immune to the psychologist's hypnotic suggestions. They had made me into a kind of conspirator against her. Even if her purposes were benign, I felt a wave of anxiety whenever I thought of confessing that I was resistant to hypnosis—especially since it meant any underlying *conditioning* hidden in our training also was affecting me less and less.

I now hid not one but two secrets, and that meant I was steadily, irrevocably, becoming estranged from the expedition and its purpose.

Estrangement, in all of its many forms, was nothing new for these missions. I understood this from having been given an opportunity along with the others to view videotape of the reentry interviews with the members of the eleventh expedition. Once those individuals had been identified as having returned to their former lives, they were quarantined and questioned about their experiences. Reasonably enough, in most cases family members had called the authorities, finding their loved one's return uncanny or frightening. Any papers found on these returnees had been confiscated by our superiors for examination and study. This information, too, we were allowed to see.

The interviews were fairly short, and in them all eight expedition members told the same story. They had experienced no unusual phenomenon while in Area X, taken no unusual readings, and reported no unusual internal conflicts. But after a period of time, each one of them had had the intense desire to return home and had set out to do so. None of them could explain how they had managed to come

back across the border, or why they had gone straight home instead of first reporting to their superiors. One by one they had simply abandoned the expedition, left
their journals behind, and drifted home. Somehow.

Throughout these interviews, their expressions were friendly and their gazes
direct. If their words seemed a little flat, then this went with the kind of general
calm, the almost dreamlike demeanor each had returned with—even the compact, wiry man who had served as that expedition's military expert, a person
who'd had a mercurial and energetic personality. In terms of their affect, I could
not tell any of the eight apart. I had the sense that they now saw the world through
a kind of veil, that they spoke to their interviewers from across a vast distance in
time and space.

As for the papers, they proved to be sketches of landscapes within Area X or
brief descriptions. Some were cartoons of animals or caricatures of fellow expedition members. All of them had, at some point, drawn the lighthouse or written
about it. Looking for hidden meaning in these papers was the same as looking for
hidden meaning in the natural world around us. If it existed, it could be activated
only by the eye of the beholder.

At the time, I was seeking oblivion, and I sought in those blank, anonymous
faces, even the most painfully familiar, a kind of benign escape. A death that
would not mean being dead.

02: INTEGRATION

In the morning, I woke with my senses heightened, so that even the rough brown bark of the pines or the ordinary lunging swoop of a woodpecker came to me as a kind of minor revelation. The lingering fatigue from the four-day hike to base camp had left me. Was this some side effect of the spores or just the result of a good night's sleep? I felt so refreshed that I didn't really care.

But my reverie was soon tempered by disastrous news. The anthropologist was gone, her tent empty of her personal effects. Worse, in my view, the psychologist seemed shaken, and as if she hadn't slept. She was squinting oddly, her hair more windblown than usual. I noticed dirt caked on the sides of her boots. She was favoring her right side, as if she had been injured.

"Where is the anthropologist?" the surveyor demanded, while I hung back, trying to make my own sense of it. *What have you done with the anthropologist?* was my unspoken question, which I knew was unfair. The psychologist was no different than she had been before; that I knew the secret to her magician's show did not necessarily mean she was a threat.

The psychologist stepped into our rising panic with a strange assertion: "I talked to her late last night. What she saw in that . . . structure . . . unnerved her to the point that she did not want to continue with this expedition. She has started back to the border to await extraction. She took a partial report with her so that our superiors will know our progress." The psychologist's habit of allowing a slim smile to cross her face at inappropriate times made me want to slap her.

"But she left her gear—her gun, too," the surveyor said.

"She took only what she needed so we would have more—including an extra gun."

"Do you think we need an extra gun?" I asked the psychologist. I was truly curious. In some ways I found the psychologist as fascinating as the tower. Her motivations, her reasons. Why not resort to hypnosis now? Perhaps even with our underlying conditioning some things are not suggestible, or fade with repetition, or she lacked the stamina for it after the events of the night before.

"I think we don't know what we need," the psychologist said. "But we definitely did not need the anthropologist here if she was unable to do her job."

The surveyor and I stared at the psychologist. The surveyor's arms were crossed. We had been trained to keep a close watch on our colleagues for signs of sudden mental stress or dysfunction. She was probably thinking what I was thinking: We had a choice now. We could accept the psychologist's explanation for the anthropologist's disappearance or reject it. If we rejected it, then we were saying the psychologist had lied to us, and therefore also rejecting her authority at a critical time. And if we tried to follow the trail back home, hoping to catch up with the anthropologist, to verify the psychologist's story . . . would we have the will to return to base camp afterward?

"We should continue with our plan," the psychologist said. "We should investigate the . . . tower." The word *tower* in this context felt like a blatant plea for my loyalty.

Still the surveyor wavered, as if fighting the psychologist's suggestion from the night before. This alarmed me in another way. I was not going to leave Area X before investigating the tower. This fact was ingrained in every part of me. And in that context I could not bear to think of losing another member of the team so soon, leaving me alone with the psychologist. Not when I was unsure of her and not when I still had no idea of the effects of my exposure to the spores.

"She's right," I said. "We should continue with the mission. We can make do without the anthropologist." But my pointed stare to the surveyor made it clear to both of them that we would revisit the issue of the anthropologist later.

The surveyor gave a surly nod and looked away.

An audible sigh of either relief or exhaustion came from the psychologist. "That's settled then," she said, and brushed past the surveyor to start making breakfast. The anthropologist had always made breakfast before.

At the tower, the situation changed yet again. The surveyor and I had readied light packs with enough food and water to spend the full day down there. We both had our weapons. We both had donned our breathing masks to keep out the spores, even though it was too late for me. We both wore hard hats with fixed beams on them.

But the psychologist stood on the grass just beyond the circle of the tower, slightly below us, and said, "I'll stand guard here."

"Against what?" I asked, incredulous. I did not want to let the psychologist out of my sight. I wanted her embedded in the risk of the exploration, not standing at the top, with all of the power over us implied by that position.

The surveyor wasn't happy, either. In an almost pleading way that suggested a high level of suppressed stress, she said, "You're supposed to come with us. It's safer with three."

"But you need to know that the entrance is secured," the psychologist said, sliding a magazine into her handgun. The harsh scraping sound echoed more than I would have thought.

The surveyor's grip on her assault rifle tightened until I could see her knuckles whiten. "You need to come down with us."

"There's no *reward in the risk* of all of us going down," the psychologist said, and from the inflection I recognized a hypnotic command.

The surveyor's grip on her rifle loosened. The features of her face became somehow indistinct for a moment.

"You're right," the surveyor said. "Of course, you're right. It makes perfect sense."

A twinge of fear traveled down my back. Now it was two against one.

I thought about that for a moment, took in the full measure of the psychologist's stare as she focused her attention on me. Nightmarish, paranoid scenarios came to me. Returning to find the entrance blocked, or the psychologist picking us off as we reached for the open sky. Except: She could have killed us in our sleep any night of the week.

"It's not that important," I said after a moment. "You're as valuable to us up here as down there."

And so we descended, as before, under the psychologist's watchful eye.

The first thing I noticed on the staging level before we reached the wider staircase that spiraled down, before we encountered again the words written on the wall . . . the tower was *breathing*. The tower *breathed*, and the walls when I went to touch them carried the echo of a heartbeat . . . and they were not made of stone but of *living tissue*. Those walls were still blank, but a kind of silvery-white phosphorescence rose off of them. The world seemed to lurch, and I sat down heavily next to the wall, and the surveyor was by my side, trying to help me up. I think I was shaking as I finally stood. I don't know if I can convey the enormity of that moment in words. The tower was a living creature of some sort. *We were descending into an organism.*

"What's wrong?" the surveyor was asking me, voice muffled through her mask. "What happened?"

I grabbed her hand, forced her palm against the wall.

"Let me go!" She tried to pull away, but I kept her there.

"Do you feel that?" I asked, unrelenting. "Can you feel that?"

"Feel *what*? What are you talking about?" She was scared, of course. To her, I was acting irrationally.

Still, I persisted: "A vibration. A kind of beat." I removed my hand from hers, stepped back.

The surveyor took a long, deep breath, and kept her hand on the wall. "No. Maybe. No. No, nothing."

"What about the wall. What is it made of?"

"Stone, of course," she said. In the arc of my helmet flashlight, her shadowed face was hollowed out, her eyes large and circled by darkness, the mask making it look like she had no nose or mouth.

I took a deep breath. I wanted it all to spill out: that I had been contaminated, that the psychologist was hypnotizing us far more than we might have suspected. *That the walls were made of living tissue.* But I didn't. Instead, I "got my shit together," as my husband used to say. I got my shit together because we were going to go forward and the surveyor couldn't see what I saw, couldn't experience what I was experiencing. And I couldn't make her see it.

"Forget it," I said. "I became disoriented for a second."

"Look, we should go back up now. You're panicking," the surveyor said. We had all been told we might see things that weren't there while in Area X. I know she was thinking that this had happened to me.

I held up the black box on my belt. "Nope—it's not flashing. We're good." It was a joke, a feeble joke, but still.

"You saw something that wasn't there." She wasn't going to let me off the hook.

You can't see what is *there*, I thought.

"Maybe," I admitted, "but isn't that important, too? Isn't that part of all of this? The reporting? And something I see that you don't might be important."

The surveyor weighed that for a moment. "How do you feel now?"

"I feel fine," I lied. "I don't see anything now," I lied. My heart felt like an animal had become trapped in my chest and was trying to crawl out. The surveyor was now surrounded by a corona of the white phosphorescence from the walls. Nothing was receding. Nothing was leaving me.

"Then we'll go on," the surveyor said. "But only if you promise to tell me if you see anything unusual again."

I almost laughed at that, I remember. *Unusual?* Like strange words on a wall? Written among tiny communities of creatures of unknown origin.

"I promise," I said. "And you will do the same for me, right?" Turning the tables, making her realize it might happen to her, too.

She said, "Just don't touch me again or I'll hurt you."

I nodded in agreement. She didn't like knowing I was physically stronger than her.

Under the terms of that flawed agreement we proceeded to the stairs and into the gullet of the tower, the depths now revealing themselves in a kind of ongoing horror show of such beauty and biodiversity that I could not fully take it all in. But I tried, just as I had always tried, even from the very beginning of my career.

My lodestone, the place I always thought of when people asked me why I became a biologist, was the overgrown swimming pool in the backyard of the rented house where I grew up. My mother was an overwrought artist who achieved some success but was a little too fond of alcohol and always struggled to find new clients, while my dad the underemployed accountant specialized in schemes to get rich quick that usually brought in nothing. Neither of them seemed to possess the ability to focus on one thing for any length of time. Sometimes it felt as if I had been placed with a family rather than born into one.

They did not have the will or inclination to clean the kidney-shaped pool, even though it was fairly small. Soon after we moved in, the grass around its edges grew long. Sedge weeds and other towering plants became prevalent. The short bushes lining the fence around the pool lunged up to obscure the chain link. Moss grew in the cracks in the tile path that circled it. The water level slowly rose, fed by the rain, and the surface became more and more brackish with algae. Dragonflies continually scouted the area. Bullfrogs moved in, the wriggling malformed dots of their tadpoles always present. Water gliders and aquatic beetles began to make the place their own. Rather than get rid of my thirty-gallon freshwater aquarium, as my parents wanted, I dumped the fish into the pool, and some survived the shock of that. Local birds, like herons and egrets, began to appear, drawn by the frogs and fish and insects. By some miracle, too, small turtles began to live in the pool, although I had no idea how they had gotten there.

Within months of our arrival, the pool had become a functioning ecosystem. I would slowly enter through the creaking wooden gate and observe it all from a rusty lawn chair I had set up in a far corner. Despite a strong and well-founded fear of drowning, I had always loved being around bodies of water.

Inside the house, my parents did whatever banal, messy things people in the human world usually did, some of it loudly. But I could easily lose myself in the microworld of the pool.

Inevitably my focus netted from my parents useless lectures of worry over my chronic introversion, as if by doing so they could convince me they were still in charge. I didn't have enough (or any) friends, they reminded me. I didn't seem to make the effort. I could be earning money from a part-time job. But when I told them that several times, like a reluctant ant lion, I had had to hide from bullies at the bottom of the gravel pits that lay amid the abandoned fields beyond the school, they had no answers. Nor when one day for "no reason" I punched a fellow student in the face when she said hello to me in the lunch line.

So we proceeded, locked into our separate imperatives. They had their lives, and I had mine. I liked most of all pretending to be a biologist, and pretending often leads to becoming a reasonable facsimile of what you mimic, even if only from a distance. I wrote down my pool observations in several journals. I knew each individual frog from the next, Old Flopper so much different from Ugly Leaper, and during which month I could expect the grass to teem with hopping juveniles. I knew which species of heron turned up year-round and which were migrants. The beetles and dragonflies were harder to identify, their life cycles harder to intuit, but I still diligently tried to understand them. In all of this, I eschewed books on ecology or biology. I wanted to discover the information on my own first.

As far as I was concerned—an only child, and an expert in the uses of solitude— my observations of this miniature paradise could have continued forever. I even jury-rigged a waterproof light to a waterproof camera and planned to submerge the contraption beneath the dark surface, to snap pictures using a long wire attached to the camera button. I have no idea if it would have worked, because suddenly I didn't have the luxury of time. Our luck ran out, and we couldn't afford the rent anymore. We moved to a tiny apartment, stuffed full of my mother's paintings, which all resembled wallpaper to me. One of the great traumas of my life was worrying about the pool. Would the new owners see the beauty and the importance of leaving it as is, or would they destroy it, create unthinking slaughter in honor of the pool's real function?

I never found out—I couldn't bear to go back, even if I also could never forget the richness of that place. All I could do was look forward, apply what I had learned from watching the inhabitants of the pool. And I never did look back, for better or worse. If funding for a project ran out, or the area we studied was suddenly bought for development, I never returned. There are certain kinds of deaths that one should not be expected to relive, certain kinds of connections so deep that when they are broken you feel the snap of the link inside you.

As we descended into the tower, I felt again, for the first time in a long time, the flush of discovery I had experienced as a child. But I also kept waiting for the snap.

Where lies the strangling fruit that came from the hand of the sinner I shall bring forth the seeds of the dead to share with the worms that . . .
The tower steps kept revealing themselves, those whitish steps like the spiraling teeth of some unfathomable beast, and we kept descending because there seemed to be no choice. I wished at times for the blinkered seeing of the surveyor. I knew now why the psychologist had sheltered us, and I wondered how she withstood it, for she had no one to shield her from . . . anything.

At first, there were "merely" the words, and that was enough. They occurred always at roughly the same level against the left-hand side of the wall, and for a time I tried to record them, but there were too many of them and the sense of them came and went, so that to follow the meaning of the words was to follow a trail of deception. That was one agreement the surveyor and I came to right away: that we would document the physicality of the words, but that it would require a separate mission, another day, to photograph that continuous, never-ending sentence.

. . . to share with the worms that gather in the darkness and surround the world with the power of their lives while from the dim-lit halls of other places forms that never could be writhe for the impatience of the few who have never seen or been seen . . .

The sense of unease in ignoring the ominous quality of those words was palpable. It infected our own sentences when we spoke, as we tried to catalogue the biological reality of what we were *both* seeing. Either the psychologist wanted us to see the words and how they were written or simply suppressing the physical reality of the tower's walls was a monumental and exhausting task.

These things, too, we experienced together during our initial descent into the darkness: The air became cooler but also damp, and with the drop in temperature came a kind of gentle sweetness, as of a muted nectar. We also both saw the tiny hand-shaped creatures that lived among the words. The ceilings were higher than we would have guessed, and by the light of our helmets as we looked up, the surveyor could see glints and whorls as of the trails of snails or slugs. Little tufts of moss or lichen dotted that ceiling, and, exhibiting great tensile strength, tiny long-limbed translucent creatures that resembled cave shrimp stilt-walked there as well.

Things only I could see: That the walls minutely rose and fell with the tower's breathing. That the colors of the words shifted in a rippling effect, like the strobing of a squid. That, with a variation of about three inches above the current words and three inches below, there existed a ghosting of *prior words*, written in the same cursive script. Effectively, these layers of words formed a watermark, for they were just an impression against the wall, a pale hint of green or sometimes purple the only sign that once they might have been raised letters. Most seemed to repeat the main thread, but some did not.

For a time, while the surveyor took photographic samples of the living words, I read the phantom words to see how they might deviate. It was hard to read them—there were several overlapping strands that started and stopped and started up again. I easily lost track of individual words and phrases. The number of such ghost scripts faded into the wall suggested this process had been ongoing for a long time. Although without some sense of the length of each "cycle," I could not give even a rough estimate in years.

There was another element to the communications on the wall, too. One I wasn't sure if the surveyor could see or not. I decided to test her.

"Do you recognize this?" I asked the surveyor, pointing to a kind of interlocking latticework that at first I hadn't even realized was a pattern but that covered the wall from just below the phantom scripts to just above them, the main strand roughly in the middle. It vaguely resembled scorpions strung end-to-end arising, only to be subsumed again. I didn't even know if I was looking at a language, per se. It could have been a decorative pattern for all I knew.

Much to my relief, she could see it. "No, I don't recognize it," she said. "But I'm not an expert."

I felt a surge of irritation, but it wasn't directed at her. I had the wrong brain for this task, and so did she; we needed a linguist. We could look at that latticework script for ages and the most original thought I would have is that it resembled the sharp branching of hard coral. To the surveyor it might resemble the rough tributaries of a vast river.

Eventually, though, I was able to reconstruct fragments of a handful of some of the variants: *Why should I rest when wickedness exists in the world . . . God's love shines on anyone who understands the limits of endurance, and allows forgiveness . . . Chosen for the service of a higher power.* If the main thread formed a kind of dark, incomprehensible sermon, then the fragments shared an affinity with that purpose without the heightened syntax.

Did they come from longer accounts of some sort, possibly from members of prior expeditions? If so, for what purpose? And over how many years?

But all such questions would be for later, in the light of the surface. Mechanically, like a golem, I just took photographs of key phrases—even as the surveyor thought I was clicking pictures of blank wall, or off-center shots of the main fungal words—to put some distance between myself and whatever I might think about these variants. While the main scrawl continued, and continued to unnerve: *. . . in the black water with the sun shining at midnight, those fruit shall come ripe and in the darkness of that which is golden shall split open to reveal the revelation of the fatal softness in the earth . . .*

Those words defeated me somehow. I took samples as we went, but half-heartedly. All of these tiny remnants I was stuffing into glass tubes with tweezers . . . what would they tell me? Not much, I felt. Sometimes you get a sense of when the truth of things will not be revealed by microscopes. Soon, too, the sound of the heartbeat through the walls became so loud to me I stopped to put in earplugs to muffle its beat, choosing a moment while the surveyor's attention lay elsewhere. Be-masked, half-deaf for different reasons, we continued our descent.

It should have been me who noticed the change, not her. But after an hour of downward progress, the surveyor stopped on the steps below me.

"Do you think the words on the wall are becoming . . . fresher?"

"Fresher?"

"More recent."

I just stared at her for a moment. I had become acclimated to the situation, had done my best to pretend to be the kind of impartial observer who simply catalogues details. But I felt all of that hard-won distance slipping away.

"Turn off your light?" I suggested, as I did the same.

The surveyor hesitated. After my show of impulsiveness earlier, it would be some time before she trusted me again. Not the kind of trust that responded unthinkingly to a request to plunge us into darkness. But she did it. The truth was, I had purposefully left my gun in its belt holster and she could have extinguished me in a moment with her assault rifle, with one fluid motion pulling on the strap and freeing it from her shoulder. This premonition of violence made little rational sense, and yet it came to me too easily, almost as if placed in my mind by outside forces.

In the dark, as the tower's heartbeat still throbbed against my eardrums, the letters, the words, swayed as the walls trembled with their breathing, and I saw that indeed the words seemed more active, the colors brighter, the strobing more intense than I remembered it from levels above. It was an even more noticeable effect than if the words had been written in ink with a fountain pen. *The bright, wet slickness of the new.*

Standing there in that impossible place, I said it before the surveyor could, to own it.

"Something below us is writing this script. Something below us may still be in the process of writing this script." We were exploring an organism that might contain a mysterious second organism, which was itself using yet other organisms to write words on the wall. It made the overgrown pool of my youth seem simplistic, one-dimensional.

We turned our lights back on. I saw fear in the surveyor's eyes, but also a strange determination. I have no idea what she saw in me.

"Why did you say something?" she asked.

I didn't understand.

"Why did you say 'something' rather than 'someone'? Why can't it be 'someone'?"

I just shrugged.

"Get out your gun," the surveyor said, a hint of disgust in her voice masking some deeper emotion.

I did as I was told because it didn't really matter to me. But holding the gun made me feel clumsy and odd, as if it were the wrong reaction to what might confront us.

Whereas I had taken the lead to this point, now it seemed as if we had switched roles, and the nature of our exploration changed as a result. Apparently, we had just established a new protocol. We stopped documenting the words and organisms on the wall. We walked much more swiftly, our attention focused on interpreting the darkness in front of us. We spoke in whispers, as if we might be overheard. I went first, with the surveyor covering me from behind until the curves, where she went first and I followed. At no point did we speak of turning back. The psychologist watching over us might as well have been thousands of miles away. We were charged with the nervous energy of knowing there might be some answer below us. A living, breathing answer.

At least, the surveyor *may* have thought of it in those terms. She couldn't feel or hear the beating of the walls. But as we progressed, even I could not see the writer of those words in my mind. All I could see was what I had seen when I had stared back at the border on our way to base camp: a fuzzy white blankness. Yet still I knew it could not be human.

Why? For a very good reason—one the surveyor finally noticed another twenty minutes into our descent.

"There's something on the floor," she said.

Yes, there was something on the floor. For a long time now, the steps had been covered in a kind of residue. I hadn't stopped to examine it because I hadn't wanted to unnerve the surveyor, uncertain if she would ever come to see it. The residue covered a distance from the edge of the left wall to about two feet from the right wall. This meant it filled a space on the steps about eight or nine feet wide.

"Let me take a look," I said, ignoring her quivering finger. I knelt, turning to train my helmet light on the upper steps behind me. The surveyor walked up to stare over my shoulder. The residue sparkled with a kind of subdued golden shimmer shot through with flakes red like dried blood. It seemed partially reflective. I probed it with a pen.

"It's slightly viscous, like slime," I said. "And about half an inch deep over the steps."

The overall impression was of something *sliding* down the stairs.

"What about those marks?" the surveyor asked, leaning forward to point again. She was whispering, which seemed useless to me, and her voice had a catch in it. But every time I noticed her becoming more panicky, I found it made me calmer.

I studied the marks for a moment. Sliding, perhaps, or *dragged*, but slowly enough to reveal much more in the residue left behind. The marks she had pointed to were oval, and about a foot long by half a foot wide. Six of them were splayed over the steps, in two rows. A flurry of indentations inside these shapes resembled the marks left by cilia. About ten inches outside of these tracks, encircling them, were two lines. This irregular double circle undulated out and then in again, almost like the hem of a skirt. Beyond this "hem" were faint indicators of further "waves," as of some force emanating from a central body that had left a mark. It resembled most closely the lines left in sand as the surf recedes during low tide. Except that something had blurred the lines and made them fuzzy, like charcoal drawings.

This discovery fascinated me. I could not stop staring at the trail, the cilia marks. I imagined such a creature might correct for the slant of the stairs much like a geo-stabilizing camera would correct for bumps in a track.

"Have you ever seen anything like that?" the surveyor asked.

"No," I replied. With an effort, I bit back a more caustic response. "No, I never have." Certain trilobites, snails, and worms left trails simple by comparison but vaguely similar. I was confident no one back in the world had ever seen a trail this complex or this large.

"What about *that*?" The surveyor indicated a step a little farther up.

I trained a light on it and saw a suggestion of a boot print in the residue. "Just one of our own boots." So mundane in comparison. So boring.

The light on her helmet shuddered from side to side as she shook her head. "No. See."

She pointed out my boot prints and hers. This imprint was from a third set, and headed back up the steps.

"You're right," I said. "That's another person, down here not long ago."

The surveyor started cursing.

At the time, we didn't think to look for more sets of boot prints.

According to the records we had been shown, the first expedition reported nothing unusual in Area X, just pristine, empty wilderness. After the second and third expeditions did not return, and their fate became known, the expeditions were shut down for a time. When they began again, it was using carefully chosen volunteers who might at least know a measure of the full risk. Since then, some expeditions had been more successful than others.

The eleventh expedition in particular had been difficult—and personally difficult for me with regard to a fact about which I have not been entirely honest thus far.

My husband was on the eleventh expedition as a medic. He had never wanted to be a doctor, had always wanted to be in first response or working in trauma. "A triage nurse in the field," as he put it. He had been recruited for Area X by a friend, who remembered him from when they had both worked for the navy, before he switched over to ambulance service. At first he hadn't said yes, had been unsure, but over time they convinced him. It caused a lot of strife between us, although we already had many difficulties.

I know this information might not be hard for anyone to find out, but I have hoped that in reading this account, you might find me a credible, objective witness. Not someone who volunteered for Area X because of some other event unconnected to the purpose of the expeditions. And, in a sense, this is still true, and my husband's status as a member of an expedition is in many ways irrelevant to why I signed up.

But how could I not be affected by Area X, if only through him? One night, about a year after he had headed for the border, as I lay alone in bed, I heard someone in the kitchen. Armed with a baseball bat, I left the bedroom and turned on all the lights in the house. I found my husband next to the refrigerator, still dressed in his expedition clothes, drinking milk until it flowed down his chin and neck. Eating leftovers furiously.

I was speechless. I could only stare at him as if he were a mirage and if I moved or said anything he would dissipate into nothing, or less than nothing.

We sat in the living room, him on the sofa and me in a chair opposite. I needed some distance from this sudden apparition. He did not remember how he had left Area X, did not remember the journey home at all. He had only the vaguest recollection of the expedition itself. There was an odd calm about him, punctured only by moments of remote panic when, in asking him what had happened, he recognized that his amnesia was unnatural. Gone from him, too, seemed to be any memory of how our marriage had begun to disintegrate well before our arguments over his leaving for Area X. He contained within him now the very distance he had in so many subtle and not so subtle ways accused me of in the past.

After a time, I couldn't take it any longer. I took off his clothes, made him shower, then led him into the bedroom and made love to him with me on top. I was trying to reclaim remnants of the man I remembered, the one who, so unlike me, was outgoing and impetuous and always wanted to be of use. The man who had been a passionate recreational sailor, and for two weeks out of the year went with friends to the coast to go boating. I could find none of that in him now.

The whole time he was inside me he looked up at my face with an expression that told me he did remember me but only through a kind of fog. It helped for a while, though. It made him more real, allowed me to pretend.

But only for a while. I only had him in my life again for about twenty-four hours. They came for him the next evening, and once I went through the long, drawn-out process of receiving security clearance, I visited him in the observation facility right up until the end. That antiseptic place where they tested him and tried without success to break through both his calm and his amnesia. He would greet me like an old friend—an anchor of sorts, to make sense of his existence—but not like a lover. I confess I went because I had hopes that there remained some spark of the man I'd once known. But I never really found it. Even the day I was told he had been diagnosed with inoperable, systemic cancer, my husband stared at me with a slightly puzzled expression on his face.

He died six months later. During all that time, I could never get beyond the mask, could never find the man I had known inside of him. Not through my personal interactions with him, not through eventually watching the interviews with him and the other members of the expedition, all of whom died of cancer as well.

Whatever had happened in Area X, he had not come back. Not really.

Ever farther down into the darkness we went, and I had to ask myself if any of this had been experienced by my husband. I did not know how my infection changed things. Was I on the same journey, or had he found something completely different? If similar, how had his reactions been different, and how had that changed what happened next?

The path of slime grew thicker and we could now tell that the red flecks were living organisms discharged by whatever lay below, for they wriggled in the viscous layer. The color of the substance had intensified so that it resembled a sparkling golden carpet set out for us to tread upon on our way to some strange yet magnificent banquet.

"Should we go back?" the surveyor would say, or I would say.

And the other would say, "Just around the next corner. Just a little farther, and then we will go back." It was a test of a fragile trust. It was a test of our curiosity and fascination, which walked side by side with our fear. A test of whether we preferred to be ignorant or unsafe. The feel of our boots as we advanced step by careful step through that viscous discharge, the way in which the stickiness seemed to mire us even as we managed to keep moving, would eventually end in inertia, we knew. If we pushed it too far.

But then the surveyor rounded a corner ahead of me and recoiled into me, shoved me back up the steps, and I let her.

"There's something down there," she whispered in my ear. "Something like a body or a person."

I didn't point out that a body could be a person. "Is it writing words on the wall?"

"No—*slumped down* by the side of the wall. I only caught a glimpse." Her breathing came quick and shallow against her mask.

"A man or a woman?" I asked.

"I *thought* it was a person," she said, ignoring my question. "I thought it was a person. I thought it was." Bodies were one thing; no amount of training could prepare you for encountering a monster.

But we could not climb back out of the tower without first investigating this new mystery. We could not. I grabbed her by the shoulders, made her look at me. "You said it's like a person sitting down against the side of the wall. That's *not* whatever we've been tracking. This has to do with the *other boot print*. You know that. We can risk taking a look at whatever this is, and then we will go back up. This is as far as we go, no matter what we find, I promise."

The surveyor nodded. The idea of this being the extent of it, of not going farther down, was enough to steady her. *Just get through this last thing, and you'll see the sunlight soon.*

We started back down. The steps seemed particularly slippery now, even though it might have been our jitters, and we walked slowly, using the blank slate of the right wall to keep our balance. The tower was silent, holding its breath, its heartbeat suddenly slow and far more distant than before, or perhaps I could only hear the blood rushing through my head.

Turning the corner, I saw the figure and shone my helmet light on it. If I'd hesitated a second longer, I never would have had the nerve. It was the body of the anthropologist, slumped against the left-hand wall, her hands in her lap, her head down as if in prayer, something green spilling out from her mouth. Her clothing seemed oddly fuzzy, indistinct. A faint golden glow arose from her body, almost imperceptible; I imagined the surveyor could not see it at all. In no scenario could I imagine the anthropologist alive. All I could think was, *The psychologist lied to us*, and suddenly the pressure of her presence far above, guarding the entrance, was pressing down on me in an intolerable way.

I put out a palm to the surveyor, indicating that she should stay where she was, behind me, and I stepped forward, light pointed down into the darkness. I walked past the body far enough to confirm the stairs below were empty, then hurried back up.

"Keep watch while I take a look at the body," I said. I didn't tell her I had sensed a faint, echoing suggestion of *something* much farther below, moving slowly.

"It *is* a body?" the surveyor said. Perhaps she had expected something far stranger. Perhaps she thought the figure was just sleeping.

"It's the anthropologist," I said, and saw that information register in the tensing of her shoulders. Without another word, she brushed past me to take up a position just beyond the body, assault rifle aimed into the darkness.

Gently, I knelt beside the anthropologist. There wasn't much left of her face, and odd burn marks were all over the remaining skin. Spilling out from her broken jaw, which looked as though someone had wrenched it open in a single act of brutality, was a torrent of green ash that sat on her chest in a mound. Her hands, palms up in her lap, had no skin left on them, only a kind of gauzy filament and more burn marks. Her legs seemed fused together and half-melted, one boot missing and one flung against the wall. Strewn around the anthropologist were some of the same sample tubes I had brought with me. Her black box, crushed, lay several feet from her body.

"What happened to her?" the surveyor whispered. She kept taking quick, nervous glances back at me as she stood guard, almost as if whatever had happened wasn't over. As if she expected the anthropologist to come back to horrifying life.

I didn't answer her. All I could have said was *I don't know*, a sentence that was becoming a kind of witness to our own ignorance or incompetence. Or both.

I shone my light on the wall above the anthropologist. For several feet, the script on the wall became erratic, leaping up and dipping down, before regaining its equilibrium.

. . . the shadows of the abyss are like the petals of a monstrous flower that shall blossom within the skull and expand the mind beyond what any man can bear . . .

"I think she interrupted the creator of the script on the wall," I said.

"And it did that to her?" She was pleading with me to find some other explanation.

I didn't have one, so I didn't reply, just went back to observing as she stood there, watching me.

A biologist is not a detective, but I began to think like a detective. I surveyed the ground to all sides, identifying first my own boot prints on the steps and then the surveyor's. We had obscured the original tracks, but you could still see traces. First of all, the *thing*—and no matter what the surveyor might hope, I could not think of it as human—had clearly turned in a frenzy. Instead of the smooth sliding tracks, the slime residue formed a kind of clockwise swirl, the marks of the "feet," as I thought of them, elongated and narrowed by the sudden change. But on top of this swirl, I could also see boot prints. I retrieved the one boot, being careful to walk around the edges of the evidence of the encounter. The boot prints in the middle of the swirl were indeed from the anthropologist—and I could follow partial imprints back up the right-hand side of the wall, as if she had been hugging it.

An image began to form in my mind, of the anthropologist creeping down in the dark to observe the creator of the script. The glittering glass tubes strewn around her body made me think that she had hoped to take a sample. But how insane or oblivious! Such a risk, and the anthropologist had never struck me as impulsive or brave. I stood there for a moment, and then backtracked even farther up the stairs as I motioned to the surveyor, much to her distress, to hold her position. Perhaps if there had been something to shoot she would have been calmer, but we were left with only what lingered in our imaginations.

Another dozen steps up, right where you could still have a slit of a view of the dead anthropologist, I found two sets of boot prints, facing each other. One set belonged to the anthropologist. The other was neither mine nor the surveyor's.

Something clicked into place, and I could see it all in my head. In the middle of the night, the psychologist had woken the anthropologist, put her under hypnosis, and together they had come to the tower and climbed down this far. At this point, the psychologist had given the anthropologist an order, under hypnosis, one that she probably knew was suicidal, and the anthropologist had walked right up to the thing that was writing the words on the wall and tried to take a sample—and died trying, probably in agony. The psychologist had then fled; certainly, as I walked back down I could find no trace of her boot prints below that point.

Was it pity or empathy that I felt for the anthropologist? Weak, trapped, with no choice.

The surveyor waited for me, anxious. "What did you find?"

"Another person was here with the anthropologist." I told the surveyor my theory.

"But why would the psychologist do that?" she asked me. "We were going to all come down here in the morning anyway."

I felt as if I were observing the surveyor from a thousand miles away.

"I have no idea," I said, "but she has been hypnotizing all of us, and not just to give us peace of mind. Perhaps this expedition had a different purpose than what we were told."

"Hypnotism." She said the word like it was meaningless. "How do you know that? How could you possibly know that?" The surveyor seemed resentful—of me or of the theory, I couldn't tell which. But I could understand why.

"Because, somehow, I have become impervious to it," I told her. "She hypnotized you before we came down here today, to make sure you would do your duty. I saw her do it." I wanted to confess to the surveyor—to tell her *how* I had become impervious—but believed that that would be a mistake.

"And you did *nothing*? If this is even true." At least she was considering the possibility of believing me. Perhaps some residue, some fuzziness, from the episode had stuck in her mind.

"I didn't want the psychologist to know that she couldn't hypnotize me." And, I had *wanted* to come down here.

The surveyor stood there for a moment, considering.

"Believe me or don't believe me," I said. "But believe this: When we go up there, we need to be ready for anything. We may need to restrain or kill the psychologist because we don't know what she's planning."

"Why would she be planning anything?" the surveyor asked. Was that disdain in her voice or just fear again?

"Because she must have different orders than the ones we got," I said, as if explaining to a child.

When she did not reply, I took that as a sign that she was beginning to acclimate to the idea.

"I'll need to go first, because she can't affect me. And you'll need to wear these. It might help you resist the hypnotic suggestion." I gave her my extra set of earplugs.

She took them hesitantly. "No," she said. "We'll go up together, at the same time."

"That isn't wise," I said.

"I don't care what it is. You're not going up top without me. I'm not waiting there in the dark for you to fix everything."

I thought about that for a moment, then said, "Fine. But if I see that she is starting to coerce you, I'll have to stop her." Or at least try.

"If you're right," the surveyor said. "If you're telling the truth."

"I am."

She ignored me, said, "What about the body?"

Did that mean we were agreed? I hoped so. Or maybe she would try to disarm me on the way up. Perhaps the psychologist had already prepared her in this regard.

"We leave the anthropologist here. We can't be weighed down, and we also don't know what contaminants we might bring with us."

The surveyor nodded. At least she wasn't sentimental. There was nothing left of the anthropologist in that body, and we both knew it. I was trying very hard not to think of the anthropologist's last moments alive, of the terror she must have felt as she continued trying to perform a task that she had been willed to do by another, even though it meant her own death. *What had she seen? What had she been looking at before it all went dark?*

Before we turned back, I took one of the glass tubes strewn around the anthropologist. It contained just a trace of a thick, fleshlike substance that gleamed darkly golden. Perhaps she had gotten a useful sample after all, near the end.

As we ascended toward the light, I tried to distract myself. I kept reviewing my training over and over again, searching for a clue, for any scrap of information that might lead to some revelation about our discoveries. But I could find nothing, could only wonder at my own gullibility in thinking that I had been told anything at all of use. Always, the emphasis was on our own capabilities and knowledge base. Always, as I looked back, I could see that there had been an almost willful intent to obscure, to misdirect, disguised as concern that we not be frightened or overwhelmed.

The map had been the first form of misdirection, for what was a map but a way of emphasizing some things and making other things invisible? Always, we were directed to the map, to memorizing the details on the map. Our instructor, who remained nameless to us, drilled us for six long months on the position of the lighthouse relative to the base camp, the number of miles from one ruined patch of houses to another. The number of miles of coastline we would be expected to explore. Almost always in the context of the *lighthouse*, not the base camp. We became so comfortable with that map, with the dimensions of it, and the thought of what it contained that it stopped us from asking *why* or even *what*.

Why this stretch of coast? *What* might lie inside the lighthouse? *Why* was the camp set back into the forest, far from the lighthouse but fairly close to the tower (which, of course, did not exist on the map)—and had the base camp always been there? *What* lay beyond the map? Now that I knew the extent of the hypnotic suggestion that had been used on us, I realized that the focus on the map might have itself been an embedded cue. That if we did not ask questions, it was because we were programmed not to ask questions. That the lighthouse, representative or actual, might have been a subconscious trigger for a hypnotic suggestion—and that it might also have been the epicenter of whatever had spread out to become Area X.

My briefing on the ecology of that place had had a similar blinkered focus. I had spent most of my time becoming familiar with the natural transitional ecosystems, with the flora and fauna and the cross-pollination I could expect to find.

But I'd also had an intense refresher on fungi and lichen that, in light of the words on the wall, now stood out in my mind as being the true purpose of all of that study. If the map had been meant solely to distract, then the ecology research had been meant, after all, to truly prepare me. Unless I was being paranoid. But if I wasn't, it meant they knew about the tower, perhaps had always known about the tower.

From there, my suspicions grew. They had put us through grueling survival and weapons training, so grueling that most evenings we went right to sleep in our separate quarters. Even on those few occasions when we trained together, we were training apart. They took away our names in the second month, stripped them from us. The only names applied to things in Area X, and only in terms of their most general label. This, too, a kind of distraction from asking certain questions that could only be reached through knowing specific details. But the *right* specific details, not, for example, that there were six species of poisonous snakes in Area X. A reach, yes, but I was not in the mood to set aside even the most unlikely scenarios.

By the time we were ready to cross the border, we knew everything . . . and we knew nothing.

The psychologist wasn't there when we emerged, blinking into the sunlight, ripping off our masks and breathing in the fresh air. We had been ready for almost any scenario, but not for the psychologist's absence. It left us adrift for a while, afloat in that ordinary day, the sky so brightly blue, the stand of trees casting long shadows. I took out my earplugs and found I couldn't hear the beating of the tower's heartbeat at all. How what we had seen below could coexist with the mundane was baffling. It was as if we had come up too fast from a deep-sea dive but it was the memories of the creatures we had seen that had given us the bends. We just kept searching the environs for the psychologist, certain she was hiding, and half-hoping we would find her, because surely she had an explanation. It was, after a time, pathological to keep searching the same area around the tower. But for almost an hour we could not find a way to stop.

Finally I could not deny the truth.

"She's gone," I said.

"Maybe she's back at the base camp," the surveyor said.

"Would you agree that her absence is a sign of guilt?" I asked.

The surveyor spat into the grass, regarded me closely. "No, I would not. Maybe something happened to her. Maybe she needed to go back to the camp."

"You saw the footprints. You saw the body."

She motioned with her rifle. "Let's just get back to base camp."

I couldn't read her at all. I didn't know if she was turning on me or just cautious. Coming up aboveground had emboldened her, regardless, and I had preferred her uncertain.

But back at base camp, some of her resolve crumbled again. The psychologist wasn't there. Not only wasn't she there, but she had taken half of our supplies and most of the guns. Either that or buried them somewhere. So we knew the psychologist was still alive.

You must understand how I felt then, how the surveyor must have felt: We were scientists, trained to observe natural phenomena and the results of human activity. We had not been trained to encounter what appeared to be the uncanny. In unusual situations there can be a comfort in the presence of even someone you think might be your enemy. Now we had come close to the edges of something unprecedented, and less than a week into our mission we had lost not just the linguist at the border but our anthropologist and our psychologist.

"Okay, I give up," the surveyor said, throwing down her rifle and sagging into a chair in front of the anthropologist's tent as I rummaged around inside of it. "I'm going to believe you for now. I'm going to believe you because I don't really have a choice. Because I don't have any better theories. What should we do now?"

There still weren't any clues in the anthropologist's tent. The horror of what had happened to her was still hitting me. To be coerced into your own death. If I was right, the psychologist was a murderer, much more so than whatever had killed the anthropologist.

When I didn't answer the surveyor, she repeated herself, with extra emphasis: "So what the hell are we going to do now?"

Emerging from the tent, I said, "We examine the samples I took, we develop the photographs and go through them. Then, tomorrow, we probably go back down into the tower."

The surveyor gave a harsh laugh as she struggled to find words. Her face seemed to almost want to pull apart for a second, perhaps from the strain of fighting off the ghost of some hypnotic suggestion. Finally she got it out: "No. I'm not going back down into that place. And it's a *tunnel*, not a tower."

"What do you want to do instead?" I asked.

As if she'd broken through some barrier, the words now came faster, more determined. "We go back to the border and await extraction. We don't have the resources to continue, and if you're right the psychologist is out there right now plotting something, even if it's just what excuses to give us. And if she's not, if she's dead or injured because something attacked her, that's another reason to get the hell out." She had lit a cigarette, one of the few we'd been given. She blew two long plumes of smoke out of her nose.

"I'm not ready to go back," I told her. "Not yet." I wasn't near ready, despite what had happened.

"You prefer this place, you really do, don't you?" the surveyor said. It wasn't really a question; a kind of pity or disgust infused her voice. "You think this is going to last much longer? Let me tell you, even on military maneuvers designed to simulate negative outcomes, I've seen better odds."

Fear was driving her, even if she was right. I decided to steal my delaying tactics from the psychologist.

"Let's just look at what we brought back, and then we can decide what to do. You can always head back to the border tomorrow."

She took another drag on the cigarette, digesting that. The border was still a four-day hike away.

"True enough," she said, relenting for the moment.

I didn't say what I was thinking: That it might not be that simple. That she might make it back across the border only in the abstract sense that my husband had, stripped of what made her unique. But I didn't want her to feel as if she had no way out.

I spent the rest of the afternoon looking at samples under the microscope, on the makeshift table outside of my tent. The surveyor busied herself with developing the photographs in the tent that doubled as a darkroom, a frustrating process for anyone used to digital uploads. Then, while the photos were resting, she went back through the remnants of maps and documents the prior expedition had left at the base camp.

My samples told a series of cryptic jokes with punch lines I didn't understand.

The cells of the biomass that made up the words on the wall had an unusual structure, but they still fell within an acceptable range. Or, those cells were doing a magnificent job of mimicking certain species of saprotrophic organisms. I made a mental note to take a sample of the wall from behind the words. I had no idea how deeply the filaments had taken root, or if there were nodes beneath and those filaments were only sentinels.

The tissue sample from the hand-shaped creature resisted any interpretation, and that was strange but told me nothing. By which I mean I found no cells in the sample, just a solid amber surface with air bubbles in it. At the time, I interpreted this as a contaminated sample or evidence that this organism decomposed quickly. Another thought came to me too late to test: that, having absorbed the organism's spores, I was causing a reaction in the sample. I didn't have the medical facilities to run the kinds of diagnostics that might have revealed any further changes to my body or mind since the encounter.

Then there was the sample from the anthropologist's vial. I had left it for last for the obvious reasons. I had the surveyor take a section, put it on the slide, and write down what she saw through the microscope.

"Why?" she asked. "Why did you need me to do this?"

I hesitated. "Hypothetically . . . there could be contamination."

Such a hard face, jaw tight. "Hypothetically, why would you be any more or less contaminated than me?"

I shrugged. "No particular reason. I was the first one to find the words on the wall, though."

She looked at me as if I had spouted nonsense, laughed harshly. "We're in so much deeper than that. Do you really think those masks we wore are going to keep us safe? From whatever's going on here?" She was wrong—I thought she was wrong—but I didn't correct her. People trivialize or simplify data for so many reasons.

There was nothing else to be said. She went back to her work as I squinted through the microscope at the sample from whatever had killed the anthropologist. At first I didn't know what I was looking at because it was so unexpected. It was brain tissue—and not just any brain tissue. The cells were remarkably human, with some irregularities. My thought at the time was that the sample *had* been corrupted, but if so not by my presence: The surveyor's notes perfectly described what I saw, and when she looked at the sample again later she confirmed its unchanged nature.

I kept squinting through the microscope lens, and raising my head, and squinting again, as if I couldn't see the sample correctly. Then I settled down and stared at it until it became just a series of squiggles and circles. Was it really human? Was it *pretending* to be human? As I said, there were irregularities. And how had the anthropologist taken the sample? Just walked up to the *thing* with an ice-cream scoop and asked, "Can I take a biopsy of your brain?" No, the sample had to come from the margins, from the exterior. Which meant it couldn't be brain tissue, which meant it was definitely not human. I felt unmoored, drifting, once again.

About then, the surveyor strode over and threw the developed photographs down on my table. "Useless," she said.

Every photograph of the words on the wall was a riot of luminous, out-of-focus color. Every photograph of anything other than the words had come out as pure darkness. The few in-between photos were also out of focus. I knew this was probably because of the slow, steady breathing of the walls, which might also have been giving off some kind of heat or other agent of distortion. A thought that made me realize I had not taken a sample of the walls. I had recognized the words were organisms. I had known the walls were, too, but my brain had still registered *walls* as inert, part of a structure. Why sample them?

"I know," the surveyor said, misunderstanding my cursing. "Any luck with the samples?"

"No. No luck at all," I said, still staring at the photographs. "Anything in the maps and papers?"

The surveyor snorted. "Not a damn thing. Nothing. Except they all seem fixated on the lighthouse—watching the lighthouse, going to the lighthouse, living in the goddamn lighthouse."

"So we have nothing."

The surveyor ignored that, said, "What do we do now?" It was clear she hated asking the question.

"Eat dinner," I said. "Take a little stroll along the perimeter to make sure the psychologist isn't hiding in the bushes. Think about what we're doing tomorrow."

"I'll tell you one thing we're not doing tomorrow. We're not going back into the tunnel."

"Tower."

She glared at me.

There was no point in arguing with her.

At dusk, the familiar moaning came to us from across the salt-marsh flats as we ate our dinner around the campfire. I hardly noticed it, intent on my meal. The food tasted so good, and I did not know why. I gobbled it up, had seconds, while the surveyor, baffled, just stared at me. We had little or nothing to say to each other. Talking would have meant planning, and nothing I wanted to plan would please her.

The wind picked up, and it began to rain. I saw each drop fall as a perfect, faceted liquid diamond, refracting light even in the gloom, and I could smell the sea and picture the roiling waves. The wind was like something alive; it entered every pore of me and it, too, had a smell, carrying with it the earthiness of the marsh reeds. I had tried to ignore the change in the confined space of the tower, but my senses still seemed too acute, too sharp. I was adapting to it, but at times like this, I remembered that just a day ago I had been someone else.

We took turns standing watch. Loss of sleep seemed less foolhardy than letting the psychologist sneak up on us unannounced; she knew the location of every perimeter trip wire and we had no time to disarm and reset them. I let the surveyor take the first watch as a gesture of good faith.

In the middle of the night, the surveyor came in to wake me up for the second shift, but I was already awake because of the thunder. Grumpily, she headed off to bed. I doubt she trusted me; I just think she couldn't keep her eyes open a moment longer after the stresses of the day.

The rain renewed its intensity. I didn't worry that we'd be blown away—these tents were army regulation and could withstand anything short of a hurricane—but if I was going to be awake anyway, I wanted to experience the storm. So I walked outside, into the welter of the stinging water, the gusting pockets of wind. I already could hear the surveyor snoring in her tent; she probably had slept through much worse. The dull emergency lights glowed from the edges of the camp, making the tents into triangles of shadow. Even the darkness seemed more alive to me, surrounding me like something physical. I can't even say it was a sinister presence.

I felt in that moment as if it were all a dream—the training, my former life, the world I had left behind. None of that mattered anymore. Only this place mattered, only this moment, and not because the psychologist had hypnotized me. In the grip of that powerful emotion, I stared out toward the coast, through the jagged narrow spaces between the trees. There, a greater darkness gathered, the confluence of the night, the clouds, and the sea. Somewhere beyond, another border.

Then, through that darkness, I saw it: a flicker of orange light. Just a touch of illumination, too far up in the sky. This puzzled me, until I realized it must originate with the lighthouse. As I watched, the flicker moved to the left and up slightly before being snuffed out, then reappeared a few minutes later much higher, then was snuffed out for good. I waited for the light to return, but it never did. For some reason, the longer the light stayed out, the more restless I became, as if in this strange place a light—any sort of light—was a sign of civilization.

There had been a storm that final full day alone with my husband after he returned from the eleventh expedition. A day that had the clarity of dream, of something strange yet familiar—familiar routine but strange calmness, even more than I had become accustomed to before he left.

In those last weeks before the expedition, we had argued—violently. I had shoved him up against a wall, thrown things at him. Anything to break through the armor of resolve that I know now might have been thrust upon him by hypnotic suggestion. "If you go," I had told him, "you might not come back, and you can't be sure I'll be waiting for you if you do." Which had made him laugh, infuriatingly, and say, "Oh, have you been waiting for me all this time? Have I arrived yet?" He was set in his course by then, and any obstruction was a source of rough humor for him—and that would have been entirely natural, hypnosis or not. It was entirely in keeping with his personality to become set on something and follow it, regardless of the consequences. To let an impulse become a compulsion, especially if he thought he was contributing to a cause greater than himself. It was one reason he had stayed in the navy for a second tour.

Our relationship had been thready for a while, in part because he was gregarious and I preferred solitude. This had once been a source of strength in our relationship, but no longer. Not only had I found him handsome but I *admired* his confident, outgoing nature, his need to be around people—I recognized this as a healthy counterbalance to my personality. He had a good sense of humor, too, and when we first met, at a crowded local park, he snuck past my reticence by pretending we were both detectives working a case and were there to watch a suspect. Which led to making up facts about the lives of the busy hive of people buzzing around us, and then about each other.

At first, I must have seemed mysterious to him, my guardedness, my need to be alone, even after he thought he'd gotten inside my defenses. Either I was a puzzle to be solved or he just thought that once he got to know me better, he could still break through to some other place, some core where another person lived inside of me. During one of our fights, he admitted as much—tried to make his "volunteering" for the expedition a sign of how much I had pushed him away, before taking it back later, ashamed. I told him point-blank, so there would be no mistake: This person he wanted to know better did not exist; I was who I seemed to be from the outside. That would never change.

Early in our relationship, I had told my husband about the swimming pool as we lay in bed, something we did a lot of back then. He had been captivated, possibly even thinking there were more interesting revelations to come. He had pushed aside the parts that spoke of an isolated childhood, to focus entirely on the pool itself.

"I would have sailed boats on it."

"Captained by Old Flopper, no doubt," I replied. "And everything would have been happy and wonderful."

"No. Because I would have found you surly and willful and grim. Fairly grim."

"I would have found you frivolous and wished really hard for the turtles to scuttle your boat."

"If they did, I would just have rebuilt it even better and told everyone about the grim kid who talked to frogs."

I had never talked to the frogs; I despised anthropomorphizing animals. "So what has changed if we wouldn't have liked each other as kids?" I asked.

"Oh, I would have liked you despite that," he said, grinning. "You would have fascinated me, and I would have followed you anywhere. Without hesitation."

So we fit back then, in our odd way. We clicked, by being opposites, and took pride in the idea that this made us strong. We reveled in this construct so much, for so long, that it was a wave that did not break until after we were married . . . and then it destroyed us over time, in depressingly familiar ways.

But none of this—the good or the bad—mattered when he returned from the expedition. I asked no questions, did not bring up any of our past arguments. I knew when I woke up beside him that morning after his return that our time to-gether was already running out.

I made him breakfast, while outside the rain beat down, lightning cracking nearby. We sat at the kitchen table, which had a view, through the sliding-glass doors, of the backyard, and had an excruciatingly polite conversation over eggs and bacon. He admired the gray shape of the new bird feeder I had put in, and the water feature that now rippled with raindrops. I asked him if he had gotten enough sleep, and how he felt. I even asked again questions from the night before, like whether the journey back had been tough.

"No," he said, "effortless," flashing an imitation of his old infuriating smile.

"How long did it take?" I asked.

"No time at all." I couldn't read his expression, but in its blankness I sensed something mournful, something left inside that wanted to communicate but couldn't. My husband had never been mournful or melancholy as long as I had known him, and this frightened me a little.

He asked me how my research was going, and I told him about some of the new developments. At the time, I worked for a company devoted to the creation of natural products that broke down plastics and other nonbiodegradable sub-stances. It was boring. Before that, I had been out in the field, taking advantage of various research grants. Before that, I had been a radical environmentalist, participating in protests and employed by a nonprofit to call potential donors on the phone.

"And your work?" I asked, tentative, not sure how much more circling I could do, ready at a moment's notice to dart away from the mystery.

"Oh, you know," he said, as if he'd only been away a few weeks, as if I were a colleague, not his lover, his wife. "Oh, you know, the same as always. Nothing really new." He drank deeply from his orange juice—really drank to savor it so that for a minute or two nothing existed in the house but his enjoyment. Then he casually asked about other improvements around the house.

After breakfast, we sat out on the porch, watching the sheets of rain, the pud-dles collecting in the herb garden. We read for a while, then went back inside and made love. It was a kind of repetitive, trancelike fucking, comfortable only because the weather cocooned us. If I had been pretending up until that point, I couldn't fool myself any longer that my husband was entirely present.

Then it was lunch, and then television—I found a rerun of a two-man sailing race for him—and more banal talk. He asked about some of his friends, but I had no answers. I never saw them. They'd never really been my friends; I didn't cultivate friends, I had just inherited them from my husband.

We tried to play a board game and laughed at some of the sillier questions. Then weird gaps in his knowledge became apparent and we stopped, a kind of silence settling over us. He read the paper and caught up on his favorite magazines, watched the news. Or perhaps he only pretended to do those things.

When the rain stopped, I woke from a brief nap on the couch to find him gone from beside me. I tried not to panic when I checked every room and couldn't find him anywhere. I went outside and eventually found him around the side of the house. He was standing in front of the boat he had bought a few years back, which we could never fit in the garage. It was just a cruiser, about twenty feet long, but he loved it.

As I came and curled my arm around his, he had a puzzled, almost forlorn look on his face, as if he could remember that the boat was important to him but not why. He didn't acknowledge my presence, kept staring at the boat with a growing blank intensity. I could feel him trying to recall something important; I just didn't realize until much later that it had to do with me. That he could have told me something vital, then, there, if he could only have recalled what. So we just stood there, and although I could feel the heat and weight of him beside me, the steady sound of his breathing, we were living apart.

After a while, I couldn't take it—the sheer directionless anonymity of his distress, his silence. I led him back inside. He didn't stop me. He didn't protest. He didn't try to look back over his shoulder at the boat. I think that's when I made my decision. If he had only looked back. If he had just resisted me, even for a moment, it might have been different.

At dinner, as he was finishing, they came for him in four or five unmarked cars and a surveillance van. They did not come in rough or shouting, with handcuffs and weapons on display. Instead, they approached him with respect, one might almost say fear: the kind of watchful gentleness you might display if about to handle an unexploded bomb. He went without protest, and I let them take this stranger from my house.

I couldn't have stopped them, but I also didn't want to. The last few hours I had coexisted with him in a kind of rising panic, more and more convinced that whatever had happened to him in Area X had turned him into a shell, an automaton going through the motions. Someone I had never known. With every atypical act or word, he was driving me further from the memory of the person I had known, and despite everything that had happened, preserving that idea of him was important. That is why I called the special number he had left me for emergencies: I didn't know what to do with him, couldn't coexist with him any longer in this altered state. Seeing him leave I felt mostly a sense of relief, to be honest, not guilt at betrayal. What else could I have done?

As I have said, I visited him in the observation facility right up until the end. Even under hypnosis in those taped interviews, he had nothing new to say, really, unless it was kept from me. I remember mostly the repetitious sadness in his words. "I am walking forever on the path from the border to base camp. It is taking a long time, and I know it will take even longer to get back. There is no one with me. I am all by myself. The trees are not trees the birds are not birds and I am not me but just something that has been walking for a very long time . . ."

This was really the only thing I discovered in him after his return: a deep and unending solitude, as if he had been granted a gift that he didn't know what to do with. A gift that was poison to him and eventually killed him. But would it have killed me? That was the question that crept into my mind even as I stared into his eyes those last few times, willing myself to know his thoughts and failing.

As I labored at my increasingly repetitive job, in a sterile lab, I kept thinking about Area X, and how I would never know what it was like without going there. No one could really tell me, and no account could possibly be a substitute. So several months after my husband died, I volunteered for an Area X expedition. A spouse of a former expedition member had never signed up before. I think they accepted me in part because they wanted to see if that connection might make a difference. I think they accepted me as an experiment. But then again, maybe from the start they expected me to sign up.

By morning, it had stopped raining and the sky was a searing blue, almost devoid of clouds. Only the pine needles strewn across the top of our tents and the dirty puddles and fallen tree limbs on the ground told of the storm the night before. The brightness infecting my senses had spread to my chest; I can describe it no other way. Internally, there was a *brightness* in me, a kind of prickling energy and anticipation that pushed hard against my lack of sleep. Was this part of the change? But even so, it didn't matter—I had no way to combat what might be happening to me.

I also had a decision to make, finding myself torn between the lighthouse and the tower. Some part of the brightness wanted to return to darkness at once, and the logic of this related to nerve, or lack of it. To plunge right back into the tower, without thought, without planning, would be an act of faith, of sheer resolve or recklessness with nothing else behind it. But now I also knew that *someone* had been in the lighthouse the night before. If the psychologist had sought refuge there, and I could track her down, then I might gain more insight into the tower before exploring it further. This seemed of increasing importance, more so than the night before, because the number of unknowns the tower represented had multiplied tenfold. So by the time I talked to the surveyor, I had decided on the lighthouse.

The morning had the scent and feel of a fresh start, but it was not to be. If the surveyor had wanted no part of a return to the tower, then she equally had no interest in the lighthouse.

"You don't want to find out if the psychologist is there?"

The surveyor gave me a look as if I had said something idiotic. "Holed up in a high position with clear lines of sight in every direction? In a place they've told us has a weapons cache? I'll take my chances here. If you were smart, you'd do the same. You might 'find out' that you don't like a bullet hole in the head. Besides, she might be somewhere else."

Her stubbornness tore at me. I didn't want to split up for purely practical reasons—it was true we had been told prior expeditions had stored weapons at the lighthouse—and because I believed it more likely that the surveyor would try to go home without me there.

"It's the lighthouse or the tower," I said, trying to sidestep the issue. "And it would be better for us if we found the psychologist before we went back down into the tower. She saw whatever killed the anthropologist. She knows more than she's told us." The unspoken thought: That perhaps if a day passed, or two, whatever lived in the tower, slowly making words on the wall, would have disappeared or gotten so far ahead of us we would never catch up. But that brought to mind a disturbing image of the tower as endless, with infinite levels descending into the earth.

The surveyor folded her arms. "You really don't get it, do you? This mission is over."

Was she afraid? Did she just not like me enough to say yes? Whatever the reason, her opposition angered me, as did the smug look on her face.

In the moment, I did something that I regret now. I said, "There's no *reward in the risk* of going back to the tower right now."

I thought I had been subtle in my intonation of one of the psychologist's hypnotic cues, but a shudder passed over the surveyor's face, a kind of temporary disorientation. When it cleared, the look that remained told me she understood what I had tried to do. It wasn't even a look of surprise; more that in her mind I had confirmed an impression of me that had been slowly forming but was now set. Now, too, I had learned that hypnotic cues only worked for the psychologist.

"You'd do anything, wouldn't you, to get your way," the surveyor said, but the fact was: She held the rifle. What weapon did I really have? And I told myself it was because I didn't want the anthropologist's death to be meaningless that I had suggested this course of action.

When I did not reply, she sighed, then said, with weariness in her voice, "You know, I finally figured it out while I was developing those useless photographs. What bothered me the most. It's not the thing in the tunnel or the way you conduct yourself or anything the psychologist did. It's this rifle I'm holding. This damn rifle. I stripped it down to clean it and found it was made of thirty-year-old parts, cobbled together. *Nothing* we brought with us is from the present. Not our clothes, not our shoes. It's all old junk. Restored crap. We've been living in the past this whole time. In some sort of *reenactment*. And why?" She made a derisive sound. "You don't even know why."

It was as much as she'd ever said to me at one time. I wanted to say that this information registered as little more than the mildest of surprises in the hierarchy of what we had thus far discovered. But I didn't. All I had left was to be succinct.

"Will you remain here until I return?" I asked.

This was now the essential question, and I didn't like the speed of her reply, or its tone.

"Whatever you want."

"Don't say anything you can't back up," I said. I had long ago stopped believing in promises. Biological imperatives, yes. Environmental factors, yes. Promises, no.

"Fuck off," she said.

So that's how we left it—her leaning back in that rickety chair, holding her assault rifle, as I went off to discover the source of the light I had seen the night before. I had with me a knapsack full of food and water, along with two of the guns, equipment to take samples, and one of the microscopes. Somehow I felt safer taking a microscope with me. Some part of me, too, no matter how I had tried to convince the surveyor to come with me, welcomed the chance to explore alone, to not be dependent on, or worried about, anyone else.

I looked back a couple of times before the trail twisted away, and the surveyor was still sitting there, staring at me like a distorted reflection of who I'd been just days before.

03: IMMOLATION

Now a strange mood took hold of me, as I walked silent and alone through the last of the pines and the cypress knees that seemed to float in the black water, the gray moss that coated everything. It was as if I traveled through the landscape with the sound of an expressive and intense aria playing in my ears. Everything was imbued with emotion, awash in it, and I was no longer a biologist but somehow the crest of a wave building and building but never crashing to shore. I saw with such new eyes the subtleties of the transition to the marsh, the salt flats. As the trail became a raised berm, dull, algae-choked lakes spread out to the right and a canal flanked it to the left. Rough channels of water meandered out in a maze through a forest of reeds on the canal side, and islands, oases of wind-contorted trees, appeared in the distance like sudden revelations. The stooped and blackened appearance of these trees was shocking against the vast and shimmering gold-brown of the reeds. The strange quality of the light upon this habitat, the stillness of it all, the sense of *waiting*, brought me halfway to a kind of ecstasy.

Beyond, the lighthouse stood, and before that, I knew, the remains of a village, also marked on the map. But in front of me was the trail, strewn at times with oddly tortured-looking pieces of heavy white driftwood flung far inland from past hurricanes. Tiny red grasshoppers inhabited the long grass in legions, with only a few frogs present to feast on them, and flattened grass tunnels marked where the huge reptiles had, after bathing in the sun, slid back into the water. Above, raptors searched the ground below for prey, circling as if in geometric patterns so controlled was their flight.

In that cocoon of timelessness, with the lighthouse seeming to remain distant no matter how long I walked, I had more time to think about the tower and our expedition. I felt that I had abdicated my responsibility to that point, which was to consider those elements found inside of the tower as part of a vast biological entity that might or might not be terrestrial. But contemplating the sheer enormity of that idea on a macro level would have broken my mood like an avalanche crashing into my body.

So . . . what did I know? What were the specific details? An . . . organism . . . was writing living words along the interior walls of the tower, and may have been doing so for a very long time. Whole ecosystems had been born and now flourished among the words, dependent on them, before dying off as the words faded. But this was a side effect of creating the right conditions, a viable habitat. It was important only in that the adaptations of the creatures living in the words could tell me something about the tower. For example, the spores I had inhaled, which pointed to a *truthful seeing*.

I was brought up short by this idea, the wind-lashed marsh reeds a wide, blurred ripple all around me. I had assumed the psychologist had hypnotized me into seeing the tower as a physical construction not a biological entity, and that an effect of the spores had made me resistant to this hypnotic suggestion. But what if the process had been more complex? What if, by whatever means, the *tower* emanated an effect, too—one that constituted a kind of defensive mimicry, and the spores had made me immune to that illusion?

Telescoping out from this context, I had several questions and few answers. What role did the *Crawler* serve? (I had decided it was important to assign a name to the maker-of-words.) What was the purpose of the physical "recitation" of the words? Did the actual words matter, or would any words do? Where had the words come from? What was the interplay between the words and the tower-creature? Put another way: Were the words a form of symbiotic or parasitic communication between the Crawler and the Tower? Either the Crawler was an *emissary* of the Tower or the Crawler had originally existed independent from it and come into its orbit later. But without the damned missing sample of the Tower wall, I couldn't really begin to guess.

Which brought me back to the words. *Where lies the strangling fruit that came from the hand of the sinner* . . . Wasps and birds and other nest-builders often used some core, irreplaceable substance or material to create their structures but would also incorporate whatever they could find in their immediate environment. This might explain the seemingly random nature of the words. It was just building material, and perhaps this explained why our superiors had forbidden high-tech being brought into Area X, because they knew it could be used in unknown and powerful ways by whatever occupied this place.

Several new ideas detonated inside me as I watched a marsh hawk dive into the reeds and come up with a rabbit struggling in its talons. First, that the words—the line of them, their physicality—were absolutely essential to the well-being of either the Tower or the Crawler, or both. I had seen the faint skeletons of so many past lines of writing that one might assume some biological imperative for the Crawler's work. This process might feed into the reproductive cycle of the Tower or the Crawler. Perhaps the Crawler depended upon it, and it had some subsidiary benefit to the Tower. Or vice versa. Perhaps words didn't matter because it was a process of *fertilization*, only completed when the entire left-hand wall of the Tower had a line of words running along its length.

Despite my attempt to sustain the aria in my head, I experienced a jarring return to reality as I worked through these possibilities. Suddenly I was just a person trudging across a natural landscape of a type I had seen before. There were too many variables, not enough data, and I was making some base assumptions that might not be true. For one thing, in all of this I assumed that neither Crawler nor Tower was intelligent, in the sense of *possessing free will*. My procreation theory would still apply in such a widening context, but there were other possibilities. The role of ritual, for example, in certain cultures and societies. How I longed for access to the anthropologist's mind now, even though in studying social insects I had gained some insight into the same areas of scientific endeavor.

And if not ritual, I was back to the purposes of communication, this time in a conscious sense, not a biological one. What could the words on the wall communicate to the Tower? I had to assume, or thought I did, that the Crawler didn't just live in the Tower—it went far afield to gather the words, and it had to assimilate them, even if it didn't understand them, before it came back to the Tower. The Crawler had to in a sense *memorize* them, which was a form of absorption. The strings of sentences on the Tower's walls could be *evidence* brought back by the Crawler to be analyzed by the Tower.

But there is a limit to thinking about even a small piece of something monumental. You still see the shadow of the whole rearing up behind you, and you become lost in your thoughts in part from the panic of realizing the *size* of that imagined leviathan. I had to leave it there, compartmentalized, until I could write it all down, and seeing it on the page, begin to divine the true meaning. And now the lighthouse had finally gotten larger on the horizon. This presence weighed on me as I realized that the surveyor had been correct about at least one thing. Anyone within the lighthouse would see me coming for miles. Then, too, that other effect of the spores, the brightness in my chest, continued to sculpt me as I walked, and by the time I reached the deserted village that told me I was halfway to the lighthouse, I believed I could have run a marathon. I did not trust that feeling. I felt, in so many ways, that I was being lied to.

Having seen the preternatural calm of the members of the eleventh expedition, I had often thought during our training of the benign reporting from the first expedition. Area X, before the ill-defined Event that locked it behind the border thirty years ago and made it subject to so many inexplicable occurrences, had been part of a wilderness that lay adjacent to a military base. People had still lived there, on what amounted to a wildlife refuge, but not many, and they tended to be the tight-lipped descendants of fisherfolk. Their disappearance might have seemed to some a simple intensifying of a process begun generations before.

When Area X first appeared, there was vagueness and confusion, and it is still true that out in the world not many people know that it exists. The government's version of events emphasized a localized environmental catastrophe stemming from experimental military research. This story leaked into the public sphere over a period of several months so that, like the proverbial frog in a hot pot, people found the news entering their consciousness gradually as part of the general daily noise of media oversaturation about ongoing ecological devastation. Within a year or two, it had become the province of conspiracy theorists and other fringe elements. By the time I volunteered and was given the security clearance to have a firm picture of the truth, the idea of an "Area X" lingered in many people's minds like a dark fairy tale, something they did not want to think about too closely. If they thought about it at all. We had so many other problems.

During training, we were told that the first expedition went in two years after the Event, after scientists found a way to breach the border. It was the first expedition that set up the base-camp perimeter and provided a rough map of Area X, confirming many of the landmarks. They discovered a pristine wilderness devoid of any human life. They found what some might call a preternatural silence.

"I felt as if I were both freer than ever before and more constrained," one member of the expedition said. "I felt as if I could do anything *as long as I did not mind being watched.*"

Others mentioned feelings of euphoria and extremes of sexual desire, for which there was no explanation and which, ultimately, their superiors found unimportant.

If one could spot anomalies in their reports, these anomalies lay at the fringes. For one thing, we never saw their journals; instead, they offered up their accounts in long recorded interviews. This, to me, hinted at some avoidance of their direct experience, although at the time I also thought perhaps I was being paranoid, in a nonclinical sense.

Some of them offered descriptions of the abandoned village that seemed inconsistent to me. The warping and level of ruination depicted a place abandoned for much longer than a few years. But if someone had caught this strangeness earlier, any such observation had been stricken from the record.

I am convinced now that I and the rest of the expedition were given access to these records for the simple reason that, for certain kinds of classified information, it did not matter what we knew or didn't know. There was only one logical conclusion: Experience told our superiors that few if any of us would be coming back.

The deserted village had so sunk into the natural landscape of the coast that I did not see it until I was upon it. The trail dipped into a depression of sorts, and there lay the village, fringed by more stunted trees. Only a few roofs remained on the twelve or thirteen houses, and the trail through had crumbled into porous rubble. Some outer walls still stood, dark rotting wood splotched with lichen, but for the most part these walls had fallen away and left me with a peculiar glimpse of the interiors: the remains of chairs and tables, a child's toys, rotted clothing, ceiling beams brought to earth, covered in moss and vines. There was a sharp smell of chemicals in that place, and more than one dead animal, decomposing into the mulch. Some of the houses had, over time, slid into the canal to the left and looked in their skeletal remains like creatures struggling to leave the water. It all seemed like something that had happened a century ago, and what was left were just vague recollections of the event.

But in what had been kitchens or living rooms or bedrooms, I also saw a few peculiar eruptions of moss or lichen, rising four, five, feet tall, misshapen, the vegetative matter forming an approximation of limbs and heads and torsos. As if there had been runoff from the material, too heavy for gravity, that had congregated at the foot of these objects. Or perhaps I imagined this effect.

One particular tableau struck me in an almost emotional way. Four such eruptions, one "standing" and three decomposed to the point of "sitting" in what once must have been a living room with a coffee table and a couch—all facing some point at the far end of the room where lay only the crumbling soft brick remains of a fireplace and chimney. The smell of lime and mint unexpectedly arose, cutting through the must, the loam.

I did not want to speculate on that tableau, its meaning, or what element of the past it represented. No sense of peace emanated from that place, only a feeling of something left unresolved or still in progress. I wanted to move on, but first I took samples. I had a need to document what I had found, and a photograph didn't seem sufficient, given how the others had turned out. I cut a piece of the moss from the "forehead" of one of the eruptions. I took splinters of the wood. I even scraped the flesh of the dead animals—a stricken fox, curled up and dry, along with a kind of rat that must have died only a day or two before.

It was just after I had left the village that a peculiar thing happened. I was startled to see a sudden double line coming down the canal toward me, cutting through the water. My binoculars were no use as the water was opaque from the glare of the sun. Otters? Fish? Something else? I pulled out my gun.

Then the dolphins breached, and it was almost as vivid a dislocation as that first descent into the Tower. I knew that the dolphins here sometimes ventured in from the sea, had adapted to the freshwater. But when the mind expects a certain range of possibilities, any explanation that falls outside of that expectation can surprise. Then something more wrenching occurred. As they slid by, the nearest one rolled slightly to the side, and it stared at me with an eye that did not, in that brief flash, resemble a dolphin eye to me. It was painfully human, almost familiar. In an instant that glimpse was gone and they had submerged again, and I had no way to verify what I had seen. I stood there, watched those twinned lines disappear up the canal, back toward the deserted village. I had the unsettling thought that the natural world around me had become a kind of camouflage.

A little shaken, I continued toward the lighthouse, which now loomed larger, almost heavy, its black-and-white stripes topped with red making it somehow authoritarian. I would have no further shelter before I reached my destination. I would stand out to whoever or whatever watched from that vantage as something unnatural in that landscape, something that was foreign. Perhaps even a threat.

It was almost noon by the time I reached the lighthouse. I had been careful to drink water and have a snack on my journey, but I still arrived weary; perhaps the lack of sleep had caught up with me. But then, too, the last three hundred yards to reach the lighthouse were tension-filled, as I kept remembering the surveyor's warning. I had a gun out, held down by my side, for all the good it would do against a high-powered rifle. I kept looking at the little window halfway up its swirled black-and-white surface, and then to the large panoramic windows at the top, alert for any movement.

The lighthouse was positioned just before a natural crest of the dunes that resembled a curled wave facing the ocean, the beach spread out beyond. Up close it gave the strong appearance of having been converted into a fortress, a fact conveniently left out of our training. This only confirmed the impression I had formed from farther out, because although the grass was still long, no trees at all grew along the trail from about a quarter mile out; I had found only old stumps. When within an eighth mile, I had taken a look with my binoculars and noticed an approximately ten-foot circular wall rising from the landward side of the light-house that had clearly not been part of the original construction.

On the seaward side, another wall, an even stouter-looking fortification high on the crumbling dune, topped with broken glass and, as I drew near, I could see crenellations that created lines of sight for rifles. It was all in danger of falling down the slope onto the beach below. But for it not to have done so already, who-ever had built it must have dug its foundations deep. It appeared that some past defenders of the lighthouse had been at war with the sea. I did not like this wall because it provided evidence of a very specific kind of insanity.

At some point, too, someone had taken the time and effort to rappel down the sides of the lighthouse and attach jagged shards of glass with some strong glue or other adhesive. These glass daggers started about one-third of the way up and continued to the penultimate level, just below the glass-enclosed beacon. At that point, a kind of metal collar extended out a good two or three feet, and this de-fensive element had been enhanced with rusty barbed wire.

Someone had tried very hard to keep others out. I thought of the Crawler and the words on the wall. I thought of the fixation with the lighthouse in the fragments of notes left by the last expedition. But despite these discordant elements, I was glad to reach the shadow of that cool, dank wall around the landward side of the lighthouse. From that angle, no one could shoot at me from the top, or the window in the middle. I had passed through the first gauntlet. If the psychologist was inside, she had decided against violence for now.

The defensive wall on the landward side had reached a level of disrepair that reflected years of neglect. A large, irregular hole led to the lighthouse's front door. That door had exploded inward and only fragments of wood clung to the rusted hinges. A purple flowering vine had colonized the lighthouse wall and curled itself around the remains of the door on its left side. There was comfort in that, for whatever had happened with such violence must have occurred long ago.

The darkness beyond, however, made me wary. I knew from the floor plan I had seen during training that this bottom level of the lighthouse had three outer rooms, with the stairs leading to the top somewhere to the left, and that to the right the rooms opened up into a back area with at least one more larger space. Plenty of places for someone to hide.

I picked up a stone and half threw, half rolled it onto the floor beyond those crushed double doors. It clacked and spun across tile and disappeared from view. I heard no other sound, no movement, no suggestion of breathing beyond my own. Gun still drawn, I entered as quietly as I was able, sliding with my shoulder along the left-hand wall, searching for the entry point to the stairs leading upward.

The outer rooms at the base of the lighthouse were empty. The sound of the wind was muffled, the walls thick, and only two small windows toward the front brought any light inside; I had to use my flashlight. As my eyes adjusted, the sense of devastation, of loneliness, grew and grew. The purple flowering vine ended just inside, unable to thrive in the darkness. There were no chairs. The tiles of the floor were covered in dirt and debris. No personal effects remained in those outer rooms. In the middle of a wide-open space, I found the stairs. No one stood on those steps to watch me, but I had the impression someone could have been there a moment before. I thought about climbing to the top first rather than exploring the back rooms, but then decided against it. Better to think like the surveyor, with her military training, and clear the area now, even though someone could always come in the front door while I was up there.

The back room told a different story than the front rooms did. My imagination could only reconstruct what might have happened in the broadest, crudest terms. Here stout oak tables had been overturned to form defensive barricades. Some of the tables were full of bullet holes and others appeared half-melted or shredded by gunfire. Beyond the remains of the tables, the dark splotches across the walls and pooled on the floor told of unspeakable and sudden violence. Dust had settled over everything, along with the cool, flat smell of slow decay, and I could see rat droppings and signs of a cot or a bed having been placed in a corner at some later date . . . although who could have slept among such reminders of a massacre? Someone, too, had carved their initials into one of the tables: "R.S. was here." The marks looked fresher than the rest of it. Maybe you carved your initials when visiting a war monument, if you were insensitive. Here it stank of bravado to drown out fear.

The stairs awaited, and to quell my rising nausea, I headed back to them and began to climb. I had put my gun away by then, since I needed that hand for balance, but I wished I had the surveyor's assault rifle. I would have felt safer.

It was a strange ascent, in contrast to my descents into the Tower. The brackish quality of the light against those graying interior walls was better than the phosphorescence of the Tower, but what I found on these walls unnerved me just as much, if in a different way. More bloodstains, mostly thick smudges as if several people had bled out while trying to escape attackers from below. Sometimes dribbles of blood. Sometimes a spray.

Words had been written on these walls, but nothing like the words in the Tower. More initials, but also little obscene pictures and a few phrases of a more personal nature. Some longer hints of what might have transpired: "4 boxes of foodstuffs 3 boxes of medical supplies and drinking water for 5 days if rationed; enough bullets for all of us if necessary." Confessions, too, which I won't document here but that had the sincerity and weight of having been written immediately before, or during, moments when the individuals must have thought death was upon them. So many needing so much to communicate what amounted to so little.

Things found on the stairs . . . a discarded shoe . . . a magazine from an automatic pistol . . . a few moldy vials of samples long rotted or turned to rancid liquid . . . a crucifix that looked like it had been dislodged from the wall . . . a clipboard, the wooden part soggy and the metal part deep orange-red from rust . . . and, worst of all, a dilapidated toy rabbit with ragged ears. Perhaps a good-luck symbol smuggled in on an expedition. There had been no children in Area X since the border had come down, as far as I knew.

At roughly the halfway point, I came to a landing, which must have been where I had first seen the flicker of light the night before. The silence still dominated, and I had heard no hint of movement above me. The light was better because of the windows to left and right. Here the blood spatter abruptly cut off, although bullet holes riddled the walls. Bullet casings littered the floor, but someone had taken the time to sweep them off to the sides, leaving the path to the stairs above clear. To the left lay a stack of guns and rifles, some of them ancient, some of them not army-issue. It was hard to tell if anyone had been at them recently. Thinking about what the surveyor had said, I wondered when I would encounter a blunderbuss or some other terrible joke.

Otherwise, there was just the dust and the mold, and a tiny square window looking down on the beach and the reeds. Opposite it, a faded photograph in a broken frame, dangling from a nail. The smudged glass was cracked and half-covered in specks of green mold. The black-and-white photograph showed two men standing at the base of the lighthouse, with a girl off to the side. A circle had been drawn with a marker around one of the men. He looked about fifty years old and wore a fisherman's cap. A sharp eagle's eye gleamed out from a heavy face, the left eye lost to his squint. A thick beard hid all but a hint of a firm chin under it. He didn't smile, but he didn't frown, either. I'd had experience enough with lighthouse keepers to know one when I saw one. But there was also some quality to him, perhaps just because of the strange way the dust framed his face, that made me think of him as the lighthouse keeper. Or perhaps I'd already spent too much time in that place, and my mind was seeking any answer, even to simple questions.

The rounded bulk of the lighthouse behind the three was bright and sharp, the door on the far right in good repair. Nothing like what I had encountered, and I wondered when the photo had been taken. How many years between the photograph and the start of it all. How many years had the lighthouse keeper kept to his schedule and his rituals, lived in that community, gone to the local bar or pub. Perhaps he'd had a wife. Perhaps the girl in the photo was his daughter. Perhaps he'd been a popular man. Or solitary. Or a little of both. Regardless, none of it had mattered in the end.

I stared at him from across the years, trying to tell from the moldy photograph, from the line of his jaw and the reflection of light in his eyes, how he might have reacted, what his last hours might have been like. Perhaps he'd left in time, but probably not. Perhaps he was even moldering on the ground floor in a forgotten corner. Or, and I experienced a sudden shudder, maybe he was waiting for me above, at the top. In some form. I took the photograph out of its frame, shoved it in my pocket. The lighthouse keeper would come with me, although he hardly counted as a good-luck charm. As I left the landing, I had the peculiar thought that I was not the first to pocket the photo, that someone would always come behind to replace it, to circle the lighthouse keeper again.

I continued to encounter additional signs of violence the higher I went, but no more bodies. The closer I came to the top, the more I began to have the sense that someone had lived here recently. The mustiness gave way to the scent of sweat, but also a smell like soap. The stairs had less debris on them, and the walls were clean. By the time I was bending over the last narrow stretch of steps out into the lantern room, the ceiling grown suddenly close, I was sure I would emerge to find someone staring at me.

So I took out my gun again. But, again, no one was there—just a few chairs, a rickety table with a rug beneath it, and the surprise that the thick glass here was still intact. The beacon glass itself lay dull and dormant in the center of the room. You could see for miles to all sides. I stood there for a moment, looking back the way I had come: at the trail that had brought me, at the shadow in the distance that might have been the village, and then to the right, across the last of the marsh, the transition to scrubland and the gnarled bushes punished by the wind off the sea. They, clinging to the soil, stopped it from eroding and helped bulwark the dunes and the sea oats that came next. It was a gentle slope from there to the glittering beach, the surf, and the waves.

A second look, and from the direction of base camp amid the swamp and far distant pines, I could see strands of black smoke, which could have meant anything. But I also could see, from the location of the Tower, a kind of brightness of its own, a sort of refracted phosphorescence, that did not bear thinking about. That I could see it, that I had an affinity to it, agitated me. I was certain no one else left here, not the surveyor, not the psychologist, could see that stirring of the inexplicable.

I turned my attention to the chairs, the table, searching for whatever might give me insight into . . . anything. After about five minutes, I thought to pull back the rug. A square trapdoor measuring about four feet per side lay hidden there. The latch was set into the wood of the floor. I pushed the table out of the way with a terrible rending sound that made me grit my teeth. Then, swiftly, in case someone waited down there, I threw open the trapdoor, shouting out something inane like "I've got a gun!" aiming my weapon with one hand and my flashlight with the other.

I had the distant sense of the weight of my gun dropping to the floor, my flashlight shaking in my hand, though somehow I held on to it. I could not believe what I was staring down at, and I felt lost. The trapdoor opened onto a space about fifteen feet deep and thirty feet wide. The psychologist had clearly been here, for her knapsack, several weapons, bottles of water, and a large flashlight lay off to the left side. But of the psychologist herself there was no sign.

No, what had me gasping for breath, what felt like a punch in the stomach as I dropped to my knees, was the huge mound that dominated the space, a kind of insane midden. I was looking at a pile of papers with hundreds of journals on top of it—just like the ones we had been issued to record our observations of Area X. Each with a job title written on the front. Each, as it turned out, filled with writing. Many, many more than could possibly have been filed by only twelve expeditions.

Can you really imagine what it was like in those first moments, peering down into that dark space, and *seeing that*? Perhaps you can. Perhaps you're staring at it now.

My third and best field assignment out of college required that I travel to a remote location on the western coast, to a curled hook of land at the farthest extremity from civilization, in an area that teetered between temperate and arctic climates. Here the earth had disgorged huge rock formations and old-growth rain forest had sprouted up around them. This world was always moist, the annual rainfall more than seventy inches a year, and not seeing droplets of water on leaves was an extraordinary event. The air was so amazingly clean and the vegetation so dense, so richly green, that every spiral of fern seemed designed to make me feel at peace with the world. Bears and panthers and elk lived in those forests, along with a multitude of bird species. The fish in the streams were mercury-free and enormous.

I lived in a village of about three hundred souls near the coast. I had rented a cottage next to a house at the top of a hill that had belonged to five generations of fisherfolk. A husband and wife, childless, owned the property, and they had the kind of severely laconic quality common to the area. I made no friends there, and I wasn't sure that even long-standing neighbors were friends, either. Only in the local pub that everyone frequented, after a few pints, would you see signs of friendliness and camaraderie. But violence lived in the pub, too, and I kept away most of the time. I was four years away from meeting my future husband, and at the time I wasn't looking for much of anything from anyone.

I had plenty to keep me busy. Every day I drove the hellish winding road, rutted and treacherous even when dry, that led me to the place they called simply Rock Bay. There, sheets of magma that lay beyond the rough beaches had been worn smooth over millions of years and become pitted with tidal pools. At low tide in the morning, I would photograph those tidal pools, take measurements, and catalogue the life found within them, sometimes staying through part of high tide, wading in my rubber boots, the spray from the waves that smashed over the lip of the ledge drenching me.

A species of mussels found nowhere else lived in those tidal pools, in a symbiotic relationship with a fish called a gartner, after its discoverer. Several species of marine snails and sea anemones lurked there, too, and a tough little squid I nicknamed Saint Pugnacious, eschewing its scientific name, because the danger music of its white-flashing luminescence made its mantle look like a pope's hat.

I could easily lose hours there, observing the hidden life of tidal pools, and sometimes I marveled at the fact that I had been given such a gift: not just to lose myself in the present moment so utterly but also to have such solitude, which was all I had ever craved during my studies, my practice to reach this point.

Even then, though, during the drives back, I was grieving the anticipated end of this happiness. Because I knew it had to end eventually. The research grant was only for two years, and who really would care about mussels longer than that, and it's true my research methods could be eccentric. These were the kinds of thoughts I'd have as the expiration date came nearer and the prospects looked dimmer and dimmer for renewal. Against my better judgment, I began to spend more and more time in the pub. I'd wake in the morning, my head fuzzy, sometimes with someone I knew but who was a stranger just leaving, and realize I was one day closer to the end of it all. Running through it, too, was a sense of relief, not as strong as the sadness, but the thought, counter to everything else I felt, that this way I would not become that person the locals saw out on the rocks and still thought of as an outsider. *Oh, that's just the old biologist. She's been here for ages, going crazy studying those mussels. She talks to herself, mutters to herself at the bar, and if you say a kind word . . .*

When I saw those hundreds of journals, I felt for a long moment that I had become that old biologist after all. That's how the madness of the world tries to colonize you: from the outside in, forcing you to live in its reality.

Reality encroaches in other ways, too. At some point during our relationship, my husband began to call me the ghost bird, which was his way of teasing me for not being present enough in his life. It would be said with a kind of creasing at the corner of his lips that almost formed a thin smile, but in his eyes I could see the reproach. If we went to bars with his friends, one of his favorite things to do, I would volunteer only what a prisoner might during an interrogation. They weren't *my* friends, not really, but also I wasn't in the habit of engaging in small talk, nor in broad talk, as I liked to call it. I didn't care about politics except in how politics impinged upon the environment. I wasn't religious. All of my hobbies were bound up in my work. I lived for the work, and I thrilled with the power of that focus but it was also deeply personal. I didn't like to talk about my research. I didn't wear makeup or care about new shoes or the latest music. I'm sure my husband's friends found me taciturn, or worse. Perhaps they even found me unsophisticated, or "strangely uneducated" as I heard one of them say, although I don't know if he was referring to me.

I enjoyed the bars, but not for the same reasons as my husband. I loved the late-night slow burn of *being out*, my mind turning over some problem, some piece of data, while able to appear sociable but still existing apart. He worried too much about me, though, and my need for solitude ate into his enjoyment of talking to friends, who were mostly from the hospital. I would see him trail off in mid-sentence, gazing at me for some sign of my own contentment, as, off to the side, I drank my whiskey neat. "Ghost bird," he would say later, "did you have fun?" I'd nod and smile.

But fun for me was sneaking off to peer into a tidal pool, to grasp the intricacies of the creatures that lived there. Sustenance for me was tied to ecosystem and habitat, orgasm the sudden realization of the interconnectivity of living things. Observation had always meant more to me than interaction. He knew all of this, I think. But I never could express myself that well to him, although I did try, and he did listen. And yet, I was *nothing but* expression in other ways. My sole gift or talent, I believe now, was that places could impress themselves upon me, and I could become a part of them with ease. Even a bar was a type of ecosystem, if a crude one, and to someone entering, someone without my husband's agenda, that person could have seen me sitting there and had no trouble imagining that I was happy in my little bubble of silence. Would have had no trouble believing I fit in.

Yet even as my husband wanted me to be assimilated in a sense, the irony was that *he* wanted to stand out. Seeing that huge pile of journals, this was another thing I thought of: That he had been wrong for the eleventh expedition because of this quality. That here were the indiscriminate accounts of so many souls, and that his account *couldn't possibly stand out*. That, in the end, he'd been reduced to a state that approximated my own.

Those journals, flimsy gravestones, confronted me with my husband's death all over again. I dreaded finding his, dreaded knowing his true account, not the featureless, generic mutterings he had given to our superiors upon his return.

"Ghost bird, do you love me?" he whispered once in the dark, before he left for his expedition training, even though he was the ghost. "Ghost bird, do you need me?" I loved him, but I didn't need him, and I thought that was the way it was supposed to be. A ghost bird might be a hawk in one place, a crow in another, depending on the context. The sparrow that shot up into the blue sky one morning might transform mid-flight into an osprey the next. This was the way of things here. There were no reasons so mighty that they could override the desire to be in accord with the tides and the passage of seasons and the rhythms underlying everything around me.

The journals and other materials formed a moldering pile about twelve feet high and sixteen feet wide that in places near the bottom had clearly turned to compost, the paper rotting away. Beetles and silverfish tended to those archives, and tiny black cockroaches with always moving antennae. Toward the base, and spilling out at the edges, I saw the remains of photographs and dozens of ruined cassette tapes mixed in with the mulch of pages. There, too, I saw evidence of rats. I would have to lower myself down into the midden by means of the ladder nailed to the lip of the trapdoor and trudge through a collapsing garbage hill of disintegrating pulp to uncover anything at all. The scene obliquely embodied the scrap of writing I had encountered on the Tower wall: . . . *the seeds of the dead to share with the worms that gather in the darkness and surround the world with the power of their lives . . .*

I overturned the table and laid it across the narrow entrance to the stairwell. I had no idea where the psychologist had gotten to, but I didn't want her or anyone else surprising me. If someone tried to move the table from below, I would hear it and have time to climb up to greet them with my gun. I also had a sensation I can in hindsight attribute to the brightness growing within me: of a *presence* pressing up from below, impinging on the edges of my senses. A prickling crept across my skin at unexpected times, for no good reason.

I didn't like that the psychologist had stashed all of her gear down with the journals, including what appeared to be most or all of her weapons. For the moment, though, I had to put the puzzle of that out of my mind, along with the still-reverberating tremors from the certain knowledge that most of the training the Southern Reach had given us had been based on a lie. As I lowered myself into that cool, dark, sheltered space beneath, I felt the pull of the brightness within me even more acutely. That was harder to ignore, since I didn't know what it meant.

My flashlight, along with the natural light from the open trapdoor, revealed that the walls of the room were rife with striations of mold, some of which formed dull stripes of red and green. From below, the way the midden spilled out in ripples and hillocks of paper became more apparent. Torn pages, crushed pages, journal covers warped and damp. Slowly the history of exploring Area X could be said to be turning into Area X.

I picked around the edges at first, chose journals at random. Most, at a glance, depicted quite ordinary events, such as those described by the first expedition . . . which could not have been the first expedition. Some were extraordinary only because the dates did not make sense. How many expeditions had really come across the border? Just how much information had been doctored and suppressed, and for how long? Did "twelve" expeditions refer only to the latest iteration of a longer effort, the omission of the rest necessary to quell the doubts of those approached to be volunteers?

What I would call pre-expedition accounts, documented in a variety of forms, also existed in that place. This was the underlying archive of audiocassettes, chewed-at photographs, and decomposing folders full of papers that I had first glimpsed from above—all of it oppressed by the weight of the journals on top. All of it suffused by a dull, damp smell that contained within it a masked sharp stench of decay, which revealed itself in some places and not others. A bewildering confusion of typewritten, printed, and handwritten words piled up in my head alongside half-seen images like a mental facsimile of the midden itself. The clutter at times brought me close to becoming frozen, even without factoring in the contradictions. I became aware of the weight of the photograph in my pocket.

I made some initial rules, as if that would help. I ignored journals that appeared to be written in a shorthand and did not try to decipher those that appeared to be in code. I also started out reading some journals straight through and then decided to force myself to skim. But sampling was sometimes worse. I came across pages that described unspeakable acts that I still cannot bring myself to set down in words. Entries that mentioned periods of "remission" and "cessation" followed by "flare-ups" and "horrible manifestations." No matter how long Area X had existed, and how many expeditions had come here, I could tell from these accounts that for years before there had ever been a border, strange things had happened along this coast. There had been a proto–Area X.

Some types of omissions made my mind itch as much as more explicit offerings. One journal, half-destroyed by the damp, focused solely on the qualities of a kind of thistle with a lavender blossom that grew in the hinterlands between forest and swamp. Page after page described encountering first one specimen of this thistle and then another, along with minute details about the insects and other creatures that occupied that microhabitat. In no instance did the observer stray more than a foot or two from a particular plant, and at no point, either, did the observer pull back to provide a glimpse of base camp or their own life. After a while, a kind of unease came over me as I began to perceive a terrible presence hovering in the background of these entries. I saw the Crawler or some surrogate approaching in that space just beyond the thistle, and the single focus of the journal keeper a way of coping with that horror. An absence is not a presence, but still with each new depiction of a thistle, a shiver worked deeper and deeper into my spine. When the latter part of the book dissolved into ruined ink and moist pulp, I was almost relieved to be rid of that unnerving repetition, for there had been a hypnotic, trancelike quality to the accounts. If there had been an endless number of pages, I feared that I would have stood there reading for an eternity, until I fell to the floor and died of thirst or starvation.

I began to wonder if the absence of references to the Tower fit this theory as well, this writing around the edges of things.

. . . in the black water with the sun shining at midnight, those fruit shall come ripe . . .

Then I found, after several banal or incomprehensible samples, a journal that wasn't the same type as my own. It dated back to before the first expedition but after the border had come down and referenced "building the wall," which clearly meant the fortification facing the sea. A page later—mixed in with esoteric meteorological readings—three words leapt out at me: "repelling an attack." I read the next few entries with care. The writer at first made no reference to the nature of the attack or the identity of the attackers, but the assault had come from the sea and "left four of us dead," although the wall had held. Later, the sense of desperation grew, and I read:

> *. . . the desolation comes from the sea again, along with the strange lights and the marine life that at high tide batters itself against our wall. At night, now, their outliers try to creep in through the gaps in our wall defenses. Still, we hold, but our ammunition is running out. Some of us want to abandon the lighthouse, try for either the island or inland, but the commander says she has her orders. Morale is low. Not everything that is happening to us has a rational explanation.*

Soon after, the account trailed off. It had a distinctly unreal quality to it, as if a fictionalized version of a real event. I tried to imagine what Area X might have looked like so long ago. I couldn't.

The lighthouse had drawn expedition members like the ships it had once sought to bring to safety through the narrows and reefs offshore. I could only underscore my previous speculation that to most of them a lighthouse was a symbol, a reassurance of the old order, and by its prominence on the horizon it provided an illusion of a safe refuge. That it had betrayed that trust was manifest in what I had found downstairs. And yet even though some of them must have known that, still they had come. Out of hope. Out of faith. Out of stupidity.

But I had begun to realize that you had to wage a guerrilla war against whatever force had come to inhabit Area X if you wanted to fight at all. You had to fade into the landscape, or like the writer of the thistle chronicles, you had to pretend it wasn't there for as long as possible. To acknowledge it, to try to name it, might be a way of letting it in. (For the same reason, I suppose, I have continued to refer to the changes in me as a "brightness," because to examine this condition too closely—to quantify it or deal with it empirically when I have little control over it—would make it too real.)

At some point, I began to panic at the sheer volume of what remained in front of me, and in my panic I refined my focus further: I would search only for phrases identical to or similar in tone to the words on the wall of the Tower. I started to assail the hill of paper more directly, to wade into the middle sections, the rectangle of light above me a reassurance that this was not the sum of my existence. I rummaged like the rats and the silverfish, I shoved my arms into the mess and came out holding whatever my hands could grasp. At times I lost my balance and became buried in the papers, wrestled with them, my nostrils full of rot, my tongue tasting it. I would have looked unhinged to anyone watching from above, and I knew it even as I engaged in this frenzied, futile activity.

But I found what I was looking for in more journals than I would have expected, and usually it was that beginning phrase: *Where lies the strangling fruit that came from the hand of the sinner I shall bring forth the seeds of the dead to share with the worms* . . . Often it appeared as a scrawled margin note or in other ways disconnected from the text around it. Once, I discovered it documented as a phrase on the wall of the lighthouse itself, which "we quickly washed away," with no reason given. Another time, in a spidery hand, I found a reference to "text in a logbook that reads as if it came out of the Old Testament, but is from no psalm I remember." How could this not refer to the Crawler's writing? . . . *to share with the worms that gather in the darkness and surround the world with the power of their lives* . . . But none of this placed me any closer to understanding *why* or *who*. We were all in the dark, scrabbling at the pile of journals, and if ever I felt the weight of my predecessors, it was there and then, lost in it all.

At a certain point, I discovered I was so overwhelmed I could not continue, could not even go through the motions. It was too much data, served up in too anecdotal a form. I could search those pages for years and perhaps never uncover the right secrets, while caught in a loop of wondering how long this place had existed, who had first left their journals here, why others had followed suit until it had become as inexorable as a long-ingrained ritual. By what impulse, what shared fatalism? All I really thought I knew was that the journals from certain expeditions and certain individual expedition members were missing, that the record was incomplete.

I was also aware that I would have to go back to base camp before nightfall or remain at the lighthouse. I didn't like the idea of traveling in the dark, and if I didn't return, I had no guarantee the surveyor wouldn't abandon me and try to recross the border.

For now, I decided on one last effort. With great difficulty, I climbed to the top of the midden, trying hard not to dislodge journals as I did so. It was a kind of roiling, moving monster beneath my boots, unwilling, like the sand of the dunes outside, to allow my tread without an equal and opposite reaction. But I made it up there anyway.

As I'd imagined, the journals on the top of that mass were more recent, and I immediately found the ones written by members of my husband's expedition. With a kind of lurch in my stomach, I kept rummaging, knowing that it was inevitable what I would stumble upon, and I was right. Stuck to the back of another journal by dried blood or some other substance, I found it more easily than I'd imagined: my husband's journal, written in the confident, bold handwriting I knew from birthday cards, notes on the refrigerator, and shopping lists. The ghost bird had found his ghost, on an inexplicable pile of other ghosts. But rather than looking forward to reading that account, I felt as if I were stealing a private diary that had been locked by his death. A stupid feeling, I know. All he'd ever wanted was for me to open up to him, and as a result he had always been there for the taking. Now, though, I would have to take him as I found him, and it would probably be forever, and I found the truth of that intolerable.

I could not bring myself to read it yet, but fought the urge to throw my husband's journal back on the pile and put it instead with the handful of other journals I planned to take back to base camp with me. I also retrieved two of the psychologist's guns as I climbed up out of that wretched space. I left her other supplies there for now. It might be useful to have a cache in the lighthouse.

It was later than I had thought when I emerged from below, the sky taking on the deep amber hue that marked the beginning of late afternoon. The sea was ablaze with light, but nothing beautiful here fooled me anymore. Human lives had poured into this place over time, volunteered to become party to exile and worse. Under everything lay the ghastly presence of countless desperate struggles. Why did they keep sending us? Why did we keep going? So many lies, so little ability to face the truth. Area X broke minds, I felt, even though it hadn't yet broken mine. A line from a song kept coming back to me: *All this useless knowledge.*

After being in that space for so long, I needed fresh air and the feel of the wind. I dropped what I'd taken into a chair and opened the sliding door to walk out onto the circular ledge bounded by a railing. The wind tore at my clothes and slapped against my face. The sudden chill was cleansing, and the view even better. I could see forever from there. But after a moment, some instinct or premonition made me look straight down, past the remains of the defensive wall, to the beach, part of which was half-hidden by the curve of the dune, the height of the wall, even from that angle.

Emerging from that space was a foot and the end of a leg, amid a flurry of disrupted sand. I trained my binoculars on the foot. It lay unmoving. A familiar pant leg, a familiar boot, with the laces double-tied and even. I gripped the railing tight to counter a feeling of vertigo. I knew the owner of that boot.

It was the psychologist.

04: IMMERSION

Everything I knew about the psychologist came from my observations during training. She had served both as a kind of distant overseer and in a more personal role as our confessor. Except, I had nothing to confess. Perhaps I confessed more under hypnosis, but during our regular sessions, which I had agreed to as a condition of being accepted for the expedition, I volunteered little.

"Tell me about your parents. What are they like?" she would ask, a classic opening gambit.

"Normal," I replied, trying to smile while thinking *distant, impractical, irrelevant, moody, useless.*

"Your mother is an alcoholic, correct? And your father is a kind of . . . con man?"

I almost exhibited a lack of control at what seemed like an insult, not an insight. I almost protested, defiantly, "My mother is an artist and my father is an entrepreneur."

"What are your earliest memories?"

"Breakfast." *A stuffed puppy toy I still have today. Putting a magnifying glass up to an ant lion's sinkhole. Kissing a boy and making him strip for me because I didn't know any better. Falling into a fountain and banging my head; the result, five stitches in the emergency room and an abiding fear of drowning. In the emergency room again when Mom drank too much, followed by the relief of almost a year of sobriety.*

Of all of my answers, "Breakfast" annoyed her the most. I could see it in the corners of her mouth fighting a downward turn, her rigid stance, the coldness in her eyes. But she kept her control.

"Did you have a happy childhood?"

"Normal," I replied. *My mom once so out of it that she poured orange juice into my cereal instead of milk. My dad's incessant, nervous chatter, which made him* seem *perpetually guilty of something. Cheap motels for vacations by the beach where Mom would cry at the end because we had to go back to the normal strapped-for-cash life, even though we'd never really left it. That sense of impending doom occupying the car.*

"How close were you to your extended family?"

"Close enough." *Birthday cards suitable for a five-year-old even when I was twenty. Visits once every couple of years. A kindly grandfather with long yellow fingernails and the voice of a bear. A grandmother who lectured on the value of religion and saving your pennies. What were their names?*

"How do you feel about being part of a team?"

"Just fine. I've often been part of teams." *And by "part of," I mean off to the side.*

"You were let go from a number of your field jobs. Do you want to tell me why?"

She knew why, so, again, I shrugged and said nothing.

"Are you only agreeing to join this expedition because of your husband?"

"How close were you and your husband?"

"How often did you fight? Why did you fight?"

"Why didn't you call the authorities the moment he returned to your house?"

These sessions clearly frustrated the psychologist on a professional level, on the level of her ingrained training, which was predicated on drawing personal information out of patients in order to establish trust and then delve into deeper issues. But on another level I could never quite grasp, she seemed to approve of my answers. "You're very self-contained," she said once, but not as a pejorative. It was only as we walked for a second day from the border toward base camp that it struck me that perhaps the very qualities she might disapprove of from a psychiatric point of view made me suitable for the expedition.

Now she sat propped up against a mound of sand, sheltered by the shadow of the wall, in a kind of broken pile, one leg straight out, the other trapped beneath her. She was alone. I could see from her condition and the shape of the impact that she had jumped or been pushed from the top of the lighthouse. She probably hadn't quite cleared the wall, been hurt by it on the way down. While I, in my methodical way, had spent hours going through the journals, she had been lying here the whole time. What I couldn't understand was why she was still alive.

Her jacket and shirt were covered in blood, but she was breathing and her eyes were open, looking out toward the ocean as I knelt beside her. She had a gun in her left hand, left arm outstretched, and I gently took the weapon from her, tossed it to the side, just in case.

The psychologist did not seem to register my presence. I touched her gently on one broad shoulder, and then she screamed, lunged away, falling over as I recoiled.

"Annihilation!" she shrieked at me, flailing in confusion. "Annihilation! Annihilation!" The word seemed more meaningless the more she repeated it, like the cry of a bird with a broken wing.

"It's just me, the biologist," I said in a calm voice, even though she had rattled me.

"Just you," she said with a wheezing chuckle, as if I'd said something funny. "Just you."

As I propped her up again, I heard a kind of creaking groan and realized she had probably broken most of her ribs. Her left arm and shoulder felt spongy under her jacket. Dark blood was seeping out around her stomach, beneath the hand she had instinctively pressed down on that spot. I could smell that she had pissed herself.

"You're still here," she said, surprise in her voice. "But I killed you, didn't I?" The voice of someone waking from dream or falling into dream.

"Not even a little bit."

A rough wheeze again, and the film of confusion leaving her eyes. "Did you bring water? I'm thirsty."

"I did," and I pressed my canteen to her mouth so she could swallow a few gulps. Drops of blood glistened on her chin.

"Where is the surveyor?" the psychologist asked in a gasp.

"Back at the base camp."

"Wouldn't come with you?"

"No." The wind was blowing back the curls of her hair, revealing a slashing wound on her forehead, possibly from impact with the wall above.

"Didn't like your company?" the psychologist asked. "Didn't like what you've become?"

A chill came over me. "I'm the same as always."

The psychologist's gaze drifted out to sea again. "I saw you, you know, coming down the trail toward the lighthouse. That's how I knew for sure you had changed."

"What did you see?" I asked, to humor her.

A cough, accompanied by red spittle. "You were a *flame*," she said, and I had a brief vision of my brightness, made manifest. "You were a flame, scorching my gaze. A flame drifting across the salt flats, through the ruined village. A slow-burning flame, a will-o'-the-wisp, floating across the marsh and the dunes, floating and floating, like nothing human but something free and floating . . ."

From the shift in her tone, I recognized that even now she was trying to hypnotize me.

"It won't work," I said. "I'm immune to hypnosis now."

Her mouth opened, then closed, then opened again. "Of course you are. You were always difficult," she said, as if talking to a child. Was that an odd sense of pride in her voice?

Perhaps I should have left the psychologist alone, let her die without providing any answers, but I could not find that level of grace within me.

A thought occurred, if I had looked so inhuman: "Why didn't you shoot me dead as I approached?"

An unintentional leer as she swiveled her head to stare at me, unable to control all of the muscles in her face. "My arm, my hand, wouldn't let me pull the trigger."

That sounded delusional to me, and I had seen no sign of an abandoned rifle beside the beacon. I tried again. "And your fall? Pushed or an accident or on purpose?"

A frown appeared, a true perplexity expressed through the network of wrinkles at the corners of her eyes, as if the memory were only coming through in fragments. "I thought . . . I thought something was after me. I tried to shoot you, and couldn't and then you were inside. Then I thought I saw something behind me, coming toward me from the stairs, and I felt such an overwhelming fear I had to get away from it. So I jumped out over the railing. I jumped." As if she couldn't believe she had done such a thing.

"What did the thing coming after you look like?"

A coughing fit, words dribbling out around the edges: "I never saw it. It was never there. Or I saw it too many times. It was inside me. Inside you. I was trying to get away. From what's inside me."

I didn't believe any part of that fragmented explanation at the time, which seemed to imply something had followed her from the Tower. I interpreted the frenzy of her disassociation as part of a need for control. She had lost control of the expedition, and so she had to find someone or something to blame her failure on, no matter how improbable.

I tried a different approach: "Why did you take the anthropologist down into the 'tunnel' in the middle of the night? What happened there?"

She hesitated, but I couldn't tell if it was from caution or because something inside her body was breaking down. Then she said, "A miscalculation. Impatience. I needed intel before we risked the whole mission. I needed to know where we stood."

"You mean, the progress of the Crawler?"

She smiled wickedly. "Is that what you call it? The Crawler?"

"What happened?" I asked.

"What do you think happened? It all went wrong. The anthropologist got too close." Translation: The psychologist had forced her to get close. "The thing *reacted*. It killed her, wounded me."

"Which is why you looked so shaken the next morning."

"Yes. And because I could tell that you were already changing."

"I'm not changing!" I shouted it, an unexpected rage rising inside of me.

A wet chuckle, a mocking tone. "Of course you're not. You're just becoming more of what you've always been. And I'm not changing, either. None of us are changing. Everything is fine. Let's have a picnic."

"Shut up. Why did you abandon us?"

"The expedition had been compromised."

"That isn't an explanation."

"Did you ever give *me* a proper explanation, during training?"

"We hadn't been compromised, not enough to abandon the mission."

"Sixth day after reaching base camp and one person is dead, two already *changing*, the fourth wavering? I would call that a disaster."

"If it was a disaster, you helped create it." I realized that as much as I mistrusted the psychologist personally, I had come to rely on her to lead the expedition. On some level, I was furious that she had betrayed us, furious that she might be leaving me now. "You just panicked, and you gave up."

The psychologist nodded. "That, too. I did. I did. I should have recognized earlier that you had changed. I should have sent you back to the border. I shouldn't have gone down there with the anthropologist. But here we are." She grimaced, coughed out a thick wetness.

I ignored the jab, changed the line of questioning. "What does the border look like?"

That smile again. "I'll tell you when I get there."

"What really happens when we cross over?"

"Not what you might expect."

"Tell me! What do we cross through?" I felt as if I were getting lost. Again.

There was a gleam in her eye now that I did not like, that promised damage. "I want you to think about something. You might be immune to hypnosis—you might—but what about the veil already in place? What if I removed that veil so you could access your own memories of crossing the border?" the psychologist asked. "Would you like that, Little Flame? Would you like it or would you go mad?"

"If you try to do anything to me, I'll kill you," I said—and meant it. The thought of hypnosis in general, and the conditioning behind it, had been difficult for me, an invasive price to be paid in return for access to Area X. The thought of further tampering was intolerable.

"How many of your memories do you think are implanted?" the psychologist asked. "How many of your memories of the world beyond the border are verifiable?"

"That won't work on me," I told her. "I am sure of the here and now, this moment, and the next. I am sure of my past." That was ghost bird's castle keep, and it was inviolate. It might have been punctured by the hypnosis during training, but it had not been breached. Of this I was certain, and would continue to be certain, because I had no choice.

I sat back on my haunches, staring at her. I wanted to leave her before she poisoned me, but I couldn't.

"Let's stick to your own hallucinations," I said. "Describe the Crawler to me."

"There are things you must see with your own eyes. You might get closer. You might be more familiar to it." Her lack of regard for the anthropologist's fate was hideous, but so was mine.

"What did you hide from us about Area X?"

"Too general a question." I think it amused the psychologist, even dying, for me to so desperately need answers from her.

"Okay, then: What do the black boxes measure?"

"Nothing. They don't measure anything. It's just a psychological ploy to keep the expedition calm: no red light, no danger."

"What is the secret behind the Tower?"

"The tunnel? If we knew, do you think we would keep sending in expeditions?"

"They're scared. The Southern Reach."

"That is my impression."

"Then they have no answers."

"I'll give you this scrap: The border is advancing. For now, slowly, a little bit more every year. In ways you wouldn't expect. But maybe soon it'll eat a mile or two at a time."

The thought of that silenced me for a long moment. When you are too close to the center of a mystery there is no way to pull back and see the shape of it entire. The black boxes might do nothing but in my mind they were all blinking red.

"How many expeditions have there been?"

"Ah, the journals," she said. "There are quite a lot of them, aren't there?"

"That doesn't answer my question."

"Maybe I don't know the answer. Maybe I just don't want to tell you."

It was going to continue this way, to the end, and there wasn't anything I could do about it.

"What did the 'first' expedition really find?"

The psychologist grimaced, and not from her pain this time, but more as if she were remembering something that caused her shame. "There's video from that expedition . . . of a sort. The main reason no advanced tech was allowed after that."

Video. Somehow, after searching through the mound of journals, that information didn't startle me. I kept moving forward.

"What orders didn't you reveal to us?"

"You're beginning to bore me. And I'm beginning to fade a little . . . Sometimes we tell you more, sometimes less. They have their metrics and their reasons." Somehow the "they" felt made of cardboard, as if she didn't quite believe in "them."

Reluctantly, I returned to the personal. "What do you know about my husband?"

"Nothing more than you'll find out from reading his journal. Have you found it yet?"

"No," I lied.

"Very insightful—about you, especially."

Was that a bluff? She'd certainly had enough time up in the lighthouse to find it, read it, and toss it back onto the pile.

It didn't matter. The sky was darkening and encroaching, the waves deepening, the surf making the shorebirds scatter on their stilt legs and then regroup as it receded. The sand seemed suddenly more porous around us. The meandering paths of crabs and worms continued to be written into its surface. A whole community lived here, was going about its business, oblivious to our conversation. And where out there lay the seaward border? When I had asked the psychologist during training she had said only that no one had ever crossed it, and I had imagined expeditions that just evaporated into mist and light and distance.

A rattle had entered the psychologist's breathing, which was now shallow and inconsistent.

"Is there anything I can do to make you more comfortable?" Relenting.

"Leave me here when I die," she said. Now all her fear was visible. "Don't bury me. Don't take me anywhere. Leave me here where I belong."

"Is there anything else you're willing to tell me?"

"We should never have come here. I should never have come here." The rawness in her tone hinted at a personal anguish that went beyond her physical condition.

"That's all?"

"I've come to believe it is the one fundamental truth."

I took her to mean that it was better to let the border advance, to ignore it, let it affect some other, more distant generation. I didn't agree with her, but I said nothing. Later, I would come to believe she had meant something altogether different.

"Has anyone ever really come back from Area X?"

"Not for a long time now," the psychologist said in a tired whisper. "Not really." But I don't know if she had heard the question.

Her head sagged and she lost consciousness, then came to again and stared out at the waves. She muttered a few words, one of which might have been "remote" or "demote" and another that might have been "hatching" or "watching." But I could not be sure.

Soon dusk would descend. I gave her more water. It was hard to think of her as an adversary the closer she came to death, even though clearly she knew so much more than she had told me. Regardless, it didn't bear much thought because she wasn't going to divulge anything else. And maybe I *had* looked to her like a flame as I came near. Maybe that was the only way she could think of me now.

"Did you know about the pile of journals?" I asked. "Before we came here?"

But she did not answer.

There were things I had to do after she died, even though I was running short of daylight, even though I did not like doing them. If she wouldn't answer my questions while alive, then she would have to answer some of them now. I took off the psychologist's jacket and laid it to the side, discovering in the process that she had hidden her own journal in a zippered inside pocket, folded up. I put that to the side, too, under a stone, the pages flapping in the gusts of wind.

Then I took out my penknife and, with great care, cut away the left sleeve of her shirt. The sponginess of her shoulder had bothered me, and I saw I'd had good reason to be concerned. From her collarbone down to her elbow, her arm had been colonized by a fibrous green-gold fuzziness, which gave off a faint glow. From the indentations and long rift running down her triceps, it appeared to have spread from an initial wound—the wound she said she had received from the Crawler. Whatever had contaminated me, this different and more direct contact had spread faster and had more disastrous consequences. Certain parasites and fruiting bodies could cause not just paranoia but schizophrenia, all-too-realistic hallucinations, and thus promote delusional behavior. I had no doubt now that she had seen me as a flame approaching, that she had attributed her inability to shoot me to some exterior force, that she had been assailed by the fear of some approaching presence. If nothing else, the memory of the encounter with the Crawler would, I imagined, have unhinged her to some degree.

I cut a skin sample from her arm, along with some of the flesh beneath, and prodded it into a collection vial. Then I took another sample from her other arm. Once I got back to base camp, I would examine both.

I was shaking a little by then, so I took a break, turned my attention to the journal. It was devoted to transcribing the words on the wall of the Tower, was filled with so many new passages:

> . . . but whether it decays under the earth or above on green fields, or out to sea or in the very air, all shall come to revelation, and to revel, in the knowledge of the strangling fruit and the hand of the sinner shall rejoice, for there is no sin in shadow or in light that the seeds of the dead cannot forgive . . .

There were a few notes scribbled in the margins. One read "lighthouse keeper," which made me wonder if she'd circled the man in the photograph. Another read "North?" and a third "island." I had no clue what these notes meant—or what it said about the psychologist's state of mind that her journal was devoted to this text. I felt only a simple, uncomplicated relief that someone had completed a task for me that would have been laborious and difficult otherwise. My only question was whether she had gotten the text from the walls of the Tower, from journals within the lighthouse, or from some other source entirely. I still don't know.

Careful to avoid contact with her shoulder and arm, I then searched the psychologist's body. I patted down her shirt, her pants, searching for anything hidden. I found a tiny handgun strapped to her left calf and a letter in a small envelope folded up in her right boot. The psychologist had written a name on the envelope; at least, it looked like her handwriting. The name started with an S. Was it her child's name? A friend? A lover? I had not seen a name or heard a name spoken aloud for months, and seeing one now bothered me deeply. It seemed wrong, as if it did not belong in Area X. A name was a dangerous luxury here. Sacrifices didn't need names. People who served a function didn't need to be named. In all ways, the name was a further and unwanted confusion to me, a dark space that kept growing and growing in my mind.

I tossed the gun far across the sand, balled up the envelope, sent it after the gun. I was thinking of having discovered my husband's journal, and how in some ways that discovery was worse than its absence. And, on some level, I was still angry at the psychologist.

Finally I searched her pants pockets. I found some change, a smooth worry stone, and a slip of paper. On the paper I found a list of hypnotic suggestions that included "induce paralysis," "induce acceptance," and "compel obedience," each corresponding to an activation word or phrase. She must have been intensely afraid of forgetting which words gave her control over us, to have written them down. Her cheat sheet included other reminders, like: "Surveyor needs reinforcement" and "Anthropologist's mind is porous." About me she had only this cryptic phrase: "Silence creates its own violence." How insightful.

The word "Annihilation" was followed by "help induce immediate suicide."

We had all been given self-destruct buttons, but the only one who could push them was dead.

Part of my husband's life had been defined by nightmares he'd had as a child. These debilitating experiences had sent him to a psychiatrist. They involved a house and a basement and the awful crimes that had occurred there. But the psychiatrist had ruled out suppressed memory, and he was left at the end with just trying to draw the poison by keeping a diary about them. Then, as an adult at university, a few months before he'd joined the navy, he had gone to a classic film festival . . . and there, up on the big screen, my future husband had seen his nightmares acted out. It was only then that he realized the television set must have been left on at some point when he was only a couple of years old, with that horror movie playing. The splinter in his mind, never fully dislodged, disintegrated into nothing. He said that was the moment he knew he was free, that it was from then on that he left behind the shadows of his childhood . . . because it had all been an illusion, a fake, a forgery, a scrawling across his mind that had falsely made him go in one direction when he had been meant to go in another.

"I've had a kind of dream for a while now," he confessed to me the night he told me he had agreed to join the eleventh expedition. "A new one, and not really a nightmare this time."

In these dreams, he floated over a pristine wilderness as if from the vantage point of a marsh hawk, and the feeling of freedom "is indescribable. It's as if you took everything from my nightmares and reversed it." As the dreams progressed and repeated, they varied in their intensity and their viewpoint. Some nights he swam through the marsh canals. Others, he became a tree or a drop of water. Everything he experienced refreshed him. Everything he experienced made him want to go to Area X.

Although he couldn't tell me much, he confessed that he already had met several times with people who recruited for the expeditions. That he had talked to them for hours, that he knew this was the right decision. It was an honor. Not everyone was taken—some were rejected and others lost the thread along the way. Still others, I pointed out to him, must have wondered what they had done, after it was too late. All I understood of what he called Area X at the time came from the vague official story of environmental catastrophe, along with rumors and sideways whispers. Danger? I'm not sure this crossed my mind so much as the idea that my husband had just told me he wanted to leave me and had withheld the information for weeks. I was not yet privy to the idea of hypnosis or reconditioning, so it did not occur to me that he might have been *made suggestible* during his meetings.

My response was a profound silence as he searched my face for what he thought he hoped to find there. He turned away, sat on the couch, while I poured myself a very large glass of wine and took the chair opposite him. We remained that way for a long time.

A little later, he started to talk again—about what he knew of Area X, about how his work right now wasn't fulfilling, how he needed more of a challenge. But I wasn't really listening. I was thinking about my mundane job. I was thinking about the wilderness. I was wondering why I hadn't done something like he was doing now: dreaming of another place, and how to get there. In that moment, I couldn't blame him, not really. Didn't I sometimes go off on field trips for my job? I might not be gone for months, but in principle it was the same thing.

The arguing came later, when it became real to me. But never pleading. I never begged him to stay. I couldn't do that. Perhaps he even thought that going away would save our marriage, that somehow it would bring us closer together. I don't know. I have no clue. Some things I will never be good at.

But as I stood beside the psychologist's body looking out to sea, I knew that my husband's journal waited for me, that soon I would know what sort of nightmare he had encountered here. And I knew, too, that I still blamed him fiercely for his decision . . . and yet even so, somewhere in the heart of me I had begun to believe there was no place I would rather be than in Area X.

I had lingered too long and would have to travel through the dark to make it back to base camp. If I kept up a steady pace, I might make it back by midnight. There was some advantage in arriving at an unexpected hour, given how I had left things with the surveyor. Something also warned me against staying at the lighthouse overnight. Perhaps it was just the unease from seeing the strangeness of the psychologist's wound or perhaps I still felt as if a presence inhabited that place, but regardless I set out soon after gathering up my knapsack full of supplies and my husband's journal. Behind me lay the increasingly solemn silhouette of what was no longer really a lighthouse but instead a kind of reliquary. As I stared back, I saw a thin green fountain of light gushing up, framed by the curve of the dunes, and felt even more resolve to put miles between us. It was the psychologist's wound, from where she lay on the beach, glowing more brightly than before. The suggestion of some sped-up form of life burning fiercely did not bear close scrutiny. Another phrase I had seen copied in her journal came to mind:

There shall be a fire that knows your name, and in the presence of the strangling fruit, its dark flame shall acquire every part of you.

Within the hour, the lighthouse had disappeared into the night, and with it the beacon the psychologist had become. The wind picked up, the darkness intensified. The ever-more distant sound of waves was like eavesdropping on a sinister, whispering conversation. I walked as quietly as possible through the ruined village under just a sliver of moon, unwilling to risk my flashlight. The shapes in the exposed remains of rooms had gathered a darkness about them that stood out against the night and in their utter stillness I sensed an unnerving suggestion of movement. I was glad to soon be past them and onto the part of the trail where the reeds choked both the canal on the seaward side and the little lakes to the left. In a while, I would encounter the black water and cypress trees, vanguard for the sturdy utility of the pines.

A few minutes later, the moaning started. For a moment I thought it was in my head. Then I stopped abruptly, stood there listening. Whatever we had heard every night at dusk was at it again, and in my eagerness to leave the lighthouse I had forgotten it lived in the reeds. This close the sound was more guttural, filled with confused anguish and rage. It seemed so utterly human and inhuman, that, for the second time since entering Area X, I considered the supernatural. The sound came from ahead of me and from the landward side, through the thick reeds that kept the water away from the sides of the trail. It seemed unlikely I could pass by without it hearing me. And what then?

Finally I decided to forge ahead. I took out the smaller of my two flashlights and crouched as I turned it on so the beam couldn't easily be seen above the reeds. In this awkward way, I walked forward, gun drawn in my other hand, alert to the direction of the sound. Soon I could hear it closer, if still distant, pushing through the reeds as it continued its horrible moaning.

A few minutes passed, and I made good progress. Then, abruptly, something nudged against my boot, flopped over. I aimed my flashlight at the ground—and leapt back, gasping. Incredibly, a human face seemed to be rising out of the earth. But when after a moment nothing further happened, I shone my light on it again and saw it was a kind of tan mask made of skin, half-transparent, resembling in its way the discarded shell of a horseshoe crab. A wide face, with a hint of pockmarks across the left cheek. The eyes were blank, sightless, staring. I felt as if I should recognize these features—that it was very important—but with them disembodied in this way, I could not.

Somehow the sight of this mask restored to me a measure of the calm that I had lost during my conversation with the psychologist. No matter how strange, a discarded exoskeleton, even if part of it resembled a human face, represented a kind of solvable mystery. One that, for the moment at least, pushed back the disturbing image of an expanding border and the countless lies told by the Southern Reach.

When I bent at the knees and shone my flashlight ahead, I saw more detritus from a kind of molting: a long trail of skin-like debris, husks, and sloughings. Clearly I might soon meet what had shed this material, and just as clearly the moaning creature was, or had once been, human.

I recalled the deserted village, the strange eyes of the dolphins. A question existed there that I might in time answer in too personal a way. But the most important question in that moment was whether just after molting the thing became sluggish or more active. It depended on the species, and I was not an expert on this one. Nor did I have much stamina left for a new encounter, even though it was too late to retreat.

Continuing on, I came to a place on the left where the reeds had been flattened, veering off to form a path about three feet wide. The moltings, if that's what they were, veered off, too. Shining my flashlight down the path, I could see it curved sharply right after less than a hundred feet. This meant that the creature was already ahead of me, out in the reeds, and could possibly circle back and emerge to block my path back to base camp.

The dragging sounds had intensified, almost equal to the moaning. A thick musk clung to the air.

I still had no desire to return to the lighthouse, so I picked up my pace. Now the darkness was so complete I could only see a few feet ahead of me, the flashlight revealing little or nothing. I felt as if I were moving through an encircling tunnel. The moaning grew still louder, but I could not determine its direction. The smell became a special kind of stench. The ground began to sag a little under my weight, and I knew water must be close.

There came the moaning again, as close as I'd ever heard it, but now mixed with a loud thrashing sound. I stopped and stood on tiptoe to shine my flashlight over the reeds to my left in time to see a great disrupting wave of motion ahead at a right angle to the trail, and closing fast. A dislocation of the reeds, a fast smashing that made them fall as if machine-threshed. The thing was trying to outflank me, and the brightness within surged to cover my panic.

I hesitated for just a moment. Some part of me wanted to see the creature, after having heard it for so many days. Was it the remnants of the scientist in me, trying to regroup, trying to apply logic when all that mattered was survival?

If so, it was a very small part.

I ran. It surprised me how fast I could run—I'd never had to run that fast before. Down the tunnel of blackness lined with reeds, raked by them and not caring, willing the brightness to propel me forward. To get past the beast before it cut me off. I could feel the thudding vibration of its passage, the rasping clack of the reeds beneath its tread, and there was a kind of expectant tone to its moaning now that sickened me with the urgency of its seeking.

From out of the darkness there came an impression of a great weight, aimed at me from my left. A suggestion of the side of a tortured, pale visage and a great, ponderous bulk behind it. Barreling toward a point ahead of me, and me with no choice but to let it keep coming, lunging forward like a sprinter at the finish line, so I could be past it and free.

It was coming so fast, too fast. I could tell I wasn't going to make it, couldn't possibly make it, not at that angle, but I was committed now.

The crucial moment came. I thought I felt its hot breath on my side, flinched and cried out even as I ran. But then the way was clear, and from almost right behind I heard a high keening, and the feeling of the space, the air, suddenly *filled*, and the sound of something massive trying to brake, trying to change direction, and being pulled into the reeds on the opposite side of the trail by its own momentum. An almost plaintive keening, a lonely sound in that place, called out to me. And kept calling, pleading with me to return, to see it entire, to acknowledge its existence.

I did not look back. I kept running.

Eventually, gasping for air, I stopped. On rubbery legs I walked until the trail opened up into forest lands, far enough to find a large oak I could climb, and spent the night in an uncomfortable position wedged into a crook of the tree. If the moaning creature had followed me there, I don't know what I would have done. I could still hear it, though far distant again. I did not want to think about it, but I could not stop thinking about it.

I drifted in and out of sleep, one watchful eye on the ground. Once, something large and snuffling paused at the base of the tree, but then went on its way. Another time, I had the sense of vague shapes moving in the middle distance, but nothing came of it. They seemed to stop for a moment, luminous eyes floating in the dark, but I sensed no threat from them. I held my husband's journal to my chest like a talisman to ward off the night, still refusing to open it. My fears about what it might contain had only grown.

Sometime before morning, I woke again to find that my brightness had become literal: My skin gave off a faint phosphorescence against the darkness, and I tried to hide my hands in my sleeves, draw my collar up high, so I would be less visible, then drifted off again. Part of me just wanted to sleep forever, through the rest of anything that might occur.

But I did remember one thing, now: where I had seen the molted mask before — the psychologist from the eleventh expedition, a man I had seen interviewed after his return across the border. A man who had said, in a calm and even tone, "It was quite beautiful, quite peaceful in Area X. We saw nothing unusual. Nothing at all." And then had smiled in a vague way.

Death, as I was beginning to understand it, was not the same thing here as back across the border.

The next morning my head was still full of the moans of the creature as I reentered the part of Area X where the trail rose to a steep incline, and on either side the swampy black water was littered with the deceptively dead-seeming cypress knees. The water stole all sound, and its unmoving surface reflected back only gray moss and tree limbs. I loved this part of the trail as I loved no other. Here the world had a watchfulness matched only by a sense of peaceful solitude. The stillness was simultaneously an invitation to let down your guard and a rebuke against letting down your guard. Base camp was a mile away, and I was lazy with the light and the hum of insects in the tall grass. I was already rehearsing what I would say to the surveyor, what I would tell her and what I would withhold.

The brightness within me flared up. I had time to take a half step to the right.

The first shot took me in the left shoulder instead of the heart, and the impact twisted me as it pushed me back. The second shot ripped through my left side, not so much lifting me off my feet as making me spin and trip myself. Into the profound silence as I hit the incline and jounced down the hill there came a roaring in my ears. I lay at the bottom of the hill, breath knocked out of me, one outstretched hand plunged into the black water and the other arm trapped beneath me. The pain in my left side seemed at first as if someone kept opening me up with a butcher knife and sewing me back together. But it quickly subsided to a kind of roiling ache, the bullet wounds reduced through some cellular conspiracy to a sensation like the slow squirming inside me of tiny animals.

Only seconds had passed. I knew I had to move. Luckily, my gun had been holstered or it would have gone flying. I took it out now. I had seen the scope, a tiny circle in the tall grass, recognized who had set the ambush. The surveyor was ex-military, and good, but she couldn't know that the brightness had protected me, that shock wasn't overtaking me, that the wound hadn't transfixed me with paralyzing pain.

I rolled onto my belly, intending to crawl along the water's edge.

Then I heard the surveyor's voice, calling out to me from the other side of the embankment: "Where is the psychologist? What did you do with her?"

I made the mistake of telling the truth.

"She's dead," I called back, trying to make my voice sound shaky and weak.

The surveyor's only reply was to fire a round over my head, perhaps hoping I'd break cover.

"I didn't kill the psychologist," I shouted. "She jumped from the top of the lighthouse."

"*Risk for reward!*" the surveyor responded, throwing it back at me like a grenade. She must have thought about that moment the whole time I'd been gone. It had no more effect on me than had my attempt to use it on her.

"Listen to me! You've hurt me—badly. You can leave me out here. I'm not your enemy."

Pathetic words, placating words. I waited, but the surveyor didn't reply. There was just the buzzing of the bees around the wildflowers, a gurgling of water somewhere in the black swamp beyond the embankment. I looked up at the stunning blue of the sky and wondered if it was time to start moving.

"Go back to base camp, take the supplies," I shouted, trying again. "Return to the border. I don't care. I won't stop you."

"I don't believe you about any of it!" she shouted, the voice a little closer, advancing along the other side. Then: "You've come back and you're not human anymore. You should kill yourself so I don't have to." I didn't like her casual tone.

"I'm as human as you," I replied. "This is a natural thing," and realized she wouldn't understand that I was referring to the brightness. I wanted to say that I was a natural thing, too, but I didn't know the truth of that—and none of this was helping plead my case anyway.

"Tell me your name!" she screamed. "Tell me your name! *Tell me your god-damn fucking name!*"

"That won't make any difference," I shouted back. "How would that make any difference? I don't understand why that makes a difference."

Silence was my answer. She would speak no more. I was a demon, a devil, something she couldn't understand or had chosen not to. I could feel her coming ever closer, crouching for cover.

She wouldn't fire again until she had a clear shot, whereas I had the urge to just charge her, firing wildly. Instead, I half crawled, half crept *toward* her, fast along the water's edge. She might expect me to get away by putting distance between us, but I knew with the range of her rifle that was suicidal. I tried to slow my breathing. I wanted to be able to hear any sound she might make, giving away her position.

After a moment, I heard footsteps opposite me on the other side of the hill. I found a clump of muddy earth, and I lobbed it low and long down the edge of the black water, back the way I had come. As it was landing about fifty feet from me with a glutinous plop, I was edging my way up the hillside so I could just barely see the edge of the trail.

The top of the surveyor's head rose up not ten feet ahead of me. She had dropped down to crawl through the long grass of the path. It was just a momentary glimpse. She was in plain view for less than a second, and then would be gone. I didn't think. I didn't hesitate. I shot her.

Her head jolted to the side and she slumped soundlessly into the grass and turned over on her back with a groan, as if she had been disturbed in her sleep, and then lay still. The side of her face was covered with blood and her forehead looked grotesquely misshapen. I slid back down the incline. I was staring at my gun, shocked. I felt as if I were stuck between two futures, even though I had already made the decision to live in one of them. Now it was just me.

When I checked again, cautious and low against the side of the hill, I saw her still sprawled there, unmoving. I had never killed anyone before. I was not sure, given the logic of this place, that I had truly killed someone now. At least, this was what I told myself to control my shakes. Because behind it all, I kept thinking that I could have tried to reason with her a little longer, or not taken the shot and escaped into the wilderness.

I got up and made my way up the hill, feeling sore all over although my shoulder remained just a dull ache. Standing over the body, her rifle lying straight above her bloody head like an exclamation mark, I wondered what her last hours had been like at base camp. What doubts had racked her. If she had started back to the border, hesitated, returned to the camp, set out again, caught in a circle of indecision. Surely some trigger had driven her to confront me, or perhaps living alone in her own head overnight in this place had been enough. Solitude could press down on a person, seem to demand that action be taken. If I had come back when I'd promised, might it all have been different?

I couldn't leave her there, but I hesitated about taking her back to base camp and burying her in the old graveyard behind the tents. The brightness within me made me unsure. What if there was a purpose for her in this place? Would burying her circumvent an ability to change that might belong to her, even now? Finally I rolled her over and over, the skin still elastic and warm, blood spooling out from the wound in her head, until she reached the water's edge. Then I said a few words about how I hoped she would forgive me, and how I forgave her for shooting at me. I don't know if my words made much sense to either of us at that point. It all sounded absurd to me as I said it. If she had suddenly been resurrected we would probably both admit we forgave nothing.

Carrying her in my arms, I waded into the black water. I let her go when I was knee-deep and watched her sink. When I could no longer see even the outstretched pale anemone of her left hand, I waded back to shore. I did not know if she was religious, expected to be resurrected in heaven or become food for the worms. But regardless, the cypress trees formed a kind of cathedral over her as she went deeper and deeper.

I had no time to absorb what had just happened, however. Soon after I stood once again on the trail, the brightness usurped many more places than just my nerve centers. I crumpled to the ground cocooned in what felt like an encroaching winter of dark ice, the brightness spreading into a corona of brilliant blue light with a white core. It felt like cigarette burns as a kind of searing snow drifted down and infiltrated my skin. Soon I became so frozen, so utterly numb, trapped there on the trail in my own body, that my eyes became fixed on the thick blades of grass in front of me, my mouth half open in the dirt. There should have been an awareness of comfort at being spared the pain of my wounds, but I was being haunted in my delirium.

I can remember only three moments from these hauntings. In the first, the surveyor, psychologist, and anthropologist peered down at me through ripples as if I were a tadpole staring up through a pool of water. They kept staring for an abnormally long time. In the second, I sat beside the moaning creature, my hand upon its head as I murmured something in a language I did not understand. In the third, I stared at a living map of the border, which had been depicted as if it were a great circular moat surrounding Area X. In that moat vast sea creatures swam, oblivious to me watching them; I could feel the absence of their regard like a kind of terrible bereavement.

All that time, I discovered later from thrash marks in the grass, I wasn't frozen at all: I was spasming and twitching in the dirt like a worm, some distant part of me still experiencing the agony, trying to die because of it, even though the brightness wouldn't let that happen. If I could have reached my gun, I think I would have shot myself in the head . . . and been glad of it.

It may be clear by now that I am not always good at telling people things they feel they have a right to know, and in this account thus far I have neglected to mention some details about the brightness. My reason for this is, again, the hope that any reader's initial opinion in judging my objectivity might not be influenced by these details. I have tried to compensate by revealing more personal information than I would otherwise, in part because of its relevance to the nature of Area X.

The truth is that in the moments before the surveyor tried to kill me, the brightness expanded within me to enhance my senses, and I could feel the shifting of the surveyor's hips as she lay against the ground and zeroed in on me through the scope. I could hear the sound of the beads of sweat as they trickled down her forehead. I could smell the deodorant she wore, and I could taste the yellowing grass she had flattened to set her ambush. When I shot her, it was with these enhanced senses still at work, and that was the only reason she was vulnerable to me.

This was, in extremis, a sudden exaggeration of what I had been experiencing already. On the way to the lighthouse and back, the brightness had manifested in part as a low-grade cold. I had run a mild fever, had coughed, and had sinus difficulties. I had felt faint at times and light-headed. A floating sensation and a heaviness had run through my body at intervals, never with any balance, so that I was either buoyant or dragging.

My husband would have been proactive about the brightness. He would have found a thousand ways to try to cure it—and to take away the scars, too—and not let me deal with it on my own terms, which is why during our time together I sometimes didn't tell him when I was sick. But in this case, anyway, all of that effort on his part would have been pointless. You can either waste time worrying about a death that might not come or concentrate on what's left to you.

When I finally returned to my senses it was already noon of the next day. Somehow I had managed to drag myself back to base camp. I was wrung out, a husk that needed to gulp down almost a gallon of water over the next hours to feel whole. My side burned, but I could tell that too-quick repair was taking place, enough for me to move about. The brightness, which had already infiltrated my limbs, now seemed in one final surge to have been fought to a draw by my body, its progress stunted by the need to tend to my injuries. The cold symptoms had receded and the lightness, the heaviness, had been replaced by a constant sustaining hum within me and for a time an unsettling sensation, as of something creeping under my skin, forming a layer that perfectly mimicked the one that could be seen.

I knew not to trust this feeling of well-being, that it could simply be the interregnum before another stage. Any relief that thus far the changes seemed no more radical than enhanced senses and reflexes and a phosphorescent tint to my skin paled before what I had now learned: To keep the brightness in check, I would have to continue to become wounded, to be injured. To shock my system.

In that context, when confronted with the chaos that was base camp my attitude was perhaps more prosaic than it might have been otherwise. The surveyor had hacked at the tents until long strips of the tough canvas fabric hung loose. The remaining records of scientific data left by prior expeditions had been burned; I could still see blackened fragments sticking out of the ash-crumbling logs. Any weapons she had been unable to carry with her she had destroyed by carefully taking them apart piece by piece; then she had scattered the pieces all around the camp as if to challenge me. Emptied-out cans of food lay strewn and gaping across the entire area. In my absence, the surveyor had become a kind of frenzied serial killer of the inanimate.

Her journal lay like an enticement on the remains of her bed in her tent, surrounded by a flurry of maps, some old and yellowing. But it was blank. Those few times I had seen her, apart from us, "writing" in it had been a deception. She had never had any intention of letting the psychologist or any of us know her true thoughts. I found I respected that.

Still, she had left one final, pithy statement, on a piece of paper by the bed, which perhaps helped explain her hostility: "The anthropologist tried to come back, but I took care of her." She had either been crazy or all too sane. I carefully sorted through the maps, but they were not of Area X. She had written things on them, personal things that spoke to remembrance, until I realized that the maps must show places she had visited or lived. I could not fault her for returning to them, for searching for something from the past that might anchor her in the present, no matter how futile that quest.

As I explored the remains of base camp further, I took stock of my situation. I found a few cans of food she had somehow overlooked. She also had missed some of the drinking water because, as I always did, I had secreted some of it in my sleeping bag. Although all of my samples were gone—these I imagined she'd flung into the black swamp on her way back down the trail to set her ambush— nothing had been solved or helped by this behavior. I kept my measurements and observations about samples in a small notebook in my knapsack. I would miss my larger, more powerful microscope, but the one I'd packed would do. I had enough food to last me a couple of weeks as I did not eat much. My water would last another three or four days beyond that, and I could always boil more. I had enough matches to keep a fire going for a month, and the skills to create one without matches anyway. More supplies awaited me in the lighthouse, at the very least in the psychologist's knapsack.

Out back, I saw what the surveyor had added to the old graveyard: an empty, newly dug grave with a mound of dirt out to the side—and stabbed into the ground, a simple cross made from fallen branches. Had the grave been meant to hold me or the anthropologist? Or both? I did not like the idea of lying next to the anthropologist for all eternity.

Cleaning up a little later, a fit of laughter came out of nowhere and made me double up in pain. I had suddenly remembered doing the dishes after dinner the night my husband had come back from across the border. I could distinctly recall wiping the spaghetti and chicken scraps from a plate and wondering with a kind of bewilderment how such a mundane act could coexist with the mystery of his reappearance.

05: DISSOLUTION

I have never done well in cities, even though I lived in one by necessity—because my husband needed to be there, because the best jobs for me were there, because I had self-destructed when I'd had opportunities in the field. But I was not a domesticated animal. The dirt and grit of a city, the unending *wakefulness* of it, the crowdedness, the constant light obscuring the stars, the omnipresent gasoline fumes, the thousand ways it presaged our destruction . . . none of these things appealed to me.

"Where do you go so late at night?" my husband had asked several times, about nine months before he left as part of the eleventh expedition. There was an unspoken "really" before the "go"—I could hear it, loud and insistent.

"Nowhere," I said. *Everywhere.*

"No, really—where do you go?" It was to his credit that he had never tried to follow me.

"I'm not cheating on you if that's what you mean."

The directness of that usually stopped him, even if it didn't reassure him.

I had told him a late-night walk alone relaxed me, allowed me to sleep when the stress or boredom of my job became too much. But in truth I didn't walk except the distance to an empty lot overgrown with grass. The empty lot appealed to me because it wasn't truly empty. Two species of snail called it home and three species of lizard, along with butterflies and dragonflies. From lowly origins—a muddy rut from truck tires—a puddle had over time collected rainwater to become a pond. Fish eggs had found their way to that place, and minnows and tadpoles could be seen there, and aquatic insects. Weeds had grown up around it, making the soil less likely to erode into the water. Songbirds on migration used it as a refueling station.

As habitats went, the lot wasn't complex, but its proximity dulled the impulse in me to just get in a car and start driving for the nearest wild place. I liked to visit late at night because I might see a wary fox passing through or catch a sugar glider resting on a telephone pole. Nighthawks gathered nearby to feast off the insects bombarding the streetlamps. Mice and owls played out ancient rituals of predator and prey. They all had a watchfulness about them that was different from animals in true wilderness; this was a jaded watchfulness, the result of a long and weary history. Tales of bad-faith encounters in human-occupied territory, tragic past events.

I didn't tell my husband my walk had a destination because I wanted to keep the lot for myself. There are so many things couples do from habit and because they are expected to, and I didn't mind those rituals. Sometimes I even enjoyed them. But I needed to be selfish about that patch of urban wilderness. It expanded in my mind while I was at work, calmed me, gave me a series of miniature dramas to look forward to. I didn't know that while I was applying this Band-Aid to my need to be unconfined, my husband was dreaming of Area X and much greater open spaces. But, later, the parallel helped assuage my anger at his leaving, and then my confusion when he came back in such a changed form . . . even if the stark truth is that I still did not truly understand what I had missed about him.

The psychologist had said, "The border is advancing . . . a little bit more every year."

But I found that statement too limiting, too ignorant. There were thousands of "dead" spaces like the lot I had observed, thousands of transitional environments that no one saw, that had been rendered invisible because they were not "of use." Anything could inhabit them for a time without anyone noticing. We had come to think of the border as this monolithic invisible wall, but if members of the eleventh expedition had been able to return without our noticing, couldn't other things have already gotten through?

In this new phase of my brightness, recovering from my wounds, the Tower called incessantly to me; I could feel its physical presence under the earth with a clarity that mimicked that first flush of attraction, when you knew without looking exactly where the object of desire stood in the room. Part of this was my own need to return, but part might be due to the effect of the spores, and so I fought it because I had work to do first. This work might also, if I was left to it without any strange intercession, put everything in perspective.

To start with, I had to quarantine the lies and obfuscation of my superiors from data that pertained to the actual eccentricities of Area X. For example, the secret knowledge that there had been a proto–Area X, a kind of *preamble* and beachhead established first. As much as seeing the mound of journals had radically altered my view of Area X, I did not think that the higher number of expeditions told me much more about the Tower and its effects. It told me primarily that even if the border was expanding, the progress of assimilation by Area X could still be considered conservative. The recurring data points found in the journals that related to repeating cycles and fluctuations of seasons of the strange and the ordinary were useful in establishing trends. But this information, too, my superiors probably knew and therefore it could be considered something already reported by others. The myth that only a few early expeditions, the start date artificially *suggested* by the Southern Reach, had come to grief reinforced the idea of cycles existing within the overall framework of an *advance*.

The individual details chronicled by the journals might tell stories of heroism or cowardice, of good decisions and bad decisions, but ultimately they spoke to a kind of *inevitability*. No one had as yet plumbed the depths of *intent* or *purpose* in a way that had obstructed that intent or purpose. Everyone had died or been killed, returned changed or returned unchanged, but Area X had continued on as it always had . . . while our superiors seemed to fear any radical reimagining of this situation so much that they had continued to send in knowledge-strapped expeditions as if this was the only option. *Feed Area X but do not antagonize it, and perhaps someone will, through luck or mere repetition, hit upon some explanation, some solution, before the world* becomes *Area* X.

There was no way I could corroborate any of these theories, but I took a grim comfort in coming up with them anyway.

I left my husband's journal until last, even though its pull was as strong as the allure of the Tower. Instead, I focused on what I had brought back: the samples from the ruined village and from the psychologist, along with samples of my own skin. I set up my microscope on the rickety table, which I suppose the surveyor had found already so damaged it did not require her further attention. The cells of the psychologist, both from her unaffected shoulder and her wound, appeared to be normal human cells. So did the cells I examined from my own sample.

This was impossible. I checked the samples over and over, even childishly pretending I had no interest in looking at them before swooping down with an eagle eye.

I was convinced that when I wasn't looking at them, these cells became something else, that the very act of observation changed everything. I knew this was madness and yet still I thought it. I felt as if Area X were laughing at me then— every blade of grass, every stray insect, every drop of water. What would happen when the Crawler reached the bottom of the Tower? What would happen when it came back up?

Then I examined the samples from the village: moss from the "forehead" of one of the eruptions, splinters of wood, a dead fox, a rat. The wood was indeed wood. The rat was indeed a rat. The moss and the fox . . . were composed of modified human cells. *Where lies the strangling fruit that came from the hand of the sinner I shall bring forth the seeds of the dead . . .*

I suppose I should have reared back from the microscope in shock, but I was beyond such reactions to anything that instrument might show me. Instead, I contented myself with quiet cursing. The boar on the way to base camp, the strange dolphins, the tormented beast in the reeds. Even the idea that replicas of members of the eleventh expedition had crossed back over. All supported the evidence of my microscope. Transformations were taking place here, and as much as I had felt part of a "natural" landscape on my trek to the lighthouse, I could not deny that these habitats were transitional in a deeply *unnatural* way. A perverse sense of relief overtook me; at least now I had proof of something strange happening, along with the brain tissue the anthropologist had taken from the skin of the Crawler.

By then, though, I'd had enough of samples. I ate lunch and decided against putting more effort into cleaning up the camp; most of that task would have to fall to the next expedition. It was another brilliant, blinding afternoon of stunning blue sky allied with a comfortable heat. I sat for a time, watched the dragonflies skimming the long grass, the dipping, looping flight of a redheaded woodpecker. I was just putting off the inevitable, my return to the Tower, and yet still I wasted time.

When I finally picked up my husband's journal and started to read, the brightness washed over me in unending waves and connected me to the earth, the water, the trees, the air, as I opened up and kept on opening.

Nothing about my husband's journal was expected. Except for some terse, hastily scribbled exceptions, he had addressed most of the entries to me. I did not want this, and as soon as it became apparent I had to resist the need to throw the journal away from me as if it were poison. My reaction had nothing to do with love or lack of love but was more out of a sense of guilt. He had meant to share this journal with me, and now he was either truly dead or existed in a state beyond any possible way for me to communicate with him, to reciprocate.

The eleventh expedition had consisted of eight members, all male: a psychologist, two medics (including my husband), a linguist, a surveyor, a biologist, an anthropologist, and an archaeologist. They had come to Area X in the winter, when the trees had lost most of their leaves and the reeds had turned darker and thicker. The flowering bushes "became sullen" and seemed to "huddle" along the path, as he put it. "Fewer birds than indicated in reports," he wrote. "But where do they go? Only the ghost bird knows." The sky frequently clouded over, and the water level in the cypress swamps was low. "No rain the entire time we've been here," he wrote at the end of the first week.

They, too, discovered what only I call the Tower on their fifth or sixth day—I was ever more certain that the location of the base camp had been chosen to trigger that discovery—but their surveyor's opinion that they must continue mapping the wider area meant they followed a different course than ours. "None of us were eager to climb down in there," my husband wrote. "Me least of all." My husband had claustrophobia, sometimes even had to leave our bed in the middle of the night to go sleep on the deck.

For whatever reason, the psychologist did not in this case coerce the expedition to go down into the Tower. They explored farther, past the ruined village, to the lighthouse and beyond. Of the lighthouse, my husband noted their horror at discovering the signs of carnage, but of being "too respectful of the dead to put things right," by which I suppose he meant the overturned tables on the ground level. He did not mention the photograph of the lighthouse keeper on the wall of the landing, which disappointed me.

Like me, they had discovered the pile of journals at the top of the lighthouse, been shaken by it. "We had an intense argument about what to do. I wanted to abort the mission and return home because clearly we had been lied to." But it was at this point that the psychologist apparently reestablished control, if of a tenuous sort. One of the directives for Area X was for each expedition to remain a unit. But in the very next entry the expedition had decided to split up, as if to salvage the mission by catering solely to each person's will, and thus ensuring that no one would try to return to the border. The other medic, the anthropologist, the archaeologist, and the psychologist stayed in the lighthouse to read the journals and investigate the area around the lighthouse. The linguist and the biologist went back to explore the Tower. My husband and the surveyor continued on past the lighthouse.

"You would love it here," he wrote in a particularly manic entry that suggested to me not so much optimism as an unsettling euphoria. "You would love the light on the dunes. You would love the sheer expansive wildness of it."

They wandered up the coast for an entire week, mapping the landscape and fully expecting at some point to encounter the border, whatever form it might take—some obstacle that barred their progress.

But they never did.

Instead, the same habitat confronted them day after day. "We're heading north, I believe," he wrote, "but even though we cover a good fifteen to twenty miles by nightfall, nothing has changed. It is all the same," although he also was quite emphatic that he did not mean they were somehow "caught in a strange recurring loop." Yet he knew that "by all rights, we should have encountered the border by now." Indeed, they were well into an expanse of what he called the Southern Reach that had *not yet been charted*, "that we had been encouraged by the vagueness of our superiors to assume existed back beyond the border."

I, too, knew that Area X ended abruptly not far past the lighthouse. How did I know this? Our superiors had told us during training. So, in fact, I knew nothing at all.

They turned back finally because "behind us we saw strange cascading lights far distant and, from the interior, more lights, and sounds that we could not identify. We became concerned for the expedition members we had left behind." At the point when they turned back, they had come within sight of "a rocky island, the first island we have seen," which they "felt a powerful urge to explore, although there was no easy way to get over to it." The island "appeared to have been inhabited at one time—we saw stone houses dotting a hill, and a dock below."

The return trip to the lighthouse took four days, not seven, "as if the land had contracted." At the lighthouse, they found the psychologist gone and the bloody aftermath of a shoot-out on the landing halfway up. A dying survivor, the archaeologist, "told us that something 'not of the world' had come up the stairs and that it had killed the psychologist and then withdrawn with his body. 'But the psychologist came back later,' the archaeologist raved. There were only two bodies, and neither was the psychologist. He could not account for the absence. He also could not tell us why then they had shot each other, except to say 'we did not trust ourselves' over and over again." My husband noted that "some of the wounds I saw were not from bullets, and even the blood spatter on the walls did not correspond to what I knew of crime scenes. There was a strange residue on the floor."

The archaeologist "propped himself up in the corner of the landing and threatened to shoot us if I came close enough to see to his wounds. Soon enough, though, he was dead." Afterward, they dragged the bodies from the landing and buried them high up on the beach a little distance from the lighthouse. "It was difficult, ghost bird, and I don't know that we ever really recovered. Not really."

This left the linguist and the biologist at the Tower. "The surveyor suggested either going back up the coast past the lighthouse or following the beach down the coast. But we both knew this was just an avoidance of the facts. What he was really saying was that we should abandon the mission, that we should lose ourselves in the landscape."

That landscape was impinging on them now. The temperature dipped and rose violently. There were rumblings deep underground that manifested as slight tremors. The sun came to them with a "greenish tinge" as if "somehow the border were distorting our vision." They also "saw flocks of birds headed inland—not of the same species, but hawks and ducks, herons and eagles all grouped together as if in common cause."

At the Tower, they ventured only a few levels down before coming back up. I noticed no mention of words on the wall. "If the linguist and the biologist were inside, they were much farther down, but we had no interest in following them." They returned to base camp, only to find the body of the biologist, stabbed several times. The linguist had left a note that read simply, "Went to the tunnel. Do not look for me." I felt a strange pang of sympathy for a fallen colleague. No doubt the biologist had tried to reason with the linguist. Or so I told myself. Perhaps he had tried to kill the linguist. But the linguist had clearly already been ensnared by the Tower, by the words of the Crawler. Knowing the meaning of the words on such intimate terms might have been too much for anyone, I realize now.

The surveyor and my husband returned to the Tower at dusk. Why is not apparent from the journal entries—there began to be breaks that corresponded to the passage of some hours, with no recap. But during the night, they saw a ghastly procession heading into the Tower: seven of the eight members of the eleventh expedition, including a doppelgänger of my husband and the surveyor. "And there before me, *myself.* I walked so stiffly. I had such a blank look on my face. It was so clearly not me . . . and yet it was me. A kind of shock froze both me and the surveyor. We did not try to stop them. Somehow, it seemed impossible to try to stop *ourselves*—and I won't lie, we were terrified. We could do nothing but watch until they had descended. For a moment afterward, it all made sense to me, everything that had happened. We were dead. We were ghosts roaming a haunted landscape, and although we didn't know it, people lived normal lives here, everything was as it should be here . . . but we couldn't see it through the veil, the interference."

Slowly my husband shook off this feeling. They waited hidden in the trees beyond the Tower for several hours, to see if the doppelgängers would return. They argued about what they would do if that happened. The surveyor wanted to kill them. My husband wanted to interrogate them. In their residual shock, neither of them made much of the fact that the psychologist was not among their number. At one point, a sound like hissing steam emanated from the Tower and a beam of light shot out into the sky, then abruptly cut off. But still no one emerged, and eventually the two men returned to base camp.

It was at this point that they decided to go their separate ways. The surveyor had seen all he cared to see and planned to return down the trail from base camp to the border immediately. My husband refused because he suspected from some of the readings in the journal that "this idea of return through the same means as our entry might in fact be a trap." My husband had, over the course of time, having encountered no obstacle to travel farther north, "grown suspicious of the entire idea of borders," although he could not yet synthesize "the intensity of this feeling" into a coherent theory.

Interspersed with this direct account of what had happened to the expedition were more personal observations, most of which I am reluctant to summarize here. Except there is one passage that pertains to Area X and to our relationship, too:

Seeing all of this, experiencing all of it, even when it's bad, I wish you were here. I wish we had volunteered together. I would have understood you better here, on the trek north. We wouldn't have needed to say anything if you didn't want to. It wouldn't have bothered me. Not at all. And we wouldn't have turned back. We would have kept going until we couldn't go farther.

Slowly, painfully, I realized what I had been reading from the very first words of his journal. My husband had had an inner life that went beyond his gregarious exterior, and if I had known enough to let him inside my guard, I might have understood this fact. Except I hadn't, of course. I had let tidal pools and fungi that could devour plastic inside my guard, but not him. Of all the aspects of the journal, this ate at me the most. He had created his share of our problems—by pushing me too hard, by wanting too much, by trying to see something in me that didn't exist. But I could have met him partway and retained my sovereignty. And now it was too late.

His personal observations included many grace notes. A description in the margin of a tidal pool in the rocks down the coast just beyond the lighthouse. A lengthy observation of the atypical use of an outcropping of oysters at low tide by a skimmer seeking to kill a large fish. Photographs of the tidal pool had been stuck in a sleeve in the back. Placed carefully in the sleeve, too, were pressed wildflowers, a slender seedpod, a few unusual leaves. My husband would have cared little for any of this; even the focus to observe the skimmer and write a page of notes would have required great concentration from him. I knew these elements were intended for me and me alone. There were no endearments, but I understood in part because of this restraint. He knew how much I hated words like *love*.

The last entry, written upon his return to the lighthouse, read, "I am going back up the coast. But not on foot. There was a boat in the ruined village. Staved in, rotting, but I have enough wood from the wall outside the lighthouse to fix it. I'll follow the shoreline as far as I can go. To the island, and perhaps beyond. If you ever read this, that is where I am going. That is where I will be." Could there be, even within all of these transitional ecosystems, one still more transitional—at the limits of the Tower's influence but not yet under the border's influence?

After reading the journal, I was left with the comfort of that essential recurring image of my husband putting out to sea in a boat he had rebuilt, out through the crashing surf to the calm just beyond. Of him following the coastline north, alone, seeking in that experience the joy of small moments remembered from happier days. It made me fiercely proud of him. It showed resolve. It showed bravery. It bound him to me in a more intimate way than we had ever seemed to have while together.

In glimmers, in shreds of thought, in the aftermath of my reading, I wondered if he kept a journal still, or if the dolphin's eye had been familiar for a reason other than that it was so human. But soon enough I banished this nonsense; some questions will ruin you if you are denied the answer long enough.

⟫⟫⟩

My injuries had receded into a constant but manageable ache when I breathed. Not coincidentally, by nightfall, the brightness was thrushing up through my lungs and into my throat again so that I imagined wisps of it misting from my mouth. I shuddered at the thought of the psychologist's plume, seen from afar, like a distress signal. I couldn't wait for morning, even if this was just a premonition of a far-distant future. I would return to the Tower *now*. It was the only place for me to go. I left behind the assault rifle and all but one gun. I left my knife. I left my knapsack, affixed a water canteen to my belt. I took my camera, but then thought better of it and abandoned it by a rock halfway to the Tower. It would just distract, this impulse to record, and photographs mattered no more than samples. I had decades of journals waiting for me in the lighthouse. I had generations of expeditions that had ghosted on ahead of me. The pointlessness of that, the pressure of that, almost got to me again. The waste of it all.

I had brought a flashlight but found I could see well enough by the green glow that emanated from my own body. I crept quickly through the dark, along the path leading to the Tower. The black sky, free of clouds, framed by the tall narrow lines formed by pine trees, reflected the full immensity of the heavens. No borders, no artificial light to obscure the thousands of glinting pinpricks. I could see everything. As a child, I had stared up at the night sky and searched for shooting stars like everyone else. As an adult, sitting on the roof of my cottage near the bay, and later, haunting the empty lot, I looked not for shooting stars but for fixed ones, and I would try to imagine what kind of life lived in those celestial tidal pools so far from us. The stars I saw now looked strange, strewn across the dark in chaotic new patterns, where just the night before I had taken comfort in their familiarity. Was I only now seeing them clearly? Was I perhaps even farther from home than I had thought? There shouldn't have been a grim sort of satisfaction in the thought.

The heartbeat came to me more distantly as I entered the Tower, my mask tied tightly in place over my nose and mouth. I did not know if I was keeping further contamination out or just trying to contain my brightness. The bioluminescence of the words on the wall had intensified, and the glow from my exposed skin seemed to respond in kind, lighting my way. Otherwise, I sensed no difference as I descended past the first levels. If these upper reaches had become familiar that feeling was balanced by the sobering fact that this was my first time alone in the Tower. With each new curve of those walls down into further darkness, dispelled only by the grainy, green light, I came more and more to expect something to erupt out of the shadows to attack me. I missed the surveyor in those moments and had to tamp down my guilt. And, despite my concentration, I found I was drawn to the words on the wall, that even as I tried to concentrate on the greater depths, those words kept bringing me back. *There shall be in the planting in the shadows a grace and a mercy that shall bloom dark flowers, and their teeth shall devour and sustain and herald the passing of an age . . .*

Sooner than expected, I came to the place where we had found the anthropologist dead. Somehow it surprised me that she still lay there, surrounded by the debris of her passage—scraps of cloth, her empty knapsack, a couple of broken vials, her head forming a broken outline. She was covered with a moving carpet of pale organisms that, as I stooped close, I discovered were the tiny hand-shaped parasites that lived among the words on the wall. It was impossible to tell if they were protecting her, changing her, or breaking her body down—just as I could not know whether some version of the anthropologist had indeed appeared to the surveyor near base camp after I had left for the lighthouse . . .

I did not linger but continued farther down.

Now the Tower's heartbeat began to echo and become louder. Now the words on the wall once again became fresher, as if only just "dried" after creation. I became aware of a hum under the heartbeat, almost a staticky buzzing sound. The brittle mustiness of that space ceded to something more tropical and cloying. I found that I was sweating. Most important, the track of the Crawler beneath my boots became fresher, stickier, and I tried to favor the right-hand wall to avoid the substance. That right-hand wall had changed, too, in that a thin layer of moss or lichen covered it. I did not like having to press my back up against it to avoid the substance on the floor, but I had no choice.

After about two hours of slowed progress, the heartbeat of the Tower had risen to a point where it seemed to shake the stairs, and the underlying hum splintered into a fresh crackling. My ears rang with it, my body vibrated with it, and I was sweating through my clothes due to the humidity, the stuffiness almost making me want to take off my mask in an attempt to gulp down air. But I resisted the temptation. I was close. I knew I was close . . . to what, I had no idea.

The words on the wall here were so freshly formed that they appeared to drip, and the hand-shaped creatures were less numerous, and those that did manifest formed closed fists, as if not yet quite awake and alive. *That which dies shall still know life in death for all that decays is not forgotten and reanimated shall walk the world in a bliss of not-knowing* . . .

I spiraled around one more set of stairs, and then as I came into the narrow straightaway before the next curve . . . I saw *light*. The edges of a sharp, golden light that emanated from a place beyond my vision, hidden by the wall, and the brightness within me throbbed and thrilled to it. The buzzing sound again intensified until it was so jagged and hissing that I felt as if blood might trickle from my ears. The heartbeat overtop boomed into every part of me. I did not feel as if I were a person but simply a receiving station for a series of overwhelming transmissions. I could feel the brightness spewing from my mouth in a half-invisible spray, meeting the resistance of the mask, and I tore it off with a gasp. *Give back to that which gave to you,* came the thought, not knowing what I might be feeding, or what it meant for the collection of cells and thoughts that comprised me.

You understand, I could no more have turned back than have gone back in time. My free will was compromised, if only by the severe temptation of the unknown. To have quit that place, to have returned to the surface, without rounding that corner . . . my imagination would have tormented me forever. In that moment, I had convinced myself I would rather die knowing . . . something, *anything*.

I passed the threshold. I descended into the light.

One night during the last months at Rock Bay I found myself intensely restless. This was after I had confirmed that my grant wouldn't be renewed and before I had any prospects of a new job. I had brought another stranger I knew back from the bar to try to distract myself from my situation, but he had left hours ago. I had a wakefulness that I could not shake, and I was still drunk. It was stupid and dangerous, but I decided to get in my truck and drive out to the tidal pools. I wanted to creep up on all of that hidden life and try to surprise it somehow. I had gotten it into my mind that the tidal pools changed during the night when no one watched. This is what happens, perhaps, if you have been studying something so long that you can tell one sea anemone from another in an instant, could have picked out any denizen of those tidal pools from a lineup if it had committed a crime.

So I parked the truck, took the winding trail down to the grainy beach, making my way with the aid of a tiny flashlight attached to my key chain. Then I sloshed through the shallows and climbed up onto the sheet of rock. I really wanted to lose myself. People my entire life have told me I am too much in control, but that has never been the case. I have never truly been in control, have never wanted control.

That night, even though I had come up with a thousand excuses to blame others, I knew I had screwed up. Not filing reports. Not sticking to the focus of the job. Recording odd data from the periphery. Nothing that might satisfy the organization that had provided the grant. I was the queen of the tidal pools, and what I said was the law, and what I reported was what I had wanted to report. I had gotten sidetracked, like I always did, because I melted into my surroundings, could not remain *separate from, apart from,* objectivity a foreign land to me.

I went to tidal pool after tidal pool with my pathetic flashlight, losing my balance half a dozen times and almost falling. If anyone had been observing—and who is to say now that they were not?—they would have seen a cursing, half-drunk, reckless biologist who had lost all perspective, who was out in the middle of nowhere for the second straight year and feeling vulnerable and lonely, even though she'd promised herself she would never get lonely. *The things she had done and said that society labeled antisocial or selfish.* Seeking something in the tidal pools that night even though what she found during the day was miraculous enough. She might even have been shouting, screaming, whirling about on those slippery rocks as if the best boots in the world couldn't fail you, send you falling to crack your skull, give you a forehead full of limpets and barnacles and blood.

But the fact is, even though I didn't deserve it—did I deserve it? and had I really just been looking for something familiar?—I found something miraculous, something that uncovered itself with its own light. I spied a glinting, wavery promise of illumination coming from one of the larger tidal pools, and it gave me pause. Did I really want a sign? Did I really want to discover something or did I just think I did? Well, I decided I did want to discover something, because I walked toward it, suddenly sobered up enough to watch my steps, to shuffle along so I wouldn't crack my skull before I saw whatever it was in that pool.

What I found when I finally stood there, hands on bent knees, peering down into that tidal pool, was a rare species of colossal starfish, six-armed, larger than a saucepan, that bled a dark gold color into the still water as if it were on fire. Most of us professionals eschewed its scientific name for the more apt "destroyer of worlds." It was covered in thick spines, and along the edges I could just see, fringed with emerald green, the most delicate of transparent cilia, thousands of them, propelling it along upon its appointed route as it searched for its prey: other, lesser starfish. I had never seen a destroyer of worlds before, even in an aquarium, and it was so unexpected that I forgot about the slippery rock and, shifting my balance, almost fell, steadying myself with one arm propped against the edge of the tidal pool.

But the longer I stared at it, the less comprehensible the creature became. The more it became something alien to me, the more I had a sense that I knew nothing at all—about nature, about ecosystems. There was something about my mood and its dark glow that eclipsed sense, that made me see this creature, which had indeed been assigned a place in the taxonomy—catalogued, studied, and described—irreducible down to any of that. And if I kept looking, I knew that ultimately I would have to admit I knew less than nothing about myself as well, whether that was a lie or the truth.

When I finally wrenched my gaze from the starfish and stood again, I could not tell where the sky met the sea, whether I faced the water or the shore. I was completely adrift, and dislocated, and all I had to navigate by in that moment was the glowing beacon below me.

Turning that corner, encountering the Crawler for the first time, was a similar experience at a thousand times the magnitude. If on those rocks those many years ago I could not tell sea from shore, here I could not tell stairs from ceiling, and even though I steadied myself with an arm against the wall, the wall seemed to cave in before my touch, and I struggled to keep from falling through it.

There, in the depths of the Tower, I could not begin to understand what I was looking at and even now I have to work hard to pull it together from fragments. It is difficult to tell what blanks my mind might be filling in just to remove the weight of so many unknowns.

Did I say I had seen golden light? As soon as I turned that corner entire, it was no longer golden but blue-green, and the blue-green light was like nothing I had experienced before. It surged out, blinding and bleeding and thick and layered and absorbing. It so overwhelmed my ability to comprehend shapes within it that I forced myself to switch from sight, to focus at first on reports from other senses.

The sound that came to me now was like a crescendo of ice or ice crystals shattering to form an unearthly noise that I had mistaken earlier for buzzing, and which began to take on an intense melody and rhythm that filled my brain. Vaguely, from some far-off place, I realized that the words on the wall were being infused with sound as well, but that I had not had the capacity to hear it before. The vibration had a texture and a weight, and with it came a burning smell, as of late fall leaves or like some vast and distant engine close to overheating. The taste on my tongue was like brine set ablaze.

No words can . . . no photographs could . . .

As I adjusted to the light, the Crawler kept changing at a lightning pace, as if to mock my ability to comprehend it. It was a figure within a series of refracted panes of glass. It was a series of layers in the shape of an archway. It was a great sluglike monster ringed by satellites of even odder creatures. It was a glistening star. My eyes kept glancing off of it as if an optic nerve was not enough.

Then it became an overwhelming *hugeness* in my battered vision, seeming to rise and keep rising as it leapt toward me. The shape spread until it was even where it was not, or *should not have been*. It seemed now more like a kind of obstacle or wall or thick closed door blocking the stairs. Not a wall of light—gold, blue, green, existing in some other spectrum—but a wall of flesh that *resembled* light, with sharp, curving elements within it and textures like ice when it has frozen from flowing water. An impression of living things lazily floating in the air around it like soft tadpoles, but at the limits of my vision so I could not tell if this was akin to those floating dark motes that are tricks of the eye, that do not exist.

Within this fractured mass, within all of these different impressions of the Crawler—half-blinded but still triangulating through my other senses—I thought I saw a darker shadow of an arm or a kind of *echo* of an arm in constant blurring motion, continuously imparting to the left-hand wall a repetition of depth and signal that made its progress laboriously slow—its message, its code of change, of recalibrations and adjustments, of transformations. And, perhaps, another dark shadow, vaguely head-shaped, above the arm—but as indistinct as if I had been swimming in murky water and seen in the distance a shape obscured by thick seaweed.

I tried to pull back now, to creep back up the steps. But I couldn't. Whether because the Crawler had trapped me or my brain had betrayed me, I could not move.

The Crawler changed or I was beginning to black out repeatedly and come back to consciousness. It would appear as if nothing was there, nothing at all, as if the words wrote themselves, and then the Crawler would tremble into being and then wink out again, and all that remained constant was a suggestion of an arm and the impression of the words being written.

What can you do when your five senses are not enough? Because I still couldn't truly *see* it here, any more than I had seen it under the microscope, and that's what scared me the most. Why couldn't I *see* it? In my mind, I stood over the starfish at Rock Bay, and the starfish grew and grew until it was not just the tidal pool but the world, and I was teetering on its rough, luminous surface, staring up at the night sky again, while the light of it flowed up and through me.

Against the awful pressure of that light, as if the entire weight of Area X were concentrated here, I changed tactics, tried to focus just on the creation of the words on the wall, the impression of a head or a helmet or . . . what? . . . somewhere above the arm. A cascade of sparks that I knew were living organisms. A new word upon the wall. And me still not seeing, and the brightness coiled within me assumed an almost hushed quality, as if we were in a cathedral.

The enormity of this experience combined with the heartbeat and the crescendo of sound from its ceaseless writing to fill me up until I had no room left. *This* moment, which I might have been waiting for my entire life all unknowing— this moment of an encounter with the most beautiful, the most terrible thing I might ever experience—was beyond me. What inadequate recording equipment I had brought with me and what an inadequate name I had chosen for it—the Crawler. Time elongated, was nothing but fuel for the words this thing had created on the wall for who knew how many years for who knew what purpose.

I don't know how long I stood at the threshold, watching the Crawler, frozen. I might have watched it forever and never noticed the awful passage of the years.

But then what?

What occurs after revelation and paralysis?

Either death or a slow and certain thawing. A returning to the physical world. It is not that I became used to the Crawler's presence but that I reached a point—a single infinitesimal moment—when I once again recognized that the Crawler was an organism. A complex, unique, intricate, awe-inspiring, dangerous organism. It might be inexplicable. It might be beyond the limits of my senses to capture—or my science or my intellect—but I still believed I was in the presence of some kind of living creature, one that practiced mimicry using my own thoughts. For even then, I believed that it might be pulling these different impressions of itself from my mind and projecting them back at me, as a form of camouflage. To thwart the biologist in me, to frustrate the logic left in me.

With an effort I could feel in the groan of my limbs, a dislocation in my bones, I managed to turn my back on the Crawler.

Just that simple, wrenching act was such a relief, as I hugged the far wall in all its cool roughness. I closed my eyes—why did I need vision when all it did was keep betraying me?—and started to crab-walk my way back, still feeling the light upon my back. Feeling the music from the words. The gun I had forgotten all about digging into my hip. The very idea of *gun* now seemed as pathetic and useless as the word *sample*. Both implied aiming at something. What was there to aim at?

I had only made it a step or two when I felt a rising sense of heat and weight and a kind of licking, lapping wetness, as if the thick light was transforming into the sea itself. I had thought perhaps I was about to escape, but it wasn't true. With just one more step away, as I began to choke, I realized that the light *had* become a sea.

Somehow, even though I was not truly underwater, I was drowning.

The franticness that rose within me was the awful formless panic of a child who had fallen into a fountain and known, for the first time, as her lungs filled with water, that she could die. There was no end to it, no way to get past it. I was awash in a brothy green-blue ocean alight with sparks. And I just kept on drowning and struggling against the drowning, until some part of me realized I would keep drowning forever. I imagined tumbling from the rocks, falling, battered by the surf. Washing up thousands of miles from where I was, unrecognizable, in some other form, but still retaining the awful memory of this moment.

Then I felt the impression from behind me of hundreds of eyes beginning to turn in my direction, staring at me. I was a thing in a swimming pool being observed by a monstrous little girl. I was a mouse in an empty lot being tracked by a fox. I was the prey the starfish had reached up and pulled down into the tidal pool.

In some watertight compartment, the brightness told me I had to accept that I would not survive that moment. I wanted to live—I really did. But I couldn't any longer. I couldn't even breathe any longer. So I opened my mouth and welcomed the water, welcomed the torrent. Except it wasn't really water. And the eyes upon me were not eyes, and I was pinned there now by the Crawler, had let it in, I realized, so that its full regard was upon me and I could not move, could not think, was helpless and alone.

A raging waterfall crashed down on my mind, but the water was comprised of fingers, a hundred fingers, probing and pressing down into the skin of my neck, and then punching up through the bone of the back of my skull and into my brain . . . and then the pressure eased even though the impression of unlimited force did not let up and for a time, still drowning, an icy calm came over me, and through the calm bled a kind of monumental blue-green light. I smelled a burning inside my own head and there came a moment when I screamed, my skull crushed to dust and reassembled, mote by mote.

There shall be a fire that knows your name, and in the presence of the strangling fruit, its dark flame shall acquire every part of you.

It was the most agony I have ever been in, as if a metal rod had been repeatedly thrust into me and then the pain distributed like a second skin inside the contours of my outline. Everything became tinged with the red. I blacked out. I came to. I blacked out, came to, blacked out, still perpetually gasping for breath, knees buckling, scrabbling at the wall for support. My mouth opened so wide from the shrieking that something popped in my jaw. I think I stopped breathing for a minute but the brightness inside experienced no such interruption. It just kept oxygenating my blood.

Then the terrible invasiveness was gone, ripped away, and with it the sensation of drowning and the thick sea that had surrounded me. There came a *push*, and the Crawler tossed me aside, down the steps beyond it. I washed up there, bruised and crumpled. With nothing to lean against, I fell like a sack, crumbling before something that was never meant to be, something never meant to invade me. I sucked in air in great shuddering gasps.

But I couldn't stay there, still within the range of its regard. I had no choice now. Throat raw, my insides feeling eviscerated, I flung myself down into the greater dark below the Crawler, on my hands and knees at first, scrabbling to escape, taken over by a blind, panicked impulse to get out of the sight of it.

Only when the light behind me had faded, only when I felt safe, did I drop to the floor again. I lay there for a long time. Apparently, I was recognizable to the Crawler now. Apparently, I was words it could understand, unlike the anthropologist. I wondered if my cells would long be able to hide their transformation from me. I wondered if this was the beginning of the end. But mostly I felt the utter relief of having passed a gauntlet, if barely. The brightness deep within was curled up, traumatized.

Perhaps my only real expertise, my only talent, is to endure beyond the endurable. I don't know when I managed to stand again, to continue on, legs rubbery. I don't know how long that took, but eventually I got up.

Soon the spiral stairs straightened out, and with this straightening, the stifling humidity abruptly lessened and the tiny creatures that lived on the wall were no longer to be seen, and the sounds from the Crawler above took on a more muffled texture. Though I still saw the ghosts of past scrawlings on the wall, even my own luminescence became muted here. I was wary of that tracery of words, as if somehow they could hurt me as surely as the Crawler, and yet there was some comfort in following them. Here the variations were more legible and now made more sense to me. *And it came for me. And it cast out all else.* Retraced again and again. Were the words more naked down here, or did I just possess more knowledge now?

I couldn't help but notice that these new steps shared the depth and width of the lighthouse steps almost exactly. Above me, the unbroken surface of the ceiling had changed so that now a profusion of deep, curving grooves crisscrossed it.

I stopped to drink water. I stopped to catch my breath. The aftershock of the encounter with the Crawler was still washing over me in waves. When I continued, it was with a kind of numbed awareness that there might be more revelations still to absorb, that I had to prepare myself. Somehow.

A few minutes later, a tiny rectangular block of fuzzy white light began to take form, shape, far below. As I descended, it became larger with a reluctance I can only call hesitation. After another half hour, I thought it must be a kind of door, but the haziness remained, almost as if it were obscuring itself.

The closer I got, and with it still distant, the more I was also certain that this door bore an uncanny resemblance to the door I had seen in my glance back after having crossed the border on our way to base camp. The very vagueness of it triggered this response because it was a specific kind of vagueness.

In the next half hour after that, I began to feel an instinctual urge to turn back, which I overrode by telling myself I could not yet face the return journey and the Crawler again. But the grooves in the ceiling hurt to look at, as if they ran across the outside of my own skull, continually being remade there. They had become lines of some repelling force. An hour later, as that shimmering white rectangle became larger but no more distinct, I was filled with such a feeling of *wrongness* that I suffered nausea. The idea of a *trap* grew in my mind, that this floating light in the darkness was not a door at all but the maw of some beast, and if I entered through it to the other side, it would devour me.

Finally I came to a halt. The words continued, unrelenting, downward, and I estimated the door lay no more than another five or six hundred steps below me. It blazed in my vision now; I could feel a rawness to my skin as if I were getting a sunburn from looking at it. I wanted to continue on, but I could not continue on. I could not will my legs to do it, could not force my mind to overcome the fear and uneasiness. Even the temporary absence of the brightness, as if hiding, counseled against further progress.

I remained there, sitting on the steps, watching the door, for some time. I worried that this sensation was residual hypnotic compulsion, that even from beyond death the psychologist had found a way to manipulate me. Perhaps there had been some encoded order or directive my infection had not been able to circumvent or override. Was I in the end stages of some prolonged form of annihilation?

The reason didn't matter, though. I knew I would never reach the door. I would become so sick I wouldn't be able to move, and I would never make it back to the surface, eyes cut and blinded by the grooves in the ceiling. I would be stuck on the steps, just like the anthropologist, and almost as much of a failure as she and the psychologist had been at recognizing the impossible. So I turned around, and, in a great deal of pain, feeling as if I had left part of myself there, I began to trudge back up those steps, the image of a hazy door of light as large in my imagination as the immensity of the Crawler.

I remember the sensation in that moment of turning away that something was now peering out at me from the door below, but when I glanced over my shoulder, only the familiar hazy white brilliance greeted me.

I wish I could say that the rest of the journey was a blur, as if I were indeed the flame the psychologist had seen, and I was staring out through my own burning. I wish that what came next was sunlight and the surface. But, although I had earned the right for it to be over . . . it was not over.

I remember every painful, scary step back up, every moment of it. I remember halting before I turned the corner where again lay the Crawler, still busy and incomprehensible in its task. Unsure if I could endure the excavation of my mind once more. Unsure if I would go mad from the sensation of drowning this time, no matter how much reason told me it was an illusion. But also knowing that the weaker I became, the more my mind would betray me. Soon it would be easy to retreat into the shadows, to become some *shell* haunting the lower steps. I might never have more strength or resolve to summon than in that moment.

I let go of Rock Bay, of the starfish in its pool. I thought instead about my husband's journal. I thought about my husband, in a boat, somewhere to the north. I thought about how everything lay above, and nothing now below.

So, I hugged the wall again. So, I closed my eyes again. So, I endured the light again, and flinched and moaned, expecting the rush of the sea into my mouth, and my head cracked open . . . but none of that happened. None of it, and I don't know why, except that having scanned and sampled me, and having, based on some unknown criteria, released me once, the Crawler no longer displayed any interest in me.

I was almost out of sight above it, rounding the corner, when some stubborn part of me insisted on risking a single glance back. One last ill-advised, defiant glance at something I might never understand.

Staring back at me amid that profusion of selves generated by the Crawler, I saw, barely visible, the face of a man, hooded in shadow and orbited by indescribable things I could think of only as his jailers.

The man's expression displayed such a complex and naked extremity of emotion that it transfixed me. I saw on those features the endurance of an unending pain and sorrow, yes, but shining through as well a kind of grim satisfaction and *ecstasy*. I had never seen such an expression before, but I recognized that face. I had seen it in a photograph. *A sharp, eagle's eye gleamed out from a heavy face, the left eye lost to his squint. A thick beard hid all but a hint of a firm chin under it.*

Trapped within the Crawler, the last lighthouse keeper stared out at me, so it seemed, not just across a vast, unbridgeable gulf but also out across the years. For, though thinner—his eyes receded in their orbits, his jawline more pronounced— the lighthouse keeper had not aged a day since that photograph was taken more than thirty years ago. This man who now existed in a place none of us could comprehend.

Did he know what he had become or had he gone mad long ago? Could he even really see me?

I do not know how long he had been looking at me, observing me, before I had turned to see him. Or if he had even existed before I saw him. But he was real to me, even though I held his gaze for such a short time, too short a time, and I cannot say anything passed between us. How long would have been enough? There was *nothing* I could do for him, and I had no room left in me for anything but my own survival.

There might be far worse things than drowning. I could not tell what he had lost, or what he might have gained, over the past thirty years, but I envied him that journey not at all.

I never dreamed before Area X, or at least I never remembered my dreams. My husband found this strange and told me once that maybe this meant I lived in a continuous dream from which I had never woken up. Perhaps he meant it as a joke, perhaps not. He had, after all, been haunted by a nightmare for years, had been shaped by it, until it had all fallen away from him, revealed as a facade. *A house and a basement and the awful crimes that had occurred there.*

But I'd had an exhausting day at work and took it seriously. Especially because it was the last week before he left on the expedition.

"We all live in a kind of continuous dream," I told him. "When we wake, it is because something, some event, some pinprick even, disturbs the edges of what we've taken as reality."

"Am I a pinprick then, disturbing the edges of your reality, ghost bird?" he asked, and this time I caught the desperation of his mood.

"Oh, is it bait-the-ghost-bird time again?" I said, arching an eyebrow. I didn't feel that relaxed. I felt sick to my stomach, but it seemed important to be normal for him. When he later came back and I saw what normal could be, I wished I'd been abnormal, that I'd shouted, that I'd done anything but be banal.

"Perhaps I'm a figment of your reality," he said. "Perhaps I don't exist except to do your bidding."

"Then you're failing spectacularly," I said as I made my way into the kitchen for a glass of water. He was already on a second glass of wine.

"Or succeeding spectacularly because you want me to fail," he said, but he was smiling.

He came up behind me then to hug me. He had thick forearms and a wide chest. His hands were hopeless man-hands, like something that should live in a cave, ridiculously strong, and an asset when he went sailing. The antiseptic rubber smell of Band-Aids suffused him like a particularly unctuous cologne. He was one big Band-Aid, placed directly on the wound.

"Ghost bird, where would you be if we weren't together?" he asked.

I had no answer for that. *Not here. Not there, either. Maybe nowhere.*

Then: "Ghost bird?"

"Yes," I said, resigned to my nickname.

"Ghost bird, I'm afraid now," he said. "I'm afraid and I have a selfish thing to ask. A thing I have no right to ask."

"Ask it anyway." I was still angry, but in those last days I had become reconciled to my loss, had compartmentalized it so I would not withhold my affection from him. There was a part of me, too, that raged against the systematic loss of my field assignments, was envious of his opportunity. That gloated about the empty lot because it was mine alone.

"Will you come after me if I don't come back? If you can?"

"You're coming back," I told him. To sit right here, like a golem, with all the things I knew about you drained out.

How I wish, beyond reason, that I had answered him, even to tell him no. And how I wish now—even though it was always impossible—that, in the end, I *had* gone to Area X for him.

A swimming pool. A rocky bay. An empty lot. A tower. A lighthouse. These things are real and not real. They exist and they do not exist. I remake them in my mind with every new thought, every remembered detail, and each time they are slightly different. Sometimes they are camouflage or disguises. Sometimes they are something more truthful.

When I finally reached the surface, I lay on my back atop the Tower, too exhausted to move, smiling for the simple, unexpected pleasure of the heat on my eyelids from the morning sun. I was continually reimagining the world even then, the lighthouse keeper colonizing my thoughts. I kept pulling out the photograph from my pocket, staring at his face, as if he held some further answer I could not yet grasp.

I wanted—I needed—to know that I had indeed seen him, not some apparition conjured up by the Crawler, and I clutched at anything that would help me believe that. What convinced me the most wasn't the photograph—it was the sample the anthropologist had taken from the edge of the Crawler, the sample that had proven to be human brain tissue.

So with that as my anchor, I began to form a narrative, as best I could, even as I stood and once again made my way back to the base camp. It was difficult because I knew nothing at all about the lighthouse keeper's life, had none of those indicators that might have allowed me to imagine him. I had just a photograph and that terrible glimpse of him inside the Tower. All I could think was that this was a man who had had a normal life once, perhaps, but not one of those familiar rituals that defined normal had had any permanence—or helped him. He had been caught up in a storm that hadn't yet abated. Perhaps he had even seen it coming from the top of the lighthouse, the Event arriving like a kind of wave.

And what had manifested? What do I believe manifested? Think of it as a thorn, perhaps, a long, thick thorn so large it is buried deep in the side of the world. Injecting itself into the world. Emanating from this giant thorn is an endless, perhaps automatic, need to assimilate and to mimic. Assimilator and assimilated interact through the catalyst of a script of words, which powers the engine of transformation. Perhaps it is a creature living in perfect symbiosis with a host of other creatures. Perhaps it is "merely" a machine. But in either instance, if it has intelligence, that intelligence is far different from our own. It creates out of our ecosystem a new world, whose processes and aims are utterly alien—one that works through supreme acts of mirroring, and by remaining hidden in so many other ways, all without surrendering the foundations of its *otherness* as it becomes what it encounters.

I do not know how this thorn got here or from how far away it came, but imagine the expeditions—twelve or fifty or a hundred, it doesn't matter—that keep coming into contact with that entity or entities, that keep becoming fodder and becoming remade. These expeditions that come here at a hidden entry point along a mysterious border, an entry point that (perhaps) is mirrored within the deepest depths of the Tower. Imagine these expeditions, and then recognize that *they all still exist* in Area X in some form, even the ones that came back, especially the ones that came back: layered over one another, communicating in whatever way is left to them. Imagine that this communication sometimes lends a sense of the uncanny to the landscape because of the narcissism of our human gaze, but that it is just part of the natural world here. I may never know what triggered the creation of the doppelgängers, but it may not matter.

Imagine, too, that while the Tower makes and remakes the world inside the border, it also slowly sends its emissaries across that border in ever greater numbers, so that in tangled gardens and fallow fields its envoys begin their work. *How does it travel and how far? What strange matter mixes and mingles?* In some future moment, perhaps the infiltration will reach even a certain remote sheet of coastal rock, quietly germinate in those tidal pools I know so well. Unless, of course, I am wrong that Area X is rousing itself from slumber, changing, becoming *different* than it was before.

The terrible thing, the thought I cannot dislodge after all I have seen, is that I can no longer say with conviction that this is a bad thing. Not when looking at the pristine nature of Area X and then the world beyond, which we have altered so much. Before she died, the psychologist said I had changed, and I think she meant I had *changed sides.* It isn't true—I don't even know if there are sides, or what that might mean—but it *could* be true. I see now that I could be persuaded. A religious or superstitious person, someone who believed in angels or in demons, might see it differently. Almost anyone else might see it differently. But I am not those people. I am just the biologist; I don't require any of this to have a deeper meaning.

I am aware that all of this speculation is incomplete, inexact, inaccurate, useless. If I don't have real answers, it is because we still don't know what questions to ask. Our instruments are useless, our methodology broken, our motivations selfish.

There is nothing much left to tell you, though I haven't quite told it right. But I am done trying anyway. After I left the Tower, I returned to base camp briefly, and then I came here, to the top of the lighthouse. I have spent four long days perfecting this account you are reading, for all its faults, and it is supplemented by a second journal that records all of my findings from the various samples taken by myself and other members of the expedition. I have even written a note for my parents.

I have bound these materials together with my husband's journal and will leave them here, atop the pile beneath the trapdoor. The table and the rug have been moved so that anyone can find what once was hidden. I also have replaced the lighthouse keeper's photograph in its frame and put it back on the wall of the landing. I have added a second circle around his face because I could not help myself.

If the hints in the journals are accurate, then when the Crawler reaches the end of its latest cycle within the Tower, Area X will enter a convulsive season of barricades and blood, a kind of cataclysmic molting, if you want to think of it that way. Perhaps even sparked by the spread of activated spores erupting from the words written by the Crawler. The past two nights, I have seen a growing cone of energy rising above the Tower and spilling out into the surrounding wilderness. Although nothing has yet come out of the sea, from the ruined village figures have emerged and headed for the Tower. From base camp, no sign of life. From the beach below, there is not even a boot left of the psychologist, as if she has melted into the sand. Every night, the moaning creature has let me know that it retains dominion over its kingdom of reeds.

Observing all of this has quelled the last ashes of the burning compulsion I had to *know everything* . . . anything . . . and in its place remains the knowledge that the brightness is not done with me. It is just beginning, and the thought of continually doing harm to myself to remain human seems somehow pathetic. I will not be here when the thirteenth expedition reaches base camp. (Have they seen me yet, or are they about to? Will I melt into this landscape, or look up from a stand of reeds or the waters of the canal to see some other explorer staring down in disbelief? Will I be aware that anything is wrong or out of place?)

I plan to continue on into Area X, to go as far as I can before it is too late. I will follow my husband up the coast, up past the island, even. I don't believe I'll find him—I don't need to find him—but I want to see what he saw. I want to feel him close, as if he is in the room. And, if I'm honest, I can't shake the sense that he is *still here*, somewhere, even if utterly transformed—in the eye of a dolphin, in the touch of an uprising of moss, anywhere and everywhere. Perhaps I'll even find a boat abandoned on a deserted beach, if I'm lucky, and some sign of what happened next. I could be content with *just that*, even knowing what I know.

This part I will do alone, leaving you behind. Don't follow. I'm well beyond you now, and traveling very fast.

Has there always been someone like me to bury the bodies, to have regrets, to carry on after everyone else was dead?

I am the last casualty of both the eleventh and the twelfth expeditions.

I am not returning home.

AUTHORITY

INCANTATIONS

000

In Control's dreams it is early morning, the sky deep blue with just a twinge of light. He is staring from a cliff down into an abyss, a bay, a cove. It always changes. He can see for miles into the still water. He can see ocean behemoths gliding there, like submarines or bell-shaped orchids or the wide hulls of ships, silent, ever moving, the size of them conveying such a sense of power that he can feel the havoc of their passage even from so far above. He stares for hours at the shapes, the movements, listening to the whispers echoing up to him . . . and then he falls. Slowly, too slowly, he falls soundless into the dark water, without splash or ripple. And keeps falling.

Sometimes this happens while he is awake, as if he hasn't been paying enough attention, and then he silently recites his own name until the real world returns to him.

001: FALLING

First day. The beginning of his last chance.

"These are the survivors?"

Control stood beside the assistant director of the Southern Reach, behind smudged one-way glass, staring at the three individuals sitting in the interrogation room. Returnees from the twelfth expedition into Area X.

The assistant director, a tall, thin black woman in her forties, said nothing back, which didn't surprise Control. She hadn't wasted an extra word on him since he'd arrived that morning after taking Monday to get settled. She hadn't spared him an extra look, either, except when he'd told her and the rest of the staff to call him "Control," not "John" or "Rodriguez." She had paused a beat, then replied, "In that case, call me Patience, not Grace," much to the stifled amusement of those present. The deflection away from her real name to one that also meant something else interested him. "That's okay," he'd said, "I can just call you Grace," certain this would not please her. She parried by continually referring to him as the "acting" director. Which was true: There lay between her stewardship and his ascension a gap, a valley of time and forms to be filled out, procedures to be followed, the rooting out and hiring of staff. Until then, the issue of authority might be murky.

But Control preferred to think of her as neither patience nor grace. He preferred to think of her as an abstraction if not an obstruction. She had made him sit through an old orientation video about Area X, must have known it would be basic and out of date. She had already made clear that theirs would be a relationship based on animosity. From her side, at least.

"Where were they found?" he asked her now, when what he wanted to ask was why they hadn't been kept separate from one another. Because you lack the discipline, because your department has been going to the rats for a long time now? The rats are down there in the basement now, gnawing away.

"Read the files," she said, making it clear he should have read them already.

Then she walked out of the room.

Leaving Control alone to contemplate the files on the table in front of him—and the three women behind the glass. Of course he had read the files, but he had hoped to duck past the assistant director's high guard, perhaps get her own thoughts. He'd read parts of her file, too, but still didn't have a sense of her except in terms of her reactions to him.

His first full day was only four hours old and he already felt contaminated by the dingy, bizarre building with its worn green carpet and the antiquated opinions of the other personnel he had met. A sense of diminishment suffused everything, even the sunlight that halfheartedly pushed through the high, rectangular windows. He was wearing his usual black blazer and dress slacks, a white shirt with a light blue tie, black shoes he'd shined that morning. Now he wondered why he'd bothered. He disliked having such thoughts because he wasn't above it all—he was *in* it—but they were hard to suppress.

Control took his time staring at the women, although their appearance told him little. They had all been given the same generic uniforms, vaguely army-issue but also vaguely janitorial. Their heads had all been shaved, as if they had suffered from some infestation, like lice, rather than something more inexplicable. Their faces all retained the same expression, or could be said not to retain any expression. Don't think of them by their names, he'd told himself on the plane. Let them carry only the weight of their functions at first. Then fill in the rest. But Control had never been good at remaining aloof. He liked to burrow in, try to find a level where the details illuminated without overwhelming him.

The surveyor had been found at her house, sitting in a chair on the back patio.

The anthropologist had been found by her husband, knocking on the back door of his medical practice.

The biologist had been found in an overgrown lot several blocks from her house, staring at a crumbling brick wall.

Just like the members of the prior expedition, none of them had any recollection of how they had made their way back across the invisible border, out of Area X. None of them knew how they had evaded the blockades and fences and other impediments the military had thrown up around the border. None of them knew what had happened to the fourth member of their expedition—the psychologist, who had, in fact, also been the director of the Southern Reach and overridden all objections to lead them, incognito.

None of them seemed to have much recollection of anything at all.

In the cafeteria that morning for breakfast, Control had looked out through the wall-to-wall paneled window into the courtyard with its profusion of stone tables, and then at the people shuffling through the line—too few, it seemed, for such a large building—and asked Grace, "Why isn't everyone more excited to have the expedition back?"

She had given him a long-suffering look, as if he were a particularly slow student in a remedial class. "Why do you think, Control?" She'd already managed to attach an ironic weight to his name, so he felt as if he were the sinker on one of his grandpa's fly rods, destined for the silt near the bottom of dozens of lakes. "We went through all this with the last expedition. They endured nine months of questions, and yet we never found out anything. And the whole time they were dying. How would that make you feel?" Long months of disorientation, and then their deaths from a particularly malign form of cancer.

He'd nodded slowly in response. Of course, she was right. His father had died of cancer. He hadn't thought of how that might have affected the staff. To him, it was still an abstraction, just words in a report, read on the plane down.

Here, in the cafeteria, the carpet turned dark green, against which a stylized arrow pattern stood out in a light green, all of the arrows pointing toward the courtyard.

"Why isn't there more light in here?" he asked. "Where does all the light go?"

But Grace was done answering his questions for the moment.

When one of the three—the biologist—turned her head a fraction, looking into the glass as if she could see him, Control evaded that stare with a kind of late-blooming embarrassment. Scrutiny such as his was impersonal, professional, but it probably didn't feel that way, even though they knew they were being watched.

He hadn't been told he would spend his first day questioning disoriented returnees from Area X, and yet Central must have known when he'd been offered the position. The expedition members had been picked up almost six weeks ago, been subjected to a month of tests at a processing station up north before being sent to the Southern Reach. Just as he'd been sent to Central first to endure two weeks of briefings, including gaps, whole days that slid into oblivion without much of anything happening, as if they'd always meant to time it this way. Then everything had sped up, and he had been given the impression of urgency.

These were among the details that had caused a kind of futile exasperation to wash over him ever since his arrival. The Voice, his primary contact in the upper echelons, had implied in an initial briefing that this was an easy assignment, given his past history. The Southern Reach had become a backward, backwater agency, guarding a dormant secret that no one seemed to care much about anymore, given the focus on terrorism and ecological collapse. The Voice had, in its gruff way, typified his mission "to start" as being brought in to "acclimate, assess, analyze, and then dig in deep," which wasn't his usual brief these days.

During an admittedly up-and-down career, Control had started as an operative in the field: surveillance on domestic terror cells. Then he'd been bumped up to data synthesis and organizational analysis—two dozen or more cases banal in their similarities and about which he was forbidden to talk. Cases invisible to the public: the secret history of nothing. But more and more he had become the fixer, mostly because he seemed better at identifying other people's specific problems than at managing his own general ones. At thirty-eight, that was what he had become known for, if he was known for anything. It meant you didn't have to be there for the duration, even though by now that's exactly what he wanted: to see something through. Problem was, no one really liked a fixer—"Hey, let me show you what you're doing wrong"—especially if they thought the fixer needed fixing from way back.

It always started well, even though it didn't always end well.

The Voice had also neglected to mention that Area X lay beyond a border that still, after more than thirty years, no one seemed to understand. No, he'd only picked up on that when reviewing the files and in the needless replication from the orientation video.

Nor had he known that the assistant director would hate him so much for replacing the missing director. Although he should have guessed; according to the scraps of information in her file, she had grown up lower-middle class, had gone to public school at first, had had to work harder than most to get to her current position. While Control came with whispers about being part of a kind of invisible dynasty, which naturally bred resentment. There was no denying that fact, even if, up close, the dynasty was more like a devolving franchise.

"They're ready. Come with me."

Grace, conjured up again, commanding him from the doorway.

There were, he knew, several different ways to break down a colleague's opposition, or their will. He would probably have to try all of them.

Control picked up two of the three files from the table and, gaze now locked in on the biologist, tore them down the middle, feeling the torque in his palms, and let them fall into the wastebasket.

A kind of choking sound came from behind him.

Now he turned—right into the full force of the assistant director's wordless anger. But he could see a wariness in her eyes, too. Good.

"Why are you still keeping paper files, Grace?" he asked, taking a step forward.

"The director insisted. You did that for a reason?"

He ignored her. "Grace, why are none of you comfortable using the words *alien* or *extraterrestrial* to talk about Area X?" He wasn't comfortable with them, either. Sometimes, since he'd been briefed on the truth, he'd felt a great, empty chasm opening up inside of him, filled with his own screams and yelps of disbelief.

But he'd never tell. He had a face for playing poker; he'd been told this by lovers and by relatives, even by strangers. About six feet tall. Impassive. The compact, muscular build of an athlete; he could run for miles and not feel it. He took pride in a good diet and enough exercise, although he did like whiskey.

She stood her ground. "No one's sure. Never prejudge the evidence."

"Even after all this time? I only need to interview one of them."

"What?" she asked.

Torque in hands transformed into torque in conversation.

"I don't need the other files because I only need to question one of them."

"You need all three." As if she still didn't quite understand.

He swiveled to pick up the remaining file. "No. Just the biologist."

"That is a mistake."

"Seven hundred and fifty-three isn't a mistake," he said. "Seven hundred and twenty-two isn't a mistake, either."

Her eyes narrowed. "Something is wrong with you."

"Keep the biologist in there," he said, ignoring her but adopting her syntax. *I know something you don't.* "Send the others back to their quarters."

Grace stared at him as if he were some kind of rodent and she couldn't decide whether to be disgusted or pitying. After a moment, though, she nodded stiffly and left.

He relaxed, let out his breath. Although she had to accept his orders, she still controlled the staff for the next week or two, could check him in a thousand ways until he was fully embedded.

Was it alchemy or a true magic? Was he wrong? And did it matter, since if he was wrong, each was exactly like the others anyway?

Yes, it mattered.

This was his last chance.

His mother had told him so before he'd come here.

Control's mother often seemed to him like a flash of light across a distant night sky. Here and gone, gone and here, and always remembered; perhaps wondered what it had been—what had caused the light. But you couldn't truly *know* it.

An only child, Jackie Severance had followed her father into the service and excelled; now she operated at levels far above anything her father, Jack Severance, had achieved, and he had been a much-decorated agent. Jack had brought her up sharp, organized, ready to lead. For all Control knew, Grandpa had made Jackie do tire obstacle courses as a child, stab flour sacks with bayonets. There weren't a whole lot of family albums from which to verify. Whatever the process, he had also bred into her a kind of casual cruelty, an expectation of high performance, and a calculated quality that could manifest as seeming indifference to the fate of others.

As a distant flash of light, Control admired her fiercely, had, indeed, followed her, if at a much lower altitude . . . but as a parent, even when she was around, she was unreliable about picking him up from school on time or remembering his lunches or helping with homework—rarely consistent on much of anything important in the mundane world on this side of the divide. Although she had always encouraged him in his headlong flight into and through the service.

Grandpa Jack, on the other hand, had never seemed fond of the idea, had one day looked at him and said, "I don't think he has the temperament." That assessment had been devastating to a boy of sixteen, already set on that course, but then it made him more determined, more focused, more tilted skyward toward the light. Later he thought that might have been why Grandpa had said it. Grandpa had a kind of unpredictable wildfire side, while his mother was an icy blue flame.

When he was eight or nine, they'd gone up to the summer cottage by the lake for the first time—"our own private spy club," his mother had called it. Just him, his mother, and Grandpa. There was an old TV in the corner, opposite the tattered couch. Grandpa would make him move the antenna to get better reception. "Just a little to the left, Control," he'd say. "Just a little more." His mother in the other room, going over some declassified files she'd brought from the office. And so he'd gotten his nickname, not knowing Grandpa had stolen it from spy jargon. As that kid, he'd held that nickname close as something cool, something his grandpa had given him out of love. But he was still astute enough not to tell anyone outside of family, even his girlfriends, for many years. He'd let them think that it was a sports nickname from high school, where he'd been a backup quarterback.

When he grew up, he took "Control" for his own. He could feel the sting of condescension in the word by then, but would never ask Grandpa if he'd meant it that way, or some other way. Wondered if the fact he'd spent as much time reading in the cottage by the lake as fishing had somehow turned his grandfather against him.

So, yes, he'd taken the name, remade it, and let it stick. But this was the first time he'd told his coworkers to call him "Control" and he couldn't say why, really. It had just come to him, as if he could somehow gain a true fresh start.

A little to the left, Control, and maybe you'll pick up that flash of light.

Why an empty lot? This he'd wondered ever since seeing the surveillance tape earlier that morning. Why had the biologist returned to an empty lot rather than her house? The other two had returned to something personal, to a place that held an emotional attachment. But the biologist had stood for hours and hours in an overgrown lot, oblivious to anything around her. From watching so many suspects on videotape, Control had become adroit at picking up on even the most mundane mannerism or nervous tic that meant a signal was being passed on . . . but there was nothing like that on the tape.

Her presence there had registered with the Southern Reach via a report filed by the local police, who'd picked her up as a vagrant: a delayed reaction, driven by active searching once the Southern Reach had picked up the other two.

Then there was the issue of terseness versus terseness.

753. 722.

A slim lead, but Control already sensed that this assignment hinged on the details, on detective work. Nothing would come easy. He'd have no luck, no shit-for-brains amateur bomb maker armed with fertilizer and some cut-rate version of an ideology who went to pieces within twenty minutes of being put in the interrogation room.

During the preliminary interviews before it was determined who went on the twelfth expedition, the biologist had, according to the transcripts in her file, managed to divulge only 753 words. Control had counted them. That included the word *breakfast* as a complete answer to one question. Control admired that response.

He had counted and recounted the words during that drawn-out period of waiting while they set up his computer, issued him a security card, presented to him passwords and key codes, and went through all of the other rituals with which he had become overly familiar during his passage through various agencies and departments.

He'd insisted on the former director's office despite Grace's attempts to cordon him off in a glorified broom closet well away from the heart of everything. He'd also insisted they leave everything as is in the office, even personal items. She clearly disliked the idea of him rummaging through the director's things.

"You are a little off," Grace had said when the others had left. "You are not all there."

He'd just nodded because there was no use denying it was a little strange. But if he was here to assess and restore, he needed a better idea of how badly it had all slipped—and as some sociopath at another station had once said, "The fish rots from the head." Fish rotted all over, cell corruption being nonhierarchical and not caste-driven, but point taken.

Control had immediately taken a seat behind the battering ram of a desk, among the clutter of piles and piles of folders, the ramble of handwritten notes and Post-its . . . in the swivel chair that gave him such a great panoramic view of the bookcases against the walls, interspersed with bulletin boards overlaid with the sediment of various bits of paper pinned and re-pinned until they looked more like oddly delicate yet haphazard art installations. The room smelled stale, with a slight aftertaste of long-ago cigarettes.

Just the size and weight of the director's computer monitor spoke to its obsolescence, as did the fact that it had died decades ago, thick dust layered atop it. It had been halfheartedly shoved to the side, two shroud-shadows on the calendar blotter beneath describing both its original location and the location of the laptop that had apparently supplanted it—although no one could now find that laptop. He made a mental note to ask if they had searched her home.

The calendar dated back to the late nineties; was that when the director had started to lose the thread? He had a sudden vision of her in Area X with the twelfth expedition, just wandering through the wilderness with no real destination: a tall, husky, forty-year-old woman who looked older. Silent, conflicted, torn. So devoured by her responsibility that she'd allowed herself to believe she owed it to the people she sent into the field to join them. Why had no one stopped her? Had no one cared about her? Had she made a convincing case? The Voice hadn't said. The maddeningly incomplete files on her told Control nothing.

Everything in what he saw showed that she had cared, and yet that she had cared not at all about the functioning of the agency.

Nudging his knee on the left, under the desk: the hard drive for the monitor. He wondered if that had stopped working back in the nineties, too. Control had the feeling he did not want to see the rooms the hardware techs worked in, the miserable languishing corpses of the computers of past decades, the chaotic unintentional museum of plastic and wires and circuit boards. Or perhaps the fish did rot from the head, and only the director had decomposed.

So, sans computer, his own laptop not yet deemed secure enough, Control had done a little light reading of the transcripts from the induction interviews with the members of the twelfth expedition. The former director, in her role as psychologist, had conducted them.

The other recruits had been uncappable, unstoppable geysers in Control's opinion: Great chortling, hurtling, cliché-spouting babblers. People who by comparison could not hold their tongues . . . 4,623 words . . . 7,154 words . . . and the all-time champion, the linguist who had backed out at the last second, coming in at 12,743 words of replies, including a heroically prolonged childhood memory "about as entertaining as a kidney stone exploding through your dick," as someone had scrawled in the margin. Which left just the biologist and her terse 753 words. That kind of self-control had made him look not just at the words but at the pauses between them. For example: "I enjoyed all of my jobs in the field." Yet she had been fired from most of them. She thought she had said nothing, but every word—even *breakfast*—created an opening. Breakfast had not gone well for the biologist as a child.

The ghost was right there, in the transcripts since her return, moving through the text. Things that showed themselves in the empty spaces, making Control unwilling to say her words aloud for fear that somehow he did not really understand the undercurrents and hidden references. A detached description of a thistle . . . A mention of a lighthouse. A sentence or two describing the quality of the light on the marshes in Area X. None of it should have gotten to him, yet he felt her there, somehow, looking over his shoulder in a way not evoked by the interviews with the other expedition members.

The biologist claimed to remember as little as the others.

Control knew that for a lie—or it would become a lie if he drew her out. Did he want to draw her out? Was she cautious because something had happened in Area X or because she was just built that way? A shadow had passed over the director's desk then. He'd been here before, or somewhere close, making these kinds of decisions before, and it had almost broken him, or broken through him. But he had no choice.

About seven hundred words after she came back. Just like the other two. But unlike them, that was roughly comparable to her terseness before she had left.

And there were the odd specifics that the others lacked. Whereas the anthropologist might say "The wilderness was empty and pristine," the biologist said, "There were bright pink thistles everywhere, even when the fresh water shifted to saline . . . The light at dusk was a low blaze, a brightness."

That, combined with the strangeness of the empty lot, made Control believe that the biologist might actually remember more than the others. That she might be more present than the others but was hiding it for some reason. He'd never had this particular situation before, but he remembered a colleague's questioning of a terrorist who had suffered a head wound and spent the interrogation sessions in the hospital delaying and delaying in hopes his memory would return. It had. But only the facts, not the righteous impulse that had engendered his action, and then he'd been lost, easy prey for the questioners.

Control hadn't shared his theory with the assistant director because if he was wrong she'd use it to shore up her negative opinion of him—but also to keep her off-balance for as long as possible. "Never do something for just one reason," his grandpa had told him more than once, and that, at least, Control had taken to heart.

The biologist's hair had been long and dark brown, almost black, before they'd shaved it off. She had dark, thick eyebrows, green eyes, a slight, slightly off-center nose (broken once, falling on rocks), and high cheekbones that spoke to the strong Asian heritage on one side of her family. Her chapped lips were surprisingly full for such a thin frown. He mistrusted the eyes, the percentages on that, had checked to confirm they hadn't been another color before the expedition.

Even sitting down at the table, she somehow projected a sense of being physically strong, with a ridge of thick muscle where her neck met her shoulders. So far, all the tests run had come back negative for cancer or other abnormalities. He couldn't remember what it said in her file, but Control thought she was probably almost as tall as him. She had been held in the eastern wing of the building for two weeks now, with nothing to do but eat and exercise.

Before going on the expedition, the biologist had received intense survival and weapons training at a Central facility devoted to that purpose. She would have been briefed with whatever half-truths the Southern Reach's command and control deemed useful, based on criteria Control still found arcane, even murky. She would have been subjected to conditioning to make her more receptive to hypnotic suggestion.

The psychologist/director would have been given any number of hypnotic cues to use—words that, in certain combinations, would induce certain effects. Passing thought as the door shut behind Control: Had the director had anything to do with muddying their memories, while they were still in Area X?

Control slid into a chair across from the biologist, aware that Grace, at the very least, watched them through the one-way glass. Experts had questioned the biologist, but Control was also a kind of expert, and he needed to have the direct contact. There was something in the texture of a face-to-face interview that transcripts and videotape lacked.

The floor beneath his shoes was grimy, almost sticky. The fluorescent lights above flickered at irregular intervals, and the table and chairs seemed like something out of a high-school cafeteria. He could smell the sour metallic tang of a low-quality cleaning agent, almost like rotting honey. The room did not inspire confidence in the Southern Reach. A room meant as a debriefing space—or meant to seem like a debriefing space—should be more comfortable than one meant always and forever for interrogation, for a presumption of possible resistance.

Now that Control sat across from the biologist, she had the kind of presence that made him reluctant to stare into her eyes. But he always felt nervous right before he questioned someone, always felt as if that bright flash of light across the sky had frozen in its progress and come down to stand at his shoulder, mother in the flesh, observing him. The truth of it was, his mother did check up on him sometimes. She could get hold of the footage. So it wasn't paranoia or just a feeling. It was part of his possible reality.

Sometimes it helped to play up his nervousness, to make the person across from him relax. So he cleared his throat, took a hesitant sip of water from the glass he'd brought in with him, fiddled with the file on her he'd placed on the table between them, along with a remote control for the TV to his left. To preserve the conditions under which she'd been found, to basically ensure she didn't gain memories artificially, the assistant director had ordered that she not be given any of the information from her personnel file. Control found this cruel but agreed with Grace. He wanted the file between them to seem like a possible reward during some later session, even if he didn't yet know if he would give it to her.

Control introduced himself by his real name, informed her that their "interview" was being recorded, and asked her to state her name for the record.

"Call me Ghost Bird," she said. Was there a twinge of defiance in her flat voice?

He looked up at her, and instantly was at sea, looked away again. Was she using hypnotic suggestion on him somehow? It was his first thought, quickly dismissed.

"Ghost Bird?"

"Or nothing at all."

He nodded, knew when to let something go, would research the term later. Vaguely remembered something in the file. Perhaps.

"Ghost Bird," he said, testing it out. The words tasted chalky, unnatural in his mouth. "You remember nothing about the expedition?"

"I told the others. It was a pristine wilderness." He thought he detected a note of irony in her tone, but couldn't be sure.

"How well did you get to know the linguist—during training?" he asked.

"Not well. She was very vocal. She wouldn't shut up. She was . . ." The biologist trailed off as Control stifled elation. A question she hadn't expected. Not at all.

"She was what?" he prompted. The prior interrogator had used the standard technique: develop rapport, present the facts, grow the relationship from there. With nothing really to show for it.

"I don't remember."

"I think you do remember." And if you remember that, then . . .

"No."

He made a show of opening the file and consulting the existing transcripts, letting the edge of the paper-clipped pages that gave her most vital statistics come clear.

"Okay, then. Tell me about the thistles."

"The thistles?" Her expressive eyebrows told him what she thought of the question.

"Yes. You were quite specific about the thistles. Why?" It still perplexed him, the amount of detail there about thistles, in an interview from the prior week, when she'd arrived at the Southern Reach. It made him think again of hypnotic cues. It made him think of words being used as a protective thicket.

The biologist shrugged. "I don't know."

He read from the transcript: "'The thistles there have a lavender bloom and grow in the transitional space between the forest and the swamp. You cannot avoid them. They attract a variety of insects and the buzzing and the brightness that surrounds them suffuses Area X with a sense of industry, almost like a human city.' And it goes on, although I won't."

She shrugged again.

Control didn't intend to hover, this first time, but instead to glide over the terrain, to map out the extent of the territory he wanted to cover with her. So he moved on.

"What do you remember about your husband?"

"How is that relevant?"

"Relevant to what?" Pouncing.

No response, so he prompted her again: "What do you remember about your husband?"

"That I had one. Some memories before I went over, like I had about the linguist." Clever, to tie that in, to try to make it seem part and parcel. A vagueness, not a sharpness.

"Did you know that he came back, like you?" he asked. "That he was disoriented, like you?"

"I'm not disoriented," she snapped, leaning forward, and Control leaned back. He wasn't afraid, but for a moment he'd thought he should be. Brain scans had been normal. All measures had been taken to check for anything remotely like an invasive species. Or "an intruder" as Grace put it, still unable to say anything to him remotely like the word *alien*. If anything, Ghost Bird was healthier now than before she'd left; the toxins present in most people today existed in her and the others at much lower levels than normal.

"I didn't mean to offend," he said. And yet she *was* disoriented, Control knew. No matter what she remembered or didn't remember, the biologist he'd come to know from the pre-expedition transcripts would not have so quickly shown irritation. Why had he gotten to her?

He picked up the remote control from beside the file, clicked twice. The flat-screen TV on the wall to their left fizzled to life, showing the pixelated, fuzzy image of the biologist standing in the empty lot, almost as still as the pavement or the bricks in the building in front of her. The whole scene was awash in the sickly green of surveillance-camera noir.

"Why that empty lot? Why did we find you there?"

A look of indifference and no answer. He let the video continue to play. The repetition in the background sometimes got to the interviewee. But usually video footage showed a suspect putting down a bag or shoving something into a trash bin.

"First day in Area X," Control said. "Hiking to base camp. What happened?"

"Nothing much."

Control had no children, but he imagined that this was more or less what he'd get from a teenager asked about her day at school. Perhaps he would circle back for a moment.

"But you remember the thistles very, very well," he said.

"I don't know why you keep talking about thistles."

"Because what you said about them suggests you remember some of your observations from the expedition."

A pause, and Control knew the biologist was staring at him. He wanted to return fire, but something warned him against it. Something made him feel that the dream of falling into the depths might take him.

"Why am I a prisoner here?" she asked, and he felt it was safe to meet her gaze again, as if some moment of danger had come and gone.

"You aren't. This is part of your debriefing."

"But I can't leave."

"Not yet," he admitted. "But you will." If only to another facility; it might be another two or three years, if all went well, before they allowed any of the return-ees back out in the world. Their legal status was in that gray area often arbitrarily defined by the threat to national security.

"I find that unlikely," she said.

He decided to try again. "If not thistles, what would be relevant?" he asked. "What should I ask you?"

"Isn't that your job?"

"What is my job?" Although he knew perfectly well what she meant.

"You're in charge of the Southern Reach."

"Do you know what the Southern Reach is?"

"Yesss." Like a hiss.

"What about the second day at base camp? When did things begin to get strange?" Had they? He had to assume they had.

"I don't remember."

Control leaned forward. "I can put you under hypnosis. I have the right to. I can do that."

"Hypnosis doesn't work on me," she said, disgust at his threat clear from her tone.

"How do you know?" A moment of disorientation. Had she given up something she didn't want to give up, or had she remembered something lost to her before? Did she know the difference?

"I just know."

"For clarity on that, we could recondition you and then put you under hypnosis." All of this a bluff, in that it was more complicated logistically. To do so, Control would have to send her to Central, and she'd disappear into that maw forever. He might get to see the reports, but he'd never have direct contact again. Nor did he particularly *want* to recondition her.

"Do that and I'll—" She managed to stop herself on the cusp of what sounded like the beginning of the word *kill.*

Control decided to ignore that. He'd been on the other end of enough threats to know which to take seriously.

"What made you resistant to hypnosis?" he asked.

"Are *you* resistant to hypnosis?" Defiant.

"Why were you at the empty lot? The other two were found looking for their loved ones."

No reply.

Maybe enough had been said for now. Maybe this was enough.

Control turned off the television, picked up his file, nodded at her, and walked to the door.

Once there, the door open and letting in what seemed like more shadows than it should, he turned, aware of the assistant director staring at him from down the hall as he looked back at the biologist.

He asked, as he had always planned to, the postscript to an opening act: "What's the last thing you remember doing in Area X?"

The answer, unexpected, surged up toward him like a kind of attack as the light met the darkness: "Drowning. I was drowning."

002: ADJUSTMENTS

J ust close your eyes and you will remember me," Control's father had told him three years ago, in a place not far from where he was now, the dying trying to comfort the living. But when he closed his eyes, everything disappeared except the dream of falling and the accumulated scars from past assignments. Why had the biologist said that? Why had she said she was drowning? It had thrown him, but it had also given him an odd sense of secret sharing between them. As if she had gotten into his head and seen his dream, and now they were bound together. He resented that, did not want to be connected to the people he had to question. He had to glide above. He had to choose when he swooped down, not be brought to earth by the will of another.

When Control opened his eyes, he was standing in the back of the U-shaped building that served as the Southern Reach's headquarters. The curve lay in the front, a road and parking lot preceding it. Built in a style now decades old, the layered, stacked concrete was a monument or a midden—he couldn't decide which. The ridges and clefts were baffling; the way the roof leered slightly over the rest made it seem less functional than like performance art or abstract sculpture on a grand and yet numbing scale. Making things worse, the area coveted by the open arms of the U had been made into a courtyard, looking out on a lake ringed by thick old-growth forest. The edges of the lake were singed black, as if at one time set ablaze, and a wretched gnarl of cypress knees waded through the dark, brackish water. The light that suffused the lake had a claustrophobic gray quality, separate and distinct from the blue sky above.

This, too, had at one time been new, perhaps back during the Cretaceous period, and the building had probably stood here then in some form, reverse engineered so far into the past that you could still look out the windows and see dragonflies as big as vultures.

The U that hugged them close inspired no great confidence; it felt less a symbol of luck than of the incomplete. Incomplete thoughts. Incomplete conclusions. Incomplete reports. The doors at the ends of the U, through which many passed as a shortcut to the other side, confirmed a failure of the imagination. And all the while, the abysmal swamp did whatever swamps did, as perfect in its way as the Southern Reach was imperfect.

Everything was so still that when a woodpecker swooped across that scene it was as violent as the sonic boom of an F-16.

To the left of the U and the lake—just visible from where he stood—a road threaded its way through the trees, toward the invisible border, beyond which lay Area X. Just thirty-five miles of paved road and then another fifteen unpaved beyond that, with ten checkpoints in all, and shoot-to-kill orders if you weren't meant to be there, and fences and barbed wire and trenches and pits and more swamp, possibly even government-trained colonies of apex predators and genetically modified poison berries and hammers to hit yourself on the head with . . . but in some ways, ever since Control had been briefed, he had wondered: To what point? Because that's what you did in such situations? Keep people out? He'd studied the reports. If you reached the border in an "unauthorized way" and crossed over anywhere but the door, you would never be seen again. How many people had done just that, without being spotted? How would the Southern Reach ever know? Once or twice, an investigative journalist had gotten close enough to photograph the outside of the Southern Reach's border facilities, but even then it had just confirmed in the public imagination the official story of environmental catastrophe, one that wouldn't be cleaned up for a century.

There came a tread around the stone tables in the concrete courtyard across which little white tiles competed with squares of clotted earth into which unlikely tulips had been shoved at irregular intervals . . . He knew that tread, with its special extra little dragging sound. The assistant director had been a field officer once; something had happened on assignment, and she'd hurt her leg. Inside the building, she could disguise it, but not on the treacherous grouted tiles. It wasn't an advantage for him to know this, because it made him want to empathize with her. "Whenever you say 'in the field,' I have this image of all of you spooks running through the wheat," his father had said to his mother, once.

Grace was joining him at his request, to assist him in staring out at the swamp while they talked about Area X. Because he'd thought a change of setting—leaving the confines of the concrete coffin—might help soften her animosity. Before he'd realized just how truly hellish and prehistoric the landscape was, and thus now pre-hysterical as well. Look out upon this mosquito orgy, and warm to me, Grace.

"You interviewed just the biologist. I still do not know why." She said this before he could extend even a tendril of an opening gambit . . . and all of his resolve to play the diplomat, to somehow become her colleague, not her enemy—even if by misdirection or a metaphorical jab in the kidneys—dissolved into the humid air.

He explained his thought processes. She seemed impressed, although he couldn't really read her yet.

"Did she ever seem, during training, like she was hiding something?" he asked.

"Deflection. You think she is hiding something."

"I don't know yet, actually. I could be wrong."

"We have more expert interrogators than you."

"Probably true."

"We should send her to Central."

The thought made him shudder.

"No," he said, a little too emphatically, then worried in the next split second that the assistant director might guess that he cared about the biologist's fate.

"I have already sent the anthropologist and the surveyor away."

Now he could smell the decay of all that plant matter slowly rotting beneath the surface of the swamp, could sense the awkward turtles and stunted fish pushing their way through matted layers. He didn't trust himself to turn to face her. Didn't trust himself to say anything, stood there suspended by his surprise.

Cheerfully, she continued: "You said they weren't of any use, so I sent them to Central."

"By whose authority?"

"Your authority. You clearly indicated to me that this was what you wanted. If you meant something else, my apologies."

A tiny seismic shift occurred inside of Control, an imperceptible shudder.

They were gone. He couldn't have them back. He had to put it out of his mind, would feed himself the lie that Grace had done him a favor, simplified his job. Just how much pull did she have at Central, anyway?

"I can always read the transcripts if I change my mind," he said, attempting an agreeable tone. They'd still be questioned, and he'd given her the opening by saying he didn't want to interview them.

She was scanning his face intently, looking for some sign that she'd come close to hitting the target.

He tried to smile, doused his anger with the thought that if the assistant director had meant him real harm, she would have found a way to spirit the biologist away, too. This was just a warning. Now, though, he was going to have to take something away from Grace as well. Not to get even but so she wouldn't be tempted to take yet more from him. He couldn't afford to lose the biologist, too. Not yet.

Into the awkward silence, Grace asked, "Why are you just standing out here in the heat like an idiot?" Breezily, as if nothing had happened at all. "We should go inside. It's time for lunch, and you can meet some of the admin."

Control was already growing accustomed to her disrespect of him, and he hated that, wanted an opportunity to reverse the trend. As he followed her in, the swamp at his back had a weight, a presence. Another kind of enemy. He'd had enough of such views, growing up nearby as a teenager after his parents' divorce, and, again, while his father slowly died. He'd hoped to never see a swamp again.

"Just close your eyes and you will remember me."

I do, Dad. I do remember you, but you're fading. There's too much interference, and all of *this* is becoming much too real.

Control's father's side of the family came originally from Central America, Hispanic and Indian; he had his father's hands and black hair, his mother's slight nose and height, a skin color somewhere in between. His paternal grandfather had died before Control was old enough to know him, but he had heard the epic stories. The man had sold clothespins door-to-door as a kid, in certain neighborhoods, and been a boxer in his twenties, not good enough to be a contender but good enough to be a paid opponent and take a beating. Afterward, he'd been a construction worker, and then a driving instructor, before an early death from a heart attack at sixty-five. His wife, who worked in a bakery, passed on just a year later. His eldest child, Control's father, had grown up to be an artist in a family mostly composed of carpenters and mechanics, and used his heritage to create abstract sculptures. He had humanized the abstractions by painting over them in the bright palette favored by the Mayans and by affixing to them bits of tile and glass— bridging some gap between professional and outsider art. That was his life, and Control never knew a time that his father was not that person and only that person.

The story of how Control's father and mother fell in love was also the happy story of how his father had risen, for a time, as a favorite in high-end art galleries. They had met at a reception for his work and, as they told it, had been enamored with each other right from the first glance, although later Control found that difficult to believe. At the time, she was based up north and had what amounted to a desk job, although she was rising fast. His father moved to be with her, and they had Control and then only a year or two later she was reassigned, from a desk job to active duty in the field, and that was the start of the end of it all, the story that anchored Control as a kid soon revealed as just a brief moment set against a landscape of unhappiness. Not unique: the kind of depressingly familiar painting you'd find in a seaside antique store but never buy.

The silence was punctuated by arguments, a silence created not just by the secrets she carried with her but by those she could not divulge, and, Control realized as an adult, by her inner reserve, which after a time could not be bridged. Her absences tore at his father, and by the time Control was ten, that was the subtext and sometimes the transcript of their dispute: She was killing his art and that wasn't fair, even though the art scene had moved on and what his father did was expensive and required patrons or grants to sustain.

She bore the recrimination, Control remembered, with calm and a chilly, aloof compassion. She was the unstoppable force that came blowing in—not there, there—with presents bought at the last minute in far-off airports and an innocent-sounding cover story about what she'd been up to, or a less innocent story that Control realized years later, when faced with a similar dilemma, had been coming to them from a time delay. Something declassified she could now share but that had happened to her long ago. The stories, and the aloofness, agitated his father, but the compassion infuriated him.

When they divorced, Control went south to live with his dad, who became embedded in a community that felt comfortable because it included some of his relatives and fed his artistic ambitions even as his bank account starved.

Yet during those hot summers in that small town not very far from the Southern Reach, as a thirteen-year-old with a rusty bike and a few loyal friends, Control kept thinking about his mother, out in the field, in some far-off city or country: that distant streak of light that sometimes came down out of the night sky and materialized on their doorstep as a human being. Exactly in the same way as when they'd been together as a family.

One day, he believed, she would take him with her, and he would become the streak of light, have secrets no one else could ever know.

Some rumors about Area X were elaborate and in their complexity seemed to Control like schools of the most deadly and yet voluminous jellyfish at the aquarium. As you watched them, in their undulating progress, they seemed both real and unreal framed against the stark blue of the water. *Invasion site. Secret government experiments.* How could such an organism actually exist? The simple ones that echoed the official story—variations on a human-made ecological disaster area—were by contrast so commonplace these days that they hardly registered or elicited curiosity. The petting-zoo versions that ate out of your hand.

But the truth did have a simple quality to it: About thirty-two years ago, along a remote southern stretch known by some as the "forgotten coast," an Event had occurred that began to transform the landscape and simultaneously caused a border or wall to appear. A kind of ghost or "permeable pre-border manifestation" as the files put it—light as fog, almost invisible except for a flickering quality—had quickly emanated out in all directions from an unknown epicenter and then suddenly stopped at its current impenetrable limits.

Since then, the Southern Reach had been established and sought to investigate what had occurred, with little success and much sacrifice of lives via the expeditions—sent in through the sole point of egress. Yet that loss of life was trifling compared to the possibility of some break in containment across a border that the scientists were still studying and trying to understand. The riddle of why equipment, when recovered, had been rendered nonfunctional, some of it decomposing at an incredibly fast rate. The teasing, inconsistent way in which some expeditions came back entirely unharmed that seemed almost more inexplicable.

"It started earlier than the border coming down," the assistant director told him after lunch in his new-old office. She was all business now, and Control chose to accept her at face value, to continue to put away, for now, his anger at her preemptive strike in banishing the anthropologist and the surveyor.

Grace rolled out the map of Area X on a corner of his desk: the coastline, the lighthouse, the base camp, the trails, the lakes and rivers, the island many miles north that marked the farthest reach of the . . . Incursion? Invasion? Infestation? What word worked? The worst part of the map was the black dot hand-labeled by the director as "the tunnel" but known to most as "the topographical anomaly." Worst part because not every expedition whose members had survived to report back had encountered it, even when they'd mapped the same area.

Grace tossed files on top of the map. It still struck Control, with a kind of nostalgia rarely granted to his generation, how anachronistic it was to deal in paper. But the concern about sending modern technology across the border had infected the former director. She had forbidden certain forms of communication, required that all e-mails be printed out and the original, electronic versions regularly archived and purged, and had arcane and confusing protocols for using the Internet and other forms of electronic communication. Would he put an end to that? He didn't know yet, had a kind of sympathy for the policy, impractical though it might be. He used the Internet solely for research and admin. He believed a kind of a fragmentation had crept into people's minds in the modern era.

"*It started earlier . . .*"

"How much earlier?"

"Intel indicates that there may have been odd . . . activity occurring along that coast for at least a century before the border came down." Before Area X had formed. A "pristine wilderness." He'd never heard the word *pristine* used so many times before today.

Idly, he wondered what *they* called it—whoever or whatever had created that pristine bubble that had killed so many people. Maybe they called it a holiday retreat. Maybe they called it a beachhead. Maybe "they" were so incomprehensible he'd never understand what they called it, or why. He'd asked the Voice if he needed access to the files on other major unexplained occurrences, and the Voice had made "No" sound like a granite cliff, with only flailing blue sky beyond it.

Control had already seen at least some of the flotsam and jetsam now threatening to buckle the desk in the file summary. He knew that quite a bit of the information peeking out at him from the beige folders came from lighthouse journals and police records—and that the inexplicable in it had to be teased out from the edges, pushed forward into the light like the last bit of toothpaste in the dehydrated tube curled up on the edge of the bathroom sink. The kind of "strange doings" alluded to by hard-living bearded fishermen in old horror movies as they stared through haunted eyes at the unforgiving sea. Unsolved disappearances. Lights in the night. Stories of odd salvagers, and false beacons, and the hundred legends that accrete around a lonely coastline and a remote lighthouse.

There had even been an informal group—the Séance & Science Brigade—dedicated to applying "empirical reality to paranormal phenomena." Members of the S&S Brigade had written several self-published books that had collected dust on the counters of local businesses. It was the S&SB that had in effect named Area X, identifying that coast as "of particular interest" and calling it "Active Site X"—a name prominent on their bizarre science-inspired tarot cards.

The Southern Reach had discounted S&SB early on as "not a catalyst or a player or an instigator" in whatever had caused Area X—just a bunch of (un)lucky "amateurs" caught up in something beyond the grasp of their imaginations. Except, almost every effective terrorist Control had encountered was an "amateur."

"We live in a universe driven by chance," his father had said once, "but the bullshit artists all want causality." Bullshit artist in this context meant his mother, but the statement had wide applications.

So was all or any of it random coincidence—or part of some vast, pre–Area X conspiracy? You could spend years wading through the data, trying to find the answer—and it looked to Control as if that's exactly what the former director had been doing.

"And you think this is credible evidence?" Control still didn't know how far into the mountain of bullshit the assistant director had fallen. Too far, given her natural animosity, and he wouldn't be inclined to pull her out of it.

"Not all of it," she conceded, a thin smile erasing the default frown. "But tracking back from the events we know have occurred since the border came down, you begin to see patterns."

Control believed her. He would have believed Grace had she said visions appeared in the swirls of her strawberry gelato on hot summer days or in the fracturing of the ice in another of her favorites, rum-and-diet with a lime (her personnel file was full of maddeningly irrelevant details). It was in the nature of being an analyst. But what patterns had colonized the former director's mind? And how much of that had infiltrated the assistant director? On some level, Control hoped that the mess the director had left behind was deliberate, to hide some more rational progression.

"But how is that different from any other godforsaken stretch of coast half off the grid?" There were still dozens of them all across the country. Places that were poison to real-estate agents, with little infrastructure and a long history of distrust of the government.

The assistant director stared at him in a way that made him feel uncomfortably like a middle-school student again, sent up for insolence.

"I know what you're thinking," she said. "Have we been compromised by our own data? The answer is: Of course. That is what happens over time. But if there is something in the files that is useful, you might see it because you have fresh eyes. So I can archive all of this now if you like. Or we can use you the way we need to use you: not because you know anything but because you know so little."

A kind of resentful pride rose up in Control that wasn't useful, that came from having a parent who *did* seem to know everything.

"I didn't mean that I—"

Mercifully, she cut him off. Unmercifully, her tone channeled contempt. "We have been here a long time . . . Control. A very long time. Living with this. Unable to do very much about this." A surprising amount of pain had entered her voice. "You don't go home at night with it in your stomach, in your bones. In a few weeks, when you have seen everything, you will have been living with it for a long time, too. You will be just like us—only more so, because it is getting worse. Fewer and fewer journals recovered, and more zombies, as if they have been mind-wiped. And no one in charge has time for us."

It could have been a moment to commiserate over the vagaries and injustices perpetrated by Central, Control realized later, but he just sat there staring at her. He found her fatalism a hindrance, especially suffused, as he misdiagnosed it at first, with such a grim satisfaction. A claustrophobic combination that no one needed, that helped no one. It was also inaccurate in its progressions.

The first expedition alone had, according to the files, experienced such horrors, almost beyond imagining, that it was a wonder that they had sent anyone after that. But they'd had no choice, understood they were in it for "the long haul" as, he knew from transcripts, the former director had liked to say. They hadn't even let the later expeditions know the true fate of the first expedition, had created a fiction of encountering an undisturbed wilderness and then built other lies on top of that one. This had probably been done as much to ease the Southern Reach's own trauma as to protect the morale of the subsequent expeditions.

"In thirty minutes, you have an appointment to tour the science division," she said, getting up and looming over him, leaning with her hands on his desk. "I think I will let you find the place yourself." That would give him just enough time to check his office for surveillance devices beforehand.

"Thanks," he said. "You can leave now."

So she left.

But it didn't help. Before he'd arrived, Control had imagined himself flying free above the Southern Reach, swooping down from some remote perch to manage things. That wasn't going to happen. Already his wings were burning up and he felt more like some ponderous moaning creature trapped in the mire.

As he became more familiar with it, the former director's office revealed no new or special features to Control's practiced eye. Except that his computer, finally installed on the desk, looked almost science-fictional next to all the rest of it.

The door lay to the far left of the long, rectangular room, so that you wandered into its length toward the mahogany desk set against the far wall. No one could have snuck up on the director or read over her shoulder. Each wall had been covered in bookcases or filing cabinets, with stacks of papers and some books forming a second width in front of this initial layering. At the highest levels, or in some ridiculous cases, balanced on the stacks, those bulletin boards with ripped pieces of paper and scribbled diagrams pinned to them. He felt as if he had been placed inside someone's disorganized mind. Near her desk, on the left, he uncovered an array of preserved natural ephemera. Dusty and decaying bits of pinecone trailed across the shelves. A vague hint of a rotting smell, but he couldn't track down the origin.

Opposite the entrance lay another door, situated in a gap between bookcases, but this had been blocked by more piles of file folders and cardboard boxes and he'd been told it opened onto the wall—detritus of an inelegant remodeling. Opposite the desk, on the far wall about twenty-five feet away, was a kind of break in the mess to make room for two rows of pictures, all in the kinds of frames cheaply bought at discount stores. From bottom left, clockwise around to the right: a square etching of the lighthouse from the 1880s; a black-and-white photograph of two men and a girl framed by the lighthouse; a long, somewhat amateurish watercolor panorama showing miles of reeds broken only by a few isolated islands of dark trees; and a color photograph of the lighthouse beacon in all its glory. No real hints of the personal, no pictures of the director with her Native American mother, her white father—or with anyone who might matter in her life.

Of all the intel Control had to work through in the coming days, he least looked forward to what he might uncover in what was now his own office; he thought he might leave it until last. Everything in the office seemed to indicate a director who had gone feral. One of the drawers in the desk was locked, and he couldn't find the key. But he did note an earthy quality to the locked drawer that hinted at something having rotted inside a long time ago. Which mystery didn't even include the mess drooping off the sides of the desk.

Ever-helpful, unhelpful spy Grandpa used to reflexively say, whether it was washing the dishes or preparing for a fishing trip, "Never skip a step. Skip a step, you'll find five more new ones waiting ahead of you."

The search for surveillance equipment, for bugs, then, was more time-consuming than he'd thought it would be, and he buzzed the science division to let them know he'd be late. There was a kind of visceral grunt in response before the line went dead, and he had no idea who had been on the other end. A person? A trained pig?

Ultimately, after a hellish search, Control to his surprise found twenty-two bugs in his office. He doubted many of them had actually been reporting back, and even if they had, if anyone had been watching or listening to what they conveyed. For the fact was, the director's office had contained an unnatural history museum of bugs—different kinds from different eras, progressively smaller and harder to unearth. The behemoths of this sort were bulging, belching metal goiters when set next to the sleek ethereal pinheads of the modern era.

The discovery of each new bug contributed to a cheerful, upbeat mood. Bugs made sense in a way some of the other things about the Southern Reach didn't. In his training as an omnivore in the service, he'd had at least six assignments that involved bugging people or places. Spying on people didn't bring him the kind of vicarious rush it gave some, or if it did, that feeling faded as he came to know his subjects better and invested in a sense of protectiveness meant to shield them. But he did find the actual devices fascinating.

When he thought his search complete, Control amused himself by arranging the bugs across the faded paper of the blotter in what he believed might be chronological order. Some of them glittered silver. Some, black, absorbed the light. There were wires attached to some like umbilical cords. One iteration—disguised within what appeared to be a small, sticky ball of green papier-mâché or colored honeycomb—made him think that a few might even be foreign-made: interlopers drawn by curiosity to the black box that was Area X. Clearly, though, the former director knew and hadn't cared they were there. Or perhaps she had thought it safest to leave them. Perhaps, too, she'd put some there herself. He wondered if this accounted for her distrust of modern technology.

As for installing his own, he'd have to wait until later: No time now. No time, either, to deploy these bugs for another purpose that had just occurred to him. Control carefully swept them all into a desk drawer and went to find his science guide.

The labs had been buried in the basement on the right side of the U, if you were facing the building from the parking lot out front. They lay directly opposite the sealed-off wing that served as an expedition pre-prep area and currently housed the biologist. Control had been assigned one of the science division's jack-of-all-trades as his tour guide. Which meant that despite seniority—he had been at the agency longer than anyone on staff—Whitby Allen was a push-me-pull-me who, in part due to staff attrition, often sacrificed his studies as a "cohesive naturalist and holistic scientist specializing in biospheres" to type up someone else's reports or run someone else's errands. Whitby reported to the head of the science division, but also to the assistant director. He was the scion of intellectual aristocracy, came from a long line of professors, men and women who had been tenured at various faux-Corinthian-columned private colleges. Perhaps to his family, he had become an outlaw: the dropout art-school student who went wandering and only later got a proper degree.

Whitby was dressed in a blue blazer with a white shirt and an oddly unobtrusive burgundy bow tie. He looked much younger than his age, with eternal brown hair and the kind of tight, pinched face that allows a fifty-something to look a boyish thirty-two from afar. His wrinkles had come in as tiny hairline fractures. Control had seen him in the cafeteria at lunch next to a dozen dollar bills fanned out on the table beside him for no good reason. Counting them? Making art? Designing a monetary biosphere?

Whitby had an uncomfortable laugh and bad breath and teeth that clearly needed some work. Up close, Whitby also looked as if he hadn't slept in years: a youth wizened prematurely, all the moisture leached from his face, so that his watery blue eyes seemed too large for his head. Beyond this, and his fanciful attitude toward money, Whitby appeared competent enough, and while he no doubt had the ability to engage in small talk, he lacked the inclination. This was as good a reason as any, as they threaded their way through the cafeteria, for Control to question him.

"Did you know the members of the twelfth expedition before they left?"

"I wouldn't say 'know,'" Whitby said, clearly uncomfortable with the question.

"But you saw them around."

"Yes."

"The biologist?"

"Yes, I saw her."

They cleared the cafeteria and its high ceiling and stepped into an atrium flooded with fluorescent light. The crunchy chirp of pop music dripped, distant, out of some office or another.

"What did you think of her? What were your impressions?"

Whitby concentrated hard, face rendered stern by the effort. "She was distant. Serious, sir. She outworked all of the others. But she didn't seem to be working at it, if you know what I mean."

"No, I don't know what you mean, Whitby."

"Well, it didn't matter to her. The work didn't matter. She was looking past it. She was seeing something else." Control got the sense that Whitby had subjected the biologist to quite a bit of scrutiny.

"And the former director? Did you see the former director interact with the biologist?"

"Twice, maybe three times."

"Did they get along?" Control didn't know why he asked this question, but fishing was fishing. Sometimes you just had to cast the line any place at all to start.

"No, sir. But, sir, neither of them got along with anyone." He said this last bit in a whisper, as if afraid of being overheard. Then said, as if to provide cover, "No one but the director wanted that biologist on the twelfth expedition."

"No one?" Control asked slyly.

"Most people."

"Did that include the assistant director?"

Whitby gave him a troubled look. But his silence was enough.

The director had been embedded in the Southern Reach for a long time. The director had cast a long shadow. Even gone, she had a kind of influence. Perhaps not entirely with Whitby, not really. But Control could sense it anyway. He had already caught himself having a strange thought: that the director looked out at him through the assistant director's eyes.

The elevators weren't working and wouldn't be fixed until an expert from the army base dropped by in a few days, so they took the stairs. To get to the stairs, you followed the curve of the U to a side door that opened onto a parallel corridor about fifty feet long, the floor adorned with the same worn green carpet that lowered the property value of the rest of the building. The stairs awaited them at the corridor's end, through wide swinging doors more appropriate for a slaughterhouse or emergency room. Whitby, out of character, felt compelled to burst through those double doors as if they were rock stars charging onto a stage—or, perhaps, to warn off whatever lay on the other side—then stood there sheepishly holding one side open while Control contemplated that first step.

"It's through here," Whitby said.

"I know," Control said.

Beyond the doors, they were suddenly in a kind of free fall, the green carpet cut off, the path become a concrete ramp down to a short landing with a staircase at the end—which then plunged into shadows created by dull white halogens in the walls and punctuated by blinking red emergency lights. All of it under a high ceiling that framed what, in the murk, seemed more a human-made grotto or warehouse than the descent to a basement. The staircase railing, under the shy lights, glittered with luminous rust spots. The coolness in the air as they descended reminded him of a high-school field trip to a natural history museum with an artificial cave system meant to mimic the modern day, the highlight of which had been non sequiturs: mid-lunge reproductions of a prehistoric giant sloth and giant armadillo, megafauna that had taken a wrong turn.

"How many people in the science division?" he asked when he'd acclimated.

"Twenty-five," Whitby said. The correct answer was nineteen.

"How many did you have five years ago?"

"About the same, maybe a few more." The correct answer was thirty-five.

"What's the turnover like?"

Whitby shrugged. "We have some stalwarts who will always be here. But a lot of new people come in, too, with their ideas, but they don't really change anything." His tone implied that they either left quickly or came around . . . but came around to what?

Control let the silence elongate, so that their footsteps were the only sound. As he'd thought, Whitby didn't like silences. After a moment, Whitby said, "Sorry, sorry. I didn't mean anything by that. It's just sometimes frustrating when new people come in and want to change things without knowing . . . our situation. You feel like if they just read the manual first . . . if we had a manual, that is."

Control mulled that, making a noncommittal sound. He felt as if he'd come in on the middle of an argument Whitby had been having with other people. Had Whitby been a new voice at some point? Was *he* the new Whitby, applied across the entire Southern Reach rather than just the science division?

Whitby looked paler than before, almost sick. He was staring off into the middle distance while his feet listlessly slapped the steps. With each step, he seemed more ill at ease. He had stopped saying "sir."

Some form of pity or sympathy came over Control; he didn't know which. Perhaps a change of subject would help Whitby.

"When was the last time you had a new sample from Area X?"

"About five or six years ago." Whitby sounded more confident about this answer, if no more robust, and he was right. It had been six years since anything new had come to the Southern Reach from Area X. Except for the forever changed members of the eleventh expedition. The doctors and scientists had exhaustively tested them and their clothing, only to find . . . nothing. Nothing at all out of the ordinary. Just one anomaly: the cancer.

No light reached the basement except for what the science division created for itself: They had their own generator, filtration system, and food supply. Vestiges, no doubt, of some long-ago imperative that boiled down to "in an emergency, save the scientists." Control found it hard to imagine those first days, when behind closed doors the government had been in panic mode, and the people who worked in the Southern Reach believed that whatever had come into the world along the forgotten coast might soon turn its attentions inland. But the invasion hadn't happened, and Control wondered if something in that thwarting of expectation had started the Southern Reach's decline.

"Do you like working here, Whitby?"

"Like? Yes. I must admit it's often fascinating, and definitely challenging." Whitby was sweating now, beads breaking on his forehead.

It might indeed be fascinating, but Whitby had, according to the records, undergone a sustained spasm of transfer requests about three years ago—one every month and then every two months like an intermittent SOS, until it had trailed off to nothing, like a flatlined EKG. Control approved of the initiative, if not the sense of desperation embedded in the number of attempts. Whitby didn't want to be stuck in a backwater and just as clearly the director or someone hadn't wanted him to leave.

Perhaps it was his utility-player versatility, because it was clear to Control that, just like every department in the Southern Reach, the science division had been "stripped for parts," as his mother would have put it, by antiterrorism and Central. According to the personnel records, there had once been one hundred and fifteen scientists in-house, representing almost thirty disciplines and several subdepartments. Now there were only sixty-five people in the whole haunted place. There had even been talk, Control knew, about relocating, except that the building was too close to the border to be used for anything else.

The same cheap, rotting scent came to him again just then, as if the janitor had unlimited access to the entire building.

"Isn't that cleaning smell a bit strong?"

"The smell?" Whitby's head whipped around, eyes made huge by the circles around them.

"The rancid honey smell."

"I don't smell anything."

Control frowned, more at Whitby's vehemence than anything else. Well, of course. They were used to it. Tiniest of his tasks, but he made a note to authorize changing cleaning supplies to something organic.

When they curved down at an angle unnecessarily precipitous, into a spacious preamble to the science division, the ceiling higher than ever, Control was surprised. A tall metal wall greeted them, and a small door within it with a sophisticated security system blinking red.

Except the door was open.

"Is this door always open, Whitby?" he asked.

Whitby seemed to believe hazarding a guess might be perilous, and hesitated before saying, "This used to be the back end of the facilities—they only added a door a year or two ago."

Which made Control wonder what this space had been used for back then. Dance hall? Weddings and bar mitzvahs? Impromptu court-martials?

They both had to stoop to enter, only to be greeted by two space-program-quality air locks, no doubt to protect against contamination. The portal doors had been cantilevered open and from within glowed an intense white light that, for whatever reason, refused to peek out beyond the unsecured security door.

Along the walls, at shoulder height, both rooms were lined with flaccid long black gloves that hung in a way that Control could only think of as dejected. There was a sense that it had been a long time since they had been brought to life by hands and arms. It was a kind of mausoleum, entombing curiosity and due diligence.

"What are those for, Whitby? To creep out guests?"

"Oh, we haven't used those for ages. I don't know why they've left them in here."

It didn't really get much better after that.

003: PROCESSING

Later, back in his office, having left Whitby in his world, Control made one more sweep for bugs. Then he prepared to call the Voice, who required reports at regular intervals. He had been given a separate cell phone for this purpose, just to make his satchel bulkier. The dozen times he'd talked to the Voice at Central prior to coming to the Southern Reach, s/he could have been somewhere nearby. S/he could have been observing him through hidden cameras the whole time. Or been a thousand miles away, a remote operative used just to run one agent.

Control didn't recall much beyond the raw information from those prior times, but talking to the Voice made him nervous. He was sweating through his undershirt as he punched the number, after having first checked the hallway and then locked the door. Neither his mother nor the Voice had told him what might be expected from any report. His mother had said that the Voice could remove him from his position without consulting with her. He doubted that was true but had decided to believe it for now.

The Voice was, as ever, gruff and disguised by a filter. Disguised purely for security or because Control might recognize it? "You'll likely never know the identity of the Voice," his mother had said. "You need to put that question out of your head. Concentrate on what's in front of you. Do what you do best."

But what was that? And how did it translate into the Voice thinking he had done a good job? He already imagined the Voice as a megalodon or other leviathan, situated in a think tank filled with salt water in some black-op basement so secret and labyrinthine that no one now remembered its purpose even as they continued to reenact its rituals. A sink tank, really. Or a stink tank. Control doubted the Voice or his mother would find that worth a chuckle.

The Voice used Control's real name, which confused him at first, as if he had sunk so deeply into "Control" that this other name belonged to someone else. He couldn't stop tapping his left index finger against the blotter on his desk.

"Report," the Voice said.

"In what way?" was Control's immediate and admittedly inane response.

"Words would be nice," the Voice said, sounding like gravel ground under boots.

Control launched into a summary of his experience so far, which started as just a summary of the summary he had received on the state of things at the Southern Reach.

But somewhere in the middle he lost the thread or momentum—had he already reported the bugs in his office?—and the Voice interrupted him. "Tell me about the scientists. Tell me about the science division. You met with them today. What's the state of things there?"

Interesting. Did that mean the Voice had another pair of eyes inside the Southern Reach?

So he told the Voice about the visit to the science division, although couching his opinions in diplomatic language. If his mother had been debriefing him, Control would have said the scientists were a mess, even for scientists. The head of the department, Mike Cheney, was a short, burly, fifty-something white guy in a motorcycle jacket, T-shirt, and jeans, who had close-cropped silver hair and a booming, jovial voice. An accent that had originated in the north but at times relaxed into an adopted southern drawl. The lines to the sides of his mouth conspired with plunging eyebrows to make of his face an X, a fate he perpetually fought against by being the kind of person who smiled all the time.

His second-in-command, Deborah Davidson, was also a physicist: a skinny jogger type who had actually smoked her way to weight loss. She creaked along in a short-sleeved red plaid shirt and tight brown corduroy pants cinched with a thick, overlarge leather belt. Most of this hidden by a worn black business jacket whose huge shoulder pads revealed its age. She had a handshake like a cold, dead fish, from which Control could not at first extricate himself.

Control's ability to absorb new names, though, had ended with Davidson. He gave vague nods to the research chemist, as well as the staff epidemiologist, psychologist, and anthropologist who had also been stuffed into the tiny conference room for the meeting. At first Control felt disrespected by that space, but halfway through he realized he'd gotten it wrong. No, they were like a cat confronted by a predator—just trying to make themselves look bigger to him, in this case by scaling down their surroundings.

None of the extras had much to add, although he had the sense they might be more forthcoming one-on-one. Otherwise, it was the Cheney and Davidson show, with a few annotations from the anthropologist. From the way they spoke, if their degrees had been medals, they would all have had them pinned to some kind of quasi-military scientist uniform—like, say, the lab coats they all lacked. But he understood the impulse, understood that this was just part of the ongoing narrative: What once had been a wide territory for the science division had, bit by bit, been taken away from them.

Grace had apparently told them—ordered them?—to give Control the usual spiel, which he took as a form of subterfuge or, at best, a possible waste of time. But they didn't seem to mind this rehash. Instead, they relished it, like overeager magicians in search of an audience. Control could tell that Whitby was embarrassed by the way he made himself small and insignificant in a far corner of the room.

The "piece of resistance," as his father used to joke, was a video of white rabbits disappearing across the invisible border: something they must have shown many times, from their running commentary.

The event had occurred in the mid-1990s, and Control had come across it in the data pertaining to the invisible border between Area X and the world. As if in a reflexive act of frustration at the lack of progress, the scientists had let loose two thousand white rabbits about fifty feet from the border, in a clear-cut area, and herded them right into the border. In addition to the value of observing the rabbits' transition from here to there, the science division had had some hope that the simultaneous or near-simultaneous breaching of the border by so many "living bodies" might "overload" the "mechanism" behind the border, causing it to short-circuit, even if "just locally." This supposed that the border *could* be overloaded, like a power grid.

They had documented the rabbits' transition not only with standard video but also with tiny cameras strapped to some of the rabbits' heads. The resulting montage that had been edited together used split screen for maximum dramatic effect, along with slow motion and fast-forward in ways that conveyed an oddly flippant quality when taken in aggregate. As if even the video editor had wanted to make light of the event, to somehow, through an embedded irreverence, find a way to unsee it. In all, Control knew, the video and digital library contained more than forty thousand video segments of rabbits vanishing. Jumping. Squirming atop one another as they formed sloppy rabbit pyramids in their efforts not to be pushed into the border.

The main video sequence, whether shown at regular speed or in slow motion, had a matter-of-fact and abrupt quality to it. The rabbits were zigging and zagging ahead of humans in baggy contamination suits, who had corralled them in a semicircle. The humans looked weirdly like anonymous white-clad riot police, holding long white shields linked together to form a wall to hem in and herd the rabbits. A neon red line across the ground delineated the fifteen-foot transition zone between the world and Area X.

A few rabbits fled around the lip of the semicircle or in crazed jumps found trajectories that brought them over the riot wall as they were pushed forward. But most could not escape. Most hurtled forward and, either running or in mid-jump, disappeared as they hit the edge of the border. There was no ripple, no explosion of blood and organs. They just disappeared. Close-up slow motion revealed a microsecond of transition in which a half or quarter of a rabbit might appear on the screen, but only a captured frame could really chart the moment between *there* and not-there. In one still, this translated into staring at the hindquarters of about four dozen jostling rabbits, most in mid-leap, disembodied from their heads and torsos.

The video the scientists showed him had no sound, just a voice-over, but Control knew from the records that an awful screaming had risen from the herded rabbits once the first few had been driven across the border. A kind of keening and a mass panic. If the video had continued, Control would have seen the last of the rabbits rebel so utterly against being herded that they turned on the herders and fought, leaping to bite and scratch . . . would have seen the white of the shields stained red, the researchers so surprised that they mostly broke ranks and a good two hundred rabbits went missing.

The cameras were perhaps even less revealing. As if the abandoned rushes from an intense movie battle scene, they simply showed the haunches and the underside of the hind paws of desperately running rabbits and some herky-jerky landscape before everything went dark. There were no video reports from rabbits that had crossed over the border, although the escapees muddied the issue, the swamps on either side looking very similar. The Southern Reach had spent a good amount of time in the aftermath tracking down escapees to rule out that they were receiving footage from across the border.

Nor had the next expedition to Area X, sent in a week after the rabbit experiment, found any evidence of white rabbits, dead or alive. Nor had any similar experiments, on a far smaller scale, produced any results whatsoever. Nor had Control missed a finicky note in one file by an ecologist about the event that read, "What the hell? This is an invasive species. They would have *contaminated* Area X." Would they have? Would whatever had created Area X have allowed that? Control tried to push away a ridiculous image of Area X, years later, sending back a human-size rabbit that could not remember anything but its function. Most of the magicians were all snickering at inappropriate places anyway, as if showing him how they'd done their most notorious trick. But he'd heard nervous laughter before; he was sure that, even at such a remove, the video disturbed many of them.

Some of the individuals responsible had been fired and others reassigned. But apparently adding the passage of time to a farce left you with an iconic image, because here was the noble remnant of the science division, showing him with marked enthusiasm what had been deemed an utter failure. They had more to show him—data and samples from Area X under glass—but it all amounted to nothing more than what was already in the files, information he could check later at his leisure.

In a way, Control didn't mind seeing this video. It was a relief considering what awaited him. The videos from the first expedition, the members of which had died, save one survivor, would have to be reviewed later in the week as primary evidence. But he also couldn't shake the echo of a kind of frat-boy sensibility to the current presentation, the underlying howl of "Look at this shit we sent out into the border! Look at this stunt we pulled!" Pass the cheap beer. Do a shot every time you see a white rabbit.

When Control left, they had all stood there in an awkward line, as if he were about to take a photograph, and shook his hand, one by one. Only after he and Whitby were back on the stairs, past the horrible black gloves, did he realize what was peculiar about that. They had all stood so straight, and their expressions had been so serious. They must have thought he was there to cull yet more from their department. That he was there to judge them. Later still, scooping up some of the bugs from his desk on his way to carry out a bad deed before calling the Voice, he wondered if instead they were afraid of something else entirely.

Most of this Control told the Voice with a mounting sense of futility. Not a lot of it made much sense or would be news; he was just pushing words around to have something to say. He didn't tell the Voice that some of the scientists had used the words *environmental boon* to describe Area X, with a disturbing and demoralizing subtext of "Should we be fighting this?" It was "pristine wilderness," after all, human-made toxins now absent.

"GODDAMMIT!" the Voice screamed near the end of Control's science report, interrupting the Voice's own persistent mutter in the background . . . and Control held the cell phone away from his ear for a moment, unsure of what had set that off, until he heard, "Sorry. I spilled coffee on myself. Continue." Coffee somewhat spoiled the image of the megalodon in Control's head, and it took him a moment to pick up the thread.

When he was done, the Voice just dove forward, as if they were starting over: "What is your mental state at this moment? Is your house in order? What do you think it will take?"

Which question to answer? "Optimistic? But until they have more direction, structure, and resources, I won't know."

"What is your impression of the prior director?"

A hoarder. An eccentric. An enigma. "It's a complicated situation here and only my first full da—"

"WHAT IS YOUR IMPRESSION OF THE PRIOR DIRECTOR?" A howl of a shout, as if the gravel had been lifted up into a storm raining down.

Control felt his heart rate increase. He'd had bosses before who had anger-management issues, and the fact that this one was on the other end of a cell phone didn't make it any better.

It all spilled out, his nascent opinions. "She had lost all perspective. She had lost the thread. Her methods were eccentric toward the end, and it will take a while to unravel—"

"ENOUGH!"

"But, I—"

"Don't disparage the dead." This time a pebbled whisper. Even with the filter, a sense of mourning came through, or perhaps Control was just projecting.

"Yes, sorry, it's just that—"

"Next time," the Voice said, "I expect you to have something more interesting to tell me. Something I don't know. Ask the assistant director about the biologist. For example. The director's plan for the biologist."

"Yes, that makes sense," Control agreed, but really just hoping to get off the line soon. Then a thought occurred. "Oh—speaking of the assistant director . . ." He outlined the issue that morning with sending the anthropologist and surveyor away, the problem of Grace seeming to have contacts at Central that could cause trouble.

The Voice said, "I'll look into it. I'll handle it," and then launched into something that sounded prerecorded because it was faintly repetitious: "And remember, I am always watching. So really *think* about what it might be that I don't know."

Click.

Control caught up with the assistant director while navigating his way through one of the many corridors he hadn't quite connected one to the other. He was trying to find HR to file paperwork but still couldn't see the map of the building entire in his head and remained a little off-balance from the phone call with the Voice.

The scraps of overheard conversation in the hallways didn't help, pointing as they did to evidence for which he as yet had no context. "How deep do you think it goes down?" "No, I don't recognize it. But I'm not an expert." "Believe me or don't believe me." Grace didn't help, either. As soon as he came up beside her, she began to crowd him, perhaps to make the point that she was as strong and tall as him. She smelled of some synthetic lavender perfume that made him stifle a sneeze.

After fielding an inquiry about the visit with the scientists, Control turned and bore down on her before she could veer off. "Why didn't you want the biologist on the twelfth expedition?"

She stopped, put some space between them to look askance at him. Good—at least she was willing to engage.

"What was on your mind back then? Why didn't you want the biologist on that expedition?"

Personnel were passing by them on either side. Grace lowered her voice, said, "She did not have the right qualifications. She had been fired from half a dozen jobs. She had some raw talent, some kind of spark, yes, but she was not qualified. Her husband's position on the prior expedition—that compromised her, too."

"The director didn't agree."

"How is Whitby working out, anyway?" she asked by way of reply, and he knew his expression had confirmed his source. Forgive me, Whitby, for giving you up. Yet this also told him Grace was concerned about Whitby talking to him. Did that mean Whitby was Cheney's creature?

He pressed forward: "But the director didn't agree."

"No," she admitted. Control wondered what kind of betrayal that had been. "She did not. She thought these were all *pluses*, that we were too concerned about the usual measurements of suitability. So we deferred to her."

"Even though she had the bodies of the prior expedition disinterred and reexamined?"

"Where did you hear that?" she asked, genuinely surprised.

"Wouldn't that speak to the director's own suitability?"

But Grace's surprise had already ossified back into resistance, which meant she was on the move again as she said curtly, "No. No, it would not."

"She suspected something, didn't she?" Control asked, catching up to her again. Central thought the files suggested that even if the unique mind-wiped condition of the prior expedition didn't signal a kind of shift in the situation in Area X, it might have signaled a shift in the director.

Grace sighed, as if tired of trying to shake him. "She suspected that they might have . . . changed since the autopsies. But if you're asking, you know already."

"And had they? Had they changed?" Disappeared. Been resurrected. Flown off into the sky.

"No. They had decomposed a little more rapidly than might be expected, but no, they hadn't changed."

Control wondered how much that had cost the director in respect and in favors. He wondered if by the time the director had told them she was attaching herself to the twelfth expedition some of the staff might have felt not alarm or concern but a strange sort of guilty relief.

He had another question, but Grace was done, had already pivoted to veer off down a different corridor in the maze.

There followed some futile, halfhearted efforts to rearrange his office, along with a review of some basic reports Grace had thrown at him, probably to slow his progress. He learned that the Southern Reach had its own props design department, tasked with creating equipment for the expeditions that didn't violate protocols. In other words, fabrication of antiquated technology. He learned that the security on the facilities that housed returning expedition members was undergoing an upgrade; the outdated brand of surveillance camera they'd been using had suffered a systemic meltdown. He'd even thrown out a DVD given to him by a "lifecycle biologist" that showed a computer-generated cross section of the forgotten coast's ecosystem. The images had been created as a series of topographical lines in a rainbow of colors. It was very pretty but the wrong level of detail for him.

At day's end, on his way out, he ran into Whitby again, in the cafeteria around which the man seemed to hover, almost as if he didn't want to be down in the dungeon with the rest of the scientists. Or as if they sent him on perpetual errands to keep him away. A little dark bird had become trapped inside, and Whitby was staring up at where it flew among the skylights.

Control asked Whitby the question he'd wanted to ask Grace before her maze-pivot.

"Whitby, why are there so few returning journals from the expeditions?" Far, far fewer than returnees.

Whitby was still mesmerized by the flight of the bird, his head turning the way a cat's does to follow every movement. There was an intensity to his gaze that Control found disconcerting.

"Incomplete data," Whitby said. "Too incomplete to be sure. But most returnees tell us they just don't think to bring them back. They don't believe it's important, or don't feel the need to. Feeling is the important part. You lose the need or impetus to divulge, to communicate, a bit like astronauts lose muscle mass. Most of the journals seem to turn up in the lighthouse anyway, though. It hasn't been a priority for a while, but when we did ask later expeditions to retrieve them, usually they didn't even try. You lose the impetus or something else intercedes, becomes more crucial and you don't even realize it. Until it's too late."

Which gave Control an uncomfortable image of someone or something in Area X entering the lighthouse and sitting atop a pile of journals and reading them *for* the Southern Reach. Or writing them.

"I can show you something interesting in one of the rooms near the science division that pertains to this," Whitby said in a dreamy tone, still following the path of the bird. "Would you like to see it?" His disconnected gaze clicked into hard focus and settled on Control, who had a sudden jarring impression of there being two Whitbys, one lurking inside the other.

"Why don't you just tell me about it?"

"No. I have to show you. It's a little strange. You have to see it to understand it." Whitby now gave the impression of not caring if Control saw the odd room, and yet caring entirely too much at the same time.

Control laughed. Various people had been showing him bat-shit crazy things since his days working in domestic terrorism. People had said bat-shit crazy things to him today.

"Tomorrow," he said. "I'll see it tomorrow." Or not. No surprises. No satisfaction for the keepers of strange secrets. No strangeness before its time. He had truly had enough for one day, would gird his loins overnight for a return encounter. The thing about people who wanted to show you things was that sometimes their interest in granting you knowledge was laced with a little voyeuristic sadism. They were waiting for the Look or the Reaction, and they didn't care what it was so long as it inflicted some kind of discomfort. He wondered if Grace had put Whitby up to this after their conversation, whether it was some odd practical joke and he'd been meant to stick his hand into a space only to find his hand covered in earthworms, or open a box only for a plastic snake to spring out.

The bird now swooped down in an erratic way, hard to make out in the late-afternoon light.

"You should see it now," Whitby said, in a kind of wistfully hurt tone. "Better late than never."

But Control had already turned his back on Whitby and was headed for the entrance and then the (blessed) parking lot.

Late? Just how late did Whitby think he was?

004: REENTRY

The car offered a little breathing room, a chance to decompress and transform from one thing to another. The town of Hedley was a forty-minute drive from the Southern Reach. It lay against the banks of a river that, just twenty miles later, fed into the ocean. Hedley was large enough to have some character and culture without being a tourist trap. People moved there even though it fell just short of being "a good town to raise a family in." Between the sputtering shops huddled at one end of the short river walk and the canopy roads, there were hints of a certain quality of life obscured in part by the strip malls that radiated outward from the edges of the city. It had a small private college, with a performing arts center. You could jog along the river or hike greenways. Still, though, Hedley also partook of a certain languor that, especially in the summers, could turn from charming to tepid overnight. A stillness when the breeze off the river died signaled a shift in mood, and some of the bars just off the waterfront had long been notorious for sudden, senseless violence—places you didn't go unless you could pass for white, or maybe not even then. A town that seemed trapped in time, not much different from when Control had been a teenager.

Hedley's location worked for Control. He wanted to be close to the sea but not on the coast. Something about the uncertainty of Area X had created an insistence inside of him on that point. His dream in a way forbid it. His dream told him he needed to be at a remove. On the plane down to his new assignment, he'd had strange thoughts about the inhabitants of those coastal towns to either side of Area X being somehow mutated under the skin. Whole communities no longer what they once were, even though no one could tell this by looking. These were the kinds of thoughts you had to both keep at bay and fuel, if you could manage that trick. You couldn't become devoured by them, but you had to heed them. Because in Control's experience they reflected something from the subconscious, some instinct you didn't want to go against. The fact was, the Southern Reach knew so little about Area X, even after three decades, that an irrational precaution might not be unreasonable.

And Hedley was familiar to him. This was the city to which he and his friends had come for fun on weekends once some of them could drive, even knowing it was kind of a shithole, too, just not as small a shithole as where they lived. Landlocked and forlorn. His mother had even alluded to it the last time he'd seen her. She'd flown in at his old job up north, which had been gradually reduced from analysis and management to a more reactive and administrative role. Due to his own baggage, he guessed. Due to the fact it always started out well, but then, if he stayed too long . . . sometimes something happened, something he couldn't quite define. He became too invested. He became too empathic, or less so. It confused him when it all went to shit because he couldn't remember the point at which it had started to go bad—was still convinced he could get the formula right.

But his mother had come from Central and they'd met in a conference room he knew was probably bugged. Had the Voice traveled with her, been set up in a saltwater tank in the adjoining room?

It was cold outside and she wore a coat, an overcoat, and a scarf over a professional business suit and black high heels. She took off the overcoat and held it in her lap. But she didn't take off the scarf. She looked as if she could surge from her chair at any moment and be out the door before he could snap his fingers. It had been five years since he'd seen her—predictably unreachable when he'd tried to get a message to her about her ex-husband's funeral—but she had aged only a little bit, her brown hair just as fashion-model huge as ever and eyes a kind of calculating blue peering out from a face on which wrinkles had encroached only around the corners of the eyes and, hidden by the hair, across her forehead.

She said, "It will be like coming home, John, won't it?" Nudging him, wanting him to say it, as if he were a barnacle clinging to a rock and she were a seagull trying to convince him to release his grip. "You'll be comfortable with the setting. You'll be comfortable with the people."

He'd had to suppress anger mixed with ambivalence. How would she know whether she was right or wrong? She'd rarely been there, even though she'd had visitation rights. Just him and his father, Dad beginning to fall apart by then, to eat too much, to drink a little too much, during a succession of flings once the divorce was final . . . then redirecting himself to art no one wanted. Getting his house in order and going off to college had been a guilty relief, to not live in that atmosphere anymore.

"And, comfortably situated in this world I know so well, what would I do?"

She smiled at him. A genuine smile. He could tell the difference, having suffered so many times under the dull yellow glow of a fake one that tried to reheat his love for her. When she really smiled, when she meant it, his mother's face took on a kind of beauty that surprised anyone who saw it, as if she'd been hiding her true self behind a mask. While people who were always sincere rarely got credit for that quality.

"It's a chance to do better," she said. "It's a chance to erase the past."

The past. Which part of the past? The job up north had been his tenth posting in about fifteen years, which made the Southern Reach his eleventh. There were a number of reasons, there were always reasons. Or one reason, in his case.

"What would I have to do?" If he had to pull it out of her, he knew it might not be something he wanted. But he was already tired of the repetitive nature of his current position, which had turned out to be less about fixing and more about repainting facades. He was tired of the office politics, too. Maybe that had always been his problem, at heart.

"You've heard of the Southern Reach?"

He had, mostly through a couple of colleagues who had worked there at one time. Vague allusions, keeping to the cover story about environmental catastrophe. Rumors of a chain of command that was eccentric at best. Rumors of significant variation, of there being more to the story. But, then, there always was.

He didn't know, on hearing his mother say those words, whether he was excited or not.

"And why me?"

The smile that prefaced her response was tinged with a bit of sadness or regret or something else that made Control look away. When she'd been on assignment, before she'd left for good, she'd had a short period when she'd been good at writing long, handwritten letters to him—almost as good as he had been at not finding the time or need to read them. But now he almost wished she was writing to him about the Southern Reach in a letter, not telling him about it in person.

"Because they're downsizing this department, although you might not know that, and you'll be on the chopping block. And this is the right fit for you."

That lurch in the pit of his stomach. Another change. Another city. Never any chance to catch his balance. The truth was that after Control had joined up, he had rarely felt like a flash of light. He had often felt heavy, and realized his mother probably felt heavy, too. That she had been feigning a kind of aloofness and lightness, hiding from him the weight of information, of history and context. All of the things that wore you down, even as that was balanced by the electric feeling of being on the side of a border where you knew things no one else knew.

"Is it the only option?" Of course it was, since she hadn't mentioned any other options. Of course it was, since she hadn't traveled all this way just to say hello. He knew that he was the black sheep, that his lack of advancement reflected poorly on her. Had no idea what internecine battles she fought at the higher levels of clandestine departments so far removed from his security clearance that they might as well exist in the clouds, among the angels.

"It might not be fair, John, I know that. But this might be your last chance," she said, and now she wasn't smiling. Not smiling at all. "At least, it's the last chance I can get for you." For a permanent posting, an end to his nomadic lifestyle, or in general? For keeping a foothold in the agency?

He didn't dare ask—the cold roiling fear she'd put into him was too deep. He hadn't known he needed a last chance. The fear ran so deep that it pushed most other questions out of his head. He hadn't had a moment then to wonder if, perhaps, she wasn't just there to do her son a favor. That perhaps she *needed* him to say yes.

The teasing hook, to balance his fear, delivered lightheartedly and at the perfect moment: "Don't you want to know more than I know? You will if you take this position."

And nothing he could do about his response. It was true. He did.

She hugged him when he said yes to the Southern Reach, which surprised him. "The closer you are, the safer you are," she whispered in his ear. Closer to what?

She smelled vaguely of an expensive perfume, the scent a bit like the plum trees in the backyard of the house they'd all shared up north. The little orchard he'd forgotten about until just this moment. The swing set. The neighbor's malamute that always halfheartedly chased him up the sidewalk.

By the time the questions arose within him, it was too late. She had put on the overcoat and was gone as if she'd never been there.

Certainly there was no record of her ever signing in or signing out.

Dusk, the start of the nightly reprieve from the heat, had settled over Hedley by the time he pulled into the driveway. The place he'd rented sat about a mile up a gentle slope of the hills that eventually ended below at the banks of the river. A small, 1,300-square-foot cedar house painted light blue, with the white shutters on the windows slightly heat-warped. It had two bathrooms, a master bedroom, a living room, a galley kitchen, and an office, with a screened-in patio in back. The interior decoration was all in a cloying yet comfortable "heirloom chic." In front, a garden of herbs and petunias that transitioned to a short stretch of lawn next to the driveway.

As he walked up the steps to the front door, El Chorizo jumped out from the bushes to the side and got underfoot. El Chorizo was a huge black-and-white cat, a draft horse of a cat, named by his father. The family had had a pig named El Gato growing up, so this was his father's way of making a joke. Control had taken him as a pet about three years ago, when the cancer had gotten bad enough that El Chorizo had become a burden. He'd always been an indoor-outdoor cat, and Control had decided to let him be that in his new surroundings, too. Apparently it had been the right decision; El Chorizo, or "Chorry" as Control called him, looked alert and confident, even if his long hair was already tangled and dirty.

Together they went inside, and Control put out some wet food in the kitchen, petted him for a few minutes, then listened to his messages, the landline just for "civilians." There was only one message: from Mary Phillips, his girlfriend until they'd broken up about six months ago, checking in to make sure the move had gone okay. She had threatened to come visit, although he hadn't told her his precise location and had just gotten used to sleeping alone again. "No hard feelings," and he couldn't even really remember if he had broken up with her or she with him. There rarely were hard feelings—which felt odd to him and wrong. Shouldn't there be? There had been almost as many girlfriends as postings; they usually didn't survive the moves, or his circumspection, or his odd hours, or maybe he just hadn't found the right person. He couldn't be sure, tried as the cycle kept repeating to wring as much intensity and intimacy out of the early months, having a sense of how it would end. "You're a strange kind of player," the one-night stand before Mary had said to him as he was going down on her, but he wasn't really a player. He didn't know what he was.

Instead of returning the call, he slipped into the living room and sat on the couch. Chorry promptly curled up next to him, and he absentmindedly rubbed the cat's head. A wren or some such rooted around outside the window. There came, too, the call of a mockingbird and a welcome chitter of bats, which weren't as common anymore.

It was so close to everything he knew from his teenage years that he decided to let that be a comfort, along with the house, which helped him believe that this job was going to last. But "always have an exit strategy" was something his mother had repeated ad nauseam from his first day of training, so he had the standard packet hidden in a false bottom to a suitcase. He'd brought more than just his standard sidearm, one of the guns stored with the passports and money.

Control had already unpacked, the idea of leaving his things in storage painful. On the mantel over a brick fireplace that was mostly for show, he had placed a chessboard with the little brightly colored wooden figurines that had been his father's last redoubt. His father had sold them in local crafts shops and worked in a community center after his career had stalled. Occasionally during the last decade of his father's life, an art collector would buy one of the huge art installations rusting under tarps in the backyard, but that was more like receiving a ghost, a time traveler, than anything like a revival of interest. The chessboard, frozen in time, reflected the progress of their last game together.

He pulled himself off the couch, went into the bedroom, and changed into his shorts and T-shirt and running shoes. Chorry looked up at him as if he wanted to come along.

"I know, I know. I just got home. But I'll be back."

He slipped out the front door, deciding to leave Chorry inside, put on his headphones, turned on some of the classical music he loved, and lit out along the street. By now full dusk had arrived and there was just a haze of dark blue remaining over the river below and the lights of homes and businesses, while above the reflected glow of the city pushed the first stars farther into the heavens. The heat had dropped away, but the insistent low chiseling noise of crickets and other insects brought back its specter.

Something immediately felt tight in his left quad, but he knew it would work itself out. He started slowly, letting himself take in the neighborhood, which was mostly small houses like his, with rows of high bushes instead of fences and streets that ran parallel to the ridge of the hill, with some connector streets running straight down. He didn't mind the winding nature of it—he wanted a good three to five miles. The thick smell of honeysuckle came at him in waves as he ran by certain homes. Few people were still out except for some swing-sitters and dog-walkers, a couple of skateboarders. Most nodded at him as he passed.

As he sped up and established a rhythm, headed ever downward toward the river, Control found himself in a space where he could think about the day. He kept reliving the meetings and in particular the questioning of the biologist. He kept circling back to all of the information that had flooded into him, that he had let keep flooding into him. There would be more of it tomorrow, and the day after that, and no doubt new information would keep entering him for a while before any conclusions came back out.

He could try to not get involved at this level. He could try to exist only on some abstract level of management and administration, but he didn't believe that's really what the Voice wanted him to do—or what the assistant director would *let* him do. How could he be the director of the Southern Reach if he didn't understand in his gut what the personnel there faced? He had already scheduled at least three more interviews with the biologist for the week, as well as a tour of the entry point into Area X at the border. He knew his mother would expect him to prioritize based on the situation on the ground.

The border in particular stuck with him as he jogged. The absurdity of it co-existing in the same world as the town he was running through, the music he was listening to. The crescendo of strings and wind instruments.

The border was invisible.

It did not allow half measures: Once you touched it, it pulled you in (or across?).

It had discrete boundaries, including to about one mile out to sea. The military had put up floating berms and patrolled the area ceaselessly.

He wondered, as he jumped over a low wall overgrown with kudzu and took a shortcut between streets across a crumbling stone bridge. He wondered for a moment about those ceaseless patrols, if they ever saw anything out there in the waves, or if their lives were just an excruciation of the same gray-blue details day after day.

The border extended about seventy miles inland from the lighthouse and approximately forty miles east and forty miles west along the coast. It ended just below the stratosphere and, underground, just above the asthenosphere.

It had a door or passageway through it into Area X.

The door might not have been created by whatever had created Area X.

He passed a corner grocery store, a pharmacy, a neighborhood bar. He crossed the street and narrowly missed running into a woman on a bicycle. Abandoned the sidewalk for the side of the road when he had to, wanting now to get to the river soon, not looking forward to the run back up the hill.

You could not get under the border by any means on the seaward side. You could not tunnel under it on the landward side. You could not penetrate it with advanced instrumentation or radar or sonar. From satellites peering down from above, you would see only wilderness in apparent real time, nothing out of the ordinary. Even though this was an optical lie.

The night the border had come down, it had taken ships and planes and trucks with it, anything that happened to be on or approaching that imaginary but too-real line at the moment of its creation, and for many hours after, before anyone knew what was going on, knew enough to keep distant. Before the army moved in. The plaintive groan of metal and the vibration of engines that continued running as they disappeared . . . into something, somewhere. A smoldering, apocalyptic vision, the con towers of a destroyer, sent to investigate with the wrong intel, "sliding into nothing" as one observer put it. The last shocked transmissions from the men and women on board, via video and radio, while most ran to the back in a churning, surging wave that, on the grainy helicopter video, looked like some enormous creature leaping off into the water. Because they were about to disappear and could do nothing about it, all of it complicated by the fog. Some, though, just stood there, watching as their ship disintegrated, and then they crossed over or died or went somewhere else or . . . Control couldn't fathom it.

The hill leveled out and he was back on sidewalks, this time passing generic strip malls and chain stores and people crossing at stoplights and people getting into cars in parking lots . . . until he reached the main drag before the river—a blur of bright lights and more pedestrians, some of them drunk—crossed it, and came into a quiet neighborhood of mobile homes and tiny cinder-block houses. He was sweating a lot by now, despite the coolness. Someone was having a barbecue and they all stopped to watch him as he ran by.

His thoughts turned again to the biologist. To the need to know what the biologist had seen and experienced in Area X. Aware of the fact the assistant director might do more than threaten to take her away. Aware that the assistant director wanted to use that uncertainty to get him to make unsound decisions.

A one-way road fringed with weeds and strewn with gravel from potholes led him down to the river. He emerged from a halo of branches onto a rickety pontoon dock, bent his knees to keep his balance. Finally came to a stop there, at the end of the dock, next to a speedboat lashed to it. Few lights across the river, just little clusters here and there, nothing compared to the roaring splash of lights to his left, where the river walk waited under the deliberate touristy feature of stupid faux-Victorian lampposts topped with globes full of blurry soft-boiled eggs.

Somewhere across the river and off to the left lay Area X—many miles away but still visible somehow as a weight, a shadow, a glimmering. Expeditions would have been coming back or not coming back while he was still in high school. The psychologist would have been transitioning to director at some point as well. A whole secret history had been playing out while he and his friends drove into Hedley, intent on scoring some beers and finding a party, not necessarily in that order.

He'd had a phone call with his mother the day before he'd boarded the plane, headed for the Southern Reach. They'd talked a little bit about his connection to Hedley. She'd said, "I only knew the area because you were there. But you don't remember that." No, he didn't. Nor had he known that she had worked briefly for the Southern Reach, a fact that both did and didn't surprise him. "I worked there to be closer to you," she said, and something in his heart loosened, even as he wasn't sure whether to believe her.

Because it was so hard to tell. At that time he would have been receiving her time-lapse stories from earlier assignments. He tried to fast-forward, figure out when, if ever, she'd told him a disguised version of the Southern Reach. He couldn't find the point, or his memory just didn't want to give it to him. "What did you do there?" he'd asked, and the only word back had been a wall: "Classified."

He turned off his music, stood there listening to the croaking of frogs, the lap and splash of water against the side of the speedboat as a breeze rippled across the river. The dark was more complete here, and the stars seemed closer. The flow of the river had been faster back in the day, but the runoff from agribusiness had generated silt that slowed it, stilled it, and changed what lived in it and where. Hidden by the darkness of the opposite shore lay paper mills and the ruins of earlier factories, still polluting the groundwater. All of it coursing into seas ever-more acidic.

There came a distant shout across the river, and an even-more distant reply. Something small snuffled and quorked its way through the reeds to his right. A deep breath of fresh air was limned by a faint but sharp marsh smell. It was the kind of place where he and his father would have gone canoeing when he was a teenager. It wasn't true wilderness, was comfortingly close to civilization, but existed just enough apart to create a boundary. This was what most people wanted: to be *close to* but not *part of.* They didn't want the fearful unknown of a "pristine wilderness." They didn't want a soulless artificial life, either.

Now he was John Rodriguez again, "Control" falling away. John Rodriguez, son of a sculptor whose parents had come to this country looking for a better life. Son of a woman who lived in a byzantine realm of secrets.

By the time he started back up the hill, he was thinking about whether he should just pursue an exit strategy now. Load everything in the car and leave, not have to face the assistant director again, or any of it.

It always started well.

It might not end well.

But he knew that when morning came, he would rise as Control and that he would go back to the Southern Reach.

RITES

005: THE FIRST BREACH

What is it? Is it on me? Where is it on me? Is it on me? Where on me? Can you see it on me? Can you see it? Where is it on me?"

Morning, after a night filled with dreams from atop the cliff, staring down. Control stood in the parking lot of a diner with his to-go cup of coffee and his breakfast biscuit, staring from two cars away at a thirty-something white woman in a purple business suit. Even gyrating to find the velvet ant that had crawled onto her, she looked like a real-estate agent, with careful makeup and blond hair in a short pageboy cut. But her suit didn't fit well, and her fingernails were uneven, her red nail polish eroded, and he felt her distress extended well back beyond the ant.

The ant was poised on the back of her neck, unmoving for a moment. If he'd told her, she would have smacked it dead. Sometimes you had to keep things from people just so they wouldn't do the first thing that came into their heads.

"Hold still," he told her as he set his coffee and biscuit atop the trunk of his car. "It's harmless, and I'll get it off you." Because no one else seemed of any use. Most were ignoring her, while some, as they got into or out of their cars and SUVs, were laughing at her. But Control wasn't laughing. He didn't find it amusing. He didn't know where Area X was on him, either, and all the questions in his head seemed in that moment as frenetic and useless as the woman's questions.

"Okay, okay," she said, still upset as he curled around and brought his hand down level with the ant, which, after a bit of gentle prodding, climbed on board. It had been struggling to progress across the field of golden hairs on the woman's neck. Red-banded and soft yet prickly, it roamed across his hand in an aimless fashion.

The woman shook her head, craned her neck as if trying to see behind her, gave him a hesitant smile, and said, "Thanks." Then bolted for her car as if late for an appointment, or afraid of him, the strange man who had touched her neck.

Control took the ant into the fringe of vegetation lining the parking lot and let it crawl from his thumb onto the wood chips there. The ant quickly got its bearings and walked off with purpose toward the green strip of trees that lay between the parking lot and the highway, governed by some sense of where it was and where it needed to be that was beyond Control's understanding.

"So long as you don't tell people you don't know something, they'll probably think you know it." That from his father, not his mother, surprisingly. Or perhaps not. His mother knew so much that maybe she thought she didn't need to pretend.

Was he the woman with no clue where the ant was or the ant, unaware it was on the woman?

Control spent the first fifteen minutes of his morning searching for the key to the locked desk drawer. He wanted to solve that mystery before his appointment with the greater mystery posed by the biologist. His stale breakfast biscuit, cooling cup of coffee, and satchel lay graceless to the side of his computer. He didn't feel particularly hungry anyway; the rancid cleaning smell had invaded his office.

When he found the key, he sat there for a moment, staring at it, and then at the locked drawer and the earthy stain across the bottom left corner. As he turned the key in the lock, he suppressed the ridiculous thought that he should have someone else present, Whitby perhaps, when he opened it.

There was something dead inside—and something living.

A plant grew in the drawer, had been growing there in the dark this whole time, crimson roots attached to a nodule of dirt. As if the director had pulled it out of the ground and then, for whatever reason, placed it in the drawer. Eight slender leaves, a deep almost luminous green, protruded from the ridged stem at irregular intervals to form a pleasing circular pattern when viewed from above. From the side, though, the plant had the look of a creature trying to escape, with a couple of limbs, finally freed, reflexively curled over the edge of the drawer.

At the base, half-embedded in the clump of dirt, lay the desiccated corpse of a small brown mouse. Control couldn't be certain the plant hadn't been feeding on it somehow. Next to the plant lay an old first-generation cell phone in a battered black leather case, and underneath both plant and phone he found stacked sedimentary layers of water-damaged file folders. Almost as if someone had, bizarrely, come in and watered the plant from time to time. With the director gone, who had been doing that? Who had done that rather than remove the plant, the mouse?

Control stared at the mouse corpse for a moment, and then reluctantly reached beside it to rescue the phone—the case looked a little melted—and, with the tip of a pen, teased open the edges of a file or two. These weren't official files, from what he could tell, but instead were full of handwritten notes, scraps of newspaper, and other secondary materials. He caught glimpses of words that alarmed him, let the pages fall back into place.

The effect was oddly as if the director had been creating a compost pile for the plant. One full of eccentric intel. Or some ridiculous science project: "mouse-powered irrigation system for data relay and biosphere maintenance." He'd seen weirder things at high-school science fairs, although his own lack of science acumen meant that when extra credit had been dangled in front of him, he'd stuck to time-honored classics, like miniature volcanoes or growing potatoes from other potatoes.

Perhaps, Control conceded as he rummaged a bit more, the assistant director had been correct. Perhaps he would have been better off taking a different office. Sidling out from behind his desk, he looked for something to put the plant in, found a pot behind a stack of books. Maybe the director had been searching for it, too.

Using a few random pages from the piles stacked around his desk—if they held the secret to Area X, so be it—Control carefully removed the mouse from the dirt and tossed it in the garbage. Then he lifted the plant into the pot and set it on the edge of his desk, as far away from him as possible.

Now what? He'd de-bugged and de-moused the office. All that was left beyond the herculean task of cleaning up the stacks and going through them was the closed second door that led nowhere.

Fortifying himself with a sip of bitter coffee, Control went over to the door. It took a few minutes to clear the books and other detritus from in front of it.

Right. Last mystery about to be revealed. He hesitated for a moment, irritated by the thought that all of these little peculiarities would have to be reported to the Voice.

He opened the door.

He stared for several minutes.

After a while, he closed it again.

006: TYPOGRAPHICAL ANOMALIES

S ame interrogation room. Same worn chairs. Same uncertain light. Same Ghost Bird. Or was it? The residue of an unfamiliar gleam or glint in her eyes or her expression, he couldn't figure out which. Something he hadn't caught during their first session. She seemed both softer and harder-edged than before. "If someone seems to have changed from one session to another, make sure you haven't changed instead." A warning from his mother, once upon a time, delivered as if she'd upended a box of spy-advice fortune cookies and chosen one at random.

Control casually set the pot on the table to his left, placed her file between them as the ever-present carrot. Was that a slightly raised eyebrow in response to the pot? He couldn't be sure. But she said nothing, even though a normal person might have been curious. On a whim, Control had retrieved the mouse from the trash and placed it in the pot with the plant. In that depressing place it looked like trash.

Control sat. He favored her with a thin smile, but still received no response. He had already decided not to pick up where they had left off, with the drowning, even though that meant he had to fight off his own sudden need to be direct. The words Control had found scrawled on the wall beyond the door kept curling through his head in an unpleasant way. *Where lies the strangling fruit that came from the hand of the sinner I shall bring forth the seeds of the dead* . . . A plant. A dead mouse. Some kind of insane rant. Or some kind of prank or joke. Or continued evidence of a downward spiral, a leap off the cliff into an ocean filled with monsters. Maybe at the end, before she shoehorned herself into the twelfth expedition, the director had been practicing for some perverse form of Scrabble.

Nor could the assistant director be entirely innocent of this devolution. Another reason Control was happy she wouldn't be watching from behind the one-way glass. Stealing a trick he'd learned from a colleague who had done it to him at his last job, Control had given Grace an afternoon time for the session. Then he had walked down to the expedition holding area, spoken to the security guard, and had the biologist brought to the debriefing room.

As he dove in, without preamble this time, Control ignored the water stains on the ceiling that resembled variously an ear and a giant subaqueous eye staring down.

"There's a topographical anomaly in Area X, fairly near base camp. Did you or any members of your expedition find this topographical anomaly? If so, did you go inside?" In actual fact, most of those who encountered it called it a tower or a tunnel or even a pit, but he stuck with "topographical anomaly" in hopes she would give it a more specific name on her own.

"I don't remember."

Her constant use of those words had begun to grate, or perhaps it was the words on the wall that grated, and the consistency of her stance was just pushing that irritation forward.

"Are you sure?" Of course she was sure.

"I think I would remember forgetting that."

When Control met her gaze now, it was always to the slightly upraised corners of her mouth, eyes that had a light in them so different from the last session. For reasons he couldn't fathom, that frustrated him. This was not the same person. Was it?

"This isn't a joke," he said, deciding to see how she would react if he seemed irritated. Except he really was irritated.

"I do not remember. What else can I say?" Each word said as if he were a bit slow and hadn't understood her the first time.

A vision of his couch in his new home, of Chorry curled up on his lap, of music playing, of a book in hand. A better place than here.

"That you do remember. That you are holding something back." Pushing. Some people wanted to please their questioners. Others didn't care or deliberately wanted to obstruct. The thought had occurred, from the first session and the transcripts of three other sessions before he'd arrived, that the biologist might float back and forth between these extremes, not know her own mind or be severely conflicted. What could he do to convince her? A potted mouse had not moved her. A change of topic hadn't, either.

The biologist said nothing.

"Improbable," he said, as if she had denied it again. "So many other expeditions have encountered this topographical anomaly." A mouthful, topographical anomaly.

"Even so," she said, "I don't remember a tower."

Tower. Not tunnel or pit or cave or hole in the ground.

"Why do you call it a tower?" he asked, pouncing. Too eager, he realized a moment later.

A grin appeared on Ghost Bird's face, and a kind of remote affection. For him? Because of some thought that his words had triggered?

"Did you know," she replied, "that the phorus snail attaches the empty shells of other snails onto its own shell. As a result, the saltwater phorus snail is very clumsy. It staggers and tumbles about because of these empty shells, which offer camouflage, but at a price."

The deep well of secret mirth behind the answer stung him.

Perhaps, too, he had wanted her to share his disdain for the term *topographical anomaly*. It had come up during his initial briefing with Grace and other members of the staff. As some "topographical anomaly" expert had droned on about its non-aspects, basically creating an outline for what they didn't know, Control had felt a heat rising. A whole monologue rising with it. Channeling Grandpa Jack, who could work himself into a mighty rage when he wanted to, especially when confronted by the stupidities of the world. His grandpa would have stood and said something like, "Topological anomaly? Topological anomaly? Don't you mean *witchcraft*? Don't you mean the end of civilization? Don't you mean some kind of spooky thing that we know nothing, absolutely fucking nothing about, to go with everything else we don't know?" Just a shadow on a blurred photo, a curling nightmare expressed by the notes of a few unreliable witnesses—made more unreliable through hypnosis, perhaps, no matter Central's protestations. A spiraling thread gone astray that might or might not be made of something else entirely—not even as scrutable in its eccentricity as a house-squatter of a snail that stumbled around like a drunk. No hope of knowing what it was, or even just blasting it to hell because that's what intelligent apes do. Just some thing in the ground, mentioned as casually, as matter-of-factly, as *manhole cover* or *water faucet* or *steak knives*. *Topographical anomaly.*

But he had said most of this to the bookshelves in his office on Tuesday—to the ghost of the director while at a snail's pace beginning to sort through her notes. To Grace and the rest of them, he had said, in a calm voice, "Is there anything else you can tell me about it?" But they couldn't.

Any more, apparently, than could the biologist.

Control just stared at her for a moment, the interrogator's creepy prerogative, usually meant to intimidate. But Ghost Bird met his stare with those sharp green eyes until he looked away. It continued to nag at him that she was different today.

What had changed in the past twenty-four hours? Her routine was the same, and surveillance hadn't revealed anything different about her mental state. They'd offered her a carefully monitored phone call with her parents, but she'd had nothing to say to them. Boredom from being cooped up with nothing but a DVD player and a censored selection of movies and novels could not account for it. The food she ate was from the cafeteria, so Control could commiserate with her there, but this still did not provide a reason.

"Perhaps this will jog your memory." Or stop you lying. He began to read summaries of accounts from prior expeditions.

"An endless pit burrowing into the ground. We could never get to the bottom of it. We could never stop falling."

"A tower that had fallen into the earth that gave off a feeling of intense unease. None of us wanted to go inside, but we did. Some of us. Some of us came back."

"There was no entrance. Just a circle of pulsing stone. Just a sense of great depth."

Only two members of that expedition had returned, but they had brought their colleagues' journals. Which were filled with drawings of a tower, a tunnel, a pit, a cyclone, a series of stairs. Where they were not filled with images of more mundane things. No two journals the same.

Control did not continue for long. He had begun the recitations aware that the selected readings might contaminate the edges of her amnesia . . . if she actually suffered from memory loss . . . and that feeling had quickly intensified. But it was mostly his own sense of unease that made him pause, and then stop. His feeling that in making the tower-pit more real in his imagination, he was also making it more real in fact.

But Ghost Bird either had not or had picked up on his tiny moment of distress, because she said, "Why did you stop?"

He ignored her, switched one tower for another. "What about the lighthouse?"

"What about the lighthouse?" First thought: She's mimicking me. Which brought back a middle school memory of humiliation from bullies before the transformation in high school as he'd put his efforts into football and tried to think of himself as a spy in the world of jocks. Realized that the words on the wall had thrown him off. Not by much, but just enough.

"Do you remember it?"

"I do," she said, surprising him.

Still, he had to pull it out of her: "What do you remember?"

"Approaching it from the trail through the reeds. Looking in the doorway."

"And what did you see?"

"The inside."

It went that way for a while, with Control beginning to lose track of her answers. Moving on to the next thing she said she couldn't remember, letting the conversation fall into a rhythm, one that she might find comfortable. He told himself he was trying to get a sense of her nervous tics, of anything that might give away her real state of mind or her real agenda. It wasn't actually dangerous to stare at her. It wasn't dangerous at all. He was Control, and he was in control.

Where lies the strangling fruit that came from the hand of the sinner I shall bring forth the seeds of the dead to share with the worms that gather in the darkness and surround the world with the power of their lives while from the dim-lit halls of other places forms that never could be writhe for the impatience of the few who have never seen or been seen. In the black water with the sun shining at midnight, those fruit shall come ripe and in the darkness of that which is golden shall split open to reveal the revelation of the fatal softness in the earth. The shadows of the abyss are like the petals of a monstrous flower that shall blossom within the skull and expand the mind beyond what any man can bear . . . And on and on it went, so that Control had the impression that if the director hadn't run out of space, hadn't added a map of Area X, she wouldn't have run out of words, either.

At first he had thought the wall beyond the door was covered in a dark design. But no, someone had obliterated it with a series of odd sentences written with a remarkably thick black pen. Some words had been underlined in red and others boxed in by green. The weight of them had made him take a step back, then just stand there, frowning.

Initial theory, abandoned as ridiculous: The words were the director's psychotic ode to the plant in her desk drawer. Then he was drawn to the slight similarities between the cadence of the words and some of the more religious anti-government militias he had monitored during his career. Then he thought he detected a faint murmur of the tone of the kinds of sloth-like yet finicky lunatics who stuck newspaper articles and Internet printouts to the walls of their mothers' basements. Creating—glue stick by glue stick and thumbtack by thumbtack—their own single-use universes. But such tracts, such philosophies, rarely seemed as melancholy or as earthy yet ethereal as these sentences.

What had burned brightest within Control as he stared at the wall was not confusion or fear but the irritation he had brought into his session with the biologist. An emotion that manifested as surprise: cold water dumped into an unsuspecting empty glass.

Inconsequential things could lead to failure, one small breach creating another. Then they grew larger, and soon you were in free fall. It could be anything. Forgetting to enter field notes one afternoon. Getting too close to a surveillance subject. Skimming a file you should have read with your full attention.

Control had not been briefed on the words on the director's wall, and he had seen nothing about them in any of the files he had so meticulously read and re-read. It was the first indication of a flaw in his process.

When Control thought the biologist was truly comfortable and feeling pleased with herself and perhaps even very clever, he said, "You say your last memory of Area X was of drowning in the lake. What do you remember specifically?"

The biologist was supposed to blanch, gaze turning inward, and give him a sad smile that would make him sad, too, as if she had become disappointed in him for some reason. That somehow he'd been doing so well and now he'd fucked up. Then she would protest, would say, "It wasn't the lake. It was in the ocean," and all of the rest would come spilling out.

But none of that happened. He received no smile of any kind. Instead, she locked everything away from him, and even her gaze withdrew to some far-off height—a lighthouse, perhaps—from which she looked down at him from a safe distance.

"I was confused yesterday," she said. "It wasn't in Area X. It was my memory from when I was five, of almost drowning in a public fountain. I hit my head. I had stitches. I don't know why, but that's what came back to me, in pieces, when you asked that question."

He almost wanted to clap. He almost wanted to stand up, clap, and hand over her file.

She had sat in her room last night, bored out of her mind from lack of stimuli, and she had anticipated this question. Not only had she anticipated it, Ghost Bird had decided to turn it into an egg laid by Control. Give away a less personal detail to protect something more important. The fountain incident was a well-documented part of her file, since she'd had to go to the hospital for stitches. It might confirm for him that she remembered something of her childhood, but nothing more.

It occurred to him that perhaps he wasn't entitled to her memories. Perhaps no one was. But he pushed himself away from that thought, like an astronaut pushing off from the side of a space capsule. Where he'd end up was anyone's guess.

"I don't believe you," he said flatly.

"I don't care," she said, leaning back in her chair. "When do I get out of here?"

"Oh, you know the drill—you've got to take one for the team," he said, using clichés to breeze past her question, trying to sound ignorant or dumb. Not so much a strategy as to punish himself for not bringing his A game. "You signed the agreement; you knew the debriefing might take a while." You knew, too, that you might come back with cancer or not come back at all.

"I don't have a computer," she said. "I don't have any of the books I requested. I'm being kept in a cell that has a tiny window high up on the wall. It only shows the sky. If I'm lucky, I see a hawk wheel by every few hours."

"It's a room, not a cell." It was both.

"I can't leave, so it's a cell. Give me books at least."

But he couldn't give her the books she wanted on memory loss. Not until he knew more about the nature of her memory loss. She had also asked for all kinds of texts about mimicry and camouflage—he'd have to question her about that at some point.

"Does this mean anything to you?" he asked to deflect her attention, pushing the potted plant–mouse across the table to her.

She sat straight in her chair, seemed to become not just taller but wider, more imposing, as she leaned in toward him.

"A plant and a dead mouse? It's a sign you should give me my fucking books and a computer." Perhaps it wasn't amusement that made her different today. Maybe it was a sense of recklessness.

"I can't."

"Then you know what you can do with your plant and your mouse."

"All right then."

Her contemptuous laughter followed him out into the hall. She had a nice laugh, even when she was using it as a weapon against him.

wenty minutes later, Control had contrived to cram Whitby, Grace, and the staff linguist, Jessica Hsyu, into cramped quarters in front of the revealed section of wall with the director's peculiar handwritten words scrawled across it. Control hadn't bothered to move books or much of anything else. He wanted them to have to sit in close, uncomfortable proximity—let us bond in this phone booth, with our knees shoved up against one another's. Little fabric sounds, mouth-breathing, shoe-squeaks, unexpected smells, all would be magnified. He thought of it as a bonding experience. Perhaps.

Only the assistant director had gotten a regular-size chair. That way she could hold on to the illusion that she was in charge; or, rather, he hoped he could forestall any complaint from her later that he was being petty. He had already ignored Grace's pointed "I am so thankful that this is correct on the schedule," which meant she already knew he'd moved up his interrogation of the biologist. She'd kept him waiting while she joked with someone in the hall, which he took as a micro-retaliation.

They were huddled around the world's smallest conference table/stool, on which Control had placed the pot with the plant and mouse. Everything in its time and place, although the director's cell phone would not be part of the conversation—Grace had already confiscated it.

"What is this," he said, pointing to the wall of words, "in my office?" Not quite willing to concede the unspoken point that continued to radiate from Grace like a force field: It was still the former director's office.

"This" included not just the words but the crude map of Area X drawn beneath the words, in green, red, and black, showing the usual landmarks: lighthouse, topographical anomaly, base camp . . . and also, farther up the coast, the island. A few stray words had been scribbled with a ball-point pen out to the sides—incomprehensible—and there were two rather daunting slash marks about half a foot above Control's head, with dates about three years apart. One red. One green. With the director's initials beside them, too. Had the director been *checking her height*? Of all of the strange things on the wall, that seemed the strangest.

"I thought you said you had read all the files," Grace replied.

Nothing in the files had mentioned a door's worth of peculiar text, but he wouldn't argue the point. He knew it was unlikely he had uncovered something unknown to them.

"Humor me."

"The director wrote it," Grace said. "These are words found written on the walls of the tunnel."

Control took a moment to digest that information.

"But why did you leave it there?" For an intense moment the words and the rotting honey smell combined to make him feel physically ill.

"A memorial," Whitby said quickly, as if to provide an excuse for the assistant director. "It seemed too disrespectful to take it down." Control had noticed Whitby kept giving the mouse strange glances.

"Not a memorial," Grace said. "It's not a memorial because the director isn't dead. I don't believe she's dead." She said this in a quiet but assured way, causing a hush from Whitby and Hsyu, as if Grace had shared an opinion that was an embarrassment to them. Control's careful manipulation of the thermostat meant they were sweating and squirming a bit anyway.

"What does it mean?" Control asked, to move past the moment. Beyond Grace's obstructionism, he could see a kind of pain growing in her that he had no wish to exploit.

"That's why we brought the linguist," Whitby said charitably, even though it was clear that Hsyu's presence had surprised the assistant director. But Hsyu had ever more influence as the Southern Reach shrank; soon enough, they might have a situation where subdepartments consisted of one person writing themselves up for offenses, giving themselves raises and bonuses, celebrating their own birthdays with custom-made Southern Reach–shaped carrot cakes.

Hsyu, a short, slender woman with long black hair, spoke.

"First of all, we are ninety-nine point nine percent certain that this text is by the lighthouse keeper, Saul Evans." A slight uprising inflection to her voice imbued even the blandest or most serious statement with optimism.

"Saul Evans . . ."

"He's right up there," Whitby said, pointing to the wall of framed images. "In the middle of that black-and-white photo." The one in front of the lighthouse. So that was Saul. He'd known that already, somewhere in the back of his mind.

"Because you found it printed somewhere else?" Control asked Hsyu. He hadn't had time to do more than glance at the file on Evans—he'd been too busy familiarizing himself with the staff of the Southern Reach and the general outline of the situation in Area X.

"Because it matches his syntax and word choice in a few of his sermons we have on audiotape."

"What was he doing preaching if he was a lighthouse keeper?"

"He was retired as a preacher, actually. He left his ministry up north very suddenly, for no documented reason, then came south and took the lighthouse keeper position. He'd been there for five years when the border came down."

"Do you think he brought whatever caused Area X with him?" Control ventured, but no one followed him into the hinterlands.

"It's been checked out," Whitby said. For the first time a sliver of condescension had entered his tone when addressing Control.

"And these words were found within the topographical anomaly?"

"Yes," Hsyu said. "Reconstructed from the reports of several expeditions, but we've never gotten a useful sample of the material the words are made of."

"Living material," Control said. Now it was coming back to him, a bit. The words hadn't been part of the summary, but he'd seen reports of words written on the tower walls in living tissue. "Why weren't these words in the files?"

The linguist again, this time with some reluctance: "To be honest, we don't like to reproduce the words. So it might have been buried in the information, like in a summary in the lighthouse keeper's file."

Grace had nothing to add, apparently, but Whitby chimed in: "We don't like to reproduce the words because we still don't know exactly what triggered the creation of Area X . . . or why."

And yet they'd left the words up behind the door that led nowhere. Control was struggling to see the logic there.

"That's superstition," Hsyu protested. "That's complete and utter superstition. You shouldn't say that." Control knew her parents were very traditional and came from a culture in which spirits manifested and words had a different significance. Hsyu did not share these beliefs—vehemently did not, practicing a lax sort of Christian faith, which brought with it inexplicable elements and phantasmagoria all its own. But he still agreed with her assessment, even if that antipathy might be leaking into her analysis.

She would have continued with a full-blown excoriation of superstition, except that Grace stopped her.

"It's not superstition," she said.

They all turned to her, swiveling on their stools.

"It is superstition," she admitted. "But it might be true."

How could a superstition be true? Control pondered that later, as he turned his attention to his trip to the border along with a cursory look at a file Whitby had pulled for him titled simply "Theories." Maybe "superstition" was what snuck into the gaps, the cracks, when you worked in a place with falling morale and depleted resources. Maybe superstition was what happened when your director went missing in action and your assistant director was still mourning the loss. Maybe that was when you fell back on spells and rituals, the reptile brain saying to the rest of you, "I'll take it from here. You've had your shot." It wasn't even unreasonable, really. How many invisible, abstract incantations ruled the world beyond the Southern Reach?

But not everyone believed in the same versions. The linguist still believed in the superstition of logic, for example, perhaps because she had only been at the Southern Reach for two years. If the statistics held true, she would burn out within the next eighteen months; for some reason, Area X was very hard on linguists, almost as hard as it was on priests, of which there were none now at the Southern Reach.

So perhaps she was only months removed from converting to the assistant director's belief system, or Whitby's, whatever that might be. Because Control knew that belief in a scientific process only took you so far. The ziggurats of illogic erected by your average domestic terrorist as he or she bought the fertilizer or made a detonator took on their own teetering momentum and power. When those towers crashed to the earth, they still existed whole in the perpetrator's mind, and everyone else's too—just for different reasons.

But Hsyu had been adamant, for reasons that didn't make Control any more comfortable about Area X.

Imagine, she had told Control next, that language is only part of a method of communication. Imagine that it isn't even the important part but more like the pipeline, the highway. A conduit only. *Infrastructure* was the word Control would use with the Voice later.

The real core of the message, the meaning, would be conveyed by the combinations of living matter that composed the words, as if the "ink" itself was the message.

"And if a message is half-physical, if a kind of coding is half-physical, then words on a wall don't mean that much at all, really, in my opinion. I could analyze those words for years—which is, incidentally, what I understand the director may have done—and it wouldn't help me to understand anything. The type of conduit helps decide how fast the message arrives, and perhaps some context, but that's all. Further"—and here Control recognized that Hsyu had slipped into the rote routine of a lecture given many times before, possibly accompanied by a PowerPoint presentation—"if someone or something is trying to jam information inside your head using words you understand but a meaning you don't, it's not even that it's not on a bandwidth you can receive, it's much worse. Like, if the message were a knife and it created its meaning by cutting into meat and your head is the receiver and the tip of that knife is being shoved into your ear over and over again . . ."

She didn't need to say more for Control to think of the expeditions come to grief before they had banned names and modern communication technology. What if the fate of the first expedition in particular had been sealed by a kind of *interference* they had brought with them that had made them simply unable to listen, to perceive?

He returned to the lighthouse keeper. "So we think that Saul Evans wrote all of this long ago, right? He can't possibly be writing anything now, though. He'd be ancient at this point."

"We don't know. We just don't know."

This, unhelpfully, from Whitby, while they all gave him a look like animals caught in the middle of the road late at night with a car coming fast.

008: THE TERROR

An hour or so later, it was time to visit the border, Grace telling him that Cheney would take him on the tour. "He wants to, for some reason." And Grace didn't, clearly. Down the corridor again to those huge double doors, led by Whitby, as if Control had no memory—only to be greeted by a cheerful Cheney, whose brown leather jacket seemed not so much ubiquitous or wedded to him as a part of him: a beetle's carapace. Whitby faded into the background, disappearing through the doors with a conspicuous and sharp intake of breath as if about to dive into a lake.

"I thought I'd come up and spare you the dread gloves," Cheney exclaimed as he shook Control's hand. Control wondered if there was some cunning to his affability, or if that was just paranoia spilling over from his interactions with Grace.

"Why keep them there?" Control asked as Cheney led him via a circuitous "shortcut" past security and out to the parking lot.

"Budget, I'm afraid. Always the answer around here," Cheney said. "Too expensive to remove them. And then it became a joke. Or, we made it into a joke."

"A joke?" He'd had enough of jokes today.

At the entrance, Whitby miraculously awaited them at the wheel of an idling army jeep with the top down. He looked like a silent-movie star, the person meant to take the pratfalls, and his pantomimed unfurling of his hand to indicate they should get on board only intensified the impression. Control gave Whitby an eye roll and Whitby winked at him. Had Whitby been a member of the drama club in college? Was he a thwarted thespian?

"Yes, a joke," Cheney continued, agreeable, as they jumped into the back; Whitby or someone had conspicuously put a huge file box in the front passenger seat so no one could sit there. "As if whatever's strange and needs to be analyzed comes to us from inside the building, not from Area X. Have you *met* those people? We're a bunch of lunatics." A bullfrog-like smile—another joke. "Whitby—take the scenic route."

But Control was hardly listening; he was wrinkling his nose at the unwelcome fact that the rotting honey smell had followed them into the jeep.

For a long time, Whitby spoke not at all and Cheney said things Control already knew, playing tour guide and apparently forgetting he was repeating things from the bunny briefing just the day before. So Control focused most of his attention on his surroundings. The "scenic route" took them the usual way Control had seen on maps: the winding road, the roadblocks, the trenches like remnants from an ancient war. Where possible, the swamp and forest had been retained as natural cover or barriers. But odd bald patches of drained swamp and clear-cut forest appeared at intervals, sometimes with guard stations or barracks placed there but often just turned into meadows of yellowing grass. Control got a prickling on his neck that made him think of snipers and remote watchers. Maybe it helped flush out intruders for the drones. Most army personnel they passed were in camouflage, and it was hard for him to judge their numbers. But he knew everyone they passed outside the last checkpoint thought what lay beyond was an area rendered hazardous due to environmental contamination.

In "cooperation with" the Southern Reach, the army had been tasked with finding new entry points into Area X, and relentlessly—or, perhaps, with growing boredom—monitored the edges for breaches. The army also still tested the border with projectiles from time to time. He knew, too, that nukes were locked in on Area X from the nearest silos, military satellites keeping watch from above.

But the army's primary job was to work hard to keep people out while maintaining the fiction of an ecological disaster area. Annexing the land that comprised Area X, and double again around it, as a natural expansion of a military base farther up the coast had helped in that regard. As did the supposed "live fire ranges" dotting the area. The army's role had arguably become larger as the Southern Reach had been downsized. All medical staff and engineers now resided with army command, for example. If a toilet broke down at the Southern Reach, the plumber came over from the military base to fix it.

Whitby whipped the jeep from side to side on a rough stretch of road, bringing Cheney alarmingly close. On further inspection, Cheney displayed the remnants of a body builder's physique, as if he had once been fit, but that this condition, like all human conditions, had receded—and then reconstituted itself in the increased thickness around his waist—but in receding had left behind a still-solid chest, jutting forward through the white shirt, out from the brown jacket, in a triumphant way that almost gave cover to his gut. He was also, according to his file, "a first-rate scientist partial to beer," the kind of mind Control had seen before. It needed dulling to slow it down or to distance itself from the possibility of despair. Beer versus scientist represented a kind of schism between the banality of speech versus the originality of thought. An ongoing battle.

Why would Cheney play the buffoon to Control when he was in fact a mighty brain? Well, maybe he was a buffoon, outside of his chosen field, but then Control wasn't exactly anyone's first invitee to a cocktail party, either.

Once they'd put the distraction of the major checkpoints behind them and entered the stretch of fifteen miles of gravel road—which seemed to take all of

Whitby's attention, so he continued to say little—Control asked, "Is this the route that the expedition would take to the border, too?"

The longer they had been traveling, the more the image in his head, of the progress of the expeditions down this very road, each member quiet, alone in the vast expanse of their thoughts, had been interrupted by the stage business of lurching to a stop at so many checkpoints. The destruction of solace.

"Sure," Cheney said. "But in a special bus that doesn't need to stop."

A special bus. No checkpoints. No limousine for the expeditions, not on this road. Were they allowed last-meal requests? Was the night before often a drunken reverie or more of a somber meditation? When was the last time they were allowed to see family or friends? Did they receive religious counsel? The files didn't say; Central descended on the Southern Reach like a many-limbed über-parasite to coordinate that part.

Loaded down or unencumbered? "And already with their backpacks and equipment?" he asked. He was seeing the biologist on that special bus, sans checkpoints, fiddling with her pack, or sitting there silent with it beside her on the seat. Nervous or calm? No matter what her state of mind at that point, Control guessed she would not have been talking to her fellow expedition members.

"No—they'd get all of that at the border facility. But they'd know what was in it before that—it'd be the same as their training packs. Just fewer rocks." Again, the look that meant he was supposed to laugh, but, always considerate, Cheney chuckled for him yet again.

So: Approaching the border. Was Ghost Bird elated, indifferent? It frustrated him that he had a better sense of what she wouldn't be than what she was.

"We used to joke," Cheney said, interrupted by a pothole poorly navigated by Whitby, "we used to joke that we ought to send them in with an abacus and a piece of flint. Maybe a rubber band or two."

In checking Control's reaction to his levity, Cheney must have seen something disapproving or dangerous, because he added, "Gallows humor, you know. Like in an ER." Except he hadn't been the one on the gallows. He'd stayed behind and analyzed what they'd brought back. The ones who did come back. A whole storeroom of largely useless samples bought with blood and careers, because hardly any of the survivors went on to have happy, productive lives. Did Ghost Bird remember Cheney, and if so, what was her impression of him?

The endless ripple of scaly brown tree trunks. The smell of pine needles mixed with a pungent whiff of decay and the exhaust from the jeep. The blue-gray sky above, through the scattered canopy. The back of Whitby's swaying head. Whitby. Invisible and yet all too visible. The cipher who came in and out of focus, seemed both near and far.

"The terror," Whitby had said during the morning meeting, staring at the plant and the mouse. *"The terror."* But oddly, slurring it slightly, and in a tone as if he were imparting information rather than reacting or expressing an emotion.

Terror sparked by what? Why said with such apparent enthusiasm?

But the linguist talked over Whitby and soon pushed so far beyond the moment that Control couldn't go back to it at the time.

"A name conveys a whole series of related associations," Hsyu had said, launching some more primordial section of her PowerPoint, created during a different era and perhaps initially pitched to an audience of the frozen megafauna Control remembered so vividly from the natural history museum. "A set of related ideas, facts, etc. And these associations exist not just in the mind of the one named—form their identity—but also in the minds of the other expedition members and thus accessible to whatever else might access them in Area X. Even if by a process unknown to us and purely speculative in nature. Whereas 'biologist'— that's a function, a subset of a full identity." Not if you did it right, like Ghost Bird, and you were totally and wholly your job to begin with. "If you can be your function, then the theory is that these associations narrow or close down, and that closes down the pathways into personality. Perhaps."

Except Control knew that wasn't the only reason to take away names: It was to strip personality away for the starker purpose of instilling loyalty and to make conditioning and hypnosis more effective. Which, in turn, helped mitigate or stave off the effects of Area X—or, at least, that was the rationale Control had seen in the files, as put forward in a note by James Lowry, the only survivor of the first expedition and a man who had stayed on at the Southern Reach despite being damaged and taking years to recover.

Overtaken by some sudden thought she chose not to share, Hsyu then performed her own pivot, like Grace through the hallway maze: "We keep saying 'it'—and by 'it' I mean whatever initiated these processes and perhaps used Saul Evans's words—is like this thing or like that thing. But it isn't—it is only itself. Whatever it is. Because our minds process information almost solely through analogy and categorization, we are often defeated when presented with something that fits no category and lies outside of the realm of our analogies." Control imagined the PowerPoint coming to a close, the series of marbled borders giving way to a white screen with the word *Questions?* on it.

Still, Control understood the point. It echoed, in a different way, things the biologist had said during their session. In college, what had always stuck with him in Astronomy 101 was that the first astronomers to think of points of light not as part of a celestial tapestry revolving around the earth but as individual stars had had to wrench their imaginations—and thus their analogies and metaphors—out of a grooved track that had been running through everyone's minds for hundreds and hundreds of years.

Who at the Southern Reach had the kind of mind needed to see something new? Probably not Cheney at this point. Cheney's roving intellect had uncovered nothing new for quite some time, possibly through no real fault of its own. Yet Control came back to one thought: Cheney's willingness to keep banging his head against a wall—despite the fact that he would never publish any scientific papers about any of this—was, in a perverse way, one of the best reasons to assume the director had been competent.

Gray moss clinging to trees. A hawk circling a clear-cut meadow under skies growing darker. A heat and humidity to the air that was trying to defeat the rush of wind past them.

The Southern Reach called the last expedition the twelfth, but Control had counted the rings, and it was actually the thirty-eighth iteration, including six "eleventh" expeditions. The hagiography was clear: After the true fifth expedition, the Southern Reach had gotten stuck like a jammed CD, with nearly the same repetitions. Expedition 5 became X.5.A, followed by X.5.B and X.5.C, all the way to an X.5.G. Each expedition number thereafter adhered to a particular set of metrics and introduced variables into the equation with each letter. For example, the eleventh expedition series had been composed of all men, while the twelfth, if it continued to X.12.B and beyond, would continue to be composed of all women. He wondered if his mother knew of any parallel in special ops, if secret studies showed something about gender that escaped him in considering the irrelevance of this particular metric. And what about someone who didn't identify as male or female?

Control still couldn't tell from his examination of the records that morning if the iterations had started as a clerical error and become codified as process (unlikely) or been initiated as a conscious decision by the director, sneakily enacted below the radar of any meeting minutes. It had just popped up as if always there. A need to somehow act as if they weren't as far along without concrete results or answers. Or the need to describe a story arc for each set of expeditions that didn't give away how futile it was fast becoming.

During the fifth, too, the Southern Reach had started lying to the participants. No one was ever told they were part of Expedition 7.F or 8.G or 9.B, and Control wondered how anyone had kept it straight, and how the truth might have eaten away at morale rather than buoyed it, brought into the Southern Reach a kind of cynical fatalism. How peculiar to keep prepping the "fifth" expedition, to keep rolling this stone up this hill, over and over.

Grace had just shrugged when asked about the transition from X.11.K to X.12.A during orientation on Monday, which already felt a month away from Wednesday. "The biologist knew about the eleventh expedition because her husband was careless. So we moved on to the twelfth." Was that the only reason?

"A lot of accommodations were made for the biologist," Control observed.

"The director ordered it," Grace said, "and I stood behind her." That was the end of that line of inquiry, Grace no longer willing to admit that there might have been any distance between her and the director.

And, as often happened, one big lie had let in a series of little lies, under the guise of "changing the metrics," of altering the experiment. So that as they got diminishing returns, the director fiddled more and more with the composition of the expeditions, and fiddled with what information she told them, and who knew if any of it had helped anything at all? You reached a certain point of desperation, perhaps thought the train was coming faster than others did, and you'd use whatever you found hidden under the seats, whether a weapon or just a bent paper clip.

If you quacked like a scientist and waddled like a scientist, soon, to nonscientists, you became the subject under discussion and not a person at all. Some scientists lived within this role, almost embraced it, transformed into walking theses or textbooks. This couldn't be said about Cheney, though, despite lapses into jargon like "quantum entanglements."

At a certain point on the way to the border, Control began to collect Cheney-isms. Much of it came to Control unsolicited because he found that Cheney, once he got warmed up, hated silence, and threw into that silence a strange combination of erudite and sloppy syntax. All Control had to do, with Whitby as his innocent accomplice, was not respond to a joke or comment and Cheney would fill up the space with his own words. Jesus, it was a long drive.

"Yeah, there's a lot of enabling of each other's dip-shittery. It's almost all we've got."

"We don't even understand how every organism on our planet works. Haven't even identified them all yet. What if we just don't have the language for it?"

"Are we obsolete? I think not, I think not. But don't ask the army's opinion of that. A circle looks at a square and sees a badly made circle."

"As a physicist, what do you do when you're faced by something that doesn't care what you do and isn't affected by your actions? Then you start thinking about dark energy and you go a little nuts."

"Yeah, it's something we think about: How do you know if something is out of the ordinary when you don't know if your instruments would register the progressions? Lasers, gravitational-wave detectors, X-rays. Nothing useful there. I got this spade here and a bucket and some rubber bands and duct tape, you know?"

"Hardly any scientists at Central, either. Am I right?"

"I guess it's kind of strange. To practically live next to this. I guess I could say that. But then you go home and you're home."

"Do you know any physics? No of course you don't. How could you?"

"Black holes and waves have a similar structure, you know? Very, very similar as it turns out. Who would've expected that?"

"I mean, you'd expect Area X to cooperate at least a little bit, right? I'd've staked my reputation on it cooperating with us enough to get some accurate readings at least, an abnormal heat signature or something."

Later, a refinement of this statement: "There is some agreement among us now, reduced though we may be, that to analyze certain things, an object must allow itself to be analyzed, must agree to it. Even if this is just simply by way of *some* response, some reaction."

These last two utterances, jostling elbows, Cheney had offered up a bit plaintively because, in fact, he had staked his reputation to Area X—in the general sense that the Southern Reach had become his career. The initial glory of it, of being chosen, and then the constriction of it, like a great snake named Area X was suffocating him, and then also what he had to know in his innermost thoughts, or even coursing across the inner rind of his brain. That the Southern Reach had indeed destroyed his career, perhaps even been the reason for his divorce.

"How do you feel about all of the misinformation given to the expeditions?" Control asked Cheney, if only to push back against the flood of Cheneyisms. He knew Cheney had had some influence in shaping that misinformation.

Cheney's frown made it seem as if Control's question were akin to criticizing the paint job on a car that had been involved in a terrible accident. Was Control a killjoy to want to snuff out Cheney's can-do, his can't-help-it brand of the jowly jovial? But jovial grated on Control most of the time. "Jovial" had always been a pretext, from the high school football team's locker room on—the kind of hearty banter that covered up greater and lesser crimes.

"It wasn't—isn't—really misinformation," Cheney said, and then went dark for a moment, searching for words. Possibly he thought it was a test. Of loyalty or attitude or moral rigor. But he found words soon enough: "It's more like creating a story or a narrative to guide them through the narrows. An anchor."

Like a lighthouse that distracted them from topographical anomalies, a lighthouse that seemed by its very function to provide safety. Maybe Cheney told himself that particular story about the tale, or tale about the story, but Control doubted the director had seen it that way, or even a biologist with only partial memory.

"Jesus, this is a long drive," Cheney said into the silence.

009: EVIDENCE

Finally they had addressed the mouse in the room, and the plant, during their meeting about the wall beyond his door.

"What about this mouse, this plant?" Control had demanded, to see what that shook loose. "Is this a memorial, too?"

Plant and mouse still resided inside the pot, had not yet leapt out and gone for their throats even though Hsyu had kept a keen eye on the pot during the entire meeting. Whitby, though, wouldn't even acknowledge it with a glance, looked like a cat ready to leap off in the opposite direction at the slightest sign of impending pot-activated danger.

"No, not really," Grace conceded after a pause. "She was trying to kill it."

"What?"

"It wouldn't die." She said it with contempt, as if breaking the natural order of things wasn't a miracle but an affront.

The assistant director made Whitby embark upon a summary of hair-raising attempts at destruction that included stabbings, careful burnings, deprivation of soil and water, introduction of parasites, general neglect, the emanation of hateful vibes, verbal and physical abuse, and much more. Whitby reenacted some of these events with overly manic energy.

Clippings had been rushed to Central, and perhaps even now scientists labored to unlock the plant's secrets. But Central had sent no information back, and nothing the director had done could kill it, not even sticking it in a locked drawer. Except, someone had taken pity on the plant and watered it, perhaps even stuck in a dead mouse for nutritional value. Control looked with suspicion upon both Whitby and Grace. The idea that one of them had been merciful only made him like them both a little more.

Hsyu had then piped up: "She took it from the samples rooms, I believe. It was from Area X originally. A very common plant, although I'm not a botanist."

Then, by all means, lead the way to the samples rooms.

Except that Hsyu, as a linguist, didn't have security clearance.

A few miles from the border the landscape changed, and Whitby had to slow down to about ten miles an hour as the road narrowed and became more treacherous. The dark pines and the patches of swamp gave way to a kind of subtropical rain forest. Control could see the curling question marks of fiddlehead ferns and a surprising density of delicate black-winged mayflies as the jeep passed over several wooden bridges that crossed a welter of creeks. The smell of the land had changed from humid and cloying to something as questing as the ferns: a hint of freshness caused by a thicker canopy of leaves. They were, he realized, making their way along the periphery of a huge sinkhole, the kind of "topographical anomaly" that created an entirely different habitat. Sinkhole parks in the area were, for whatever reason, favorite teen hangouts, and sometimes after leaving Hedley with their ill-gotten six-packs they had headed for rendezvous with girls there. The sinkholes he remembered had been litter grounds of crushed beer cans and a scattering of condom wrappers. The kinds of places the local police kept an eye on because it was a rare weekend someone didn't get into a fight there.

More surprising still, white rabbits could be seen, nimbly negotiating the edges of pools of standing water and brown-leaf-littered moist spaces where the rotting of the earth proceeded apace and red-tipped mushrooms rose primordial.

Which caused Control to interrupt one of Cheney's stutter-step monologues: "Are those what I think they are?"

Cheney, clearly relieved that Control had said something: "Yes, those are the true descendants of the experiment. The ones that got away. They breed . . . well, just like rabbits. There was an eradication effort, but it was taking up too many resources, so we just let it happen now."

Control followed the progress of one white brute, larger than his fellows—or larger than her fellows—who sought the higher ground in limitless leaps and bounds. There was something defiant in its stride. Or Control was projecting that onto the animal, just as he was projecting onto most of the other rabbits a peculiar stillness and watchfulness.

Whitby chimed in unexpectedly: "Rabbits have three eyelids and can't vomit." For a moment Control, startled that Whitby had spoken, assigned more significance to the statement than it deserved.

"You know, it's a good reminder to be humble," Cheney said, like a rumbling steamroller intent on paving over Whitby, "to be humbled. A humbling experience. Something like that."

"What if some of them are returnees?" Control asked.

"What?"

Control thought Cheney had heard, but he repeated the question.

"You mean from across the border—they got across and came back? Well, that would be bad. That would be sloppy. Because we know that they've spread fairly far. The ones savvy enough to survive. And as happens, some of them have gotten out of the containment zone and been trapped by enterprising souls and sold to pet stores."

"So you're saying that it's possible that some of the progeny of your fifteen-year-old experiment are now residing in people's homes? As pets?" Control was astonished.

"I wouldn't put it quite that way, but that's the gist, I guess," Cheney conceded.

"Remarkable" was Control's only comment, aghast.

"Not really," Cheney replied, pushing back gently but firmly. "Way of the world. Or at least of invasive species everywhere. I can sell you a python from the dread peninsula that's got the same motivations."

Whitby, a few moments later, the most he said in one gulp during the whole trip: "The few white-and-brown ones are the offspring of white rabbits mating with the native marsh rabbits. We call them Border Specials, and the soldiers shoot and eat them. But not the pure white ones, which I don't think makes sense. Why shoot any of them?"

Why not shoot *all* of them? Why *eat* any of them?

Fifty thousand samples languished in the long rooms that formed the second floor of the left-hand side of the U, assuming an approach from the parking lot. They'd gone before lunch, left Hsyu behind. They had to don white biohazard suits with black gloves, so that Control was actually wearing a version of the gloves that had so unsettled him down in the science division. This was his revenge, to plunge his hands into them and make them his puppets, even if he didn't like their rubbery feel.

The atmosphere was like that inside a cathedral, and as if the science division had been some kind of rehearsal for this event, the sequence of air locks was the same. An ethereal, heavenly music should have been playing, and the way the light struck the air meant that in certain pools of illumination Control could see floating dust motes, and certain archways and supporting walls imbued the rooms with a numinous feeling, intensified by the high ceilings. "This is my favorite place in the Southern Reach," Whitby told him, face alight through his transparent helmet. "There's a sense of calm and safety here."

Did he feel unsafe in the other sections of the building? Control almost asked Whitby this question, but felt that doing so would break the mood. He wished he had his neoclassical music on headphones for the full experience, but the notes played on in his mind regardless, like a strange yearning.

He, Whitby, and Grace walked through in their terrestrial space suits like remote gods striding through a divinely chosen terrain. Even though the suits were bulky, the lightweight fabric didn't seem to touch his skin, and he felt buoyant, as if gravity operated differently here. The suit smelled vaguely of sweat and pep-permint, but he tried to ignore that.

The rows of samples proliferated and extended, the effect enhanced by the mirrors that lined the dividing wall between each hall. Every kind of plant, pieces of bark, dragonflies, the freeze-dried carcasses of fox and muskrat, the dung of coyotes, a section from an old barrel. Moss, lichen, and fungi. Wheel spokes and the glazed eyes of tree frogs staring blindly up at him. He had expected, some-how, a Frankenstein laboratory of two-headed calves in formaldehyde and some hideous manservant with a hunchback lurching ahead of them and explaining it all in an incomprehensible bouillabaisse of good intentions and slurred syntax. But it was just Whitby, and it was just Grace, and in that cathedral neither felt inclined to explain anything.

Analysis by Southern Reach scientists of the most recent samples, taken six years ago and brought back by expedition X.11.D, showed no trace of human-created toxicity remained in Area X. Not a single trace. No heavy metals. No in-dustrial runoff or agricultural runoff. No plastics. Which was impossible.

Control peeked inside the door the assistant director had just opened for him. "There you are," she said, inanely he thought. But there he was, in the main room, with an even higher ceiling and more columns, looking at endless rows and rows of shelves housed inside of a long, wide room.

"The air is pure here," Whitby said. "You can get high just from the oxy-gen levels."

Not a single sample had ever shown any irregularities: normal cell structures, bacteria, radiation levels, whatever applied. But he had also seen a few strange comments in the reports from the handful of guest scientists who had passed the security check and come here to examine the samples, even as they had been kept in the dark about the context. The gist of these comments was that when they looked away from the microscope, the samples changed; and when they stared again, what they looked at had reconstituted itself to appear normal. "There you are." To Control, in that brief glance, staring across the vast litter of objects spread out before him, it mostly looked like a cabinet of curiosities: desiccated beetle husks, brittle starfish, and other things in jars, bottles, beakers, and boxes of assorted sizes.

"Has anyone ever tried to eat any of the samples?" he asked Grace. If they'd just devoured the undying plant, Control was fairly sure it wouldn't have come back.

"Shhhh," she said, exactly as if they were in church and he had spoken too loudly or received a cell-phone call. But he noticed Whitby looking at him quizzically, head cocked to one side within his helmet. Had *Whitby* sampled the samples? Despite his terror?

Parallel to this thought, the knowledge that Hsyu and other non-biologists had never seen the samples cathedral. He wondered what they might have read in the striations of the fur of a dead swamp rat or in the vacant glass eyes of a marsh hawk, its curved beak. What susurrations or utterances might verbalize all unexpected from a cross section of tree moss or cypress bark. The patterns to be found in twigs and leaves.

It was too absurd a thought to give words to, not when he was so new. Or, perhaps, even when he was old in this job, should he be that lucky or unlucky.

So there he was.

When the assistant director closed the door and they moved on to the next section of the cathedral, Control had to bite his thumb to stop a giggle from escaping. He'd had a vision of the samples starting to dance behind that door, freed of the terrible limitations of the human gaze. "Our banal, murderous imagination," as the biologist had put it in a rare unguarded moment with the director before the twelfth expedition.

In the corridor afterward, with Whitby, a little drained by the experience: "Was that the room you wanted me to see?"

"No," Whitby said, but did not elaborate.

Had he insulted the man with his prior refusal? Even if not, Whitby had clearly withdrawn his offer.

Glimpses of towns now under kudzu and other vines, moldering in the moss: a long-abandoned miniature golf course with a pirate theme. The golf greens had been buried in leaves and mud. The half decks of corsairs' ships rose at crazy angles as if from choppy seas of vegetation, masts cracked at right angles and disappearing into the gloom as it began to rain. A gas station lay next door, the roof caved in by fallen trees, the pavement so cracked by gnarled roots that it had crumbled into water-ripe pieces with the seeming texture and consistency of dark, moist brownies. The fuzzy, irregular shapes of houses and two-story buildings through the trees proved that people had lived here before the evacuation. This close to the border as little as possible was disturbed, and so these abandoned places could only be broken down by the natural process of decades of rain and decay.

The final stretch to the border had Whitby circling ever lower until Control was certain they were below sea level, before they came up again slightly to a low ridge upon which sat a drab green barracks, a more official-looking brick building for army command and control, and the local Southern Reach outpost.

According to a labyrinthine hierarchical chart that resembled several thick snakes fucking one another, the Southern Reach was under the army's jurisdiction here, which might be why the Southern Reach facility, closed down between expeditions, looked a bit like a row of large tents that had been made of lemon meringue. Which is to say, it looked like any number of the churches Control had become familiar with in his teenage years, usually because of whatever girl he was dating. The calcification of revivalists and born-agains often took this form: as of something temporary that had hardened and become permanent. And thus it was either a series of white permafrost tents that greeted them or the white swell of huge waves, frozen forever. The sight was as out of place and startling as if the facility had resembled a fossilized herd of huge MoonPies, a delicacy of those youthful years.

Army HQ was in a dome-shaped section of the barracks after the final checkpoint, but no one seemed to be around except a few privates standing in the churned mud bath that was the unofficial parking lot. Loitering with no regard for the light rain falling on them, talking in a bored but intense way while smoking cherry-scented filtered cigarettes. "Whatever you want." "Fuck off." They had the look of men who had no idea what they guarded, or knew but had been trying to forget.

Border commander Samantha Higgins—who occupied a room hardly larger than a storage closet and just as depressing—was AWOL when they called on her. Higgins's aide-de-camp—"add the camp" as his punning father would've put it—relayed an apology that she'd had to "step out" and couldn't "receive you personally." Almost as if he were a special-delivery signature-required package.

Which was just as well. There had been awkwardness between the two entities after the final eleventh expedition had turned up back home—procedures changed, the security tapes scrutinized again and again. They had rechecked the border for other exit points, looking for heat signals, fluctuations in air flow, anything. Found nothing.

So Control thought of "border commander" as a useless or misleading title and didn't really care that Higgins wasn't there, no matter how Cheney seemed to take it as a personal affront: "I told her this was important. She knew this was important."

While Whitby took the opportunity to fondle a fern, revealing a hitherto unobserved sensitivity to texture.

Control had felt foolish asking Whitby what he meant by saying "the terror," but he also couldn't leave it alone. Especially after reading over the theories document Whitby had handed him that morning, which he also wanted to talk about. Control thought of the theories as "slow death by," given the context: Slow death by aliens. Slow death by parallel universe. Slow death by malign unknown time-traveling force. Slow death by invasion from an alternate earth. Slow death by wildly divergent technology or the shadow biosphere or symbiosis or iconography or etymology. Death by this and by that. Death by indifference and inference. His favorite: "Surface-dwelling terrestrial organism, previously unknown." Hiding where all of these years? In a lake? On a farm? At slots in a casino?

But he recognized his bottled-up laughter for the onset of hysteria, and his cynicism for what it was: a defense mechanism so he wouldn't have to think about any of it.

Death, too, by arched eyebrow: a fair amount of implied or outright "your theory is ridiculous, unwarranted, useless." Some of the ghosts of old interdepartmental rivalries resurrected, and coming through in odd ways across sentences. He wondered how much fraternization had taken place over the years—if an archaeologist's written wince at an environmental scientist's seemingly reasonable assertion represented a fair opinion or meant he was seeing an endgame playing out, the final consequence of an affair that had occurred twenty years earlier.

So before the trip to the border, giving up his lunchtime, Control had summoned Whitby to his office to have it out with him about "the terror" and talk about the theories. Although as it turned out they barely touched on the theories.

Whitby had perched on the edge of the chair opposite Control and his huge desk, intent and waiting. He was almost vibrating, like a tuning fork. Which made Control reluctant to say what he had to say, even though he still said it: "Why did you say 'the terror' earlier? And then you repeated it."

Whitby wore an expression of utter blankness, then lit up to the extent that he seemed to levitate for a moment. He had the busy look of a hummingbird in the act of pollination as he said, "Not 'terror.' Not 'terror' at all. *Terroir.*" And this time he drew out and corrected the pronunciation of the word, so Control could tell it was not "terror."

"What is . . . terroir then?"

"A wine term," Whitby said, with such enthusiasm that it made Control wonder if the man had a second job as a sommelier at some upscale Hedley restaurant along the river walk.

Somehow, though, the man's sudden animation animated Control, too. There was so much obfuscation and so much rote recital at the Southern Reach that to see Whitby excited by an idea lifted him up.

"What does it mean?" he asked, although still unsure whether it was a good idea to encourage Whitby.

"What doesn't it mean?" Whitby said. "It means the specific characteristics of a place—the geography, geology, and climate that, in concert with the vine's own genetic propensities, can create a startling, deep, original vintage."

Now Control was both confused and amused. "How does this apply to our work?"

"In all ways," Whitby said, his enthusiasm doubled, if anything. "Terroir's direct translation is 'a sense of place,' and what it means is the sum of the effects of a localized environment, inasmuch as they impact the qualities of a particular product. Yes, that can mean wine, but what if you applied these criteria to thinking about Area X?"

On the cusp of catching Whitby's excitement, Control said, "So you mean you would study everything about the history—natural and human—of that stretch of coast, in addition to all other elements? And that you might—you just might—find an answer in that confluence?" Next to the idea of terroir, the theories that had been presented to Control seemed garish and blunt.

"Exactly. The point of terroir is that no two areas are the same. That no two wines can be exactly the same because no combination of elements can be exactly the same. That certain varietals cannot occur in certain places. But it requires a deep understanding of a region to reach conclusions."

"And this isn't being done already?"

Whitby shrugged. "Some of it. Some of it. Just not all of it considered together, in my opinion. I feel there is an overemphasis on the lighthouse, the tower, base camp—those discrete elements that could be said to jut out of the landscape— while the landscape itself is largely ignored. As is the idea that Area X could have formed nowhere else . . . although that theory would be highly speculative and perhaps based mostly on my own observations."

Control nodded, unable now to shake a sturdy skepticism. Would terroir really be more useful than another approach? If something far beyond the experience of human beings had decided to embark upon a purpose that it did not intend to allow humans to recognize or understand, then terroir would simply be a kind of autopsy, a kind of admission of the limitations of human systems. You could map the entirety of a process—or, say, a beachhead or an invasion—only after it had happened, and still not know the *who* or the *why*. He wanted to say to Whitby, "Growing grapes is simpler than Area X," but refrained.

"I can provide you with some of my personal findings," Whitby said. "I can show you the start of things."

"Great," Control said, nodding with exaggerated cheerfulness, and was relieved that Whitby took that single word as closure to the conversation and made a fairly rapid exit, less relieved that he seemed to take it as undiluted affirmation.

Grand unified theories could backfire—for example, Central's overemphasis on trying to force connections between unconnected right-wing militia groups. Recalled that his father had made up stories about how one piece in his ragtag sculpture garden commented on that one, and how they were all part of a larger narrative. They had all occupied the same space, were by the same creator, but they had never been meant to communicate, one to another. Just as they had never been meant to molder and rust in the backyard. But that way at least his father could rationalize them remaining out there together, under the hot sun and in the rain, even if protected by tarps.

The border had come down in the early morning, on a day, a date, that no one outside of the Southern Reach remembered or commemorated. Just that one inexplicable event had killed an estimated fifteen hundred people. How did you factor ghosts into any terroir? Did they deepen the flavor, or did they make things dry, chalky, irreconcilable? The taste in Control's mouth was bitter.

If terroir meant a confluence, then the entrance through the border into Area X was the ultimate confluence. It was also the ultimate secret, in that there were no visual records of that entry point available to anyone. Unless you were there, look-ing across at it, you could never experience it. Nor did it help if you were peering at it through a raging thunderstorm, shoes filling up with mud, with only one umbrella between the three of you.

They stood, soaked and cold, near the end of a path that wound from the bar-racks across the ridge above the giant sinkhole and then on to more stable land. They were looking at the right side of a tall, sturdy, red wooden frame that delin-eated the location, the width and height, of the entrance beyond. The path ran parallel to a paint line perpetually refreshed to let you know the border lay fifteen feet beyond. If you went ten feet beyond the line, the lasers from a hidden secu-rity system would activate and turn you into cooked meat. But otherwise, the army had left as small a footprint as possible; no one knew what might change the terroir. Here the toxicity levels almost matched those inside of Area X, which was to say: nil, nada, nothing.

As for terror, his personal level had been intensified by deltas of lightning that cracked open the sky and thunder that sounded like a giant in a bad mood rip-ping apart trees. Yet they had persevered, Cheney holding the blue-and-white-striped umbrella aloft, arm fully extended toward the sky, and Control and Whitby huddled around him, trying to shuffle in a synchronized way along the narrow path without tripping. All of it useless against the slanted rain.

"The entrance isn't visible from the side," Cheney said in a loud voice, his forehead flecked with bits of leaf and dirt. "But you'll see it soon. The path circles around to meet it head-on."

"Doesn't it project light?" Control smacked away something red with six legs that had been crawling up his pants.

"Yes, but you can't see it from the side. From the side it doesn't appear to be there at all."

"It is twenty feet high and twelve feet wide," Whitby added.

"Or, as I say, sixty rabbits high and thirty-six rabbits wide," Cheney said.

Control, struck by a sudden generosity, laughed at that one, which he imag-ined brought a flush of happiness to Cheney's features although they could barely recognize each other in the slop and mire.

The area had the aspect of a shrine, even with the downpour. Especially be-cause the downpour cut off abruptly at the border even though the landscape continued uninterrupted. Somehow Control had expected the equivalent of the disconnect when a two-page spread didn't quite line up in a coffee-table book.

But instead it just looked like they were slogging through a huge terrarium or greenhouse with invisible glass revealing a sunny day on the grounds beyond.

They continued to the end amid a profusion of lush plant life and an alarmingly crowded landscape of birdlife and insects, with deer visible in the middle distance through the veil of rain. Hsyu had said something during their meeting about making assumptions about terminology, and he had replied, to a roaring silence, "You mean like calling something a 'border'?" Tracking back from stripping names from expedition members: What if when you accreted personality and other details around mere function, a different picture emerged?

After a few minutes of sloshing through mud, they curved around to come to a halt in front of the wooden structure.

He had not expected any of it to be beautiful, but it was beautiful.

Beyond the red wooden frame, Control could see a roughly rectangular space forming an arch at the top, through which swirled a scintillating, questing white light, a light that fizzed and flickered and seemed always on the point of being snuffed out but never was . . . There was a kind of spiraling effect to it, as it continually circled back in on itself. If you blinked quickly it almost looked as if the light consisted of eight or ten swiftly rotating spokes, but this was an illusion.

The light was like nothing he had ever seen. It was neither harsh nor soft. It was not twee, like faery lite from bad movies. It was not the darkish light of hucksters and magicians or anyone else looking to define light by use of shadows. It lacked the clarity of the all-revealing light of the storage cathedral, but it wasn't murky or buttery or any other descriptor he could think of right then. He imagined trying to tell his father about it, but, really, it was his father who could have described the quality of that light to him.

"Even though it's such a tall corridor and so wide, you have to crawl with your pack as close to the middle as possible. As far away from the sides as possible." Cheney, confirming what Control had already read in summaries. Like cats with duct tape on their backs, slinking forward on their bellies. "No matter how you feel about enclosed or open spaces, it'll be strange in there, because you will feel simultaneously as if you are progressing across a wide-open field and as if you're on a narrow precipice without guardrails and could fall off at any moment. So you exist in a confined and limitless space all at once. One reason we put the expedition members under hypnosis."

Not to mention—and Cheney never did—that the expedition leader in each case had to endure the experience without benefit of hypnosis, and that some experienced strange visions while inside. "It was like being in one of those aquariums with the water overhead, but murkier, so that I could not really tell what was swimming there. Or it wasn't the water that was murky but instead the creatures." "I saw constellations and everything was near and far all at once." "There was a vast plain like where I grew up, and it just kept expanding and expanding, until I had to look at the ground because I was getting the sense of being filled up until I would have burst." All of which could just as easily have occurred inside the subjects' minds.

Nor did the length of the passageway correspond to the width of the invisible border. Some reports from returning expeditions indicated that the passageway meandered, while others described it as straight. The point was, it varied and the time to travel through it into Area X could not be estimated except within a rough parameter of a "norm" of three hours to ten hours. Indeed, because of this, one of the earliest fears of Central had been that the entry point might disappear entirely, even if other opinions differed. Among the files on the border, Control had found a relevant quote from James Lowry: ". . . the door when I saw it looked like it had always been there, and would always be there even if there was no Area X."

The director had apparently thought the border was advancing, but there was no evidence to support that view. An interceding note in the files from far up the chain of command had offered the comment that perhaps the director was just trying to get attention and money for a "dying agency." Now that he saw the entrance, Control wondered how anyone would know what an "advance" meant.

"Don't stare at it directly for too long," Whitby offered. "It tends to draw you in."

"I'll try not to," Control said. But it was too late, his only solace that surely if he started walking toward it, Whitby or Cheney would stop him. Or the lasers would.

The swirling light defeated his attempts to conjure up the biologist. He could not get her to stand beside him, to follow the other three members of the twelfth expedition into that light. By then, by the time she had arrived at this spot, she would already have been under hypnotic influence. The linguist would already have left the expedition. There would have been just the four of them, with their packs, about to crawl through that impossible light. Only the director would have been seeing it all with clear eyes. If Control went through her scribbled notes, if he excavated the sedimentary layers and got to the core of her . . . could he come back here and reconstruct her thoughts, her feelings, at that moment?

"How did the members of the last eleventh and the twelfth get out of Area X without being seen?" Control asked Cheney.

"There must be another exit point we haven't been able to find." The object, observed, still not cooperating with him. A vision of his father in the kitchen when he was fourteen, shoving rotting strawberries into the bottom of a glass and then adding a cone of curled-up paper over the top, to trap the fruit flies that had gotten into the house.

"Why can we see the corridor?" Control asked.

"Not sure what you mean," Cheney said.

"If it's visible, then we were meant to see it." Maybe. Who really knew? Every off-the-cuff comment Control made came, or so he thought, with a built-in echo, as if the past banal observations of visitors and new employees lingered in the air, seeking to merge, same with same, and finding an exact match far too often.

Cheney sucked on his cheek a second, grudgingly admitted, "That's a theory. That's definitely a theory, all right. I can't say it isn't."

Staggering thought: What might come out into the world down a corridor twenty feet tall by twelve feet wide?

They stood there for long moments, bleeding time but not acknowledging it, heedless of the rain. Whitby stood apart, letting the rain soak him, contemptuous of the umbrella. Behind them, through the thunder, the hard trickle of water from the creeks gurgling back down into the sinkhole beyond the ridge. Ahead, the clarity of a cloudless summer day.

While Control tried to stare down that sparkling, that dancing light.

010: FOURTH BREACH

The terroir" infiltrated his thoughts again, when, late in the day, drying off, Control received the transcripts from his morning session with the biologist, the trip to the border kaleidoscoping through his head. He had just reluctantly re-tossed the mouse into the trash and repatriated the plant with the storage cathedral. It had taken an effort of will to do that and to close the door on the weird sermon scrawled on his wall. He hated to engage in superstition, but the doubt remained—that he had made a mistake, that the director had left both mouse and plant in her desk drawer for a reason, as a kind of odd protection against . . . what?

He still didn't know as he performed an Internet search on Ghost Bird's reference to the phorus snail, which revealed she was quoting almost word for word from an old book by an obscure amateur "parson-naturalist." Something she would have encountered in college, with whatever associated memories that, too, might bring. He didn't believe it had significance, except for the obvious one: The biologist had been comparing him to an awkward snail.

Then he thumbed through the transcript, which he found comforting. At one point during the session, fishing, Control had pivoted away from both tower and lighthouse, back to where she had been picked up.

Q: *What did you leave at the empty lot?*

What if, he speculated there at his desk—still ignoring the water-stained pages in the drawer next to him—the empty lot was a terroir related to the terroir that was Area X? What if some confluence of person and place meant something more than just a return home? Did he need to order a complete historical excavation of the empty lot? And what about the other two, the anthropologist and the surveyor? Mired in the arcana of the Southern Reach, he wouldn't have time to check on them for another few days. Grudging gratitude to Grace for simplifying his job by sending them away.

Meanwhile, the biologist was answering his question on the page.

A: *Leave? Like, what? A necklace with a crucifix? A confession?*
Q: *No.*
A: *Well, why don't you tell me what you thought I might've left there?*
Q: *Your manners?*

That had earned him a chuckle, if a caustic one, followed by a long, tired sigh that seemed to expel all the air from her lungs.

A: *I've told you that nothing happened there. I woke up as if from an endless dream. And then they picked me up.*

Q: *Do you ever dream? Now, I mean.*
A: *What would be the point?*
Q: *What do you mean?*
A: *I'd just dream of being out of this place.*
Q: *Do you want to hear about my dreams?*

He didn't know why he had said this to her. He didn't know what he'd tell her. Would he tell her about the endless falling into the bay, into the maw of leviathans?

To his surprise, she said:

A: *What do you dream of, John? Tell me.*

It was the first time she'd used his name, and he tried to hate how it had sent a kind of spark through him. *John.* She had brought her feet up onto the chair so she was hugging her knees and peering at him almost impishly.

Sometimes you had to adjust your strategy, give up something to get something. So he did tell her his dream, even though he felt self-conscious and hoped Grace wouldn't see it in the official record, use it against him somehow. But if he'd lied, if he'd made something up, Control believed that Ghost Bird would know, that even as he'd been trying to interpret her tells, she had been processing *him* the whole time. Even when he asked the questions he was hemorrhaging data. He had a sudden image of information floating out the side of his head in a pixelated bloodred mist. These are my relatives. This is my ex-girlfriend. My father was a sculptor. My mother is a spy.

But she had relented, too, during the conversation, for a moment.

A: *I woke in the empty lot and I thought I was dead. I thought I was in purgatory, maybe, even though I don't believe in an afterlife. But it was quiet and so empty . . . so I waited there, afraid to leave, afraid there might be some reason I was meant to be there. Not sure I wanted to know anything else. Then the police came for me, and then the Southern Reach after that. But I still believed I wasn't really alive.*

What if the biologist had just that morning decided she was alive, not dead? Perhaps that accounted for the change in her mood.

When he had finished reading, he could feel Ghost Bird still staring at him, and she would not let his gaze drop, held him there, or he let her do it. For whatever reason.

On the way back from the border, a silence had come over Control, Whitby, and Cheney, perhaps overloaded by the contrast between sun/heat and rain/cold. But it had seemed to Control like the companionable silence of shared experience, as if he had been initiated into membership in an exclusive club without having been asked first. He was wary of that feeling; it was a space where shadows crept in that shouldn't creep in, where people agreed to things that they did not actually agree with, believing that they were of one purpose and intent. Once, in such a space, a fellow agent had called him "homey" and made an offhand comment about him "not being your usual kind of spic."

When they were about a mile from the Southern Reach, Cheney said, too casually, "You know, there's a rumor about the former director and the border."

"Yes?" Here it came. There it was. How comfort led to overreach or to some half reveal of what should be hidden.

"That she went over the border by herself once," Cheney said, staring off into the distance. Even Whitby seemed to want to distance himself from that statement, leaning forward in his seat as he drove. "Just a rumor," Cheney added. "No idea if it's true."

But Control didn't care about that, despite the addition being disingenuous. The truth clearly didn't worry Cheney, or he already knew it was true and wanted Control on the scent.

"Does this rumor include when this might have happened?" Control asked.

"Before the final eleventh expedition."

Part of him had wanted to take that to the assistant director and see what she might or might not know. Another part decided that was a premature idea. So he'd chewed on the information, wondering why Cheney had fed it to him, especially in front of Whitby. Did that mean Whitby had the spine, despite the evidence, to withhold even when Grace wanted him to share?

"Have you ever been over the border, Cheney?"

An explosive snort. "No. Are you crazy? No."

In the parking lot at day's end, Control sat behind the wheel, keys in the ignition, and decompressed for a moment. The rain had passed, leaving oily puddles and a kind of verdant sheen on the grass and trees. Only Whitby's purple electric car remained, at an angle across two spaces, as if it had washed up there.

Time to call the Voice and file his report. Getting it over with was better than letting work bleed into his evening.

The phone rang and rang.

The Voice finally answered with a "Yes—what?" as if Control had called at a bad time.

He had meant to ask about the director's clandestine border trip, but the Voice's tone threw him off. Instead, he started off with the plant and the mouse: "I found something odd in the director's desk . . ."

Control blinked once, twice, three times. As they were talking, he had noticed something. It was the smallest thing, and yet it rattled him. There was a squashed mosquito on the inside of his windshield, and Control had no idea how it had gotten there. He knew it hadn't been there in the morning, and he had no memory of swatting one anyway. Paranoid thought: Carelessness on the part of someone searching his car . . . or did someone want him to know he was being watched?

Attention divided, Control became aware of wobbles in his conversation with the Voice. Almost like air pockets that pushed an airplane up and forward, while the passenger inside, him, sat there strapped in and alarmed. Or as if he were watching a TV show where the cable hiccupped and brought him five seconds forward every few minutes. Yet the conversation picked up where it had left off.

The Voice was saying, with more than usual gruffness, "I'll get you more information—and don't you worry, I'm still working on the goddamn assistant director situation. Call me tomorrow."

A ridiculous image snuck into his head of the assistant director walking into the parking lot while he was at the border, forcing the lock, rummaging through his glove box, sadistically squashing the mosquito.

"I don't know if that's a good idea at this point, about Grace," Control said. "It might be better to . . ."

But the Voice had already hung up, leaving Control to wonder how it had gotten dark so quickly.

Control contemplated the tangled geometry of blood and delicate limbs. He couldn't stop staring at the mosquito. He had meant to say something else to the Voice, but he'd forgotten it because of the mosquito and now it would have to wait until tomorrow.

Was it possible he *had* squashed the mosquito reflexively and didn't remember? He found that unlikely. Well, just in case he hadn't, he'd leave the damn thing there, along with its splotch of blood. That might send some kind of message back. Eventually.

011: SIXTH BREACH

At home, Chorry waited on the step. Control let him inside, put out some cat food he'd bought at the store along with a chicken sandwich, ate in the kitchen, even though Chorry's meal made the space stink of greasy salmon. He watched the cat chow down but his thoughts were elsewhere, on what he considered the failures of his day. He felt as if most of his passes had been behind his receivers and his high school coach was yelling at him. The wall behind the door had thrown him off. The wall and the meetings had taken up too much of his time. Even the border trip hadn't put things right, just stabilized them while opening new lines of inquiry. The idea that the director had been across the border before the final eleventh expedition had returned to worry at him. Cheney, during their border trip: "I never had the idea that the director agreed with us much, you know? Or, she kept her own counsel, or had some other council, along with Grace. Or I don't know much about people. Which is possible, I guess."

Control reached into his satchel for some of his notes from the border trip, and in doing so was shocked to find three cell phones there instead of two—the sleek one used for communication with the Voice, the other one for regular use, and another, bulkier. Frowning, Control pulled them out. The third was the old, nonfunctioning phone from the director's desk. He stared at it. How had it gotten in there? Had Grace put it in there? An old black beetle of a phone, the rippled, pitted burn across the leather cover a bit like a carapace. Grace couldn't have done it. She must have left it in his office after all and he must have absentmindedly picked it up. But then why hadn't he noticed it in the parking lot, after he finished talking to the Voice?

He set the phone on the kitchen counter, giving it a wary stare or two before he settled into the living room. What was he missing?

After a few sets of halfhearted push-ups, he turned on the television. Soon he was being bombarded by a montage of reality shows, news of another school massacre, a report on another garbage zone in the ocean, and some announcer screaming out the prelims of an MMA match. He dithered between a cooking show and a mystery, two of his favorites, because they didn't require him to think, before deciding on the mystery, the cat purring on his lap like a revving engine.

As he watched the TV, he remembered a lecture in his second year of college by a professor of environmental science. The gist had been that institutions, even individual departments in governments, were the concrete embodiments of not just ideas or opinions but also of attitudes and emotions. Like hate or empathy, statements such as "immigrants need to learn English or they're not really citizens" or "all mental patients deserve our respect." That in the workings of, for example, an agency, you could, with effort, discover not just the abstract thought behind it but the concrete emotions. The Southern Reach had been set up to investigate (and contain) Area X, and yet despite all the signs and symbols of that mission—all of the talk and files and briefs and analysis—some other emotion or attitude also existed within the agency. It frustrated him that he could not quite put his finger on it, as if he needed another sense, or a sensitivity, that he lacked. And yet as Grace had said, once he became too comfortable within the Southern Reach, once he was cocooned by its embrace, he would be too indoctrinated to perceive it.

That night, he did not dream. He did remember being woken well before dawn by something small crawling across the roof in fits and starts, but soon enough it stopped moving. It hadn't been enough to wake the cat.

012: SORT OF SORTING

In the morning, back at work, he discovered that a fluorescent rod had burned out in his office, dulling the light. Control's chair and desk in particular lay under a kind of gloom. He moved a lamp from the bookcases and set it up on a shelf jutting out toward the desk on his left. The better to see that Whitby had followed through on his threat and left a thick, somewhat worn-looking document on his desk entitled "Terroir and Area X: A Complete Approach." Something about the rust on the massive paper clip biting into the title page, the yellowing nature of the typed pages, the handwritten annotations in different-color pens, or maybe the torn-out taped-in images, made him reluctant to go down that particular rabbit hole. It would have to wait its turn, which might at this point mean next week or even next month. He had another session with the biologist, as well as a meeting with Grace about his agency recommendations, and then, on Friday, an appointment to view the videos from the first expedition. Among other pressing things on his mind . . . like a little redecorating. Control opened the door with the words hidden behind it. He took some photographs. Then, using a can of white paint and a brush requisitioned from maintenance, he meticulously painted over all of it: every last word, every detail of the map. Grace and the others would have to get by without a memorial because he couldn't live with the pressure of those words pulsing out from behind the door. Also the height measurements, if that's what they were. Two coats, three, until only a shadow remained, although the height marks, written using a different kind of pen, continued to shine through. If they were height marks, then the director had grown by a quarter inch between measurements, unless she'd been wearing higher heels the second time.

After painting, Control set out two of his father's carvings from the chessboard at home, meaning for them to replace the missing talismans of plant and mouse. A tiny red rooster and a moon-blue goat, they came from a series entitled simply *Mi Familia*. The rooster had the name of one of his uncles, the goat an aunt. His dad had photographs from his youth of playing in the backyard with his friends and cousins, surrounded by chickens and goats, a garden stretching out of sight along a wooden fence. But Control only remembered his father's chickens— generously put, tradition or legacy chickens, named and never slaughtered. "Homage chickens" as Control had teased his father.

Chess was a hobby he had developed that could be shared during his father's chemo treatments and that his father could ponder and worry at when Control wasn't there in the room. Their shared affliction before the cancer had been pool, at which they were both mediocre, even though they enjoyed it. But his dad's physical ailments had outstripped the mental deterioration, so that hadn't been an option. Books as a salve to the boredom of TV? No, because the bookmark just began to separate one sea of unread words from another. But with a reminder of whose turn it was, chess left some evidence of its past even when his dad got confused toward the end.

Control had press-ganged his dad's carvings into being pieces; they were a motley bunch that didn't much correlate to their function, since they were being twice reinterpreted—first as people into animals and then into chess pieces. But he became a better player, his interest raised because abstraction had been turned into something real, and the results, although comical to them, seemed to matter more. "Abuela to bishop" as a move had set them both to giggling. "Cousin Humberto to La Sobrina Mercedez."

Now these carvings were going to help him. Control set the rooster on the far left corner of his desk and the goat on the right, with the rooster facing out and the goat staring back at him. He had glued to each a nearly invisible nano-camera that would transmit wirelessly to his phone and laptop. If nothing else, he meant for his office to be secure, to make of it a bastion, to take from it all unknowns, and to substitute only that which might be a comfort to him. Who knew what he might discover?

He was then free to consider the director's notes.

The preamble to reading the director's notes had much of the ritual of a spring cleaning. He cleared all of the chairs except his own from the office, setting them up in the hallway. Then he started to make piles in the middle of the floor. He tried to ignore the ambivalent stains revealed on the carpet. Coffee? Blood? Gravy? Cat vomit? Clearly the janitor and any cohorts had been banned from the director's office for quite some time. He had a vision of Grace ordering that the office be kept as is, in much the same way that on cop shows the parents of slain children allowed not a single new dust mote to enter the hallowed ground of their lost ones' bedrooms. Grace had kept it locked until his arrival, had held on to the spare key, and yet he didn't think she'd be showing up on his surveillance video.

So he sat on a stool, his favorite neoclassical composer playing on his laptop, and let the music fill the room and create a kind of order out of chaos. Skipping no step, Grandpa, even if there was a skip to his step. He already had received files that morning from Grace—conveyed via a third-party administrative assistant so they could avoid talking to each other. These files detailed all of the director's official memos and reports—against which he would have to check every doodle and fragment. An "inventory list" as Control thought of it. He had considered asking Whitby to sort through the notes, but with each item the security clearance fluctuated from secret to top secret to what-the-fuck-is-this-secret like some volatile stock market dealing in futures.

Grace's title for the list was too functional: DIRECTOR FILES—DMP OF MAJOR AND MINOR MEMOS AND REPORTS. DMP, or Data Management Program, referred to the proprietary imaging and viewing system the Southern Reach had paid for and implemented in the nineties. Control would have gone with something pithier than Grace had, like THE DIRECTOR DOCUMENTS, or more dramatic, like TALES FROM A FORGOTTEN AGENCY or THE AREA X DOSSIER.

The piles had to be organized by topic so that they would at least loosely match up to Grace's DMP: border, lighthouse, tower, island, base camp, natural history, unnatural history, general history, unknown. He also decided to make a pile for "irrelevant," even though what might seem irrelevant to him might to someone else be the Rosetta stone—if such a stone, or the pebble version, even existed among all the debris.

This was a comfortable place for him, a comfortable task, familiar as penance during a period of shame and demotion, and he could lose himself in it almost as thoughtlessly as doing the dishes after dinner or making the bed in the morning— emerge in some ways refreshed.

But with the crucial difference that these piles looked in part as if he had tracked in dirt on his shoes from outside. The former director was making him into a new kind of urban farmer, building compost piles with classified material that had originated out in the world, bringing with it a rich backstory. Oak and magnolia trees had provided some of the raw material in the form of leaves, to which the director had added napkins, receipts, even sometimes toilet paper, creating a thick mulch.

The diner where Control ate breakfast had yielded several noteworthy receipts, as did a corner grocery store, where the former director had at various times shopped as a convenient last resort. The receipts indicated straggler items, not quite a formal outing for groceries. A roll of paper towels and beef jerky one time, fruit juice and breakfast cereal another time, hot dogs, a quart of skim milk, nail scissors, and a greeting card the next. The napkins, receipts, and advertising brochures from a barbecue place in her hometown of Bleakersville figured prominently, and induced in Control a hunger for ribs. Bleakersville was only about fifteen minutes from the Southern Reach, right off the highway that led to Hedley. According to Grace, the house there had been swept clean of anything related to the Southern Reach, the results catalogued in a special DIRECTOR'S HOUSE section of the DMP file.

Panicked thought after about an hour: What if the seemingly random surfaces on which the director had written her notes had significance? What if the words were not the whole message, just as the lighthouse keeper's deranged sermon wasn't the whole story? The storage cathedral came to mind, and although it seemed improbable he wondered, paranoid, if some of the leaves came from Area X, then dismissed the thought as speculative and counterproductive.

No, the director's vast array of textures revealed "only" that she had been absorbed in her task, as if she had been desperate to write down her observations in the moment, had wanted neither to forget nor to have an internal editor interrupt her search for understanding. Or no hacker to peer into the inner workings of her mind, distilled down to a DMP or otherwise.

He had, as a result, to sort through not just piles of primary "documents" but also a haphazard record of the director's life and her wanderings through the world outside of the Southern Reach buildings. This helped, because he had only dribs and drabs from the official file—either due to Grace's interference or because the director herself had managed to winnow it terse. She had no siblings and had grown up with her father in the Midwest. She had studied psychology at a state college, been a consultant for about five years. She had then applied for the Southern Reach through Central, where she had endured a grueling schedule designed to force her to prove herself over and over—and thus make up for her undistinguished career to date. The Southern Reach must have seemed a more attractive posting back then—and where the sparse information turned into the roiling mass of notes in her office. His request for further intel had been offered up to the labyrinthine and terse maw of Central, which had clamped shut on it. Someday a file might be spat out in his direction.

So he was left with trying to build a true terroir vision of the director—her motivations and knowledge base—from everything he was sorting through and by creating a whole layering of other, non-DMP categories in his mind. She had a subscription to a table television guide, as well as a selection of culture and art magazines, judging not just from torn pages but from subscription renewal forms. She had owed the dentist $72.12 at one point for a cleaning not covered by her insurance and didn't care who knew it. A bowling alley outside of town was a frequent haunt. She got birthday cards from an aunt, but either wasn't sentimental about cards or wasn't that close to the woman. She liked pork chops and shrimp with grits. She liked to dine alone, but one receipt from the barbecue place had two dinner orders on it. Company? Perhaps, like him, she sometimes ordered food to go so she'd have a lunch for the next day.

There was not much about the border in her notes, but that white spiral, that enormous space, did not leave him completely. There was an odd synchronicity as he worked that linked the spiral to his mother's flash of light across the sky, the literal and the metaphoric joined together across an expanse of time and context so vast that only thoughts could bridge the gap.

The sedimentary layers that had existed under the plant and mouse proved the most difficult to separate out. Some pages were brittle and thin, and the scraps of paper and ragged collages of leaves had a tendency to stick together, while being infiltrated and bound more tightly by the remains of translucent roots touched by lines of crimson left behind by the plant. As Control painstakingly separated one page from another, a musty smell that had lain dormant rose up, became strong and pungent. He tried not to compare it to the stench of dirty socks.

The layers continued to support that the director liked both nature and a cold breakfast. As he liberated the proof of purchase cut out of a box of bran flakes from an oak leaf stained blue by words thickened into almost unreadable ink blots, he knew that the cardboard had never before been unwedded from its brittle bride. "Review transcripts from X.10.C, esp. anthro on LH landing" read the cardboard. "Recommend discontinuing use of black boxes for conditioning purposes" read the leaf. He placed the oak leaf on the unknown pile, as in "unknown value."

Other intriguing fragments revealed themselves, too, some peeking out between books on the stacks or just shoved roughly between pages, less like bookmarks and more as if she had become irritated with them and was punishing the very words she had scribbled down. It was between the pages of a basic college biology textbook that looked worn enough to have been the director's own that Control found, on real paper, bizarrely printed on a dot matrix printer despite a date of only eighteen months ago, a note on the twelfth expedition.

In the note, which hadn't made it into Grace's DMP file, the director called the surveyor "someone with a strong sense of reality, a good, bracing foil to the others." The linguist discarded in the border prep area she called "useful but not essential; possibly a dangerous addition, a sympathetic but narrow character who might deflect attention." Sympathetic to whom? Deflect attention from what?

And was this deflection desirable or . . . ? The anthropologist was referred to by her first name, which confused Control until he suddenly recognized it. "Hildi will be on board, will understand." He stared at that note for a while. On board with what? Understand what?

Beyond a frustrating lack of context, the notes conveyed a sense that the director had been casting a play or movie. Notes for actors. Teams needed cohesion, but the director didn't seem as concerned with morale and the group dynamic as with . . . some other quality.

The note on the biologist was the most extensive and caused Control to vibrate with additional questions.

> Not a very good biologist. In a traditional sense. Empathic more toward environments than people. Forgets the reasons she went, who is paying her salary. But becomes embedded to an extraordinary extent. Would know Area X better than I do from almost the first moment sets foot there. Experience with similar settings. Self-sufficient. Unburdened. Connection through her husband. What would she be in Area X? A signal? A flare? Or invisible? Exploit.

Another note, found nearby in volume 2 of a slim three-pamphlet set on xenobiology, came to mind: "bio: expo to TA contam?" Biologist exposure to topographical anomaly contamination was his best guess—an easy guess. But without a date, he could not even be sure it pertained to the same expedition. Similarly, when had "Keep from L" and "L said no—no surprise" been written on two separate scraps, and did "L" stand for Lowry or in some esoteric and less likely way mean "lighthouse keeper"?

He let all of this settle in, knew he had to be patient. There were a lot of notes, and a lot of pages to Grace's DMP file, nothing yet on a prior trip by the director across the border. But already he was getting the sense of undercurrents, was finding now in Whitby's terroir theory something that might apply more to the Southern Reach than to Area X, perhaps framed by a single mind. The idea that a dysfunctional thought could take root in a vacuum, the individual anonymous and wraithlike, unknowable because, especially at first, he or she had no interaction with other people. Because more and more in the modern Internet era you came across isolated instances of a mind virus or worm: brains that self-washed, bathed in received ideologies that came down from on high, ideologies that could remain dormant or hidden for years, silent as death until they struck.

Almost anything could happen now, and did. The government could not investigate every farmer's purchase of fertilizer and fireworks—could not self-police every deviant brain within its own ranks.

The thought had occurred while sorting through the scraps that if you ran an agency devoted to understanding and combating a force that constituted an insurgency, and you believed the border was, in some sense at least, advancing, then you might deviate from official protocols. That if your supervisors and colleagues did not agree with your assessment, you might come up with an alternative plan and begin to enact it on your own. That, wary and careful, you might then and only then reach out to recruit the help of others who did believe you, or at least weren't hostile, to implement that plan. Whether you let them in on the details or not. Just possibly, you might begin to work out this plan on the back of receipts from your favorite restaurants, while watching TV or reading a magazine.

When it came time to leave for his appointment with Grace, Control looked up to realize he had boxed himself in with piles of paper and stacked folders. Past that, the doorway full of chairs and a small collapsible table required so much effort to navigate that he wondered if he'd subconsciously been trying to keep something out.

013: RECOMMENDATIONS

Control had wanted to impose himself on Grace's territory, to show her he was comfortable there, but that meant when he arrived she was in the middle of a ridiculously cheerful conversation with her administrative assistant.

While he waited, Control reviewed the basics, the basics being all that had been given to him, for whatever reason. Grace Stevenson. *Homo sapiens*. Female. Family originally from the West Indies. She was third-generation in this country and the eldest of three daughters. The parents had worked hard to put all three through college, and Grace had graduated valedictorian of her class with dual degrees in political science and history, followed by training at Central. Then, during a special op, she'd injured her leg—no details on how—and washed up on the shores of the Southern Reach. No, that wasn't right. The director had picked her name out of a hat? Cheney had made some noises to that effect at one point on their border trip.

But she had to have harbored larger ambitions at some point, so what had kept her here—just the director? For from the start of her stint at the Southern Reach, Grace Stevenson had entered a kind of holding pattern, if not a slow slide into stagnation—the personal depths of that pit probably her messy, drawn-out divorce almost eight years ago, that event timed almost to the month of the college graduation of her twin boys. A year later she had informed Central about her relationship with a Panamanian national—a woman—so that she could again be fully vetted and deemed no security risk, which she wasn't. A planned mess, then, but still traumatic. Her boys were doctors now, and also immortalized in a desk photo of them at a soccer game. Another photo showed her arm in arm with the director. The director was a big woman, with the kind of frame where you couldn't tell if she ran to fat or was muscular. They were at some Southern Reach company picnic, a barbecue station jutting into the frame from the left and people in flowery beach shirts in the backgrouund. The idea of agency social events struck Control as absurd for some reason. Both photos were already familiar to him.

After the divorce, the assistant director's fate had been ever more joined to that of the director, whom she'd had to cover for several times, if he was reading between the lines correctly. The story ended with the director's disappearance and Grace landing the booby prize: getting to be the Assistant Director for Life.

Oh, yes, and as a result of all of this, and more, Grace Stevenson fostered an overwhelming sense of hostility toward him. An emotion he sympathized with, although only to a point, which was probably his failing. "Empathy is a losing game," his father had liked to say, sometimes worn down by the casual racism he encountered. If you had to think about it, then you were doing it wrong.

The assistant finally gone, Control sat down opposite Grace while she held the printout of his initial list of recommendations at arm's length, not so much because it smelled or was otherwise offensive but because she refused to get progressive lenses.

Would she take the recommendations as a challenge? They were deliberately premature, but he hoped so. Although it certainly didn't bode well that a mini tape recorder lay whirring in front of him, her response to his presence in her space. But he had practiced his mannerisms in the mirror that morning, just to see how nonverbal he could be.

In truth, most of his admin and managerial recommendations could apply to any organization that had been rudderless—or to be generous, operating with half a rudder—for a few years. The rest were stabs in the dark, but whatever they cut was as likely to flense lard as hamstring anyone. He wanted the flow of information to go in multiple directions, so that, for example, Hsyu the linguist had access to classified information from other agency departments. He also wanted to approve long-forbidden overtime and nighttime working hours, since the electricity in the building had to stay on twenty-four hours a day anyway. He had noticed most of the staff left early.

Some other things were unnecessary, but with any luck Grace would waste time and energy fighting him on them.

"That was fast," she said finally, tossing the paper-clipped pages of his list back across the desk at him. The pages slid into his lap before he could catch them.

"I did my homework," Control said. Whatever that meant.

"A conscientious schoolboy. A star pupil."

"The first part." Control half agreed, not sure he liked the way she said it.

Grace didn't bother wasting even an insincere smile in response. "Let me get to the point. Someone has been interfering with my access to Central this week—making inquiries, poking around. But whoever is doing you this favor has no tact—or whatever faction is behind it doesn't have quite enough pull."

"I don't know what you're talking about," Control said, his nonverbal mannerisms sagging in surprise along with the rest of him, despite his best efforts.

Faction. Despite his daydream about the Voice having a black-ops identity, it had not occurred to him that his mother might be heading up a faction, which led him automatically to the idea of true shadow ops—along with an opposition. It threw him, a little, that Central might be that fragmented. Just how elephantine, how rhinoceroscrutian, had the Voice's efforts been in following up on Control's request? And: What did Grace use her contacts for when she wasn't turning them against him?

Grace's look of disgust told him what she thought about his answer. "Then, in that case, John Rodriguez, I have no comment on your recommendations, except to say that I will begin to implement them in as excruciatingly slow a fashion as possible. You should begin to see a few of them—like, 'buy new floor cleaner,' in place by next quarter. Possibly. Maybe."

He had a vision, again, of Grace spiriting away the biologist, of multiple mutual attempted destructions, until somewhere up in the clouds, atop two vast and blood-drenched escalators, they continued to do battle years from now.

Control's stiff nod—gruffly acknowledging defeat—wasn't the mannerism he'd been hoping to use.

But she wasn't done. Her eyes glittered as she opened a drawer and pulled out a mother-of-pearl jewelry box.

"Do you know what this is?" she asked him.

"A jewelry box?" he replied, confused, definitely back on his heels now.

"This is a box full of accusations," Grace said, holding it toward him like an offering. With this jewelry box, I thee despise.

"What is a box of accusations?" Although he didn't want to know.

With a clink-and-tinkle, the yawning velvet mouth sent a handful of bugs Control recognized all too well rolling and skittering across her blotter at him. Most of them came to a stop before the edge, but a couple followed the list onto his lap. The rotting honey smell had intensified again.

"*That* is a box of accusations."

Attempting a comeback, aware it was feeble: "I see only one accusation there, made multiple times."

"I haven't emptied it yet."

"Would you like to empty it now?"

She shook her head. "Not yet. But I will if you continue to interfere with Central. And you can take your spies with you."

Should he lie? That would defeat the purpose of sending the message.

"Why would I bug you?" With a look that he knew undercut his innocence, even as indignation rose in him as ardently as if he *were* innocent. Because in a way he thought he was innocent: Action bred reaction. Lose a few expedition members, gain a few bugs. She might even recognize some of them.

But Grace persisted: "You did. You also rifled through my files, looked in all of my drawers."

"No, I didn't." This time his anger was backed by something real. He hadn't ransacked her office, only placed the bugs there, but now even that act troubled him the more he thought about it. It was out of character, had served no real purpose, had been counterproductive.

Grace continued on patiently. "If you do it again, I'll file a complaint. I've already changed the pass-key combination on my door. Anything you need to know, you can just ask me."

Easily said, but Control didn't think it was true, so he tested it: "Did you put the director's cell phone in my satchel?" Couldn't bring himself to ask the even more ludicrous question "Did you squash a mosquito in my car?" or anything about the director and the border.

"Now, why would I do that?" she asked, echoing him, but she looked serious, puzzled. "What are you talking about?"

"Keep the bugs as souvenirs," he said. Put them in the Southern Reach Olde Antique Shoppe and sell them to tourists.

"No, I mean it—what are you talking about?"

Rather than respond, Control got up, retreated into the corridor, not sure if he heard laughter from behind him or some distorted echo through the overhead vent.

014: HEROIC HEROES OF THE REVOLUTION

Later, as he was wallowing in the notes, plugging his ears and eyes with them, to forget about Grace—if he hadn't ransacked Grace's office, who had?—the expedition wing buzzed him and an excitable-sounding male voice told Control that the biologist was "not feeling good at all—she says she's not up for an interview today." When he asked what was wrong, the man told him, "She's been complaining of cramps and fever. The doctor says it's a cold." A cold? A cold was nothing.

"Hit the ground running." The notes and these sessions were still firmly within his domain. He didn't want to postpone, so he'd go to her. With any luck, he wouldn't bump into Grace. Whitby he could've used help from, but even though he'd buzzed him, the man was making himself scarce.

As he said that he'd stop by soon, Control realized that it might be some ploy—the obvious one of not playing along, but also that by going he might be giving up some advantage or confirming that she held some power over him. But his head was full of scraps of notes and the puzzle of a possible clandestine trip by the director across the border and the deadly echo of muffled interiors of jewelry boxes. He wanted to clear it out, or fill it up with something else for a while.

He left his office, headed down the corridor. Of the smattering of personnel in the hall beyond some were actually in lab coats for once. For his benefit? "Bored?" a pale gaunt man who looked vaguely familiar murmured to the black woman walking beside him as they passed. "Eager to get on with it," came the reply. "You prefer this place, you really do, don't you?" Should he be playing it by the book more? Perhaps. He couldn't deny that the biologist had gotten lodged inside of his head: a faint pressure that made the path leading to the expedition wing narrower, the ceilings lower, the continuous seeking tongue of rough green carpet curling up around him. They were beginning to exist in some transitional space between interrogation and conversation, something for which he could not quite find a name.

Every time the biologist spoke something changed in his world, which he found suspicious on some level, resented it for the distraction. But not a flirtation, no, nor even the ordinary emotional bond. He knew with absolute certainty that he would *not* become overly fixated or obsessional, enter into some downward spiral, if they continued to talk, to share the same space. That had no place in his plans, didn't fit his profile.

The expedition wing featured four layers of obvious security, with the debriefing room they usually used perched on the edge of the outer layer—right after you passed through a decontamination zone that scanned you for everything from bacteria to the ghost of that rusty nail that had risen up through your foot on the rocky beach when you were ten. Considering the biologist had stood in a festering empty lot full of weeds, rusted metal, cracked concrete, and dog shit for hours before arriving, this seemed pointless. But still they did it, with an unsmiling and calm efficiency. Beyond that, all was rendered in an almost blinding white that contrasted with the washed-out teal-and-copper textures of the rooms off the corridor. Three more locked doors lay between the rest of the Southern Reach and the "suites," aka the holding areas. A texture and tone that might once have been futurist but now felt retro-futurist clung to white-and-black furniture that had an abstract modernist quality.

In the minimalist foyer and rec rooms that served as preamble to the suites you could also find a novel's worth of photographs and portraits that had no relationship to reality. The photographs had been carefully chosen to suggest post-mission success, complete with grins and cheers, when they actually depicted pre-mission prep, often for expeditions gone disastrously wrong, or actors from photoshoots. The portraits, a long procession of them ending at the suites, were worse, in Control's estimation. They depicted all twenty-five "returning" members of the first expedition, the triumphant pioneers who had encountered the "pristine wilderness" that in fact had killed all but Lowry. This was the alternative reality any staff that came into contact with expedition members had to support. This was the fiction that came with its own made-up or tailored stories of bravery and endurance meant to evoke these same qualities in the current expedition. Like some socialist dictatorship's glorious heroes of the revolution.

What did it mean? Nothing. Had the biologist believed it all? Perhaps. The tale wanted to be believed, begged to be believed: a story of good old national can-do pride. Roll up your sleeves and get down to work, and if you try hard enough you'll come back alive and not a broken-down zombie with a distant gaze and cancer in place of a personality and an intact short-term memory.

He found Ghost Bird in her room, on her cot—or, someone other than him might have reported back, her bed. The place combined the ambiance of a whitewashed barracks, a summer camp, and a failing hotel. The same pale walls—although here you could see painted-over graffiti, the same as in a prison cell. The high ceiling included a skylight, and on the side wall a narrow window, too high for the biologist to peer out of it. The bed had been built into the far wall, and opposite it a TV with DVD player: approved movies only and a couple of approved channels. Nothing too realistic. Nothing that might fill in the amnesia. It was mostly ancient science-fiction and fantasy movies or melodramas. Documentaries and news programs were on the No list. Animal shows could go either way.

"I thought I would visit you this time, since you don't feel well," he said, through his surgical mask. The attendant had already said she had given her permission.

"You thought you'd crash my sickness party and take advantage of me not being at full strength," she said. Her eyes were bloodshot and hooded with shadow, her face drawn. She was still wearing the same odd janitorial-military outfit, this time with red socks. Even sick, she looked strong. She must do push-ups and pull-ups at a ferocious rate, was all he could think.

"No," he said, spinning an ovoid plastic chair so, before he'd thought through the visual, he could lean against the back, legs awkwardly splayed to either side. Did they not allow real chairs for the same reason airports only had plastic knives? "No, I was concerned. I didn't want to drag you to the debriefing room." He wondered if the medication for her sickness had made her fuzzy, if he should come back later. Or not at all. He had become uncomfortably aware of the power imbalance between them in this setting.

"Of course. Phorus snails are known for their courtesy."

"If you'd read further in your biology text, you would have discovered this is true."

That earned him half a laugh, but also her turning away from him on the bed-cot as she hugged an extra yellow pillow. Her V of a back faced him, the fabric of her shirt pulled tight, the delicate hairs on the smooth skin of her neck revealed to him with an almost microscopic precision.

"We could go into the common area if you would prefer?"

"No, you should see me in my unnatural environment."

"It seems nice enough," he said, then wished he hadn't.

"The Ghost Bird has a usual daily range of ten to twenty square miles, not a cramped space for pacing of, say, forty feet."

He winced, nodded in recognition, changed the subject. "I thought maybe today we'd talk about your husband and also the director."

"We won't talk about my husband. And *you're* the director."

"Sorry. I meant the psychologist. I misspoke." Cursing and forgiving himself at the same time.

She swiveled enough to give him a raised eyebrow, right eye hidden by the pillow, then fell back into contemplating the wall. "Misspoke?"

"I meant the psychologist."

"No, I think you meant director."

"Psychologist," he said stubbornly. Perhaps with too much irritation. There was something about the casualness of the situation that alarmed him. He should not have come anywhere near her private quarters.

"If you say so." Then, as if playing on his discomfort, she turned again so she was on her side facing him, still clutching the pillow. She peered up at him and said with a kind of sleepy cheekiness, "What if we share information?"

"What do you mean?" He knew exactly what she meant.

"You answer a question and I'll answer a question."

He said nothing, weighing the threat of that versus the reward. He could lie to her. He could lie to her all day long, and she'd never know.

"Okay," he said.

"Good. I'll start. Are you married or ever been married?"

"No and no."

"Zero for two. Are you gay?"

"That's another question—and no."

"Fair enough. Now ask away."

"What happened at the lighthouse?"

"Too general. Be more specific."

"When you went inside the lighthouse, did you climb to the top? What did you find?"

She sat up, back to the wall. "That's two questions. Why are you looking at me that way?"

"I'm not looking at you in any particular way." He'd just become aware of her breasts, which hadn't happened during prior sessions, and now was trying to become unaware of them again.

"But that's two questions." Apparently, he'd given the correct response.

"Yes, you're right about that."

"Which one do you want answered?"

"What did you find?"

"Who says I remember any of it?"

"You just did. So tell me."

"Journals. Lots of journals. Dried blood on the steps. A photograph of the lighthouse keeper."

"A photograph?"

"Yes."

"Can you describe it?"

"Two middle-aged men, in front of the lighthouse, a girl out to the side. The lighthouse keeper in the middle. Do you know his name?"

"Saul Evans," he said without thinking. But couldn't see the harm, was already mulling over the significance of a photograph that hung in the director's office also existing in the lighthouse. "That's your question."

He could tell she was disappointed. She frowned, shoulders slumped. Could tell as readily that the name "Saul Evans" meant nothing to her.

"What else can you tell me about the photo?"

"It was framed, hanging on the wall at the middle landing, and the light-house keeper's face was circled."

"Circled?" Who had circled it, and why?

"That's another question."

"Yes."

"Now tell me what your hobbies are."

"What? Why?" It seemed like a question for the wider world, not the Southern Reach.

"What do you do when you're not here?"

Control considered that. "I feed my cat."

She laughed—chortled, actually, ending in a short coughing fit. "That's not a hobby."

"More like a vocation," he admitted. "No, but—I jog. I like classical music. I play chess sometimes. I watch TV sometimes. I read books—novels."

"Nothing very distinctive there," she said.

"I never claimed to be unique. What else do you remember from the expedition?"

She squinted, eyebrows applying pressure to the rest of her face as if that might help her memory. "That's a very broad question, Mr. Director. Very broad."

"You can answer it however you like."

"Oh, thank you."

"I just mean that—"

"I know what you mean," she said. "I almost always know what you mean."

"Then answer the question."

"It's a voluntary game," she explained. "We can stop at any time. Maybe I want to stop now." That recklessness again, or something else? She sighed, crossed her arms. "Something bad happened at the top. I saw something bad. But I'm not quite sure what. A green flame. A shoe. It's confused, like it's in a kaleidoscope. It comes and it goes. It feels as if I'm receiving someone else's memories. From the bottom of a well. In a dream."

"Someone else's memories?"

"It's my turn. What does your mother do?"

"That's classified."

"I bet it is," she said, giving him an appraising look.

He ended the session soon thereafter. What was true empathy anyway but sometimes turning away, leaving someone alone? Tired and in her room, she had become not so much less sharp as almost too relaxed.

She was confusing him. He kept seeing sides of her that he had not known existed, that had not existed in the biologist he had known from the files and transcripts. He felt as if he'd been talking to someone younger today, someone more glib and also more vulnerable, if he'd chosen to exploit that. Perhaps it *was* because he had invaded her territory, while she was sick—or perhaps she was, for some reason, trying out personalities. Some part of him missed the more confrontational Ghost Bird.

As he went back through the layers of security, passing the faked portraits and photos, he acknowledged that at least she had admitted some of her memories of the expedition were intact. That was a kind of progress. Although it still felt too slow, felt every now and then as if everything was happening too slow, and that he was taking too long to understand.

One day her portrait would be up on the wall. When the subject was still alive, did they have to sit for those, or were they created from existing photographs? Would she have to recount some fiction about her experiences in Area X, without ever having a complete memory of what had actually happened?

015: SEVENTH BREACH

Photographs had also been buried in the sedimentary layers of the director's desk. Many were of the lighthouse from different angles, a few from various expeditions but also reproductions of ancient daguerreotypes taken soon after the lighthouse had first been built, along with etchings and maps. The topographical anomaly as well, although fewer of these. Among them was a second copy of one of the photographs that hung on the wall opposite his desk—almost certainly the photograph the biologist had seen. That black-and-white photograph of the last lighthouse keeper, Saul Evans, with one of his assistants to his left, and on the right, hunched over as she clambered up some rocks in the background, a girl whose face was half-obscured by the hood of her jacket. Was her hair black, brown, or blond? Impossible to tell from the few strands visible. She was dressed in a practical flannel shirt and jeans. The photo had a wintry feel to it, the grass in the background faded and sparse, the waves visible beyond the sand and rocks cresting in a cold kind of way. A local girl? As with so many others, they might never know who she had been. The forgotten coast had not been the best place to live if you cared about anyone finding you from census records.

The lighthouse keeper was in his late forties or early fifties, except Control knew you could only serve until fifty, so he must have been in his forties. A weathered face, bearded as you might expect. A sea captain's hat, even though the man had never been any kind of sailor. Control couldn't intuit much from looking at Saul Evans. He looked like a walking, talking cliché, as if he'd tried hard for years to mimic first an eccentric lay preacher whose sermons referenced hellfire and then whatever one might expect from a lighthouse keeper. You could become invisible that way, as Control knew from his few operations in the field. Become a type, no one saw you. Paranoid thought: What better disguise? But disguise for what?

The photo had been taken by a member of the Séance & Science Brigade about a week or two before the Event that had created Area X. The photographer had gone missing when the border came down. It remained the only photo of Saul Evans they had, except for some shots from twenty years earlier, well before he'd come to the coast.

By the late afternoon, Control felt as if he hadn't gotten much further—just given himself a respite from governance of the Southern Reach—although even that was interrupted (again) by the sound of his reconstituted chair barricade being encountered by an apparition who turned out to be Cheney ambitiously leaning forward across the clattery chairs so he could peer around the corner.

". . . Hello, Cheney."

"Hello . . . Control."

Perhaps because of his precarious position, Cheney seemed at a loss, even though he was the intruder. Or as if he had thought the office might be empty, the chairs foreshadowing some shift in hierarchy?

"Yes?" Control said, not wanting to invite Cheney all the way in.

The X of his face tightened, the lines unsuccessfully trying to break free and become either parallel or one line. "Oh, yes, well, I guess I just wondered if you'd followed up about, you know, the director's *trip*." This last bit delivered in a low voice backed up by a quick glance away down the hall. Did Cheney have a faction, too? That would be tiresome. But no doubt he did: He was the one true hope of the nervous scientists huddled in the basement, waiting to be downsized, plucked one by one from their offices and cubicles by the giant, invisible hand of Central and then tossed into a smoldering pit of indifference and joblessness.

"Since I've got you here, Cheney, here's a question for you: Anything out of the ordinary about the second-to-last eleventh expedition?" Another thing Control hated about the iterations: a metric mouthful to enunciate, harder still to remember the actual number. "X.11.H, it was, right?"

Cheney, stabilized by some crude chair rearrangement, appeared in full, motorcycle jacket and all, in the doorway. "X.11.J. I don't think so. You have the files."

But that was just it. Control had a fairly crude report, including the intel that the director had conducted the exit interviews . . . which were astonishingly vague in their happy-happy nothing-bad-happened message. "Well, it was the expedition before the director's *special trip*. I thought you might have some insight."

Cheney shook his head, seemed now to very much regret his intrusion. "No, nothing much. Nothing that comes to mind." Did the director's office somehow make him uncomfortable? His gaze couldn't seem to fix on one thing, ricocheted from the far wall to the ceiling and then, ever so briefly, like the brush of a moth's wings, touched upon the mounds of unprofessional evidence circling Control. Did Cheney think of them as piles of gold Control would steal or piles of shit sandwiches he was being forced to eat?

"Let me ask you about Lowry, then," Control said, thinking about the ambiguous "L." notes he'd found and the video he'd be watching all too soon. "How did Lowry and the director get along?"

Cheney seemed just as uncomfortable with this question but more willing to answer. "How does anyone get along, when you think about it, really? Lowry didn't like me personally but we got along fine professionally. He had an appreciation for our role. He knew the value of having good equipment." Which probably meant Lowry had approved every purchase order Cheney ever wrote.

"But what about him and the director?" Control asked. Again.

"Bluntly? Lowry admired her in his way, tried to make her his protégé, but she didn't want to be. She was very much her own person. And I think she thought he got too much credit for just surviving."

"Wasn't he a hero?" A glorious hero of the revolution plastered on a wall, remade in the image created by a camera lens and doctored documents. Rehabilitated from his awful experiences. Made productive. Booted up to Central after a while.

"Sure, sure," Cheney said. "Sure enough. But, you know, maybe overrated. He liked to drink. He liked to throw his weight around. I remember the director once said something unkind, compared him to a prisoner of war who thinks just because he suffered he knows a lot. So, some friction. But they worked together, though. They did work together. Respect in opposition." Quick flash of a smile, as if to say, "We're all comrades here."

"Interesting." Although not really. Another tactical discovery: Evidence of infighting in the Southern Reach, a breakdown in organizational harmony because people weren't robots, couldn't be made to act like robots. Or could they?

"Yes, if you say so," Cheney said, and trailed off.

"Is there anything else?" Control asked, a pointed stare beneath a frozen smile daring Cheney to ask again about his investigation into the director's trip.

"No, I guess not. Nope. Not that I can think of," Cheney said, clearly relieved. He tossed his goodbyes in classic convoluted Cheneyesque fashion as he backed out, amble-stumbling over the chairs and out of sight down the corridor.

After that, Control concentrated on nothing but basic sorting, until all the bits of paper had been accounted for and the piles safely stored in separate filing boxes for further categorizing. Although Control had noticed numerous references to the Séance & Science Brigade, he had found only three brief mentions of Saul Evans to go with the photo. As if the director's interests had led her elsewhere.

He had, however, uncovered and set aside a sheet handwritten by the director, of seemingly random words and phrases, which he eventually realized, by taking a cross-referencing peek at Grace's DMP file, had been used as hypnotic commands on the twelfth expedition. Now *that* was interesting. He almost buzzed Cheney to ask him about it, but something made him put the phone receiver down before punching in the extension.

At a quarter past six, Control felt a compulsion to wander out into the corridor for a good stretch. Everything lay under a hush and even a distant radio sounded like a garbled lullaby. Roaming farther afield, he was crossing the end of the now-empty cafeteria when he heard sounds coming from a storage room close to the corridor that led to the science division. Almost everyone had left, and he'd planned to leave soon himself, but the sounds distracted him. Who was in there? The elusive janitor, he hoped. The horrible cleaning product needed to be switched out. He was convinced it was a health hazard.

So he grasped the knob, receiving a little electric shock as he turned it, and then wrenched outward with all of his strength.

The door flew open, knocking Control back.

A pale creature was crouched in front of shelves of supplies, revealed under the sharp light of a single low-swinging lightbulb.

An unbearable yet beatific agony deformed its features.

Whitby.

Breathing heavily, Whitby stared up at Control. The look of agony had begun to evaporate, leaving behind an expression of combined cunning and caution.

Clearly Whitby had just suffered some kind of trauma. Clearly Whitby had just heard that a family member or close friend had died. Even though it was Control who had received the shock.

Control said, idiotically, "I'll come back later," as if they'd had a meeting scheduled in the storage room.

Whitby jumped up like a trap-door spider, and Control flinched and took a step back, certain Whitby was attacking him. Instead Whitby pulled him into the storage room, shutting the door behind them. Whitby had a surprisingly strong grip for such a slight man.

"No, no, please come in," he was saying to Control, as if he hadn't been able to speak and guide his boss inside at the same time, so that now there was a lip-synch issue.

"I really can come back later," Control said, still rattled, preserving the illusion that he hadn't just seen Whitby in extreme distress . . . and also the illusion that this was Whitby's office and not a storage space.

Whitby stared at him in the dull light of the low-hung single bulb, standing close because it was crowded with the two of them in there, narrow with a high ceiling that could not be seen through the darkness above the bulb, a shield directing its light downward only. The shelves to either side of the central space displayed several rows of a lemon-zest cleaning product, along with stacked cans of soup, extra mop heads, garbage bags, and a few digital clocks with a heavy layer of dust on them. A long silver ladder led up into darkness.

Whitby was *still* composing his expression, Control realized, having to consciously wrench his frown toward a smile, wring the last clenched fear from his features.

"I was just getting some peace and quiet," Whitby said. "It can be hard to find."

"You looked like you were having a breakdown, to be honest," Control said, not sure he wanted to continue playing pretend. "Are you okay?" He felt more comfortable saying this now that Whitby clearly wasn't going to have a psychotic break. But he was also embarrassed that Whitby had managed to so easily trap him in here.

"Not at all," Whitby said, a smile finally fitted in place, and Control hoped the man was responding to the first part of what he had said. "What can I help you with?"

Control went along with this fiction Whitby continued to offer up, if only because he had noticed that the inside lock on the door had been disabled with a blunt instrument. So Whitby had wanted privacy, but he had also been utterly afraid of being trapped in the room, too. There was a staff psychiatrist—a free resource for Southern Reach employees. Control didn't remember seeing anything in Whitby's file to indicate that he had ever gone.

It took Control a moment longer than felt natural, but he found a reason. Something that would run its course and allow him to leave on the right note. Preserve Whitby's dignity. Perhaps.

"Nothing much, really," Control said. "It's about some of the Area X theories."

Whitby nodded. "Yes, for example, the issue of parallel universes," he said, as if they were picking up a conversation from some other time, a conversation Control did not remember.

"That maybe whatever's behind Area X came from one," Control said, stating something he didn't believe and not questioning the narrowing of focus.

"That, yes," Whitby said, "but I've been thinking more about how every decision we make theoretically splits off from the next, so that there are an infinite number of other universes out there."

"Interesting," Control said. If he let Whitby lead, hopefully the dance would end sooner.

"And in some of them," Whitby explained, "we solved the mystery and in some of them the mystery never existed, and there *never was* an Area X." This said with a rising intensity. "And we can take comfort in that. Perhaps we could even be *content* with that." His face fell as he continued: "If not for a further thought. Some of these universes where we solved the mystery may be separated from ours by the thinnest of membranes, the most insignificant of variations. This is something always on my mind. What mundane detail aren't we seeing, or what things are we doing that lead us away from the answer."

Control didn't like Whitby's confessional tone because it felt as if Whitby was revealing one thing to hide another, like the biologist's explanation of the sensation of drowning. This simultaneous with parallel universes of perception opening between him and Whitby as he spoke because Control felt as if Whitby were talking about *breaches*, the same breaches so much on his mind on a daily basis. Whitby talking about breaches angered him in a territorial way, as if Whitby was commenting on Control's past, even though there was no logic to that.

"Perhaps it's your presence, Whitby," Control said. A joke, but a cruel one, meant to push the man away, close down the conversation. "Maybe without you here we would have solved it already."

The look on Whitby's face was awful, caught between knowing that Control had expressed the idea with humor and the certainty that it didn't matter if it was a joke or serious. All of this conveyed in a way that made Control realize the thought was not original but had occurred to Whitby many times. It was too insincere to follow up with "I didn't mean it," so some version of Control just left, running down the hall as fast as he was able, aware that his extraction solution was unorthodox but unable to stop himself. Running down the green carpet while he stood there and apologized/laughed it off/changed the subject/took a pretend phone call . . . or, as he actually did, said nothing at all and let an awkward silence build.

In retaliation, although Control didn't understand it then, Whitby said, "You have seen the video, haven't you? From the first expedition?"

"Not yet," as if he were admitting to being a virgin. That was scheduled for tomorrow.

A silent shudder had passed through Whitby in the middle of delivering his own question, a kind of spasmodic attempt to fling out or reject . . . something, but Control would leave it up to some other, future version of himself to ask Whitby why.

Was there a reality in which Whitby had solved the mystery and was telling it to him right now? Or a reality in which he was throttling Whitby just for being Whitby? Perhaps sometimes, at this moment, he met Whitby in a cave after a nuclear holocaust or in a store buying ice cream for a pregnant wife or, wandering farther afield, perhaps in some scenarios they had met much earlier—Whitby the annoying substitute teacher for a week in his freshman high school English class. Perhaps now he had some inkling as to why Whitby hadn't advanced farther, why his research kept getting interrupted by grunt work for others. He kept wanting to grant Whitby a localized trauma to explain his actions, kept wondering if he just hadn't gotten through enough layers to reach the center of Whitby, or if there was no center to reach and the layers defined the man.

"Is *this* the room you wanted to show me?" Control asked, to change the subject.

"No. Why would you think that?" Whitby's cavernous eyes and sudden expression of choreographed puzzlement made him into an emaciated owl.

Control managed to extricate himself a minute or so later.

But he couldn't get the image of Whitby's agony-stricken face out of his head. Still had no idea why Whitby had hidden in a storage room.

The Voice called a few minutes later, as Control was trying desperately to leave for the day. Control was ready despite Whitby. Or, perhaps, because of Whitby. He made sure the office door was locked. He took out a piece of paper on which he had scribbled some notes to himself. Then he carefully put the Voice on speakerphone at medium volume, having already tested to make sure there was no echo, no sense of anything being out of the ordinary.

He said hello.

A conversation ensued.

They talked for a while. Then the Voice said, "Good," while Control kept looking, at irregular intervals, at his sheet. "Just stabilize and do your job. Paralysis is not a cogent option, either. You will get good sleep tonight."

Stabilize. Paralysis. Cogent. As he hung up, he was alarmed to realize that he did feel as if he *had* been stabilized. That now the encounter with Whitby seemed like a blip, inconsequential when seen in the context of his overall mission.

016: TERROIRS

At the diner counter the next morning, the cashier, a plump gray-haired woman, asked him, "You with the folks working at that government agency on the military base?"

Guarded, still shaking off sleep and a little hungover: "Why do you ask?"

"Oh," she said sweetly, "they all have the same look about them, that's all."

She wanted him to ask "What look is that?" Instead, he just smiled mysteriously and gave her his order. He didn't want to know what look he shared, what secret club he'd joined all unsuspecting. Did she have a chart somewhere so she could check off shared characteristics?

Back in the car, Control noticed that a white mold had already covered the dead mosquito and the dried drop of blood on his windshield. His sense of order and cleanliness offended, he wiped it all away with a napkin. Who would he present the evidence of tampering to, anyway?

The first item on his agenda was the long-awaited viewing of the videotape taken by the first expedition. Those video fragments existed in a special viewing room in an area of the building adjacent to the quarters for expedition members. A massive white console sat against the far wall in that cramped space. It jutted more sharply at the top than the bottom and mimicked the embracing shape of the Southern Reach building. Within that console—dull gray head recessed inside a severe cubist cowl—a television had been embedded that provided access to the video and nothing else. The television was an older model dating back to the time of the first expedition, with its bulky hindquarters recessed into an alcove in the wall. Control's back still retained the groaning memory of a similar ungainly weight as a college student struggling to get a TV into his dorm room.

A low black marble desk with glints of Formica stood in front of the television, old-fashioned buttons and joy sticks allowing for manipulation of the video content—almost like an antiquated museum exhibit or one of those quarter-fed séance machines at the carnival. A phalanx of four black leather conference chairs had been tucked in under the desk. Cramped quarters with the chairs pulled out, although the ceiling extended a good twenty feet above him. That should have alleviated his slight sense of claustrophobia, but it only reinforced it with some minor vertigo, given the slant of the console. The vents above him, he noticed, were filthy with dust. A sharp car-dashboard smell warred with a rusty mold scent.

The names of twenty-four of the twenty-five members of the first expedition had been etched on large gold labels affixed to the side walls.

If Grace denied that the wall of text written by the lighthouse keeper was a memorial for the former director, she could not deny either that this room *did* serve as a memorial for that expedition or that she served as its guardian and curator. The security clearance was so high for the video footage that of the current employees at the Southern Reach only the former director, Grace, and Cheney had access. Everyone else could see photo stills or read transcripts, but even then only under carefully controlled conditions.

So Grace served as his liaison because no one else could, and as she wordlessly pulled out a chair and through some arcane series of steps prepped the video footage, Control realized a change had come over her. She prepared the footage not with the malicious anticipation he might have expected but with loving devotion and at a deliberate pace more common to graveyards than AV rooms. As if this were a neutral space, some cease-fire agreed to between them without his knowledge.

The video would show him dead people who had become darkly legendary within the Southern Reach, and he could see she took her job as steward seriously. Probably in part because the director had, too—and the director had known these people, even if her predecessor had sent them to their fates. After a year of prep. With all of the best high-tech equipment that the Southern Reach could acquire or create, dooming them.

Control realized his heart rate had leapt, that his mouth had become dry and his palms sweaty. It felt as if he were about to take a very important test, one with consequences.

"It's self-explanatory," Grace said finally. "The video is cued up to the beginning and proceeds, with gaps, chronologically. You can move from clip to clip. You can skip around—whatever you prefer. If you are not finished by the end of one hour, I will come in here and your session will be over." They had recovered more than one hundred and fifty fragments, most of the surviving footage lasting between ten seconds and two minutes. Some recovered by Lowry, others by the fourth expedition. They did not recommend watching the footage for more than an hour at any one time. Few had spent that long with it.

"I will also be waiting outside. You can knock on the door if you are done early."

Control nodded. Did that mean he was to be locked in? Apparently it did.

Grace relinquished her seat. Control took her place, and as she left there came an unexpected hand on his shoulder, perhaps putting more weight into the gesture than necessary. Then came the click of the door lock from the outside as she left him alone in a marble vault lined with the names of wraiths.

Control had asked for this experience, but now did not really want it.

The earliest sequences showed the normal things: setting up camp, the distant lighthouse jerkily coming into view from time to time. The shapes of trees and tents showed up dark in the background. Blue sky wheeled across the screen as someone lowered the camera and forgot to turn off the camcorder. Some laughter, some banter, but Control was, like a seer or a time traveler, suspicious already. Were those the expected, normal things, the banal camaraderie displayed by human beings, or instead harbingers of secret communiqués, subcutaneous and potent? Control hadn't wanted the interference, the contamination, of someone else's analysis or opinions, so he hadn't read everything in the files. But he realized right then that he was too armored with foreknowledge anyway, and too cynical about his caution not to find himself ridiculous. If he wasn't careful, everything would be magnified, misconstrued, until each frame carried the promise of menace. He kept in mind the note from another analyst that no other expedition had encountered what he was about to see. Among those that had come back, at least.

A few segments from the expedition leader's video journal followed at dusk—caught in silhouette, campfire behind her—reporting nothing that Control didn't already know. Then about seven entries followed, each lasting four or five seconds, and these showed nothing but blotchy shadow: night shots with no contrast. He kept squinting into that murk hoping some shape, some image, would reveal itself. But in the end, it was just the self-fulfilling prophecy of black dust motes floating across the corners of his vision like tiny orbiting parasites.

A day went by, with the expedition spreading outward in waves from the base camp, with Control trying not to become attached to any of them. Not swayed by the charm of their frequent joking. Nor by the evident seriousness and competence of them, some of the best minds the Southern Reach could find. The clouds stretched long across the sky. A sobering moment when they encountered the sunken remains of a line of abandoned jeeps and pickup trucks, their drivers, trapped inside the border, nowhere to be found. The equipment had already been covered over in loam and vines. By the time of the fourth expedition, Control knew, all traces of it would be gone. Area X would have requisitioned it for its own purposes, privilege of the victor. But there were no human remains to disturb the first expedition, although Control could see frowns on some faces. By then, too, if you listened carefully, you could begin to hear the disruption of transmissions on the walkie-talkies issued to the expedition members, more and more queries of "Come in" and "Are you there" followed by static.

Another evening, the dawn of another day, and Control felt as if he were moving along at a rapid clip, almost able to relax into the closed vessel formed by each innocuous moment and to live there in blissful ignorance of the rest. Even though by now the disruption had spread, so that queries via walkie-talkie had become verbal miscues and misunderstandings. Listener and listened-to had begun to be colonized by some outside force but had not yet realized it. Or, at least, not voiced concerns for the camera. Control chose not to rewind these instances. They sent a prickling shiver across the back of his neck, gave him a faint sensation of nausea, increased the destabilizing sense of vertigo and claustrophobia.

Finally, though, Control could no longer fool himself. The famous twenty-second clip had come up, which the file indicated had been shot by Lowry, who had served as both the team's anthropologist and its military expert. Dusk of the second day, with a lisp of sunset. Dull dark tower of the lighthouse in the middle distance. In their innocence, they had not seen the harm in splitting up, and Lowry's group had decided to bivouac on the trail, among the remains of an abandoned series of houses about halfway to the lighthouse. It had hardly been enough to constitute a village, with no name on the maps, but had been the largest population center in the area.

A rustling sound Control associated with sea oats and the wind off the beach, but faint. The wreckage of the old walls formed deeper shadows against the sky, and he could just see the wide line that was the stone path running through. In the clip, Lowry shook a bit holding the camera. In the foreground, a woman, the expedition leader, was shouting, "Get her to stop!" Her face was made a mask by the light from the recorder and the way it formed such severe shadows around her eyes and mouth. Opposite, across a kind of crude picnic table that appeared fire-burned, a woman, the expedition leader, shouted, "Get her to stop! Please stop! Please stop!" A lurch and spin of the camera and then the camera steadied, presumably with Lowry still holding it. Lowry began to hyperventilate, and Control recognized that the sound he had heard before was a kind of whispered breathing with a shallow rattle threading through it. Not the wind at all. He could also just hear urgent, sharp voices from off-camera, but he couldn't make out what they were saying. The woman on the left of the screen then stopped shouting and stared into the camera. The woman on the right also stopped shouting, stared into the camera. An identical fear and pleading and confusion radiated from the masks of their faces toward him, from so far away, from so many years away. He could not distinguish between the two manifestations, not in that murky light.

Then, sitting bolt upright, even knowing what was to come, Control realized it was not dusk that had robbed the setting behind them of any hint of color. It was more as if something had interceded on the landscape, something so incredibly large that its edges were well beyond the camera's lens. In the last second of the videotape, the two women still frozen and staring, the background seemed to shift and keep shifting . . . followed by a clip even more chilling to Control: Lowry in front of the camera this time, goofing off on the beach the next morning, and whoever was behind the camera laughing. No mention of the expedition leader. No sign of her on any of the subsequent video footage, he knew. No explanation from Lowry. It was as if she had been erased from their memories, or as if they had all suffered some vast, unimaginable trauma while off-camera that night.

But the dissolution continued despite their seeming happiness and ease. For Lowry was saying words that had no meaning and the person holding the camera responded as if she could understand him, her own speech not yet deformed.

Carnage followed him from the video screening, when he finally left, escorted by Grace back into the light, or a different kind of light. Carnage might follow him for a while. He wasn't sure, was having difficulty putting things into words, had done little more than mumble and nod to Grace when she asked him if he was okay, while she held his arm as if she were holding him up. Yet he knew that her compassion came with a price, that he might pay for it later. So he extricated himself, insisted on leaving her behind and walking the rest of the way back in solitude.

He had a full day ahead of him still. He had to recover. Next was his scheduled time with the biologist, and then status meetings, and then . . . he forgot what was next. Stumbled, tripped, leaned on one knee, realized he was in the cafeteria area and its familiar green carpet with the arrow pattern pointing in from the courtyard. Caught by the light streaming from those broad, almost cathedral-like windows. It was sunny outside, but he could already see the angry gray in the middle of white clouds that signaled more afternoon showers.

In the black water with the sun shining at midnight, those fruit shall come ripe and in the darkness of that which is golden shall split open to reveal the revelation of the fatal softness in the earth.

A lighthouse. A tower. An island. A lighthouse keeper. A border with a huge shimmering door. A director who might have gone AWOL across that border, through that door. A squashed mosquito on his windshield. Whitby's anguished face. The swirling light of the border. The director's phone in his satchel. Demonic videos housed in a memorial catafalque. Details were beginning to overwhelm him. Details were beginning to swallow him up. No chance yet to let them settle or to know which were significant, which trivial. He'd "hit the ground running" as his mother had wanted, and it wasn't getting him very far. He was in danger of incoming information outstripping his prep work, the knowledge he'd brought with him. He'd exhausted so many memorized files, burned through tactics. And he'd have to dig into the director's notes in earnest soon, and that would bring with it more mysteries, he was sure.

The screaming had gone on and on toward the end. The one holding the camera hadn't seemed human. Wake up, he had pleaded with the members of the first expedition as he watched. Wake up and understand what is happening to you. But they never did. They couldn't. They were miles away, and he was more than thirty years too late to warn them.

Control put his hand on the carpet, the green arrows up close composed of threads of a curling intertwined fabric almost like moss. He felt its roughness, how threadbare it had become over the years. Was it the original carpet, from thirty years ago? If so, every major player in those videos, in the files, had strode across it, had crisscrossed it hundreds and hundreds of times. Perhaps even Lowry, holding his camcorder, joking around before their expedition. It was as worn down as the Southern Reach, as the agency moved along its appointed grooves on this fun-house ride that was called Area X.

People were staring at him, too, as they crisscrossed the cafeteria. He had to get up.

From the dim-lit halls of other places forms that never could be writhe.

Control went from bended knee to the interrogation room with the biologist— after a brief interlude in his office. He had needed some form of relief, some way to cleanse. He'd called up the information on Rock Bay, the biologist's longest assignment before she'd joined the twelfth expedition. From her field notes and sketches, he could tell it was her favorite place. A rich, northern rain forest with a verdant ecosystem. She'd rented a cottage there, and in addition to photographs of the tidal pools she'd studied, he had shots of her living quarters—Central's routine thorough follow-up. The cot-like bed, the comfortable kitchen, and the black stove in the corner that doubled as a fireplace, the long spout going up into a chimney. There were aspects of the wilderness that appealed to him, that calmed him, but so too did the simple domesticity of the cottage.

Once seated in the room, Control placed a bottle of water and her files between them. A gambit he was bored with, but nevertheless . . . His mother had always said the repetition of ritual made pointing to the thing that had been rendered invisible all the more dramatic. Someday soon he might point to the files and make an offer.

The fluorescent lights pulsed and flickered, something beginning to devolve in them. He didn't care if Grace watched from behind the glass or not. Ghost Bird looked terrible today, not so much sick but like she had been crying, which was how he felt. There was a darkness around her eyes and a slump to her posture. Any recklessness or amusement had been burned away or gone into hiding.

Control didn't know where to start because he didn't want to start at all. What he wanted to talk about was the video footage, but that was impossible. The words would linger, form in his mind, but never become sound, trapped between his need and his will. He couldn't tell any human being, ever. If he let it out, contaminated someone else's mind, he would not forgive himself. A girlfriend who had gleaned some sense of his job had once asked, "Why do you do it?"— meaning why serve such a clandestine purpose, a purpose that could not be shared, could not be revealed. He'd given his standard response, in a portentous manner, to poke fun at himself. To disguise the seriousness. "To know. To go beyond the veil." Across the border. Even as Control said it, he had known that he was also telling her he didn't mind leaving her there, alone, on the other side.

"What would you like to talk about?" he asked Ghost Bird, not because he was out of questions but because he wanted her to take the lead.

"Nothing," she said, listless. The word came out at a muttering slant.

"There must be something." Pleading. Let there be something, to distract from the carnage in my head.

"I am not the biologist."

That brought Control out of himself, forced him to consider what she meant.

"You are not the biologist," he echoed.

"You want the biologist. I'm not the biologist. Go talk to her, not me."

Was this some kind of identity crisis or just metaphorical?

Either way, he realized that this session had been a mistake.

"We can try again in the afternoon," he said.

"Try what?" she snapped. "Do you think this is *therapy*? Who for?"

He started to respond, but in one violent motion she swept his files and water off the table and grabbed his left hand with both of hers and wouldn't let go. Defiance and fear in her eyes. "What do you want from me? What do you *really* want?"

With his free hand, Control waved off the guards plunging into the room. From the corner of his eye, their retreat had a peculiar suddenness, as if they'd been sucked back into the doorway by something invisible and monstrous.

"Nothing," he said, to see how she'd respond. Her hand was clammy and warm, not entirely pleasant; something was definitely going on beneath her skin. Had her fever gotten worse?

"I won't assist in charting my own pathology," she hissed, breathing hard, shouting: "I am not the biologist!"

He pulled himself loose, pushed away from the table, stood, and watched as she fell back into her seat. She stared down at the table, wouldn't look up at him. He hated to see her distress, hated worse that he seemed to have caused it.

"Whoever you are, we'll pick this up later," he said.

"Humoring me," she muttered, arms folded.

But by the time he'd picked up the bottle of water and his scattered files and made it to the door, something had changed in her again.

Her voice trembled on the cusp of some new emotion. "There was a mating pair of wood storks in the holding pond out back when I left. Are they still there?"

It took a moment to realize she meant when she'd left on the expedition. Another moment to realize that this was almost an apology.

"I don't know," he said. "I'll find out."

What had happened to her out there? What had happened to him in here?

The last fragment of video remained in its own category: "Unassigned." Everyone was dead by then, except for an injured Lowry, already halfway back to the border.

Yet for a good twenty seconds the camera flew above the glimmering marsh reeds, the deep blue lakes, the ragged white cusp of the sea, toward the lighthouse.

Dipped and rose, fell again and soared again.

With what seemed like a horrifying enthusiasm.

An all-consuming joy.

017: PERSPECTIVE

Steps had begun to go missing. Steps had begun to occur out of step. Lunch followed a status meeting that, the moment it was done, Control barely remembered no matter how hard he tried. He was here to solve a puzzle in some ways, but he felt as if it were beginning to solve him instead.

Control had talked for a while, he knew that, about how he wanted to know more about the lighthouse and its relationship to the topographical anomaly. After which Hsyu said something about the patterns in the lighthouse keeper's sermon, while the sole member of the props department, a hunched-over elderly man named Darcy with a crinkly tinfoil voice, added commentary throughout her talk, referring to the "crucial role, now and in the future, of the historical accuracy division."

Trees framed the campfire, the members of the expedition around the campfire. Something so large you couldn't see its outline, crawling or lumbering through the background, obscenely threaded between the trees and the campfire. He didn't like to think about what could be so huge and yet so lithe as to thread like that, to conjure up the idea of a fluid wall of ribbony flesh.

Perhaps he could have continued to nod and ask questions, but he had become more and more repulsed by the way Hsyu's assistant, Amy-something, chewed on her lip. Slowly. Methodically. Without thought. As she scribbled notes or whispered some piece of information in Hsyu's ear. The off-white of her upper left cuspid and incisors would appear, the pink gum exposed as the upper lip receded, and then with almost rhythmic precision, she would nip and pincer, nip and pincer, the left side of her lower lip, which over time became somewhat redder than her lipstick.

Something had *brushed* through or *interceded* across the screen for a moment in the background, while in the middle a man with a beard squatted—not Lowry but a man named O'Connell. At first, Control had thought O'Connell was mumbling, was saying something in a language he didn't understand. And, trying to find logic, trying to grasp, Control had almost buzzed Grace right then to tell her about his discovery. But by another few frames, Control could tell that the man was actually chewing on his lip, and continued chewing until the blood came, the whole time resolutely staring into the camera because there was, Control slowly realized, no other place safe enough to look. O'Connell was speaking as he chewed, but the words weren't anything unique now that Control had read the wall. It was the most primal and thus most banal message imaginable.

Predictable lunch to follow, in the cafeteria. Stabilizing lunch, he'd thought, but *lunch* repeated too many times became a meaningless word that morphed into *lunge* that became *lunged* that became a leaping white rabbit that became the biologist at the depressing table that became an expedition around a campfire, unaware of what they were about to endure.

Control followed a version of Whitby he was both wary of and concerned about, and who muddled his way through the tables, with Cheney, Hsyu, and Grace trailing behind him. Whitby hadn't been in the status meeting, but Grace had seen him ducking into a side corridor as they'd walked downstairs and roped him into their lunch. Then it had just been a case of everyone deferring to Whitby in his natural habitat. Whitby couldn't like the cafeteria for the food. It had to be the open-air quality of the space, the clear lines of sight. Perhaps it was simply that you could escape in any direction.

Whitby led them to a round faux-wooden table with low plastic seats—all of it jammed up against the corner farthest from the courtyard, which abutted stairs that led to the largely empty space known as the third level that they had just vacated, really a glorified landing with a few conference rooms. Control realized Whitby had chosen the table so he could cram his slight frame into the semicircle closest to the wall—a wary if improbable gunslinger with his back to the stairs, looking out across the cafeteria to the courtyard and the fuzzy green of a swamp dissolving in humid bubbles of condensation against the glass.

Control sat facing Grace, with Whitby and Hsyu flanking Grace to right and left. Cheney plopped into the seat next to Control, opposite Whitby. Control began to suspect some of them weren't there by chance, or voluntarily, the way Grace seemed to be commandeering the space. The huffing X of Cheney's face leaned in, solicitous as he said, "I'll hold down the fort while you get your food and go after."

"Just get me a pear or an apple and some water, and I'll stay here instead," Control said. He felt vaguely nauseated.

Cheney nodded, withdrew his thick hands from the table with a slap, and left along with the others, while Control contemplated the large framed photo hanging on the wall. Old and dusty, it showed the core of the Southern Reach team at the time. Control recognized some faces from his various briefings, zeroing in on

Lowry, come back for a visit from Central, still looking haggard. Whitby was there, too, grinning near the center. The photo suggested that at one time Whitby had been inquisitive, quick, optimistic—perhaps even impishly proactive. The missing director was just a hulking shadow off at the left edge. She loomed, committed to neither a smile nor a frown.

At that time, she would have been a relatively new hire, an apprentice to the staff psychologist. Grace would have joined about five years later. It could not have been easy for either of them to make their way up the hierarchy and hold on to their power. That had taken toughness and perseverance. Perhaps too much. But at least they had both missed the crazier manifestations of the early days, of which the hypnosis was the only surviving remnant. Cryptozoologists, an almost séance, the bringing in of psychics, given the bare facts and asked to produce . . . what? Information? No information could be extracted from their divinations.

The others returned from the buffet, Cheney with a pear on a plate and the asked-for water. Control reflected that if something terrible happened later that day and forensics tried to reconstruct events from the contents of their stomachs, Cheney would look like a fussy bird, Whitby like a pig, Hsyu a health nut, and Grace a mere nibbler. She sat back in her seat, glaring at him now, with her two packets of crackers and coffee arranged in front of her as if she planned to use it as evidence against him. He braced himself, trying to clear his head with a sip of water.

"Status meetings every Thursday or every other Thursday?" he asked, just to test the waters and make conversation. He clamped down on an automatic impulse to use the question to begin a sly exploration of department morale.

But Grace didn't want to make conversation.

"Do you want to hear a story," she said, and it wasn't a question. She looked as if she had made up her mind about something.

"Sure," Control said. "Why not?" While Cheney fidgeted next to him, and Whitby and Hsyu simultaneously seemed to flatten and become smaller, looking away from Grace, as if she'd become a repelling magnet.

Her stare bore down on him and he lost the urge to gnaw on his pear. "It concerns a domestic terrorism operative." Here it comes, there it goes.

"How interesting," Control said. "I was in domestic terrorism for a while."

Continuing on as if Control hadn't said a word: "The story is about a blown field assignment, this operative's third out of training. Not his first or his second, but his third, so no real excuses. What was his job? He was to observe and report on separatist militia members on the northwest coast—based in the mountains but coming down into two key port cities to recruit." Central had believed that the radical cells in this militia had the will and resources to disrupt shipping, blow up a building, many things. "No coherent political views or vision. Just ignorant white men mostly, college age but not in college. A few radicalized women, and then the usual others unaware of what their ignorant men were up to. None of them as stupid as the operative."

Control sat very still. He began to feel as if his face were cracking. He was getting warmer and warmer, a tingling flame spreading slowly throughout his body. Was she trying to tear him down, stone by stone? In front of the few people at the Southern Reach with whom he already had some kind of rapport?

Cheney had gotten in some huffing sounds to express his disapproval of where this might be going. Whitby looked as if a stranger walking toward him from very far away was trying to give him the details of an interesting conversation, but he wasn't quite close enough to hear about it yet—so sorry, not his fault.

"Sounds familiar," Control said, because it did, and he even knew what came next.

"The operative infiltrates the group, or the edges of the group," Grace said. "He gets to know some of the friends of the people at the core of it."

Hsyu, frowning, focused on something of interest on the carpet as she got up with her tray, managed a cheerful if abrupt goodbye, and left the table.

"Not fair, Grace, you know that," Cheney whispered, leaning forward, as if somehow he could direct his words solely to her. "An ambush." But by Control's own reckoning, it *was* fair. Very fair. Given that they hadn't agreed to ground rules ahead of time.

"This operative starts following the friends and, eventually, they lead him to a bar. The girlfriend of the second-in-command likes to have a drink at this bar. She is on the list; he has memorized her photograph. But instead of just observing her and reporting back, this clever, clever operative ignores his orders and starts to talk to her, there in the bar—"

"Do you want me to tell the rest of the story?" Control interrupted. Because he could. He could tell it—wanted to tell it, had a fierce desire to tell it—and felt a perverse gratitude toward Grace, because this was such a human problem, such a banal, human problem compared to all the rest.

"Grace . . ." Cheney, imploring.

But Grace waved them both off, faced Whitby so that Whitby had no choice but to look at her. "Not only does he have a conversation with this woman, Whitby"—Whitby as startled by the complicity of his name as if she had put her arm around him—"but he seduces her, telling himself that he is doing it to help the cause. Because he is an arrogant man. Because he is too far off his leash." Mother had typified that as hearsay, as she had typified a lot of things, but in this case she had been right.

"We used to have forks and spoons in the cafeteria," Whitby said, mournfully. "Now we just have sporks." He turned to the left, then the right, looking either for alternative cutlery or for a quick way to exit.

"Next time you tell this story, you should leave out the seduction, which didn't happen," Control said, a spiral of ash in his head and a faint ringing in his ears. "You could also add that the operative didn't have clear orders from his superior."

"You heard the man. You heard him." The Cheney murmur, as subtle as a donkey burp.

Grace kept speaking directly to Whitby, with Whitby now swiveling toward Cheney, the expression asking Cheney what he should do, and Cheney unable or unwilling to give him guidance. Let it play out to the bitter end. Draw the poison. This was trench warfare. This was always going to continue.

"So the operative beds the girlfriend"—no triumph in her voice at least—"although he knows it is dangerous, knows that the members of the militia might find out. His supervisor does not know what he is doing. Yet. And then one day—"

"One day," Control interrupted, because if she was going to tell this story she should get the rest of it right, godfucking dammit. "One day he goes to the bar—this is only the third time—and gets made by surveillance cameras put in overnight by the boyfriend." Control hadn't spoken to her the second time in the bar. That third and final time, yes. How he wished he hadn't. He couldn't even remember what he'd said to her, or her to him.

"Correct," Grace said, a momentary confused expression adding weight to her face. "Correct."

It was an old scar by now for Control, even if it seemed like a fresh wound to every scavenger that tried to dip their beak or snout into it, to tear away some spoiled meat. The routine of telling the story transformed Control from a person into an actor dramatizing an ancient event from his own life. Every time he had to reenact it, the monologue became smoother, the details less complex and more easily fitted together, the words like stuffing puzzle pieces into his mouth and spewing them out in the perfect order to form a picture. He disliked the performance more each time. But the only other choice was to be blackmailed by a part of his past now more than seventeen years and five months gone by. Even though it followed him around to each new job because his supervisor at the time had decided Control deserved, forever, more punishment than he'd received at the point of impact.

In the worst versions, like the one Grace had started to tell, he'd slept with the girlfriend, Rachel McCarthy, and had compromised operations beyond repair. But the truth had been bad enough. He had come out of private college as his mother's protégé; excellent grades, a kind of unthinking swagger, and completion of training at Central with high marks. He'd had great success in the field the first two times out, tracking good ole boys across flat plains and gentle hills in the middle of the country—pickups and chewing tobacco and lonely little town squares, snacking on fried okra while he watched guys in baseball caps load suspicious boxes into the backs of vans.

"I made a terrible mistake. I think about it every day. It guides me in my job now. It makes me humble and keeps me focused." But he didn't think about it every day. You didn't think about it every day or it would rise up and consume you. It just remained there, nameless: a sad, dark thing that weighed you down only some of the time. When the memory became too faint, too abstract, it would transform itself into an old rotator cuff injury, a pain so thin yet so sharp that he could trace the line of it all the way across his shoulder blade and down his back.

"So then," Control said, Whitby beginning to be crushed by their tandem attention and Cheney gone, having orchestrated a subtle jailbreak right under Control's nose. "So then, the boyfriend has it on tape that some stranger was talking to his girlfriend, which would probably be enough for a beating. But then he has a comrade follow this stranger to a café about twenty minutes away by car. The operative doesn't notice—he's forgotten to take the steps to see if he was being tailed, because he's so thrilled with himself and so confident in his abilities." Because he was part of a dynasty. Because he knew so much. "And guess who the operative is talking to? His supervisor. Only, members of this militia had a run-in with the supervisor a few years back, which, it turns out, is why it's me in the field rather than him in the first place. So now they know the person talking to his girlfriend is comparing notes with a known government agent."

Here he deviated from the script long enough to remind Grace of what he had endured just that morning: "It was like I was floating above it all, above everyone, looking down, gliding through the air. Able to do anything I wanted to." Saw the connection register with her, but not the guilt.

"Now they know that a member of their militia has had contact with the government—and on top of that, the boyfriend, as noted, is the possessive, controlling, jealous type. And that boyfriend works himself into a rage, watching the operative come back the next day, not doing much more than nodding at McCarthy, but for all he knows they've got a secret method of communication. It's enough that the operative has come back. The boyfriend gets it into his head that his girlfriend might be part of it, that maybe McCarthy is spying on them. So what do you think they do?"

Whitby took the opportunity to give an answer to a different question: He slid out from behind the table and ran away down the curve of the wall, headed for the science division without even a hurried goodbye.

Leaving Control with Grace.

"Are you going to guess?" Control asked Grace, turning the full weight of his anger and self-loathing on the assistant director, not caring that all eyes in the cafeteria were on them.

To reanimate the emotions of a dead script, he had started thinking of things like *topographical anomalies* and *video of the first expedition* and *hypnotic conditioning*—inverse to the extreme where ritual decreed he hold words in his head like *horrible goiter* and *math homework* to stop from coming too soon during sex.

"Are you going to fucking guess?" he hissed in a kind of mega-whisper, wanting to confess not to anyone in the audience, but to the biologist.

"They shoot Rachel McCarthy," she said.

"Yes, that's right!" Control shouted, knowing that even the people serving the food at the far-distant buffet could hear him, were looking at him. Maybe fifteen people remained there, in the cafeteria, most trying to pretend none of this was happening.

"They shoot Rachel McCarthy," Control said. "Although by the time they're searching for me, I'm already safe at home. After, what? Two or three conversations? A standard surveillance operation from my perspective. I'm being pulled in for a debriefing while other, more seasoned, agents are brought in to follow up on the lead. Except by then the militia has beaten McCarthy half senseless and driven her to the top of an abandoned quarry. And they want her to tell the truth, to just tell the truth about the person in the bar. Which she can't do, because she's innocent and didn't know I was an operative. But that's the wrong answer—any answer is the wrong answer by then." Will always be the wrong answer. And around the time that he's excited he helped crack the case wide open, and a judge is issuing warrants, the boyfriend has shot McCarthy in the head and let her fall, dead, into the shallow water below. To be found three days later by the local police.

Anyone else might have been finished, although he'd been too green to know that. He hadn't known until years later that his mother had rescued him, for better or worse. Called in favors. Pulled strings. Greased palms. All the usual clichés that masked every unique collusion. Because—she told him when she finally confessed, when it no longer mattered one way or the other—she believed in him and knew that he had much more to offer.

Control had spent a year on suspension, going to therapy that couldn't repair the breach, endured a retraining program that cast a broad net to catch a tiny mistake that kept escaping anyway over and over in his mind. Then he had been given an administrative desk job, from which he'd worked his way up through the ranks again, to the exalted non-position of "fixer," with the clear understanding that he'd never be deployed in the field again.

So that one day he could be called upon to run a peculiar backwater agency. So that what he couldn't bring himself to confess to any of his girlfriends he could shout out loudly in a cafeteria, in front of a woman who appeared to hate him.

The little bird he'd seen flying darkly against the high windows of the cafeteria flew there still, but the way it flitted reminded him now more of a bat. The rain clouds gathered yet again.

Grace still sat in front of him, guarded from on high by cohorts from the past. Control still sat there, too, Grace now going through his lesser sins, one by one, in no particular order, with no one else left to hear. She had read his file and gotten her hands on more besides. As she reeled it off, she told him other things—about his mother, his father, the litany a lurching parade or procession that, curiously, no longer hurt about halfway through. A kind of numb relief, instead, began to flood Control. She was telling him something, all right. She saw him clearly and she saw him well, from his skills right down to his weaknesses, from his short relationships to his nomadic lifestyle to his father's cancer and ambiva-

lence about his mother. The ease with which he had embraced his mother's substitution of her job for family, for religion. And all of the rest of it, all of it, her
tone of voice managing the neat trick of mixing grudging respect with compas-
sionate exasperation at his refusal to retreat.

"Have you never made a mistake?" he asked, but she ignored him.

Instead she gave him the gift of a motive: "This time, your contact tried to cut
me off from Central. For good." The Voice, continuing to help him in the same
way as a runaway bull.

"I didn't ask for that." Well, if he had, he didn't want it anymore.

"You went into my office again."

"I didn't." But he couldn't be sure.

"I'm trying to keep things the way they are for the *director*, not for me."

"The director's dead. The director's not coming back."

She looked away from him, out through the windows at the courtyard and
the swamp beyond. A fierce look that shut him out.

Maybe the director was flying free over Area X, or scrabbling with root-broken
fingernails into the dirt, the reeds, trying to get away . . . from something. But she
wasn't here.

"Think about how much worse it could get, Grace, if they replace me with
someone else. Because they're never going to make you director." Truth for truth.

"You know I did you a favor just now," she said, pivoting away from what
he'd said.

"A favor? Sure you did."

But he did know. That which was uncomfortable or unflattering she had now
off-loaded pointlessly, ordnance wasted, a gun shot into the air. She had let out
the rest of the items in her jewelry box of condemnation, and by not hoarding
told him she would not be using it in the future.

"You're a lot like us," she said. "Someone who has made a lot of mistakes.
Someone just trying to do better. To be better."

Subtext: *You can't solve what hasn't been solved in thirty years. I won't let you
get out ahead of the director.* And what misdirection in that? What was she pushing him toward or away from?

Control just nodded, not because he agreed or disagreed but because he was
exhausted. Then he excused himself, locked the cafeteria bathroom, and vom-
ited up his breakfast. He wondered if he was coming down with something or if
his body was rejecting, as viciously as possible, everything in the Southern Reach.

heney came back to prowl around outside the bathroom—concerned, whispering "Do you think you're all right, man?" as if they'd become best buddies. But eventually Cheney went away, and a little while later Control's cell phone rang just as he'd propped himself up on the toilet seat. He pulled the phone out of his pocket. The Voice. The bathroom seemed like the perfect place to take this call. Cold porcelain after having slammed the bathroom door shut was a relief. So were the tiny cool blue tiles of the floor. Even the faint whiff of piss. All of it. Any of it.

Why were there no mirrors in the men's room?

"Next time, take my call *when* I call," the Voice warned, with the implication that s/he was a busy wo/man, just as Control noticed the flashing light that meant he had a message.

"I was in a meeting." I was watching videotape. I was talking to the biologist. I was getting my ass handed to me by the assistant director because of you.

"Is your house in order?" the Voice asked. "Is it in order?"

Two thousand white rabbits herded toward an invisible door. A plant that didn't want to die. Impossible video footage. More theories than there were fish in the sea. Was his house in order? An odd way for the Voice to phrase it, as if they spoke using a code to which Control did not have the key. Yet it made him feel secure even though that was counterintuitive.

"Are you there?" the Voice asked brusquely.

"Yes. Yes, my house is in order."

"Then what do you have for me?"

Control gave the Voice a brief summary.

The Voice considered that for a moment, then asked, "So do you have an answer now?"

"To what?"

"To the mystery behind Area X." The Voice laughed an oddly tinny metallic laugh. Haw haw haw. Haw.

Enough of this. "Stop trying to cut Grace off from her contacts at Central. It isn't working and it's making it harder," Control said. Remembering her care with setting up the videos of the first expedition, too wrung out by lunch to process it yet. Twinned to Control's disgust at the Voice's clearly inadequate and extreme tactics was the sudden conviction, admittedly irrational, that somehow the Voice was responsible for sticking him in the middle of the Southern Reach. If the Voice actually was his mother, then he'd be correct about that.

"Listen, John," the Voice growled, "I don't report to you. You report to me, and don't forget that." Meant to be delivered with conviction, and yet somehow failing.

"Stop trying," Control repeated. "You're doing harm to me—she knows you're trying. Just stop."

"Again, I don't report to you, Control. Don't tell me what to do. You asked me to fix it, and I'm trying to fix it." Feedback made Control take the phone away from his ear.

"You know I saw the video of the first expedition this morning," he said. "It threw me." By way of halfhearted apology. Grandpa had taught him that: Redirect while seeming to address the other party's grievance. It'd been done enough to him in the past.

But for some reason that set the Voice off. "You think that's a fucking excuse for not doing your goddamn job. Seeing a video? Get your head out of your asshole and give me a real report next time—and then maybe I'll be a lot more willing to do your bidding the way you want me to do your bidding. Got it, fuckface?"

The swear words were delivered in a peculiar, halting way, as if the Voice were completing a Mad Lib where the only scripted parts were the words *fucking*, *goddamn*, *asshole*, and *fuckface*. But Control got it. The Voice was a shithead. He'd had shithead bosses before. Unless the real Voice was taking a break and this was the sub's attempt at improv. Megalodon mad. Megalodon not happy. Megalodon have tantrum.

So he gave in and made some conciliatory sounds. Then he elaborated and told the tale of his "progress," the story structured and strung together not as the plaintive, halting start-stop of what-the-hell that it was, but instead as an analytical and nuanced "journey" that could only be interpreted as having a beginning and a middle pushing out toward a satisfying end.

"Enough!" the Voice said at some point.

Later: "That's better," the Voice said. Control couldn't really tell if the severity of that rushed cheese-grater-on-cheese-grater tone had lightened. "For now, continue to collect data and continue to question the biologist, but press her harder." Had already done that, and it had gone poorly. Uncovering useful intel was often a long-term project, a matter of listening for what didn't matter to fall away for just a moment.

After another pause, the Voice said, "I have that information you asked for."

"Which information?" Plant, mouse, or . . . ?

"I can confirm that the director did cross the border."

Control sat up straight on the toilet seat. Someone was knocking timidly at the door. They'd have to wait.

"When? Right before the last eleventh expedition?"

"Yes. Completely unauthorized and without anyone's knowledge or permission."

"And she got away with it."

"What do you mean?"

"She wasn't fired."

A pause, then the Voice said, "No doubt she should have been terminated. But, no, she got probation. The assistant director took her place for six months." Impatient, as if it didn't matter.

What was he supposed to do with that? Probably a question for his mother. Because surely someone higher up must have known the director was going across the border and then someone had protected her when she came back.

"Do you know how long she was gone? Is there a report of what she found?"

"Three weeks. No report."

Three weeks!

"She must have been debriefed. There must be a record."

A much longer pause. Was the Voice consulting with another Voice or Voices?

Finally the Voice conceded the point: "There is a debriefing statement. I can have a copy sent to you."

"Did you know that the director thought the border was advancing?" Control asked.

"I am aware of that theory," the Voice said. "But it is no concern of yours."

How was that no concern of his? How did someone go from calling him a fuckface to using a phrase like "no concern of yours"? The Voice was a bad actor, Control concluded, or had a bad script, or it was deliberate.

At the end of their conversation, for no good reason, he told a joke. "What's brown and sticky?"

"I know that one," the Voice said. "A stick."

"A turd."

Click.

"Go ahead and check the seats for change, John." Control, back in his office, exhausted, ambushed by odd flashes of memory. A colleague at his last position coming up to him after a presentation and saying in an accusing tone, "You contradicted me." No, I *disagreed* with you. A woman in college, a brunette with a broad face and beautiful brown eyes that made him ache, whom he'd fallen for in Fundamentals of Math but when he'd given her a poem had said to him, "Yes, but do you dance?" No, I write poetry. I'm going to be some kind of spy. One of his college professors in political science had made them write poetry to "get your juices flowing." Most of the time, though, he'd been studying, going to the shooting range, working out, using parties to get in practice for a lifetime of short-term relationships.

"Go ahead and check the seats for change, John," said Grandpa Jack. Control had been twelve, visiting his mother up north for a rare trip that didn't include going to the cabin or fishing. They were still getting the balance right; the divorce was still being finalized.

On a weekend afternoon, in the freezing cold, Jack had rolled up in what he called a "muscle car." He'd taken it out of hibernation because he had hatched a secret plan to drive Control to a lingerie show at a local department store. Control only had a vague idea of what that meant, but it sounded embarrassing. Mostly he didn't want to go because the next-door neighbor's daughter was his age and he'd had a crush on her since the summer. But it was hard to say no to Grandpa. Especially when Grandpa had never taken him anywhere without his mother there.

So Control checked the seats for change while Grandpa fired up the bright blue muscle car, which had sat cold for two hours while Grandpa talked to his mother inside. But Control also thought Grandpa was reacquainting himself with the mysteries of its workings, too. The heat was blasting away and Control was sweating in his coat. He checked the seats eagerly, wondering if Grandpa had left some money there on purpose. With money, he could buy the neighbor girl an ice cream. He was still in summer mode.

No money, just lint, paper clips, a scrap of paper or two, and something cold, smooth, sticky, and shaped like a tiny brain from which he recoiled: old bubble gum. Disappointed, he broadened his search from the long backseat to the dark cavern under the front passenger side. He extended his arm awkwardly forward so his hand could curl around to search, came up against something bulky yet soft taped there. No, not soft—whatever it was had been wrapped in cloth. With a bit of coaxing, he managed to pull it free, the awkward weight a muffled thud on the car floor. There was a dull metal-and-oil smell. He picked it up, unwrapped it from the cloth, and sat back, the rough coldness of it cupped in both hands . . . only to find his grandpa staring at him intently.

"What've you got there?" the old man asked. "Where'd you find that?" Which Control thought were dumb questions and then, later, disingenuous questions. The eager look on Grandpa Jack's face as he turned to stare, one arm still on the steering wheel.

"A gun," Control said, although Grandpa could see that. He remembered later mostly the darkness of it, the darkness of its shape and the stillness it seemed to bring with it.

"A Colt .45, it looks like. It's heavy, isn't it?"

Control nodded, a little afraid now. He was sweating from the heat. He'd already found the gun, but his grandpa's expression was that of someone waiting for the gift they'd given to be unwrapped and held high—and him too young to sense the danger. But he'd already made the wrong decision: He should never have gotten in the car.

What kind of psycho gave a kid a gun, even unloaded? This was the thought that occurred now. Perhaps the kind of psycho who wouldn't mind coming out of retirement at his remote cabin to work for Central again as the Voice, to run his own grandson.

Midafternoon. *Try. Try again.*

Control and the biologist stood together, leaning on the sturdy wooden fence that separated them from the holding pond. The Southern Reach building lay at their backs, a gravel path like a rough black river leading across the lawn. Just the two of them . . . and the three members of security who had brought her. They had spread out at a distance of about thirty feet and chosen angles that took into account all escape routes.

"Do they think I'll run away?" Ghost Bird asked him.

"No," Control said. If she did, Control would put the blame on them.

The holding pond was long and roughly rectangular. Inside the fence, on the far shore, a rotting shed lay on the side nearest the swamp. A scrawny pine tree half-throttled by rusted Christmas lights stood beside the shed. The water was choked with duckweed and hydrangea and water lilies. Dragonflies patrolled ceaselessly over the gray, sometimes black water. The frogs made such raucous forecasts of rain that they drowned out the crickets and, from the fringe of grass and bushes on the opposite side of the pond, came the chatter and bustle of wrens and warblers.

A lone great blue heron stood solemn and silent in the middle of the pond. Thunderclouds continued to gather, its feathers dull in the fading light.

"Should I thank you for this?" Ghost Bird asked. They were leaning on the top of the fence. Her left arm was too close to his right arm; he moved a little farther away.

"Don't thank anyone for what you should already have," he said, which brought a half turn of her head toward him and the view of one upraised eyebrow above a thoughtful eye and a noncommittal mouth. It was something his grandfather on his father's side had said, back when he was selling clothespins door-to-door. "I didn't make the wood storks disappear," he added, because he had not meant to say the first thing.

"Raccoons are the worst predators of their nests," she said. "Did you know that they pre-date the last ice age? Farther south, they roost in colonies, but in this region they're endangered, so they're more solitary."

Control had looked it up and the wood storks should have returned by now if they were going to. They tended to be creatures of habit.

"I can only give you thirty or forty minutes," he said. Bringing her here felt now like a terrible indulgence, possibly even a kind of danger, although he did not know to whom. But he also knew he couldn't have left things as they were after the morning session.

"I hate it when they mow it and try to take out the duckweed," she said, ignoring him.

He wasn't sure what to say to that. It was just a holding pond, like thousands of others. It wasn't meant to be a habitat. But, then, they'd found her in an empty lot.

"Look—there are still some tadpoles," she said, pointing, something approaching contentment on her face. He was beginning to understand that keeping her inside had been cruel. Perhaps now she wouldn't see the conversation between them solely as an interrogation.

"It is nice out here," he said, just to say something, but it was nice. It felt even better than he'd thought to get out of the building. He'd had some idea of questioning her, but the strong smell of rain and the way that the distant sky formed dark curtains of downpours fast approaching had defeated that impulse.

"Ask her about the director," the Voice said. "Ask her if the director mentioned having been across the border before." Pushed that away. You're a hologram. You're a construct. I'm going to throw chum overboard until you're so blood-enraged you can't swim properly.

Ghost Bird nudged a large black beetle with her shoe. It was frantic, ceaselessly caroming through the links of the fence and back over. "You know why they do that?"

"No, I don't," Control said. Over the past four days, he had realized there were many things he didn't know.

"They just sprayed insecticide here. I can smell it. You can see the hint of foam on its carapace. It disorients them as it kills them; they can't breathe because of it. They become what you might call panicked. They keep searching for a way to get away from what's already inside of them. Toward the end, they settle down, but that's only because they don't have enough oxygen to move anymore."

She waited until the beetle was over a piece of flat ground and then brought her shoe down, hard and fast. There was a crunch. Control looked away. Forgiving a friend who had done something to upset him, his father had once said that she heard a different kind of music.

"Ask her about the empty lot," the Voice said.

"Why do you think you ended up at the empty lot?" Control asked, mostly to placate the audience. Any one of the three might report back to Grace.

"I ended up here, at the Southern Reach." A guarded note had entered her voice.

"What does it mean to you, that place?" The same as this place, or more?

"I don't think it was where I was meant to be," she said after a pause. "Just a feeling. I remember waking up and not recognizing it for a moment and then when I did, being disappointed."

"Disappointed how?"

Ghost Bird shrugged.

Lines of lightning created fantastical countries in the sky. Thunder came on like an accusing voice.

Ask her if she left anything in the empty lot. Was it his question or the Voice's?

"Did you leave anything there?"

"Not that I remember," she said.

Control said something he had rehearsed beforehand. "Soon you'll need to be candid about what you remember and what you don't remember. They'll take you away from here if I don't get results. And I'll have no say in where they send you if that happens. It might be worse than here, a lot worse."

"Didn't I tell you I wasn't the biologist?" She said it soft, but with bite.

Ask her what she really is.

He couldn't suppress a wince, even though he had meant it when he had said she didn't owe him anything for bringing her out to the pond.

"I'm trying to be honest. I'm not her . . . and there's something inside of me I don't understand. There's a kind of . . . brightness . . . inside."

Nothing in the medical updates, except an elevated temperature.

"That's called life," Control said.

She didn't laugh at that, but said, quietly, "I don't think so."

If she had a "brightness" inside of her, there was a corresponding darkness inside of him. The rain approached. The humidity was driven away by a wild breeze. Ripples spread across the pond, and the shed wheezed as the wind pushed against it. The little Christmas pine whipped back and forth.

"You're all alone out here, aren't you, John?"

He didn't have to answer because it had started to rain—hard. He wanted to hurry back in so they wouldn't get soaked, but Ghost Bird wouldn't cooperate. She insisted on taking slow, deliberate steps, let the water needle her face, run down her neck, and soak her shirt.

The blue heron moved not at all, intent on some prey beneath the surface.

HAUNTINGS

000

In his dreams now, the sky is deep blue with just a twinge of light. He stares from the water up at the cliff far above him. He can see the silhouette of someone peering down at him from the top . . . can see the way the person leans far over the edge to stare—farther than any human could, yet keeps leaning at a more severe angle, pebbles dislodged and peppering the water around him. While he lies in wait, there, at the bottom of the cliff, swimming vast and un-knowable among the other monsters. Waiting in the darkness for the soundless fall, without splash or ripple.

020: SECOND RECOVERY

Sunday. An ice pick lodged in a brain already suffused with the corona of a dull but persistent headache that radiated forward from a throbbing bolus at the back of his skull. A kind of pulsing satellite defense shield protecting against anything more hostile that might sag into its decaying orbit.

A cup of coffee. A crumb-strewn Formica countertop with a view of the grimy street through a clean window. A wobbly wooden stool to go with shaky hands trying to hold it steady. The faint memory of a cheap disinfectant rising from the floor, tightening his throat. A woman repeated orders behind him, while he tried to spread out across the counter so none of the customers in line could join him. From the look of the coatrack to his left, some people had come in during the winter and never left.

The Voice, a weak but persistent drumbeat, from centuries ago: "Is your house in order? Is your house in order? Tell me, please, is your house in order?"

Was his house in order?

Control hadn't changed his clothes or showered in two days. He could smell his own rich stink like the musk rising off some animal prized by trappers. The sweat was being drawn through his pores onto his forehead again, reaching out in supplication to the ever-hotter Hedley sun through the window, the fans inside the coffee shop not strong enough. It had rained from the previous afternoon until the middle of the night, left large puddles full of tiny brown shrimp-like things that curled up and died in rust-colored agonies as the water evaporated.

Control had come to a halt there at the end of Empire Street, where it crossed the far end of Main Street. When he was a teenager, the coffee shop had been a retro soda joint, which he missed. He'd sit at the air-conditioned window counter with a couple of friends and be grateful for ice cream and root beer, while they talked a lot of crap about girls and sports. It had been nice then, a kind of refuge. But over time the straightlaced bohemian leanings of the so-called railroad district had been usurped by hustlers, con artists, drug addicts, and homeless people with nowhere else to go.

Through the window, waiting for the phone call he knew would come, Control dissected the daily terroir playing out across the street, in front of the discount liquor store. Two skateboarders, so preternaturally lean they reminded him of malnourished greyhounds, stood on that opposite corner in T-shirts and ragged jeans with five-year-old sneakers on their feet but no socks. One of them had a brown mutt on a hemp leash meant for a much larger dog. He'd seen two skateboarders while out jogging Tuesday night, hadn't he? It had been dark, couldn't be sure this was them. But possibly.

Within minutes of Control watching, they'd been joined by a woman he definitely hadn't seen before. Tall, she wore a blue military cap over dyed-red short hair, and a long-sleeved blue jacket with gold fringe at the shoulders and cuffs. The white tank top under the jacket didn't cover her bare midriff. The blue dress pants with a more muted gold stripe on the side ended halfway down her calves and then in bare, dirty feet, with the bright red dots of nail polish visible. It reminded Control of something a rock star might have worn in the late 1980s. Or, idle strange thought: She was some decommissioned officer of the S&S Brigade, missing, forgotten, memory shot, doomed to play out the endgame far from anywhere conducive to either science or superstition.

She had a flushed, ruddy aspect to her face, and talked in an animated way to the skateboarders, a bit too manic, and at the same time pointing down the street, but then breaking off to approach any pedestrian who walked by, hands expressive as she delivered some complex tale of hardship or the logic behind a need. Or perhaps even suggesting more. She shrugged off the first two who ignored her, but the skateboarders got on her about it and the third she yelled after, as if he'd been rude. Roused to action by this, a fat black man in a gray plastic-bag trench coat too hot for Hedley in any season popped up like a stage prop from behind a large garbage can at the far end of the liquor store's frontage. He harangued the man who had shunned the redheaded woman; Control could hear the obscenities through the glass. Then the fat man collapsed back into his former post, evaporating as fast as he'd been conjured up.

The woman could be wearing a wig. The man in the trench coat might have nothing to do with their little charade. He could be utterly out of practice in surveillance, too.

The redheaded woman, shrugging off the affront, walked around the corner to stand facing the traffic on Empire in the shade of the liquor store's side wall. She was joined by one of the skateboarders, who offered her a cigarette, both of them leaning against the brick and continuing to talk in an animated fashion. The second skateboarder now came out of the liquor store with an opened can of wet dog food—Control had missed something vital about that store—and banged it with a scrap and clatter out of the can and into a left-leaning can-shaped pile on the sidewalk right in front of the store. He then pushed the tower into pieces using the can, and for some reason threw the empty can at the fat black man half-hidden from Control's view by the garbage. There was no response to that, nor did the mutt seem enthusiastic about the food.

Although they'd accosted a few customers from the coffee shop, even come up close to the glass on his side of the street, they seemed oblivious to his presence. Which made Control wonder if he had become a wraith or if they were enacting a ritual, meant for an audience of one. Which implied a deeper significance to it all, even though Control knew that might be a false thought, and a dangerous one. Central rarely employed amateurs, but that didn't mean it wasn't possible. Nothing much seemed impossible now. "Is there something in the corner of your eye that you cannot get out?" Another thing the Voice had said to him, which he had taken as a kind of oblique taunt.

If the scene in front of him was innocent, could he disappear into it, transition from one side of the glass to the other? Or were there conspiracies even in buying dog food, begging money for a drink? Intricacies that might escape him.

First thing Saturday morning, Control had called the Voice, from his house. He had placed an electronic bullhorn rigged with a timer on one side of his desk, set the timer. He had placed a neon orange sheet of paper with his reminders on it to the right, along with a pen. He drank a shot of whiskey. He smashed his fists down on the desk, once, twice, three times. He took a deep breath. Then he made the call, putting the Voice on speakerphone.

Sounds of creaking and shuffling before the Voice debuted. No doubt downstairs in the study of his/her mansion. Or in the basement of a flophouse. Or the barn of a farm, undercover with the chickens.

"Is your house in order?" the Voice asked. A sluggish quality to the Voice, as if the megalodon had been roused from slumber in icy waters. The Voice's tone felt like an insult; it made Control even colder, began to leach away the trepidation in favor of a form of disgust shot through with stubbornness.

Deep breath. Then, preempting anything the Voice might say, Control launched into a shouted string of obscenities of the most vile kind, contorting his throat, hurting it. After a surprised pause, the Voice shouted, "Enough!" then muttered something long and quivery and curling. Control lost the thread. The bullhorn went off. Control shook himself out of it, read the words on the orange sheet of paper. Checked off the first line. Launched again into a string of obscenities. "Enough!" Again, persistent, stubborn, the Voice muttered something, this time moist and short and darting. Control floated and floated and forgot. The bullhorn went off. Control saw the words on the orange sheet of paper. Checked off the second line. Obscenities. Mutters. Floating. Bullhorn ripping through. Control saw the words on the orange sheet of paper. Check mark. Repeat. Rinse. Repeat. Fifth time. Sixth time. The seventh time the script changed. He fed back to the Voice all the muttering glottal, moist, soft words he'd gleaned from the director's cheat sheet. Heard the wet gasp and shriek of hitting the target, then an awkward lunge of words toward him, but feeble, disconnected, unintelligible.

That had left a scar. He doubted his incantation had had the full effect, but the point was that the Voice knew and had had a very unpleasant experience.

The bullhorn went off. Control saw the words on the orange sheet of paper. He was done. The Voice was done. They'd have to get another handler, one not quite so manipulative.

"Here's a joke for you," Control said. "What's the difference between a magician and a spy?" Then he hung up.

He had reviewed the surveillance of his Wednesday and Thursday conversations with the Voice on Friday night after a vigorous jog. He'd been suspicious, hadn't trusted the way he seemed to fade in and out during those conversations, or how the Voice had infiltrated his thoughts. With Chorizo on his lap, and the feed piped in from his phone to the television, Control had seen the Voice execute hypnotic commands, seen himself become unfocused, head floating a bit on his neck, eyelids fluttering, while the Voice, never dropping the metallic, guttural disguise, gave him orders and suggestions. The Voice told him not to worry about Whitby, to put his concern aside, minimize it, because "Whitby's never mattered." But then later backtracked and expressed interest in him finding Whitby's strange room. Had he been drawn to that hidey-hole because of some subliminal intel? A reference to Grace, along with an order to go back to her office, then some dithering about "too risky" when the Voice learned about the new locks. A lot of exasperation about the director's notes and the slow progress in sorting through them. That this was mostly due to the director's disorganized process made him wonder if that had been the point of the chaos. Had the Voice even *told* Control to go by "Control" at the agency? Resisted the madness of such thoughts.

The Voice, while Control languished under hypnosis, had a sharpness and focus not as present otherwise, and a kind of casual perversity, telling Control s/he wanted a joke to end their next phone call, "one with a punch line." As far as he could tell, he also had been serving as a living tape recorder for the Voice. The Voice had pulled out of Control verbatim conversations, which explained why he had been so late getting home Wednesday even though the conversation had seemed short.

He'd been on an expedition sent into the Southern Reach and just like the expeditions into Area X, not told the truth. He had been right to feel that he was getting information coming in with an extra stutter-step. What else had he done that he might never know?

So he'd written on the neon orange sheet that he could not possibly miss:

CONTROL, YOU ARE BEING SUBJECTED TO HYPNOTIC SUGGES-
TION BY THE VOICE
___ Check this line and scream obscenities. Move down one line.
___ Check this line and scream obscenities. Move down one line.

Rinse, repeat, brought out of it by the bullhorn, pulled back into it. Until, finally, he reached the end: "Check this line and repeat these phrases"—all of the
phrases he'd found in the director's desk. Shout them, actually.

*Are you excited, too? . . . The possibility of significant variation . . . Paralysis
is not a cogent analysis . . . Consolidation of authority . . . There's no reward in
the risk . . . Floating and floating, like nothing human but something free and
floating . . .*

Overload the system as the scientists with the white rabbits had been unable
to. Push the Voice into some kind of collapse.

He had been betrayed, would not now have a moment when he would not be
looking over his shoulder. Saw the biologist by the holding pond, the two of them
looking at the shed. Leading her back into the Southern Reach, as it swallowed
them. His mother leading him by the hand up the path to the summer cottage,
Grandpa waiting for them, an enigmatic smile making a mystery of his face.

The cure for his discoveries, for not having to think about them, had been a kind
of self-annihilation as he trekked undaunted from Saturday afternoon to Sunday
morning, through the small but plump underbelly of Hedley—which as far as he
could tell had forgotten there was a Southern Reach. He recalled a pool hall—
the crack of ball against ball, the *thud* and *thack*, the comfort of the felt-lined
pockets, the darkness, the smell of chalk and cigarettes. Hitting the cue ball with
the eight ball as a joke, and a handprint slapped in chalk on the ass of a woman's
jeans—or as he thought of it later, although she'd placed it there, a hand too far.
He had withdrawn soon after, not as interested as he'd thought in the banality of
a grainy morning sun seen through the windows of a cheap motel, an imprint of
a body on the sheets, a used condom in the wastebasket. These were visions for
others, at least in that moment—because it just seemed like too much work. He'd
still be in the same place. He'd still be hearing Lowry from the videos. He'd still
be seeing, in slow motion no less, Grace offering him the contents of her box of

complaints. His mind would still be whirring as it contracted and expanded, grappling with Area X.

He had three shots of cheap whiskey in a place so run down it didn't have a name. He had a gulp of some local moonshine at a party not far from the pier where ages ago he'd looked out across the river. Told himself over and over that the hypnosis was a small thing, not a large thing, and that it meant nothing. Nothing at all. Too big a deal. Too little. He thought about calling his mother. Couldn't. Wanted to call his father. Impossible.

He went into another bar already drunk, found himself confronted by a ghost. Earlier that night he had glimpsed hints of them—in the curl of a lip that sparked a memory, a flicker of an eyelid, the way someone's hand lingered on a tabletop. Those shoes. That dress. But when you encountered a real ghost—the Thing Entire—it was a shock . . . it took your breath. Not away. It didn't take your breath away—your breath wasn't *going* anywhere. Your breath was still in you, locked up, not of use to you. Took your pulse only to mutter dire predictions for the future. So when you came back into the moment, you doubted at first who you were, because the Ghost Entire trapped Control somewhere between the person he had been and the person he had become. And yet it was still just a wraith. Just a woman he had known in high school. Intensely. For the first time. Close enough that Control felt somehow like he was being disrespectful to the biologist, that the overlay of the ghost was disrupting his impression of Ghost Bird. Even if that was ridiculous. And all of it taking him farther and farther from the Southern Reach.

Trying to escape the residue of that, at another point on the carousel compass of his adventures—utterly shitfaced and giddy—he had spun onto a stool in a biker bar, winding up next to the assistant director. The whole place was still raucous and ill-behaved at two in the morning. It stank of piss, as thick as if cats had been marking their territory. Control gave her a leaky lantern of a grin, to go with an emphatic nod. She gave him a look of blank neutrality.

"The file is empty. There's nothing on her." On who? Who was he talking about? "If you could put me in your own special hell, it'd be working at the old S.R. anyway—for a lifetime, right?"

Halfway through, he realized that it couldn't really be Grace and that the words might not even be coming out of his mouth.

She unnerved him with the candor of her unblinking gaze.

"You don't have to look like that," he added. Must've said it this time.

"Like what?" she said, her head turned a little to the side. "Like a man's fucked up outta his mind and in my bar? Go to hell."

He'd reared back on his stool at that suggestion, trying to assemble his wits like pieces on a game board. A weight on his chest, in the dark and the light. He'd thought he was smarter. He'd thought she'd gotten mired in old ways of thinking. But it turned out new ways of thinking didn't help, either. Time for another drink, somewhere else. A kind of oblivion. Then regroup.

Control met her doubtful stare as he left with a bleary smile. He was making progress. She receded from him, pushed back by a waft of wind from the bar door opening and the judgmental stare of the streetlamps.

Control rubbed his face, didn't like the feel of stubble. He tried to wipe the fuzziness from his mind, the sourness from his tongue, the soreness from his joints. He was convinced the Voice had said to him, at one point, "Is there something in the corner of your eye that you cannot get out? I can help you get it out." Easy, if you'd put it there in the first place.

The woman in the uniform was probably a drug addict and definitely homeless or a squatter. You used amateurs for surveillance when the target was "in the family," when you wanted to use the natural landscape—the natural terroir—to its best advantage or when your faction was dead broke or incompetent. It occurred to him that she didn't notice him because she'd been paid to pretend not to notice him.

The skateboarder with the dog had clearly staked out the corner as his territory, sharing it with the fat drunk man. There was something about both of them that seemed more natural, perhaps because an element of theater—smashing out dog food on the curb—didn't fit with the idea of not drawing attention. The other skateboarder had left and come back several times, but Control hadn't seen him pass drugs or money or food to the other two. Maybe he was slumming it for a day, or served as a lookout for some larger con, or he was Mother's watcher, part of the tableau but not. Or perhaps there was nothing going on except three people who knew one another and helped one another out, and just happened to be down on their luck.

The thing about staying in one place for so long was that you began to get a sense, while watching, of being watched, so it didn't startle him when the cell phone rang. It was the call he'd been expecting.

"I understand you've been behaving badly," she said.

"Hello to you, too, Mother."

"Are you rough right now? You sound rough."

"I'm fine. I have complete control of my faculties."

"Then why do you seem to have lost your mind." This said in the brisk, professional tone she used to disguise emotional tells. A sense that she was as "on" with him as with any other agent she ran.

"I've already thrown the phone away, Mother. So don't think about reinstating the Voice." If she had called yesterday, he would have been yelling at her by now.

"We can always get you another one."

"Quick question, Ma." She hated *ma* or *mom*, barely tolerated *mother*, would have preferred the severe Severance even though he was her precious only child. That he knew of. "If you were to send someone on an expedition into somewhere dangerous—let's say, into the Southern Reach—how would you keep them calm and on track? What kinds of tools might you use?"

"The usual things, really, John. Although I'm not sure I like your tone."

"The usual things? Like hypnosis, maybe, backed up by conditioning beforehand at Central." He was keeping his voice low, much as he wanted to lash out. He liked the coffee shop counter. He didn't want to be asked to leave.

A pause. "It might have come into play, yes, but only with strict rules and safeguards—and only in the subject's absolute best interests."

"The subject might have preferred to have had the choice. The subject might've preferred not to be a drone." The subject might prefer to know that his hopes and desires and impulses were all definitely his *own* hopes, desires, impulses.

"The subject might not have had the intel or perspective to be involved in that decision. The subject might have needed an inoculation, a vaccine."

"Against what?"

"Against any number of things. Although at the first sign of something serious happening, we would pull you out and send a team in."

"Like what? What would you consider serious?"

"Whatever might happen."

Infuriatingly opaque, as always. Making decisions for him, as always. He was channeling his father's irritation now as much as his own, the specters of so many arguments at the dinner table or in the living room. He decided to take the conversation onto the street after all, stood in the mouth of the alley just to the left of the coffee shop. Not many people were out walking around—most of them were probably still in church, or scoring drugs.

"Jack used to say that if you don't give an operative all the information they need, you might as well cut your own leg off," he said. "Your operation is screwed."

"But your operation isn't screwed, John," she said, with some force. "You're still there. You're still in touch with us. Me. We're not going anywhere."

"Good point, except I don't think that 'we' means Central. I think you mean some faction within Central, and not an effective one. Your Voice made a mess trying to take the assistant director out of the mix. Give her another week and I'll be Grace's administrative assistant." Or was the point to waste a lot of Grace's time and attention?

"There are no factions, just Central. The Voice is under a lot of stress, John. Even more now. We all are."

"The hell there aren't factions." Now he was Jack, hard to throw off topic. "The hell there aren't." "The hell there isn't." "The hell you say."

"You won't believe me, John, but I've done you a favor placing you at the Southern Reach."

Everyone had forgotten the definition of *favor*. First Whitby, then Grace, now his mother. He didn't trust himself to respond, so he didn't.

"A lot of people would've killed for that position," she said.

He had no answer for that, either. While they'd been talking, the woman had disappeared, and the storefront was deserted. Back in the day the liquor store had been a department store. Long before Hedley was built, there had been an indigenous settlement here, along the river—something his father had told him—and the remains of that lay beneath the facade of the liquor store.

Down below the store, too, a labyrinth of limestone cradling the aquifer, narrow caves and blind albino crawfish and luminescent freshwater fish. Surrounded by the crushed remains of so many creatures, loamed into the soil, pushed down by the foundations of the buildings. Would that be the biologist's understanding of the street—what she would see? Perhaps she would see, too, one possible future of that space, the liquor store crumbling under an onslaught of vines and weather damage, becoming akin to the sunken, moss-covered hills near Area X. A loss she might not mourn. Or would she?

"Are you there, John?"

Where else would he be?

For a long time now, Control had suspected his mother had taken someone else under her wing as a protégé—it seemed almost inevitable. Someone sculpted, trained, and deployed to correct the kinds of mistakes made by Control. The thought reoccurred whenever he was feeling particularly insecure or vulnerable, or sometimes just because it could be a useful mental exercise. Now he was trying to visualize the perfectly groomed protégé walking in and taking over the Southern Reach from him. What would this person have done differently? What would this person do *right now*?

While his mother continued to talk, plunging ahead with what seemed like a lie.

"But I was mostly calling for an update, to see if you think you're making progress"—this his mother's attempt to subvert his silence with an apology. Slight emphasis on *progress*.

"You know exactly how it's going." The Voice would have told her everything It knew up to the point he had derailed It.

"True, but I haven't heard your side."

"My side? My side is that I've been dropped into a pit of snakes with a blindfold on and my hands tied behind my back."

"That's just a bit dramatic, don't you think?" said the streak of light.

"Not as dramatic as whatever you did to me at Central. I've got missing hours, maybe a missing day."

"Nothing much," she said in a bland tone that let him know she was bored with the topic. "Nothing much. Prepared you, stiffened your resolve, that's all. Made you see some things more clearly and others less so."

"Like introduce fake memories or—"

"No. That kind of thing would make you such an expensive model that no one here could *afford* you. Or afford to send you to the Southern Reach."

Because everyone would kill for this position.

"Are you lying to me?"

"You'd better hope not," she said with an in-rushing verve, "because I'm all you've got now—by your own actions. Besides, you'll never really know for sure. You've always been the kind of person who peels away the layers, even when there are no layers left. So just take it at face value, from your poor long-suffering mother."

"I can see you, Mother. I can see your reflection in the glass. You're right around the corner, watching, aren't you? It's not just your proxies. You're in town, too."

"Yes, John. That's why there's that kind of tinny echo. That's why my words seem to be falling on deaf ears, because you're hearing them twice. I'm interrupting myself, apparently."

A kind of rippling effect spread through him. He felt elongated and stretched, and his throat was dry. "Can I trust you?" he asked, sick of the sparring.

Something sincere and open in his voice must have reached her, because she dropped the distant tone and said, "Of course you can, John. You can't trust *how* I'll get somewhere, but you have to trust I know where I'm going. I always know where I'm going."

That didn't help him at all. "You want me to trust you? Then tell me, Mother. Tell me who the Voice was." If she wouldn't, the impulse in him to just disappear into the underbelly of Hedley, to fade into that landscape and not come back, might return. Might be too strong to suppress.

She hesitated, and her hesitation scared him. It felt real, not staged.

Then: "Lowry. God's honest truth, John. Lowry was the Voice."

Not thirty years distant at all. But breathing in Control's ear.

"Son of a bitch."

Banished and yet returned via the videos that would play forever in his head. Haunting him still.

Lowry.

"Go ahead and check the seats for change, John." Grandpa Jack staring at him as he held the gun.

There had come a sharp rapping at the window. It was his mother, leaning over to look in the window. Even through the condensation, Control could tell when she saw the gun on his lap. The door was wrenched open. The gun suddenly vanished, and Jack, on the other side, was out on his ear, Mother standing over him while he sat on the curb in front of the car. Control took the risk of lowering the left rear window a bit, then leaned forward so he could observe them better through the front windshield. She was talking quietly to Grandpa while she stood in front of him, arms folded and her gaze straight ahead, as if he stood at eye level. Control couldn't see where the gun had gone.

A sense of menace radiated out from his mother that he had never seen in such a concentrated form before. Her voice might be low, and he couldn't hear most of what she was saying, but the tone and quickness of it was like a sharpened butcher knife slicing, effortless, through raw meat. His grandpa gave a peculiar nod in response, one that was almost more like he was being pushed back by some invisible force or like she was shoving him.

She unfolded her arms and lowered her head to look at Grandpa, and Control heard, "Not this way! Not this way. You can't force him into it." For some reason, he wondered if she was talking about the gun or Grandpa's secret plan to take him to the lingerie show.

Then she walked back to the car to collect him, and Grandpa got in and drove off slowly. Relief swept over Control as they went back inside the house. He didn't have to go to the lingerie show. He might be able to go next door later.

Mother only talked about the incident once, when they got back in the house. They took off their coats, went into the living room. She took out a pack of cigarettes and lit one. With her big, wavy hair and her slight features and her white blouse, red scarf, crisp black pants, and high heels she looked like a magazine model, smoking. An agitated model. Now he had experienced another unknown thing beyond the fact that she could fight fiercely for him: He hadn't known she was a smoker.

Except, she'd turned it back on him, as if he had been responsible. "What the hell were you thinking, John? What the hell were you thinking?"

But he hadn't been. He'd seen his grandpa's wink when he mentioned the department-store show, had liked that the man who could be stern or even disapproving was confiding in him, trusting him to keep a secret from his mother.

"Don't touch guns, John," she said, pacing back and forth. "And don't do every stupid thing your grandpa tells you to do." Later he decided to abide by the second commandment but to ignore the first, which he doubted she had meant—even nicknamed his various guns "Gramps" or "Grandpa." He used guns, but he didn't like them and didn't like relying on them. They smelled like their perspective.

Control never told his father about the incident, for fear it would be used against his mother. Nor did he recognize until later that the whole trip had actually been about the gun, or about finding the gun. That, perhaps, it had been evolving into a kind of test.

Sitting there in the coffee shop after his mother hung up the thought crept in that perhaps his mother's anger about the gun had itself been a tableau, a terroir, with Jack and Jackie complicit, actors in a scene meant already, at that young age, to somehow influence him or correct his course. To begin a kind of indoctrination in the family empire.

He wasn't sure he knew the difference anymore between what he was meant to find and what he'd dug up on his own. A tower could become a pit. Questioning a biologist could become a trap. An expedition member might even return thirty years later in the form of a voice whispering strange nothings in his ear.

When he got home Sunday night, he checked his recording of the conversation with his mother, felt an overload of relief when there were no gaps, no evidence that his mother, too, was deceiving him.

He believed that Central was in disarray, and that he'd been run by a faction, under hypnotic control. Now the ceiling was no doubt falling in on the clandestine basement, and the megalodon was feeling nervous within the cracked glass of its tank. Grace had bloodied It. Him. And then Control had delivered a follow-up punch.

"Only Lowry had enough experience of the Southern Reach and Area X to be of use," his mother had told him, but fear leaked out of her words, too, and she went on and on about Lowry while Control felt as if a historical figure had popped out from a portrait alive to announce itself. A broken, erratic, rehabilitated historical figure who claimed to remember little not already captured by the videos. Someone who had leveraged a promotion, received due to a tangled knot of pity and remorse or some other reason than competence.

"Lowry is an asshole." To stop her talking about him. Just because you survived, just because you were labeled a hero, didn't mean you couldn't also be an asshole. She must have been desperate, had no choice. Rearing up behind that, whispers he remembered now that might have come from Lowry's direction: of shadow facilities, of things allied with the hypnosis and conditioning efforts but more hideous still.

"I knew there might be things you'd tell him you wouldn't tell me. We knew it might be better if you didn't know . . . some of the things we needed you to do."

Anger had warred with satisfaction that he'd smoked them out, that at least one variable had been removed. A need to know more balanced against already feeling overwhelmed. While trying to ignore an unsettling new thought: that his mother's power had boundaries.

"Is there anything you're hiding from me?"

"No," she said. "No. The mission is still the same: Focus on the biologist and the missing director. Dig through the notes. Stabilize the Southern Reach. Find out what has been going on that we don't know about."

Had that been the mission? That fragmented focus? Maybe the Voice's mission, which was his now, he supposed. He chose to take the lie that she had told him everything at face value, thought perhaps the worst of it was now behind him. He'd shaken off the chains. He'd taken everything Grace could throw at him. He'd seen the videos.

Control went into the kitchen and poured a whiskey, his only one of the day, and downed it in one gulp, magical thinking behind the idea that it would help him sleep. As he put the empty glass back on the counter, he noticed the director's cell phone by the landline. In its case, it still looked like a large black beetle.

A premonition came to him, and a memory of the scuttling on the roof earlier in the week. He got a dish towel, picked up the phone, opened the back door with Chorry at his heels, and tossed the phone deep into the gloom of the backyard. It hit a tree, caromed off into the darkness of the long grass at the edge of the property. Fuck you, phone. Don't come back. It could join the Voice/Lowry phone in some phone afterlife. He would rather feel paranoid or stupid than be compromised. He felt vindicated when Chorry-Chorrykins refused to follow the phone, wanted to stay inside. A good choice.

021: REPEATING

When Monday morning arrived, Control didn't go into the Southern Reach right away. Instead he took a trip to the director's house—grabbed the driving instructions from the Internet and holstered his gun and got on the highway. It had been on his list to do once the notes in his office were categorized, just to make sure Grace's people had cleaned out the house as thoroughly as she claimed. The confirmation of the Voice's/Lowry's manipulation, and by extension his mother's, remained a listless feeling, something buzzing around in the background. As answers went, Lowry got him no further, gave him no real leverage—he'd been manipulated by someone untouchable and ethereal. Lowry, shadowing himself as the Voice, haunting the Southern Reach from afar. Control now trying to merge them into one person, one intent.

There was also an impulse, once he was on his way, not to return to the Southern Reach at all—to bypass the director's house, too—and detour onto a rural road, take it over to his father's house, some fifty miles west.

But he resisted it. New owners, and no sculptures left in the backyard. After his dad's death, they'd gone to good homes with aunts and uncles, nieces and nephews, even if he'd felt as if the landscape of his formative years was being dismantled, piece by piece. So no solace there. No real history. Some of his relatives still lived in the area, but his father had been the bond between them, and he'd last known most of them as a teenager.

Bleakersville had a population of about twenty thousand—just big enough to have a few decent restaurants, a small arts center, and the three blocks of historic district. The director lived in a neighborhood with few white faces in evidence. Lots of overhanging pines, oaks, and magnolia trees, hung heavy with moss, sodden branches from the storms lying broken on the potholed road. Solid cedar or cement houses, some with brick accents, mostly brown and blue or gray, with one or two cars in gravel or pine-needle driveways. He drove past a couple of communal basketball hoops and some black and Latino kids on bicycles, who stopped and stared until he was gone. School had been out for a couple of weeks.

The director's house lay at the end of a street named Standiford, at the top of a hill. Choosing caution, Control parked a block away, on the street below, then walked into the backyard, which slanted up the hill toward her house. The backyard was overgrown with untrimmed azalea bushes and massive wisteria vines, some of them wrapped tight around the pine trees. A couple of halfhearted compost islands languished behind circles of staked chicken wire. Much of the grass had yellowed and died over time, exposing tree roots.

Three cement semicircles served in lieu of a deck, covered over with leaves and what looked like rotted birdseed alongside a pie pan filled to the top with dirty water. The white French doors stained green with mold beyond them would be his entry point. One problem—he would have to pick the lock, since he hadn't put in a formal request to visit. Except he wanted to pick the lock, he realized. Didn't want to have a key. As he worked on it with the tools he'd brought, the rain began to fall. Thick drops that clacked and thunked against last winter's fallen magnolia leaves.

He sensed he was being watched—some hint of movement from the corner of his eye, perhaps—just as he'd managed to open the door. He stood up and turned to his left.

In the neighbor's yard, well back from the chain-link fence, a black girl, maybe nine or ten, with beaded cornrows, stared warily at him. She wore a sunflower dress and white plastic sandals with Velcro straps.

Control smiled and waved. In some other universe, Control fled, abandoning his mission, but not in this one.

The girl didn't wave back, but she didn't run away, either.

He took that as a sign and went inside.

No one had been here in months, but there was a kind of swirling movement to the air that he wanted to attribute to a fan he couldn't see, or an air-conditioning unit that had just cut out. Except that Grace had had the electricity turned off until the director returned, "to save money for her." The rain was coming down hard enough now that it added to the gloom, so he turned on his flashlight. No one would notice—he was too far away from the windows, and the glass doors had a long dark curtain across them. Most people would be at work anyway.

Seen through the tunnel of the flashlight beam, the small living room soon gave up its secrets: a couch, three lounge chairs, a fireplace. What looked like a library lay beyond it, behind a dividing wall and through worn saloon-style doors. The kitchen was to the left and then a hallway; a massive refrigerator festooned with magnet-fixed photos and old calendars guarded the corner. To the right of the living room was a door leading to the garage, and beyond that probably the master bedroom. The entire house was about 1,700 square feet.

Why had the director lived here? With her pay grade, she could have done much better; Grace and Cheney both lived in Hedley in upper-middle-class subdivisions. Perhaps there was debt he didn't know about. He needed better intel. Somehow the lack of information about the director seemed connected to her clandestine trip across the border, her ability to keep her position for so long.

No one had lived here for over a year. No one except Central had come in. No one was here now. And yet the emptiness made him uneasy. His breath came shallow, his heartbeat elevated. Perhaps it was just the reliance on the flashlight, the unsettling way it reduced anything not under its bright gaze to a pack of shadows. Maybe it was some part of him acknowledging that this was as close to a field assignment as he'd had in years.

A half-empty water glass stood by the sink, reflecting his light as a circle of fire. A few dishes lay in the sink, along with forks and knives. The director had left this clutter the day she'd gotten in her car and driven to the Southern Reach to lead the twelfth expedition. Central apparently had not been instructed to clean up after the director—nor after themselves. The living-room carpet showed signs of boot prints as well as tracked-in leaves and dirt. It was like a diorama from a museum devoted to the secret history of the Southern Reach.

Grace might have had Central come here and retrieve anything classified, but in terms of the director's property theirs had been a light touch. Nothing *looked* disturbed even though Control knew they had removed five or six boxes of material. It just looked cluttered, which was no doubt the way they'd found it, if the office he'd inherited was any indication. Paintings and prints covered the walls above a few crowded CD stands, a dusty flat-screen television, and a cheap-looking stereo system on which had been stacked dozens of rare old-timey records. None of the paintings or photographs seemed personal in nature.

An elegant gold-and-blue couch stood against the wall dividing the living room from the library, a pile of magazines taking up one cushion, while the antique rosewood coffee table in front of the couch looked as if it had been requisitioned as another desk: books and magazines covered its entire surface— same as the beautifully refinished kitchen table to the left. Had she done most of her work in these rooms? It was homier than he'd thought it would be, with good furniture, and he couldn't quite figure out why that bothered him. Did it come with the house, or was it an inheritance? Did she have a connection to Bleakers-ville? A theory was forming in his head, like a musical composition he could hum from vague memories but not quite yet name or play.

He walked through the hallway beside the kitchen, encountered another fact that seemed odd for no particular reason. Every door had been closed. He had to keep opening them as if going through a series of air locks. Each time, even though there was no prickle of threat, Control prepared to jump back. He discovered an office, a room with some filing cabinets and an exercise bike and free weights, and a guest bedroom with a bathroom opposite it. There were a lot of doors for such a small house, as if the director or Central had been trying to contain something, or almost as if he were traveling between different compartments of the director's brain. Any and all of these thoughts spooked him, and after the third door, he just said the hell with it and entered each with a hand on Grandpa in its holster.

He circled around into the library area and looked out one of the front windows. Saw a branch-strewn overgrown lawn, a battered green mailbox at the end of a cement walkway, and nothing suspicious. No one lurking in a black sedan with tinted windows, for example.

Then back through the living room, through the other hallway, past the garage door, and into the master bedroom on the left.

At first, he thought the bedroom had been flooded and all of the furniture had washed up against the nearest walls. Chairs were stacked atop the dressers and armoire. The bed had come to rest against the dressers. About seven pairs of shoes—from heels to trainers—had been tossed as flotsam on top of the bed. The covers were pulled up, but sloppily. On the far side of the room, in the flashlight's gleam, a mirror shone crazily from beyond a bathroom door.

He took out Grandpa and aimed wherever his flashlight roved. From the dressers now over the bed, now to the wall against which the bed had previously rested, which was covered in thick purple curtains. Cautious, he pulled them back, revealing all-too-familiar words beneath a high horizontal window that let in a stagnant light.

Where lies the strangling fruit that came from the hand of the sinner I shall bring forth the seeds of the dead.

Written in thick dark marker, the same wall of text, with the same map beside it that he had painted over in his office. As if the moment he had rid himself of it, it had appeared in the director's bedroom. Irrational sight. Irrational thought. Now a hundred Controls were running from the room and back to the car in a hundred pocket universes.

But it had been here for a while. It had to have been. Sloppy of Grace's people not to remove it. Too sloppy.

He turned toward the bathroom. "If anyone's there, come out," he said. "I have a gun." Now his heart was beating so fast and his hand was so tight on the flashlight he didn't think it could be pried loose.

But no one came out.

No one was there, as he confirmed by forcing himself to breathe more slowly. By forcing himself to check every corner, including a small closet that seemed more cavernous the farther he progressed into it. In the bathroom, he found the usual things—shampoo, soap, a prescription for blood pressure drugs, a few magazines. Brown hair dye and a hairbrush with gray strands snarled in it. So the director had felt self-conscious about reaching middle age. The brush gleamed when his flashlight struck it, seemed to want to communicate, akin to the scribbled-on receipts and torn magazine pages that had laid bare parts of her life to him, more meaningful to him than his own.

He returned to the bedroom and played the flashlight beam over the wall again. No, not the exact same tableau. The same words, the exact same words. But no height marks. And the map—it was different, too. This version showed the island and its ruined lighthouse, along with the topographical anomaly and the lighthouse on the coast. This version also showed the Southern Reach. A line had been drawn between the ruined and functional lighthouses and the topographical anomaly. That line had then been extended to the Southern Reach. They looked very much like outposts on a border, like on ancient maps of empires.

Control backed away and then down the hall into the living room, feeling cold, feeling distant. He could not think of a scenario in which Central had seen those words, that map, and not removed it.

Which meant that it had been created after they had searched the house. Which meant . . . which probably meant . . .

He didn't allow himself the thought. Instead, he went to the front door to confirm a sudden suspicion.

The knob turned easily in his hand. Unlocked.

Which meant nothing.

Yet now his foremost idea, his only real idea, was to get out of the house. But he still had the presence of mind to lock the front door and return to the back.

Pushed open the French doors, out into the rain.

Walked-ran back to the car.

Not until he was parked well away, on Bleakersville's main street, did he call his mother, tell her what he had found, and ask her to send a team in to investigate. If he'd done it from the site, they'd have kept him there for far too long. As they talked, Control tried to convince himself of benign interpretations, almost as much as his mother did. "Don't make leaps, John, and *don't tell Grace* because she'll overreact," which was correct. Anyone from the Southern Reach could have drawn that on the wall—Whitby as prime suspect other than the former director. Pushing against that relative comfort: A disturbing vision of the director wandering through neighborhoods and parks, across fields, into forests. Revisiting old haunts.

"But, John, there *is* something I need to tell you."

"Tell me, then." Had she given up Lowry's identity as the Voice so she could hide something else?

"You know the places where we picked up the anthropologist and the surveyor?"

"A front porch, the back of a medical practice."

"We've noticed some . . . inconsistencies in those places. The readings are different."

"How? How are they different?"

"We're still sorting through the data, but we've quarantined the areas, even though it's difficult."

"But not in the empty lot? Not where the biologist was?"

"No."

022: GAMBIT

Late morning. An attempt to regain . . . control. The old familiar debriefing room whose deficiencies he had become oblivious to, expecting a call from his mother with a report about the director's house that couldn't possibly come until hours from now.

He had told Grace he was about to interview the biologist and wanted her there, in the room, this time. A few minutes later, Grace came in wearing a bright yellow dress in a flower pattern, black belt at the waist—some kind of Sunday best—not peering around the doorway, not looking like he might lob a grenade at her. He was immediately suspicious.

"Where's the biologist?" Grace asked, in a kind of conspiratorial way. Control was sitting by himself.

Control pushed out the chair opposite with his foot by way of reply, pretending to busy himself looking over some notes.

"I'm sorry," he said. "You just missed the biologist. But she had some very interesting things to say. Do you want to know what she said about you, for example?"

Somehow Control had expected Grace would see it as a trap, get up and try to leave, and he'd have to convince her to stay. But she remained sitting there, appraising him.

"Before I tell you, you should know that all recording devices have been turned off. This is just between the two of us."

Grace folded her arms. "That is fine with me. Continue."

Control felt wrong-footed. He had expected she would go check, make sure he wasn't lying. Maybe she had checked before coming into the room. Grandpa Jack's advice had been that for this kind of work you needed "a second guy, always." Well, he didn't have a second guy or gal. He plunged on anyway.

"Let me get to the point. Before the final eleventh expedition, the director crossed over the border secretly, by herself. Did you know about this in advance? And did you provide material aid? Did you provide command-and-control decision-making? Were you, in fact, *complicit* in making sure she got back across the border? Because this is what the biologist says the director told her." None of this was in the official report on the incident, which the Voice had sent via e-mail before their abrupt leave-taking over the phone. There, in the report, the director had claimed to have acted on her own.

"Interesting. What else did the biologist tell you?" No heat behind the words.

"That the director gave you instructions to wait at the border every night for a week on very specific dates about three weeks after she snuck across. To help her with her return." According to security records, each of those days Grace had left the Southern Reach early, although there was no record of her at the border checkpoints.

"This is all in the past," Grace said. "What are you trying to prove? Exactly."

Control had begun to feel like a chess player who thinks he has a great move, but the opponent is either brilliant or bluffing or has something untouchable four moves ahead.

"Really? That's your reaction? Because both of those accusations would be enough to file an addendum to the report with Central. That you colluded with the director to violate regulations and security protocols. That you provided material support. She was put on probation. What do you think you'd get for lying?"

Smiling, Grace asked, "What do you want?"

Not exactly an admission, but it allowed him to continue on with the script in his head, muffled the alarm bells. "Not what you think, Grace. I'm not pushing for you to resign, and I don't want to report this information to Central. I'm not out to get the director. I want to understand her, that's all. She went over the border. I need to know exactly why and how, and what she found. The report on file is vague." Wondered now if Grace had written the report, or overseen its writing.

The report had mostly focused on the director's punishment and the steps taken to once again tighten border security. There was a brief statement from the director that appeared to have been written by a lawyer: "Although I meant to act in the best interests of the Southern Reach and the requirements of my position, I deeply apologize for my actions and recognize that they were reckless, endangering, and not in keeping with the agency's mission statement. If allowed to return, I will endeavor to adhere to the standard of conduct expected of me, and of this position." "Measurements and samples" were also mentioned in the report, but Control had as yet been unable to track them down. They had not been placed in the storage cathedral, that much he knew. Unless that boiled down to a plant and a mouse and an old cell phone.

"The director did not share her every thought with me," Grace said in an irritated tone, as if this fact bothered her, but with a strange half-smile on her face.

"I find it hard to believe that you don't know more than you're telling me."

This did not move Grace to respond, so he prodded her with "I'm not here to destroy the director's legacy, or yours. I brought you here not just because of what the biologist said but also because I think we could *both* have autonomy here. That we could run the agency in a way that means your position remains unchanged." Because as far as he was concerned, the agency was fucked and he was now an undercover agent in the field, entering hostile territory. So use whatever you don't care about as a bargaining chip. Maybe before he found a way out he'd even give Whitby that transfer he'd once wanted. Maybe he'd return to Central and have a beer with Lowry.

"How gracious of you," Grace said. "The schoolboy is offering to share the power with the teacher."

"That's not the analogy I would have made. I would have—"

"Anything the director did, she did because she believed it was important."

"Yes, but what did she do? What was she up to?"

"Up to?" Grace said, with a little snort of disbelief.

He chose his words very carefully. "Grace, I am already here. I am already in the middle of this. You should just tell me what's going on." What was the look that could convey without the reinforcement of words that he had already seen some very strange shit? "Remember, none of this is on the record."

Grace considered that for a second with what seemed like amusement. Then she began to talk.

"You have to understand the director's position," Grace said. "The first expedition had set the tone within the organization. Even though the original director, by the time Cynthia got here, was trying to change that." Cynthia? For a moment, Control wondered who Cynthia was because he'd thought of her as "the director" for so long. "The personnel here felt that the first expedition failed because the Southern Reach did not know what it was doing. That we had sent them in, and they had died because we did not know what we were doing, and we could never really make up for that." The first expedition: a sacrifice to a lack of context. A lament unrecognized as such until it was too late. "And Lowry's presence here at the agency"—was she reading his mind, did she somehow know?—"from my understanding, only made that worse. He was a living ghost, a reminder held up as a hero when he had just been a survivor. So his advice was given more weight, even when it was wrong. The director only really had a chance to pursue her own agenda after Lowry had been promoted to Central, even though that, too, was a problem. Lowry pushed for more expeditions even though the director wanted fewer, and whereas before she could control Lowry, now he was beyond her control. So we kept sending people in, throwing them up against a complete unknown. This did not sit well with the director, although she followed orders because she had to."

He found himself being swept along by her narrative. "How did the director get her own agenda through? In what ways?"

"She became obsessed with metrics, with changing the context. If she could have her metrics, then Lowry could, grudgingly, have his expeditions, the conditioning and hypnosis he championed, although over time she came to understand why Lowry pushed the hypnosis."

Control kept seeing Lowry in the context of the camera flying through the air: Lowry crawling, the camera soaring, and the truth perhaps somewhere in the middle. And then Lowry making Control crawl and soar.

None of this really spoke to the director's secret mission across the border, though. Was Grace just tossing information at him to avoid talking about it? It was more than she'd ever said to him before.

"What else?" he asked. "What else did she do?"

She spread her hands as if for emphasis and the smile on her face was almost beatific. "She became obsessed with making it react."

"Area X?"

"Yes. She felt that if she could make Area X react, then she would somehow throw it off course. Even though we didn't know what course it was on."

"But it *had* reacted: It killed a lot of people."

"She believed that nothing we had done had *pushed* whatever is behind Area X. That it had handled anything we did too easily. Almost without thought. If thought could be said to be involved."

"So she went across the border to make Area X react."

"I will not confirm that I knew about her trip or helped in any way," Grace said. "I will tell you my belief, based on what she said to me after she came back."

"It wasn't the reaction she wanted," Control said.

"No. No, it was not. And she blamed herself. The director can be very harsh, but never harsher than with herself. When Central decided to go ahead with the last eleventh expedition, I am sure the director hoped that she had made a difference. And maybe she had. Instead of the usual, what came back were cancer-ridden ciphers."

"Which is why she forced herself onto the twelfth expedition."

"Yes."

"Which is why her methods had become suspect."

"I would not agree with that assessment. But, yes, others would say that."

"Why did Central let her go on the twelfth expedition?"

"For the same reason they reprimanded her after she went across by herself but did not fire her."

"Which was?"

Grace smiled, triumphant. At knowing something he should have known? For some other reason?

"Ask your mother. Your mother had a hand in both things, I believe."

"They had lost confidence in her anyway," Grace said next, bitterness bleeding into her voice. "What did they care if she never came back? Maybe some of them at Central even thought it solved a problem." Like Lowry.

But Control was still stuck on Jackie Miranda Severance, Severance for short, Grandpa always "Jack." His mother had placed him in the Southern Reach, in the middle of it all. She had worked for the Southern Reach briefly, when he was a teenager, to be close to him, she had said. Now, as he questioned Grace, he was trying to make the dates synch up, to get a sense of who had been at the Southern Reach and who had not, who had left by then and who was still incoming. The director—no. Grace—no. Whitby—yes. Lowry—yes, no? Where had his mother gone when she left? Had she kept ties? Clearly she had, if he were to believe Grace. And did her sudden appearance to him with a job offer correspond to knowing she had some kind of emergency on her hands? Or was it part of a more intricate plan? It could make you weary, untangling the lines. At least Grandpa had been more straightforward. Oh, look. There's a gun. What a surprise. I want you to learn how to use a gun. Make everything do more than one thing. Some-times you had to take shortcuts after all. Wink wink. But his mother never gave you the wink. Why should she? She didn't want to be your friend, and if she couldn't convince you in some more subtle way, she'd find someone she could convince. He might never know how much other residue he'd already encoun-tered from her passage through the Southern Reach.

But the idea that the director might have reached out to others in the agency, and at Central, comforted Control. It made the director less an eccentric, less a "single-celled plot" as his mother put it, than someone genuinely trying to solve a problem.

"What happened on her trip across the border?" Control, pressing again.

"She never told me. She said it was for my own protection, in case the inves-tigators subpoenaed me." He made a note to return to that later.

"Nothing at all?"

"Not a single thing."

"Did she give you any special instructions before she went on leave or after she came back?" From what Control could intuit from the files he'd read, Grace was more constrained by rules and regulations than the director, and the director might have felt slightly undermined by her assistant director's adherence to them. Or perhaps that was the point: that Grace had kept her grounded. In which case, Grace would almost certainly have been in charge of operational details.

Grace hesitated, and Control didn't know if that meant she was debating tell-ing him more or was about to feed him a line of bullshit.

"Cynthia asked me to reopen an investigation into the so-called S&S Bri-gade, and to assign someone to report in more detail on the lighthouse."

"And who did the research?"

"Whitby." Whitby the loon. It figured.

"What happened to this research?" He couldn't recall seeing this information in the files he had been given before he'd come to the Southern Reach.

"Cynthia held on to it, asked for a hard copy and for the electronic copies not to be entered into the record . . . Are you planning to go down the same rabbit holes?"

"So you thought it was a waste of time?"

"For us, not necessarily for Cynthia. It seemed irrelevant to me, but nothing we gathered would make much sense without knowing what was in the director's mind. And we did not always know what was in the director's mind."

"Is there anything else you want to tell me?" Being bold now that Grace was finally opening up to him.

A sympathetic expression, guided or pushed his way. "Do you smoke?"

"Sometimes." This past weekend. Banishing demons and voices.

"Then let's go out to the courtyard and have a smoke."

It sounded like a good idea. If he was completely honest with himself, it sounded like bliss.

They reconvened out at the edge of the courtyard, nearest the swamp. The short jaunt from room to open air had not been without revelation: He'd finally seen the janitor, a wizened little white guy with huge glasses who wore light green overalls and held a mop. He couldn't have been more than five feet tall. Control resisted the urge to break ranks with Grace to tell him to switch cleaners.

Grace in the courtyard seemed even more relaxed than inside, despite the humidity and the annoying chorus of insect voices rising from the undergrowth. He was already sweating.

She offered him a cigarette. "Take one."

Yes, he would take one, had been missing them ever since his weekend binge. The harsh, sharp taste of her unfiltered menthols as he lit up was like a spike through the eyeball to cure a headache.

"Do you like the swamp?" he asked.

She shrugged. "I like the quiet out here, sometimes. It can be peaceful." She gave him a wry smile. "If I stand with my back to the building, I can pretend it isn't there."

He nodded, was silent for a moment, then said, "What would you do if the director came back and she was like the anthropologist or the surveyor?" Just adding to the light conversation. Just a gaffe, he realized as soon as he'd said it.

Grace remained unfazed. "She won't."

"How can you be so sure?" He almost broke his promise to his mother then and told Grace about the writing on the wall in the director's house.

"I have to tell you something," Grace said, changing direction on him. "It will be a shock, but I don't mean it to be that way."

Somehow, even though it was too late, he could see the hit coming before the impact, almost as if it were in slow-motion. It still knocked him off his feet.

"Here's what you should know: Central took the biologist away late Friday evening. She's been gone the whole weekend. So you must have been talking to a ghost, because I know you would not lie to me, John. You wouldn't lie to me, would you?" Her look was serious, as if there were a bond between them.

Control wondered if the woman in the military jacket was back in front of the liquor store. He wondered if the skateboarder was in the process of dumping another can of dog food on the sidewalk, the plastic-bag man about to pop up to shout at passersby. He wondered if he should go join them. There was within him a generous affection for all of them, matched by a wide and growing sadness. A shed out back. Christmas lights wound around a pine. Wood storks.

No, he had not talked to the biologist that morning. Yes, he had thought she was still at the Southern Reach, had depended on that fact. He had already planned his next session in detail. It would be back in the interrogation room, not outside. She would sit there, maybe in a different mood from the other times but perhaps not, waiting for his now-familiar questions. But he wouldn't ask any questions. Time to change the paradigm, the hell with procedures.

He would have pushed her file over to her, said, "This is everything we know about you. About your husband. About your past jobs and relationships. Including a transcript of your initial interview sessions with the psychologist." This wouldn't be an easy thing for him to do: Afterward, she might become a different person than he knew; he might be letting Area X farther into the world, in some odd way. He might be betraying his mother.

She would make some remark about having outlasted him already, and he would reply that he didn't want to play games anymore, that Lowry's games had already made him weary. She would repeat the same line he had said to her out by the holding pond: "Don't thank people for giving you what you should already have." "I'm not looking for thanks," he would reply. "Of course you are," she would say, without reproach. "It's the way human beings are built."

"You had her sent away?" Said so quietly that Grace asked him to repeat it.

"You had formed too much of an attachment. You were losing your perspective."

"That wasn't your call!"

"I am not the one who sent her away."

"What do you mean?"

"Ask your supervisor, Control. Ask your cabal at Central."

"It's not my cabal," he said. Cabal versus faction. Which was worse? This was a record for not-fixing. A record for being sent in only to be shut out. He wondered what kind of bloodbath had to be occurring at Central right now.

He took a long drag on the cigarette, stared out at the god-awful swamp, heard from a distance Grace asking him if he was all right, his reply of "Give me a second."

Was he all right? In the long line of things he could legitimately be not all right about, this ranked right up there. He felt as if something had been severed far too prematurely, that there had been much more to say. He tamped down the impulse to walk back inside and call his mother, because, of course, she must already know and would just give him an amplified echo of what Grace had said, no matter how much this could be seen as Lowry punishing him: "You were getting too close to her in too short a time. You went from an interrogation scenario to having conversations with her in her cell to chewing on sedge weeds while you gave her a guided tour of the outside of the building—*in just four days*. What would have come next, John? A birthday party? A conga line? Her own private suite at the Hilton? Perhaps a little voice inside starts to say, 'Give her her files,' hmm?"

Then he would have lied and said that wasn't true or fair and she'd have fallen back on Grandpa Jack's offensive old-school line about fair being "for losers and pussies," and he wouldn't be talking about Chorry. Control would claim she was interfering with his ability to do the job she had sent him to do and she'd counter with the idea of getting him transcripts of any subsequent interviews, which would be "just as good." After which he might say, lamely, that's not the point. That he needed the support, and then he'd trail off awkwardly because he was on thin ice talking about support, and she wouldn't help him out, and he'd be stuck. They never spoke about Rachel McCarthy, but it was always there.

"So we should talk about division of duties," Grace said.

"Yes, we should." Because they both knew she now had the upper hand.

But his mind was elsewhere the whole time that Grace was massacring his troops, before she left the courtyard. Grace would run most things going forward, with John Rodriguez abdicating responsibility for all but figurehead duties at the most important status meetings. He would resubmit his recommendations through Grace, leaving out the pointless ones, and she would decide which to implement and which not to implement. They would coordinate so that eventually his working hours and Grace's working hours overlapped as little as possible. Grace would assist him in making sense of the director's notes, and as he acclimated himself to the new arrangements, that would be his major responsibility, although in no way did Grace acknowledge that the director might be dead or have gone completely off the tracks and hurtled through the underbrush over a cliff in her last days at the Southern Reach. Even as she did acknowledge that mouse-and-plant were eccentric, and also accepted the ex post facto reality that he had already painted over the director's wall beyond the door.

None of which in this rout—this retreat that had no vanguard or rearguard, but was just a group of desperate men hacking at the muck and mire of a swamp with outdated swords while Cossacks waited for them on the plain—went completely against Control's true wishes anyway, but this was not how he had seen it coming, with Grace dictating the terms of his surrender. And none of which saved him from a kind of grieving not at the power he was losing but at the person he had lost.

Still out there, smoking, after Grace had left, with a pat on his shoulder that was meant as sympathy but felt like failure. Even as he now counted her a colleague if not quite a friend. Trying to resurrect the idea of the biologist, the image of her, the sound of her voice.

"What should I do now?"

"I'm the prisoner," the biologist said to him from her cot, facing the wall. "Why should I tell you anything?"

"Because I'm trying to help you."

"Are you? Or are you just trying to help yourself?"

He had no answer to that.

"A normal person might give up. That would be very normal."

"Would you?" he asked.

"No. But I'm not normal."

"Neither am I."

"Where does that leave us?"

"Where we've always been."

But it didn't. Something had occurred to him, finally seeing the janitor. Something about a ladder and a lightbulb.

023: BREAK DOWN

ontrol found a flashlight, tested it out. Then he walked past the cafeteria that had by now become an irritating repetition, as if he had navigated across the same airport terminal for several days while chewing the same piece of gum. At the door to the storage room, he made sure the corridor was clear then quickly ducked inside.

It was dark. He fumbled for the lightbulb cord, pulled it. The light came on but didn't help much. As he'd remembered, the metal shade above the bulb and its low position, just an inch or so above his head, meant all you could see were the lower shelves. The only shelves the janitor could reach anyway. The only shelves that weren't empty, as the shadows revealed as his eyes adjusted.

He had a feeling that Whitby had been lying. That this *was* the special room Whitby had offered to show him. If he could solve no other mystery, he would solve this one. A puzzle. A diversion. Had Lowry's magical interference hastened this moment or postponed it?

Slowly the beam of his flashlight panned across the top of the shelves, then onto the ceiling, maybe nine feet above him. It had an unfinished feeling, that ceiling. Irregular and exposed, of different shades, the wooden planks were crossed by an X of two beams, and appeared to have been built around the shelves. The shelves continued to rise, empty, all the way up to the ceiling and then beyond. He could just see the gap where the next row of shelves continued, beyond the ceiling. After a moment more of inspection, Control noticed a thin, nearly invisible cut along the two beams that formed a square. A trapdoor? In the ceiling.

Control considered that. It could just lead to an air duct or more storage space, but in trying to imagine where this room existed in the layout of the building, he had to take into account that it lay just opposite Whitby's favorite spot in the cafeteria, and that this meant, if the stairs to the third level lay between them, that there could be considerable space up above, tucked in under the stairs.

He went to work looking for the ladder, found it, retractable, hidden in a back corner, under a tarp. He hit the bulb as he moved the ladder into position, dislodging dust, and the space came alive with a wild and flickering light.

At the top of the ladder, he turned on his flashlight again and, awkwardly, with his other hand, pushed against the ceiling at the center of the half-hidden square. This high, he could see that the "ceiling" was clearly a platform fitted around the shelves.

The door gave with a creak. He exhaled deeply, felt apprehensive, the ladder rungs a little slippery. He opened the door. It fell back on its coil hinges smoothly, without a sound, as if just oiled. Control shone his flashlight across the floor, then up to the shelves that rose another eight feet to either side. No one was there. He returned to the central space: the far wall and then the slant of a true ceiling.

Faces stared back at him, along with the impression of vast shapes and some kind of writing.

Control almost dropped the flashlight.

He looked again.

Along the wall and part of the ceiling, someone had painted a vast phantasmagoria of grotesque monsters with human faces. More specifically, oils splotched and splashed in a primitive style, in rich, deep reds and blues and greens and yellows, to form approximations of bodies. The pixelated faces were blown-up security head shots of Southern Reach staff.

One image dominated, extending up the wall and with the head peering down with a peculiar three-dimensional quality from the slanted ceiling. The others formed constellations around this image, and then much-worried sentences and phrases existing in a rich patina of cross-outs and paint-overs and other markings, as if someone had been creating a compost of words. There was a border, too: a ring of red fire that transformed at the ends into a two-headed monster, and Area X in its belly.

Reluctantly Control pulled himself up into the space, keeping low to distribute his weight until he was sure the platform could hold him. But it seemed sturdy. He stood next to the shelves on the left side of the room and considered the art in front of him.

The body that dominated the murals or paintings or whatever word applied depicted a creature that had the form of a giant hog and a slug commingled, pale painted skin mottled with what was meant to be a kind of mangy light green moss. The swift, broad strokes of arms and legs suggested the limbs of a pig, but with three thick fingers at their ends. More appendages were positioned along the midsection.

The head, atop a too-small neck rendered in a kind of gauzy pink-white, was misshapen but anchored by the face pasted onto it, the glue glistening in the flashlight beam. The face Control recognized from the files: the psychologist from the final eleventh expedition, a man who, before his death from cancer, had said in the transcripts, "It was quite beautiful, quite peaceful in Area X." And smiled in a vague way.

But here he had been portrayed as anything but peaceful. Using a pen, someone—Whitby? Whitby—had given the man a mask of utter, uncomprehending anguish, the mouth open in a perpetual O.

Arrayed to the right and left were more creatures—some private pantheon, some private significance—with more faces he recognized. The director had been rendered as a full-on boar, stuffed with vegetation; the assistant director as a kind of stout or ferret; Cheney as a jellyfish.

Then he found himself. Incomplete. His face taken from his recent serious-looking mug shot, and the vague body of not a white rabbit but a wild hare, the fur matted, curling, half penciled in. Around which Whitby had created the outlines of a gray-blue sea monster, a whalelike leviathan, with purple waves pushing out from it, and a huge circle of an eye that tunneled out from his face, making of him a cyclops. Radiating from the monster-body were not just the waves but also flurries of unreadable words in a cramped, crabby scrawl. As surprising and disturbing walls went, it beat the director's office by quite a lot. It made his skin prickle with sudden chills. It made him realize that he still had been half relying on Whitby's analysis to provide him with answers. But there were no answers here. Only proof that in Whitby's head was something akin to a sedimentary layer of papers bound by a plant, a dead mouse, and an ancient cell phone.

On the floor opposite him, near the right-hand shelves, a trowel, a selection of paints, a stand that allowed Whitby to reach the ceiling. A few books. A portable stove. A sleeping bag, bundled up. Had Whitby been *living* here? Without anyone knowing about it? Or guessing but not wanting to really know? Instead, just foist off Whitby on the new director. Disinformation and obfuscation. Whitby had put this together over a fairly long period of time. He had patiently been working at it, adding to it, subtracting from it. Terroir.

Control had been standing there with his back to the shelves for only about a minute.

He had been standing there recognizing that there was a draft in the loft. He had been standing there without realizing that it wasn't a draft.

Someone was breathing, behind him.

Someone was *breathing* on his neck. The knowledge froze him, froze the cry of "Jesus fuck!" in his throat.

He turned with incredible slowness, wishing he could seem like a statue in his turning. Then saw with alarm a large, pale, watery-blue eye that existed against a backdrop of darkness or dark rags shot through with pale flesh, and which resolved into Whitby.

Whitby, who had been there the entire time, crammed into the shelf right behind Control, at eye level, bent at the knees, on his side.

Breathing in shallow sharp bursts. Staring out.

Like something incubating. There, on the shelf.

At first, Control thought that Whitby must be sleeping with his eyes open. A waxwork corpse. A tailor's dummy. Then he realized that Whitby was wide awake and staring at him, Whitby's body shaking ever so slightly like a pile of leaves with something underneath it. Looking like something boneless, shoved into a too-small space.

So close that Control could have leaned over and bit his nose or kissed it.

Whitby continued to say nothing, and Control, terrified, somehow knew that there was a danger in speaking. That if he said anything that Whitby might lunge out of his hiding place, that the stiff shifting of the man's jaw hid something more premeditated and deadly.

Their eyes locked, and there was no way around the fact that each had seen the other, but still Whitby did not speak, as if he too wanted to preserve the illusion.

Slowly Control managed to direct his flashlight away from Whitby, stifling a shudder, and with a gritting of teeth overrode his every instinct not to turn his back on the man. He could feel Whitby's breath pluming out.

Then there was a slight movement and Whitby's hand came to rest on the back of his head. Just resting there, palm flat against Control's hair. The fingers spread like a starfish and slowly moved back and forth. Two strokes. Three. Petting Control's head. Caressing it in a gentle, tentative way.

Control remained still. It took an effort.

After a time, the hand withdrew, with a kind of reluctance. Control took two steps forward, then another. Another. Whitby did not erupt out of his space. Whitby did not make some inhuman sound. Whitby did not try to pull him back into the shelves.

He reached the trapdoor without succumbing to a shudder, lowered himself legs-first into that space, found the ladder with his feet. Slowly pulled the door closed, not looking toward the shelves, even in the dark. Felt such relief with it closed, then scrambled down the ladder. Hesitated, then took the time to lower and fold away the ladder. Forced himself to listen at the door before he left the room, leaving the flashlight in there. Then walked out into the bright, bright corridor, squinting, and took in a huge breath that had him seeing dark spots, a convulsion he could not control and wanted no one to see.

After about fifty steps, Control realized that Whitby had been up in the space without using the ladder. Imagined Whitby crawling through the air ducts. His white face. His white hands. Reaching out.

In the parking lot, Control bumped into a jovial apparition who said, "You look like you've seen a ghost!" He asked this apparition if he had heard anything strange in the building over the years, or seen anything out of the ordinary. Inserted it as small talk, as breathing space, in what he hoped was just a curious or joking way. But Cheney flunked the question, said, "Well, it's the high ceilings, isn't it? Makes you see things that aren't there. Makes the things you do see look like other things. A bird can be a bat. A bat can be a piece of floating plastic bag. Way of the world. To see things as other things. Bird-leafs. Bat-birds. Shadows made of lights. Sounds that are incidental but seem more significant. Never going to seem any different wherever you go."

A bird can be a bat. A bat can be a piece of floating plastic bag. But could it?

It struck Control—hard—that he might not have Cheney any more sussed out than Whitby—a hastily prepared facade that was receding across the parking lot, walking backward to speak a few more words at him, none of which Control really heard.

Then, starting the engine and released past the security gate, almost without a memory of the drive, or of parking along the river walk, Control was mercifully free of the Southern Reach and found himself down by the Hedley pier. He explored the river walk for a while, so far inside his head he didn't really see the shops or people or the water beyond.

His trance, his bubble of no-thought, was punctured by a little girl shouting, "You're getting here too late!" Relief when he realized she wasn't talking to him, her father walking past him then to claim her.

Where he wound up was little better than a dive bar, but dark and spacious, with pool tables in the back. Somewhere nearby was the pontoon dock from his Tuesday jog. Up a hill lay his house, but he wasn't ready to go back yet. Control ordered a whiskey neat, once the bartender had finished being hit on by a good old boy who looked a little like an aging version of the first-string quarterback from high school.

"He was a smooth talker, but way too many neck folds," Control said, and she laughed, although he'd said it with venom.

"I couldn't hear what he was saying—the wattles were too loud," she said.

He chuckled, drawn out of his thoughts for a moment. "What're you doin' tonight, honey? Am I right that you're doin' it with me?" Imitating the man's terrible pickup line.

"I'm sleeping tonight. Falling asleep now."

"Me, too," he said, still chuckling. But he could feel her gaze on him, curious, as she turned back to washing glasses. Their conversation hadn't been any longer than the ones he'd had with Rachel McCarthy, so many years ago. Or about anything more substantial.

The TV was on low, showing the aftermath of massive floods and a school massacre in between commercials for a big basketball series. Behind him he could hear a group of women talking. "I'm going to believe you for now . . . because I don't have any better theories." "What do we do now?" "I'm not ready to go back. Not yet." "You prefer this place, you really do, don't you?" He couldn't have said why their chatter bothered him, but he moved farther down the bar. The divide between their understanding of the world and his, perhaps already wide, had grown exponentially in the last week.

He knew if he went home, he'd start thinking about Whitby the Deranged, except he couldn't stop thinking about Whitby anyway, because he had to do something about Whitby tomorrow. It was just a matter of how to handle it.

Whitby had been at the Southern Reach for so long. Whitby had not hurt anyone at any point during his service for the Southern Reach. *Service* preamble to thinking about how to say "Thank you for your service, for your many years. Now take your weird art and get the fuck out."

Even as he had so many other things to do, and still no call from his mother about the director's house. Even as he nursed the wound of losing the biologist. The Voice had said Whitby was unimportant, and remembering that, Control felt that Lowry had said it with a kind of familiarity, like how you'd dismiss someone you'd worked with for a length of time.

Before leaving the Southern Reach for Hedley, he had taken a closer look at Whitby's document on terroir. Found that when you did that—trained an eye that did not skim—it began to fall apart. That the normal-sounding subsection titles and the preambles that cited other sources hid a core where the imagination became unhinged, unconcerned with the words that had tried to fence it in, to guide it along. Monsters peered out with a regularity that seemed earned given the video from the first expedition, but perhaps not earned in the right direction. He stopped reading at a certain point. It was at a section where Whitby described the border as "invisible skin," and those who tried to pass through it without using the door trapped forever in a vast stretch of *otherwhere* hundreds of miles wide. Even though the steps by which Whitby had gotten to this point had seemed, for a time, sobering and deliberate.

And then there was Lowry. He'd asked Cheney about Lowry in the parking lot, too, Cheney giving Control a rare frown. "Lowry? Come back here? Not now. Not ever, I would think." Why? A pause, like questing static on the line. "Well, he's damaged. Saw things that none of us will hopefully ever see. Can't get close to it, can't escape it. He's found his appropriate distance, you could say." Lowry, creating a web of incantations, spells, whatever, could create more of a shield between himself and Area X, because he couldn't ever forget, either. Needing to see, but too afraid to look, passing his fear on to others. Whitby's distance much closer, his spells of a more visceral nature.

By contrast, all of the ceaseless, restless notes from the director were staid, practical, stolid, and yet in the end—ordering a boilermaker after his shot, to make his next shot go down easy—they were probably meaningless, as useless as Whitby's terroir that would never explain a goddamn thing, that amounted to a kind of religion, because even with all of her additional context, the director still had not found the answer as far as he could tell.

He rasped out a request for another drink.

That would probably be his fate: to catalogue the notes of others and create his own, ceaselessly and without effect. He would develop a paunch and marry some local woman who had already been married once. They would raise a family in Hedley, a son and a daughter, and on weekends he would be fully present with his family, work a distant memory that lay across the border known as Monday. They would grow old in Hedley, while he worked at the Southern Reach, putting in his hours and counting the years, the months, the days until retirement. They would give him a gold watch and a few pats on the back and by then his knees would be shot from all the jogging so he would be sitting down, and he'd be balding a little.

And he still wouldn't know what to do about Whitby. And he would still miss the biologist. And he might still not know what was going on in Area X.

The drunk man came up and shook him out of his thoughts with a slap on his back. "You look like I know you. You look kinda familiar. What's your name, pardner?"

"Rat Poison," Control said.

The truth was, if the man who looked like the high school quarterback had responded by turning into something monstrous and torn him out into the night, part of Control wouldn't have minded because he would have been closer to the truth about Area X, and even if the truth was a fucking maw, a fanged maw that stank like a cave full of putrefying corpses, that was still closer than he was now.

00X

When Control left the house on Tuesday morning, the director's beetle-phone lay on his welcome mat. It had returned to him. Looking down at it, hand on the half-open front door, he could not help seeing it as a sign . . . but a sign of what?

Chorry jumped past him and into the bushes while Control squatted down to get a closer look. Days and nights out in the yard hadn't helped it much. The grotesquery of the thing . . . some animal had gnawed at the casing and it was smeared with dirt and grass stains. Now it looked more like something alive than it had before. It looked like something that had gone exploring or burrowing and come back to report in.

Under the phone, thankfully, was a note from the landlord. In a quivering scrawl she had written, "The lawn man found this yesterday. Please dispose of phones in the garbage if you are done with them."

He tossed it into the bushes.

In the morning light, during that ever-longer walk through the doors and down the corridor to his office, Control's recollection of Whitby on the rack, stuffed into a shelf, the disturbing art on the wall, took on a slightly changed, more forgivable texture: a long-term disintegration whose discovery had urgency to him personally but for the Southern Reach was just one symptom of many seeking ways to take Whitby out of the "sinister" file and place him under "needs our help."

Still, in his office, he wrestled with what to do about Whitby—did the man fall under his jurisdiction or Grace's? Would she be resistant, slough it off, say something like "Oh, that Whitby"? Maybe together, he and Grace would go up into Whitby's secret room and have a good laugh about the grotesqueries to be found there, and then jointly paint it all white again. Then they'd go have lunch with Cheney and Hsyu and play board games and share their mutual love of water polo. Hsyu would say, as if he'd already disagreed with her, "We shouldn't take the meaning of words for granted!" and he would shout back, "You mean a word like *border*?" and she would reply, "Yes, that's exactly what I mean! You get it! You understand!" Followed by an impromptu square dance, dissolving into a chaos of thousands of glowing green ferns and black glittering mayflies gusting across their path.

Or not.

With a snarl of frustration, Control put aside the question of Whitby and buried himself again in the director's notes, kept Grace's intel about the director's focus in mind while trying to divine from those dried entrails more than they might actually contain. From Whitby, he wanted for the moment only distance and time so that there would be no hand reaching out to him.

He returned to the lighthouse, based on what Grace had told him. What was the purpose of a lighthouse? To warn of danger, to guide coastal vessels, and to provide landfall for ships. What did it mean to the Southern Reach, to the director?

Among the layers in the locked drawer, the most prominent concerned the lighthouse, and that included pages he had confirmed with Grace came from an investigation that was inextricably tied to the history of the island to the north. That island had had numerous names, as if none would stick, until now it was simply known as Island X at the Southern Reach, although some called it "Island Y," as in "Why are we bothering to research this?"

What did fascinate—even resonate—was the fact that the beacon in the lighthouse on the coast had originally been placed in a lighthouse built on Island X. But shipping lanes had shifted and no one needed a lighthouse that helped ships navigate the shallows. The old lighthouse fell into ruin, but its eye had been removed long before.

As Grace had noted, the beacon interested the director the most: a first-order lens that constituted not just a remarkable engineering feat but also a work of art. More than two thousand separate lenses and prisms had been mounted inside a brass framework. The light from at first a lamp and then a lightbulb was reflected and refracted by the lenses and prisms to be cast seaward.

The entire apparatus could be disassembled and shipped in sections. The "light characteristics" could be manipulated in almost every conceivable way. Bent, straightened, sent bouncing off surfaces in a recursive loop so that it never reached the outside. Sent sideways. Sent down onto the spiraling steps leading up to the top. Beamed into outer space. Slanted past the open trapdoor, where lay so many journal accounts from so many expeditions.

An alarming note that Control dismissed because he had no room left in his brain for harmful speculation, x-ed out and crumpled on the back of a ticket for a local Bleakersville production of some atrocity called *Hamlet Unbound*: "More journals exist than accounted for by expedition members." He hadn't seen anywhere a report on the number of journals, no count on that.

The Séance & Science Brigade, which had operated along that coast since the fifties, had been obsessed with the twin lighthouses. And as if the S&SB had shared something personally with her, the director had zeroed in on the beacon's history, even though the Southern Reach as an institution had already ruled it out as "evidence pertaining to the creation of Area X." The number of ripped-out pages and circled passages in a book entitled *Famous Lighthouses* noted that the beacon had been shipped over just prior to the states dissolving into civil war, from a manufacturer whose name had been lost along the way. The "mysterious history" included the beacon being buried in the sand to keep it away from one side or another, then sent up north, then appearing down south, and eventually popping up at Island X on the forgotten coast. Control didn't find the history mysterious so much as hectic, overbusy, thinking of the amount of effort that had gone into carting and dragging this beacon, even in its constituent pieces, all over the country. The number of miles the beacon had traveled before finding a permanent home—that was really the only mystery, along with why anyone had thought to describe the fog signal as sounding like "two large bulls hung up by their tails."

Yet this had captivated the director, or seemed to have, roughly around the time of the planning for the twelfth expedition, if he could trust the dates on the article excerpts. Which did not interest Control as much as the fact that the director kept annotating, amending, adding data and fragments of accounts from sources she did not accredit—these sources maddeningly not in Grace's DMP archive and not alluded to in any of the notes he had looked through. This frustrated him. The banality of it, too, as if ceaselessly reviewing what she already knew for something she felt she had missed. Was the message coming down to Control from the director that he should resurrect old lines of inquiry, or that the Southern Reach had run out of ideas, had begun to endlessly recycle, feeding on itself?

How Control hated his own imagination, wished it would just shrivel up and turn brown and fall out of him. He was more willing to believe that something was staring out at him from the notes, something hidden looking at him, than to accept that the director had been pursuing dead ends. And yet he couldn't see it; he could still only see her searching, and wonder why she was searching so hard.

On impulse, he took down all of the framed images on the far wall and searched them for anything hidden—took off the back mats, disassembled them entirely. But he found nothing. Just the reeds, the lighthouse, the lighthouse keeper, his assistant, and the girl staring out at him from more than thirty years ago.

In the afternoon, he turned to Grace's DMP file, cross-checking it against the piles of notes. Which, because it was a proprietary program, meant that he was clicking Ctrl to go from page to page. Ctrl was beginning to seem the only control he actually had. Ctrl only had one role, and it performed that role stoically and without complaint. He hit Ctrl with ever more malice and force, even though every hour that he looked at the notes rather than dealt with Whitby seemed a kind of blessing. Every hour that Whitby didn't show his face, even though his car remained in the parking lot. Did Whitby want help? Did he know he needed help? Someone needed to tell Whitby what he had become. Could Grace tell him? Could Cheney? No. They had not told him yet.

Ctrl Ctrl Ctrl. Always too many pages. Ctrl this. Ctrl that. Ctrl crescendos and arias. Ctrl always clicking past information, because the information he found on the screen seemed to lead nowhere anyway, while the vast expanse of clutter that spread out in waves from his desk to the far wall contained too much.

His office began to close in on him. Listless pushing around of files and pretend efforts to straighten bookshelves had given way to further Internet searches on the places the biologist had worked before joining the twelfth expedition. This activity had proven more calming, each vista of wilderness more beautiful than the last. But eventually the parallels to the pristine landscape of Area X had begun to encroach and the bird's-eye view of some of the photographs reminded him of that final video clip.

He took a break around five, then went back to his office for a while, after short, friendly conversations with Hsyu and Cheney in the corridor. Although Hsyu seemed flushed, talking a bit too fast for some reason, her aspect ratio skewed. Cheney's big catcher's mitt of a hand had rested on Control's shoulder for an uncomfortable second or two, as the man said, "A second week! Which is a good sign, surely? We hope you find it all to your liking. We're open to change. We're open to changes, if you know what I mean, once you've heard what we have to say. And how we say it." The words almost made sense, but somehow Cheney was off today, too. Control had had days like that.

That left only the problem of Whitby; he hadn't seen him the whole afternoon, and Whitby hadn't responded to e-mails, either. It felt important to get it over with, not to let it slide into Wednesday. The *how* had become clear to him, along with what was fair and what wasn't fair. He would do it in front of Cheney in the science division, and leave Grace out of it. This had become his responsibility, his mess, and Cheney would just have to go along with his decision. Whitby would be forced to accept a leave of absence and psychiatric counseling, and with any luck the strange little man would never return.

It was late, already after six. He had lost track of time, or it had lost track of him. The office was still a mess corresponding to the contours of the director's brain, Grace's DMP files not changing those contours in any useful way.

He took Whitby's terroir manuscript with him, feeling that perhaps selective readings from it would convince Whitby of the problem. He again crossed the wide expanse of the cafeteria. The huge cafeteria windows gathered up the gray of the sky and pushed it down onto the tables, the chairs; it would rain again before long. The tables were empty. The little dark bird or bat had stopped flying and sat perched high up on a steel beam near the windows. "There's something on the floor." "Have you ever seen anything like that?" Fragments of conversation as he passed by the door to the kitchen, and then a kind of sharp but faint weeping sound. For a moment, it puzzled Control. Then he realized it must come from some machine being operated by the cafeteria staff.

Something else had been gnawing at Control for much longer, as if he'd forgotten his wallet or other essential item when he'd left the house. But it now resolved, the weeping sound pushing it into his conscious mind. An absence. The rotting honey smell was gone. In fact, he realized he hadn't smelled rotting honey the entire day, no matter where he had been. Had Grace at least passed on that recommendation?

He turned the corner into the corridor leading to the science division, kept walking under the fluorescent lights, immersed in a rehearsal of what he would say to Whitby, anticipating what Whitby might say back, or not say, feeling the weight of the man's insane manuscript.

Control reached out for the large double doors. Reached for the handle, missed it, tried again.

But there were no doors where there had always been doors before. Only wall.

And the wall was soft and breathing under the touch of his hand.

He was screaming, he thought, but from somewhere deep beneath the sea.

AFTERLIFE

ontrol, at the heart of a different tragedy, could see nothing but Rachel McCarthy with a bullet in her head, falling endlessly into the quarry. The sense of nothing being real during that time. That the room they had put him in, and the investigator assigned to him, were both constructs, and if he just kept holding on to that thought eventually the investigator would dissolve into nothing and the walls of his cell would fall away, and he would walk out into a world that was real. Then and only then would he wake up to continue with his life, which would follow the path it had followed to that point.

Even though the chair for the long hours of questioning cut into the back of his thigh and left a mark. Even though he smelled the bitter cigarette smoke on the investigator's jacket, and heard the hiccupping whir of the tape in the recorder the man had brought in as a backup for the room's video recording.

Even though the texture of the wall felt like a manta ray from the aquarium: firm and smooth, with a serrated roughness but with more give, and behind it the sense of something vast, breathing in and out. A rupture into the world of the rotted honey smell, fading fast but hard to forget. Like the swirling flourish of a line of balsamic on a chef's plate. The line of dark blood leading to a corpse on a cop show.

His parents had read "Tiger, Tiger, burning bright" to him as a child. They had collaborated on a social studies project with him, his mother on research and his father on cut-and-paste. They had taught him how to ride a bike. The pathetic little Christmas tree next to the shed linked forever now to the first holiday season he could remember. Standing on the pier in Hedley, looking across the river led to the lake by the cottage where he would fish with his grandpa. Naming the sculptures in his father's backyard became a chess set on the mantel. The wall was still breathing, though, no matter what he did. The impact of a long-ago linebacker's helmet to the chest during a scrimmage, surfacing only now so that he had trouble breathing, all the air knocked out of his lungs.

Control didn't remember leaving the corridor but had recovered himself in mid-sprint toward the cafeteria. Whitby's terroir manuscript clenched in a viselike grip. He meant to retrieve some other things from his office. He meant to go into his office and retrieve some other things. His office. His other things.

He was pulling every fire alarm he passed. He was shouting over the klaxon at people who weren't there to leave. Disbelief. Shock. Trapped inside his head the way some were trapped in the science division.

But in the cafeteria he was running so fast he slipped and fell. When he got up, he saw Grace, holding open the door leading to the courtyard. Someone to tell. Someone to tell. There was only wall. There was only wall.

He shouted her name, but Grace did not turn, and as he came up on her, he saw that she stared at someone slowly walking up from the edge of the courtyard through a thick rain, against the burnt umber of the singed edges of the swamp beyond. A tall, dark outline lit by the late-afternoon sun, shining through the downpour. He would recognize her anywhere by now. Still in her expedition clothes. So close to a gnarled tree behind her that at first she had merged with it in the gray of the rain. And she was still making her way to Grace. And Grace, in three-quarter profile there in front of her, smiling, body taut with anticipation. This false return, this corrupted reunion. This end of everything.

For the director trailed plumes of emerald dust and behind her the nature of the world was changing, filling with a brightness, the rain losing its depth, its darkness. The thickness of the layers of the rain getting lost, taken away, no longer there.

The border was coming to the Southern Reach.

In the parking lot, shoving the key into the ignition, office forgotten, not wanting to look back. Not wanting to see if an invisible wave was about to overtake him. Still cars in the parking lot, still people inside, but he didn't care. He was leaving. He was done. A scrabbling, broken-nail panic at the thought of being trapped there. Forever. Shouting at the car to start after it had already started.

He raced for the gates—open, no security, no sound from behind him at all. Just a vast silence, snuffing out thought. His hands were curled, clawlike, finger-nails dragging into his palms as he clutched the wheel.

Speeding, not caring about anything but making it to Hedley, even though he knew that might not be any kind of choice at all. Pulling out his phone, dropping it, but not stopping, groping for it as he reached the highway, screeched onto the on-ramp, relieved to see normal traffic. He stifled a dozen impulses—to stop the car and use it to block off the exit, to roll down his window in the rain and shout out a warning to the other motorists. Stifled any impulse that impeded the deep and impervious instinct to get away.

Two fighter jets roared overhead, but he couldn't see them.

He kept changing the radio channels to current news reports. Not sure what would be reported, but wanting something to be reported even though it was still happening, hadn't finished yet. Nothing. No one. Kept trying to get the feel of the wall off his hand, wiping it against the seats, the steering wheel, his pants. Would have plunged it into dog shit to get the feeling off.

When he'd turned away from Grace, he'd seen that Whitby occupied his usual seat in the back of the cafeteria, under the photograph of the old days. But Whitby came in only intermittently now, the transmission garbled. Some of the words in tone and texture still recalled human speech. Others recalled the video from the first expedition. Whitby had failed some fundamental test, had crossed some Rubicon and now sat there, jaw oddly elongated as he tried to get words out, alone, beyond Control's help. He realized then, or at some point later, that maybe Whitby wasn't just crazy. That Whitby had become a breach, a leak, a door into Area X, expressed as an elongated equation over time . . . and if the director had now come back to the Southern Reach, it wasn't because of or for Grace, it was because Whitby had been calling out to her like a human beacon. This version of her that had returned.

Trapped by his thoughts. That the Southern Reach hadn't been a redoubt but instead some kind of slow incubator. That finding Whitby's shrine might have triggered something. That placing trust in a word like *border* had been a mistake, a trap. A slow unraveling of terms unrecognized until too late.

Whitby's gaze had followed him in his flight toward the front entrance, and Control had run almost sideways to make sure Whitby never left his view until the corner took him. He could see the leviathans from his dream clearly now, staring at him, seeing him with an awful clarity. He had not escaped their attention.

Calling his mother. Hypnotize me. Hypnotize this out of me. Unable to reach her. Leaving messages shouted out, half-coherent.

The corridor leading into Hedley in the banality of rush-hour traffic. The mundane quality of the rain coming down, feeling the pressure behind him. Tried to control his breathing. Every bit of advice his mother had ever given him had gotten knocked out of his head.

Had it stopped? Had the director stopped? Or was it still onrushing?

Was an invisible blot now seeping out across the world?

Already reviewing in his mind, as he began to recover, began to function, what he could have done differently. What, if anything, might have made a difference, or if it was always going to happen like this. In this universe. On this day.

"I'm sorry," he said inside the car—to no one, to Grace, to Cheney, even to Whitby. "I'm sorry." But for what? What was his role in this?

As he reached the bottom of the hill, leading up to his house, the radio reports began to reflect his reality in slivers and glints of light. Something had occurred at the military base, perhaps related to the "continuing environmental clean-up efforts." There had been an odd glow and odd sounds and gunfire. But no one knew anything. Not for sure.

Except that Control now knew the thing that had been eluding him, hiding in the deeper waters for him to recognize it. Revealed now, too late to do any good. For, in the stooped shoulders and the tilt of the director's head—there, approaching, in the flesh—Control had finally realized that the girl in the photograph with the lighthouse keeper was the director as a child. There was a kind of slouch or lurch to the shoulders that, despite the different perspectives and the difference in years, was unmistakable if you were looking for it. Now that he could see it, he couldn't unsee it. There, hiding in plain sight in the photograph from the director's wall, was a photograph of the director as a child, taken by the S&S Brigade, standing side by side with Saul Evans, whose words decorated the wall of the topographical anomaly in living tissue. She had looked at that photo every day in her office. She had chosen to place that photograph there. She had chosen to live in Bleakersville, in a house full of heirlooms probably owned by someone on her mother's side of the family. Who at the Southern Reach had known? Or had this been another conspiracy of one, and the director had hidden that connection all on her own?

Assuming he was right, she had been at the lighthouse right before the Event. She had gotten out before the border came down. She knew the forgotten coast like she knew herself. There were things that she'd never had to put down on paper, just because of who she was, where she came from.

For all Control knew, the director had been one of the last people to see Saul Evans alive.

He pulled up in front of the house, sat there a moment, feeling beat-up, drained, unable to process what was happening. Sweat dripped off him, his shirt drenched, his blazer lost, back at the Southern Reach. He got out of the car, searched the hidden horizon beyond the river. Was that a faint flare-up of light? Was that the muffled echo of explosions, or his imagination?

When he turned to the porch, a woman was standing on the steps next to the cat. He felt relief more than surprise.

"Hello, Mother."

She looked almost the same as always, but the high fashion had a slight bulk to it, which meant under the chic dark red jacket she probably had on some sort of light body armor. She'd also be carrying. Her hair was pulled back in a pony-tail, which made the lines of her face more severe. Her features bore the stress of an ongoing puzzlement and pain of some kind.

"Hello, Son," she said, as he brushed by her.

Control let her talk at him as he opened the front door, then went into the bed-room and began to pack. Most of his clothes were still clean and folded in the draw-ers. It was easy to fit some of them quickly and neatly into his suitcase. To pack his toiletries from the adjoining bathroom, to get out the briefcase full of money, passports, guns, and credit cards. Wondering what to bring with him from the living room, in terms of personal effects. Definitely a piece from the chessboard. He wasn't hearing much of what his mother was saying, stayed focused on the task in front of him. In doing it perfectly.

Grace had stood there waiting to receive the director and he had pleaded with her to leave, pleaded with her to turn from the door and to run like hell for some kind of safety. But she wouldn't do it, wouldn't let him pull her away, had summoned a reserve of strength that was too much against his panic. But let him see the gun concealed in a shoulder holster, as if that might be a comfort. "I have my orders and they are no concern of yours." As he fell out of her orbit, fell free of everything at the Southern Reach.

His mother forced him to stop packing, closed the suitcase, which he had piled too high anyway, and took his hand, put something in it.

"Take this," she said.

A pill. A little white pill.

"What is it?"

"Just take it."

"Why not just hypnotize me?"

She ignored him, guided him to a chair in the corner. He sat there, heavy and cold in his own sweat. "We will talk after you take the pill. After you take a shower." Said in a sharp tone, the one she used with him to cut off discussion or debate.

"I don't have time for a shower," he said. Staring at the wallpaper, which began to blur. Now he would inhabit the very center of corridors. He would put no hand to any surface. He would behave like a ghost that knew if it made contact with anyone or anything its touch would slide through and that creature would then know that it existed in a state of purgatory.

Severance slapped him hard across the face, and he could hear right again.

"You've had a shock. I can see that you've had a shock, Son. I've had a few myself the last few hours. But I need you to start thinking again. I need you *present*."

He looked up at her, so like and unlike his mother.

"Okay," he said. "Okay." He took the pill, lurched to his feet while he had the will, headed for the bathroom. There had been nothing recognizable in the director's eyes. Nothing at all.

In the shower, he started to cry because he still couldn't get the feel of the wall off his hand, no matter how hard he tried. Couldn't shake the thinning of the rain, the look on Whitby's face, Grace's rigid stance, or the fact it had all happened only an hour ago and he was still trying to piece it together.

But when he stumbled out, dried himself off, and put on a T-shirt and jeans, he felt calmer, almost normal. There was still a slight wobble, but the pill must have kicked in.

He used hand sanitizer, but the texture remained on his hand like an unshakable phantom.

His mother was making coffee in the kitchen, but he went past her without a word, through the sudden cold of the air-conditioning vent, and opened the front door, letting in a blast of humidity and heat.

It had stopped raining. He could see down to the river, to a horizon that held, somewhere, the Southern Reach. Everything was quiet and still, but there were vague coronas of green light, of purple light, that shouldn't be there. A vision of whatever was in Area X spilling out over the land, spreading out across the river to Hedley.

"You won't see much from here," his mother said from behind him. "They're still attempting containment."

"How far has it spread?" he asked, shaking a bit as he closed the door and entered the kitchen. He took a sip of the coffee she had set in front of him. It was bitter but it took his mind off his hand.

"I won't lie, John. It's bad. The Southern Reach is lost. The new border isn't far beyond the gates. They're all trapped in there." The suggestion of the rain *thinning* behind the director. Grace, Whitby, who knew who else, caught up in a true nightmare now. "It might stop there, for a very long time."

"You're full of shit," he said. "You don't know what it will do."

"Or it might speed up. You're right—we can't know."

"That's right—we can't. I was there, right in the middle of it. I saw it coming." Because *you put me there*. A howl inside of betrayal, and then a thought that struck him when he saw the tired, worried look on her face. "But there's more, isn't there? Something more you haven't told me." There always was.

Even now she hesitated, didn't want to divulge a secret classified in a country that might not exist in a week. Then said in a flat voice, "The contamination at the sites from which we extracted the surveyor and the anthropologist has broken through quarantine and continued to grow, despite our best efforts."

"Jesus Christ," he said.

Even through the dulling effects of the pill, he wanted to be rid of his itching brain, his ignited skin, the flesh beneath, to in some way become so ethereal and unbound to the earth that he could unsee, disavow, disavow.

"What kind of contamination?" Although he thought he knew.

"The kind that cleanses everything. The kind you can't see until it's too late."

"There's nothing you can do?"

A rasping laugh escaped her, like she was trying to cough something up. "What are we going to do, John? Are we going to combat it by starting a mining operation there? Pollute those places to hell and back? Put traces of heavy metals in the water supply?"

He just stared at her, unbelieving. "Why the *fuck* did you station me at the Southern Reach if you knew this could happen?"

"I wanted you close to it. I wanted you to know, because that protects you."

"That *protects* me? Against the end of the world?"

"Maybe. Maybe it does. *And* we needed fresh eyes," she said, leaning beside him against the kitchen counter. He always forgot how slight she was, how thin. "I needed *your* fresh eyes. I couldn't know that things would change this fast."

"But you had a clue it might."

She kept letting drop bits of information. Was he meant to pick them up, like the gun under the seat, just because she was unraveling?

"Yes, I had a clue, John. It's why we sent you. Why a few of us thought we needed to do something."

"Like Lowry."

"Yes, like Lowry." Lowry, hiding back at Central, unable to face what had happened, as if the videos were now spilling into real life.

"You let him hypnotize me. You let them *condition* me." Unable to suppress his resentment at that, even now. He might never know the extent of it.

"I'm sorry, but that was the trade-off, John," she said, resolute, sticking to her story. "That was the trade-off. I got the person I want for the job, Lowry got some kind of . . . control. And you got protection, in a way."

Derisive, thinking he knew the answer: "How many others are there at Central, Mother? In this faction?"

"Mostly just us, John—Lowry and me—but Lowry has allies, many," she said in a small voice.

Just them. A cabal of two against a cabal of one, the director. And none of them seeming to have it right. And now all of it in ruins.

"What else?" Pushing to punish her, because he didn't want to think about the idea of localized Area Xs.

A bitter laugh. "We back-checked the extraction locations of the members of the last eleventh expedition to see if they exhibit a similar effect. We found nothing. So now we think they probably had a different purpose. And that purpose was to contaminate the Southern Reach itself. We had clues before. We just didn't interpret them the right way, couldn't agree on what it all meant. We just needed a little more time, a little more data." Bodies that had decomposed "a little faster" as Grace had put it, when the director had ordered them exhumed.

There was in his mother's fragmentation the admission that Central's was a soul-crushing failure. That they had been unable to conceive of a scenario in which Area X was smarter, more insidious, more resourceful.

None of this could obliterate the look on Grace's face, in the rain, as the director approached—the elation, the vindication, the abstract idea, viscerally expressed across her features, that sacrifice, that loyalty, that diligence would now be rewarded.

As if the physical manifestation of a friend and colleague long thought dead could erase the recent past. The director, followed by that unnatural silence. Were her eyes closed, or did she not have eyes anymore? The emerald dust splashed off her into the air, onto the ground, with each step. This person who should not have been there, this shell of a soul of whom he had uncovered only fragments.

His mother started over, and he let her because he had no choice, needed time to acclimate, to adjust. "Imagine a situation, John, in which you are trying to contain something dangerous. But you suspect that containment is a losing game. That what you want to contain is escaping slowly, inexorably. That what seems impermeable is, in fact, over time becoming very permeable. That the divide is more perforated than unperforated. And that whatever this thing is seems to want to destroy you but has no leader to negotiate with, no stated goals of any kind." It was almost a speech he could imagine the director giving.

"You mean the Southern Reach, the place you sent me into. With the wrong tools."

"I mean that the group I've been part of has believed for a while now that the Southern Reach might be compromised, but the majority have believed, until today, that this wasn't just wrong but laughably ridiculous."

"How did you get involved?"

"Because of you, John. Long ago. Because of needing an assignment to a place near where you and your father lived." Volunteered: "It was a side project. Something to watch, to keep an eye on. That became the main course."

"But why did it have to be me?"

"I told you." Pleading for him to understand: "I know you, John. I know who you are. I'd know if you . . . changed."

"Like the biologist changed." Burning now, that she'd put him in harm's way without telling him, without giving him the choice. Except, he'd had a choice: He could have stayed where he was, continued to believe he lived beyond the border when that was a lie.

"Something like that."

"Or just changed as in became more cynical, jaded, paranoid, or burned-out."

"Stop it."

"Why should I?"

"I did the best I could."

"Yeah."

"Growing up, I mean, John. I did the best I could, considering. But you're still angry. Even now, you're still angry. It's too much. It's too much." Talking around the edge of a catastrophe. But wasn't that what people did, if you were still alive?

He put his coffee down. There was a knot in his shoulders that might never come out. "I'm not thinking about that. That doesn't matter. It doesn't matter now."

"It matters most of all now," she said, "because I may never see you again." Her voice, for the only time he could remember, breaking up.

The weight of that hit him hard, and he knew it was true, and he felt for a moment as if he were falling. The enormity, the impossibility of it, was too much. How it had come to this point, he barely knew, even though he had been there every step of the way.

He brought her close, held her, as she whispered in his ear: "*I took my eye off things. I thought the director agreed with us. I thought I could handle Lowry. I thought we would work through it. I thought we had more time.*" That the problem was smaller. That somehow it was containable. That somehow she wouldn't be hurting him.

His mother. His handler. But after a moment he had to let her go. No way to fully cross that divide, to heal everything that needed to be healed. Not now.

She told him one more thing, then, delivered to him like a penance.

"John, you should know that the biologist escaped our custody over the weekend. She's been AWOL for the past three days."

An elation, a surge of an unwarranted, selfish euphoria that came in part from having banished her from his thoughts as the nightmare at the Southern Reach played out—and now his reward, that she had, in a way, been returned to him.

All of the rest of the answers to his questions rose up later, long after his mother had left in his car, after he had packed, reluctantly abandoned the cat, took her car, as she had suggested. But he stopped on a quiet street a few blocks away and hot-wired another car because he didn't trust Central. Soon he was outside of Hedley, in the middle of nowhere. He felt the absence of his father terribly as he passed where they had lived. Because his father might have been a comfort now. Because now it didn't matter what secrets he told or didn't tell.

At the airport about ninety miles away, in a city big enough to have international connections, he left his vehicle in the parking lot along with his guns and booked two tickets. One was to Honduras, with a layover on the west coast. The other had two layovers and wound up about two hundred miles from the coast. The second he bought under an alias. He checked in for Honduras, then sat in the airport bar, nursing a whiskey, waiting for the puddle jumper. Apocalyptic visions of what Area X would absorb if it moved forward came to him. Buildings, roads, lakes, valleys, airports. Everything. He scanned the closed-caption televisions for any news, trying to outthink the people from Central who might be on her trail, might already have picked up her trail. If he was the biologist, he would have train-hopped to start, which meant he might easily catch up with her. From where she'd escaped, she had just as far to travel as he did.

A blond woman at the bar asked him what he did and he said, recklessly, without thought, "A marine biologist." "Oh, with the government." "No, freelance," which sounded absurd after he'd said it. Then spent long minutes putting distance between himself and the subject. Because he wanted to stay there, at the bar, around people but not involved with them.

"How'd she escape?" he'd asked his mother.

"Let's just say she's stronger than she looks, and very resourceful." Had his mother given her the resources? The time? The opportunity? He hadn't wanted to ask. "Central suspects she will return to the empty lot because of the lack of contamination at that site."

But he knew that wasn't where she would go.

"Is that what you think?" his mother asked.

"Yes," he said.

No, she would go north, she would go to the wilderness above the town of Rock Bay, even if she didn't believe she was the biologist. She would go somewhere personal to her. Because she felt the urge, not because Area X wanted her to. If she had been right, if she'd been their true soldier, she would have been as mind-wiped as the others.

At least, that's what he chose to believe. To have a reason for his packing, and a place to think of as a sanctuary. Or a hiding place.

They announced boarding for his flight. He was headed west, yes, but he'd step out at the first connecting flight, rent a car from there, take that rental to another, then perhaps steal a car, always the arc going south, south, suggesting a slow descent. But then he'd go dark completely and head north.

He'd actually pulled at Grace to get her away, had taken her hand and pulled her off-balance, would have dragged her if he'd been able. Shouted at her. Given her all the reasons, the primal, visceral reasons. But Grace couldn't see any of it, wrenched away from him with a stare that made him give up. Because it was self-aware. Because she was going to see it through to the end, and he couldn't do that. Because he really wasn't the director. So he let Grace fade away into the rain as the director came up toward the door and he retreated in mindless panic to the cafeteria and then out to his car. And he didn't feel guilty about any of it.

A beep from his phone told him that, coming in over some unimaginable distance, he had received the last, useless videos from the Southern Reach, from the chicken and the goat.

The footage told him nothing, gave him no closure, no sense of what might have happened to Grace. The quality was grainy, indistinct. Each clip was about six seconds in duration and each cut off at the same time. In the first, his chair sat empty until the very end, when something blurred appeared to sit down. It might have been the director but the outline was ill-defined. The other video showed a slumped Whitby in the chair opposite, doing something peculiar with his hands that made his fingers look like soft coral swaying in a sea current. A wordless droning in the background. Was Whitby now in the world of the first expedition? And if so, did he know it?

Control watched both video clips twice, thrice, and then deleted them. This act did not delete the subjects, but it made him more distant from them, and that would have to be good enough.

The usual influx of heat and then frigid cold on the airplane. The grappling with frayed seat belts. As they rose, Control kept waiting for something to swat the plane out of the sky, wondered if Central would be there to greet him when he touched down, or something odder still. He wondered why the stewardesses were looking at him funny by mid-flight, and realized he'd been responding to their rote kindness with the intensity of someone who has never experienced courtesy, or never expects to experience it again.

The couple in the seats next to him were of the annoying yet ordinary type who said almost everything for their audience, or to affirm their own couple-hood. Yet even them he wanted to warn, in a sudden, unexpected outpouring of raw and almost uncontainable emotion. To somehow articulate what was happening, what was going to happen, without sounding crazy, without scaring them or him. But, ultimately, he popped another calm pill and leaned back in his seat and tried to banish the world.

"How do I know that going after the biologist isn't an idea you've put in my head?"

"The biologist was the director's weapon, I believe. You said in your reports she doesn't act like the others. Whatever she knows, she represents a kind of chance. Some kind of chance." Control hadn't shared with his mother the full experience of his last moments at the Southern Reach. Not everything he had seen, or that whatever the director was now or wherever she'd grown up, she was less herself than at any point in the past. That whatever plan she'd had was probably irrelevant.

"And you are my weapon, John. You're the one I chose to *know everything*."

The comfort of the scratched metal armrests with the fat, torn padding on top. The compartmentalized scoops of sky captured by the oval windows. The captain's unnecessary progress reports, interspersed with the stupid but comforting jokes over the intercom. He wondered where the Voice was, if Lowry was having flashbacks or freaking out in a more general way. Lowry, his buddy. Lowry, the pathetic megalodon. This is your last chance, Control. But it wasn't. It was, instead, an immolation. If he was remembered at all, it would be as the harbinger of disaster.

He ordered a whiskey with ice, to see it gleam, to keep the ice in his mouth and experience the smooth cold with the hint of bite. It helped him fall into a lull, a trough of self-induced tiredness, trying to slow the wheels of his mind. Trying to wreck those wheels.

"What will Central do now?" he'd asked his mother.

"They'll come after you because of your association with me." Would have come after him anyway, for not reporting in and for going after the biologist.

"What else will they do?"

"Try to send in a thirteenth expedition, if a door still exists."

"And what about you?"

"I'll keep making the case for the course I think is right," she said, which she had to know was a huge risk. Did that mean she'd go back, or keep some distance from Central until the situation stabilized? Because Control knew that she would keep fighting until the world disappeared around her. Or Central got rid of her. Or Lowry used her as a scapegoat. Did she think Central wouldn't try to blame the messenger? He could have asked why she didn't just liquidate her savings and head for the most remote place possible . . . and wait. But if he had, she would have asked him the same thing.

At the end of the flight, a woman in the aisle seat opposite told him and his two seatmates to open their window for landing. "You gotta open the window for landing. You gotta open it. For landing."

Or what? Or what? He just ignored her, did not pass the message on, closed his eyes.

When he opened them, the plane had landed. No one waited for him as he disembarked. No one called out his name. He rented a car without incident.

It was as if a different person put the key in the ignition and drove away from everything that was familiar. There was no going back now. There was no going forward, either. He was going in sideways, sort of, and as frightening as that was, there was the thrill of excitement, too. You couldn't feel dead this way, or as if you were just waiting for the next thing to happen to you.

Rock Bay. The end of the world. If she wasn't there, it was a better place than most to wait for whatever happened next.

Dusk of the next day. In a crappy motel on the coast with the word *Beach* in its name, Control obsessively stripped and cleaned his Glock, bought off a dealer using a fake name not thirty minutes after he'd cleared the airport, in the back lot of a car dealership. Then reassembled it. Having to focus on a repetitive and detailed task kept his mind off the void looming outside.

The television was on, but nothing made sense. The television, except for the vaguest of footnotes about a possible problem at the "Southern Reach environmental recovery site," did not tell the truth about what was going on. But it hadn't made sense for a very long time, even if no one knew that, and he knew his contempt would mirror that of the biologist, if she had been sitting where he was sitting. And the light from the curtains was just a stray truck barreling by in the dark. And the smell was of rot, but he thought perhaps he'd brought that with him. Even though he was far away from it now, the invisible border was close—the checkpoints, the swirling light of the door. The way that light seemed almost beveled, almost formed an image in that space between the curtains, and then fell away again into nothing.

On the bed: Whitby's terroir manuscript, which he hadn't looked at since leaving Hedley. All he'd done was put it in a sturdy waterproof plastic case. He kept realizing, with a kind of resigned surprise, a kind of slow registering or re-imagining meant to cushion the blow, that the invasion had been under way for quite some time, had been manifesting for much longer than anyone could have guessed, even his mother. And that perhaps Whitby had figured something out, even if no one had believed him, even if figuring it out had exposed him to something that had then figured *him* out.

When he was finished with the Glock, he sat in a chair facing the door, clenching the grip tight even though it made his fingers throb. It was another way to keep from being overwhelmed by it. Pain as distraction. All of his familiar guides had gone silent. His mother, his grandparents, his father—none of them had anything to say to him. Even the carving in his pocket seemed inert, useless now.

And the whole time, sitting in the chair and then lying in the bed with its worn blanket and yellowing sheets with cigarette burns in them, Control could not get the image of the biologist out of his head. The look on her face in the empty lot—that blankness—and then, later, in the sessions, the warring of contempt, wildness, casual vulnerability, and vehemence, strength. That had laid him low. That had expanded until it hooked into the whole of him, no part of him not committed. Even though she might never know, could give two shits about him. Even though he would be content should he never meet her again, just so long as he could believe she was still out there, alive and on her own. The yearnings in him now went in all directions and no direction at all. It was an odd kind of affection that needed no subject, that emanated from him like invisible rays meant for everyone and everything. He supposed they were normal feelings once you'd pushed on past a certain point.

North is where the biologist had fled, and he knew where she would end up: It was right there in her field notes. A precipice she knew better than almost anyone, where the land fell away into the sea, and the sea rushed up onto the rocks. He just had to be prepared. Central might catch up to him before he got there. But lurking behind them might be something even darker and more vast, and that was the killing joke. That the thing catching up with all of them would be even less merciful—and would question them until, like a towel wrung dry and then left out in the sun, they were nothing but brittle husks and hollows.

Unless he made it north in time. If she was there. If she knew anything.

He left the motel early, just as the sun appeared, grabbed breakfast at a café, and continued north. Here it was all cliffs and sharp curves and the sense that you might dive off into the sky around each upward bend. That the little thought you always overrode—to stop turning the wheel to match the road—might not be stifled this time and you'd gun the engine and push on into the air, and snuff out every secret thing you knew and didn't want to know. The temperature rarely rose above seventy-five, and the landscape soon became lush—the greens more intense than in the south, the rain when it came a kind of mist so unlike the hellish downpours he'd become used to.

At a general store in a tiny town called Selk that had a gas station whose antiquated pumps didn't take credit cards, he bought a large knapsack, filled it with about thirty pounds of supplies. He bought a hunting knife, plenty of batteries, an ax, lighters, and a lot more. He didn't know what he'd need or how much she'd need, how long he might be out there in the wilderness, searching for her. Would her reaction be what he wanted it to be—and what reaction was that? Assuming she was even there. He imagined himself years from now, bearded, living off the land, making carvings like his father, alone, slowly fading into the backdrop from the weight of solitude.

The cashier asked him his name, as part of a sales pitch for a local charity, and he said "John," and from that point on, he used his real name again. Not Control, not any of the aliases that had gotten him this far. It was a common name. It didn't stand out. It didn't mean anything.

He continued the tactics he'd been using, though. Domestic terrorism had made him familiar with a lot of rural areas. For his second assignment out of training, he had spent time in the Midwest on the road between county health departments, under the guise of helping update immunization software. But he'd really been tracking down data on members of a militia. He knew back roads from that other life and took to them as if he'd never left, used all the tricks with no effort although it had been a long time since he'd used them. There was even a kind of stressful freedom to it, an exhilaration and simplicity he hadn't known for a long time. Then, like now, he'd doubted every pickup truck, especially if it had a mud-obscured license plate, every slow driver, every hitchhiker. Then, as now, he'd picked local roads with dirt side roads that allowed him to double back. He used detailed printed maps, no GPS. He had almost wavered on his cell phone, but had thrown it into the ocean, hadn't bought a temporary to replace it. He knew he could have bought something that couldn't be traced, but anyone he called would no doubt be bugged by now. The urge to call any of his relatives, to try his mother one last time, had faded with the miles. If he'd had something to say, he should have picked up the phone a long time ago.

Sometimes he thought of the director as he drove. Along the banks of a glistening, shallow lake in a valley surrounded by mountains, ripping off pieces of sausage bought at a farmers' market. The color of the sky so light a blue yet so untroubled by clouds that it didn't seem real. The girl in the old black-and-white photo. The way she had fixated on the lighthouse but never referred to the lighthouse keeper. Because she had been there. Because she had been there until almost the end. What had she seen? What had she known? Who had known about her? Had Grace known? The hard work to find the levers and means to eventually be hired by the Southern Reach. Had anyone along the way known her secret and thought it was a good idea, as opposed to a compromising of the agency? Why was she hiding what she knew about the lighthouse keeper? These questions worried at him—missed opportunities, being behind, too much focus on plant-and-mouse, on the Voice, on Whitby, or maybe he would have seen it earlier. The files he still had with him didn't help, having the photograph there in the passenger seat didn't help.

Driving through the night now, he came back to the coast again and again, his headlights reflecting orange dashes and white reflectors and, sometimes, the silver-gray of a railing. He had stopped listening to the news on the radio. He didn't know if the subtle hints of impending catastrophe he gleaned existed only in his imagination. He wanted more and more to pretend that he existed in a bubble without context. That the drive would last forever. That the journey was the point.

When he grew too tired, he stopped in a town whose name he forgot as soon as he left, having coffee and eggs at a twenty-four-hour diner. The waitress asked him where he was headed, and he just said, "North." She nodded, didn't ask him anything else, must have seen something in his face that discouraged it.

He didn't linger, cut his meal short, nervous about the black sedan with the tinted windows in the parking lot, the battered old Volvo with the rain forest stickers on it whose owner had been slouched out there smoking a cigarette for a little too long.

The rain from off the sea thickened into fog, brought him to a twenty-mile-an-hour crawl in the dark, never sure what would come out of the haze at him.

Once a truck rattled his frame to the core, once a deer danced briefly past the headlights like a moving canvas, then was gone.

He came to the conclusion in the early dawn that it didn't matter if his mother had lied to him. It was a tactical detail, not strategic. He was always going to pursue this course, convinced himself that once he had gone to the Southern Reach that he was always going to be on this road in the middle of nowhere, headed north. The gnarled, wind-torn trees became a dark haphazard smoke in the mist, self-immolating into ash, as if he were seeing some version of the future.

The night before he would reach the town of Rock Bay, John let himself have a last meal. He pulled into a fancy restaurant in a town that lay in the shadow of the coastal mountains, cupped by the curve of a river that looked anemic next to the waves and striations of different-colored sand radiating out from the water. Scattered piles of driftwood and dead trees looked as if they'd been placed there to hold it all down.

He sat at the bar, ordered a bottle of good red wine, a petite filet with garlic mashed potatoes and mushroom gravy. He listened to the humble-brag of Jan, the experienced bartender, with a deliberately naïve enthusiasm—entertaining stories from stints working overseas in cities John had never visited. The man stared furtively at John at times, from a craggy Nordic face bordered by long yellow hair. Wondering, perhaps, if John would ask him what he was doing among the driftwood here at the butt end of the world.

A family came in—rich, white, in Polo shirts and sweaters and khaki pants as if from a clothing catalogue. Oblivious of him. Oblivious of the bartender, ordering burgers and fries, the father sitting directly to John's left, shielding his kids from the stranger. Exactly how strange, they could not know. They existed in their own bubble: They had just about everything and knew almost nothing. Their conversation was all about sitting up straight and chewing what they ate and a football game they'd watched and some tourist shop down in the village. He didn't envy them. He didn't hate them. He felt a curious nothing about them. All of the history here, everything encoded, rendered meaningless. None of it could mean anything next to the secret knowledge he carried with him.

The bartender shot John a roll of the eyes as he patiently put up with the kids' changing orders and the subtle condescension in the way the father talked to him. While the woman in the military uniform and her two skateboarder friends from Empire Street gathered ethereal to either side of John, staring at the family's meal with unabashed hunger. How many operatives went unremarked upon, never registered, were never heard from, never sustained. Snuffed out in darkness and crappy safe houses and dank motels. Made invisible. Made irrelevant. And how many could have been him. Were still him, laboring here, unbeknownst to this family or even the bartender, still trying, even though it wasn't just the border to Area X that negated people but everyone in the world beyond.

When the family had left, and along with them his companions, he asked the bartender, "Where can I get a boat?" in an agreeably conspiratorial way. A fellow world-weary traveler, his tone implied. A fellow adventurer who sometimes ignored legality in the same way as the bartender did in his stories. You're the man. You can hook me up.

"You know boats?" Jan asked.

"Yes." On lakes. Close to shore. Anything more and he'd be the punch line of one of Jack's jokes.

"Maybe I can help," the bartender said, with a grin. "Maybe I could arrange that." The fractured light from a chandelier composed of glass globes lit up his face as he leaned in to whisper, "How soon do you need it?"

Now. Immediately. By the morning.

Because he wasn't going to drive into Rock Bay.

The *Living with Salt* was a modified flat-bottom skiff, with a shallow bow and a stubborn reluctance to turn starboard with any kind of grace. It had a tiny shed of a cabin that would give him some relief from the strong ocean winds and a powerful if seasoned motor. It was ancient and the white paint had flaked, exposing the wood beneath. It almost looked like a tugboat to John, but had been used as a fishing vessel by the grizzled, barrel-bellied, bowlegged walking cliché of a fisherman who sold it to him for twice what it was worth. He almost thought the man had some illegal side business, must also be playing a part. He bought enough gasoline to either blow him sky high or last until the end of the world and loaded in the rest of his supplies.

It came with oars "for if the motor should give out" and nautical maps "though God help you if you don't seek shelter, there's a storm" and a flare gun. After a little persuading that involved more money, it also came with the skipper's old raincoat, hat, pipe, galoshes, and a fishing net with a hole in it. The pipe felt weird in his mouth, and the galoshes were a bit too big, but it made him believe that from a distance his disguise might hold.

The motor had a ragged hiccupping mutter he didn't like, but he had little choice—and he believed the boat might be as fast as the car on the treacherous roads that lay ahead, and harder to trace. As he lurched downriver toward the sea, he had a sense of impending apocalypse, the beached and blackened driftwood evidence not of bonfires and storms but of some more radical catastrophe.

Old houses lay among the rocks of the coast and the few crude beaches as he chugged along through choppy waters and calm waters, struggling to learn the jump and list of the boat, slowly adjusting to the current. Most of the houses were falling apart, and even those awake with lights at dusk seemed only temporarily resurrected. Smoke from grills. People on piers below. They all looked like they'd be gone by winter.

He passed an abandoned lighthouse, a low, squat white tower with a black crown. It slid past in silence, the fitted stones showing through the ruined paint, the beacon dark, and he had a startled sense of doubling, as if he were somehow traveling up the coast of an alternative Area X. The sense that he had passed beyond some boundary.

Somewhere in the fog, if he looked closely, he'd see Lowry and Whitby, wandering lost. Somewhere, too, the Séance & Science Brigade taking their measurements, and Saul Evans walking up the spiral steps of the lighthouse, with a girl, oblivious, playing on the rocks below. Perhaps even Grace, gathering the remnants of the Southern Reach around her.

By midafternoon, he had reached the part of the coast where the land curved sharply, an inlet that led to the town of Rock Bay. What the biologist called "Rock Bay" was actually the tidal pools and reefs that lay about twenty miles north of town. But her former cottage had been right outside of the town. Or village, if you wanted to be specific. Because it only had about five hundred residents.

The *Living with Salt* wasn't the kind of boat that John could pull up onto the shore and hide under branches. But he wanted to do a recon of Rock Bay before moving on. He chanced going a little ways up the wide inlet, half-hidden by rock islands that jutted out from the water. Soon he spotted a rotten old pier where he could tie up. According to the maps it was close enough to the local wildlife refuge that he could walk from there and intersect a hiking trail, following it close to the town. He left behind his hat and pipe and, taking his raincoat, binoculars, and gun, made his way inland through scrubland and then forest. The smell of fresh cedar invigorated him. Soon enough, he was looking down from a bluff at the wooden bridge leading into town and the tiny main street beyond. He'd come across a roadblock manned by local police well before the bridge, but he'd seen nothing suspicious on the trails—just a jogger and a couple of teenagers clearly looking for a place to smoke pot. From his vantage now, looking down with his binoculars through the intense tree cover, though, he could see half a dozen black sedans and SUVs with tinted windows parked on the main street. The vehicles reeked of Central, as did the too-coiffed would-be lumberjacks who stood near the vehicles in bright plaid shirts and jeans and boots that looked too new to have yet been through a slog.

If they had come in such small numbers, then either this location was one of many being searched or the biologist was by now only part of a much larger problem, Central fully occupied elsewhere. Somewhere in the south, perhaps.

Depending on how well they knew the biologist's habits, they might believe that she'd prefer to hide somewhere farther north, along the coastline. But they'd have to rule out the town and its environs first. All around was dense coastal scrubland or even denser rain forest, none of it easy to traverse. The kind of terroir even experienced locals could get lost in, once you went beyond the town, especially during the rainy season.

On a hunch, he abandoned his position on the bluff and took a trail down and across the stream straddled by the wooden bridge, then up the opposite side back onto a rise that eventually led him over a series of moss-covered, cedar-rich hills, into a position near the water. Opposite him, across the narrow inlet, lay the cottage where the biologist had lived. He crept in hunched-over zigzag fashion through the breaks in the sharp bramble, lay among twisted black trees with thorny leaves at a good vantage point.

The cottage was only a little larger than his boat, and just enough forest had been cleared for a tiny lawn in front and to let a dirt road curl up the rise to the left. Beyond that rise, hidden, lay a larger settlement: a main house, from which he could see a tendril of white smoke rising via an obscured chimney.

But no smoke rose from the cottage. Nothing stirred around the cottage, either, in a way that he found unnatural. He kept scanning the woods to either side until after about an hour, after about fifty sweeps of the area, he realized that a patch of ground had moved: camouflage. Which, after a few moments, resolved into a man with a rifle and scope stretched out beneath a military-style blind, covering the cottage. Once he'd spotted one operative, others came clear to him: in trees, behind logs, even staring out in one uncareful moment from the cottage itself. He knew the biologist would not now come anywhere near the cottage, if she'd ever wanted to.

So he retreated into the wilderness and made his way back to his boat by a circuitous and tiring route. He didn't think he had been spotted, but he didn't want to leave it to chance. Thankful, too, to be back at the boat. He'd exhausted his small store of rusty woodcraft and felt he had been lucky. Lucky, too, that his boat was still there and the area still seemed deserted.

He ate a can of cold beans and cast off, hugging the coast until the last moment—and then making a calm and steady run across the mouth of the inlet, certain that somehow he would be uncovered from afar and Central would swoop down on him.

Yet despite how wide the expanse seemed in those moments, there were only the seagulls and the pelicans, the cormorants and, high above, what he thought might be an albatross. Only the choppy waves and a distant foghorn and the dim shapes of boats closer in and farther out. Nothing that didn't look local, no fishermen who looked newly minted.

Easier, better, to go farther away from all of this. She would be in the most desolate, isolated place she could find, daring anyone to follow her.

Either there or not. If not, it was all useless anyway.

Pursuit felt like an intermittent pulse. It died away and then picked up again. Through binoculars he saw a speedboat far off curving fast toward him. He heard a helicopter, although he couldn't see it, and spent a nervous twenty minutes in pointless fishing with his ripped, useless net, his formless hat pulled down over his forehead. Pretending with everything he had to be a fisherman. Then the sounds faded, the speedboat looped back down the coast. Everything was as before, for a very long time.

This new landscape above the Rock Bay inlet was even more foreign to him, and colder—and a relief, as if Area X were just a climate, a type of vegetation, a simple terroir, even if he knew this wasn't true. So many shades and tones of gray—the gray that shone down from the sky, a ceaseless and endless gray that was so still.

The mottled matte gray of the water, before the rain, broken by the curls of wavelets, the gray of the rain itself, prickles and ripples against the ocean's surface. The silver gray of the real waves farther out, which came in and hit the bow as he guided the boat into them, rocking and the engine whining. The gray of something large and ponderous passing underneath him and making the boat rise as he tried to keep it still and motorless for those moments, holding his breath, life too close to dream for him to exhale.

He understood why the biologist liked this part of the world, how you could lose yourself here in a hundred ways. How you could even become someone very different from who you thought you were. His thoughts became still for hours of his search. The frenetic need to analyze, to atomize the day or the week fell away from him—and with it the weight and buzz of human interaction and interference, which could no longer dwell inside his skull.

He thought about the silence of fishing on the lake as a child, the long pauses, what his grandpa might say to him in a hushed tone, as if they were in a kind of church. He wondered what he would do if he couldn't find her. Would he go back, or would he melt into this landscape, become part of what he found here, try to forget what had happened before and become no more or less than the spray against the bow, the foam against the shore, the wind against his face? There was a comfort to this idea almost as strong as the urge to find her, a comfort he had not known for a very long time, and many things receded into the distance behind him, seemed ridiculous or fantastical, or both. Were, at their core, unimportant.

During the nights of his journey farther north, tied up as best he could where the coastline allowed it—the lee of a rock island large enough to shield him, the bottom able to hold the anchor despite slippery kelp—he began to see strange lights far behind him. They rose and fell and glided across the sea and the sky, some white and some green or purple-tinged. He could not tell if they were searching or defined a purpose less purposeful. But the lights broke the spell and he turned on the radio that night, holding it to his ear to keep the volume down as he huddled in his sleeping bag. But he only heard a few unintelligible words until static set in, and he did not know if this was because of some catastrophe or the remoteness of his location.

The stars above were large and fixed. They existed against a fabric of night as vast and deep as his sleep, his dream. He was tired now, and hungry for something beyond cans and protein bars. He was sick of the sound of the waves and the sound of his boat's engine. It had been three days since leaving Rock Bay, and he had caught no sign of her along the coast, would soon come to the most remote part of the area. He had long since passed the point where anything inland could be reached by road, but only by hiking trail or helicopter or boat. The very edge of anything that could be called Rock Bay.

If he kept conserving food and water, he had enough to last another week before he had to turn back.

The morning of another day. In a lull, drifting, he rowed into an inlet surrounded by black rocks as sharp as shark fins, as craggy as any mountainside. He'd decided to get close because it looked similar to the coastline sketched in the biologist's field entries.

The rocks were covered in limpets and starfish, and in the shallows the hundred bristling dark shapes of sea urchins like miniature submerged mines. He had seen no one for two days. His arms were sore and aching from rowing. He wanted a hot meal, a bath, some landmark to tell him for certain where he was. The boat had begun to take on water; he spent some time now bailing, his fear of moving even a little ways from shore greater than that of running aground on something jagged.

The rocks formed a rough line or ridge all the way back to shore, and it was hard to navigate around them. A swell carried him too close, and he rammed up against them, felt the jarring in his bones. He put out an oar to push off; it slid off smoothly at first, and he had to try again, then frantically rowed until he was a safe distance from the suck and roll.

It took him a moment to realize why his oar had slid, why there had been no usual grinding crunch. Someone had been eating the limpets and mussels. The rock had been almost bare except for some kelp. He looked through his binoculars, saw that rocks a little farther in were bare, too, and closer to shore, a few showed pale circular marks where the limpets had resisted their picking.

No sign of a fire or of habitation nearby, but someone or something had been grazing on them. If a person, he knew it could have been anyone. Yet it was more than he'd had to go on yesterday. Trepidation and relief and a certain indecisiveness warred within him. If a person, whoever it was might have already seen the boat. He thought to make landfall there, then reversed himself and rowed back the way he'd come, back down the coast by just one cove, hidden by another of the huge rocks that rose from the ocean to form an inhospitable island.

By then, the boat had taken on more water and he realized that he was going to spend most of his time bailing, not rowing, or worrying about sinking, not rowing. So he brought the boat up close to shore, dropped anchor, and waded to a little black sand beach sheltered by overhanging trees, sat there gasping for long minutes. This was his last chance. He could try to fix the boat. He could try to turn back, limp back down the coast to Rock Bay. Be done with this, be done with the idea of this forever. Leave the vision of the biologist in his head, never manifesting in front of him, and then just face whatever had been growing there, behind him. He wondered what his mother was doing in that moment, where she was. Then a flash of Whitby reaching out a hand from the shelf struck him sideways, and of Grace at the door, waiting for the director.

He went back out to the boat, took everything useful he could fit into the backpack, including Whitby's terroir manuscript. Staggering a little under the weight of that, he began to make his way back toward the line of black rocks, trying to stay concealed by the tree line. Soon the boat was just a memory, something that had once existed but not any longer.

That night, he noticed lights in the sky, again distant but coming nearer. He imagined he could hear the sound of a ship's engine, but the lights faded, the sound faded, and he went to sleep to the hush and whisper of the surf.

At dusk of the next day, John saw a movement on the rocks, and he trained his binoculars on it. He wanted to believe that the figure was the biologist, that he knew her outline against the worn sky, the way that she moved, but he had only seen her captive. Inert. Deactivated. Different.

The first time, he lost her almost immediately from his vantage some distance from the rocks, couldn't tell if she was coming back in or going farther out. Rocks and form merged and blurred, and then it was night. He waited for the appearance of a light or a fire, but saw neither. If it was the biologist, she was in full survivalist mode.

Another day passed, and he saw nothing except seagulls and a gray fox that came to an abrupt halt when it saw him and then evaporated into the mist that coated everything for far too long. He worried that whoever he had seen had passed on, that this wasn't an outpost but just another marker on a longer journey. He ate another can of beans, drank sparingly from the water canteen. Huddled, shivering, beneath deep cover. He was reaching the edge of his woodcraft again, was made more for back roads and small-town surveillance than for living out in the wild. He thought he'd probably lost about five pounds. He kept taking in deep breaths of cedar and every green, living thing as a temporary antidote.

The figure came out at dusk again, crawling and hopping across the sheets of black rock with an expertise John knew would be beyond him. As he identified her as the biologist through the binoculars, his heart leapt and his blood stirred and the little hairs on his arms rose. A flood of emotion came over him, and he stifled tears—of relief or of something deeper? He had been existing inside himself for long enough now that he wasn't sure. But he righted himself immediately. He knew that if she got back to shore, she'd disappear into the rain forest. He did not like his odds of tracking her there.

If she saw him clambering after her, though, and he didn't get a chance to confront her, she'd slip through his fingers and he'd never see her again. This, too, he knew.

The tide had begun to come in. The light was dull and flat and gray. Again. The wind had become harsh. Out at sea, there was nothing to indicate human beings existed except for the rising and falling figure of the biologist, and a deep vein of black smoke opening up into the sky from some vessel so far out at sea that it wasn't visible even with the binoculars.

He waited until she was more than halfway out, wondering if she'd lost some natural caution because it was still easier to cut her off than it should have been. Then he snuck along the other side of the ridge of rock, hunched over, trying to keep his silhouette off her horizon, although he'd be framed by forest, not the fading light. He had brought the knapsack with him out of paranoia that she or someone else might steal it while he was gone. Although he had stripped it down somewhat, it threw off his balance, made it harder to hold his gun and climb the rocks. He could have left Whitby's manuscript behind, but this had seemed more and more important to keep in view at all times.

He tried to keep his steps short and to bend his knees, but even so slipped many times on the uneven rocks, slick with seaweed and rough and sharp from the edges of the shells of limpets and clams and mussels. Had to reach out to keep his balance and cut himself despite the cloth he'd tied over his palms. Very soon his ankles and knees felt weak.

By the time he was halfway out, the ridge of rocks had narrowed, and he had no choice but to clamber atop them. When he looked up from that vantage for the first time, the biologist was nowhere to be seen. Which meant she had either found some miraculous way back to shore, or she was hidden somewhere ahead of him.

No matter how he hunched and bent, she was going to have a clear line of sight at him. He didn't know what options she had—rock, knife, homemade spear?—if she wasn't glad to see him. He took off his hat, shoved it in the pocket of his raincoat, hoping that if she was watching she would at least recognize that it was him. That this recognition might mean more to her than "interrogator" or "captor." That it might make her hesitate should she be lying in wait.

Three-quarters of the way and he wondered if he should just head back. His legs were rubbery, matched the feel of the rocks where the kelp swelled over them. The waves to either side struck with more force, and although he could still see now—the sun a quiver of red against the far horizon, illuminating the distant smoke—he'd have to use his flashlight going back. Which would alert anyone on the shore to his presence; he hadn't come all this way just to betray her to others. So he continued on with a sense of fatalism. He'd sacrificed all his pawns, his knights, bishops, and rooks. Abuela and Abuelo were facing an onslaught from the other side of the board.

In the tiring, repetitious work of climbing on, of continuing on and not going back, a grim satisfaction spread in a last surge of energy through his body. He had pursued this line of inquiry to the end. He had come very far, this thought mixed with sadness for what lay behind, so many people with whom he'd forged such slight connections. So many people that, as he neared the end of the rocks, he wished he had known better, tried to know better. His caring for his father now seemed not like a selfless effort but something that had been for him, too, to show him what it meant to be close to someone.

At the end of the ridge, he came upon a deep lagoon of ever-rippling encircled water, roughly cradled by the rocks. Lagoon was perhaps too gentle a word for it—a gurgling deep hole, whose sharp and irregular sides could cut hand or head easily. The bottom could not be seen.

Beyond, just the endless ocean, frothing to get in, smashing against the closed fist of the rocks so that spray flecked his face and the force of the wind buffeted him. But in the lagoon, all was calm, if unknowable in its dark reflection.

She appeared so close, from concealment on his left, that he almost jumped back, caught himself in time by bending and putting out a hand.

In that moment, he was helpless and in steadying himself he found that she had a gun trained on him. It looked like a Glock, like his own, standard-issue. He hadn't expected that. Somehow, somewhere, she had found a gun. She was thinner, her cheekbones as cutting as the rocks. Her hair had begun to grow out, a dark fuzz. She wore thick jeans and a sweater too big for her but heavy, and high-quality brown hiking boots. There was a defiance on her face that warred with curiosity and some other emotion. Her lips were chapped. In this, her natural environment, she seemed so sure of herself that he felt awkward, ungainly. Something had clicked into place. Something had sharpened her, and he thought it might be memory.

"Throw your gun into the sea," she said, motioning to his holster. She had to raise her voice for him to hear her, even this close—close enough that with a few steps he could have reached out and touched her shoulder.

"We might need it later," he said.

"We?"

"Yes," he said. "More are coming. I've seen the lights." He did not want to share what had happened to the Southern Reach. Not yet.

"Toss it, now, unless you want to get shot." He believed her. He'd seen the reports from her training. She said she wasn't good with guns, but the targets hadn't agreed.

So there went Grandpa version 4.9 or 5.1. He hadn't kept track of the expeditions. The sea made it disappear with a smack that sounded like one last comment from Jack.

John looked over at her, standing across from him while the waves blasted the rocks and despite the gray and despite the wet and the cold, despite the fact he might die sometime in the next few minutes, he started to laugh. It surprised him, thought at first someone else was laughing.

Her grip tightened on the gun. "Is the idea of me shooting you funny?"

"Yes," he said. "It's very, very funny." He was laughing hard enough now that he had to bend to his knees to keep his balance on the rocks. A fierce joy or hysteria had risen inside of him, and he wondered in an idle, distant way if perhaps he should have sought out this feeling more often. The look of her, against the backdrop of the swell and the fall of the sea, was almost too much for him. But for the first time he knew he had done the right thing in coming here.

"It's funny because there have been many other times . . . so many other times when I would've understood why someone wanted to shoot me." That was only part of it, the other part being that he had felt almost as if Area X was about to shoot him, and that Area X had been trying to shoot him for a very long time.

"You followed me," she said, "even though I clearly don't want to be followed. You've come to what most people consider the butt end of the world and you've cornered me here. You probably want to ask more questions, although it should be clear that I'm done with questions. What did you think would happen?"

The truth was, he didn't know what he had thought would happen, had perhaps unconsciously fallen back on an idea of their relationship at the Southern Reach. But that didn't apply here. He sobered up, hands held high now as if surrendering.

"What if I said *I* had answers," he said. But all he had to show her that was tangible was Whitby's manuscript.

"I'd say you're lying and I'd be right."

"What if I said you still hold some of the answers, too." He was as serious as he had been giddy just moments before. He tried to hold her with his gaze, even through the murk, but he couldn't. God, but the coast here was painfully beautiful, the dark lush greens of the fir trees piercing his brain, the half-raging sky and sea, the surge of salt water against the rocks twinned to the urgent wash of blood through his arteries as he waited for her to kill him or hear him out. Seditious thought: There would be nothing too terrible about dying out here, about becoming part of all of this.

"I'm not the biologist," she said. "I don't care about my past as the biologist, if that's what you mean."

"I know," he said. He'd figured it out on the boat, even if he hadn't articulated it yet. "I know you're not. You're some version, though. You have her memories, to some extent, and somewhere back in Area X, the biologist may still be alive. You're a replica, but you're your own person."

Not an answer she had expected. She lowered the gun. A little. "You believe me."

"Yes." It had been right there. In front of him, in the video, in the very mimicry of cells, the difference in personality. Except she'd broken the mold. Something had been different in her creation.

"I've been trying to remember this place," she said, almost plaintively. "I love it here, but the entire time I've felt like it was the one remembering me."

A silence that John didn't know if he wanted to break, so he just stood there.

"Are you here to take me back?" she said. "Because I'm not going back."

"No, I'm not," he said, and realized it was true. Whatever impulse in that regard that might have lived within him had been snuffed out. "The Southern Reach doesn't exist anymore," he admitted. "There may not be anything we'd recognize out there very soon."

There in the twilight, no birds now overhead, the smoke fading into the dusk, the raucous surf the only thing that seemed alive besides the two of them.

"How did you know I'd be here?" she asked, deep in thought. "I was so careful."

"I didn't. I guessed." Somehow his face must have given something of his thoughts away, because she looked a little startled, a little wrong-footed.

"Why would you do that if you don't want to take me back?"

"I don't know." To try to save the world? To save her? To save himself? But he did know. Nothing had changed since the interrogation room. Not really.

When he looked up again, she was saying, "I thought I could just stay here. Build the life she didn't build, that she messed up. But I can't. It's clear I can't. Someone will be after me no matter what I do."

Now that the sun had truly set there was a glimmer of a light dimly familiar to him coming from deep in the lagoon below.

"What's down there?" he asked.

"Nothing." Said too quickly.

"Nothing? It's too late to lie—there's no point." It was never too late to lie, to obscure, to delay. Control knew this too well.

But she didn't. She hesitated, then said, "I was sick when I got here. One night I came out here and I had a dizzy spell and I was unconscious for a while. I woke up with the tide rising and I wasn't sick anymore. The brightness was done with me. But there was something at the bottom of that hole."

"What?" Although he thought he already knew. The swirling light was too familiar, despite being broken by ripples and the thickness of the water.

"It's a way into Area X, I think," she said, and now she looked scared. "I think I brought it with me." He didn't know how she knew this. He thought it might be true, remembered what Cheney had said about how difficult and enervating that travel could be. Whitby's horrible description of the border.

Now that the darkness was complete and she was just a shadow standing in front of him, they could both see the lights farther down the coast. Bobbing. Floating. Trudging. Dozens of them. And so far down below, that glimmer, that hint of an impossible light.

"I don't think we have much longer," he said. "I don't even know if we have the night. We'll have to find a place to hide." Not wanting to think about the other possibility. Not wanting even a hint of it in his thoughts to invade her thoughts.

"It will be high tide soon," she said. "You have to get off the rocks." But not her? Even though he could not see her face, he knew the expression that must be etched there.

"We *both* have to get off the rocks." He wasn't sure he meant it. He could hear the helicopter now, could hear boats again, too. But if she was unhinged, if she was lying, if she didn't actually know anything at all . . .

"I want to know who I am," she said. "I can't do that here. I can't do that locked up in a cell."

"I know who you are—it's all in my head, your file. I can give you that."

"I'm not going back," she said. "I'm never going back."

"It's dangerous," he told her, pleading, as if she didn't know. "It's unproven. We don't know where you'll come out." The hole was so deep and so jagged, and the water beginning to churn from the waves. He had seen wonders and he had seen terrible things. He had to believe that this was one more and that it was true and that it was knowable.

Her stare took the measure of him. She was done talking. She threw her gun away. She dove into the water, down deep.

He took one last look back at the world he knew. He took one huge gulp of it, every bit of it he could see, every bit of it he could remember.

"Jump," said a voice in his head.

Control jumped.

ACCEPTANCE

000X: THE DIRECTOR, TWELFTH EXPEDITION

J ust out of reach, just beyond you: the rush and froth of the surf, the sharp smell of the sea, the crisscrossing shape of the gulls, their sudden, jarring cries. An ordinary day in Area X, an extraordinary day—the day of your death—and there you are, propped up against a mound of sand, half sheltered by a crumbling wall. The warm sun against your face, and the dizzying view above of the lighthouse looming down through its own shadow. The sky has an intensity that admits to nothing beyond its blue prison. There's sticky sand glittering across a gash in your forehead; there's a tangy glottal *something* in your mouth, dripping out.

You feel numb and you feel broken, but there's a strange relief mixed in with the regret: to come such a long way, to come to a halt here, without knowing how it will turn out, and yet . . . *to rest*. To come to rest. Finally. All of your plans back at the Southern Reach, the agonizing and constant fear of failure or worse, the price of that . . . all of it leaking out into the sand beside you in gritty red pearls.

The landscape surges toward you, curling over from behind to peer at you; it flares in places, or swirls or reduces itself to a pinprick, before coming back into focus. Your hearing isn't what it once was, either—has weakened along with your balance. And yet there comes this impossible thing: a magician's trick of a voice rising out of the landscape and the suggestion of eyes upon you. The whisper is familiar: *Is your house in order?* But you think whoever is asking might be a stranger, and you ignore it, don't like what might be knocking at the door.

The throbbing of your shoulder from the encounter in the tower is much worse. The wound betrayed you, made you leap out into that blazing blue expanse even though you hadn't wanted to. Some communication, some trigger between the wound and the flame that came dancing across the reeds betrayed your sovereignty. Your house has rarely been in such disarray, and yet you know that no matter what leaves you in a few minutes something else will remain behind. Disappearing into the sky, the earth, the water, is no guarantee of death here.

A shadow joins the shadow of the lighthouse.

Soon after, there comes the crunch of boots, and, disoriented, you shout, "Annihilation! Annihilation!" and flail about until you realize the apparition kneeling before you is the one person impervious to the suggestion.

"It's just me, the biologist."

Just you. Just the biologist. Just your defiant weapon, hurled against the walls of Area X.

She props you up, presses water to your mouth, clearing some of the blood as you cough.

"Where is the surveyor?" you ask.

"Back at the base camp," she tells you.

"Wouldn't come with you?" Afraid of the biologist, afraid of the burgeoning flame, just like you. "A slow-burning flame, a will-o'-the-wisp, floating across the marsh and the dunes, floating and floating, like nothing human but something free and floating." A hypnotic suggestion meant to calm her, even if it will have no more effect than a comforting nursery rhyme.

As the conversation unspools, you keep faltering and losing track of it. You say things you don't mean, trying to stay in character—the person the biologist knows you as, the construct you created for her. Maybe you shouldn't care about roles now, but there's still a role to play.

She's blaming you, but you can't blame her. "If it was a disaster, you helped create it. You just panicked, and you gave up." Not true—you never gave up—but you nod anyway, thinking of so many mistakes. "I did. I did. I should have recognized earlier that you had changed." True. "I should have sent you back to the border." Not true. "I shouldn't have gone down there with the anthropologist." Not true, not really. You had no choice, once she slipped away from base camp, intent on proving herself.

You're coughing up more blood, but it hardly matters now.

"What does the border look like?" A child's question. A question whose answer means nothing. There is nothing but border. There is no border.

I'll tell you when I get there.

"What really happens when we cross over?"

Not what you might expect.

"What did you hide from us about Area X?"

Nothing that would have helped you. Not really.

The sun is a weak halo with no center and the biologist's voice threads in and out, the sand both cold and hot in your clenched right hand. The pain that keeps returning in bursts is attacking every couple of microseconds, so present that it isn't even there anymore.

Eventually, you recognize that you have lost the ability to speak. But you are still there, muffled and distant, as if you're a kid lying on a blanket on this very beach, with a hat over your eyes. Lulled into drowsiness by the constant surging sound of the water and the sea breezes, balancing the heat that ripples over you, spreads through your limbs. The wind against your hair is a sensation as remote as the ruffling of weeds sprouting from a head-shaped rock.

"I'm sorry, but I have to do this," the biologist tells you, almost as if she knows you can still hear her. "I have no choice."

You feel the tug and pull on your skin, the brief incisive line, as the biologist takes a sample from your infected shoulder. From a great and insurmountable distance, searching hands descend as the biologist goes through your jacket pockets. She finds your journal. She finds your hidden gun. She finds your pathetic letter. What will she make of them? Maybe nothing at all. Maybe she'll just throw the letter into the sea, and the gun with it. Maybe she'll waste the rest of her life studying your journal.

She's still talking.

"I don't know what to say to you. I'm angry. I'm frightened. You put us here and you had a chance to tell me what you knew, and you didn't. You wouldn't. I'd say rest in peace, but I don't think you will."

Then she's gone, and you miss her, that weight of a human being beside you, the perverse blessing of those words, but you don't miss her for long because you are fading further still, fading into the landscape like a reluctant wraith, and you can hear a faint and delicate music in the distance, and something that whispered to you before is whispering again, and then you're dissolving into the wind. A kind of alien regard has twinned itself to you, easily mistaken for the atoms of the air if it did not seem somehow concentrated, purposeful. Joyful?

Taken up over the still lakes, rising up across the marsh, flickering up in green-glinting reflections against the sea and the shore in the late-afternoon sun . . . only to wheel and bank toward the interior and its cypress trees, its black water. Then sharply up into the sky again, taking aim for the sun, the lurch and spin of it, before free fall, twisting to stare down at the onrushing earth, stretched taut above the quick flash and slow wave of reeds. You half expect to see Lowry there, wounded survivor of the long-ago first expedition, crawling toward the safety of the border. But instead there is just the biologist trudging back down the darkening path . . . and waiting beyond her, mewling and in distress, the altered psychologist from the expedition before the twelfth. Your fault as much as anyone's, your fault, and irrevocable. Unforgivable.

As you curve back around, the lighthouse fast approaches. The air trembles as it pushes out from both sides of the lighthouse and then re-forms, ever questing, forever sampling, rising high only to come low yet again, and finally circling like a question mark so you can bear witness to your own immolation: a shape huddled there, leaking light. What a sad figure, sleeping there, dissolving there. A green flame, a distress signal, an opportunity. Are you still soaring? Are you still dying or dead? You can't tell anymore.

But the whisper isn't done with you yet.

You're not down there.

You're up here.

And there's still an interrogation going on.

One that will repeat until you have given up every answer.

PART I

RANGE LIGHT

0001: THE LIGHTHOUSE KEEPER

Overhauled the lens machinery and cleaned the lens. Fixed the water pipe in the garden. Small repair to the gate. Organized the tools and shovels etc. in the shed. S&SB visit. Need to requisition paint for daymark—black eroded on seaward side. Also need nails and to check the western siren again. Sighted: pelicans, moorhens, some kind of warbler, blackbirds beyond number, sanderlings, a royal tern, an osprey, flickers, cormorants, bluebirds, pigmy rattlesnake (at the fence— remember), rabbit or two, white-tailed deer, and near dawn, on the trail, many an armadillo.

That winter morning, the wind was cold against the collar of Saul Evans's coat as he trudged down the trail toward the lighthouse. There had been a storm the night before, and down and to his left, the ocean lay gray and roiling against the dull blue of the sky, seen through the rustle and sway of the sea oats. Driftwood and bottles and faded white buoys and a dead hammerhead shark had washed up in the aftermath, tangled among snarls of seaweed, but no real damage either here or in the village.

At his feet lay bramble and the thick gray of thistles that would bloom purple in the spring and summer. To his right, the ponds were dark with the muttering complaints of grebes and buffleheads. Blackbirds plunged the thin branches of trees down, exploded upward in panic at his passage, settled back into garrulous communities. The brisk, fresh salt smell to the air had an edge of flame: a burning smell from some nearby house or still-smoldering bonfire.

Saul had lived in the lighthouse for four years before he'd met Charlie, and he lived there still, but last night he'd stayed in the village a half mile away, in Charlie's cottage. A new thing this, not agreed to with words, but with Charlie pulling him back to bed when he'd been about to put on his clothes and leave. A welcome thing that put an awkward half smile on Saul's face.

Charlie'd barely stirred as Saul had gotten up, dressed, made eggs for breakfast. He'd served Charlie a generous portion with a slice of orange, kept hot under a bowl, and left a little note beside the toaster, bread at the ready. As he'd left, he'd turned to look at the man sprawled on his back half in and half out of the sheets. Even into his late thirties, Charlie had the lean, muscular torso, strong shoulders, and stout legs of a man who had spent much of his adult life on boats, hauling in nets, and the flat belly of someone who didn't spend too many nights out drinking.

A quiet click of the door, then whistling into the wind like an idiot as soon as he'd taken a few steps—thanking the God who'd made him, in the end, so lucky, even if in such a delayed and unexpected way. Some things came to you late, but late was better than never.

Soon the lighthouse rose solid and tall above him. It served as a daymark so boats could navigate the shallows, but also was lit at night half the week, corresponding to the schedules of commercial traffic farther out to sea. He knew every step of its stairs, every room inside its stone-and-brick walls, every crack and bit of spackle. The spectacular four-ton lens, or beacon, at the top had its own unique signature, and he had hundreds of ways to adjust its light. A first-order lens, over a century old.

As a preacher he thought he had known a kind of peace, a kind of calling, but only after his self-exile, giving all of that up, had Saul truly found what he was looking for. It had taken more than a year for him to understand why: Preaching had been *projecting out*, imposing himself on the world, with the world then projecting onto him. But tending to the lighthouse—that was a way of looking inward and it felt less arrogant. Here, he knew nothing but the practical, learned from his predecessor: how to maintain the lens, the precise workings of the ventilator and the lens-access panel, how to maintain the grounds, how to fix all the things that broke—scores of daily tasks. He welcomed each part of the routine, relished how it gave him no time to think about the past, and didn't mind sometimes working long hours—especially now, in the afterglow of Charlie's embrace.

But that afterglow faded when he saw what awaited him in the gravel parking lot, inside the crisp white fence that surrounded the lighthouse and the grounds. A familiar beat-up station wagon stood there, and beside it the usual two Séance & Science Brigade recruits. They'd snuck up on him again, crept in to ruin his good mood, and even piled their equipment beside the car already—no doubt in a hurry to start. He waved to them from afar in a halfhearted way.

They were always present now, taking measurements and photographs, dictating statements into their bulky tape recorders, making their amateur movies. Intent on finding . . . what? He knew the history of the coast here, the way that distance and silence magnified the mundane. How into those spaces and the fog and the empty line of the beach thoughts could turn to the uncanny and begin to create a story out of nothing.

Saul took his time because he found them tiresome and increasingly predictable. They traveled in pairs, so they could have their séance and their science both, and he sometimes wondered about their conversations—how full of contradictions they must be, like the arguments going on inside his head toward the end of his ministry. Lately the same two had come by: a man and a woman, both in their twenties, although sometimes they seemed more like teenagers, a boy and girl who'd run away from home dragging a store-bought chemistry set and a Ouija board behind them.

Henry and Suzanne. Although Saul had assumed the woman was the superstitious one, it turned out she was the scientist—of what?—and the man was the investigator of the uncanny. Henry spoke with a slight accent, one Saul couldn't place, that put an emphatic stamp of authority on everything he said. He was plump, as clean-shaven as Saul was bearded, with shadows under his pale blue eyes, black hair in a modified bowl cut with bangs that obscured a pale, unusually long forehead. Henry didn't seem to care about worldly things, like the winter weather, because he always wore some variation on a delicate blue button-down silk shirt with dress slacks. The shiny black boots with zippers down the side weren't for trails but for city streets.

Suzanne seemed more like what people today called a hippie but would've called a communist or bohemian when Saul was growing up. She had blond hair and wore a white embroidered peasant blouse and a brown suede skirt down below the knee, to meet the calf-high tan boots that completed her uniform. A few like her had wandered into his ministry from time to time—lost, living in their own heads, waiting for something to ignite them. The frailty of her form made her somehow more Henry's twin, not less.

The two had never given him their last names, although one or the other had said something that sounded like "Serum-list" once, which made no sense. Saul didn't really want to know them better, if he was honest, had taken to calling them "the Light Brigade" behind their backs, as in "lightweights."

When he finally stood in front of them, Saul greeted them with a nod and a gruff hello, and they acted, as they often did, like he was a clerk in the village grocery store and the lighthouse a business that offered some service to the public. Without the twins' permit from the parks service, he would have shut the door in their faces.

"Saul, you don't look very happy even though it is a beautiful day," Henry said.

"Saul, it's a *beautiful* day," Suzanne added.

He managed a nod and a sour smile, which set them both off into paroxysms of laughter. He ignored that.

But they continued to talk as Saul unlocked the door. They always wanted to talk, even though he'd have preferred that they just got on with their business. This time it was about something called "necromantic doubling," which had to do with building a room of mirrors and darkness, as far as he could tell. It was a strange term and he ignored their explanations, saw no way in which it had any relationship to the beacon or his life at the lighthouse.

People weren't ignorant here, but they were superstitious, and given that the sea could claim lives, who could blame them. What was the harm of a good-luck charm worn on a necklace, or saying a few words in prayer to keep a loved one safe? Interlopers trying to make sense of things, trying to "analyze and survey" as Suzanne had put it, turned people off because it trivialized the tragedies to come. But like those annoying rats of the sky, the seagulls, you got used to the Light Brigade after a while. On dreary days he had almost learned not to begrudge the company. *Why do you see the speck in your neighbor's eye but not notice the log in your own eye?*

"Henry thinks the beacon could operate much like such a room," Suzanne said, as if this was some major and astounding discovery. Her enthusiasm struck him as serious and authentic and yet also frivolous and amateurish. Perhaps she believed it as surely as every new convert to Christ—the newness and closeness removed any sense of doubt. But perhaps they were less like new converts than like traveling preachers who set up tents at the edges of small towns and had the fervor of their convictions but not much else. Maybe they were even charlatans. The first time he'd met them, Saul thought Henry had said they were studying the refraction of light in a prison.

"Are you familiar with these theories?" Suzanne asked as they started to climb; she was lightly adorned with a camera strapped around her neck and a suitcase in one hand. Henry was trying not to seem winded, and said nothing. He was wrestling with heavy equipment, some of it in a box: mics, headphones,

UV light readers, 8mm film, and a couple of machines featuring dials, knobs, and other indicators.

"No," Saul said, mostly to be contrary, because Suzanne often treated him like someone without culture, mistook his brusqueness for ignorance, his casual clothes as belonging to a simple man. Besides, the less he said, the more relaxed they were around him. It'd been the same with potential donors as a preacher. And the truth was, he didn't know what she was talking about, just as he hadn't known what Henry meant when he'd said they were studying the "taywah" or "terror" of the region, even when he'd spelled it out as t-e-r-r-o-i-r.

"Prebiotic particles," Henry managed in a jovial if wheezy tone. "Ghost energy."

As Suzanne backed that up with a longish lecture about mirrors and things that could peer out of mirrors and how you might look at something sideways and know more about its true nature than head-on, he wondered if Henry and Suzanne were lovers; her sudden enthusiasm for the séance part of the brigade might have a fairly prosaic origin. That would also explain their hysterical laughter down below. An ungenerous thought, but he'd wanted to bask in the afterglow of the night with Charlie.

"Meet you up there," he said finally, having had enough, and leapt up the stairs, taking them two at a time while Henry and Suzanne labored below, soon out of sight. He wanted as much time at the top without them as possible. The government would retire him at fifty, mandatory, but he planned to be as in shape then as now. Despite the twinge in his joints.

At the top, hardly even breathing heavy, Saul was happy to find the lantern room as he'd left it, with the lens bag placed over the beacon, to avoid both scratching and discoloration from the sun. All he had to do was open the lens curtains around the parapet to let in light. His concession to Henry, for just a few hours a day.

Once, from this vantage, he'd seen something vast rippling through the water beyond the sandbars, a kind of shadow, the grayness so dark and deep it had formed a thick, smooth shape against the blue. Even with his binoculars he could not tell what creature it was, or what it might become if he stared at it long enough. Didn't know if eventually it had scattered into a thousand shapes, revealed as a school of fish, or if the color of the water, the sharpness of the light, changed and made it disappear, revealed as an illusion. In that tension between what he could and couldn't know about even the mundane world, he felt at home in a way he would not have five years ago. He needed no greater mysteries now than those moments when the world seemed as miraculous as in his old sermons. And it was a good story for down at the village bar, the kind of story they expected from the lighthouse keeper, if anyone expected anything from him at all.

"So that's why it's of interest to us, what with the way the lens wound up here, and how that relates to the whole history of both lighthouses," Suzanne said from behind him. She had been having a conversation with Saul in his absence, apparently, and seemed to believe he had been responding. Behind her, Henry was about ready to collapse, although the trek had become a regular routine.

When he'd dropped the equipment and regained his breath, Henry said, "You have a marvelous view from up here." He always said this, and Saul had stopped giving a polite response, or any response.

"How long are you here for this time?" Saul asked. This particular stint had already lasted two weeks, and he'd put off asking, fearing the answer.

Henry's shadow-circled gaze narrowed. "This time our permit allows us access through the end of the year." Some old injury or accident of birth meant his head was bent to the right, especially when he spoke, right ear almost touching the upward slope of his shoulder. It gave him a mechanical aspect.

"Just a reminder: You can touch the beacon, but you can't in any way interfere with its function." Saul had repeated this warning every day since they'd come back. Sometimes in the past they'd had strange ideas about what they could and could not do.

"Relax, Saul," Suzanne said, and he gritted his teeth at her use of his first name. At the beginning, they'd called him Mr. Evans, which he preferred.

He took more than the usual juvenile pleasure in positioning them on the rug, beneath which lay a trapdoor and a converted watch room that had once held the supplies needed to maintain the light before the advent of automation. Keeping the room from them felt like keeping a compartment of his mind hidden from their experiments. Besides, if these two were as observant as they seemed to think they were, they would have realized what the sudden cramping of the stairs near the top meant.

When he was satisfied they had settled in and were unlikely to disturb anything, he gave them a nod and left. Halfway down, he thought he heard a breaking sound from above. It did not repeat. He hesitated, then shrugged it off, continued to the bottom of the spiral stairs.

Below, Saul busied himself with the grounds and organizing the toolshed, which had become a mess. More than one hiker wandering through had seemed surprised to find a lighthouse keeper walking the grounds around the tower as if he were a hermit crab without its shell, but in fact there was a lot of maintenance required due to the way storms and the salt air could wear down everything if he wasn't vigilant. In the summer, it was harder, with the heat and the biting flies.

The girl, Gloria, snuck up on him while he was inspecting the boat he kept behind the shed. The shed abutted a ridge of soil and coquina parallel to the beach and a line of rocks stretching out to sea. At high tide, the sea flowed up to reinvigorate tidal pools full of sea anemones, starfish, blue crabs, snails, and sea cucumbers.

She was a solid, tall presence for her age, big for nine—"Nine and a half!"— and although Gloria sometimes wobbled on those rocks there was rarely any wobble in her young mind, which Saul admired. His own middle-aged brain sometimes slipped a gear or two.

So there she was again, a sturdy figure on the rocks, in her winter-weather gear—jeans, hooded jacket and sweater underneath, thick boots for wide feet—as he finished with the boat and brought compost around back in the wheelbarrow. She was talking to him. She was always talking to him, ever since she'd started coming by about a year ago.

"You know my ancestors lived here," she said. "Mama says they lived right here, where the lighthouse is." She had a deep and level voice for one so young, which sometimes startled him.

"So did mine, child," Saul told her, upturning the wheelbarrow load into the compost pile. Although truth was, the other side of his family had been an odd combination of rumrunners and fanatics who he liked to say, down at the bar, "had come to this land fleeing religious freedom."

After considering Saul's assertion for a moment, Gloria said, "Not before mine."

"Does it matter?" He noticed he'd missed some caulking on the boat.

The child frowned; he could feel her frown at his back, it was that powerful. "I don't know." He looked over at her, saw she'd stopped hopping between rocks, had decided that teetering on a dangerously sharp one made more sense. The sight made his stomach lurch, but he knew she never slipped, even though she seemed in danger of it many times, and as many times as he'd talked to her about it, she'd always ignored him.

"I think so," she said, picking up the conversation. "I think it does."

"I'm one-eighth Indian," he said. "I was here, too. Part of me." For what that was worth. A distant relative had told him about the lighthouse keeper's job, it was true, but no one else had wanted it.

"So what," she said, jumping to another sharp rock, balancing atop it, arms for a moment flailing and Saul taking a couple of steps closer to her out of fear.

She annoyed him much of the time, but he hadn't yet been able to shake her loose. Her father lived in the middle of the country somewhere, and her mother worked two jobs from a bungalow up the coast. The mother had to drive to far-off Bleakersville at least once a week, and probably figured her kid could manage on her own every now and again. Especially if the lighthouse keeper was looking after her. And the lighthouse held a kind of fascination for Gloria that he hadn't been able to break with his boring shed maintenance and wheelbarrow runs to the compost pile.

In the winter, too, she would be by herself a lot anyway—out on the mudflats just to the west, poking at fiddler crab holes with a stick or chasing after a half-domesticated doe, or peering at coyote or bear scat as if it held some secret. Whatever was on offer.

"Who're those strange people, coming around here?" she asked.

That almost made him laugh. There were a lot of strange people hidden away on the forgotten coast, himself included. Some were hiding from the government, some from themselves, some from spouses. A few believed that they were creating their own sovereign states. A couple probably weren't in the country legally. People asked questions out here, but they didn't expect an honest answer. Just an inventive one.

"Who exactly do you mean?"

"The ones with the pipes?"

It took Saul a moment, during which he imagined Henry and Suzanne skipping along the beach, pipes in their mouths, smoking away furiously.

"Pipes. Oh, they weren't pipes. They were something else." More like huge translucent mosquito coils. He'd let the Light Brigade leave the coils in the back room on the ground floor for a few months last summer. How in the heck had she seen that, anyway?

"Who are they?" she persisted, as she balanced now on two rocks, which at least meant Saul could breathe again.

"They're from the island up the coast." Which was true—their base was still out on Failure Island, home to dozens of them, a regular warren. "Doing tests," as the rumors went down at the village bar, where they did indeed like a good story.

Private researchers with government approval to take readings. But the rumors also insinuated that the S&SB had some more sinister agenda. Was it the orderliness, the precision, of some of them or the disorganization of the others that led to this rumor? Or just a couple of bored, drunk retirees emerging from their mobile homes to spin stories?

The truth was he didn't know what they were doing out on the island, or what they had planned to do with the equipment on the ground floor, or even what Henry and Suzanne were doing at the top of the lighthouse right now.

"They don't like me," she said. "And I don't like them."

That did make him chuckle, especially the brazen, arms-folded way she said it, like she'd decided they were her eternal enemy.

"Are you laughing at *me*?"

"No," he said. "No, I'm not. You're a curious person. You ask questions. That's why they don't like you. That's all." People who asked questions didn't necessarily like being asked questions.

"What's wrong with asking questions?"

"Nothing." Everything. Once the questions snuck in, whatever had been certain became uncertain. Questions opened the way for doubt. His father had told him that. "Don't let them ask questions. You're already giving them the answers, even if they don't know it."

"But you're curious, too," she said.

"Why do you say that?"

"You guard the light. And light sees everything."

The light might see everything, but he'd forgotten a few last tasks that would keep him out of the lighthouse for longer than he liked. He moved the wheelbarrow onto the gravel next to the station wagon. He felt a vague urgency, as if he should check on Henry and Suzanne. What if they had found the trapdoor and done something stupid, like fallen in and broken their strange little necks? Staring up just then, he saw Henry staring down from the railing far above, and that made him feel foolish. Like he was being paranoid. Henry waved, or was it some other gesture? Dizzy, Saul looked away as he made a kind of wheeling turn, disoriented by the sun's glare.

Only to see something glittering from the lawn—half hidden by a plant rising from a tuft of weeds near where he'd found a dead squirrel a couple of days ago. Glass? A key? The dark green leaves formed a rough circle, obscuring whatever lay at its base. He knelt, shielded his gaze, but the glinting thing was still hidden by the leaves of the plant, or was it part of a leaf? Whatever it was, it was delicate beyond measure, yet perversely reminded him of the four-ton lens far above his head.

The sun was a whispering corona at his back. The heat had risen, but there was a breeze that lifted the leaves of the palmettos in a rattling stir. The girl was somewhere behind him singing a nonsense song, having come back off the rocks earlier than he'd expected.

Nothing existed in that moment except for the plant and the gleam he could not identify.

He had gloves on still, so he knelt beside the plant and reached for the glittering thing, brushing up against the leaves. Was it a tiny shifting spiral of light? It reminded him of what you might see staring into a kaleidoscope, except an intense white. But whatever it was swirled and glinted and eluded his rough grasp, and he began to feel faint.

Alarmed, he started to pull back.

But it was too late. He felt a sliver enter his thumb. There was no pain, only a pressure and then numbness, but he still jumped up in surprise, yowling and waving his hand back and forth. He frantically tore off the glove, examined his thumb. Aware that Gloria was watching him, not sure what to make of him.

Nothing now glittered on the ground in front of him. No light at the base of the plant.

Slowly, Saul relaxed. Nothing throbbed in his thumb. There was no entry point, no puncture. He picked up the glove, checked it, couldn't find a tear.

"What's wrong?" Gloria asked. "Did you get stung?"

"I don't know," he said.

He felt other eyes upon him then, turned, and there stood Henry. How had he gotten down the stairs so fast? Had more time passed than he'd imagined?

"Yes—is something wrong, Saul?" Henry asked, but Saul could find no way to reconcile the concern expressed with any concern in the tone of his voice. Because there was none. Only a peculiar eagerness.

"Nothing is wrong," he said, uneasy but not knowing why he should be. "Just pricked my thumb."

"Through your gloves? That must have been quite the thorn." Henry was scanning the ground like someone who had lost a favorite watch or a wallet full of money.

"I'm fine, Henry. Don't worry about me." Angry more at looking silly over nothing, but also wanting Henry to believe him. "Maybe it was an electric shock."

"Maybe . . ." The gleam of the man's eyes was the light of a cold beacon coming to Saul from far off, as if Henry were broadcasting some other message entirely.

"Nothing is wrong," Saul said again.

Nothing was wrong.

Was it?

0002: GHOST BIRD

On the third day in Area X, with Control as her sullen companion, Ghost Bird found a skeleton in the reeds. It was winter in Area X now, and this had become more apparent once the trail meandered away from the sea that had been their entry point. The wind was cold and pushed against their faces, their jackets, the sky a watchful gray-blue that held back some essential secret. The alligators and the otters and the muskrats had retreated into the mud, ghosts somewhere beneath the dull slap and gurgle of water.

Far above, where the sky became a deeper blue, she caught a hint of some reflective surface, identified it as a wheeling cone of storks, the sun glinting silver from their white-and-gray feathers as they spun up into the sky at a great distance and with a stern authority, headed . . . where? She could not tell if they were testing the confines of their prison, able to recognize that invisible border before they crossed it, or like every other trapped thing here, simply operating on half-remembered instinct.

She stopped walking, and Control stopped with her. A man with prominent cheekbones, large eyes, an unobtrusive nose, and light brown skin. He was dressed in jeans and a red flannel shirt, along with a black jacket and a brand of boots that wouldn't have been her first choice for walking through the wilderness. The director of the Southern Reach. The man who had been her interrogator. An athlete's build, perhaps, but as long as they'd been in Area X, he'd been stooped over, muttering, as he examined forever and always a few water-stained, wrinkled pages he'd saved from some useless Southern Reach report. Flotsam from the old world.

He barely noticed the interruption.

"What is it?" he asked.

"Birds."

"Birds?" As if the word was foreign to him, or held no meaning. Or significance. But who knew what held significance here.

"Yes. Birds." Further specificity might be lost on him.

She took up her binoculars, watched the way the storks turned this way and then that way but never lost their form: a kind of living, gliding vortex in the sky. The pattern reminded her of the circling school of fish into which they'd emerged in shock, their surprising entrance into Area X from the bottom of the ocean.

Staring down at her, did the storks recognize what they saw? Were they reporting back to someone or something? Two nights running, she had sensed animals gathering at the edge of their campfire, dull and remote sensors for Area X. Control wanted more urgency, as if a destination meant something, while she wanted more data.

There had already been some misunderstandings about their relationship since reaching the beach—especially about who was in charge—and in the aftermath he'd taken back his name, asked that she call him Control again rather than John, which she respected. Some animals' shells were vital to their survival. Some animals couldn't live for long without them.

His disorientation wasn't helped by a fever and a sense, from her own accounts of "a brightness," that he too was being assimilated and might soon be something not himself. So perhaps she understood why he buried himself in what he called "my terroir pages," why he had lied about wanting to find solutions when it was so clear to her that he just needed something familiar to hold on to.

At one point on the first day, she had asked him, "What would I be to you back in the world—you at one of your old jobs, me at my old job?" He had not had an answer, but she thought she knew: She would be a suspect, an enemy of the right and the true. So what were they to each other here? Sometime soon she would have to force a real conversation, provoke conflict.

But for now, she was more interested in something off in the reeds to their left. A flash of orange? Like a flag?

She must have stiffened, or her demeanor gave her away, because Control asked, "What's wrong? Is something wrong?"

"Nothing, probably," she said.

After a moment, she found the orange again—a scrap, a tattered rag tied to a reed, bending back and forth in the wind. About three hundred feet out in the reed-ocean, that treacherous marsh of sucking mud. There seemed to be a shadow or depression just beyond it, the reeds giving way to something that couldn't be seen from their vantage.

She loaned him the binoculars. "See it?"

"Yes. It's a . . . a surveyor's mark," he said, unimpressed.

"Because that's likely," she said, then regretted it.

"Okay. Then it's 'like' a surveyor's mark." He handed back the binoculars. "We should stay on the trail, get to the island." A sincere utterance of *island* for once, proportional to his dislike of the unspoken idea that they investigate the rag.

"You can stay here," she said, knowing he wouldn't. Knowing she would have preferred he remain behind so she could be alone in Area X for a few moments.

Except: Was anyone ever truly alone out here?

For a long time after she had woken in the empty lot, then been taken to the Southern Reach for processing, Ghost Bird had thought she was dead, that she was in purgatory, even though she didn't believe in an afterlife. This feeling hadn't abated even when she'd figured out that she had come back across the border into the real world by unknown means . . . that she wasn't even the original biologist from the twelfth expedition but a copy.

She had admitted as much to Control during the interrogation sessions: "It was quiet and so *empty* . . . I waited there, afraid to leave, afraid there might be some reason I was meant to be there."

But this didn't encompass the full arc of her thoughts, of her analysis. There was not just the question of whether she was really alive but, if so, *who* she was, made oblique by her seclusion in her quarters at the Southern Reach. Then, examining the sense that her memories were not her own, that they came to her secondhand and that she could not be sure whether this was because of some experiment by the Southern Reach or an effect caused by Area X. Even through the intricacies of her escape on the way to Central, there was a sense of *projection*, of it happening to someone else, that she was only the interim solution, and perhaps that distance had aided her in avoiding capture, added a layer of absolute calm to her actions. When she'd reached the remote Rock Bay, so familiar to the biologist who had been there before her, she'd had peace for a while, let the landscape subsume her in a different way—let it break her down so she could be built up again.

But only when they had burst through into Area X had she truly gained the upper hand on her unease, her purposelessness. She had panicked for a second as the water pressed in on her, surrounded her, evoked her own drowning. But then something had *turned on*, or had come back, and raging against her own death, she had exulted in the sensation of the sea, welcomed having to fight her way to the surface—bursting through such a joyful hysteria of biomass—as a sort of proof that she was not the biologist, that she was some new thing that could, wanting to survive, cast out her fear of drowning as belonging to another.

In the aftermath, even resuscitating Control on the beach had seemed undeniable proof of her own sovereignty. As had her insistence on heading for the island, not the lighthouse. "Wherever the biologist would have gone, that is where I will go." The truth, the *rightness*, in that had given her hope, despite the sense that everything she remembered she had observed through a window opening onto another person's life. Not truly experienced. Or not experienced yet. "You want a lived-in life because you don't have one," Control had said to her, but that was a crude way to put it.

There had been little new to experience since. Nothing monstrous or unusual had yet erupted from the horizon in almost three full days of walking. Nothing unnatural, except for this hyperreal aspect to the landscape, these processes working beneath the surface. At dusk, too, an image of the biologist's starfish came to her, dimly shining, like a compass in her head that drew her on, and she realized again that Control couldn't feel what she felt here. He couldn't navigate the dangers, recognize the opportunities. The brightness had left her, but something else had stepped in to replace it.

"Counter-shading," she'd said when he'd confessed his confusion that Area X looked so normal. "You can know a thing and not know a thing. A grebe's markings from above are obvious. You cannot miss a grebe from above. Seen from below, though, as it floats in the water, it is practically invisible."

"Grebe?"

"A bird." Another bird.

"All of this is a disguise?" He said it with a kind of disbelief, as if the reality were strange enough.

Ghost Bird had relented, because it wasn't his fault. "You've never walked through an ecosystem that wasn't compromised or dysfunctional, have you? You may think you have, but you haven't. So you might mistake what's right for what's wrong anyway."

That might not be true, but she wanted to hold on to the idea of authority—didn't want another argument about their destination. Insisting on heading for the island was protecting not just her life but his, too, she believed. She had no interest in last chances, last desperate charges into the guns of the enemy, and something in Control's affect made her believe he might be working toward that kind of solution. Whereas she was not yet committed to anything other than wanting to know—herself and Area X.

The light in that place was inescapable, so bright yet distant. It brought a rare clarity to the reeds and the mud and the water that mirrored and followed them in the canals. It was the light that made her feel as if she glided because it tricked her into losing track of her own steps. It was the light that kept replenishing the calm within her. The light explored and questioned everything in a way she wasn't sure Control would understand, then retreated to allow what it touched to exist apart from it.

Perhaps it was the light that got in the way, too, for theirs was a kind of back-tracking, stuttering progress, using a stick to prod the ground in front of them for treachery, the thick reeds forming clumps that at times were impenetrable. Once, a limpkin, grainy brown and almost invisible against the reeds, rose so near and so silent it startled her almost more than it did Control.

But eventually they reached the rag tied to the reeds, saw the yellowing cathedral beyond, stuck in the mud and sunk halfway.

"What the hell is that?" Control asked.

"It's dead," she said. "It can't harm us." Because Control continued to overreact to what she considered insufficient stimuli. Skittish, or damaged from some other experience entirely.

But she knew all too well what it was. Sunken into the middle were the remains of a hideous skull and a bleached and hardened mask of a face that stared sightless up at them, fringed with mold and lichen.

"The moaning creature," she said. "The moaning creature we always heard at dusk." That had chased the biologist across the reeds.

The flesh had sloughed off, runneled down the sides of the bones, vanished into the soil. What remained was a skeleton that looked uncannily like the confluence of a giant hog and a human being, a set of smaller ribs suspended from the larger like a macabre internal chandelier, and tibias that ended in peculiar nub-like bits of gristle scavenged by birds and coyotes and rats.

"It's been here awhile," Control said.

"Yes, it has." Too long. Prickles of alarm made her scan the horizon for some intruder, as if the skeleton were a trap. Alive just eighteen months ago, and yet now in a state of advanced decay, the face plate all that saved it from being unidentifiable. Even if this creature, this transformation of the psychologist from what Control called "the last eleventh expedition," had died right after the biologist had encountered it alive . . . the rate of decomposition was unnatural.

Control hadn't caught on, though, so she decided not to share. He just kept pacing around the skeleton, staring at it.

"So this was a person, once," he said, and then said it again when she didn't respond.

"Possibly. It might also have been a failed double." She didn't think she was a failed double like this creature. She had purpose, free will.

Perhaps a copy could also be superior to the original, create a new reality by avoiding old mistakes.

"I have your past in my head," he'd told her as soon as they'd left the beach, intent on trading information. "I can give it back to you." An ancient refrain by now, unworthy of him or of her.

Her silence had forced him to go first, and although she thought he still might be holding things back, his words, infused with urgency and a kind of passion, had a sincerity to them. Sometimes, too, a forlorn subtext crept in, one that she understood quite well and chose to ignore. She had identified it easily from the time he had visited her in her quarters back at the Southern Reach.

The news that the psychologist from the twelfth expedition had been the former director of the Southern Reach and that she had thought the biologist was her special project, her special hope, made Ghost Bird laugh. She felt a sudden affection for the psychologist, remembering their skirmishes during the induction interviews. The devious psychologist/director, trying to combat something as wide and deep as Area X with something as narrow and blunt as the biologist. As her. A sudden wren, quick-darting through brambles to flit out of sight, seemed to share her opinion.

When it was her turn, she conceded that she now remembered everything up to the point at which she had been scanned or atomized or replicated by the Crawler that lived in the tunnel/tower—the moment of her creation, which might have been the moment of the biologist's death. The Crawler and the lighthouse keeper's face, burning through the layered myths of its construction, made disbelief shine through Control as if he were a translucent deep-sea fish. Among all the impossible things he had already witnessed, what were a few more?

He asked no questions that had not been asked in some form by the biologist, the surveyor, the anthropologist, or the psychologist during the twelfth expedition.

Somehow that created an uncomfortable doubling effect, too, one that she argued about in her own head. Because she did not agree with her own decisions at times—the biologist's decisions. Why had her other self been so careless with the words on the wall? For example. Why hadn't she confronted the psychologist/director as soon as she knew about the hypnosis? What had been gained by going down to find the Crawler? Some things Ghost Bird could forgive, but others grated and drove her into spirals of might-have-beens that infuriated her.

The biologist's husband she rejected entirely, without ambivalence, for there came with the husband the desolation of living in the city. The biologist had been married but Ghost Bird wasn't, released from responsibility for any of that. She didn't really understand why her double had put up with it. Among the misunderstandings between her and Control: having to make clear that her need for lived-in experience to supplant memories not her own did not extend to their relationship, whatever image of her he carried in his head. She could not just plunge into something physical with him and overlay the unreal with the ordinary, the mechanical, not when her memories were of a husband who had come home stripped of memories. Any compromise would just hurt them both, was somehow beside the point.

Standing there in front of the skeleton of the moaning creature, Control said: "Then I might end up like this? Some version of me?"

"We all end up like this, Control. Eventually."

But not quite like this, because from those eye sockets, from the moldering bones, came a sense of a brightness still, a kind of life—a questing toward her that she rebuffed and that Control could not sense. Area X was looking at her through dead eyes. Area X was analyzing her from all sides. It made her feel like an outline created by the regard bearing down on her, one that moved only because the regard moved with her, held her constituent atoms together in a coherent shape. And yet, the eyes upon her felt familiar.

"The director might have been wrong about the biologist, but perhaps you're the answer." Said only half sarcastically, as if he almost knew what she was receiving.

"I'm not an answer," she said. "I'm a question." She might also be a message incarnate, a signal in the flesh, even if she hadn't yet figured out what story she was supposed to tell.

She was thinking, too, about what she had seen on the journey into Area X, how it had seemed as if to both sides there lay nothing around them but the terrible blackened ruins of vast cities and enormous beached ships, lit by the roaring red and orange of fires that did nothing but cast shadow and obscure the distant view of mewling things that crawled and hopped through the ash. How she had tried to block out Control's rambling confessions, the shocking things he said without knowing, so that she did not think he had a secret she did not now know. *Pick up the gun . . . Tell me a joke . . . I killed her, it was my fault . . .* Had whispered hypnotic incantations in his ear to shut out not only his words but also the horror show around them.

The skeleton before them had been picked clean. The discolored bones were rotting, the tips of the ribs already turned soft with moisture, most of them broken off, lost in the mud.

Above, the storks still banked and wheeled this way and that in an intricate, synchronized aerial dance more beautiful than anything ever created by human minds.

0003: THE DIRECTOR

On the weekends, your refuge is Chipper's Star Lanes, where you're not the director of the Southern Reach but just another customer at the bar. Chipper's lies off the highway well out of Bleakersville, one step up from being at the end of a dirt road. Jim Lowry's people back at Central might know the place, might be watching and listening, but you've never met anyone from the Southern Reach there. Even Grace Stevenson, your second-in-command, doesn't know about it. For a disguise, you wear a T-shirt for a local construction company or a charity event like a chili cook-off and an old pair of jeans from the last time you were fat, sometimes topped off with a baseball cap advertising your favorite barbecue joint.

You usually start out front, on Chipper's rotting but still functional Safari Adventure miniature golf course, like you used to with your dad when you were a kid. The lions at the ninth hole are a sleeping huddle of dreamy plastic melted and blackened at the edges from some long-ago disaster. The huge hippo bestride the course-ending eighteenth has dainty ankles, and flaked-off splotches reveal bloodred paint beneath, as if its makers had been too obsessed with making it real.

Afterward you'll go inside and bowl a few pickup games with anyone who needs a fourth, under the fading universe painted on the ceiling—there's Earth, there's Jupiter, there's a purpling nebula with a red center, all of it lit up at night with a cheesy laser show. You're good for four or five games, rarely top two hundred. When done, you sit at the dark, comfortable bar. It's been shoved into a back corner as far from the room of stinking shoes as possible, and somehow the acoustics muffle the squeak, bump, and rumble of the bowling. Everything here is still too close to Area X, but as long as no one knows, that information can keep on killing the customers as slowly as it has over the past decades.

The Chipper's bar attracts mostly stalwart regulars, because it's really a dive, with dark felt stapled to the ceiling that's meant to be sprinkled with stars. But whatever the metal that's nailed up there, looking more like an endless series of sheriff's badges from old Westerns, it's been rusting for a long time, so now it's become a dull black punctuated by tiny reddish-brown starfish. A sign in the corner advertises the Star Lanes Lounge. The lounge part consists of half a dozen round wooden tables and chairs with black fake-leather upholstery that look like they were stolen long ago from a family-restaurant chain.

Most of your comrades at the bar are heavily invested in the sports leaking out of the silent, closed-caption TV; the old green carpet, which climbs the side walls, soaks up the murmur of conversations. The regulars are harmless and rarely raucous, including a Realtor who thinks she is the knower of all things but makes up for it by being able to tell a good story. Then there's the silver-bearded seventy-year-old man who's almost always standing at the end of the bar drinking a light beer. He's a veteran of some war, veers between laconic and neighborly.

Your psychologist cover story feels wrong here, and you don't like using it. Instead, you tell anyone who asks that you're a long-haul trucker between jobs and take a drag on your bottle of beer to end that part of the conversation. People find the idea of that line of work plausible; maybe something about your height and broad frame sells them on it. But most nights you can almost believe you *are* a trucker, and that these people are your sort-of friends.

The Realtor says the man's not a veteran, just "an alcoholic looking for sympathy," but you can tell she's not without sympathy for that. "I'm just going to opt out" is a favorite phrase of the veteran. So is "the hell there isn't." The rest are a cross-section of ER nurses, a couple of mechanics, a hairdresser, a few receptionists and office managers. What your dad would've called "people who're never allowed to see behind the curtain." You don't bother investigating them, or the oft-revolving bartenders, because it doesn't matter. You never say anything seditious or confidential at Chipper's.

But some nights, when you stay late and the bar crowd thins, you write down on a napkin or coaster a point or two you can't leave alone—some of the continual puzzle-questions thrown at you by Whitby Allen, a holistic environments expert who reports to Mike Cheney, the overly jovial head of the science division. You never asked for these questions, but that doesn't stop Whitby, who seems like his head's on fire and the only way to put the fire out is to douse it with his ideas.

"What's outside the border when you're inside it?" "What's the border when you're inside it?" "What's the border when someone is outside it?" "Why can't the person inside see the person outside?"

"My statements aren't any better than my questions," Whitby admitted to you once, "but if you want easy, you should check out what they serve up over at Cheney's Science Shack."

An impressive document backs up Whitby's ideas, shining out from underneath the glossy invisible membrane of a piece of clear plastic. In a brand-new three-ring black binder, exquisitely hole-punched, not a typo in the entire twelve-page printout, with its immaculate title page: a masterpiece entitled "Combined Theories: A Complete Approach."

The report is as shiny, clever, and quick as Whitby. The questions it raises, the recommendations made, insinuate with little subtlety that Whitby thinks the Southern Reach can do better, that he can do better if he is only given the chance. It's a lot to digest, especially with the science department ambushing it and taking potshots in memos sent to you alone: "Suppositions in search of evidence, head on backward or sideways." Or, maybe even sprouting from his ass.

But to you it's deadly serious, especially a list of "conditions required for Area X to exist" that include

- an isolated place
- an inert but volatile trigger
- a catalyst to pull the trigger
- an element of luck or chance in how the trigger was deployed
- a context we do not understand
- an attitude toward energy that we do not understand
- an approach to language that we do not understand

"What's next?" Cheney says at one status meeting. "A careful study of the miracles of the saints, unexplained occurrences writ large, two-headed calves predicting the apocalypse, to see if anything rings a bell?"

Whitby at the time is a feisty debater, one who likes hot water, who leaps in with a rejoinder that he knows will not just get Cheney's goat but pen it up, butcher it, and roast it: "It acts a bit like an organism, like skin with a million greedy mouths instead of cells or pores. And the question isn't *what* it is but is the motive. Think of Area X as a murderer we're trying to catch."

"Oh great, that's just great, now we've got a detective on staff, too." Cheney muttering while you give him the hush-hand and Grace helps out with her best pained smile. Because the truth is, you told Whitby to act like a detective, in an attempt to "think outside the Southern Reach."

For a while, too, with Whitby's help, you are arrows shot straight at a target. Because it's not as if you don't have successes at first. Under your watch, there are breakthroughs in expedition equipment, like enhanced field microscopes and weaponry that doesn't trigger Area X's defenses. More expeditions begin to come back intact, and the refinements in making people into their functions—the tricks you've learned from living in your own disguise—seem to help.

You chart the progress of Area X's reclamation of the environment, begin to get some small sense of its parameters, and even create expedition cycles with shared metrics. You may not always control those criteria, but, for a while, the consensus is that the situation has stabilized, that the news is improving. The gleaming silver egg you imagine when you think of Central—those seamless, high-level thoughts so imperfectly expressed through your superiors there—hums and purrs and pulses out approval over all of you . . . even if it also emanates the sense that the Southern Reach is some kind of meat-brain corruption of a beautiful elegant algorithm Central has hidden deep inside itself.

But as the years pass, with Lowry's influence more and more corrosive, there's no solution forthcoming. Data pulled out of Area X duplicates itself and declines, or "declines to be interpreted," as Whitby puts it, and theories proliferate but nothing can be proven. "We lack the analogies," the linguists keep saying.

Grace starts to call them the "languists" as they falter, can't keep up, and as the grim joke goes, "fell by the side of a road that was like a mixed metaphor of a tongue that curled up and took them with it," Area X muddying the waters. Except it wasn't muddying waters or a tongue by the side of the road or anything else, muddled or not, that they could understand. "We lack the analogies" was itself somehow deficient as a diagnosis, linguists burning up during reentry into the Earth's atmosphere after encountering Area X. Making you think of all the dead and dying satellites sent hurtling down into the coordinates that comprised Area X, because it was easy, because space debris winking out of existence made a perverse kind of sense, even as turning Area X into a garbage can seemed like the kind of disrespect that might piss off an insecure deity. Except Area X never responded, even to that indignity.

The linguists aren't really the problem, nor even Central. Lowry's the problem because Lowry keeps your secret—that you grew up in what became Area X—and in return you have to try to give him what he wants, within reason. Lowry has invested other people's blood and sweat in the idea of the expeditions, and implied by that the idea of the border as an impenetrable barrier, which means he's safe on the right side of the divide. While Whitby keeps pushing against the traditional: "Whatever we think of the border, it's important to recognize it as a *limitation* of Area X." Was that important?

What seemed more important to you: The truth to rumors about Lowry's ruthlessness once he reached Central, that he had carved out his own soundproof shop. The whispers that came back to you distant but clear over the years, like hiking in a dark, still forest and hearing the faint sound of wind chimes. Something that beckons, promising all the comforts of civilization, but once the seeker reaches the end of that particular path, all she finds is a slaughterhouse piled high with corpses. The proof of it in the way he so easily overrules Pitman, your nominal boss at Central, and presses you harder for results.

By the time you're on the eleventh cycle of expeditions, you're more and more drained, and Central's plan has begun to change. The flow of new personnel, money, and equipment has been reduced to a trickle as Central spends most of its time crushing domestic terrorism and suppressing evidence of impending ecological destruction.

You return after long days to the house in Bleakersville, which is no refuge. The ghosts follow, sit on the couch or peer in through the windows. Thoughts you don't want creep in at odd moments—in the middle of status meetings, sitting down for lunch with Grace in the cafeteria, searching idly for Central's latest bugs in your office—that maybe none of this is worth it, that you're not getting anywhere. The weight of each expedition leaning in on you.

"I could've been director," Lowry boasted once, "but a warning light came on in the cockpit and I took the hint." The warning light is a fear that you know lives inside of him, but Lowry will never admit to it. The cruel jocularity to his goading, as if he knows he keeps asking you for the impossible.

Always worried, in a continual low-grade-fever sort of way, that someone at the Southern Reach or Central will discover your secret, that Lowry won't be able to bury the information forever—or he'll divulge it himself, having decided you're disposable. Security risk. A liar. Too emotionally invested. And yet compassion is what you most distrust, what you thrust away from you, preferring to project with everyone but Grace that you're cold, distant, even harsh, so that you can be clearheaded and objective . . . even if acting the part has made you a little cold, distant, and harsh.

In some unquantifiable way, too, you believe Lowry's approach is pushing the Southern Reach farther away from the answers. Like an astronaut headed into the oblivion of vast and empty space who, in flailing about, only speeds up the moment when he is beyond rescue. And worse, to your way of thinking, reliving without nostalgia the thrust of your days as a psychologist, Lowry has doomed himself to finding countless ways to relive his own horrifying experience in Area X, so he can never be entirely free, the seeming attempt to cast it away turned into an endless embrace.

Your other sanctuary is the roof of the Southern Reach building—protected from view from below by the weird baffling, the wandering ridge, that circles the roof. Beyond Reach, BR for short, "Brr" in the winter and "Burr" or sometimes "Bee-arr!" or "Bear!" in the summer. Always "Bar" when you sneak up for drinks after work.

You share this sacred space with only one person: Grace. You bat around the ideas that pop up at Star Lanes, "shoot the shit," protected by the fact that only you, Grace, and the janitor have the key. Many times people will try to track you down, only to find you have evaporated, reappearing, unbeknownst to them, in Beyond Reach.

It's there, staring out at the prehistoric swamp, the miles of dark pine forest, that you and Grace come up with all the nicknames. The border you call "the moat" and the way in is "the front door," although both of you are always hoping you'll find a "side door" or a "trapdoor." The tunnel or topographical anomaly in Area X you refer to as "El Topoff," riffing on a strange film Grace once saw with her girlfriend.

A lot of it is stupid, but funny in the moment, especially if you've got a bottle of brandy, or if she brings cherry-flavored cigarettes, and you pull up a couple of lawn chairs and brainstorm or talk about the weekend to come. Grace knows about Chipper's, like you know about her canoe trips with her friends, "your addiction to paddles." You don't need to tell her not to show up at Chipper's, and you never invite yourself downriver. The circumference of your friendship is the length and breadth of the Southern Reach.

It's on the roof that you first mention to Grace your idea of sneaking across the border into Area X. Over time it has become more than a thought tingling at the edge of things—metastasizing as code, as "a road trip with Whitby," since the expeditions during the tenth and eleventh cycles have fared much better, even if there aren't any answers, either.

You can't take Grace, although you need her counsel. Because that would be like cutting off two heads at once if anything went wrong, and you've never thought Grace had the temperament for it; too many connections to the world. Children. Sisters. An ex-husband. A girlfriend. It's Grace who you joke is your "external moral compass" and knows better than you where the boundaries are. "Too normal," you wrote on a napkin once.

"Why do you let Lowry tell you what to do?" Grace says to you one afternoon, after you've directed the conversation that way. You deflect/refract. Lowry isn't your direct boss, is more like slant rhyme, not there at the end of things but still in control. Grace would have to know how Lowry's gotten his hooks in at Central, and how he got his hooks into you, and you've managed to shield her from that.

You remind Grace that there is a part of the kingdom you *do* control, that Lowry doesn't get to influence: what comes out of Area X from the expeditions. It's all processed through the Southern Reach, and so when the latest eleventh expedition came back with nothing to show for it except some blurry photographs left behind at base camp by the prior expedition, or perhaps one even earlier, you took them away and stared at them for hours. A collection of shadows against a black background. But was that a wall? Was that a texture that reminded you of another photograph from another expedition? So you pulled all of the photographs taken inside El Topoff. All thirteen of them, and, yes, these new ones could have been taken in the tunnel, too. That shadow, that faint outline of a face . . . is that familiar? Would it be wrong of you to believe it means something?

Confessing your simple plan to Grace, showing her some of the evidence, you're betting that she won't betray you to Central, but you know she might, out of a respect for the rules. Because behind all of your reasons, your data, you worry that it just boils down to being tired of the feeling in the pit of your stomach every time another expedition doesn't come back, or only half comes back, or comes back with nothing. Needing to somehow change the paradigm.

"It's just a quick jaunt over to El Topoff and back. No one will ever find out." Although Lowry might. What will he do if he finds out you crossed the border without his approval? Would his anger be directed just at you?

After a pause, Grace says, "What do you need from me?" Because she can see it is important, and that you'll do it whether she helps you or not.

The next thing she says is, "Do you think you can convince Whitby?"

"Yes, I do," you say, and Grace looks skeptical.

But Whitby's not a problem. Whitby's eager, like a yipping terrier wanting to go for a long, long walk. Whitby wants out of the science department for a while. Whitby's the one reassuring you by citing the survival rate of the last few expeditions. Whitby's so invigorated by the opportunity that you can almost forget the whole idea is dangerous.

It's a relief, because you realize that weekend, as you exchange small talk with the Realtor, that you were terrified of going alone. Realize, watching a football game on the bar TV, below that canopy of transfixed and rusting heavens, that if Whitby hadn't said yes, you might've called the whole thing off.

Through the door, on your way to Area X, you feel a kind of pressure that bends you low, see a black horizon full of shooting stars, their trails bleeding so rich and deep across the non-sky that you squint against the brilliance of that celestial welder's torch. A sense of teetering, of vertigo, but each time you lurch too far to one side or the other, something nudges you back toward the center, as if the edges, closer than they seem, curl up at a more severe angle. Your thoughts dart quick then slow, something stitching between them you cannot identify. The impulse comes to stop walking, to just stand there, in the corridor between the real world and Area X, for an eternity.

While hypnotized Whitby shuffles along, eyes closed, his face a twitching mass of tics as if he's having an intense dream. Whatever haunts him inside his own head, you've made sure he won't get lost, won't just come to a halt somewhere in transit. He's tied to you by the wrists with a nylon rope, and he stumbles along behind.

The molasses feeling Whitby told you to expect comes next, the sense of wading through thigh-high water, the resistance that means you are close to the end, a hint of the deep, spiraling door of light far ahead, and just in time, because stoic as you could be, Whitby's dream-walking has begun to get to you, makes you think *things* look in at you. You lose the sense of where you are in relation to anything, even your own body . . . Are you really walking, or are you standing still and your brain just thinks that your feet are lifting up, falling down, lifting up again?

Until the resistance falls away like a breath held too long and then released, and you both stumble through the door and out into Area X. With Whitby on all fours, hugging the ground, shaking convulsively, and you pulling him free and past, so he won't accidentally stagger in the wrong direction and disappear forever. He's gasping like you both are gasping, from the freshness of the air, acclimating to it.

Such a blue, cloudless sky. A trail that should be so familiar, but it has been decades since you saw the forgotten coast. It will take more than a moment to think of it as home. You recognize the trail more from photographs and the accounts of expedition members, know it was here before the first invaders, was used by some of your long-ago ancestors, and has even now survived, overgrown, as part of Area X.

"Can you walk?" you ask Whitby, once you've brought him back to his senses.

"Of course I can walk." Enthusiastic, but a kind of brittle sheen behind it, as if something has already been stripped away underneath.

You don't ask him what he dreamed, what he saw. You don't want to know until you're back across.

You had reviewed those toxic Area X video clips from the doomed first expedition not to seek answers but, with some measure of guilt, to seek a connection with the wilderness you'd known as a child. To reinforce your memories, to recall what you could not recall—pushing past the screams, the disorientation, and the lack of comprehension, past Lowry's weeping, past the darkness.

There you can see the line of rocks near the lighthouse, the shore already a little different then, as if Whitby's terroir could be traced through the patterns left by the surf. As if down there, amid the sand-crab holes and the tiny clams digging in every time the water reveals them, some sample might hold all the answers.

The trails, too: a dark stillness of the pine trees and thick underbrush mottled by a strangled light. The memory of being disoriented and lost in a thunderstorm at the age of six, of emerging from that forest not knowing where you were—brought out of you by the cautious quiet way the expedition leader noted looming clouds, as if they presaged something more than a need to find shelter.

After the storm, in the startling revelation of open space and sunlight, you'd encountered a huge alligator blocking the narrow path, with water on both sides.

You'd taken a running start and jumped over it. Never told your mother about the exhilaration, the way you had in mid-leap dared a glance down to see that yellow eye, that dark vertical pupil, appraise you, take you in like Area X had taken in the first expedition, and then you were over and past, running for a long time out of sheer joy, sheer adrenaline, like you'd conquered the world.

The running on the screen toward the end is away from something, not toward something, and the screams later not of triumph but of defeat—tired screams, as of weariness at fighting against something that would not properly show itself. In your more cynical moments you thought of them as perfunctory screams: an organism that knows there is no point in fighting back, the body capitulating and the mind letting it. They were not lost as you were lost that day; they had no cottage by the sea to return to, no mother pacing on the deck, worried out of her mind, grateful for your sudden grimy, soaked appearance.

Something on your face must have retained the memory of your joy because she didn't punish you, just got you in dry clothes and fed you, and asked no questions.

Bypassing the route to base camp, you head for the topographical anomaly with the urgency of a ticking clock driving you. The knowledge—never discussed with Whitby—that the longer you stay, the longer you seem to linger, the greater the opportunity for disaster. That alligator eye staring up at you, with more awareness behind its piercing gaze than you remember. Someone off-camera on the second day of the first expedition saying, "I want to go home," and Lowry, goofing around, so confident, saying, "What do ya mean? This is our home now. We've got everything here. Everything we need. Right?"

Nowhere is this sense of urgency more intense than while passing through the swampy forest that lies a mile or two from the border, where the woods meet a dank black-water gutter. The place where you most often saw evidence of bears and heard things rustling in the darkness of the tree cover.

Whitby's often silent, and when he speaks his questions and concerns do nothing to alleviate the pressure of that gloom, the sense of *intent* eternal and everlasting that occupies this stretch of land, that predates Area X. The still, standing water, the oppressive blackness of a sky in which the blue peers down through the trees at startling intervals, only to be taken away again, and only ever seeming to come to you from a thousand miles off anyway. Is this the clearing where three men died during the fifth expedition? Does that pond hold the bodies of men and women from the first eighth? Sometimes, immersed in these overlays, Whitby's pale whispering form is a jolting shock to you, inseparable from these echoes of prior last days.

Eventually, though, you cross into a more optimistic landscape, one in which you can adapt, reconcile past and present into one vision. Here, a wider path separates the continuing dank swamp forest from open ground, allows you a horizon of a few tall pines scattered among the wild grass and palmetto circles. The lean of that forest means that the darkness ends at an angle casting half the trail in a slanted shade.

There are other borders within Area X, other gauntlets, and you have passed through one to get to the topographical anomaly.

Once there, you know immediately the tower isn't made of stone—and so does Whitby. Does he wish now, his expression unreadable, that you had put him through conditioning, that he'd been given all the training Central could bestow, not your half measures, your shoddy hypnotism?

The tower is breathing. There is no ambiguity about it: The flesh of the circular top of the anomaly rises and falls with the regular rhythm of a person deep in sleep. No one mentioned this aspect in the reports; you aren't prepared for it, but how easily you acclimate, give yourself up to it, can already imagine descending even as a part of you is floating, ascending to look down on the foolishness of this decision.

Will it wake up while you're inside it?

The opening leading into darkness resembles a maw more than a passageway, the underbrush around it pushed back, squashed in a rough framing circle, as if some now-absent serpent had once curled around it in a protective mode. The stairs form a curling snarl of crooked teeth, the air expelled smelling of thick rot.

"I can't go down there," Whitby says, in such a final way that he must be thinking that in the descent he would no longer be Whitby. The hollows of his face, even in that vibrant, late-summer light, make him look haunted by a memory he hasn't had yet.

"Then I'll go," you offer—down into the gullet of the beast. Others have, if rarely, and come back, so why not you? Wearing a breathing mask, just to be safe.

There is a dazed panic and coiled restraint behind your every movement that will come out later through the flesh, the bone. Months from now you will wake sore and bruised, as if your body cannot forget what happened, and this is the only way it can express the trauma.

Inside, it's different than in the fragmentary reports brought back by other expeditions. The living tissue curling down the wall is almost inert, the feeble wanderings of the tendrils that form the words so slow you think for a moment it's all necrotic tissue. Nor are the words a vibrant green as reported but a searing blue, almost the color of a flame on a stove top. The word *dormant* comes to mind, and with it a wild hope: that everything beneath you will be inert, normal, even if at the outer boundary of what that word means.

You keep to the middle, do not touch either wall, try to ignore the shuddering breath of the tower. You don't read the words because you have long seen that as a kind of trap, a way to become distracted . . . and still the sense that whatever will disorient and destabilize lies below you, deciding whether to be seen or remain unseen—around a corner, beyond the horizon, and with each new empty reveal, each curve of the steps lit by the blue flames of dead words, toward an unknown become shy, you are wound ever tighter, even though there is nothing to be seen. The hell of that, the hell of nothing at all, which feels as if you are reliving every moment of your life at the Southern Reach—descending for no reason, for nothing, to find nothing. No answers, no solution, no end in sight, the words on the wall not getting fresher but darker, seeming to wink out as you come upon them . . . until, finally, you glimpse a light far, far below—so far below it's like a glowing flower in a hole at the bottom of the sea, a glimmering, elusive light that through some magician's trick also hovers right in front of your face, giving you the illusion that you can reach out and touch it if you only can find the courage to extend your hand.

But that's not what makes your legs ropy, a rush of blood surging through your brain.

A figure sits hunched along the side of the left-hand wall, staring down the steps.

A figure with head bowed, turned away from you.

A prickling engulfs your head under your mask, a kind of smooth, seamless insertion of a million cold, painless needles, ever so subtle, ever so invisible, so that you can pretend it is just a spreading heat against your skin, a taut feeling across the sides of your nose, around your eyes, the quiet soft entry of needles into a pincushion, the return of something always meant to be there.

You tell yourself this is no less or more real than bowling at Chipper's, than the hippo with the red paint under the skin, than living in Bleakersville, working at the Southern Reach. That this moment is the same as every other moment, that it makes no difference to the atoms, to the air, to the creature whose walls breathe all around you. That you gave up the right to call anything impossible when you decided to enter Area X.

You come closer, drawn by this impossible thing, sit on the step next to him.

His eyes are shut. His face is illuminated by a dark blue glow that emanates from within, as if his skin has been taken over, and he is as porous as volcanic rock. He's fused to the wall, or jutting out from it, like an extension of the wall, something that protrudes but might be retracted at any moment.

"Are you real?" you ask, but he says nothing in reply.

Reaching out to him, extending a trembling hand, awestruck by this apparition, wanting to know what that skin feels like, even as you're afraid your touch will turn him to powder. Your fingers graze his forehead, a rough, moist feel, like touching sandpaper under a thick layer of water.

"Do you remember me?"

"You shouldn't be here," Saul Evans says under his breath. His eyes are closed; he cannot see you, and yet you know he sees you. "You need to get off the rocks. The tide's coming in."

You don't know what to say. You won't know what to say for a long time. Your reply was so many years ago.

Now you can hear the vast, all-consuming hum of some mighty engine from below, the swift revolving of strange orbits, and the light below, that impossible flowering light, is fluctuating, shifting, turning into something else.

His eyes snap open, white against the darkness. He's no different than when you last saw him, has not aged, and you're nine again and the light below is coming up toward you, coursing up the steps toward you, fast, and from above you can hear the distant echo of Whitby screaming, from the top of the tower, as if he's screaming for both of you.

0004: THE LIGHTHOUSE KEEPER

Armadillos ruining the garden, but don't really want to put out poison. Sea grape bushes must be pruned back. Will make a list of maintenance issues by tomorrow. Fire on Failure Island, but already reported and not major. Sighted: albatross, unidentified terns, bobcat (peering out of the palmetto grove to the east, staring at a hiker who didn't see him), flycatcher of some kind, pod of dolphins headed east in a frenzy as they chased a school of mullet through the sea grass in the shallows.

Bodies could be beacons, too, Saul knew. A lighthouse was a fixed beacon for a fixed purpose; a person was a moving one. But people still emanated light in their way, still shone across the miles as a warning, an invitation, or even just a static signal. People opened up so they became a brightness, or they went dark. They turned their light inward sometimes, so you couldn't see it, because they had no other choice.

"That's bullshit," Charlie said during the night, when Saul expressed something similar to him, after they'd had sex. "Don't ever become a poet." For once, Saul had convinced Charlie to come to the lighthouse, a rare event because Charlie still had a skittish, flighty quality to him. Beaten by his father and kicked out by his family, and in the twenty years since he'd not entirely come out of his shell. So this was a halting step forward—something that made Saul happy, that he could provide a small sense of security.

"An idea in one of my father's sermons. The best he ever gave." Flexing his hand, trying to sense any residual discomfort from the incident with the plant. None to be found.

"Ever miss it? Being a preacher?" Charlie asked.

"No, I'm just working out something about the Light Brigade," he said. They still elicited in him a distant but sharp alarm. What were they projecting that he couldn't see?

"Oh, *them*, huh?" Charlie said with a simulated yawn as he turned over on his back. "You can't leave those Brigaders alone, can you? Bunch of crackpots. You, too." But said with affection.

Later, when he was drifting off, Charlie murmured, "It's not stupid. The beacon thing. It's kind of a nice thought. Maybe."

Maybe. Saul found it hard to tell when Charlie was sincere about such things. Sometimes their life between the sheets seemed mysterious, to have no relationship to life out in the world.

Sometimes, too, other people gave you their light, and could seem to flicker, to be hardly visible at all, if no one took care of them. Because they'd given you too much and had nothing left for themselves.

At the end, with his church, he'd felt like a beacon that had been drained of light, except for some guttering glimmer in the heart of him—the way the words shone out from his mouth, and it almost didn't matter what light they created, not to his congregation, because they were looking at him, not listening. At best, anyway, his ministry had been an odd assortment, attracting hippies and the straitlaced alike, because he'd pulled from the Old Testament and from deism, and the esoteric books available to him in his father's house. Something his father hadn't planned on: the bookshelves leading Saul to places the old man would rather he'd never gone. His father's library had been more liberal than the man himself.

The shock of going from being the center of attention to being out of it entirely—that still pulled at Saul at unexpected times. But there had been no drama to his collapsed ministry in the north, no shocking revelation, beyond the way he would be preaching one thing and thinking another, mistaking that conflict, for the longest time, as a manifestation of his guilt for sins both real and imagined. And one awful day he'd realized, betrayed by his passion, that *he* was becoming the message.

By the time Saul woke up, Charlie was gone, without even a note. But, then, a note might have seemed sentimental, and Charlie was the kind of beacon that wouldn't allow that kind of light.

In the afternoon, he saw Gloria walking up the beach, waved to her, wasn't sure she'd seen him until she corrected her course to slowly tack closer. It wouldn't do to seem too interested in talking to him, he knew. Might violate some girl code.

He was filling in holes from armadillos that had been rooting around in the garden. The holes, which roughly matched the shape of their snouts, amused him. He couldn't say why. But the work made him happy in a formless, motiveless way. Even better, the twins, Henry and Suzanne, were very late.

It had become a stunning day after a cloudy start. The sea had an aquamarine sheen to it, vibrant against the dull shadows of submerged seaweed. At the very edge of a seamless, ever-deepening blue sky, the contrail of an airplane, showing its disdain for denizens of the forgotten coast. Much closer to home, he tried to ignore rocks slick with the white shit of cormorants.

"Why don't you do something about those armadillos?" Gloria asked when she'd finally reached the lighthouse grounds. She must have meandered, distracted by the treasures to be found in the seaweed washed up on the beach.

"I like armadillos," he told her.

"Old Jim says they're pests."

Old Jim. Sometimes he thought she made up a reference to Old Jim every time she wanted to get her way. Old Jim lived down one of the dozens of dirt roads, at the end of a maze of them, in a glorified shack near an illegal drop site for barrels of chemical waste. No one knew what he'd done before he'd washed up on the forgotten coast, but now he served as the ad hoc proprietor of the on-again, off-again village bar.

"Is that what Jim says, huh?" Making sure to pack the soil tight, even though he was already feeling strangely tired. Another storm and he'd have eroded divots all over instead.

"They are armored rats."

"Like seagulls are winged rats?"

"What? You know, you could set traps."

"They're much too smart for traps."

Slowly, staring at him sideways: "I don't think that's true, Saul."

When she called him Saul, he knew he might be in trouble. So why not get in a lot of trouble. Besides, he needed a break, was sweating too much.

"One day," he said, leaning on the shovel, "they got in through the kitchen window by standing on top of each other and jiggling the latch."

"Armadillo pyramid!" Then, recovering her youthful caution: "I don't think that's true, either."

Truth was, he did like the armadillos. He found them funny—bumbling yet sincere. He'd read in a nature guide that armadillos "swam" by walking across the bottoms of rivers and holding their breath, a detail that had captivated him.

"They can be a nuisance," he admitted. "So you're probably right." He knew if he didn't make some small concession, she'd drive the point into the ground.

"Old Jim said you were crazy because you saw a kangaroo around here."

"Maybe you need to stop hanging out with Old Jim."

"I wasn't. He lives in a dump. He came to see my mother."

Ah—gone to see the doctor. A sense of relief came over him, or maybe it was just the cold sweat of his exertion. Not that there was anything wrong with Jim, but the thought of her roving so widely and boldly bothered him. Even though Charlie had told Saul more than once that Gloria knew the area better than he did.

"So did you see a kangaroo?"

My God, is this what it would've been like having kids?

"Not exactly. I saw something that *looked* like a kangaroo." The locals still joked about it, but he swore he'd seen it, just a glimpse that first year, exhilarated from the rush of exploring so many new and unfamiliar hiking trails.

"Oh, but I forgot. I came over here for a reason," she said.

"Yes?"

"Old Jim said he heard on his radio that the island's on fire, and I wanted to see it better from the top of the lighthouse. The telescope?"

"What?" Dropping his shovel. "What do you mean the island's on fire?" No one was over there now except members of the Light Brigade, as far as he knew, but part of his job was reporting incidents like fires.

"Not the *whole thing*," she said, "just part of it. Let me take a look. There's smoke and everything."

So up they went, Saul insisting she take his hand, her grip strong and clammy, telling her to be careful on the steps, while wondering if he should have called someone about the fire before he confirmed it.

At the top, after pulling back the lens curtain and peering through the telescope, mostly meant for stargazing, Saul discovered that she was right: The island was on fire. Or, rather, the top of the ruined lighthouse was in flames—several miles away, but clear through the telescope's eye. A hint of red, but mostly dark smoke. Like a funeral pyre.

"Do you think anyone died?"

"No one's over there." Except the "strange people," as Gloria had put it.

"Then who set the fire?"

"No one had to set it. It might have just happened." But he didn't believe that. He could see what looked like bonfires, too, black smoke rising from them. Was that part of a controlled burn?

"Can I look some more?"

"Sure."

Even after he had let Gloria take his position at the telescope, Saul thought he could still see the thin fractures of smoke tendrils on the horizon, but that had to be an illusion.

Strangeness was nothing new for Failure Island. If you listened to Old Jim, or some of the other locals, the myths of the forgotten coast had always included that island, even before the latest in a series of attempts at settlement had failed. The rough, unfinished stone and wood of the town's buildings, the island's isolation, the way the sea lanes had already begun to change while the lighthouse was under construction so long ago had seemed to presage its ultimate fate.

The lens in his lighthouse had previously graced the ruined tower on the island. In some people's eyes that meant some essential misfortune had followed the lens to the mainland, perhaps because of the epic story of moving the four-ton lens, with a sudden storm come up and lightning breaking the sky, how the lens had almost sunk the ship that carried it, run aground carrying the light that might have saved it.

While Gloria was still glued to the telescope, Saul noticed something odd on the floor near the base of the lens, on the side facing away from the sea. A tiny pile of glass flakes glinted against the dark wood planks. What the heck? Had the Light Brigade broken a bulb up here or something? Then another thought occurred, and stooping a bit, Saul pulled up the lens bag directly above the glass shavings. Sure enough, he found a fissure where the glass met the mount. It was almost like what he imagined the hole from a bullet might look like, except smaller. He examined the "exit wound," as he thought of it. The hairline cracks pushing out from that space resembled the roots of a plant. He saw no other damage to that smooth fractal surface.

He didn't know whether he should be angry or just add it to the list of repairs, since it wouldn't harm the functioning of the lens. Had Henry and Suzanne done this, deliberately or through some clumsiness or mistake? Unable to shake the irrational feeling of hidden connections, the sense that something had escaped from that space.

The reverberation of steps below him, the sound of voices—two sets of footsteps, two voices. The Light Brigade, Henry and Suzanne. On impulse, he pulled down the lens bag, dispersed the glass flakes with his boot, which made him feel oddly complicit.

When they finally appeared, Saul couldn't blame Gloria for the way she looked at them—staring like a feral cat with hackles up from her position at the telescope. He felt the same way.

Henry was again dressed like he was going out on the town. Suzanne looked tense, perhaps because this time she was carrying the bulk of the equipment.

"You're late," he said, unable to keep an edge of disapproval out of his voice. Henry held the handle of what looked like a metal tool kit in his left hand, was rocking it gently back and forth. "And what's that?" Saul hadn't seen it before.

"Oh, nothing, Saul," Henry said, smile as big as ever. "Just some tools. Screwdrivers, that kind of thing. Like a handyman." Or someone taking samples from a first-order lens that had managed to escape vandalism for more than a century.

Apparently noting Gloria's hostility, Suzanne put down the suitcase and cardboard box she was carrying, leaned over the telescope as she said, "You're such a sweet kid. Would you like a lollipop?" Which she produced as if by magic from Gloria's ear with the over-flourish of an amateur magician.

An appraising, hostile stare from Gloria. "No. We're watching the island burn." She dismissively put her eye to the telescope again.

"There's a fire, yes," Henry said, unperturbed, as Suzanne returned to his side. A tinny rattle as he set his tool kit next to the other equipment.

"What do you know about it?" Saul asked, although so many other questions now rose up.

"What would I know about it? An unfortunate accident. I guess we never got the right badges in the Boy Scouts, yes? No one has been hurt, luckily, on this glorious day, and we'll be gone from there very soon anyway."

"Gone?" Saul suddenly hopeful. "Closing up shop?"

Henry's expression was less friendly than it had been a moment ago. "Just on the island. What we're looking for isn't there."

Smug, like he enjoyed holding on to a secret that he wasn't going to share with Saul. Which rubbed Saul the wrong way, and then he *was* angry.

"What are you looking for? Something that would make you damage the lens?" His directness made Suzanne wince. She wouldn't meet Saul's gaze.

"We haven't touched the lens," Henry said. "You haven't, have you, Suzanne?"

"No, we'd never touch the lens," Suzanne said, in a horrified tone of voice. The thought occurred that Suzanne was protesting too much.

Saul hesitated. Should he show them the spot on the lens that had been damaged? He didn't really want to. If they'd done it, they'd just lie again. If they hadn't done it, he'd be drawing their attention to it. Nor did he want to get into an argument with Gloria around. So he relented and with difficulty tore Gloria away from the telescope, knowing she'd been listening the whole time.

Down below, in his kitchen, he called the fire department in Bleakersville, who told him they already knew about the fire on the island, it wasn't a threat to anything, and making him feel a little stupid in the process because that's how they treated people from the forgotten coast. Or they were just terminally bored.

Gloria was sitting in a chair at the table, absentmindedly gnawing on a candy bar he'd given her. He figured she probably had wanted the lollipop.

"Go home. Once you've finished." He couldn't put words to it, but he wanted her far away from the lighthouse right now. Charlie would've called him irrational, emotional, said he wasn't thinking straight. But in the confluence of the fire, the lens damage, and Suzanne's strange mood . . . he just didn't want Gloria there.

But Gloria held on to her stubbornness, like it was a kind of gift she'd been given along with the candy bar.

"Saul, you're my friend," she said, "but you're not the boss of me." Matter-of-fact, like something he should've already known, that didn't need to be said.

He wondered if Gloria's mother had said that—more than once. Wryly, he had to admit that it was true. He wasn't the boss of Henry, either, or, apparently, anyone. The tedious yet true cliché came to mind. *Tend to your own garden.*

So he nodded, admitting defeat. She was going to do whatever she wanted to do. They all would, and he would just have to put up with it. At least the weekend was approaching fast. He'd drive to Bleakersville with Charlie, check out a new place called Chipper's Star Lanes that a friend of Charlie's liked a lot. It had the miniature golf Charlie enjoyed and he didn't mind the bowling, although what Saul liked most was that they had a liquor license and a bar in the back.

Only an hour later, Henry and Suzanne were downstairs again—he noticed first the creaking of their steps and then through the kitchen window their repetitive pacing as they roved across the lighthouse grounds.

He would have stayed inside and left them to it, but a few minutes later Brad Delfino, a volunteer who sometimes helped out around the lighthouse, pulled in to the driveway in his truck. Already, even before he'd come to a stop, Brad was waving to Henry, and somehow Saul didn't want Brad talking to the Light Brigade without him there. Brad was a musician in a local band who liked to drink and talked a lot, to anyone who'd listen. Sometimes he got into trouble; his spotty work at the lighthouse was what passed for community service on the forgotten coast.

"You heard about the fire?" Brad said as Saul headed him off in the parking lot.

"Yes," Saul said curtly. "I heard about it." Of course Brad knew; why else would he have come out?

Now he could see that Henry and Suzanne were ceaselessly snapping shots of every square inch of the grounds inside the fence. Adding to the chaos, Gloria had noticed him and was bounding toward him making barking noises like she sometimes did. Because she knew he hated it.

"Know what's going on?" Brad asked.

"Not any more than you do. Fire department says there's no problem, though." Something in his tone changed when he talked to Brad, a kind of southern twang entering, which irritated him.

"Can I go up and look through the telescope anyway?" As eager as Gloria to get a peek at the only excitement going on today.

But before Saul could respond to that, Henry and Suzanne bore down on them.

"Photo time," Suzanne said, smiling broadly. She had a rather bulky tele-photo lens attached to her camera, the wide strap around her neck making her look even more childlike.

"Why do you want a photo?" Gloria asked.

That was Saul's question, too.

"It's just for our records," Suzanne said, with a wide, devouring smile. "We're creating a photo map of the area, and a record of the people who live here. And, you know, it's such a beautiful day." Except it was a little overcast now, the en-croaching gray from clouds that would probably rain inland, not here.

"Yes, how about a photograph of you, your assistant—and the girl, I guess," Henry said, ignoring Gloria. He was studying Saul with an intensity that made him uncomfortable.

"I'm not sure," Saul said, reluctant if for no other reason than their insistence. He also wanted to find a way to extricate himself from Brad, who wasn't anything as formal as an "assistant."

"*I'm* sure," Gloria muttered, glaring at them. Suzanne tried to pat her head. Gloria looked at first as if she might bite that hand, then, in character, just growled and leaned away from it.

Henry stepped in close to Saul. "What would a photograph of the lighthouse be without its keeper?" he asked, but it wasn't really a question.

"A better picture?"

"You used to be a preacher up north, I know," Henry said. "But if you're worrying about the people you left behind, don't—it's not for publication."

That threw him off-balance.

"How do you know that?" Saul said.

But Brad had gotten a kick out of this revelation, waded in before Henry could answer. "Yeah, that Saul, man. He's a real desperado. He's wanted in ten states. If you take his picture, it's all over for him."

Did a picture really matter? Even though he'd left unfinished business up north, it wasn't like he'd fled, exactly, or as if this photo would wind up in the newspapers.

The wind had taken to gusting. Rather than argue, Saul pulled his cap out of his back pocket, figured wearing it might disguise him a bit, although why did he need a disguise? An irrational thought. Probably not the first irrational thought from a lighthouse keeper on the forgotten cost.

"Say 'cheese.' Say 'no secrets.' Count of three."

No secrets?

Brad had decided to assume a stoic pose that Saul supposed might be a way of poking fun at him. Gloria, seeking the dramatic, made them wait while she drew the hood of her jacket over her head and then ran to the rocks as her protest, certain Suzanne wouldn't be able to get her in the frame. Once at the rocks, she climbed away from them, and then turned around and began to climb back, shrieking with delight and shouting, for no good reason, "I'm a monster! I'm a monster!"

The count of three came, Suzanne grown still and silent, bending at the knees as if she were on the deck of a ship at sea. She gave the signal.

"No secrets!" Brad said prematurely, with an enthusiasm he might regret, given his drug record.

Then came the flash from the camera, and in the aftermath black motes drifted across the edges of Saul's vision, gathered there, lingered for longer than seemed normal.

0005: CONTROL

hey had exploded through and up out of that terrible corridor between the world and Area X into a lack of air that had shocked Control, until the solid push of Ghost Bird's body against his, the weight of his backpack pulling him down, forced him to fight against the slapping pressure of what his burning eyes, strangled throat, told him was salt water. He had managed to shut his mouth against his surprise, to ignore the rush of bubbles pushing up and around the top of his head. Managed to clamp down on both his panic and his scream, to adjust as well to the ripping feel of a thousand rough-smooth surfaces against him, too much like the door that had become a wall cutting through his fingers, slashing against his arms, his legs, sure he had materialized into the middle of a tornado of shining knives—Whitby and Lowry and Grace and his mother the spy, the whole damned congregation of the Southern Reach calling out the word *Jump!* through those thousand silvery reflections. Even as his lungs flooded with water. Even as he struggled to lose the treacherous knapsack but still hold on to Whitby's document inside it, grappling, flailing for the pages, some of which exploded out into the water, the rest plummeting into the murk below with the knapsack: a slab of pulp, a soggy tombstone.

Ghost Bird, he recognized dimly, had already shot up and past him, toward a kind of glistening yellow egg of a reflected halo that might, or might not, be the sun. While he was still sucking water among the converging circles of the many swirling knives that stared at him with flat judgmental eyes. Confused by the swirl of pages that floated above or below, that stuck to his clothes, that came apart in miniature whirlpools to join the vortex. For a fading second, he was peering at a line of text and suffocating while blunt snouts bumped up against his chest.

Only when a true leviathan appeared did his oxygen-starved brain understand that they had emerged into a roiling school of some kind of barracuda-like fish now being disrupted by a larger predator. There came an awful free-falling emptiness . . . the quickly closing space where the enormous shark had sped through the vortex, annihilating fish in a crimson cloud. A megalodon of a kind. Lowry in yet another form . . . the air trickling out of his mouth like a series of tiny lies about the world that had decided to extinguish him.

"Lowry" left offal in its wake, so close to Control as he rose and it descended that the side of his face slid half raw against its gills. The frill and flutter sharper and harder than he could have imagined as it sculpted him, the expulsion of water a roaring, gushing piston in his ear, and the huge yet strangely delicate eye away to his left staring into him. Then his stomach was banging into its body, his bruised waist smacked by a swipe of the tail, and his head was ringing and he was drifting and he couldn't keep his mouth from beginning to open, the dot of the sun smaller and smaller above him. *"Pick up the gun, Control,"* said his grandfather. *"Pick it up from under the seat. Then jump."*

Did Lowry, or anyone, have a phrase that could save him?

Consolidation of authority.

There's no reward in the risk.

Floating and floating.

Paralysis is not a cogent analysis.

Except it was. And from the wash and churn, the thrashing around him, a familiar hand grasped his drifting wrist and yanked him upward. So that he was not just a swirl of confused memory, a bruised body, a cipher, but apparently something worth saving, someone in the process of being saved.

His feet had kicked out against nothing, like a hanging victim, while the fish again converged, his body buffeted by a hundred smooth-rough snouts as he rose, as he blacked out amid the torrent of upward-plunging bodies, the rough rebuke of continuous flesh that formed one wide maw from which he might or might not escape.

Then they were on the shore and Ghost Bird was kissing him for some reason. Kissing him with great, gulping kisses that bruised his lips, and touching his chest and, when he opened his eyes and looked up into her face, making him turn onto his side. Water gushed, then dribbled, from him, and he had propped himself up with both arms, staring down into the wet sand, the tiny bubbles of worm tunnels as the edge of the surf brushed against his hands and receded.

Lying there on his side, he could see the lighthouse in the distance. But as if she could tell his intent, Ghost Bird said, "We're not going there. We're going to the island."

And just like that, he'd lost control.

Now, on their fourth day in Area X, Control followed Ghost Bird through the long grass, puzzled, confused, sick, tired—the nights so alive with insects it was hard to sleep against their roar and chitter. While in his thoughts, a vast, invisible blot had begun to form across the world outside of Area X, like water seeping from the bottom of a leaky glass.

Worse still, the gravitational pull Ghost Bird exerted over him, even as she was indifferent to him, even as they sometimes huddled together for warmth at night. The unexpected delicacy and delirium of that accidental touch. Yet her message to him, the moment he had crossed a kind of border and she'd moved away from him, had been unmistakable and absolute. So he'd retreated to thinking of himself as Control, from necessity, to try to regain some distance, some measure of the objective. To reimagine her in the interrogation room at the Southern Reach, and him watching her from behind the one-way glass.

"How can you be so cheerful?" he'd asked her, after she had noted their depleted food, water, in an energetic way, then pointed out a kind of sparrow she said was extinct in the wider world, an almost religious ecstasy animating her voice.

"Because I'm alive," she'd replied. "Because I'm walking through wilderness on a beautiful day." This with a sideways glance he took to mean that she wondered if he was holding up. One that made him realize that her goals might not be his, that they might converge only to diverge, and he had to be ready for that. Echoes of field assignments gone wrong. Of his mother saying, "The operational damage from an event can linger in the mind like a ghost." While he wondered if even the more banal things she had said had a hidden meaning or agenda.

Freedom could take you farther from what you sought, not closer. Something he was learning out here, beyond any standard intel, in a wilderness he didn't understand. About as prepared for Area X, he realized, as for Ghost Bird, and perhaps that was, in the end, the same thing. Because they existed alone together, walked a trail that threaded its way between reed-choked lakes that could be tar-black or as green as the reflected trees that congregated in islands among the reeds . . . and he was finally free to ask her anything he wanted to, but he didn't. Because it didn't really matter.

So, instead, he shoved his hand into his jacket pocket from time to time, clenched his fist around his father's carving, taken from the mantel in the little house on the hill in Hedley. The smooth lines of it, the way the grain of the wood under the paint threatened a splinter, soothed him. A carving of a cat, chosen to remind him of long-lost Chorry, no doubt blissfully hunting rats among the bushes.

So, instead, he dove, resentful at their pull, into reexamining over and over his rescued Whitby pages, the "terroir pages," although they were more personal than that. An anchor, a bridge to his memory of the rest of the manuscript, lost at sea. If he used those pages to talk to Ghost Bird, it was in part to bring relief or distraction from the closeness of her and the way that the endless reeds, the fresh air, the blue sky, all conspired to make the real world remote, unimportant, a dream. When it was the most important thing.

Somewhere back there his mother was fighting for her career at Central, that act synonymous with fighting against the encroachment of Area X. Somewhere, too, new fronts had opened up, Area X expanding in ways that might not even match its prior characteristics. How could he know? Planes might be falling from the skies, this non-mission, this *following* of his, already a failure.

Quoting Whitby's report as he remembered it, paraphrasing: "Had they, in fact, passed judgment without a trial? Decided there could be no treaty or negotiation?"

"That might be closer to the truth, to a kind of truth," Ghost Bird replied. It was now early afternoon and the sky had become a deeper blue with long narrow clouds sliding across it. The marsh was alive with rustlings and birdsong.

"Condemned by an alien jury," Control said.

"Not likely. Indifference."

"He covers that, too: 'Would that not be the final humbling of the human condition? That the trees and birds, the fox and the rabbit, the wolf and the deer . . . reach a point at which they do not even notice us, as we are transformed.'" Another half-remembered phrasing, the real becoming half real. But his father had never valued authenticity so much as boldness of expression.

"See that deer over there, beyond the canal? She's definitely noticing us."

"Is she noticing us or is she *noticing* us?"

Either scenario might have horrified his mother the spy, who had never gotten along with nature. No one in his family had, not really. He couldn't remember any real outings into the woods, just fishing around lakes and sitting by fireplaces in cabins during the winter. Had he ever even been lost before?

"Pretend the former since we can't do anything about the latter."

"Or this," Control said. "Or this: 'Or are we back in time, some creature or impulse from the past replenishing us as we grind to a halt.'"

"A stupid thing to say," Ghost Bird said, unable to resist the bait. "Natural places are no different than human cities. The old exists next to the new. Invasive species integrate with or push out native species. The landscape you see around you is the same as seeing an old cathedral next to a skyscraper. You don't believe this crap, do you?"

He gave her what he hoped was a defiant expression, one that didn't hint at how he had begun to doubt Whitby even as he continued to recite the gospel of Whitby. He had held back the quotes that might lead to something more substantial so he could think on them a little longer, contaminate them with his own opinions.

"I'm trying to separate out the pointless from the useful. I'm trying to make some progress as we trudge on over to the island." Unable to avoid infusing the word *island* with venom. Grandpa Jack would've felt the same about the island, would be restless and pushing, for all the good it would've done against Ghost Bird.

"Did any expedition ever make it to the island?" she asked, Control recognizing her attempt at deflection.

"If they did, nothing came back to the Southern Reach about it," he said. "It wasn't a priority." Perhaps too much else to wonder about.

"Why all the focus on the lighthouse, the topographical anomaly, and not the island?"

"You'd have to ask the former director about that. Or you'd have to ask Lowry."

"I never met Lowry," she said, as if this disproved his existence.

Truth was, Lowry sounded unreal to Control when he said the name in this place. But Lowry also resisted being cast aside, disregarded, kept floating there at the edges of his vision like some majestic, demonic dust mote. Manifesting every time he worried he might still be on a mission that had lodged so deep inside his skull he couldn't draw it out. Unknown commands, messages, imperatives, impulses that were not his own, that could be activated by others.

"We think in terms of machines, not animals. The enemy doesn't acknowledge machines." He liked the word *enemy*—it crystallized and focused his attention more than "Area X." Area X was just a phenomenon visited upon humanity, like a weather event, but an *enemy* created intent and focus.

She laughed at *machines, not animals*. "It definitely understands and acknowledges machines. It understands them better than we do." She stopped to face him, to lend emphasis, and something like anger pulsed out from her. "Have you not understood yet that whatever's causing this can manipulate the genome, works miracles of mimicry and biology? Knows what to do with molecules and membranes, can *peer through things*, can surveil, and then withdraw. That, to it, a smartphone, say, is as basic as a flint arrowhead, that it's operating off of such refined and intricate senses that the tools we've bound ourselves with, the ways we record the universe, are probably evidence of our own primitive nature. Perhaps it doesn't even think that we have consciousness or free will—not in the ways it measures such things."

"If that's true, why does it pay us any attention at all?"

"It probably extends to us the least attention possible."

Is there something in the corner of your eye that you cannot get out?

"So we give up. We live on the island, make ourselves hats out of leaves, take bounty from the sea." Build a house from the ribs of one of the leviathans from his dreams. Listen to homemade dance music while drinking moonshine distilled from poisonous weeds. Turn away from the real world because it doesn't exist anymore.

Ignoring him, she said: "A whale can injure another whale with its sonar. A whale can speak to another whale across sixty miles of ocean. A whale is as intelligent as we are, just in a way we can't quite measure or understand. Because we're these incredibly blunt instruments." That idea again. "Or at least, you are." Maybe she hadn't muttered that under her breath, he'd only imagined it.

"You sympathize with It," he said. "You like It." A cheap shot that he couldn't help.

Too often over the past four days, he had felt like he was crossing one of the dioramas from the natural history museum he had loved so much—intriguing, fascinating, but not quite real, or not quite real to him. Even if the effects had not yet manifested, he was being invaded, infected, remade. Was it his fate to become a moaning creature in the reeds and then food for worms?

"There was a lot about fakes in Whitby's notes," he said a little later, slyly, to test her. Especially as her attention seemed elsewhere, always glued to the sky. To perhaps see just how dispassionate she could be about her own condition. With, he knew, just a sliver of payback in there, too, which he couldn't help. Because it made no sense to go to the island.

When she said nothing, he made up a quote, feeling guilty even as the words left his mouth: "'The sense in which the perfect fake becomes the thing it mimics, and this through some strange yet static process reveals some truth about the world. Even as it can't, by definition, be original.'"

Still no response. "No? How about 'When you meet yourself and see a double that is you, would you feel sympathy, or would the impulse be to destroy the copy? To judge it unreal and to tear it down like any cardboard construct?'" Another fake, because Whitby hadn't discussed doubles—not once in the whole damn document.

She stopped walking, faced him. As ever, he had trouble not looking away.

"Is that what you're afraid of, Control?" She said it with no particular cruelty or passion. "Because I could use hypnosis on you."

"You might be susceptible, too," he said, wanting to warn her off, even as he knew there might come a time when he would *need* her to use hypnosis just as she had in the tunnel leading into Area X. *Take my hand. Close your eyes.* It had felt as if he were continually crawling out of the mouth of a vast inky-black snake, that he could "see" a rasping sound from deep in its throat, and from all sides, through the infinite dark bruise that encircled him, leviathans stared in at him.

"I'm not."

"But you're the double—the copy," he said, pressing. "Maybe the copy doesn't have the same defenses. And you still don't know why." This much she had told him.

"Test me," she said, a snarl from deep in her throat. She stopped, faced him, threw down her pack. "Go ahead and test me. Say it. Say the words you think will destroy me."

"I don't want to destroy you," he said quietly, looking away.

"Are you sure?" she said, coming very close. He could smell her sweat, see the rise of her shoulders, the half-curled left hand. "Are you sure?" she repeated. "Why not inoculate me, if you're unsure? You're already caught between wanting me and not being sure I'm all human, is that it? Made by the enemy. Must be the enemy. But can't help yourself anyway."

"I helped you back at the Southern Reach," he said.

"Don't thank people for doing what they're supposed to. You told me that."

He took a stumbling step back. "I'm out here, Ghost Bird, traveling to a place

I didn't want to go. Having followed someone I'm not sure I know." A beacon to him still, and he resented that, didn't want it. Couldn't help it.

"That's bullshit. You know exactly who I am—or you should have. You're afraid, just like me," she said, and he knew that he was. Had no defenses out here, for anything.

"I don't think you're with the enemy," he said, *enemy* sounding harsh and unreasonable now. "And I don't think of you as a copy. Not really."

Exasperation, even as she was relenting, or he thought she was: "I *am* a copy, John. But not a perfect one. I'm not her. She's not me. Do you know what I'd say if I came face-to-face with her?"

"What?"

"I'd tell her, 'You made a lot of fucking mistakes. You made a lot of mistakes, and yet I love you. You're a mess and a revelation, but I can't be any of that. All I can do is work out things myself.' And then, knowing her, she'd probably look at me funny and take a tissue sample from me."

A roaring laughter came out of him at that. He banged his hand on his knee. "You're right. You're probably right. She'd do exactly that." He sat on the ground, while she remained where she was, stiff as a sentinel. "I'm beyond my skill set out here. I'm totally fucked. Even if we'd gone to the lighthouse."

"Totally fucked," she said, smiling.

"Strange, isn't it? A strange place to be." Being drawn out of himself, even though he didn't want to be. Suddenly calmer than he'd been since he'd gotten here, all of his failures muffled and indistinct behind another kind of border.

She stared at him, appraising him.

"We should keep going," she said. "But you can keep reading."

She offered him a hand up, the strength of her grip as he got to his feet a greater reassurance than any words.

"But it's a fucking disaster," he said. "I'm reading you the last will and testament of a fool."

"What other entertainment do we have out here?"

"True."

Control hadn't told her about Whitby's strange room or his suspicions about Whitby as a conduit for Area X. He hadn't told her about those last desperate moments at the Southern Reach as the border shifted. And in not telling Ghost Bird these things, he had come to understand his mother's lies better. She had wanted to cover up the core of her decisions by hiding facts or watering them down. But she must have been wise enough to realize, no matter her motivations, no matter the labyrinth, every omission left some sign of its presence.

"'How does It renew Itself if not through our actions? Our lives?'" Whitby asked, living on through Control when the man himself was probably dead or worse.

But she wasn't listening; something in the sky had caught her attention again, something he knew couldn't be storks, and he had the binoculars this time, scrambled to find what she was staring at. When he found it, he adjusted the focus a few times, not sure he'd seen correctly.

But he had.

Across the deepening blue, high up, something drifted that resembled ripped and tattered streamers. Long and wide and alien. Its progress so far up, so far away . . . Control thought of an invisible shredded plastic bag, eviscerated to elongate and drift through the sky . . . except it was thicker than that and *part* of the sky, too. The texture of it, the way it existed and didn't exist, made him recoil, made his hand twitch, become numb, skin cold, remembering a wall that was not a wall. A wall that had been breathing under his touch.

"Get down!" Ghost Bird said, and forced him to his knees beside her in a stand of reeds. He could feel the brightness in him now—tight, taut, pulling like it was his skin being pulled, drawn toward the sky that wasn't just the sky anymore. Drawn to it so much that he would have gotten up if Ghost Bird hadn't forced him down again. He lay there grateful for her weight beside him, grateful he wasn't out here alone.

Stitching through the sky, in a terrifying way—rippling, diving, rising again, and there came a terrible whispering that pierced not his ears but all of him, as if small particles of something physical had shot through him. He cursed, frozen there, watching, afraid. "The wavery lines that are there and not there." A line from Whitby's report he hadn't shared because he hadn't understood it. Images from the video of the first expedition coming back to him.

"Stay still," Ghost Bird whispered in his ear. "Stay still." She was sheltering his body with hers, she was trying to make it seem as if he wasn't there.

He tried not even to breathe, to become so motionless that he was no longer alive. As it curled in and through the sky, he could hear it rippling, diving, rising again, like traces of a sail until, as he risked a look, he saw some impact in the air freeze it in place, and for a moment it was stretched as taut as skin, almost brittle, unyielding.

Then, with a final plunge and ascent, coming far too close, the *presence* winked out of existence, or slipped out of the air, and the sky was the same as before.

He had no words for it, Whitby's or his own. This was no dead diorama. This was no beastly skeleton of a man he'd never known. Anything now seemed possible. Anything could happen. He clutched the carving of Chorry tight. So tight he almost punctured his skin.

They remained that way until a storm slipped across a sky Control now thought of as treacherous, and through the dark gray light there came lightning, thunder, and in amongst the raindrops that drenched them, dark, slippery tadpole-like things hurtled down and disappeared into the soil all around them while they tried to take shelter as best they could, soaked under a gnarled, blackened copse of trees with leaves like daggers. The tadpole things were more like living rivulets, about the size of his little finger. He could not help thinking of them as coming from the stitching in the sky, that somehow it had disintegrated into a million tiny pieces, and this, too, was somehow part of the ecosystem of Area X.

"What do you think that will become?" he asked her.

"Whatever everything else is becoming here," she said, and that was no answer at all.

When the storm passed, the marsh came alive with birdsong and the gurgle of water in the canals, nothing at all amiss. Perhaps the reeds seemed more vibrant, the trees greener, but this was just the quality of the light, from a sun that seemed as distant as the rest of the world.

After a time, they stood. After a time, in silence, they continued on, walking closer together than before.

0006: THE DIRECTOR

There's a place that as a kid you called the farthestmost point—the most distant you could get, the place that when you stood there you could pretend you were the only person in the world. Being there made you wary, but it also put a kind of peace into you, a sense of security. Beyond that point, in either direction, you were always returning, and are returning still. But for that moment, even now with Whitby by your side, you're so remote that there's nothing for miles—and you feel that. You feel it strongly. You've gone from being a little on edge to being a little tired, and you've come out on this perfectly still scene where the scrublands turn to wetlands, with a freshwater canal serving as a buffer to the salt marsh and, ultimately, the sea. Where once you saw otters, heard the call of curlews. You take a deep breath and relax into the landscape, walk along the shore of this lower heaven rejuvenated by its perfect stillness. Your legs are for a time no longer tired and you are afraid of nothing, not even Area X, and you have no room for memory or thought or anything except this moment, and this one, and the next.

Soon enough, though, that feeling falls away again, and you and Whitby—survivors of the topographical anomaly—stand in the remains of your mother's cottage. It's just a floor and a couple of supporting walls with the wallpaper so faded you can't figure out the pattern. On the sunken splintered deck, a battered and smashed rot of wide planks that used to be the walkway leads to the dunes, and from there to a metallic-blue sea that tosses up whitecaps and drags them down again. Perhaps you shouldn't have come here, but you needed something like normalcy, some evocation of those days before it all went wrong—days that had seemed so ordinary at the time.

"Don't forget me," Saul had said back then, as if speaking not just for him but for your mother, too, and the rest of the forgotten coast. Now truly forgotten, Whitby standing at one end and you at the other, needing the space. He's unsure of you, and you're definitely unsure of him. Whitby wanted to abort the mission after the tower, but at no point did you think you should just leave. This was your home, and Whitby isn't going to stop you, though he might protest, though he might whimper and try to get free, though he might plead with you to return across the border immediately.

"Where's your optimism now?" you want to ask, but wherever he's wound up he's still not in your world.

Long ago, a fire or two was kindled on the cottage floor, in what used to be the living room, under the shelter of one sagging wall. Blackened splotches left behind provide the evidence, tell you that even after Area X, people lived here for a time. Did your mother make those fires?

Dead beetles litter the floor, crushed into glossy emerald pieces, teal moss and thick vines creating a chaotic green sea. Wrens and warblers hop through the underbrush outside, settle on the gaping window frame that looks out landward, then are gone again. The window you'd look through when expecting your dad to come for visits, driveway outside erased by a proliferation of bushes and weeds.

Cans of food, long since rusted and rotted, along with a thick layer of soil erupting out of the corners, through the insect-chewed floorboards, what's left of them. The anomaly of cracked, ancient dishes barely recognizable, and stacked in a sink that has fallen in on itself and been transformed by mold and lichen, the cupboards below rotted away.

There's a regret in you, a kind of daymark you've let become obscured. The expeditions are never told that people had lived here, worked here, got drunk here, and played music here. People who lived in mobile homes and bungalows and lighthouses. Better not to think of people living here, of it being empty . . . and yet now you want someone to remember, to understand what was lost, even if it was little enough.

Whitby stands there like an intruder as you explore, knows you're hiding something from him about the cottage. The flat, grim line of his mouth, the resentment in his gaze—is it natural, or is Area X already turning him against you? When you burst out of the tower, escaping whatever had risen up with such speed, you found him still screaming, babbling about something that had attacked him. "There wasn't any sound. Nothing. Then . . . a *wall* behind me, running through me. Then it was gone." But since then he hasn't said more, nor have you shared what you saw right before you leapt up those last steps into the light.

Perhaps neither thinks the other would believe. Perhaps you both just want to be back in the world first.

No bodies here in the cottage, but what did you think? That you would find her huddled inside this place, cocooned from disaster somehow as the world changed around her? That was never your mother's nature. If there had been something to fight, she would have fought it. If there had been someone to help, she would have helped them. If she could have struck out for safety, she would have. In your daydreams, she held on, like you have held on, hoping for rescue.

Sitting there at the Star Lanes Lounge, scribbling, you found the cottage coming back to you at odd moments, along with the lighthouse. Always that rip-tide compulsion dragging you down into the water, that need to know overriding the fear. The sound of the midnight waves at high tide, how from the window of your room in your mother's bungalow back then you could see the surf under the moonlight as a series of metallic-blue lines, dark water squeezed between them. Sometimes those lines had been broken by her figure as she walked the beach late at night, kept awake by thoughts she never shared, her face turned away from you. As if searching even then for the answer you seek now.

"What is this place?" Whitby asks, again. "Why are we here?" His voice giving away his stress.

You ignore him. You want to say, "This is where I grew up," but he's endured one shock too many already, and you still have to deal with Lowry, with the Southern Reach, when you get back. If you get back.

"That vine-strewn shadow there—that was my room," you would tell him if you could. "My parents divorced when I was two. My dad left—he's kind of a small-time crook—and my mom raised me, except I spent the winter holidays with him every year. Until I stayed with him for good because I couldn't go home anymore. And he lied to me about the reason why until I was older, which was probably the right thing to do. And I've been wondering my whole life what it would be like to come back here, to this place. Wondered what I would feel, what I would do. Sometimes even imagined there would be some message, something my mom had had the foresight to put in a metal box or under a rock. Some sign, because even now I need a message, a sign."

But there is nothing in the cottage, nothing you didn't already know, and there's the lighthouse at your back—laughing at you, saying, "I told you so."

"Don't worry, we'll go home soon," you say. "Just the lighthouse, and we'll go home." Saving the best for last, or the worst for last? How much of a childhood can be destroyed or twisted before the overlay replaces the memories?

You push past Whitby—abruptly—because you don't want him to see that you're upset, that Area X is closing in on you all over again.

The few remaining floorboards of the cottage creak and sigh, making a rough music. The birds chirp urgently in the bushes, chasing each other, spiraling up into the sky. It will rain soon, the horizon like a scowling forehead, a battering ram headed for the coast. Could they see it coming, even Henry? Was it visible? Did it sweep over them? All you could process as a child was that your mother was dead; it had taken you years to think of her death in other ways.

All you can see is the expression on Saul's face the last time you saw him as a child—and your last long look at the forgotten coast through the dusty back window of the car as you turned off the dirt road onto a paved state road, and the distant ripple of the sea passed from view.

0007: THE LIGHTHOUSE KEEPER

Two freighters and a coast guard vessel sighted last night. Something bigger out on horizon—oil tanker? "There is the sea, vast and spacious, and there the ships go to and fro." Western siren still not right—loose wire? Feeling a little sick, so visited doctor. Went on a hike late in the day. Sighted: a horned owl atop a tortoise, trying to eat it. Didn't know what I was seeing. Disturbed me at first. Thought it was something odd with a feathery body and an armored stump. The owl looked up at me and just stared, didn't fly away until I shooed it off the tortoise.

Acts of loving-kindness. The uselessness of guilt.

Sometimes Saul did miss the sermons, the cadence of them, the way he could raise the words up from within him and send them out, never severing the deep connection between them. Could name a thing and in naming it enter so many minds. But there had come a day during his ministry when he had no words left, when he knew he was enjoying the cadence of the sentences he spoke more than the meaning—and then he was lost for a time, swimming across an endless sea of doubt, certain he had failed. Because he had failed. Hellfire and apocalyptic visions, the coming destruction of the world by demons, could not sustain a man for long without robbing him of something, too. At the end, he did not know what he meant or what he believed, and so he had given it up in one prolonged shudder that cast off an entire life and fled as far south as he could, as far remote as well. Fleeing, too, his father, who had fed off that growing cult of personality, had been at once manipulative and envious, and that had been too much to bear for long: that a man so distant, who had projected so little light, should now reveal to Saul only those emotions he did not want.

Everything had shifted when he'd moved. There were ways in which he felt so different in the south than in the north, ways in which he was different because he was happier, and he didn't want to acknowledge sickness or anything that might hint at a change in what had been so ideal.

Yet there was a slight numbness when he lay in bed with Charlie a week after the incident in the yard, an episode of perhaps ten minutes during which his body seemed disconnected from him. Or the disconcerting moments on the walks he took along the coast near the lighthouse, supposedly to patrol for trespassers but that were really just about his joy in bird-watching.

He would look out to sea and find things swimming in the corners of his eyes that he could not quite explain away as black sun dots. Was this paranoia or some nagging doubt, some part of his brain trying to ruin everything, wanting him to be unhappy—to force him to deny himself the life he'd made here?

Next to these developments, the presence of the Light Brigade had become less and less real, and in the days since the photograph there had been a kind of truce, a mutual agreement not to accuse the other. He'd fixed the hole in the lens, cleaned up the glass, and told himself everyone deserved a second chance.

But their encounters were still fraught at times.

Today, he had walked into his own kitchen to find Suzanne making a sandwich there without any shame or embarrassment at being found out. His ham and his cheese slices in a pile on the counter, along with his wheat bread, his onion, and a tomato from the garden. Perched on the kitchen stool at such an extreme angle, one leg straight, foot on the floor, and the other bent, Suzanne and her posture had compounded his irritation. Because it almost looked as if she was clenched there, rigid, holding a position as artificial to her as it looked to him.

Henry had come in then and forestalled Saul's own questions, his lecture about not taking people's things for granted. About not making a sandwich without asking first, which seemed both invasive and ridiculously trivial later.

Henry said, almost conversationally, "There isn't any spooky action here, is there, Saul? Near or far?"

All that warranted was a pained smile. Everybody knew the ghost stories about the forgotten coast.

"And it's probably just a coincidence, but ever since your freak-out in the yard, our readings are off—distorted. Sometimes it is like the equipment is junk, doesn't work, but we've tested it. There's nothing wrong with it. I'm right, am I not, Saul?"

His "freak-out" in the yard. Henry definitely was trying to get a rise out of him.

"Oh yes, it's working, all right." Saul tried to sound cheery.

Anyone would have thought Henry, especially, a kind of buffoon and his stilted attempts at conversation signs of social awkwardness. But he was often unnerving to Saul, even just standing there.

So he kicked them both out, called Charlie to ask him if he could have lunch, locked up his living quarters, and drove to the village bar to take a break.

The village bar was an impromptu place, ad hoc style depending on who was around. Today it was a barbecue station out back and a cooler full of domestic beer. Paper plates from some kid's birthday party, cake with candles against a pink background. Saul and Charlie sat outside, on the worn deck that faced the sea, at a table under a faded blue umbrella.

They talked about Charlie's day on the boat and a new resident who'd bought a house half demolished by a hurricane, and how Old Jim really needed to refurbish the village bar because "it's not cool to have a dive bar in a place with no decent bars to compare it to." How maybe they'd check out that rock band Charlie'd been telling him about. How maybe instead they'd just stay in bed all day.

How the Light Brigade was getting on Saul's nerves.

"Henry's a freak," he said to Charlie. "He's got a stare like some kind of uncanny undertaker. And Suzanne just follows him everywhere."

"They can't come around forever," Charlie said. "One day they'll be gone. Little freaks. Freak Brigade." Testing out words for the fun of it, perhaps because they'd both had some beers already.

"Maybe, but in the meantime they're giving me the creeps."

"Could be they're undercover agents from forestry or environmental protection?"

"Sure, because I'm dumping chemicals all night long."

Charlie was joking, but the forgotten coast had suffered from a decade or two of lax regulations in what was an "unincorporated area." The wilderness hid its share of rotting barrels, some of them hidden on old abandoned farmsteads, half sunk into the pine loam.

They took up the conversation later, at Charlie's two-room cottage just down the street. A couple of photographs of his family, some books, not much in the fridge. Nothing Charlie couldn't toss in a knapsack if he ever decided to take off, or move in with someone.

"Are you sure they're not escapees from an insane asylum?"

Which made Saul laugh, because just the summer before two sanitarium residents had escaped from outside of Hedley and made their way down to the forgotten coast, managing to remain free for almost three weeks before being caught by the police.

"If you took away the insane people, no one would be left."

"Except me," Charlie said. "Except me and, maybe, you."

"Except the birds and the deer and the otters."

"Except the hills and the lakes."

"Except the snakes and the ladders."

"What?"

Except by then they had so lit each other up under the sheets that they could have been saying anything, and were.

It was Gloria who changed his mind about seeing a doctor. The next day, with Henry and Suzanne back up in the lighthouse, him down below, she appeared in the early afternoon to shadow him. He was so used to her that if she'd not shown up, he would've thought something was wrong.

"You're different," Gloria said, and he chewed on that for a bit.

This time she was leaning against the shed, watching him as he resodded part of the lawn. Volunteer Brad had promised to come in and help, but hadn't shown up. The sun above was a huge gob of runny yellow. The waves were a rushing vibration in his awareness, but muffled. One of his ears had been blocked since he'd woken up, no doubt because he'd slept on it funny. Maybe he was getting too old for this kind of work after all. Maybe there was a reason why lighthouse keepers had to retire at fifty.

"I'm a day older and wiser," he replied. "Shouldn't you be in school? Then you'd be wiser, too."

"Teacher work day."

"Lighthouse-keeper work day here," he said, grunting as he broke the soil with a shovel. His skin felt elastic, formless, and a tic under his left eye kept pulsing in and out.

"Then show me how to do your work and I'll help."

At that he stopped and, leaning on the shovel, took a good long look at her. If she kept growing, she might make a decent linebacker someday.

"You want to become a lighthouse keeper?"

"No, I want to use a shovel."

"The shovel is bigger than you."

"Get another one from the shed."

Yes. The mighty shed, which held all things . . . except when it did not. He took a glance up at the lighthouse tower where the Light Brigade was no doubt doing unimaginable things to his beacon.

"Okay," he said, and he got her a small shovel, more of a glorified spade.

Shaking off his attempt at shovel instruction, she stood beside him and awkwardly scuffed bits of dirt around, while he was careful to keep well away. He'd once been smacked in the head by a shovel handle wielded by a too-close, over-enthusiastic helper.

"Why are you different?" she asked, direct as ever.

"I told you, I'm not different." A little grumpier than he'd meant to be.

"But you are," she said, ignoring his tone.

"It's because of the splinter," he said, finally, to keep it simple.

"Splinters hurt but they just make you bleed."

"Not this one," he said, putting his back into his work. "This one was different. I don't really understand it, but I'm seeing things in the corner of my eye."

"You should go to the doctor."

"I will."

"My mother's a doctor."

"So she is." Her mother was, or had been, a pediatrician. Not quite the same thing. Even if she did give unlicensed advice to residents of the forgotten coast.

"If I was different, I'd go see her." Different. But different in what way?

"You live with her."

"So?"

"Why are you really here? To interrogate me?"

"You think I don't know what 'interrogate' means, but I do," she told him, walking away.

When Henry and Suzanne left for the day, Saul climbed to the top of the lighthouse and looked out onto the rich contrast of sea and beach, the deep bronze glint of afternoon sun. From this spot, a light had shone out through storms and human-made disasters, in calms and in crises. Light that cascaded or even interrupted itself. Light that pulsed and trembled, that pulled the darkness toward it and then cast it out.

He'd been standing in the lantern room the first time he'd seen Henry, so many months ago. Henry's trudging across the sand toward the lighthouse had been a kind of travesty of progress, as he sagged and lurched and fought for purchase. Henry squinting against the glare, the wind half ripping his shirt from him—so big on him that the back of it surged right and left off his shoulders like a sail, as if mad to get free. It obscured the lagging Suzanne, whom Saul hadn't even noticed at first. The sandpipers had hardly bothered with the usual nervous pitter-patter-glide away from Henry, choosing instead to poke around in the sand until the last moment and then take wing to escape the clumsy monster. Henry had looked in that moment like an awkward supplicant, a pilgrim come to worship.

They'd left their equipment—the metal boxes with the strange dials and readings. Almost like a threat. Squatters' rights. We will return. He didn't understand half of what he was looking at, even up close. And he didn't want to—didn't want to know what was on the séance side and what was on the science side. Prebiotic particles. Ghost energy. Mirror rooms. The lens was miraculous enough in what it could do without trying to find some further significance in it.

Saul's knee was acting up, putting too much creak in his step as he went through the Light Brigade's equipment. As he searched for something he knew he probably wouldn't recognize, he was reflecting that a man could fall apart from any number of ailments, and a bit of maintenance couldn't hurt. Especially since Charlie was seven years younger. But that just hid the thought that came now in little surges of panic: that something *was* wrong, that he was more and more a stranger in his own skin, that perhaps something was beginning to look out through his eyes. *Infestation* was a thought that crept in at moments between wakefulness and sleep, sleep and wakefulness, drifting down the passageway between the two.

There was the sense of something sliding more completely into place, and the feeling confused and frightened him.

Thankfully, Gloria's mother, Trudi Jenkins, agreed to see him on short notice about an hour before nightfall. She lived to the west, in a secluded bungalow, and Saul took his pickup truck. He parked on the dirt driveway, under oak and magnolia trees and a few palmettos. Around the corner, a deck peeked out that was almost as large as her home and had a view of the beach. If she'd wanted to, she could have rented a room to tourists in the summers.

It was rumored Trudi had come to the forgotten coast after plea-bargaining a drug-trafficking charge, this more than a decade ago. But whatever her past, she had a steady hand and a level head, and going to her was better than going to the clinic another fifty miles inland, or to the medical intern who visited the village.

"I had this sliver . . ." Another thing about Trudi was that he could talk about the sliver. He'd tried with Charlie, but, for reasons he couldn't quite figure out, the more he talked about it with Charlie, the more he felt like he was somehow putting it on Charlie, and he didn't yet know how much weight Charlie could take.

Thinking about that depressed him, though, and after a while he trailed off, without having mentioned the sensation of things floating at the edge of his vision.

"You believe something *bit* you?"

"Maybe not a bite so much as stuck me. I had a glove on my hand, but I still shouldn't have reached down. It might not have anything to do with how I've been feeling." Yet how could he have known? The moment of sensation, non-sensation, he kept returning to.

She nodded, said, "I understand. It's normal to worry, what with all of the mosquito- and tick-borne illnesses. So I can check your hand and arm, and take your vitals, and maybe put your fears to rest."

She might have been a pediatrician, but she didn't speak to him as if he were a child. She just had a way of simplifying things and getting to the point that made him grateful.

"Your kid wanders over the lighthouse quite a bit," he said, to make conversation as he took off his shirt and she examined him.

"Yeah, I know," she said. "I hope she's not a problem."

"No—she just climbs on the rocks a lot."

"She's a climber, all right. Gets into everything."

"Could be dangerous."

She gave him a sharp look. "I'd rather she go to the lighthouse and be around people I know than wander off on some trail or something."

"Yeah, true," he said, sorry he'd brought it up. "She's got a talent for identifying poop."

Trudi smiled. "She gets that from me. I taught her all about different kinds of poop."

"If a bear craps in the woods, she knows about it."

She laughed at that. "I think she might be a scientist when she grows up."

"Where is she now?" He'd assumed she would have walked home right after leaving the lighthouse.

"Grocery store. That girl likes to walk everywhere. So she might as well walk down to the grocery store and get us milk and some things for dinner." The grocery store adjacent to the village bar was pretty ad hoc, too.

"She calls me the defender of the light." He didn't know where that had come from, but he had liked it when she'd called him that.

"Mmm-hmm." Back to examining him.

At the end, she said, "I can't find any indication of anything abnormal on your arm or hand. I can't even find a mark. But if it's been a week it could've faded."

"So, nothing?" Relieved, and glad he hadn't gone into Bleakersville, thinking about how much time off he had coming, and how he'd prefer to spend it with Charlie. Peeling shrimp at some roadside café. Drinking beer and playing darts. Checking into a motel, careful to ask for double beds.

"Your blood pressure's elevated and you're running a slight fever, but that's all. Eat less salt. Have more vegetables. See how you are in a few days."

He felt better when he left, after having worked out a barter-and-money payment of twenty bucks and a promise to hammer down some loose boards in the deck, maybe a couple of other things.

But as he headed back to the lighthouse, reviewing the checklist for the lens in his mind, the relief that had invigorated him faded away and doubt crept in. Underlying everything was the thought that he had gone to the doctor as a kind of half measure for a larger problem, that he'd only confirmed there would be no easy diagnosis, that this wasn't as simple as a tick bite or the flu.

Something told him to look back as he drove, toward Failure Island, which was a shadow to the west, appearing at that distance as if it were just a sharp curve to the coastline. A faint pulse of red light blinked on and off, too high to be coming from anything other than a container ship. But too irregular to be anything but handheld or jury-rigged. In the right location on the horizon to be coming from Failure Island, perhaps from the ruined lighthouse.

Blinking out a code he didn't recognize, a message from Henry that he didn't want to receive.

After he got back, he called Charlie but there was no answer, then remembered that Charlie'd signed up for a night shift, hunting octopus and squid and flounder—the kind of adventure Charlie liked best. So he made a quick dinner, cleaned up, and then prepped the beacon. No ship traffic was expected during the night and the weather report was for calm seas.

With sunset came a premonition of beauty: The pre-dusk sky already had so many stars in it. Before he activated the lens, he sat there for a few minutes, staring up at them, at the deep blue of the sky that framed them. At such moments, he felt as if he really did live on the edge of the known world. As if he was alone, in the way he wanted to be alone: when he chose to be and not when the world imposed it on him. Yet he could not ignore that tiny dot of pulsing light still coming from Failure Island, even overshadowed as it was by so many distant suns.

Then the beam came on and obliterated it, with Saul retreating to sit on the top step to monitor the functioning of the lens for a few minutes before going back down to attend to other duties.

He wasn't supposed to sleep on nights when the lighthouse lens was on, but at some point he knew that he had fallen asleep on the top step, and that he was dreaming, too, and that he could not wake up and should not try. So he didn't.

The stars no longer shone but flew and scuttled across the sky, and the violence of their passage did not bear scrutiny. He had the sense that something distant had come close from far away, that the stars moved in this way because now they were close enough to be seen as more than tiny points of light.

He was walking toward the lighthouse along the trail, but the moon was hemorrhaging blood into its silver circle, and he knew that terrible things must have happened to Earth for the moon to be dying, to be about to fall out of the heavens. The oceans were filled with graveyards of trash and every pollutant that had ever been loosed against the natural world. Wars for scant resources had left entire countries nothing but deserts of death and suffering. Disease had spread in its legions and life had begun to mutate into other forms, moaning and mewling in the filthy, burning remnants of once mighty cities, lit by roaring fires that crackled with the smoldering bones of strange, distorted cadavers.

These bodies lay strewn across the grounds approaching the lighthouse. Visceral were their wounds, bright the red of their blood, loud the sound of their moans, as abrupt and useless as the violence they still visited upon one another. But Saul, as he walked among them, had the sense that they existed somewhere else, and it was only some hidden pull, like a celestial riptide, that drew them to manifest in that place, while the darkened tower of the lighthouse rose shrouded in a spiral of shadow and flame.

Out of this landscape Henry rose, too, at the lighthouse door, with a beatific smile on his face that kept growing larger until it curled off the edges of his jaw. Words erupted from him, but not aloud. *And God said, Let there be light. God said that, Saul, and He has come from so far away, and His home is gone, but His purpose remains. Would you deny Him His new kingdom?* There came with these words such a sense of sadness that Saul recoiled from them, from Henry. They spoke to all that he had put behind him.

Inside the lighthouse, Saul found not stairs leading up but a vast tunneling into the earth—an overwhelming spiral that wound down and down.

At his back, the moon had filled utterly with blood and was plummeting to the Earth, descending in the midst of a flame so hot he could feel it at his back. The dead and the dying had taken up the cry of approaching oblivion.

He slammed the door shut behind him, took that sudden path traveling down, his hand trailing against an ice-cold wall, and saw the steps so very far below him, so that he was either watching himself from a great height or his body had become as tall as the lighthouse, and each footfall occurred stories below him.

But Henry remained at his side, unwanted, and the stairs were also filling with water with a great rush and growl of fury, and soon most of him was submerged, Henry's fine shirt billowing with water, while Saul still walked down, down, until his head was beneath water, taking no breath, teetering, and he opened his eyes to see the fiery green-gold of words on the wall, being wrought before his eyes by an invisible scribe.

Even as he knew the words came from him, had always come from him, and were being emitted soundlessly from his mouth. And that he had been speaking already for a very long time, and that each word had been unraveling his brain a little more, a little more, even as each word also offered relief from the pressure in his skull. While what lay below waited for his mind to peel away entirely. A blinding white light, a plant with leaves that formed a rough circle, a splinter that was not a splinter.

When he woke up, he was sitting in a chair outside the lighthouse, with no idea how he'd gotten there. The words still lived inside of him, a sermon now coming out whether he wanted it to or not. Whether it would destroy him or not.

Where lies the strangling fruit that came from the hand of the sinner I shall bring forth the seeds of the dead to share with the worms.

0008: GHOST BIRD

Soon after the storm, the trail they followed wound back to the sea along a slope of staggered hills running parallel to the water. The wet ground, the memory of those dark rivulets, made the newly seeded soil seem almost mirthful. Ahead lay the green outline of the island, illumined by the dark gold light of late afternoon. Nothing had returned to haunt the sky, but now they walked through a world of broken things, of half-destroyed silhouettes against that gleaming horizon.

"What happened here?" Ghost Bird asked him, pretending it was his domain. Perhaps it was.

Control said nothing, had said nothing for quite some time, as if he didn't trust words anymore. Or had begun to cherish the answers silence gave him.

But something bad had happened here.

Seeking a path down to the shore that didn't require lacerating themselves on rushes and sticker cactus, they had no choice but to encounter the memory of carnage. An old tire rut filled with mud, an abandoned boot sticking out from it. Dull glint of an automatic rifle hidden by the moist grass. Evidence of fires started and then hastily put out, tents raised and struck, then smashed apart—clear that command and control had been shattered into pieces.

"The storm didn't do this," she said. "This is old. Who were they?"

Still no answer.

They came to the top of a slight rise. Below lay the remains of a truck; two jeeps, one burned down almost to the wheels; a rocket launcher in a state of advanced decomposition. All of it gently cupped by, submerged in, moss and weeds and vines. Disturbing hints of yellowing bones amid rags of faded green uniforms. The only scent was a faint sweet tang from purple-and-white wildflowers nodding furious in the wind.

It was peaceful. She felt at peace.

Finally, Control spoke. "It couldn't be personnel trapped in Area X when it expanded, unless Area X somehow sped up the rate of decay."

She smiled, grateful to hear his voice.

"Yes, too old." But she was more interested in another feature of the tableau spread out before them.

The beach and the land directly parallel had been subject to some catastrophic event, gouged and reworked, so that a huge rut on the shore had filled with deep water, and across the grass-fringed soil beyond lay what could be enormous drag marks or just the effects of an accelerated erosion. She had a vision of something monstrous pulling itself ashore to attack.

He pointed to the huge gouges. "What did that?"

"A tornado?"

"Something that came out of the sea. Or . . . what we saw in the sky?"

The wind whipped a little ragged orange flag stuck via a stake into the ground near the ruined tents.

"Something very angry, I'd say," she said.

Curious. Down on the shore, they found a boat hidden against a rise of sea oats, a rowboat pulled up past the high-tide mark, complete with oars. It looked as if it had been there for a long time, waiting. A commingled sadness and nervousness came over Ghost Bird. Perhaps the boat had been left for the biologist to find, but instead they had found it. Or the biologist's husband had never made it to the island and this boat was proof of that. But regardless, she could not really know what it meant, except that it offered a way across.

"We have just enough time," she said.

"You want to cross now?" Control said, incredulous.

Perhaps it was foolish, but she didn't want to wait. They might have another hour of real light and then that halo of shadows before true darkness dropped down upon them.

"Would you rather spend the night sleeping next to skeletons?"

She knew he didn't much like sleeping at all anymore, had started having hallucinations. Shooting stars became white rabbits, the sky full of them, with smudges of darkness interrupting their leaping forms. Afraid his mind was playing tricks to disguise something even more disturbing that only she could see.

"What if whatever did this came from the island?"

Throwing it back at him: "What if whatever did this is somewhere behind us in the marshes? The boat's seaworthy. And there's time."

"You don't find it suspicious that a boat's just waiting for us?"

"Maybe it's the first piece of good luck we've had."

"And if something erupts out of the water?"

"We row back—very fast."

"Bold moves, Ghost Bird. Bold moves."

But she was just as afraid, if not of the same things.

By the time they cast off, over that enormous scooped-out part of the shoreline, and then past a series of sandbars, the sun had begun to set. The water was a burnished dark gold. The sky above shone a deep pink, the blue-gray of dusk encroaching at the edges. Pelicans flew overhead, while terns carved the air into sharp mathematical equations and seagulls hovered, pushing against the wind.

The slap and spray of their rowing sent little whirlpools of golden water swirling off to disappear into the reflecting current. The prow of the boat had a blunt pragmatism to it that, set against all of that light, seemed serious to Ghost Bird, as if what they were doing had substance. Patterns could suffice as purpose, and the synchronicity of their rowing reassured her. They were *meant* to be rowing toward the island—to be here, in this place. The anxiety she felt about possibly finding the biologist and her husband on the island, of standing there and facing them, reversed or erased itself, lost, at least for a time, in the water.

The long, wide swathe of green that was the island at that distance was made irregular and disheveled-looking by the few tall oaks and pines that, along with the shattered spire of the lighthouse, broke through into the skyline. Trapped between: the calm motionless sky and the always restless sea, the island shimmering in the middle distance, surrounded by distortion as if it emanated heat. Sliding in between them from either side, rangy, scruffy islets with pine trees contorted low upon them, the silhouettes of these outposts extended by the rough gray-black line of oyster beds shot through with a startling iridescent white from dead shells pried open by birds.

They did not speak, even when they needed a course correction slightly to the west to avoid a sudden shallows, or when a surge in the current—waves breaking over the bow—required that they row with vigor. There was just the leaky roar of his grunting, her heavy breathing, in rhythm with the motion of her oar, the slight tapping of his oar against the frame as Control couldn't match the fluidity of her strokes. There was in the smell of his sweat and the brine of the water, the sudden tangy smell, almost a flavor, a sense of honest effort. The tautness she felt in her triceps, her forearms as she put her back into it. The pleasing soreness that came after, letting her know this was effort, this was real.

As the light faded and the sea shed its golden glitter, the rough charcoal shadow of the boat merged with the deeper blue overtaking the waves, the stained and streaked purple of the sky. With dusk, something loosened in her chest, and her rowing became even more relaxed and powerful, so that Control glanced over with a frown. She felt his gaze upon her in little appraising glances, and sometimes she turned to blunt it or neutralize it.

The shattered lighthouse grew as the light deepened still further into night. Even ruined and ravaged and torn at by wind and erosion and storms, it was a beacon to them, had a sense of life she could not ignore. There was something almost noble about it, something about the cold and the shadows of the trees and yet this place still existing that made her both sad and proud—an unexpected feeling. Had the biologist felt this way, if she had come here? Ghost Bird didn't think so. The biologist would have seen everything that surrounded it first.

The lesser darkness between the lines of the island and sea had resolved into the wreckage of the dock, at a slight raised angle from the sea so the right half of it lay submerged, the shore to either side a human-made welter of broken concrete pilings and rocks. There was no hint of a beach, until a dull off-white grin became visible along the curve of the shore farther to the west.

No light came from the lighthouse, but raucous clusters of birds settling in for the night on the trees competed with the waves, their rude cries coming to her now over the wind. The trajectories of bats in the sky above seemed like something planned by a drunk navigator, their bodies obliterating stars in haphazard and unpredictable fashion.

"Do you feel like someone is watching us?" she whispered.

"No, I don't." His voice was hoarse, as if he'd been talking to her the whole time, some effect of the wind and the salt air.

"*I* feel like someone is watching us."

"Birds. Bats. Trees." But said with too much dismissal. He didn't believe it was just birds, bats, trees, either.

The gulping slosh under the dock as they lashed the rowboat to the pier, the lap-licking wash and retreat over the rocks below, the creak of the planks as they came up the causeway. The anonymous birds in the trees fell silent, but a throbbing series of croaks continued from various parts of the overgrown grounds of the lighthouse. Somewhere beyond that the deliberate footfalls of some medium-size mammal making its way through the underbrush. While above them the pale, almost luminous jagged spire of the lighthouse rose, framed by the dark sky and the stars arrayed around it as if it was the center of the universe.

"We'll spend the night in the lighthouse, and then forage in the morning." It was warmer here than on the sea, but still cold.

She knew it could not have escaped his notice—the worn little path through the long weeds, visible by the starlight. Only regular traffic or maintenance would cause the weeds not to grow there.

Control nodded, face unreadable in the darkness, and stooped to pick up a stick, brandished it. They had no guns—had long ago discarded their few modern supplies, acknowledgment of Area X's strange effects, keeping just one flashlight. Turning on that flashlight now would have felt unwise and foolish. But she had a gutting knife, and she took that out.

The lighthouse door lay on the landward side, and the path led right to it. The original door was missing, but in its place leaned a massive wooden barricade that she slowly realized was the door from a stable or something similar. With some effort, they moved it to the side, stood in the threshold. The inside smelled of decay and driftwood. It smelled fresher than she'd expected.

She lit a match, saw, obscured by shadows surging against the walls, that the central spiral staircase lay naked, like a giant stone corkscrew, in the middle of the ground floor, and that it ascended into a giant hole above. Unstable at best. At worst, all of it about to come down.

As if reading her thoughts, Control said, "It could probably still hold our weight. They built it in such a way that the supporting walls take most of the burden. But that's pretty raw."

She nodded, could see the steel rods running through it now, a skeleton that inspired a little more confidence.

The match went out. She lit another.

The ground floor was covered in dead leaves and a smattering of branches, a catacomb of smaller rooms hidden from view at the back. A bare concrete floor, with the scars to show that someone had ripped up the floorboards.

The match went out. She thought she heard a sound.

"What was that?"

"The wind?" But he didn't seem certain.

She lit another match.

Nothing. No one.

"Only the wind." He sounded relieved. "Should we just sleep here, or explore the rooms in back?"

"Explore—I don't want any surprises."

The match went out from a gust of wind coming from the stairwell.

"We need to make these matches last longer," Control complained.

She lit another match, screamed, Control startled beside her.

A shadow sat halfway up the steps of the staircase, a rifle aimed at them. The shadow resolved into a black woman wearing army fatigues—compactly built, curly hair cut close to her head.

"Hello, Control," the woman said, ignoring her.

Ghost Bird recognized her from her first debriefing at the Southern Reach.

Grace Stevenson, the assistant director.

0009: THE DIRECTOR

Lowry's secret facility, on a dreary part of the east coast, with gravel beaches and stark yellowing grass, has been set up on the bones of an old military base. Here, Lowry has been perfecting his neurology and conditioning techniques—some would say brainwashing. From atop a mossy hill hollowed out for his command and control, he rules a strange world of decommissioned silver harbor mines lolling on the lawn below and rusting gun emplacements from wars fought seventy years ago. Lowry has had a replica of Area X's lighthouse built and a replica of the expedition base camp, and even a hole in the ground meant to approximate the little known about the "topographical anomaly." You knew this before you were summoned, and in your imagination this false lighthouse and false base camp were foreboding and almost supernatural in their effect. But, in truth, standing there with Lowry, looking out across his domain through a long plate of tinted glass, you feel more as if you're staring at a movie set: a collection of objects that without the animation of Lowry's paranoia and fear, his projection of a story upon them, are inert and pathetic. No, not even a movie set, you realize. More like a seaside carnival in the winter, in the off-season, when even the beach is a poem about loneliness. How lonely is Lowry out here, surrounded by all of this?

"Sit down and I'll get you a drink."

Very Lowry, but you don't sit and you politely decline the drink, staring out at the shore, the sea. It's a gray, crappy day and the weather reports say it may even snow. The water has an oily quality from offshore pollution, the dull light creating rainbows across its still surface.

"No? Well, I'll make you one anyway." Also very Lowry, and you're tenser than you were a moment ago.

The room is narrow, and you're standing at the window, behind you a long, low lime-green couch with a steel frame covered by psychedelic orange pillows.

Shaped like crude downward-diving breasts, porcelain light fixtures hang in rows of twenty from a ceiling slanted to the curve of the hill. Their glow melts across the couches, tables, and wooden floor in soft overlapping circles. The whole back plate of glass sealing off the room from behind is a mirror, projecting your images and protecting you from the truth that this isn't really a lounge and you're here not by invitation but by order. That this is an interrogation room of sorts.

The refined Lowry, so unlike the uncouth Lowry—leaning forward from a chair catty-corner to the couch—has been spending a deliberate eternity prying ice cubes from a bowl on the glass table in front of you into the glasses, one by one, clink by clink. He opens a bottle of scotch with care, and, with a tap of the bottle neck against glass, pours out two fingers.

Lowry, bent over his task, letting the moment elongate further. The mane of golden hair now silver, grown long. The determined, solid head on a thick neck, the landmarks of features upon a face that had served him well: craggy good looks, people say, like an astronaut or old-fashioned movie star. People who have never seen the photographs of Lowry after the first expedition into Area X, that dehydrated unshaven face still imprinted with an encounter with the horrific unknown, Lowry gone somewhere no one else had ever gone. "An honorable guy" back then, charismatic and direct. Even gone to fat a little, a thickness around the stomach, he retains some charm. Even with a left eye prone to wandering as if a tiny planet is straining out of alignment, being pulled to the side by the attraction of something just out of the frame. Those bright, piercing blue eyes. One scintilla more brilliant and all of his charisma would be wasted—the determined nose, the resolute jaw almost a parody, like the coastline of a confident country— undermined by a stare too glacial. But there is just enough warmth in that gaze to preserve the rest of the illusion.

"There, done," he says, and you're nervous to the inverse of his calm and reverential care for the drinks.

Lowry's replaced the bunkers hidden in the adjacent hills with secret labs. Full of higher-order animals, is the ridiculous rumor, brought here to bear the brunt of Lowry's imagination, as if to punish nature for having punished him. Experiments on neurons, neural linkage, synapse control. Boring, impossible things like that. You doubt he ever brings his fourth wife here, or his children, even though the family's summer house is conveniently nearby. No tours of Daddy's workplace.

You wonder what Lowry does for fun. Or maybe he's doing it now.

He turns, a drink in each hand, dressed in his expensive dark blue suit, his gold-tipped dress shoes. He smiles, holds both the drinks outstretched, the motion doubled, tripled, by the mirror at his back. The gleam of perfect teeth. The wide politician's smile. A dangerous smile.

It's hardly even a flick of the wrist, there's such economy of motion. So compact a movement of elbow and arm that for a moment you don't realize that your drink is being thrown at you.

The glass that was in his left hand smashes against the window near your head, shatters. As you recoil, sidestep, gaze never leaving Lowry, liquid splashes your shoes and splinters of glass needle your ankles. The window's bulletproof glass, reinforced. It doesn't even reverberate. The drink in Lowry's right hand isn't even trembling. But, then, neither are you.

Lowry's still smiling.

He says, "Now that you've had your drink, maybe we can get the fuck down to it."

You recline, uncomfortable against the pillows, looking out at the sea, the lighthouse, the remains of the glass of scotch on the floor. You wonder if he has them specially made so they break easier. Lowry sits in his chair, leaning forward like a predator. You remain very still. Your heart is beating out some secret code you can't decrypt. Lowry's broad face up close, the ruddiness caused by alcohol, the abrupt lowering of the thick shoulders, the way the stomach spills onto his lap as he leans forward, his own drink still in hand. You haven't seen any sign of his staff, but you know security waits right outside the door.

"So you thought you'd take a closer look, huh, Cynthia? Thought you'd use my own security codes and bypass your superiors and take a quick peek. Couldn't resist seeing what's beyond the curtain."

It was a good plan; it should have worked. You should have been invisible coming back across. But Lowry had spies among the border command, had been alerted, and the best Grace could do was confiscate the materials they brought back, put them in the Southern Reach storage cathedral, mislabeled as from a prior expedition. Lowry'd had you held at the military base, top secret, before flying you up here. Whitby had been debriefed and then placed under a kind of house arrest.

"I already knew what was there."

A gigantic snort—of contempt, of disbelief. "Typical desk jockey. Thinks just because they've read the reports, just because they're in charge, they know something." Said without irony.

His breath is sweet, too sweet, as if something's on the verge of rotting inside him. The eyes are unstable, hostile, but otherwise his expression is unreadable. He looks like a man who, with just one more drink, is capable of almost anything.

"So you saunter across and have yourselves a great little holiday. Relax on the beach, right? Once you were across, got a little kinky thinking about being in that place with your boy toy, Whitby? Wanted a bit of lighthouse on the lighthouse steps?"

Silence is the best response. Central sees the sophisticated version of Lowry. You see the dregs, whatever he can get away with.

"You've got nothing to say to me, then. Nothing? No annotation? No further explanation?"

"I turned in my report."

He's half up out of his seat at that, but you don't move at all. Even at the age of nine on the forgotten coast you knew better than to run from a bear or wild dog. You stand your ground, face them down. Maybe even growl. Would you have done the same when the rules changed, when it became Area X? You don't know. You're sweating under all those ridiculous lights.

"I'm trying to get inside your head without getting inside your head, if you know what I mean," Lowry says. "I'm trying to understand how we got here. Trying to see if there's a good fucking reason I shouldn't just let Central fire you."

The Central egg opening up like a mouth to issue an order to make you spontaneously combust or, more likely, evaporate like mist. But this means Lowry's the main reason you haven't been fired yet, which gives you back a sense of hope.

"I couldn't keep sending in expeditions under my orders without going myself." You couldn't let them be the only ones to have the experience.

"*Your* orders? *My* orders, not *your* orders. You get that straight." He slams his glass down on the table between you. An ice cube escapes, slides across the surface onto the floor. You resist the urge to pick it up, put it back in his glass.

"And Whitby—you just had to recruit him for your sad little expedition, too?"

You could reveal that Whitby wanted to go, but you can't predict how Lowry would react. Whitby's always been beyond Lowry, a fundamental misunderstanding between tragically different life-forms.

"I didn't want to go alone. I needed backup."

"*I'm* your backup. And involving the assistant director in all of this—that was a good idea, too?"

Grace might hate Lowry, but for some reason Lowry half liked Grace. Which, if she ever found out, would disgust her.

"None of it was a good idea. It was a lapse in judgment . . . But it's hard to send men into battle without going into battle yourself." Grace's idea for a defense. Keep it simple. Keep it old school.

"Cut the bullshit. Did Grace suggest you say that? I bet she did."

Have you missed a bug this time around, or is this just a guess?

Again: "You've got our reports."

Lowry is the only one who does have them. The army's border command knows this but Grace has concealed it from the Southern Reach, at Lowry's request—"for reasons of morale and security clearance"—pending a final decision. Officially you're still taking a very long vacation, and Whitby's on administrative leave.

"Fuck your reports. You're trying to hide Whitby from me"—not strictly true—"and your findings seem flimsy, incomplete. You were in there almost three weeks and your report is four pages long?"

"Nothing that unusual happened. Considering."

"Considering bullshit. What did Whitby see? Something real or just another fucking hallucination? Do you understand what could've happened by going there? Do you understand what you could've stirred up?" The words coming out of his mouth slur together so it sounds like *stirrups*.

"I understand." A toy lighthouse suddenly come to life.

Lowry, leaning in then, lurching in, to whisper, in a miasma of that sweet rotting breath, "You want to know what's funny. What's so fucking funny?"

"No." Here it comes. As if he's somebody's gramps at a holiday gathering. The same story almost every time.

"Back in the day. Back then, you got it all wrong. If you'd 'fessed up' to the old Ess Arr during the interview, the kicker is they might've taken you anyway. You might've gotten hired. They might have done it, knowing the old director. True, maybe a sick kind of fascination attached, like with some special, intelligent lab animal—a special, particularly magnificent white rabbit, say. True, you'd never have made director, but, fuck, that job sucks, right? As you're finding out. As you're going to keep finding out. Problem now, though, is the deception's gone on too long. So what the hell do we do."

The problem, from your point of view, is less the past than the present. The time when you could somehow have tried to contain Lowry or influence him is long gone. As soon as he'd ascended to Central, been canonized, you couldn't touch him.

The person, the person you'd been back before Ess Arr, had been careful—so careful trying to get to the point where you could do something reckless like cross the border into Area X.

Your father had been paranoid about the government, every once in a while took on something shady to supplement the day job as a part-time bartender—a low-level grifter. He didn't want any involvement. He didn't want any trouble. So he kept the government out of it, didn't tell you your mother was probably dead and that you weren't going back to the forgotten coast ever again until he absolutely had to. Told you to give vague answers to the men who came to interview you about your mother—it would be better for your mother that way. Anything to avoid a light shining on his "business ventures."

"You don't know this, 'cause you're too young," came the usual lecture, "but politicians run all the big scams. Government's the thief of all time. That's why it tries so hard to catch thieves—it doesn't like the competition. You don't want *that* on your back your whole life just because you were in the wrong place at the wrong time."

When he did tell you that she was gone, you cried for a month, even as that look on your father's face, the gruff warning, the way everything in your constantly moving household operated on caution, indoctrinated you in the merits of silence.

Over time your memory of your mother faded, in the way of not knowing if an image or moment was something you'd experienced or seen going through the photographs your dad kept in a shoe box in the closet. Not in the way of keeping something close rather than pushing it away. You would stare at pictures of your mother—on the deck with friends, a drink in her hand or on the beach with your dad—and imagine that she was the one saying, "Don't forget me," feel ashamed when it was the lighthouse keeper's face that kept coming back to you.

Tentative and then with more determination, you started your own investigation. You learned there was something called the Southern Reach, devoted to cleaning up the "environmental devastation" in what had been the forgotten coast and was now Area X. Your scrapbook grew so fat it was hard to open, filled with clippings from books, newspapers, magazines, and, later, websites. Conspiracy theories dominated, or speculative recastings of the government's official story. The truth always something vague and out of focus that had nothing to do with what you'd seen, with the sense you'd had of the lighthouse keeper becoming *different*.

In your first year of college, you realized that you wanted to work for the Southern Reach, no matter what their role, and, with your grifter's sense of the truth, that your past would be a liability. So you changed your name, hired a private investigator to help you hide the rest, and went on to pursue a degree. Cognitive psychology, focused on perceptual psychology, with a minor in organizational psychology as well. You married a man you never really loved, for a variety of reasons, divorced him fifteen months later, and spent close to five years working as a consultant, applying and reapplying to Central with application-form answers tailor-made to give you a shot at the Southern Reach.

The director at the time, a navy man, loved by all but not hard enough by far, hadn't interviewed you. Lowry had—still at the Southern Reach back then and with his own agenda. He liked to acquire his power sideways. There had been the formal meeting in his office, and then you'd gone out to the edge of the courtyard and had a different kind of interview.

"We can't be overheard out here," he'd said, and alarm bells had gone off. Irrational thought that he was going to proposition you, like some of Dad's friends. Something beyond his polite demeanor, his well-made clothes, his air of authority, must have warned you.

But Lowry had something more long-term in mind.

"I had my own people check you out. It was a good effort there, all that work to disguise yourself. A solid B for effort, all of that, sure. Not bad at all, considering. But I still found out, and that means Central would have, too, if I hadn't covered up your tracks. What was left of them." A broad smile, a genial manner. You could have been talking about sports or the swamp sweltering there in front of you, seeming to simmer in its own thick broth.

You cut to the important bit: "Are you going to turn me in?" Throat dry, it seeming hotter than it had a moment before. Memories of your father being taken off to jail for petty fraud, always with the bravado of a smile and a blown kiss, as if the point after all was to get caught, to have an audience, to be noticed.

A chuckle from Lowry, and you intimidated by what struck you back then as his sophistication despite his failings. His verve. The way he filled out the suit, and the way his face reflected experience, like he'd seen what you wanted to see, been where you wanted to be.

"Turn you in, Gloria . . . I mean, Cynthia. Turn you in? To whom? The guys in charge of keeping track of fake names and false identities? The forgotten coast truthers? No, I don't think so. I don't think I'm going to turn you in to anyone." The unspoken thought: *I'm going to keep you all for myself.*

"What do you want?" you asked. Thankful, for once, that being your father's daughter meant sometimes you could cut right through the bullshit.

"Want?" Disingenuous to the core. "Nothing. Nothing yet, anyway. In fact, it's all about you . . . Cynthia. I'm going to walk back in there with you and recommend you for the job. And if you pass training at Central, then we'll see. As for all the rest of it . . . that'll just be our secret. Not really a little secret, but a secret."

"Why would you do that?" Incredulous, not sure you had heard right.

With a wink: "Oh, I only really trust people who've been to Area X. Even pre–Area X."

At first, the price wasn't so bad. All he wanted, off the record, told to him and him alone, was an account of your last days on the forgotten coast. The lighthouse keeper, the Séance & Science Brigade. "Describe the man and the woman," he said, meaning Henry and Suzanne, and all of his questions about the S&SB sounded as if you were filling in pieces of some story he'd already heard part of before.

Within months, the favors asked for and reluctantly given multiplied—support for this or that initiative or recommendation, and when you had more influence, to push against certain things, to be less than enthusiastic, to stall. Mostly, you realize, on certain committees connected to the science division, to undermine or curtail Central's influence within the Southern Reach. All of it clever and by degrees so that you didn't really notice the escalation until you were so mired in it that it was just part of your job.

Eventually, Lowry supported your bid to become director. Coming to the Southern Reach had been like being allowed to listen to the heartbeat of a mysterious beast. But as director you came even closer—terrifyingly closer, trapped within the chamber walls, needing time to adjust. Time exploited by Lowry, of course.

Tossed onto the table: the latest satellite footage from above Area X, images from on high reduced to $8\frac{1}{2} \times 11$ glossies. Glamour shots of an inexhaustible resource. This blank mimicry of the normal, marred only by the blurs you might expect to find on photos taken by ghost hunters. Definitive proof of a change, this blurring. As if somehow the Southern Reach is losing the ability to see even the lie.

"Evil advances with good. But these terms have no meaning in Area X. Or to Area X. So why should they always apply to us in pursuit of an enemy to whom they go unrecognized? An indifferent context deserves equal indifference from us—if we want to survive."

You're not expected to answer, Lowry taking a break to philosophize as he fills up his drink for a second time. Nor would you know *what* to answer, for you would never characterize Lowry as *indifferent*, or as expressing indifference through his actions. As ever, this is part of the deception: the ability to convey authority by instilling in others his own confidence.

Lowry's already threatened to put you under hypnosis, but the one thing you have resolved, having lived on the outskirts of Lowry's experiments, is that you will never allow him that. Always hoping that Lowry must have limits, can't be untouchable, can't operate without some constraint from above. Surely every action he takes reveals something about his motives to someone somewhere with the power to intervene?

So you're at what appears to be an impasse.

Then he surprises you.

"I want you to meet someone else who has a stake in this. Someone you know already. Jackie Severance."

Not a name you expected to hear. But there she is—escorted in by Mary Phillips, one of Lowry's assistants, through the mirror door to your side of the glass, Severance oblivious to the way her heels are crunching broken glass. Dressed as impeccably as always, still addicted to scarves.

Has she been listening the whole time? The dynastic successor to the legendary Jack Severance. Jackie, about fifteen years removed from her last stint with the Southern Reach—a bright star still shining in the firmament of Central's personal cosmology, despite a dark star of a son in the service that she's had to rescue more than once. Lowry the outlaw and Severance the insider seem unlikely allies. One's holding the silver egg in her hand and petting it. The other is trying to smash it with an invisible hammer.

What's the play, here? Does Lowry hold something over her, or does she hold something over Lowry?

"Jackie is going to be my adviser on this situation. She's going to be *involved* from now on. And before we make a final decision on what to do with you, I want you to repeat for her everything that's in the report—everything that happened to you across the border. One last time."

Severance smiles the way a crocodile smiles and sits on the couch next to you while Lowry shuffles off to make her a drink. "Nothing too formal, Cynthia. Nothing you need to prep. And in no particular order. You can tell it in whatever order you like."

"That's kind of you, Jackie." It's not kind—it's just an attempt to get a different version. Which makes this a ritual of sorts, with a preordained outcome.

So you go back over it all again with Severance, who stops you from time to time with questions blunter than you expect, coming from someone you've always thought of as a political animal.

"You didn't go anywhere else? No shortcuts or other excursions?"

"Excursions?"

"It's easy to omit what doesn't seem relevant."

The same flat smile.

You don't bother to answer.

"Did you bring anything back with you?"

"Just the usual recovery along the way, of past expedition equipment, as happens with many expeditions." The story you and Whitby have decided on, because you want to hold on to the plant and phone, test them at the Southern Reach, not have them taken by Central. You're the experts, not Central.

"What sense did you get of the journals in the lighthouse? Was there an impression or idea you had about them, seeing them all like that? If that's not too vague."

No particular sense or impression or idea, you tell her. They were just journals. Because you don't want to go there, don't yet want to relive the end of your trip, the things that happened in the lighthouse.

"And nothing there seemed unusual or out of order?"

"No." You're selling the simpler story of danger in the tunnel.

Later, leaning in, conspiratorial, just you girls: "Gloria. Cynthia. Why'd you do it? Really?" As if Lowry's not in the room.

You shrug, give a pained smile.

At the end of your account, Severance smiles and says, "It's possible that we'll file this under 'never happened' and move on. And if so, you have Lowry to thank." A hand on your arm, though, as if to say, "Don't forget I helped." You get to keep Whitby, too, she says, if Whitby passes a psych eval you personally help conduct at Central, off the books. But. "You are vouching for him. You are responsible for him." Like you're a child asking to keep a pet.

The new border commander will be handpicked by Lowry and report to both Lowry and Severance, and they will institute procedures so that, as Lowry puts it, "You and Whitby and any other son of a bitch stupid enough to try another jailbreak thinks twice."

A few useless pleasantries and Jackie's left the room as fast as she got there, the encounter so brief you wonder why else she's here, what other business she has with Lowry. Has she walked into a trap, or has Lowry? Trying to remember the exact date when Severance came to the Southern Reach. Going through a list of her tasks, her duties, and where she was when. Thinking that there is some part of the puzzle you can't see, that you *need* to see.

Lowry, there at the center of his secret headquarters, overlooking the sea as snow in thick flakes begins to cover the grass, the sea mines, the little paths. With the geese and seagulls that will never care about Lowry's plans or your own huddled by the fake lighthouse, as deceived by it as the expeditions have been by the real one. But Severance is out there now, walking by the rocks, staring across the water. She's on her phone, but Lowry doesn't see her—just his own reflection, and she's trapped there, within his outline.

Lowry, pumping himself up, pacing in front of the glass, smacking his chest with one hand. "And what I want is this: The next expedition, they don't go to Central. They come here. They receive their training *here*. You want Area X to react? You want something to change? I'll change it. I'll coil things so far up inside Area X's brain, things that'll have a sting in the tail. That'll draw blood. That'll fucking make the enemy know we're the resistance. That we're onto them."

Some trails go cold fast; some trails take a long time to pick up and follow. Seeing Severance walking along the ridge of black rocks near the lighthouse, even a fake lighthouse, raises your hackles, makes you want to say, "That is *mine*, not yours."

Lowry's still standing over you and ranting about what will happen and how it's going to happen. Of course he wants more control. Of course he is going to get it.

But now you know, too, what you've only guessed at before: Beneath Lowry's bluster, he feels that your fates are intertwined. That he's more bound to you than ever.

After six months, you will be able to return to the Southern Reach. No one there will know why you were gone so long, and Grace won't tell them, promises she'll have pushed them so hard in the interim that "they won't have time to think about it."

While you wait out your suspension at home, you have this image in your head of Grace as a tall, stern black woman in a white lab coat and the tricornered hat of a general, holding a saber at arm's length, for some reason standing in the prow of a rowboat, crossing a strategically important river. When it's time for her to drop the hat, get rid of the boat, cede control back to you, how will she feel about that?

Single dim thought most nights, after a doctor's appointment or buying groceries for dinner: Which world am I really living in? The one in which you can hear Whitby's screams in the lighthouse intermingling with the screams from the first expedition, or the one in which you're putting cans of soup in the cupboard. Can you exist in both? Do you want to? When Grace calls to ask how your day is going, should you say "Same as usual" or "Awful, like conducting autopsies over and over again for no reason"?

Sitting on a stool in the bar at Chipper's—that's the same, isn't it, after you come back? Perhaps even more so, given you have more time to spend there. The Realtor's around a lot, too. She talks all the time—about a trip up north to visit her family, about a movie she saw, about local politics. Sometimes the veteran with the perpetual beer in hand dredges up a long-ago memory of his kids, trying to be part of the conversation.

As the Realtor and the drunk talk past and through you, you're nodding as if you know what they're talking about, as if you can relate, when all you can see now are two images of the lighthouse keeper superimposed, saying the same thing at different times, to two different versions of you. One in darkness and one in light.

"You're thinking of your own children, aren't you?" says the Realtor. "I can tell."

Your mind must have wandered. The mask must have slipped.

"Yes, you're right," you say. "Sure."

You have another beer, start to tell the Realtor all about your kids—where they go to school, how you wish you saw them more often, that they're studying to be doctors. That you hope to see them around the holidays. That they seem to belong to a different world now that they're all grown up. The veteran, standing at the end of the bar, staring past the Realtor at you, has a strange look on his face. A look of recognition, as if he knows what you're doing.

Hell, maybe you should play some songs on the jukebox, too. Maybe go take a turn at karaoke later, have a few more beers, make up a few more details of your life. Only, the Realtor left at some point, and it's just you and the veteran and some people trickling in late who you don't know, won't ever know. The floor's sticky, dark with old stains. The bottles behind the bar have water-cooler cups over them, to keep the fruit flies out. There's a sheen off the bar top that's not entirely natural. Behind you, the lanes are dark and the faded heavens have risen again, unimaginable wonders across the ceiling, some of them requiring a moment to recognize.

Because the other world always bleeds into this one. Because no matter how you try to keep what happened at the lighthouse between you and Whitby, you know it will leak out eventually, in some form, will have consequences.

At the lighthouse, Whitby had wandered, and you were still drifting through the downstairs when you realized that you couldn't hear him moving around in the next room anymore. In the stillness and the dust, the way the light through the broken front door made the darkness murky, you expected to find him standing in a corner, a figure luminous in shadow.

But soon enough you realized he'd gone up the lighthouse stairs, headed for the very top. There came the sounds of fighting and the splintering of wood. One voice rising above the other, both curiously similar, and how could there be a second voice at all? So you followed fast, and as you climbed, there was both a doubling and a dissonance, for in memory, the steps had been much wider, the trek much longer, the space inside the lighthouse conveying a kind of weightlessness, the walls once painted white, the windows open to receive the sky, the scent of cut grass brought by Saul. But in the darkness, worried about Whitby, you had become a giant or the lighthouse had become lost or *diminished*, not just undone by time, but contracting, like the spiraling fossil of a shell, leading you to a place no longer familiar. Erasing, with each step, what you thought you knew.

At the top, you discovered Whitby down in the watch room panting like an animal, his clothes torn and blood on his hands, and the strange impression that the edges of the journals were rippling, enveloping Whitby, trying to drown him. No one else there, just Whitby with an impossible story of encountering his doppelgänger, False Whitby, on the landing, chasing him up to the lantern room, until they had fallen through the open trapdoor onto the mound of journals, off-balance and awkward. The smell of them. The bulk of them. The feel of them around Real Whitby and False Whitby as they toiled in their essential opposition, now in and now out of the light coming through the open trapdoor.

How to verify this story of not one but two Whitbys? Not Whitby punching himself, kicking himself, biting himself, awash in flapping paper, but doing this to another version. His wounds were inconclusive.

But the tableau fascinates you, returns to you during your six months off, even while chopping onions for chili in your kitchen or mowing the lawn.

Sometimes you try to imagine what it would have been like if you had arrived earlier, not in the aftermath, and stopped there, at the top of the steps, peering down into that space, unable to move, watching the two Whitbys struggle. You can almost believe that Whitby birthed Whitby, that in exploring Area X, something in Whitby's own nature created this paradox, with one version, one collection of impulses, thoughts, and opinions, trying, once and for all, to exterminate the other.

Until two pale hands reach out to choke one pale throat, and two faces stare at each other, inches apart, the face above deformed by a paroxysm of rage while the face below remains calm, so calm, surrounded by the ripped and crumpled journals. The white paper with the red line of the margin, the blue lines to write on. The pages and pages of sometimes incomprehensible handwritten text. All of those journals without names but only functions noted, and sometimes not even that, as if Area X has snuck in its own accounts. Are they shifting and settling as if something huge sleeps beneath them, breathing in and out?

Is that a glow surrounding them, or surrounding Whitby? The Whitbys?

Until there is the crack. Of a neck? Of a spine? And the Whitby pinned against the mound goes slack and his head lolls to the side and the Whitby atop him, frozen, emits a kind of defeated sob and slides off Dead Whitby, awkwardly manages to wriggle and roll his way free . . . and sits there in the corner, staring at his own corpse.

Then, and only then, are you drawn to wonder whether your Whitby won—and who this other Whitby might have been, who in death would have seemed preternaturally calm, face smooth and unwrinkled, eyes wide and staring, only the angle of the body suggesting that some violence has been perpetrated upon it.

Afterward, you forced Whitby to come out of that space, to take some air by the railing, to look out on that gorgeous unknowable landscape. You pointed out old haunts disguised as your exhaustive encyclopedic knowledge of the forgotten coast. Whitby saying something to you—urgently, but you not really hearing him. You more intent on filling up the space between with your own script, your own interpretation—either to calm Whitby or to negate his experience. To forget about the mound of journals. A thing you don't want to consider for too long, that you put out of your mind because isn't that the way of things? To ignore the unreal so it doesn't become more real.

On the way down, you searched for Dead Whitby, but he still wasn't anywhere. You may never know the truth.

But in what Whitby swore was Dead Whitby's backpack, you found two curious items: a strange plant and a damaged cell phone.

0010: CONTROL

Control woke to a boot and a foot, just six inches from where he lay on his side under some blankets. The black tread of the army-issue boot was worn down in tired ridges like the map of a slope of hills. Dried mud and sand commingled there and in the sporadic black studs meant to provide a better grip. A dragonfly wing had been broken along the axis of that tread, pulverized into rounded panes and an emerald glitter. Smudges of grass, a smear of seaweed that had dried on the side of the boot.

The landscape struck him as evidence of a lack of care not reflected by the tidy stacking of provisions, the regular sweeping out of leaves and debris from the landing. Next to the boot: the pale brown sole of a muscular foot that seemed to belong to a different person, the toenails clipped, the big toe wrapped tight in fresh gauze with a hint of dried blood staining through.

Both boot and foot belonged to Grace Stevenson.

Above the rise of her foot, he could see she held the three weathered, torn pages he'd rescued from Whitby's report. In her army fatigues, including a short-sleeved shirt, Grace looked thinner, and gray had appeared at her temples. She looked as if she had endured a lot in a short time. A pistol lay in a holster by her side, along with a knapsack.

He twisted onto his back, sat up, and shoved up against the wall catty-corner to her, the window between them. The raucous birds that had briefly woken him at dawn were quiet now, probably out foraging or doing whatever birds did. Could it be as late as noon? Ghost Bird lay curled up in a camo-patterned sleeping bag, had throughout the night made little jerking motions and sounds that reminded Control of his cat in the grip of some vision.

"Why the hell did you go through my pockets?" Somehow the accusatory tone abandoned the words as he said them, relieved to find his dad's carving still in his jacket.

She ignored him, leafing through Whitby's last words, lingering between a smile and a frown, intense but uncommitted. "This has not changed since the last time I saw it. It's even more full of shit now . . . probably. Except back then the author was a crackpot. Singular. Now we're all fucking crackpots."

"Fuck?"

A quizzical look. "What's wrong with 'fuck'? Area X doesn't give a crap if I swear."

She continued to read and reread the pages, shaking her head at certain parts, while Control stared, still feeling possessive. He was more attached to those pages than he'd thought, afraid she might just ball them up and chuck them out the window.

"Can I have those back?"

A weary amusement, something in her smile that told him he was transparent. "Not yet. Not just yet. Get some breakfast. Then file a formal request." She went back to reading again.

Frustrated, he looked around the space. Compulsively tidy, as he'd thought on first glance. Lock-action rifles in a precise row against the far wall, next to her sleeping space, which was a mattress covered with a sheet and blanket she had tucked in tight. A creased wallet photo of her girlfriend, propped on a ledge, curling edges smoothed out. Cans of food lined up against the long side wall, and protein bars. Cups and bottles of drinking water that she must have gotten from a stream or well. Knives. A portable stove. Pots, pans. Lugged all the way from the Southern Reach building or scavenged from the ambushed convoy on the shore? How much she had found on the island he wouldn't want to guess.

Control was just about to get up and pick out a can when she spilled the pages on the floor between them, right on a spot damp from rainwater.

"Dammit." He scrambled forward on all fours to retrieve them.

The muzzle of Grace's gun dug into the side of his head near his ear.

He remained extremely still, looking across at where Ghost Bird slept.

"Are you real?" she asked, in a kind of rasp, as if her voice had gone gray along with her hair. Should he have divined something more profound from her boot, her bandaged toe?

"Grace, I—"

She smacked him across the forehead with the muzzle, shoved the mouth of the gun harder into his skin, whispered in his ear, "Don't use my fucking name. Don't ever use my name! No names. It may still know names."

"*What* may know names?" Stifling the word *Grace*.

"Shouldn't you already know?" Contemptuous.

"Put the gun down."

"No."

"Can I sit up?"

"No. *Are you real?*"

"I don't know what that means," he said, as calmly as he could. Wondered if he could move fast enough to get out of the line of fire, push the gun from his temple before she blew his brains out.

"I think you do. Tampered with. Spoiled goods. A hallucination. An apparition."

"I'm as real as you," he said. But the secret fear behind that, the one he didn't want to voice. Along with the thought that he didn't know what Grace had endured since he'd seen her last. That he wasn't sure he knew her now. Any more than he knew himself now.

"What script are you running off of? Central or the L-word?"

"The L-word?" Absurd thoughts. *Lie? Lighthouse? Lesbian?* Then realized she meant Lowry. "Neither. I cut off hypnotic suggestion. I freed myself." Not sure he believed that.

"Should we run a test?"

"Don't try it. I really mean it—*don't.*"

"I wouldn't," Grace said, as if he'd accused her of high crimes. "That's L's kink. But I know the signs by now. There is a pinched look you all get, a paleness. The hands curling into claws. His signature, written all over you."

"Residual. Just residual."

"Still, you admit it."

"I admit I don't know why the living fuck you're holding a gun to my head!" he shouted. Had Ghost Bird heard *nothing*, or was she pretending to sleep? And there, as if to call him a liar anyway: what Ghost Bird called "the brightness," curious, interested, questing. It rose now as a tightness in his chest, a spasm in his left thigh as he remained on all fours being interrogated by his assistant director.

A pause, an increased pressure of the muzzle at his head; he flinched. Then the pressure was gone, along with her shadow. He looked over. Grace was back against the wall, gun still in her hand.

He sat up, hands on his thighs, forced a deep breath in, out, and considered his options. It was the kind of field situation his mother would've called "an either without the or." He could either find some way to smooth it over or go for the rifles against the wall. Not a real choice. Not with Ghost Bird out of action.

Slowly, carefully, he picked his three Whitby pages off the floor, willed himself to move past the danger of the moment: "Is that your usual welcome?"

Her face a kind of impassive mask now, daring him to challenge her. "Sometimes it ends with me pulling the trigger. Control, I am not interested in bullshit. You don't have any idea what I've been through. What might be real . . . and what might not be real."

He slumped against the wall, holding Whitby's pages against his chest. Was there something in the corner of his eye?

"There's nothing to this world," he said, "but what our senses tell us about it, and all I can do is the best I can based on that information." Even though he didn't trust the world anymore.

"There was a time I would have shot first, before you even left the boat."

"Thank you?" Putting as much punch into that as possible.

A curt nod, like he was serious, and Grace shoved the gun back in its holster on her right side, away from him. "I always have to be careful." He noted the tension in her upper arm and heard the sharp click as she toyed with the clasp on the holster. Opening it. Closing it.

"Sure," he said. "I see someone got to your big toe. That kind of thing could make a person paranoid."

She ignored that, said, "When did you get here?"

"Five days ago."

"How long since the border shifted?"

Had Grace lost track of the days out here, by herself? "No more than two weeks."

"How did you get across?"

He told her, omitting any detail about where the door under the sea might lie. Omitting, too, that Ghost Bird had created it.

Grace considered all of that for a long moment, nursing a bitter smile that rejected interpretation. But he was on high alert again; she'd taken out her gutting knife with her left hand and was creating circles in the dust beside her. This wasn't just a paranoid debriefing. There were higher stakes and his own analysis to undertake: Had Grace just been rattled by something here on the island, or suffered the kind of shock that rearranged your thought processes, forever impaired your judgment?

With as much gentleness as he could muster: "Do you mind if I wake up Ghost Bird now?"

"I gave her a sedative with her water last night."

"You *what?*" Echoes of a dozen domestic terrorism interrogations, all the symbols and signs.

"Are you her new best friend now? Do you trust her? And do you even know what I mean?"

Trusted her not to be the enemy. Trusted her to be human. Wanted to say, *I trust her as much as I trust myself,* but that wouldn't satisfy Grace. Not this version of Grace.

"What has happened here?" He felt betrayed, sad. To have come so far, but that old dynamic—sharing a smoke in the courtyard of the Southern Reach—had turned to ash.

A shudder passed through Grace, some hidden stressor coming to the surface, moving through and past, as if waking only now from a nightmare.

"It takes getting used to," she said, staring down at the patterns she'd made in the dust. "It takes getting used to, knowing that everything we did meant nothing. That Central abandoned us. That our new director abandoned us."

"I tried to—" *I tried to stay; you told me to go.* But that clearly wasn't how she saw it. And now they were at the very edge of the world, and she was taking it out on him.

"I tried to blame you, at first, when I was getting things straight in my head. I did blame you. But what could you have done? Nothing. Central probably programmed you to do what they wanted."

Going over those horrific moments again, jammed together in his memory, wedged in there at odd angles. The look on Grace's face in that moment of extremes, as the border advanced on the Southern Reach, weighing the possibility that he'd said nothing to her at all. Hadn't been as close to her and hadn't put his hand on her arm. Just thought he had.

"Your face, Control. If you could have seen the expression on your face," she said, as if they were talking about his reaction to a surprise party. The wall of the building becoming flesh. The director returned in a wave of green light. The weight of that. The fingers of his left hand had curled around the carving of Chorry in his jacket pocket. He released his grip, pulled his hand out, let his fingers open up. Examined the white curved indentations, fringed with pink.

"What happened to the people in the science division?"

"They decided to barricade the basement. But that place was changing very fast. I didn't stay long." Said so casually, too casually, talking about the disappearance of the world they had both known. *I didn't stay long.* One sentence disguising a multitude of horrors. Control doubted the staff had had a choice about what happened to them, sealed off by that sudden wall.

And Whitby? But, remembering the last transmission from his spy cameras, he didn't want to know about the W-word yet, or perhaps ever.

"What about . . . the director?"

That level gaze, even in this new context, even with her on edge, twitchy, tired, and underfed. That unbreakable ability to take responsibility, for anything and everything, and to keep pressing forward.

"I put a bullet in its head. As per prior orders. Once I determined that what had returned was an intruder, a copy, a fake."

She could not continue or had thought of something that had distracted her from the narrative, or was just trying to hold it together. What it had cost her to kill even a version of the person she had been so devoted to, could be said to have loved, Control couldn't guess.

After a while, he asked the inevitable question: "And what then?"

A shrug, as she stared at the ground. "I did what I had to. I scavenged what I could, took along those who were willing, and, per orders, I headed for the lighthouse. I went where she said. I did exactly what she said and we accomplished nothing. We made no difference. So she was wrong, just wrong, and she had no plan. No plan at all."

Raw hurt, an intensity to all of it, everything she had told him in such a calm voice. He focused on the bottom of her boot. The disembodied thorax of a velvet ant lay somewhere south of five o'clock.

"Is that why you didn't go back across the border?" he asked. Because of the guilt?

"There is *no way back* across the border!" Shouting it at him. "There is no *door* anymore."

Choking on seawater, buffeted by fish. A vision of drowning all over again.

No door. Not anymore.

Just whatever lay at the bottom of the sea. Maybe.

Lost in the thought of that, while Grace continued to talk about grotesque and impossible things.

From the windows of the landing of the ruined lighthouse, the world looked different, and not just because Grace had reentered it. A thin wall of fog had crept in from the sea to obscure the view, and the temperature had plummeted. They would need a fire by nightfall if that didn't change. Vague through both fog and tree cover: the ghostlike remains of houses, walls like warped slabs of flesh sagging into other, even more rotted, flesh. Running parallel to the sea, a road, then hills covered in a dense pine-and-oak forest.

There was no door in the border, leading home.

Grace had terminated the director's doppelgänger.

Grace had felt the border move through and past her. "It was like being *seen*. Being naked. Being reduced. Down to nothing." As she stared with a fierce devotion at the fragile photo, so carefully repaired, of the woman she loved back in the world.

She had retreated in good order with a number of Southern Reach personnel, security and otherwise, to the lighthouse, per the director's prior directive, an order unknown to him and somehow reaching out of the past to be given validity. At the lighthouse, some of the soldiers had begun to change and could not handle that change. Some had struck out for the tunnel and never been seen again. A few had spoken of vast shadows approaching from the seaward side. A schism between factions, including an argument with the border commander, had made their position worse. "None of them survived, I don't think. None of them knew how to survive."

But she remained vague about her actions in the lighthouse, her retreat to the island. "I did what I had to do." "That's all in the past. I have made my peace with it." "I don't sleep much." All of that a jumbled mess. *In the past?* It had just happened.

He had held on to some hope or delusion of last redoubts, of hardened siege mentality, of making common cause to fight the enemy. But that had been a sick fantasy, a kind of abject denial. The Southern Reach was done even if they hunkered down in the science division for the next century, became the subterranean seeds for pale cave-dwelling people who lived in fear and whose children's children heard cautionary tales of the fucked-up surface world waiting for them above.

"You had expedition training?" A guess, but an educated one based on her supplies.

"The basic protection package, we called it," Grace said. "The director came up with it for department heads, management." Because she'd valued their safety so much, had hoped the head of their props department would survive the apocalypse. He was willing to bet "the basic protection package" had applied only to Cynthia and Grace. She'd never shared it with him.

"If you planned for this, that means there's a mission?"

"Does it look like there's a mission?" A terse, ironic grin. Her tone of voice different, as if aware Ghost Bird, who had begun to stir, might be listening. "The mission is survival, John. The mission is to take it day by day. I keep to myself. I follow certain protocols. I am careful and quiet." Grace was prepared to live out her days here. She had already resigned herself to that paradigm.

Ghost Bird propped herself up on one arm. She didn't look groggy. Her stare seemed like a weapon, as if she had no need of a gun or knife. Ghost Bird didn't look like someone who would appreciate being told she had been drugged, so Control didn't. A respectful, fearful look Grace gave her, now that she wasn't a sleeping lump on the floor.

"What attacked the convoy?" Ghost Bird asked.

No *Good morning* or even an interest in what they'd been discussing. How much had she overheard, lying there? What had seeped into her half-conscious mind about fakes and the director's doppelgänger?

A grim chuckle from Grace, followed by a shrug, but no other answer.

Ghost Bird shrugged, fell upon a protein bar, gutted it with her knife, wolfed down the contents. Between bites: "This is horrible and stale. Have you encountered anything unusual on the island?"

"It's all unusual here," Grace said, with a kind of exhaustion, as if the question had been asked too often before.

"Have you seen the biologist?" Direct speaking to direct, and Control tense, waiting for that answer.

"Have I seen the biologist?" Turning that question over and over, examining it from all angles. "Have I seen the biologist?" Grace's clicking of the holster strap came quicker now, the pattern in the dust drawn at knife point more complex. Was that a helix? Was that two intertwining spirals? A starfish or just a star?

"Well, answer me, Grace," Ghost Bird said, rising now, standing in front of them with her hands at her sides, in the kind of relaxed yet perfectly balanced stance someone took if they expected trouble. If they'd had combat training.

The light through the landing window faded into shadow as a cloud crossed over. A bird outside was muttering or whispering in time to the circling of the knife blade. Far distant came the suggestion of something sonorous, mournful, perhaps an echo off the lighthouse stones. A gecko scuttled up the wall. Control didn't know if he should be worried about the foreground or something in the background. This was the only question that mattered to Ghost Bird, and Control didn't know what she would do if Grace wouldn't answer.

Grace stared over at Control, said, "If I sat here and told this copy"—pointing at Ghost Bird—"everything I've found, we would still be sitting here when hell froze over."

"Just *answer* the question," Ghost Bird muttered.

"Are we just passing through?" Control asked. "Should we be moving on?" That's what this came down to, in a way. Not Ghost Bird's question but Grace's attitude, the constant suspicion that wore on him.

"Do you know how long I've been on this island? Did you ever ask me that?"

"Have you seen the biologist?" Ghost Bird demanded in a kind of staccato growl.

"Ask me." The knife stabbed, vibrating, into the wooden floor of the landing. The hand on the holster had gone still, resting on the gun.

Control gave Ghost Bird a quick look. Had he misread something vital?

"How long have you been on the island?" he asked.

"Three years. I've been here *three* years."

Outside, all seemed still, so impossibly still. The gecko frozen on the wall. Control frozen in his thoughts. Satisfaction, that Grace could not quite suppress, etched into her worn face. To have told them something they couldn't have known, couldn't have seen coming.

"Three *years*," Control said, a plea for her to recant.

"I don't believe you," Ghost Bird said.

A generous laugh. "I don't blame you much. I don't blame you at all. You're right. I must just be some crazy bitch who went mad out here all on her own. I must be unable to cope with my situation. I must be fucking nuts. Sure. Must be. Except for this . . ."

Grace pulled a sheaf of pages out of her knapsack. Brittle, yellowing, they had handwriting on them. A rusting clasp in the corner.

She flung the pages at Ghost Bird's feet. "Read it. Read it before I waste time telling you anything else. Just read it."

Ghost Bird picked it up, looked at the first page in confusion.

"What is it?" Control asked. Some part of him not wanting to know. Not wanting another dislocation.

"The biologist's last will and testament," Grace said.

PART II
FIXED LIGHT

Writing, for me, is like trying to restart an engine that has rested for years, silent and rusting, in an empty lot—choked with water and dirt, infiltrated by ants and spiders and cockroaches. Vines and weeds shoved into it and sprouting out of it. A kind of coughing splutter, an eruption of leaves and dust, a voice that sounds a little like mine but is not the same as it was before; I use my actual voice rarely enough.

A great deal of time has passed since I placed words on paper, and for so long I felt no urge to do so again. I have felt more acutely than ever that here on the island I should *never be taken out of the moment*. To be taken out of the moment is dangerous—that is when things sneak their way in and then there is no present moment to return to. Only very recently have I begun to feel something like a *lack*, or anything beyond the thought that I would in this place simply exist and live out whatever span was allotted to me. Neither have I had any interest in *recounting*, in *setting down*, in *communicating* in what has come to seem such a mundane way. Perhaps it's no surprise, then, that I have started to write this several times, and that I abandoned three or four drafts of this . . . this document? This letter? This . . . whatever *this* is.

Perhaps, too, hesitance overtakes me because when I think of writing I glimpse the world I left behind. The world beyond, that when my thoughts drift toward it at all, is a hazy, indistinct sphere radiating a weak light, riddled through with discordant voices and images that cut across eyes and minds like a razor blade, and none of us able to even blink. It seems a myth, a kind of mythic tragedy, a lie, that I once lived there or that anyone lives there still. Someday the fish and the falcon, the fox and the owl, will tell tales, in their way, of this disembodied globe of light and what it contained, all the poison and all the grief that leaked out of it. If human language meant anything, I might even recount it to the waves or to the sky, but what's the point?

Still, having decided to finally let the brightness take me, after holding out against it for so many years, I am giving it one more try. Who will read this? I don't know, nor do I really care. Perhaps I am just writing for myself, that some further record exist of this journey, even if I can only tell the first part of a much longer story. But if someone does read it, know that I didn't live here waiting for rescue, hoping for a thirteenth expedition. If the world beyond appears to have abandoned the entire idea of expeditions, perhaps that's evidence of the sudden appearance of sanity. But the world beyond, or even the dangers of this one I live in, will be even less of a concern in a few days.

01: THE BRIGHTNESS

At first, there was always the island ahead of me, somewhere, along the coast, and my husband's presence in the bread-crumb notes I thought I found along the way, that I hoped came from him. Under rocks, stabbed on branches, curling dead on the ground. They were all important to me, no matter which might be real and which nothing more than chance or coincidence. Making it to the island meant something to me then. I was still holding on to the idea of causality, of *purpose* as that word might be recognizable to the Southern Reach. But what if you discover that the price of purpose is to render invisible so many other things?

According to his journal, it took my husband six days to reach the island the first time. It took me somewhat longer. Because the rules had changed. Because the ground I found purchase on one day became the next uncertain, and at times seemed to fall away beneath me. Behind me at the lighthouse, a luminescence was growing in strength and a burnt haze had begun to dominate the sky, and through my binoculars for more days than should have been possible, there came the suggestion of something enormous rising from the sea in a continuous, slow-motion wave. Something I was not yet ready to see.

Ahead, the birds that shot through the sky trailed blurs of color that resembled other versions of themselves, that might have been hallucinations. The air seemed malleable, or like it could be *convinced* or *coerced*. I felt stuck in between, forever traveling, never arriving, so that soon I wanted a place to pretend was "base camp" for a while—a place that might quell the constant frustration of feeling that I couldn't trust the landscape I traveled through, my only anchor the trail itself, which, although it became ever more overgrown and twisty, never faltered, never petered out into nothing.

If it had led me to a cliff, would I have stood there or would I have followed it over the edge? Or would that lack have been enough that I might have turned back and tried to find the door in the border? It's difficult to predict what I might have done. The trajectories of my thoughts were scattered on that journey, twisted this way and that, like the swallows in the clear blue sky that, banking and circling back for a split second, would then return to their previous course, their fleeting digression a simple hunt for a speck of insect protein.

Nor do I know how much of these phenomena, these thoughts, I should attribute to the brightness within me. Some, but not all, based on everything that happened later, that is still happening. Just when I thought the brightness was one thing, it would become another. The fifth morning I rose from the grass and dirt and sand, the brightness had gathered to form a hushed second skin over me, that skin cracking from my opening eyes like the slightest, the briefest, touch of an impossibly thin layer of ice. I could hear the fracturing of its melting as if it came from miles and years away.

As the day progressed, the brightness manifested in my chest like a hot, red stone that pulsed next to my heart, unwelcome company. The scientist in me wanted to self-anesthetize and operate, remove the obstruction, even though I wasn't a surgeon and the brightness no tumor. I remember thinking that I might be talking to the animals by the next morning. I might be rolling in the dirt, laughing hysterically under that merciless blue sky. Or I might find the brightness rising curious out of the top of my head, like a periscope—independent and lively, with nothing left beneath it but a husk.

By dusk of that day, having ignored the biting flies and the huge reptiles that stared from the water, grinning up at me like the mindless carnivores they were . . . by then the brightness had come up to my head and lay behind all of my thoughts like a cooling piece of coal covered in icy ash. And I no longer could be sure that the brightness was a feeling, an impulse, an infection. Was I headed toward an island that might or might not give me answers because I *meant* to go there or because I was being directed somewhere by an invisible stranger? A companion. Was the brightness more *separate* than I knew? And why did the psychologist's words appear in my mind so often, and why could I not pry them out?

These were not speculative questions, a matter for idle debate, but concrete worries. At times, I felt as if those words, my final conversation with the psychologist, lay like a shield or wall between me and aspects of the brightness, that an intended peculiarity of those words had activated something in me. But no matter how I turned that exchange over and over in my thoughts, I came no closer to a conclusion. Some things you can be so close to that you never grasp their true nature.

That night, I made camp, started a fire, because I didn't care who saw me. If the brightness existed separate, and if every part of Area X saw me anyway, what did it matter? A kind of giddy recklessness was coming back to me again—and I welcomed it. The lighthouse had long since faded, but I found I looked for it still, that great anchor, that great trap. Here, too, grew the purple thistles, in a greater abundance, which I could not help thinking of as spies for Area X. Even if everything here spied and was spied upon.

The wind came up strong from the shore, I remember, and it was cold. I held on to such details back then as a way of warding off the brightness—as superstitious as anyone else. Soon, too, a moaning came out of and through the dusk, along with a familiar thrashing, as something ponderous fought against the reeds. I shuddered, but I also laughed, and said aloud, "It's just an old friend!" Not so old, and not really a friend. Hideous presence. Simple beast. In that fearless moment, or maybe just in this one, I felt a deep affection for and kinship with it. I went out to meet it, my brightness muttering the whole way in a surly, almost petulant fashion. A monster? Yes, but after the monster that was the Crawler, I embraced this simpler source of mystery.

02: THE MOANING CREATURE

I'll spare you the search for this creature I had once fled; it was absurd trying to differentiate wind-blown reeds from those rattled by some force more specific, of sloshing through the muck and mire without breaking an ankle or getting stuck.

Eventually I came out into a kind of clearing, an island of dirt covered in anemic grass and bounded by yet more reeds. At the far end, something pale and grub-like and monstrous flailed and moaned, its limbs pummeling the reed floor, the speed I had witnessed in the past seemingly now unavailable to it. I realized soon enough that it was sleeping.

The head was small compared to the body, but faced away from me, so all I could see was a thick wrinkled neck morphing into the skull. I still had a chance to leave. I had every reason to leave. I felt shaky, the resolve that had made me veer off the main trail evaporating. But something in its obliviousness made me stay.

I advanced, keeping my gun trained on the beast. This close, the moaning was deafening, the strange guttural tolling of a living cathedral bell. There was no way to be stealthy—the ground was strewn with dried reeds over the dirt and grass that crackled with my steps—and yet still it slept. I trained my flashlight on its bulk. The body had the consistency and form of a giant hog and a slug commingled, the pale skin mottled with mangy patches of light green moss. The arms and legs suggested the limbs of a pig but with three thick fingers at their ends. Positioned along the midsection near what I supposed was the stomach were two more appendages, which resembled fleshy pseudopods. The creature used them to help lurch its bulk along, but they often writhed pathetically and beat at the ground as if not entirely under its control.

I shone the flashlight on the creature's head, that small pink oval backed by the too-thick neck. As the molting mask I'd found during my prior encounter suggested, it had the face of the psychologist from my husband's expedition. And this face in its slumber formed a mask of utter uncomprehending anguish, the mouth open in a perpetual O as it moaned out its distress, as its limbs gouged at the ground, as it made its wounded, halting progress in what amounted to circles. Its eyes had a white film over them that told me it was blind.

I should have felt something. I should have been moved or disgusted by this encounter. Yet after my descent into the tower, my annihilation by the Crawler, I felt nothing. No emotion at all, not even simple, common pity, despite this raw expression of trauma, some agony beyond comprehension.

This beast should have been a dolphin with an uncanny eye, a wild boar that acted as if it were new to its body. And perhaps it was part of an intentional pattern, and I just could not see those outlines. But it *looked* like a mistake, a misfire by an Area X that had assimilated so much so beautifully and so seamlessly. Which made me wonder if my brightness was a harbinger of some form of *this*. To disappear into the coastline, into the anonymous reaches of the beach and the wind, or the marshes, did not really disturb me, perhaps never had. But this did—this blind, relentless questing. Had I tricked myself into believing that letting the brightness overtake me would be a painless, even beautiful, process? There was nothing beautiful about the moaning creature, nothing that didn't seem a ghastly intervention.

In that context, I could not intervene, either, even as I watched the writhing of its perpetual distress. I would not end its misery, in part because I worked from incomplete data. I could not be sure of what it represented or what it was going through. Beneath what seemed to be pain might lie ecstasy—what remained of the human dreaming, and in that dream, comfort. There also came to me the thought that perhaps what this expedition member had *brought* to Area X had contributed to this final state.

This is what I can remember now, when memory begins to be interwoven with so many other considerations. In the end, I took a hair sample that proved as useless as any other—a consistency I suppose I should have admired but did not—and went back to my sad little fire out in the middle of a nowhere that was everywhere.

But this encounter did affect me in one way. I became resolved not to give in to the brightness, to give up my identity—not yet. I could not come to terms with the possibility that one day I might put aside my vigilance and become the moaning creature in the reeds.

Perhaps this was weakness. Perhaps this was just fear.

03: THE ISLAND

Soon enough, the island became a shadow or smudge on the seaward horizon, so I knew it was only a matter of days, even if I had trouble telling how much time was passing. The island that was as blank to me now as my husband had been upon his return. I knew nothing of what I might encounter there, and the reality of this sobered me, made me monitor the brightness more closely, fight it harder, as if, ridiculously, by the time I made it across, I had to be at my best, my most alert. For what? For a corpse I might find if I were lucky? For some memory of a life back in the world that we could now misremember as more placid and comfortable than it had been? I don't know the answer to those questions, except that an organism's primary directive is to continue to exist—to breathe and to eat and to shit and to sleep and to fuck, and to otherwise carry on with the joyous repetitions of its days.

I secured my backpack, and I dove into the water.

Anyone reading who likes stories about characters huddled around guttering fires with the wolves waiting just beyond will be disappointed to learn that I was not attacked by leviathans from the depths as I swam over to the island. That, although tired and cold, I easily set up living quarters in the ruined lighthouse waiting on the shore. That I found enough food there, over time, by catching fish and foraging for berries, digging up tubers that while bland were edible. I trapped small animals when I had to, planted my own garden using seeds from the fruit I found, fertilized it with homemade compost.

At first, the lighthouse perplexed me more than anything on the island. It kept striking me as a mirror of the lighthouse on the coast—the way the light glanced off of it—and that seemed to me like some kind of obscure and potentially ruthless joke. It could be just another detail in a host of them that brought me no closer to answers about Area X. Or this confluence, this incomplete synonym, the top caved in and the landing I chose as my stronghold languishing under a trough of wet dead leaves . . . it could be an unmistakable and massive indicator of some kind.

I took my time, later, exploring the lighthouse, the buildings nearby, the abandoned town, with a systematic and scientific thoroughness, but I felt that my first reconnaissance should be broader: to scour the island for threats, for food and water sources, for any sign of other human life. Not wanting to hope, for I had found no evidence of recent occupation of the lighthouse, which seemed the most likely shelter because most of the other buildings were, even at first glance, dilapidated, had rotted with astonishing swiftness once Area X had imposed its will on this place. There were also signs of pollution, of old scars, but faded so fast into the firmament that I could not gauge how long ago they had been inflicted. Whether Area X was accelerating the erasure of their effects.

This island is about fourteen miles long, six broad, and forty in circumference, containing what I would estimate as about eighty-four square miles or more than fifty thousand acres. The pine-and-oak forest comprises most of the interior, sprawling down toward the shore on the landward side, but the side facing the sea has been assaulted by storms, and there you will find mostly scrub and moss and gnarled bushes. Fresh springwater occurs more frequently than I had expected, from rivulets meandering down from the hills toward the shore. This probably explains the placement of the abandoned town, along with protection from storms blowing in from the sea. But I also found one faucet on the lighthouse grounds that, although spewing forth brown rust at first, eventually settled down to a trickle of something brackish but drinkable, from some hidden aquifer.

Farther afield, I found a rich ecosystem in which a wary rabbit population was held in check by raptors and island foxes, these latter the scrappy small sort that suggested an isolated initial breeding pair or pairs had adapted to the limited range and opportunities of their surroundings. The birdlife was robust as well, from tree swallows and purple martins to vireos and wrens, woodpeckers and nighthawks—along with too many types of shorebirds to catalog. At dusk, the sound of avian life triumphant forms a mighty bursting chorus of voices, such a contrast with the silence of the marshes, whose own richness is more muted, almost watchful.

I wandered the island for many days, both its perimeter and the interior, getting a feel for it and what it contained. As I recorded my observations, I cursed the Southern Reach for not providing us with a map, even if I also knew that I would have tested any map provided to me and wound up doing almost as much work. Not just because I distrusted the Southern Reach, but also because I distrusted Area X. Yet when I was done with this initial inspection, I could not say there was anything preternatural or unusual about the island itself.

Other, perhaps, than the owl.

04: THE OWL

Did I find my husband? In a way, if not in the form in which I had known him. On the far side of the island, in the late afternoon, after I had burst through nettles and scrub and sticker, lacerating long grasses, all of it overshadowed by close-knit copses of wind-gnarled black pines—burst through to a tranquil cove that cupped a white-sand beach and shallows that extended a fair distance before the darkness of deep water took over. On the beach, a scattering of low-lying concrete pilings and rocks, all that remained of an abandoned pier from another age, created a perch for more than a dozen cormorants.

A single stunted pine the height of a person stood defiant amid rocks and cormorants alike, blackened and almost bare of needles. On one outstretched branch, the unlikely silhouette of a common horned owl with sharp tufted ears: rust-brown face with white feathers at chin and throat, mottled gray-and-brown body. My loud approach should have alarmed it, but this owl just perched there, surrounded by the cormorants sunning themselves. An unnatural scene, to me, and it brought me up short.

I thought at first the owl must be hurt, more so when I came closer and it still didn't move, unlike the whirling circle of cormorants that, complaining bitterly, flew away, a long low line over the water, exiled to rove, restless. Any other owl would have taken wing and disappeared back into the forest. But instead, it remained glued to the ridged, scaly bark of the branch, staring out at the fading sun with enormous eyes.

Even when I stood right beside the tree, awkward on the rocks, the owl did not fly, did not look over at me. Injured or dying, I thought again, but cautious, ready to retreat, because an owl can be a dangerous animal. This one was huge, four pounds at least, despite its hollow bones, lightweight feathers. But nothing I had done had yet provoked it, and so I stood there as the sun began to set, the owl beside me.

I had studied owls early in my career and knew that neuroses were unknown among them as opposed to other, more intelligent bird species. Most owls are also beautiful, along with another quality that is hard to define but registers as calm in the observer. There was such a hush upon that beach, and one that didn't register with me as sinister.

At dusk, the owl turned its fierce yellow gaze upon me at last, and with the tip of its outstretched wing brushing against my face, the bird launched itself into the air in a smooth, silent arc that sent it off toward the forest behind me. Forever gone, or so I believed, with any of a number of reasons to account for its odd behavior. The lines between the eccentricities of wildlife and the awareness imposed by Area X are difficult to separate at times.

I needed to seek shelter for the night, and I found on the far western edge of the beach a small circle of rocks around the blackened ash of an old fire—above the high-tide mark, set back almost into the beginning of the forest. I found, too, in the last glimmers of light, an old tent, faded by the sun, weathered and crumpled by storms. Someone had lived here for a time, and without daring to think who it might have been, I made camp there, started my own fire, cooked a rabbit I had killed earlier that afternoon. Then, tired, I fell asleep to the sound of the waves, under a soft and subdued canopy of stars.

I woke only once during the night and saw the owl perched opposite me across the fire, atop my backpack. It had brought me another rabbit. I dozed again, and it was gone when I woke.

I stayed there three days, and I admit I did so because of the owl, and because the cove was near-perfect; I could see spending my life there. But also because I wanted to know more about the person who had made the fire, lived in the tent. Even in disarray and so old, it was clearly a standard-issue tent, although it carried no Southern Reach logo on it.

A little ways into the forest behind the tent, I found an expedition-issue sidearm, much like my own, in a rotting holster, amid wildflowers and sedge weeds and moss. I found the undershirt from an expedition uniform, and then the jacket and socks, strewn across that expanse as if given up willingly, even joyously . . . or as if some animal or person had thrown them there. I did not bother to gather them up, to try to re-create this exoskeleton of a person. I would not find a name, I knew that, and I did not find a letter, either. I would never really know if it might have been my husband who had camped there or some other person even more anonymous to me.

And yet there was the owl, always watching over me, always nearby. Always a little closer, a little tamer, but never completely tame. It would drop twigs at my feet, at random, more as if through some absentmindedness than on purpose. It would bow at me, a typical owl behavior, then spend the next hours distant, almost sullen. Once or twice, it would perch at close to my height, and I would approach as an experiment, only for the owl to hiss at me almost like a cat, and beat its wings and fluff out its feathers until I had retreated. Other times, on a branch high up, the owl would sway and bob, bob and sway, moving its body from side to side while gripping its perch in the same place. Then look down at me stupidly.

I moved on, following the shore, sometimes also shadowed by the cormorants. I did not expect the owl to join me, but I am unashamed to say I was glad when it did. By the end of the second week, it ate from my hands at dusk, before going off to its nocturnal life. During the night I would hear its curious hollow hooting—a sound many find mysterious or threatening but that I have always found playful or deeply irreverent. The owl would reappear briefly toward dawn—once, in a tangle of feathers as it plunged its head into the sand and ruffled out its plumage, giving itself a dry bath and then picking at lice and other parasites.

The thought crept into my head when I wasn't careful, and then I would banish it. Was this my husband in altered form? Did he recognize me, or was this owl simply responding to the presence of a human being? Unlike the uncanny presence of other animals, there was no such feeling here—no sense of it to me, at least. But, I reasoned, perhaps I had become acclimated by then. Perhaps I'd reached a kind of balance with the brightness that normalized such indicators.

When I came full circle, back to the ruined lighthouse, the owl stayed with me. He tried even less for my attention, but in the twilight would appear in the branches of a tree outside the lighthouse, and we would stand there together. Sometimes he would already be there by midafternoon, if I walked through the shade of the dark trees, and follow me, making great hoot-hoots to warn of my coming. But never earlier, as if he remembered that I hated the unnatural in animals, as if he understood me. Besides, he had his own business—hunting. After a week, though, he roosted in the shattered upper spire of the lighthouse. The cormorants, too, reappeared there, or perhaps they were not the same cormorants, but I had not seen so many of the birds in that place before my explorations.

During the day, the owl would sun himself up there before falling into a sleep that sometimes was accompanied by a low and nasal snore. During the night, I would fall asleep on the landing and above me hear, so faint, the whisper as his wings caressed the air on his flight to the forest to seek prey. In those transitional moments, between day and night, when anything seemed possible, or I tricked myself into believing that this was true, I began to talk to the owl. Even though I dislike anthropomorphizing animals, it did not seem important to withhold this communication because the evidence of his eccentric behavior was self-evident. Either he understood or did not, but even if not, sound is more important to owls than to human beings. So I spoke to him in case he was other than what he seemed, and as common courtesy, and as a way to help with the welling up of the brightness.

Despite this, which might be foolishness, how could I ever truly recognize in him the one I'd sought, ever cross that divide? Yet there grew to be a useful symbiosis in our relationship. I continued to hunt for him, and he continued to hunt for me, although with a kind of sloppiness, as if unintentional—rabbits and squirrels falling from his perch down to mine. In some ways, wordless on his end and based on the most basic principles of friendship and survival, this arrangement worked better than anything back in the wider world. I had still seen no person on the island, but now I found more evidence of a prior presence.

It was not what I'd expected.

05: THE SEEKER & SURVEILLANCE BANDITS

Returned from my exploration, with the owl as my companion, I now slowly took the measure of my immediate surroundings: the lighthouse, the buildings around it, and the town beyond. The town, which must have been abandoned long before the creation of Area X, consisted of a main street and a few side streets that then faded into the impression of dirt roads, the tire ruts overgrown with weeds. All of it empty; I could be the ruler of this place by default, if I wanted to be.

"Main Street" had become a kind of facade, having fallen to a disheveled army of vines and flowering trees and bushes and weeds and wildflowers. Squirrels and badgers, skunks and raccoons, had taken over the remains, ospreys nesting on the ruins of rooftops. In the upper story of a house or former business pigeons and starlings perched on gaping windows, the glass broken and fallen inside. It all had the rich scent of the reclaimed, of sweet blossoms and fresh grass in the summer, with the pungent underlying odor of animals marking their territory. It had also a hint of the unexpected for me, a kind of lingering shock to see these rough, rude memorials to the lives of human beings in a place I had thought largely free of them.

Here and there, I found more signs of expeditions that had reached the island and either gone back across the water or died here and been transformed here. An abandoned backpack with the usual map in it. A flashlight. A rifle scope. A water canteen. These were tantalizing remnants—indicators that I tried to read too much into, for reasons that revealed a weakness in me. It should have been enough to know others had come here first, and that others had sought answers, whether they had found them or not.

But there were sedimentary layers to this information, and some of the older materials, which I believed dated back to just before and right after the creation of Area X, interested me more. People had taken up residence here within that narrow spectrum, and those people went by the initials of S&SB, although I never once found a fragment that told me what these initials stood for. Nor could I recall, either back in the world or during our training for the expedition, ever hearing of such an organization. Not, of course, that the island had been given any thought or attention in that training. By then, any betrayal by the Southern Reach struck me as just more of the same.

In lieu of any other evidence, I called them the Seeker & Surveillance Bandits. It suited what I knew about them from the scraps they'd left behind, and for a time, it occupied my days to try to reconstruct their identity and their purpose on the island.

The leavings of the S&SB, their detritus, took the form of damaged equipment that I identified as meant to record radio waves, to monitor infrared and other frequencies, along with more esoteric machines that defeated my attempts to decode their purpose. Along with such broken flotsam, I uncovered weathered (often unreadable) papers and photographs, and even a few recordings that croaked out incomprehensible too-slow words as I plugged them into a failing generator that gave me only about thirty seconds of power at a time before cutting out.

All of this I found inside the abandoned buildings on Main Street, remains protected by fallen-in supporting walls or in basements where certain corners had escaped flooding. Burn marks existed in places where controlled fires had been started indoors. But I couldn't tell if the S&SB had started these fires or if they had come later, during some desperate phase before everything had been assimilated by Area X. Looking at all of that ash, I realized that any attempt to reconstruct a sequence of events would be forever incomplete because someone had wanted to hide something.

I took what I found to the lighthouse and began to sort through it, such as it was, all under the watchful but unhelpful eye of the owl. Despite the oblique nature of what I had recovered, I began to piece together hints of purpose, suggestions of conspiracy. All of what I relate here is highly speculative but, I think, supported by the fragile evidence available to me.

The S&SB had begun their occupation of this island not with a mapping of the perimeter but with a thorough investigation of the ruined lighthouse, which meant they had come here with a specific purpose. That investigation had been twinned to establishing a kind of link between the lighthouse on the island and the one on the mainland. There were references to something that "might or might not" have been transferred, suggesting that perhaps the lens in the lighthouse I knew so well had originally come from here. But in context, this "might or might not" seemed almost certain to exist separate from the lens itself—or could exist separate. Torn pages from a book on the history of famous lighthouses, the lineage of lens manufacture and shipping, helped me little.

There also was debate as to whether they sought "an object or a recordable phenomenon," which seemed to return to the idea of linking the two lighthouses; if a "phenomenon," then this linkage was important. If an "object," then the linkage might not be important, and either the island or the lighthouse on the mainland would no longer be of interest. Further, the nature of these fragments was contradictory as to their organization and sophistication. Some S&SB members seemed to lack even a rudimentary understanding of science and wasted my time with scrawlings about ghosts and hauntings and copied-down passages from books about demonic possession. The listing of stages interested me only inasmuch as I could transfer it to the biological world of parasitic and symbiotic relationships. Others among them lay out under the stars at night and recorded their dreams as if they were transmissions from beyond. As a kind of fiction, it enlivened my reading but was otherwise worthless.

Along with this ephemeral superstition, I would also group the lesser scientific observations, which reflected the involvement of third- or fourth-rate minds. Here, it was not so much the accuracy of the observations but the banality of the conclusions. Into this category fell extrapolations about "prebiotic" materials and "spooky action at a distance," along with already debunked experiments from decades past.

What stood out from what I tossed on the compost heap seemed to come from a different sort of intelligence entirely. This mind or these minds asked questions and did not seem interested in hasty answers, did not care if one question birthed six more and if, in the end, none of those six questions led to anything concrete. There was a patience that seemed imposed and not at all a part of the swirling quicksilver consciousness that surrounded it. If I understood the scraps correctly, my pathetic attempt at playing oracle, this second type not only kept tabs on people living on the mainland, but on certain of its own fellow S&SB members. It did not have only experimentation on its collective mind.

Does the residue of a presence leave an identifiable trace? Although I could not be sure, I felt I had identified such a presence regardless—one that had infiltrated the S&SB late. A shift in command and control toward something more sophisticated, staring out at me from the pages I had found.

In among this detritus, these feeble guesses, the word *Found!* Handwritten, triumphant. Found what? But with so little data, even *Found!*, even the awareness of some more intelligent entity peering out from among the fragments led nowhere. Someone, somewhere had additional information, but the elements—Area X?—had so accelerated the decay of the documents that I could not glean much more, even though this was enough. Enough to suggest that there had been a kind of tampering with this coast before the creation of Area X, and my own experience to tell me that the Southern Reach had deliberately excised knowledge of the island from our expedition maps and briefings. These two data points, although more to do with absence than with positive confirmation, made me redouble my efforts looking for S&SB scraps amid the rubble. But I never found anything more than what I uncovered on my first, thorough investigation.

06: THE PASSAGE OF TIME, AND PAIN

I never had a country, never had the choice; I was born into one. But over time, this island has become my country, and I need no other. I never thought to seek the way out, back into the world. As the years passed and no one else reached my island refuge, I began to wonder if the Southern Reach existed anymore—or if it had ever existed, that perhaps there had never been another world or an expedition, and I had suffered a delusion or trauma, a kind of memory loss. One day, perhaps, I would wake up and recall it all: some cataclysm that had left me the only person in this place, with just an owl to talk to.

I survived storms that gusted in suddenly, and drought, and a nail through my foot when I wasn't careful. I survived being bitten by many things, including a poisonous spider and a snake. I learned to become so attuned to my environment that after a time no animal, natural or unnatural, shied away at my presence, and for this reason I no longer hunted anything but fish unless forced to, relying more and more on vegetables and fruit. Although I thought I grew attuned to their messages as well.

In the lengthening silence and solitude, Area X sometimes would reveal itself in unexpected ways. I began to perceive infinitesimal shifts in the sky, as if the pieces did not quite fit together . . . and to acquire from the habitat around me a sense of invisible things stitching through, phantoms that almost made me reconsider my antipathy for the S&SB's emphasis on the supernatural.

Standing in a clearing one evening, as still as possible, I felt a kind of *breath* or thickness of molecules from behind that I could not identify, and I willed my heartbeat to slow so that for every one of mine the hearts of the tree frogs throating out their song might beat twenty thousand times. Hoping to be so quiet that without turning I might hear or in some other way glimpse what regarded me. But to my relief it fled or withdrew into the ground a moment later.

Once, the sky broke open with rain in an unnatural way, and through the murk an odd light burned at the limits of my vision. I imagined it was the far-off lighthouse, that other expeditions had been sent in after me. But the longer I stared the more the light appeared to be cracking open the darkness, through which I glimpsed for a moment dissipating shadows that could have been peculiar storm clouds or the reverse quickening of some type of vast organism. Such phenomena, experienced off and on these past thirty years, have also been accompanied by a changing of the night sky. On such nights, presaged only by a kind of tremor in the brightness within me, there is never a moon. There is never a moon, and the stars above are unfamiliar—they are foreign, belonging to a cosmology I cannot identify. On such nights, I wish I had decided to become an astronomer.

On at least two occasions, I would define this change as more significant, as a kind of celestial cataclysm, accompanied by what might be earthquakes, and cracks or rifts appearing in the fabric of the night, soon closing, and with nothing but a greater darkness seen shining through. Somewhere, out in the world or the universe, something must be happening to create these moments of dysfunction. At least, this is my belief. There is a sense of the world around me strengthened or *thickened*, the weight and waft of reality more focused or determined. As if the all-too-human dolphin eye I once glimpsed staring up at me is with each new phase further subsumed in the flesh that surrounds it.

Beyond these observations, I have a single question: What is the nature of my delusion? Am I hallucinating when I see the night sky that I know? Or when I see the one that is strange? Which stars should I trust and navigate by? I stand in the ruined lighthouse some nights and look out to sea and realize that in this form, this body, I will never know.

ACCEPTANCE

My survival has also, to put it bluntly, been predicated by hurting myself. By the time I stood on the shore opposite the island, about to swim over, I was using pain to push the brightness back. The ways were myriad and I was precise. You can find methods to almost drown, to almost suffocate, that are not as onerous as the thought might suggest. Ways to suggest the infliction of pain that can fool whatever lies within you. A rusty nail. A snake's venom. As a result, pain does not much bother me anymore; it gives me evidence of my ongoing existence, has saved me from those times when, otherwise, I might have stared so long at wind and rain and sea as to become nothing, to just disappear.

In a separate document, I have listed the best, least intrusive approaches, which I realize may seem morbid, even though I consider it an absurd method of chronicling my days. I have also noted the rotation of cycles that has proven most effective. Although, given the choice, I would not recommend this approach—you become acclimated to it, like doing the chores or foraging for food.

After so much time, pain has become such a familiar and revisited friend that I wonder if I will notice him more now that I have stopped my regimen. Will an absence of pain be harder to get used to? I suspect that this concern will be forgotten amid so many other adjustments that must be made. For, having found so many ways to put it off, I believe that my transformation will be more radical than it might have been, that I might indeed become something like the moaning creature. Will I see the real stars then?

Sometimes, too, pain comes at you unexpectedly; you don't have to generate it, don't have to will it consciously upon yourself. It's just there. The owl that has been my companion these thirty years died a week ago, without my being able to help, without knowing until too late. He had become an old owl, and although his eyes were still enormous and bright, his colors had faded, his camouflage tattered; he slept more and did not go out to hunt as often. I fed him mice by hand in his redoubt at the top of the ruined lighthouse.

I found him in the forest, after he had been missing for a few days, and I had finally gone out to search for him. From what I can reconstruct, he had become injured, perhaps from frailty or the onset of blindness, broken his wing, and settled on the forest floor. A fox or pair of foxes had probably gotten to him. He lay there splayed out in a mottled flurry of brown and dark red, eyes shut, head fallen to the side, all the life having left him.

My microscope had long since been abandoned in a corner of the lighthouse grounds, overtaken by mold, half buried there by the simple passage of years. I had no heart to take samples, to discover what I already knew: that, in the end, there was nothing a microscope could tell me about the owl that I had not learned from my many years of close interactions and observation.

What am I to say? That I do not miss him?

PART III

OCCULTING LIGHT

0011: GHOST BIRD

What kind of life was this, where you could read a letter from your own haunted twin? That you could live within the memories of another and think of them as real, a second skin, and yet so utterly false. This is who she had been. This is what she had thought, and how she had lived. Should that now be Ghost Bird's life, too, her thoughts? Anger and awe warred within—and no one to push either emotion onto, except herself. She had to let them battle like a second heartbeat and trust that her reaction was not just the mirror reflecting what it saw. That even if she was a mistake, she had become a viable mistake—a mutation, not an anomaly like the moaning creature. Long-moldering bones trapped in the marshes.

There were questions she did not want to ask, because if she did they would take on detail and weight and substance, flesh and skin reclothing the arch of ribs. Wonders and horrors alike she could compartmentalize, but Control, at least, might never be ready, and on some level it was wearying to push, to have that kind of purpose. It seemed to push against the reality of Area X, to say that even *she* had learned nothing from being her. Should she even try, knowing that it wasn't fair, that they had all traveled too far, too fast, even Grace with her three-year head start?

It was dusk now, almost nightfall, and into the silence and gathering shadows, Grace took the lead, said: "We're astronauts. All of the expedition members have been astronauts."

That should have been comforting in its way, a kind of anchor, but Control's face had become a resolute mask that said he didn't want to deal with this, that, defiantly, he wanted only to bury his nose in what was comfortable. He clutched the yellowing pages of the biologist's letter tight in his left hand, while the biologist's journal, which Grace had rescued from the lighthouse, lay on his lap. It had interested Ghost Bird to read it, to fill in the final gaps, and yet what gaps remained despite it. *The white light at the bottom of the tower. The manifestation of the lighthouse keeper within the Crawler.* These were things she distrusted without seeing them for herself. But to Control she knew it would just register as new evidence, new hope—information that might provide a solution, a sudden fix. As if Grace's scrutiny and thoughts about them were not enough.

"We're not on Earth," Ghost Bird said. We cannot be on Earth. "Not with that much distortion of time. Not with the things the biologist saw." Not if they wanted to pretend that there were rules in place, even if the rules had been obscured, made unclear, withheld. But was that true? Or had time just become irrational, inconsistent?

Still that reluctance, and the distance it created between her and them, until Grace finally said, "That was my conclusion, one of the theories put forward by the science division."

"A kind of wormhole," Control said. The limit of how far he could go; anything more would be pulled out of him by the brightness.

A disbelieving stare from Grace. "Do you think Area X builds spaceships, too? Do you think Area X traverses interstellar space? Wormholes? Think of something more subtle, something peering through what we think of as reality."

Flat, clipped words, stripped of the awe that should have animated them. Because she'd had those extra three years? Because she was thinking of loved ones back home?

Control, so slowly, almost as if in a hypnotized state: "Everything in Area X that we thought was degrading too rapidly . . . most of it was just getting old."

Some things were very old indeed—the remnants of the village and the various sedimentary layers of those journals under the trapdoor in the lighthouse. So much more time had passed in Area X after the border came down, before the first expedition had gone in. People could have *lived* in Area X for much, much longer after the border came down than anyone had thought.

"How was this not known before," Control said. "How was this not clear *before*." As if some elemental force of repetition might bring about a swift justice against those who had obstructed his access to the truth. Instead, repetition just underscored their ignorance.

"Corrupted data," Grace said. "Skewed samples. Incomplete information."

"I don't know how—"

"She means," Ghost Bird said, "that so many expeditions came back disoriented, damaged, or not at all, that the SR had no reliable samples." She meant that the time dilation must be more severe when Area X shifted or underwent a change, and otherwise must be almost unmeasurable.

"She's right," Grace said. "We never had anyone who lived long enough in Area X or saw so clearly and managed to write down their observations." Conflicting data, conflicting purposes. An opponent that didn't make it easy.

"But do we believe the biologist?" Control asked. Because the theories of the biologist's copy might be suspect? Because he wasn't built for this and Ghost Bird was.

"Do you believe *me*?" Grace said. "I've seen strange stars in the sky at night, too. I have seen the rifts in the sky. I have lived here *three years*."

"Then tell me—how can the sun shine, the stars, the moon? If we are not on Earth?"

"That's not the critical question," Ghost Bird said. "Not for organisms that are so masterful at camouflage."

"Then what is?" Control frustrated, trying to take in the enormity of the idea, and Ghost Bird found it painful to watch.

"The critical question," Grace said, "is what is the *purpose* of this organism or organisms. And how do we survive."

"We know its purpose," Control said. "Which is to kill us, to transform us, to get rid of us. Isn't that what we try to avoid thinking about? What the director, you"—pointing at Grace—"and Cheney and all the rest had to keep suppressing? The thought that it just wants to kill us all."

"You think we didn't have these conversations a thousand times?" Grace said. "You think we didn't go around and around trying to get out of our circles?"

"People make patterns all the time without realizing it," Ghost Bird said. "An organism can have a purpose and yet also make patterns that have little to do with that purpose."

"So fucking what," Control snarled, a trapped animal. "So fucking what?"

Ghost Bird exchanged a stare with Grace, who looked away. Control wasn't prepared to receive this knowledge. It was eating him from the inside out. Maybe something specific would distract him.

"There's a lot of energy being generated and discharged," she said. "If the border is a kind of membrane, it could be a case of dumping it somewhere else—think of how things disappear when they come into contact with the border."

"But they don't disappear, do they?" Grace said.

"I don't think so. I think they get sent somewhere."

"Where?" Control asked.

Ghost Bird shrugged, thinking about the journey into Area X, and the devastation and destruction she had seen. The ruined cities. Was that real? Something that gave them a clue? Or just a delusion?

Membranes and dimensions. Limitless amounts of space. Limitless amounts of energy. Effortless manipulation of molecules. Continual attempts to transform the human into the non-human. The ability to move an entire biosphere to another place. Right now, if the outside world existed, it would still be sending radio-wave messages into space and monitoring radio-wave frequencies to seek out other intelligent life in the universe. But Ghost Bird didn't think those messages were being received. Another way people were bound by their own view of consciousness. What if an infection was a message, a brightness a kind of symphony? As a defense? An odd form of communication? If so, the message had not been received, would probably never be received, the message buried in the transformation itself. Having to reach for such banal answers because of a lack of imagination, because human beings couldn't even put themselves in the mind of a cormorant or an owl or a whale or a bumblebee.

Did she want to ally herself to such a lack, and did she have a choice?

From the window the low buildings were revealed as facades: bruised and ruined cinder-block houses with the roofs gone, vines bursting out, and the worn white paint of the sides that lay in grainy despondency, unable to contain the tangled green. In among that unintended terrarium: a row of little crosses stuck in the soil, fresh enough to have been bodies buried by Grace. Perhaps she'd lied and a handful of others had followed her over to the island, only to meet some fate Grace had avoided. She'd heard almost the entire conversation between Control and Grace, had been ready to intervene if Grace had not taken the gun from Control's head. No one could drug her if her body didn't want it done. She wasn't built like that. Not anymore.

But she didn't like the view, felt some kind of instinctual discomfort at the sight of the damaged road, the "scrapes" on the forested hills that looked less like clearings in the late-afternoon sun and more like a kind of violence. The seaward window looked out on calm seas and a mainland rendered normal and perhaps even ordinary. Yet the distance disguised the havoc wreaked on the convoy.

Behind her, Grace and Control talked, but Ghost Bird had disengaged. It was a circular discussion, a loop that Control was creating to trap himself inside of, to dig the trenches, the moat, that would keep things out. How is this possible, how is that possible, and why—agonizing over both what he knew or thought he knew and what he could never, ever know.

She knew where it would all lead, what it always led to in human beings—a decision about what to do. What are we going to *do*? Where do we *go* from here? How do we *move forward*? What is our *mission* now? As if purpose could solve everything, could take the outlines of what was missing and by sheer will invoke it, make it appear, bring it back to life.

Even the biologist had done it, creating a pattern out of what might be random—correlating eccentric owl behavior with her lost husband. When it might have been the evidence of, the residue of, some other ritual entirely—and thus her account of the owl no more on target than her assertions about the S&SB. You could know the what of something forever and never discover the why.

The allure of the island lay in its negation of why—both for the biologist and, Ghost Bird guessed, for Grace, who had lived here with this knowledge for almost three years, as it ate at her. Ate at her still, the relief of companions having done nothing to take the edge off, Ghost Bird observing her from the window and wondering if she still withheld some vital piece of information—that her watchfulness and the evidence that she didn't sleep well provided the outline of a different, undisclosed *why*.

She felt so apart from both of them in that moment, as if the knowledge of how far they might be from Earth, of how time passed, ruthless, had pushed them away, and she was looking at them from the border—peering in through the shimmering door.

Control had started to return to safe ground of subjects like the lighthouse keeper, like Central. So there wouldn't be galaxies bursting in his brain like fireworks and the Southern Reach become a redoubt of Area X and humans turning into creatures with a purpose known only to the stitching in the sky, perhaps.

"Central kept the island a secret all this time. Central buried it, buried the island, just kept sending expeditions out here, to this . . . this fucking ugly place, this place that isn't really even where it's supposed to be, this fucking place that just keeps killing people and doesn't fucking even give you the chance to fight back because it's always going to win anyway and the . . ." Control couldn't stop. He wasn't going to stop. All he might do is pause, trail off, and then take it up again.

So after a time, Ghost Bird stopped him. She knelt beside him, gently took the biologist's letter and journal from him. She placed her arms around Control and held him, while Grace looked elsewhere in embarrassment, or a suppression of her own need for comfort. He thrashed in Ghost Bird's arms, resisting, her feeling the preternatural warmth of him, and then eventually he subsided, stopped fighting, held her loosely, then held her tightly while she said not a word because to say anything—anything at all—would be to humiliate him, and she cared more about him than that. And it cost her nothing.

When he was still, she disengaged, stood, directed her attention to Grace. There was still a question to ask. With no sound from the querulous nesting birds or, indeed, much sound at all intruding beyond the waves and wind, their own breathing, and Grace rolling a can of beans back and forth with her foot.

"Where is the biologist now?" Ghost Bird asked.

"Not important," Control said. "The least thing now. A fly or a bird or something. Or nothing. Dead?"

Grace laughed at that, in a way Ghost Bird didn't like.

"Grace?" Not about to let her get out from under an answer.

"Yes, she is definitely still alive."

"And where is she?"

"Somewhere out there."

The sonorous sound now rising. The distant sense of weight and movement and bulk and substance and intent, and something in Ghost Bird's mind linked to it, and no way to undo that.

"Not *somewhere* out there," Ghost Bird said.

Grace, nodding now, frightened now. This thing she couldn't tell them on top of all the impossible things she'd had to tell them.

"The biologist is coming here." Coming back to where the owl had once roosted. Coming down to the place where her doppelgänger now stood. That sound. Louder now. The snapping of tree branches, of tree trunks.

The biologist was coming down the hillside.

In all her glory and monstrosity.

Ghost Bird saw it from the landing window. How the biologist coalesced out of the night, her body flickering and stitching its way into existence, in the midst of a shimmering wave that imposed itself on the reality of forested hillside. The vast bulk seething down the hill through the forest with a crack and splinter as trees fell to that gliding yet ponderous and muffled darkness, reduced to kindling by the muscle behind the emerald luminescence that glinted through the black. The smell that presaged the biologist: thick brine and oil and some sharp, crushed herb. The sound that it made: as if the wind and sea had been smashed together and in the aftershock there reverberated that same sonorous moan. A seeking. A questing. A communication or communion. That, Ghost Bird recognized; that, she understood.

The hillside come alive and sliding down to the ruined lighthouse, at a steady pace like a lava flow. This intrusion. These darknesses that re-formed into a mighty shape against the darkness of the night sky, lightened by the reflections of clouds and the greater shadow of the tree line and the forests.

It bore down on the lighthouse, that strange weight, that leviathan, still somehow half here and half not, and Ghost Bird just stood at the window waiting for it, while Grace and Control screamed at her to come away, to get away, but she would not come, would not let them pull her from the window, and stood there like the captain of a ship facing a monumental storm, the waves rising huge against the window. Grace and Control gone, running down the stairs, and then that great bulk was shoved up against the window and smashing into the doorway below in a crack and crumble of stone and brick. Leaning against the lighthouse, and the lighthouse resisting, but only just.

The song had grown so loud as to be almost unbearable. Now like deep cello strings, now like guttural clicking, now eerie and mournful.

The great slope of its wideness was spread out before Ghost Bird, the edges wavery, blurred, sliding off into some *other place*. The mountain that was the biologist came up almost to the windowsill, so close she could have jumped down onto what served as its back. The suggestion of a flat, broad head plunging directly into torso. The suggestion, far to the east, already overshooting the lighthouse, of a vast curve and curl of the mouth, and the flanks carved by dark ridges like a whale's, and the dried seaweed, the kelp, that clung there, and the overwhelming ocean smell that came with it. The green-and-white stars of barnacles on its back in the hundreds of miniature craters, of tidal pools from time spent motionless in deep water, time lost inside that enormous brain. The scars of conflict with other monsters pale and dull against the biologist's skin.

It had many, many glowing eyes that were also like flowers or sea anemones spread open, the blossoming of many eyes—normal, parietal, and simple—all across its body, a living constellation ripped from the night sky. Her eyes. Ghost Bird's eyes. Staring up at her in a vast and unblinking array.

As it smashed into the lower floor, seeking something.

As it sang and moaned and hollered.

Ghost Bird leaned out the window, reached out and pushed through the shimmering layer, so like breaking the surface of a tidal pool to touch what lay within . . . and her hands found purchase on that slick, thick skin, among all of those eyes, her eyes, staring up at her. She buried both hands there, felt the touch of thick, tough lashes, felt the curved, smooth surfaces and the rough, craggy ones. All of those eyes. In the multiplicity of that regard, Ghost Bird saw what they saw. She saw herself, standing there, looking down. She saw that the biologist now existed across locations and landscapes, those other horizons gathering in a blurred and rising wave. There passed between the two something wordless but deep. She understood the biologist in that moment, in a way she had not before, despite their shared memories. She might be stranded on a planet far from home. She might be observing an incarnation of herself she could not quite comprehend, and yet . . . there was connection, there was *recognition*.

Nothing monstrous existed here—only beauty, only the glory of good design, of intricate planning, from the lungs that allowed this creature to live on land or at sea, to the huge gill slits hinted at along the sides, shut tightly now, but which would open to breathe deeply of seawater when the biologist once again headed for the ocean. All of those eyes, all of those temporary tidal pools, the pockmarks and the ridges, the thick, sturdy quality of the skin. An animal, an organism that had never existed before or that might belong to an alien ecology. That could transition not just from land to water but from one remote *place* to another, with no need for a door in a border.

Staring up at her with her own eyes.

Seeing her.

0012: THE LIGHTHOUSE KEEPER

Repainted black daymark, seaward side; ladder may need to be replaced, rickety. Tended to the garden most of the day, ran errands. Went on a hike late in the day. Sighted: a muskrat, possum, raccoons, red foxes up a tree at dusk, resting in crooks like crooks. Downy woodpecker. Redheaded woodpecker.

A thousand lighthouses burned to columns of ash along the coastline of an endless island. A thousand blackened candles trailing white smoke from atop the broad, broken head of a monster rising from the sea. A thousand dark cormorants, wings awash in crimson flames, taking flight from the waves, eyes reflecting the wrath of their own extinction. *Who maketh his angels spirits; his ministers a flaming fire.*

Saul woke coughing in the darkness, sweating from a thin, flat heat that flared up in wings across the bridge of his nose and over his eyes. Leaning forward through his skull to kiss that heat came the now-familiar pressure, which he'd described to the doctor in Bleakersville a couple of days ago as "dull but intense, somehow like a second skin on the inside." That sounded bizarre, wasn't accurate, but he couldn't find the right words. The doctor had looked at him for a moment, almost as if Saul had said something offensive, and then diagnosed his condition as "an atypical cold, with a sinus infection," sent him on his way with useless medicine to "clear up your sinus cavity." *His word was in mine heart as a burning fire shut up in my bones.*

There came a whispering again, and instinctually he reached a hand out to find his lover's shoulder, chest, but gripped only the sheets. Charlie wasn't there, wouldn't be back from his night gig for another week at the earliest. Unable to tell him the truth: that he still didn't feel right, not a sickness in the normal way, not what the doctor had diagnosed, but something hiding inside, waiting for its moment. A paranoid thought, Saul knew. It was a cold, or maybe a sinus infection, like the doctor had said. A winter cold, like he'd had in the past, just with night sweats, nightmares, and verse spilling out of him, this strange sermon that spiraled up into his thoughts when he wasn't vigilant, was coiled there now. *And the hand of the sinner shall rejoice, for there is no sin in shadow or in light that the seeds of the dead cannot forgive.*

He sat up abruptly in bed, stifled another cough.

Someone was in his lighthouse. More than one person. Whispering. Or maybe even shouting, the sound by the time it infiltrated the brick and stone, the wood and steel, brought to him through a distance, a time, that he couldn't know. The irrational thought that he was hearing the ghosts of dozens of lighthouse keepers all at once, in a kind of threnody, the condensed chorus of a century. Another phantom sound?

The whispering, the mumbling, continued in a matter-of-fact way, without emotion, and this convinced him to investigate. He roused himself from bed, put on jeans and a sweater, and taking up the ax on the wall—a monstrous and unwieldy pendulum—he padded up the stairs in his bare feet.

The steps were cold and the spiral dark, but he didn't want to risk turning on the lights in case a real intruder waited above. At the landing, the moon shone in at an angle, making the chairs there, the table, look like angular creatures frozen by its glow. He paused, listening. The waves below, their soft hush, stitched through with the sudden chatter of bats, close and then gone, as their echolocation pushed them away from the lighthouse walls. There should have been a hum in the background, too, a kind of purr from above, but he could not hear it. Which meant no light shot out across twenty miles to guide the ships.

He continued up as fast as he could, fueled by an anger that cut through the haze of his sickness, wanted confrontation. *And he said unto me, My grace is sufficient for thee: for my strength is made perfect in weakness.*

When he barged into the lantern room, it was to the sight of the blue-black sky filled with stars—and to three figures, two standing, one bent over in front of the extinguished lens. All three holding tiny flashlights, the pinpricks of that illumination only intensifying his sense of their guilt, their complicity, but in what?

All three were staring at him.

He raised his ax in a threatening way and hit the switch, flooding the room with light.

Suzanne and a woman he didn't know stood by the door to the railing, dressed all in black, with Henry on his knees in front of them, almost as if he'd been dealt a blow. Suzanne looked offended, as if he'd burst in on them in their own home. But the stranger hardly acknowledged his presence, stood there with arms crossed, oddly relaxed. Her hair was long and coiffed. She was dressed in an overcoat, dark slacks, and a long red scarf. Taller and older than Suzanne, she had a way of staring at him that made him concentrate on Henry instead.

"What the *hell* are you doing here?"

Their calm faced by a man with an ax baffled him, took some of the ire out of him, this delay between accusatory question and any response. Even Henry had composed himself, gone from a look almost of fear to a thin smile.

"Why don't you go back to sleep, Saul," Henry said, unmoving. "Why don't you go back to bed and let us finish up. We won't be long now."

Finish up with what? Henry's ritual humiliation? His usually perfect hair was mussed, his left eye twitching. Something had happened here, right before Saul had burst in. The condescension hit Saul hard, turned bewilderment and concern back into anger.

"The hell I will. You're trespassing. You broke in. *You turned off the light.* And who is *this*?" What was the woman to Suzanne and Henry? She did not seem to even belong to the same universe. He was more than sure that the bulge under her overcoat was a gun.

But he wasn't going to get an answer.

"We have a key, Saul," Henry said in a cloying tone, as if trying to soothe Saul. "We have a permit, Saul." Head turned a little to the side. Appraising. Quizzical. Telling Saul that he was the unreasonable one—the one interrupting Henry in his important studies.

"No, you *broke in*," he said, retreating to an even safer position, confused by Henry's inability to admit this basic fact, confused by the way the strange woman now regarded him with a kind of gunslinger's sangfroid. "You turned off the light, for Chrissake! And your permit says *nothing* about sneaking around at night while I'm asleep. Or bringing . . . guests . . ."

Henry ignored all of that, got up, and, with a quick glance at the woman and Suzanne, came closer than Saul wanted. If Saul took even two steps back he'd be stumbling down the stairwell.

"Go back to sleep." An urgency there, a whispered quality to the words, almost as if Henry was pleading with him, as if he didn't want the woman or Suzanne to see the concern on his face.

"You know, Saul," Suzanne said, "you really don't look well. You are sick and need to rest. You are sick and you want to put down that very heavy ax, this ax that just looks so heavy and hard to hold on to, and you want to put it down, this ax, and take a deep breath and relax, and turn around and go back to sleep, go to sleep . . ."

A sense of drifting, of sleepiness, began to overtake Saul. He panicked, took a step back, swung the ax over his head, and, as Henry brought his hands up to protect himself, buried the axhead in the floorboards. The impact reverberated through his hands, jamming one of his wrists.

"Get out. Now. All of you." Get out of the lighthouse. Get out of my head. *In the darkness of that which is golden, the fruit shall split open to reveal the revelation of the fatal softness in the earth.*

Another long silence spread, and the stranger seemed to grow taller and straighter and somehow more serious, as if he had her full attention. Her coldness, her calm, scared the shit out of him.

"We're studying something unique, Saul," Henry said finally. "So perhaps you can forgive our eagerness, our need to go the extra mile—"

"Just *get the hell out*," Saul said, and wrenched the ax free, although it cost him. Held it high on the handle, because in such close quarters it would be no use to him otherwise. There was such a terror in him now—that they wouldn't go, that he couldn't make them *get the hell out*. While still in his head a thousand lighthouses burned.

But Henry just shrugged, said, "Suit yourself."

Staunch though he felt weak, to fill the silence they kept leaving like a trap: "You're done here. I'm calling the police if I ever see you here again." Curious, the words that came out of his mouth, that he meant them and yet was examining them already for their truth.

"But it is going to be a beautiful morning," Suzanne said, the words hurled at him with a knife's blade of sarcasm?

Henry almost contorted himself to avoid brushing against Saul as they passed by, as if Saul were made of the most delicate crystal. The woman gave him a mysterious smile as she turned into the spiral leading down, a smile full of teeth.

Then they disappeared down the steps.

When he was sure they weren't coming back, Saul leaned over to switch on the lens. It would need some time to warm up, and then he would have to go through the checklist of tests to ensure Henry and his acolytes hadn't changed the direction of the main reflective surfaces within the lens. In the meantime, still holding the ax, he decided he would go downstairs to make sure the odd three hadn't lingered.

When he reached the bottom, he found no sign of them. Opening the front door, he expected to see them walking across the lighthouse grounds or getting into a car. But even when he turned on the lawn lights, there was no sign of them or of a vehicle. Not enough time had passed. Had they run part of the way and disappeared into the hazy gloom of the beach? Or scattered into the pines, hidden in the marshes, become one with the shadows there?

Then he heard the faint sound of a motorboat over the waves. A boat that must be running without lights. The only illumination now besides the moon and stars came from the faint red dot still pulsing from the island.

Back at the front door, though, a shadow waited for him. Henry.

"Don't worry, it's just me," Henry said. "The other two are gone."

Saul sighed, leaned on his ax. "Will you never just leave, Henry? Will you continue to be *such* a burden?" But he was relieved Suzanne and the unknown woman hadn't remained behind.

"A burden? I'm a kind of gift, Saul. Because I *understand*. I know what's going on."

"I've told you I don't know what you're talking about."

"Saul, I made the hole in the lens, while Suzanne was away. I'm the one."

Saul almost laughed. "And that's why I should listen to you? Because you vandalized my lighthouse?"

"I did it because I knew something must be in there. Because there was this one spot where none of my equipment registered . . . anything."

"So what?" Didn't that just mean that trying to find strange things with uncertain instruments was a losing game?

"Saul, why would you look so haunted if this place wasn't haunted also? You know, just as I know. Even if no one else believes."

"Henry . . ." Should he launch into an explanation of why faith in a God did not automatically mean a faith in spirits?

"You don't need to say anything. But you know the truth—and I'll track it down, too. I'll find it."

The eagerness in Henry, the way he fairly thrummed with it, shocked Saul. It was as if Henry had thrown aside a disguise, laid bare his soul, and beneath that guarded exterior Saul had discovered one of the more virulently rigid of his flock from back north. The chosen ones who would never be dissuaded, the "Séance" side of their little brigade. He didn't want a follower.

"I still don't know what you're talking about." Obstinate, because he didn't want to be dragged into this, because he felt so ill. Because a few strange dreams did not add up to what Henry wanted them to add up to.

Henry ignored him, said, "Suzanne thinks the catalyst was something *they* brought with *them*. But that's not true, even if I can't tell you what combination of steps or processes brought us to this point. And yet, it happened. After we've spent so many years of searching in so many places with so little to show for it."

Against his better judgment, because more and more Henry looked like a victim to him, Saul said, "Do you need help? Tell me what's going on, and maybe I can help you. Tell me who that woman was."

"Forget you saw her, Saul. You'll never see her again. She doesn't care about the supernatural world or getting to the truth, not really."

Then Henry smiled and walked away, toward what destination Saul had no idea.

0013: CONTROL

Half the wall exploded and a thousand eyes peered in as Control sprawled from the impact in the dust and debris. His head throbbed and there was pain in his side and his left leg, but he forced himself to lie still. He was playing dead just to keep his head. He was playing dead to keep his head. A line from a book about monsters his father had read to him as a child. Rising out of a place long forgotten like a flare shot into the sky. Knocked into his brain, it kept looping. Playing dead to keep his head. The brick dust settling now, those eyes still an awful pressure. Even as the crunch of glass—the obliterating sound of that, the questing horror of that—sounded near his ear, and then the weight shifting near his legs. He fought the impulse to open his eyes, because he had to play dead to keep his head. Somewhere to his right, the knife he'd dropped, and his father's carving falling out of his pocket. Even sprawled as he was sprawled, seeking it with a trembling hand, reflexively. He was shivering, he was shaking, the reverberations of the creature's passage creating a pain like cracks and fissures in his bones, the brightness trying to escape, the part of him that was lonely, that wanted to reach out. Playing dead. To keep his head.

The glass crunch, the crunch glass, and its source beyond the wall, exploring inward, held his full attention. Boot? Shoe? Foot? No. Claws? Hooves? Cilia? Fins? Suppressed a shudder. Could he reach his knife? No. If he could have reached his knife in time, if his knife had been any help, it wouldn't have happened like this, except, yes, it was always going to be like this. Border breach, but there was no border here. It had all been moving so slow, like a journey that meant something, and now so fast. Too fast. Like breath that had become light, gone from mist to a ray, slashing out toward the horizon but not taking him with it. On the other side of the half-demolished wall, a new thing? An old thing? But not a mistake. Was there anything in it now of what he'd once known through its surrogate? Because he recognized its eyes.

Some part of it enveloped him, held him there, against the floor, while he screamed. Something like an eclipse in his head, a thick, tactile eclipse, pushing out his own intent. Questing through his mind for something else entirely, making him turn inward to see the things Lowry had put there, the terrible, irrevocable things, and how his mother must have helped Lowry. "Check the seats for loose change," Grandpa Jack had said, or had he? The heavy shape of the gun in his hands, Grandpa Jack's greedy gaze, and yet even that childhood memory seemed as hazy as smoke curling up from the cigarette of someone who stood in shadow at the far end of a long, darkened room.

Those thousands of eyes regarding him, *reading* him from across a vast expanse of space, as if the biologist existed simultaneously halfway across the universe. The sensation of being *seen* and then relief and a stabbing disappointment as it withdrew, spit him out. Rejected him.

There came a sound like a weight leaving the sky, a plunging toward the waves, and the awful weight of a pushing against the air lessened, and the restless agony in his bones receded, and he was just a dirty, spent figure weeping on the floor of a ruined lighthouse. With words like *collateral damage* and *containment* and *counterattacks* blossoming like old spells, incantations that worked in other, far distant, lands but not here. He was back in control, but control was meaningless. His father's sculptures in his old backyard were tipping over, one after the other. The chess moves between them in those last days before his father had died. The pressure of the piece between his fingers as he moved it, and the empty air as he let go.

Silence then. An absence into which the brightness again took up sentinel duty, swung around with ever-greater confidence to peer at him like the leviathans from his dreams. Perhaps unaware of what it protected, what it lived within.

Except *he* would never forget now.

Later, much later, familiar steps, and a familiar voice—Grace, extending a hand.

"Can you walk?"

Could he walk? He felt like an old man leveled by a blow from an invisible fist. He had fallen into a deep, dark, narrow fissure and now had to crawl up out of it.

"Yes, I can walk."

Grace handing him his father's carving, him taking it.

"Let's go back up to the landing."

There was a huge hole in the side of the first-floor wall. The night peered in from it. But the lighthouse had held.

"Yes, the landing."

He would be safe there.

He wouldn't be safe there.

Control lay there, back on the landing, sprawled across a blanket, looking up at the paint-peeled ceiling mottled by candlelight. Everything seemed so far away. Such an overwhelming psychic sense of their distance from Earth, that there might not now be astronomers, might never be astronomers who, all-knowing, could even make out the speck that was the star around which they must revolve. He found it hard to breathe, kept calling forth another passage from the pages of Whitby where the man almost waxed poetic: "Area X has been created by an organism left behind by a civilization so advanced and so ancient and so alien to us and our own intent and our own thought processes that it has long since left us behind, left everything behind."

Wondering, too, because of all that the biologist's intrusion had knocked loose in his head . . . if there was any evidence he'd ever sat in the backseat of his grandfather's muscle car—if somewhere at Central you would find black-and-white photos shot from farther down the street, through the windshield of a car or a van. An investment. A divestment. The start of it all. He'd had dreams of cliffs and leviathans and falling into the sea. But what if the leviathans were back at Central? The shadowy forms mere outlines of memories he could not quite recall, overlaid with those that he should not remember because they had never occurred. *Jump*, a voice had said, and he had jumped. Two days lost at Central before he came to the Southern Reach, and only his mother's word for it that he was being paranoid . . . But it was such a weight, so exhausting to analyze, as if the Southern Reach and Area X both interrogated him.

Hello, John, said some version of Lowry in his head. *Surprise.*

Fuck you.

Seriously, John? And here I thought you knew all along, the game we were playing. The game we've always been playing.

His lungs felt heavy, thick, as Grace checked him out, bandaged his elbow, told him, "You've bruised some ribs and your hip is bruised, too, but you seem able to move everything."

"The biologist . . . she's really gone?" *This leviathan that has taken the terroir of a place and made it its own.* Every moment that passed, the gospel of Whitby made more and less sense to him. Such an inconsistent heartbeat. Such simplicity to concentrate on those three pages, to focus on the parts so smudged he had to interpret the words or to smooth out a curled corner, than on the fact that the sun should not be shining above, that the sky could peel back to reveal a celestial landscape perhaps never dreamed of by humankind, the weight of that oppressive, a beast bearing down on the very center, which must be protected from that which did not bear contemplating.

"She's been gone for a while," Grace said. "You've been a little gone, for a while."

She stood next to the seaward window, along with Ghost Bird. Ghost Bird had her back to Control, staring out at the night. Was she charting her original's progress? Was that vast form now in open water, seeking depth and distance? Or had she departed for someplace stranger and more remote? He didn't want to know.

When Ghost Bird finally turned, the shadows made of her face an impression of a fading smile and wide, curious eyes.

"What did it share with you?" Control asked. "What did it take?" More caustic than he'd meant, but he was still in a kind of shock, knew that on some level. Wanted his experience to be the common one.

"Nothing. Nothing at all."

What side are you on? Lowry asked.

"What side are you on?" he asked.

"Enough!" Grace said. "Enough! Just shut the fuck up. That's not helping."

But he couldn't shut up. "No wonder you're on edge," he said. "No wonder you didn't tell us."

"The biologist took out the convoy," Ghost Bird said.

"Yes, she did," Grace admitted. "But I have been careful and quiet and not provoked her. I know when to stay away from the lighthouse or the shore. I know when to fade into the forest. Sometimes there's a kind of *foreshadowing* in the air. Sometimes she will make landfall where she found the owl, then push on through the interior, headed here. As if she remembers. Most times, I can avoid her. Most times, she isn't here."

"Remembers what? This place?"

"I don't know what she remembers or doesn't remember," Grace said. "I just know your presence here attracted her, made her curious." Not Control's presence, that much he knew. Ghost Bird's presence. The biologist was drawn to her as surely as he had been drawn to her.

"We could be just like the biologist," Control said. "Stay here. Wait it out. Wait her out. Just give in." Goading them.

But it was Ghost Bird who answered: "She earned the right to choose her fate. She earned the right."

"We're not her," Grace said. "I don't want to become her, or anything like her."

"Isn't that all you've been doing? Waiting?" Wanting to see just how well Grace had adjusted to living on an island with a monster.

"Not exactly. But what do you want me to do? Tell me what I should do, and I will do it!" Shouting now. "Do you think I *want* to wait here, die here? Do you think I like it?" The thought occurred that Grace had made use of the biologist's list of pain-inducers, that her thinness, the hollowed-out quality to her face, wasn't just about being haunted by a monster.

"You need a way out," Ghost Bird said.

"Through a hole in the sea that may not be there?"

"No. Another way out."

Control propped himself up with a groan. His side was on fire. "Are you sure the ribs are just bruised?"

"I can't be sure without an X-ray."

Another impossible thing. Yet another moment in his decline. A wall changing to the touch of his hand, the touch of the biologist in his head. Enough of this. Enough.

He took up Whitby's pages, read by candlelight even as he began to tear the corners off. Slowly.

We must trust our thoughts while we sleep. We must trust our hunches. We must begin to examine all of those things that we think of as irrational simply because we do not understand them. In other words, we must distrust the rational, the logical, the sane, in an attempt to reach for something higher, for something more worthy. Brilliance and bullshit both. A binary trapped in its single-minded focus on solutions.

"What?" he asked. He could feel the other two staring at him.

Ghost Bird said, "You need to rest."

"What I'd suggest isn't going to be popular anyway," he said. Tearing one full page into shreds. Letting the pieces fall to the floor. It felt good to tear something apart.

"Say it." Challenging him.

A pause, preparing himself. Aware of the conflicting voices in his head.

"What you call the Crawler—we have to try. We have to go back down into the tower and find some way to neutralize it."

Ghost Bird: "Have you been paying attention? Have you been listening?"

"Or we stay here."

"Staying here isn't going to work," Grace admitted. "Either the biologist will get us, or Area X will."

"There's a lot of open, vulnerable space for us between here and the tower," Ghost Bird said.

"There's a lot of everything between here and there."

"Control," Ghost Bird said, and he didn't want to look at her, didn't want to see those eyes that now reminded him of the creature the biologist had become. "Control, there's no reset. There's never going to be a reset. That's a suicide mission." Unspoken, that she thought it was a suicide mission for them. Who knew what it might be for her?

"But the director thought you could change its direction," he said. "That you could change it, if you tried hard enough." A halting kind of hope. A childish thrashing against the dictates of the real. *If you wished upon a star.* He was thinking of the light at the bottom of the tower, this new thing he hadn't known about before entering Area X. He was thinking about being sick, and now sicker, and what that meant. At least they were all out in the open now, clear to him. The brightness, Lowry, all of it. Everything in the mix, including the core he still thought of as John Rodriguez. The Rodriguez who didn't belong to anyone. Who clasped his father's carving tight in his pocket. Who remembered something beyond the wreck and ruin of all this.

"It's true we have one thing no one else had," Grace said.

"What?" Ghost Bird asked in a skeptical, doubting tone.

"You," Grace said. "The only photocopy of the director's last plan."

0014: THE DIRECTOR

When, eventually, you return to the Southern Reach, you find a gift waiting for you: a framed black-and-white photograph of the lighthouse keeper, his assistant, and a little girl playing on the rocks—head down, jacket hood disguising her features. The blood rushes to your head, and you almost black out, seeing that this photo you didn't know still existed.

"It's for your office," reads the pointed note that comes with it. "You should hang it on the wall there. In fact, you must keep it on the wall. As a reminder of how far you've come. For your years of service and for your loyalty. Love and Kisses, Jimmy Boy."

That's when you realize there is something very much more wrong with Lowry than you'd ever thought before. That he creates ever more spectacular and grandiose dysfunctions to test what the system might bear before it finds him out. He seems, year after year, to revel in his clandestine operations not because they are secret but for those tantalizing moments when, either by his own hand or by fate, the edges of them almost become known.

But where had the photograph come from?

"Pull everything we have on Jackie Severance," you tell Grace. "Pull every file that mentions *Jack* Severance. And the son—*John Rodriguez*. Even if it takes a year. We're looking for something that connects Severance—any Severance— to Lowry." You've got a sense of an unholy alliance, a devilish foundation. An inkling of bad faith. Something hidden in the grout between the stones.

Meanwhile, you have a plant and a cell phone, very early model, to deal with—all you have to show for your journey. Other than a new sense of being separate, remote, set apart from the staff.

When you see Whitby in the hallway now, sometimes you meet his gaze and nod and there is a sense of a secret shared. Other times, you must look away, stare at that worn green carpet that meanders through everything. Make some polite comment in the cafeteria, try to immerse yourself in meetings as they prep another expedition. Try to pretend everything is normal. Is Whitby broken? His smile flickers back into place at times. His old confident stance, the wit in Whitby, will reappear but not for long, and then a light winks out in his eyes and darkness comes back in.

There's nothing you could say to Whitby except "I'm sorry," but you can't even say that. You can't change the moments that changed him except in your memory, and even in memory that attempt is obscured by the fast-rising *thing* from below, the thing that terrified you so much you abandoned Saul there, on the tunnel steps. Said to yourself afterward that Saul wasn't real, couldn't be real, so you hadn't abandoned anyone. "Don't forget about me," he'd said, so long ago, and you won't ever forget him, but you might have to leave him behind. That apparition. The hallucination that, as you sit at the bar in Chipper's Star Lanes or debate policy with Grace on the Southern Reach rooftop, you still try to rationalize as not a hallucination at all.

In part because you came back with the plant. For a time, you are obsessed with each dark green leaf, the way looking at it from above it forms a kind of fan-like circle, but from the side the effect fades completely. If you focus on the plant, maybe you can forget Lowry, waiting out there, for a while. Maybe Saul won't matter. Maybe you can salvage something out of . . . nothing.

The plant will not die.

No parasites will touch the plant.

The plant will not die.

No extremes of temperature will affect it. Freeze it, it will thaw. Burn it, it will regenerate.

The plant will not die.

No matter what you try, no matter the experiments performed on it in the sterile, the blinding white environs of the storage cathedral . . . the plant won't die. It's not that you mean to order its execution, but that in the course of the samples taken, the researchers inform you that the plant refuses to die. That cutting—you could chop it up into five dozen tiny pieces, put those in a measuring cup, sprinkle it on a steak for seasoning . . . and in theory it would grow inside of you, eventually burst forth seeking sunlight.

So, relenting, you let samples be whisked away to Central, so that experts can solve the mystery of this simple, ordinary plant that looks like any number of temperate-climate perennials. Samples, too, to Lowry's secret headquarters, per-

haps to reside next to cages in experimental bunkers, although none of their findings ever come back to you. All of this in the midst of a frenzied slicing and dicing
of other specimens in the storage cathedral, just to make sure there hasn't been
some domino effect, or something's been missed. But nothing has been missed.

"I don't think we're looking at a plant," Whitby says, tentative, at one status
meeting, risking his new relationship with the science division, which he has
embraced as a kind of sanctuary.

"Then why are we *seeing* a plant, Whitby?" Cheney, managing to convey an
all-consuming exasperation. "Why are we seeing a plant that *looks like* a plant
being a plant. Doing plant things, like photosynthesis and drawing water up
through its roots. Why? That's not a tough question, is it, really? Or is it? Maybe
it is a tough question, I don't know, for reasons beyond me. But that's going to be
a problem, don't you think? Having to reassert that things we think are the things
they are actually are in fact the things they are and not *some other thing entirely.*
Just think of all the fucking things we will have to reevaluate if you're right,
Whitby—starting with you!" Cheney's blistered, reddening expression bears
down on Whitby as if he were the receptacle of every evil thing that has ever
afflicted Cheney since the day he was born. "Because," Cheney says, lowering his
voice, "if that's a tough question, don't we have to reclassify all the *really* tough
questions?"

Later Whitby will regale you with information on how quantum mechanics
impacts photosynthesis, which is all about "antenna receiving light and antenna
can be hacked," about how "one organism might *peer out* from another organism
but not live there," of how plants "talk" to one another, how communication can
occur in chemical form and through processes so invisible to human beings that
the sudden visibility of it would be "an irreparable shock to the system."

For the Southern Reach? For humanity?

But Whitby's close-lipped about that, changes the subject. Abruptly.

You're less obsessed with the cell phone, which has been living with the techs
down in the hardware department, the ones who have the right security clearance. But the techs can't make it work, are confused by it, perhaps even unnerved. Nothing about it indicates a malfunction. It should work. It just doesn't.
It should reveal who owned it. It just doesn't.

"As if it's not really made of the parts it should be made of. But it looks exactly
that way—like a normal phone. Really old, though."

A bulky veteran of a phone, scarred and scraped and worn. It looks like you feel sometimes.

You offer it to Lowry during one of your calls, as a kind of sacrifice of a pawn. Give Lowry an exclusive, let him worry at it like a dog with a new bone, so the old bone can get some rest. But he doesn't want it—insists you keep it.

Something an expedition member had snuck in with them or inadvertently brought along? Something perhaps from a recent expedition that someone had thought was old enough not to disturb Area X's slumber? During the cycles that predated Lowry's intervention, your stewardship, techniques primitive and untested.

Recalling the very earliest photographs and video—of Lowry and the others in what amounted to deep-sea diving outfits to traverse the border, before they realized it was unnecessary. Lowry, returned, disoriented, babbling on videotape, words he would later recant, about how nothing would ever come out of the passage in the border, nothing, because they were waiting for ghosts, for something long dead, Area X a memorial, a gravestone.

"What made Area X spit it back up?" you ask Grace, safe on the roof in Beyond Reach.

"What made Whitby the one to find it?"

"A good question." A gift from Dead Whitby.

"Why did it allow itself to be found?"

That sounds like the right question, and some days you want to tell Grace . . . everything. But most days you want to shield her from information that will make no difference to her job, her life. Somehow Dead Whitby and the Saul apparition fall on the same side as telling her that your name is not your name. That all of the unimportant things about you are a lie.

Eventually, into the middle of all this comes the call you've been dreading: Lowry, with a purpose. While you're staring at the incriminating photograph on the wall: you on the rocks, shouting either before or after the shot was taken, "I'm a monster! I'm a monster!"

"Another eleventh expedition is a go."

"Already."

"Three months. We're almost there."

You want to say, but don't say, "It's time to stop tampering, not time to intensify the tampering." The fiddling. All the ways Lowry tries to control what cannot really be controlled.

"That's too soon," you say. Too soon by far. Nothing has changed, except that you interfered and went over the border and brought back two objects you can't explain.

"Maybe it's time for you to stop being a fucking coward," Lowry says. "Three months. Get ready, *Cynthia*." He bangs the phone down, and you imagine him banging it down into a housing that's a polished human skull.

They implant into the brain of the psychologist—on what will turn out to be the last eleventh—what Lowry calls "a pearl of surveillance and recall." Some tiny subset of the silver egg that is Central, passing first through Lowry's deforming grip. They make a man *not himself*, and you go along with it to keep your job, to stay close to what is important to you.

Twelve months later, the last eleventh expedition comes back, acting almost like zombies, memories cloudier than the drunk veteran's at the Star Lanes Lounge. Eighteen months later, they're all dead of cancer, and Lowry's back on the phone talking about the "next eleventh" and "making refinements to our process" and you realize something has to change. Again. And short of putting a gun to Lowry's head and pulling the trigger, it's going to come down to influencing the composition of the expeditions, how they are deployed, and a host of lesser factors. None of which may make a difference, but you have to try. Because you never want to see such lost, vacant faces ever again, never again want to see people who have been stripped of something so vital that it can't be expressed through words.

Morale at the Southern Reach becomes worse after the last eleventh returns and then, so quickly, passes on to the next place, wherever that might be. Numbness? A sense of having gone through so many crises that emotion must be hoarded, that it might not run out.

From the transcripts: "It was a beautiful day." "The expedition was uneventful." "We had no problems in completing the mission."

What was the mission, in their eyes? But they'd never answer that question. Grace spoke of them in reverential tones, almost as if they'd become saints. Down in the science division, Cheney became more muted and subdued for a long time, as if the color TV of his commentary had been replaced by a black-and-white model with a single channel of pixelated fuzz. Ephemeral, ethereal Pitman called from Central with oblique condolences and a kind of calculated indifference to his tone that suggested misdirection.

But you were the one who had seen the curling worm of Lowry's corruption at work—that what he'd done, the bargain you had made that had allowed him to be so invasive and controlling, hadn't been worth it.

Even worse, Jackie Severance visits regularly afterward, as if maybe Central is concerned about something, takes to pacing around your office and gesticulating as she talks, rather than just sitting still. This emissary of Central you have to deal with in the flesh rather than just Lowry.

"She's my parole officer," you tell Grace.

"Then who is Lowry?"

"Lowry's the parole officer's partner? Boss? Employee?" Because you don't know.

"A riddle wrapped in a puzzle," Grace says. "Do you know what her father, Jack Severance, is up to?"

"No, what?"

"Everything." So much everything that Grace is still wading through all of it.

When Severance comes calling, there's a sense she's checking up on her investment, her shared risk.

"Does it ever get to you?" Severance asks you more than once, and you're fairly sure she's just making conversation.

"No," you lie, shoot back your own cliché: "We all have our jobs to do."

Back when she worked for the Southern Reach, you'd liked her—sharp, charming, and she'd done a good job of fine-tuning logistics, of diving in and getting work done. But since she's chained to Lowry, you can't risk that her presence isn't his presence. Sharing a swig of brandy with Grace: "A living bug—can't exactly just pull her out of the ceiling tiles." And the glamour has begun to fade: At times, Severance looks to you like a tired, faded clerk at a makeup counter in a department store.

Severance sits with you, observing the returnees through closed-circuit cameras for long minutes, coffee in hand, checking her phone every few minutes, often drawn off into some side conversation about some other project altogether, then coming back into focus to ask questions.

"You're sure they're not contaminated with something?"

"When do you send in the next expedition?"

"What do you think of Lowry's metrics?"

"If you had a bigger budget, what would you spend it on?"

"Do you know what you're looking for?"

No, you don't know. She knows you don't know. You don't even know what you're looking at, these people who became ever more gaunt until they were living skeletons, and then not even that. The psychologist perhaps even blanker than the rest, like a kind of warning to you, as if it were a side effect of his profession, encountering Area X. But a closer look at his history reveals Lowry probably leaned on him the most, thought, maybe, that his profession made him stronger than the rest. The bindings, the reconditioning sessions, the psychological tricks—surely a psychologist could absorb them, armed with foreknowledge. Except the man hadn't, and as far as they knew this "coiled sting" inside his brain had made no difference at all to Area X.

"There must be things you would have done differently," Severance says.

You make some noncommittal sound and pretend you're scribbling something on your notepad. A grocery list, maybe. A blank circle that's either a representation of the border or of Central. A plant rising out of a cell phone. Or maybe you should just write *Fuck you* and be done with it. Gnaw your way out of Lowry's trap.

At some point after the last of the last eleventh passes away, you get black paint from maintenance, along with thick black markers, and you open the useless door that gives you access to the blank wall—casualty of a clumsy corridor redesign. You write out the words collected from the topographical anomaly, the words that you know must have been written by the lighthouse keeper (this flash of intuition, unveiled at a status meeting, allowing you to order a deeper investigation into Saul's background than ever before).

You draw a map, too, of all the landmarks in Area X. There's the base camp, or, as you call it now, the Mirage. There's the lighthouse, which should be some form of safety but too often isn't, the place that journals go to die. There's the topographical anomaly, the hole in the ground into which all initiative and focus descended, only to become hazy and diffuse. There, too, is the island and, finally, the Southern Reach itself, looking either like the last defense against the enemy or its farthestmost outpost.

Lowry, drunk out of his mind at his going-away party, headed for Central, only three years after you had been hired, had said, "How goddamn boring. Fucking boring if they win. If we gotta live in that world." As if people would be living in "that world" at all, which wasn't what any of the evidence foretold, or kept foretelling, as if there were nothing worse than being bored and the only point of the world people already lived in was to find ways to combat boredom, to make sure "all the moments," as Whitby put it when he went on about parallel universes, might be accounted for in some way, so minds wouldn't fill up with emptiness that they bifurcated simply to have more capacity to be bored.

And Grace, fearless, an opposing voice from years later at some other party where a member of the staff had voiced an equally cynical, depressing opinion, but as if answering Lowry: "I'm still here because of my family. Because of my family and because of the director, and because I don't want to give up on them or you." Even if Grace could never share with her family the struggles she faced at the Southern Reach, being your "right-hand gal" as Lowry puts it, sarcastically. The profane voice of reason when yours is perceived as too esoteric, too distant.

Halfway through drawing the map, you feel eyes on you, and there's Grace, arms folded, giving you the stink eye. She closes the office door behind her, just keeps staring at you.

"Is there something I can help you with?" you ask, paint can in one hand and brush in the other.

"You can reassure me that everything is okay." For one of the first times, you sense doubt from her. Not disagreement but doubt, and given how much things rely on faith at the late-era Southern Reach, this worries you.

"I'm fine," you say. "I'm just fine. I just want a reminder."

"Of what? To the staff? That you're getting a little eccentric?"

A surge of anger at that, a faint echo of hurt, too. Lowry, for all of his faults, might not think it was strange. He'd understand. But also, if it were Lowry painting a map on the wall of his office, no one would be questioning him. They'd be asking if they could hold the brush, touch up this spot, that spot, get him more paint.

Going for the cumulative effect, to put more pressure on the breaking point, you say to Grace, "After I'm done here, I'm going to order the bodies of the last eleventh exhumed."

"Why?" Aghast, something in her background averse to such desecrations.

"Because I think it's necessary. Which is enough of a reason." Having what Grace will call "your Lowry moment," and it's not even that volcanic, just stubbornness.

"Cynthia," Grace says. "Cynthia, what I think or don't think doesn't matter, but the rest of the staff has to *want* to follow you."

More stubborn thought still: that all you really need is Lowry to follow you and Severance, and you could hold on here forever. Hideous thought, though, the image of another thirty-six expeditions being sent out, only some coming back, of you and Grace and Whitby, progressively more jaded and cynical, becoming ancient, going through motions that wouldn't help anyone, not even yourselves.

"I'm going to finish this up," you tell her in a conciliatory way. "Because I started it."

"Because it will look fucking stupid if you don't finish it now," she says, relenting as well.

"Yes, exactly. It will look fucking stupider if I don't finish."

"So let me help," she says, and something in the emphasis she puts on the words gets to you. Will always get to you.

Let me help.

"All right, then," you say gruffly, and hand her the extra brush.

But you're still going to dig up the dead, and you're still wondering how to change the paradigm like Lowry keeps trying to change the paradigm. Lost in the thought of that the next weekend at Chipper's while bowling, while home clipping coupons for the grocery store, while taking a bath, while going out for a ballroom dancing lesson because it's the kind of thing you would never do. So you do it, aware that if Severance has eyes on you, she'll find it evidence of being "erratic," but not caring. You put yourself here, set this trap for yourself, so if you feel trapped by it now, it's your own fault.

The day after painting the door, Grace follows up, as she always does, unable to leave it alone, but privately, on the rooftop, which by now you're pretty sure Cheney suspects exists, just as he suspects the involvement of "dark energy" in the maintenance of the invisible border . . . Grace saying, "You have a plan, right? This is all part of a plan. I'm relying on you to have a plan."

So you nod, smile, say, "Yes, Grace, I have a plan," because you don't want to betray that trust, because what's the good of saying "All I have is a feeling, an intuition, and a brief conversation with a man who should be dead. I have a plant and a phone."

In your dreams you stand on the sidelines, holding the plant in one hand and the cell phone in the other, watching a war between Central and Area X. In some fundamental way, you feel, they have been in conflict for far longer than thirty years—for ages and ages, centuries in secret. Central the ultimate void to counteract Area X: impersonal, antiseptic, labyrinthine, and unknowable. Against the facade, you cannot help but express a kind of terrible betrayal: Sometimes you admire Lowry's fatal liveliness next to *that*, a silhouette writhing against a dull white screen.

0015: THE LIGHTHOUSE KEEPER

Western siren finally fixed; touched up the white part of the daymark, seaward side; fixed the ladder, too, but still feels rickety, unsafe. Something knocked down a foot of fence and got into the garden, but couldn't tell what. No deer tracks, but likely culprit. S&SB? The shadows of the abyss are like the petals of a monstrous flower. Didn't feel up to a hike, but seen from lighthouse grounds, of note: flycatcher (not sure what kind), frigate birds, least terns, cormorants, black-throated stilt(!), a couple of yellowthroats. On the beach, found a large pipefish had washed up, a few sail jellyfish rotting in the sand.

There came an incandescent light. There came a star in motion, the sun plummeting to Earth. There fell from the heavens a huge burning torch, thick flames dripping out behind it. And this light, this star, shook the sky and the beach where he had walked a second ago under a clear blue sky. The scorched intensity of the sudden object hurtling down toward him battered his senses, sent him sprawling to his knees as he tried to run, and then dove face-first into the sand. He screamed as the rays, the sparks, sprayed out all around, and the core of the light hit somewhere in front of him, his teeth smashed in his mouth, his bones turned to powder. The reverberation lived within him as he tried to regain his footing, even as the impact conjured up an enormous tidal wave like a living creature, aimed at the beach. When it fell upon him the weight, the immensity, destroyed him once more and washed away anything he could have recognized, could have known. He gasped and thrashed and hurt, dug his tortured hands into the shocking cold sand. The sand had a different texture, and the tiny creatures living there were different. He didn't want to look up, take in his surroundings, frightened that the landscape, too, might have changed, might be so different he would not recognize it.

The tidal waves faded. The burning lights receded.

Saul managed to get to his feet, to stagger a step or two, and as he did, he realized that everything around him had been restored. The world he knew, the world he loved: tranquil, unchanged, the lighthouse up the shore undamaged by the wave. Seagulls flew by, and far in the distance someone walked, looking for shells. He brushed the sand from his shirt, his shorts, stood there for a long moment bent over with his hands on his thighs. The impact was still affecting his hearing, still making him shake with the memory of its power. Yet it had left no evidence behind except melancholy, as if he held within him the only memory of some lost world.

He could not stop trembling in the aftermath, wondered if he were going insane. That took less hubris than thinking this was a message from on high. For in the center of the light that had come storming down, an image had appeared, a pattern that he recognized: the eight leaves of the strange plant, each one like another spiraling step down into oblivion.

Midmorning. The rocks were slippery and sharp, encrusted with limpets and barnacles. Sea lice, ancient of days, traveled across those rocks on quests to scavenge whatever they could, and the seaweed that gathered there, in strands thin and thick and sometimes gelatinous, brought a tangy, moldy smell.

It was a relief to sit there, trying to recover—peering into the tidal pool that lay at his feet as the rock dug into his posterior. As he tried to control his shaking. There had been other visions, but none as powerful as this one. He had a perverse urge for Henry to appear, to confess all of his symptoms to a man who, once revealed as a passionate, delusional ghost-hunter, he recalled almost with fondness. But Saul hadn't seen Henry or Suzanne since the incident in the night, nor the strange woman. Sometimes he thought he was being watched, but that was probably nothing more than a reflection of believing Henry when he said he would "find it," implying a return.

The tidal pool directly in front of him became frustratingly occluded when a cloud passed overhead and changed the quality of the light, or when the wind picked up and created ripples. But when the sun broke through again and it wasn't just the reflection of his face and knees he saw, the pool became a kind of living cabinet of curiosities. He might prefer to hike, to bird-watch, but he could understand a fascination with tidal pools, too.

Fat orange starfish, either lumbering or slumbering, lay half in, half out of the water. Some bottom-dwelling fish contemplated him with a kind of bulging, jaded regard—a boxy, pursed-lipped creature whose body was the same color as the sand, except for bejeweled sapphire-and-gold eyes. A tiny red crab sidled across that expanse toward what to it must be a gaping chasm of a dark hole leading down, perhaps into an endless network of tiny caverns carved into the rocks over the years. If he stared long enough into the comforting oblivion of that microcosm, it washed away everything else, even the shadow of his reflection.

It was there, some minutes later, that Gloria found him, as Saul perhaps had known she would, the rocks to her what the lighthouse had become to him.

She dropped down beside him as if indestructible, corduroy-clad rump sliding hardly at all on the hard surface. Not so much perched as a rock atop another rock. The solid weight of her forced him a little to the side. She was breathing hard from clambering fast over the rocks, managed a kind of "uh-huh" of approval at his choice of entertainment and he gave her a brief smile and a nod in return.

For a long while, they just sat together, watching. He had decided he could not talk to her about what he had seen, that pushing that onto her was wrong. The only one he could tell was Charlie. Maybe.

The crab sifted through something in the sand. The camouflaged fish risked a slow walk on stickery fins like drab half-opened fans, making for the shadow-shelter of a tiny ledge of rock. One of the starfish, as if captured via time-lapse photography, withdrew at a hypnotically slow speed into the water, until only the tips of two arms lay exposed and glistening.

Finally Gloria said, "Why are you down here and not working by the shed or in the tower?"

"I don't feel like working today." Images from old illuminated manuscripts, of comets hurtling through the sky, from the books in his father's house. The reverberation and recoil of the beach exploding under his feet. The strange creatures in the sand. What message should he take from that?

"Yeah, I don't always want to go to school," she said. "But at least you get money."

"I do get money, that's true," he said. "And they're never going to give you money to go to school."

"They should give me money. I have to put up with a lot." He wondered just how much. It might well be a lot.

"School's important," he said, because he felt he should say it, as if Gloria's mother stood right behind them, tapping her foot.

Gloria considered that a moment, nudged him in the ribs in a way as familiar as if they were drinking buddies down at the village bar.

"I told my mom this is a school, too, but that didn't work."

"What's 'this'?"

"The tidal pools. The forest. The trails. All of it. Most of the time it's true I'm just goofing off, but I'm learning things, too."

Saul could imagine how that conversation had gone. "You're not going to get any grades here." Warming to the idea: "Although I guess the bears might give you grades for watching out for them."

She kind of leaned back to get a better look at him, as if reappraising him. "That's stupid. Are you feeling okay?"

"Yeah, this whole conversation is stupid."

"Are you still feeling different?"

"What? No. No, I'm fine, Gloria."

They watched the fish for a bit after that. Something about their conversation, the way they'd moved too fast or been too loud, had made the fish retreat into the sand so now only its eyes looked up at them.

"There are things the lighthouse teaches me, though," Gloria said, wrenching Saul out of his thoughts.

"To stand up straight and tall and project light out of your head toward the sea?"

She giggled at that, giving him too much credit for an answer he'd meant at least half ironically.

"No. Here's what the lighthouse teaches me. Be quiet and let me tell you. The lighthouse teaches me to work hard, to keep my room clean, to be honest, and to be nice to people." Then, reflecting, looking down at her feet. "My room is a mess and I lie sometimes and I'm not always nice to people, but that's the idea."

A little embarrassed, he said, "That fish down there sure is frightened of you."

"Huh? It just doesn't know me. If it knew me, that fish would shake my hand."

"I don't think there's anything you could say to convince it of that. And there are all kinds of ways you could hurt it without meaning to." Watching those unblinking blue eyes with the gold streaks—the dark vertical pupil—that seemed like a fundamental truth.

Ignoring him: "You like being a lighthouse keeper, don't you, Saul?" Saul.

That was a new thing. When had they become Saul and Gloria rather than Mr. Evans and Gloria?

"Why, do you want my job when you grow up?"

"No. I never want to be a lighthouse keeper. Shoveling and making tomatoes and climbing all the time." Was that how it seemed he spent his time? He guessed it did.

"At least you're honest."

"Yep. Mom says I should be less honest."

"There's that, too." His father could have been less honest, because honesty was often just a way of being cruel.

"Anyway, I can't stay long." There was real regret in her voice.

"A shame, given how honest you're being."

"I know, right? But I gotta go. Mom's going to come by in the car soon. We're driving into town to meet my dad."

"Oh, he's picking you up for the holidays?" So this was the day.

A shadow had passed over the tidal pool again and all he could see were their two faces, peering down. He could've passed for her father, couldn't he? Or was he too old? But such thoughts were a form of weakness.

"It's longer this time," she said, clearly not happy about it. "Mom wants me up there for a couple of months at least. Because she's lost her second job and needs to look for another one. But that's only eight weeks. Or maybe sixty days."

He looked over at her, saw the serious expression on her face. Two months. That was an impossibly long time.

"You'll have fun. When you get back, you'll appreciate this place even more."

"I appreciate it now. And it won't be fun. Dad's girlfriend is a bitch."

"Don't use that word."

"Sorry. But she is."

"Did your mom say that?"

"No. I made it up myself. It wasn't hard."

"Well, try to get along," Saul said, having reached the end of any advice a lighthouse could convey. "It's just for a little while."

"Sure. And then I'll be back. Help me up, I think my mom's here." He couldn't hear a car, but that didn't mean anything.

He took her hand, braced himself so she could lean on him and get to her feet. She stood there, balanced against him, hand on his shoulder, and said, "Goodbye, Saul. Save this tidal pool for me."

"I'll put up a sign." He tried to smile.

She nodded, and then she was gone, scampering across the rocks like some kind of deranged daredevil—showing off.

On impulse he turned and shouted "Hey, Gloria!" at her before she was out of earshot.

She turned, balanced with both arms outstretched, waiting.

"Don't forget about me! Take care of yourself!" He tried to make it sound without weight, sentences that could float away into the air. Nothing that mattered.

She nodded and waved, and said something he couldn't hear, and then she was running up the lighthouse lawn and around the curve of the lighthouse wall, out of sight.

Below, the fish had its mouth around the small red crab, which was struggling in a slow, meditative way, almost like it didn't want to get free.

0016: GHOST BIRD

The lighthouse rose from fog and reflections like a mirror of itself, the beach gray and cold, the sand rasping against the hull of the boat as they abandoned it in the shallows. The waves came in small and half curling like the froth of malformed questions. The lighthouse did not resemble Ghost Bird's memory of it, for its sides had been scoured by fire. Discoloration extended all the way to the top, where the lens, the light within, lay extinguished. The fire had erupted from the landing windows as well, and in combination with the bits of broken glass, and all of the other talismans human beings had rendered up to it over the years, gave the lighthouse the appearance of something shamanistic. Reduced now to a daymark for their boat, the simplest of its functions, the one task that, unperformed, made a lighthouse no longer of use to anyone. Made it into a narrow, haunted redoubt.

"Burned by the border commander," Grace had told them. "Burned because they didn't understand it—and the journals with it."

But Ghost Bird caught the hesitation in Grace's voice, how she still would not tell them exactly what had happened within the lighthouse, what *slaughter* and *deception* consisted of, any detailed accounting of what had come at them from the seaward side.

All Grace could offer in its place was a localized pathology—the origin of the orange flags. The doing of the border commander, a cataloging of all that was unknowable to her. Perhaps the commander had been trying to keep separate the real from the imagined. If so, she had failed. Even common thistles had been so marked. Given more time, the commander might have marked the entire world.

Ghost Bird had a vision of the journals impervious, still up there, reconstituted, were they now to enter, walk up into the lantern room, undo the trapdoor, stare down as had the biologist, as had she, so many years ago. Would the reflected light from those frozen accounts irradiate their thoughts, contaminate their dreams, forever trap them? Or was there just a mountain of ashes in there now? Ghost Bird did not want to find out.

It was late afternoon already. They had left the island in the early morning, in a bigger boat Grace had hidden out of sight of the pier. The biologist had not reappeared, although Control had searched those waters with a kind of nervous anxiety. Ghost Bird would have sensed her presence long before there was any danger. She could not tell him, for his own sake, that the oceans through which the biologist now traveled were wider and deeper than the one that led them to the lighthouse.

They trudged up the beach toward the lighthouse, taking a path that minimized the possibility of sniper fire from above. Grace believed everyone was dead, or long since had moved on, but there was always the chance. Nothing arose from the seaward side, ghostlike or otherwise. *Things came out of the sea, things like the biologist, but less kind.*

From the lip of the dunes, they came up to the level ground next to the lighthouse without incident, lingered at the edge of the overgrown, long-wild lawn beside it. Where nettle weed and snarls of blackberry plants grew: a thorny thicket for them, but a natural shelter for the wrens and sparrows that darted betwixt, between, their cheerful song a discordant element against the overcast quality of the light. The ever-present thistles looked to Ghost Bird like some kind of natural microphone, the stickery domes there to pick up and transmit sound instead of disseminate seeds.

A broken door yawned, beckoned to them with darkness, while the gray sky above, the way it could glint or waver at odd moments, made Control in particular jittery. He could not stand still, did not want Ghost Bird or Grace standing still, either. Ghost Bird could see the brightness flaring out from him like a halo of jagged knives, wondered if he would still be himself by the time they reached the tower. Perhaps he would, if nothing preternatural stitched its way through that sky.

"No point in going up," Grace said.

"Not even the least bit curious?"

"Do you like walking through charnel houses and cemeteries, too?"

Still evaluating her, and Ghost Bird unable to tell what she was thinking. Had Grace thrown in her lot with them, hoping Ghost Bird was indeed a secret weapon, or for some other purpose? What she did know was that with Grace there she'd had little time to talk to Control in private—any conversations were of necessity between the three of them. This disturbed her, because she knew Grace even less than she knew Control.

"I don't want to go up," Control said. "I don't. I want to cover the open ground as fast as possible. Get to where we're going as fast as possible."

"At least no one appears to be here," Grace said. "At least it appears as if Area X may have thinned out the opposition."

Yes, that was good, if a cold thing to say, but the look Control gave Grace indicated he could not jettison some essential sentimentality that was of no use here, some mechanism that belonged to the world outside.

"Well, let me add to the collection," Grace said, and tossed the biologist's island account and her journal through the open front door.

Control stared into that darkness as if she had committed a terrible act that he was thinking of setting right. But Ghost Bird knew that Grace was just trying to set them free.

"Never has a setting been so able to live without the souls traversing it." A sentence Ghost Bird remembered from a college text, one that had lingered with the biologist after her transition to the city, come back to her as she stood in the empty lot, following the silent launch of a sugar glider from one telephone pole to another. The text had been referring to urban landscapes, but the biologist had interpreted it as applying to the natural world, or at least what could be interpreted as wilderness, even though human beings had so transformed the world that even Area X had not been able to completely reduce those signs and symbols. The shrubs and trees that constituted invasive species were only one part of that; the other, how even the faint outline of a human-made path changed the topography of a place. "The only solution to the environment is neglect, which requires our collapse." A sentence the biologist had excised from her thesis, but one that had burned bright in her mind, and now in Ghost Bird's, where, even analyzed and kept at arm's length like all received memories, it had a kind of power. In the presence of the memory of a thousand eyes staring up at her.

As they headed inland, the larger things fell away, revealing the indelible: the dark line of a marsh hawk flying low over the water, the delicate fractures in the water where a water moccasin swam, the strangely satisfying long grass that cascaded like hair from the ground.

She was content with silence, but Grace and Control were less so.

"I miss hot showers," Control said. "I miss not itching all over."

"Boil water," Grace said, as if it provided the solution to both problems. As if Control's misses were wishes, and he should think bigger.

"Not the same thing."

"I miss standing on the roof of the Southern Reach and looking out over the forest," Grace said.

"You used to do that? How did you get up there?"

"The janitor let us go up. The director and me. We would stand up there and make our plans."

That catch in Grace's throat, that invisible connection, Ghost Bird contemplated it. What did *she* miss? There had been so little time to miss anything. Their conversation existed so apart from her that she wondered again what she might do when she met the Crawler. What if she was a sleeper cell for a cause much older than either the Southern Reach or Area X? Did her allegiance lie with the former director, or the director as a child, playing on those black rocks near the lighthouse? And what master did the lighthouse keeper serve? It would have been better if she could have thought of each person in the equation as just one thing, but none of them were that simple.

Perhaps the biologist's final response was the only response that mattered, and her entire letter a sop to expectations, to the reaction human beings were hardwired to have. A kind of final delay before she had come to embody that correct answer? Perhaps so many journals had piled up in the lighthouse because on some level most came, in time, to recognize the futility of language. Not just in Area X but against the rightness of the lived-in moment, the instant of touch, of connection, for which words were such a sorrowful disappointment, so inadequate an expression of both the finite and the infinite. Even as the Crawler wrote out its terrible message.

Back on the island, there had been one last, unanswerable question, and the weight of it had settled over each of them in different ways. If they now traversed a landscape transplanted from somewhere far remote, then what existed within the coordinates of the *real* Area X, back on Earth?

Grace had put forward the idea, had clearly been thinking about it, possibly for years now, haunted and frustrated by it.

"We are," Control had replied—distant, coming to her from afar with an unfocused stare. "We are. That's where we are." Although he wasn't stupid, must know Grace was right.

"If you go through the door, you come to Area X," Grace said. "If you walk across the border, you go to the other place. Whatever it is."

Grace's tone did not admit to doubt, or that she cared whether they believed her or not, an essential indifference to questions, as if Area X had worn her down. A pragmatism that meant she knew the conclusions she had reached would please no one.

But Ghost Bird knew what she had seen in the corridor leading into Area X, the detritus and trash she had seen there, the bodies, and wondered if it might be real and not summoned from her mind. Wondered what might have come through the twenty-foot door that Control had described to her, the door lost to them. What might still come through such a door? And her thought: Nothing, because if so, it would have happened long ago.

The marsh lakes had become such a deep, perfect blue in that uncertain light that the reflections of the surrounding scrub forest on that surface seemed as real as their root-bound doppelgängers. Their mud-encrusted boots churned up amid the rich sediment and plant roots a smell almost like crisp hay.

Control leaned against Ghost Bird more than once to keep his balance, almost pulling her down in the process. Ahead of them now came the smell of burning, and from above, something the others could not see stitched its way through the overcast sky, and Ghost Bird was not surprised.

0017: THE DIRECTOR

One spring day at the Southern Reach, you're taking a break, pacing across the courtyard tiles as you worry at a problem in your head, and you see something strange out by the swamp lake. At the edge of the black water, a figure squats, hunched over, hands you cannot see busy at some mysterious task. Your first impulse is to call security, but then you recognize the slight frame, the tuft of dark hair: It's Whitby, in his brown blazer, his navy slacks, his dress shoes.

Whitby, playing in the mud. Washing something? Strangling something? The level of concentration he displays, even at this distance, is of working on something that requires a jeweler's precision.

Instinct tells you to be silent, to walk slow, to take care with fallen branches and dead leaves. Whitby has been startled enough in the past, by the past, and you want your presence known by degrees. Halfway there, though, he turns long enough to acknowledge you and go back to what he's doing, and you walk faster after that.

The trees are as sullen as ever, looking like hunched-over priests with long beards of moss, or as Grace says, less respectfully, "Like a line of used-up old drug addicts." The water carries only the small, patient ripples made by Whitby, and your reflection as you come close and lean over his shoulder is distorted by widening rings and wavery gray light.

Whitby is washing a small brown mouse.

He holds the mouse, careful but firm, between the thumb and index finger of his left hand, the mouse's head and front legs circled by this fleshy restraint, the pale belly, back legs, and tail splayed out across his palm. The mouse seems hypnotized or for some other reason preternaturally calm while Whitby with his cupped right hand ladles water onto the mouse, then extends his little finger and rubs the water into the fur of the underbelly, the sides, then the furry cheeks, followed by anointment of the top of the head.

Whitby has draped a little white towel across his left forearm; it is mono-grammed with a large cursive W in gold thread. Brought from home? He pinches the towel from his forearm and, using a single corner, delicately daubs the top of the mouse's head while its tiny black eyes stare off into the distance. There's a kind of febrile extremity of care here, as Whitby proceeds to wipe off one pink-clawed paw and then the other, before moving to the back paws and the thin tail. Whitby's hand is so pale and small that there is a sort of symmetry on display, an absurd yet somehow touching suggestion of a shared ancestry.

It has been four months since the last member of the last eleventh expedition died of cancer, six weeks since you had them exhumed. It has been more than two years since you came back across the border with Whitby. Over the past seven or eight months, you have had a sense of Whitby recovering—fewer trans-fer requests, more engagement in status meetings, a revival of self-interest in his "combined theories document," which he now calls "a thesis on terroir," evoking a "comprehensive ecosystem" approach based on an advanced theory of wine pro-duction. There has been nothing in the execution of his duties to indicate any-thing more than his usual eccentricity. Even Cheney has, grudgingly, admitted this, and you don't care that the man often uses Whitby as a wedge against you now. You don't care about reasons so long as it brings Whitby back closer to the center of things.

"What do you have there, Whitby?" Breaking the silence is sudden and intru-sive. Nothing you say will sound like anything other than an adult talking to a child, but Whitby's put you in that position.

Whitby stops washing and drying the mouse, throws the towel over his left shoulder, stares at the mouse, examining it as if there might still be a spot of dirt here or there.

"A mouse," he says, as if it should be obvious.

"Where did you find her?"

"*Him.* In the attic. I found him in the attic." His tone like someone about to be reprimanded, but defiant, too.

"Oh—at home?" Bringing the safety of home to the dangerous place, the workplace, in physical form. You're trying to suppress the psychologist in you, not overanalyze, but it's difficult.

"In the attic."

"Why did you bring him out here?"

"To wash him."

You don't mean for it to seem like an interrogation, but you're sure it does. Is this a bad thing or a good thing in the progression of Whitby's recovery? There is no base score assigned to owning a mouse or washing a mouse that can confer an automatic rating of fit or unfit for duty.

"You couldn't wash him inside?"

Whitby gives you an upturned sideways glance. You're still stooping. He's still hunched. "That water's contaminated."

"Contaminated." An interesting choice of words. "But you use it, don't you?"

"Yes, I do . . ." Relenting, giving in a little, relaxing so that you're less concerned he's going to strangle the mouse by accident. "But I thought maybe he'd like to be outside for a while. It's a nice day."

Translation: Whitby needed a break. Just like you needed a break, pacing the courtyard tiles.

"What's his name?"

"He doesn't have a name."

"He doesn't have a name?"

"No."

Somehow this bothers you more than the washing, but it's an unease you can't put into words. "Well, he's a handsome mouse." Which sounds stupid even as you say it, but you're at a loss.

"Don't talk to me like I'm an idiot," he says. "I'm aware this looks strange, but think about some of the things you do for stress."

You'd gone across the border with this man. You'd sacrificed his peace of mind on the altar of your insatiable fascination, your curiosity, and your ambition. He doesn't deserve condescension on top of that.

"Sorry." You awkwardly lower yourself in the dead leaves and half-dried mud next to him. The truth is you don't want to go back inside yet, and Whitby doesn't seem to want to, either. "The only excuse I've got is that it's been a long day. Already."

"It's okay," Whitby says after a pause, and returns to cleaning his mouse. Then volunteers, "I've had him about five weeks. I had a dog and a cat growing up, but no pets since."

You've tried to imagine what Whitby's house looks like, and failed. You can only imagine an endless white space with white, modern furniture, and a computer screen in the corner as the only spot of color. Which probably means

Whitby's house is an opulent, decadent free-for-all of styles and periods, all offered up in bright, saturated colors.

"The plant bloomed," Whitby says into the middle of your musings.

The sentence has no meaning at first. But when it takes on meaning, you sit up straighter.

Whitby looks over at you. "There's no emergency. It's already over."

You're quelling the impulse to pull Whitby to his feet and march him back inside to show you what *no emergency* means.

"Explain," you say, putting just enough pressure on the word to hold it there like an egg about to crack. "Be specific."

"It happened in the middle of the night. Last night," he says. "Everyone else had left. I work very late sometimes, and I like to spend time in the storage cathedral." He looks away, continues as if you've asked him something: "I just like it in there. It calms me down."

"And?"

"And last night, I came in and I just decided to check on the plant"—said too casually, as if he always checked on the plant—"and there was a flower. The plant was blooming. But it's gone now. It all happened very fast."

It's important to just keep talking, to keep Whitby calm and answering your questions.

"How long?"

"Maybe an hour. If I had thought it would disintegrate, I would have called someone."

"What did the blossom look like?"

"Like an ordinary flower, with seven or eight petals. Translucent, almost white."

"Did you take any photographs? Any video?"

"No," he says. "I thought it would still be there for a while. I didn't tell anyone because it's gone." Or because, with no evidence, it would be more evidence against *him*, against his state of mind, his suitability, when he is just now getting out from under that reputation.

"What did you do then?"

He shrugs, the mouse's tail twitching, as he transfers the animal to his right hand. "I scheduled a purification. Just to be sure. And I left."

"You were in a suit the whole time, right?"

"Sure. Yes. Of course."

"No strange readings after?"

"No, no strange readings. I checked."

"And nothing else I need to know?" Like, the possible connection between the plant having bloomed and Whitby, the next day, coming out here with his mouse.

"Nothing you don't already know."

A shade defiant again, a lifting of his gaze to tell you he's thinking about the trip into Area X, the one he can't tell anyone about, the one that made him unreliable to the rest of the staff. How to evaluate hallucinations that might be real? A paranoia that might be justified? Right after you came back, you remember Whitby saying wistfully to himself, as if something had been lost, "They didn't notice us at first. But, then, gradually, they began to peer in at us . . . because we just couldn't stop."

You get to your feet, look down at Whitby, say, "Give me a more extensive report on the plant—for my eyes only. And you cannot keep sneaking a mouse into the building, Whitby. For one thing, security will catch you eventually. Take it home."

Whitby and the mouse are both looking up at you now, Whitby harder to read than the mouse, which just wants to get out of Whitby's grasp and be on its way.

"I'll keep him in the attic," Whitby says.

"Do that."

Back inside, you visit the storage cathedral, putting on a purification suit so you don't contaminate that environment or it doesn't contaminate you. You find the plant, which has a false tag that designates it as belonging to the first eighth expedition. You examine the plant, the area around it, the floor, searching for any evidence of a dried-up flower. You find none, just a residue beside it that later comes back from testing as pine resin from some other sample that had sat there previously.

You look at those test results in your office and you wonder if the plant had only blossomed in Whitby's mind, and, if so, what that meant. Wonder for a good long while, before the thought becomes buried in the memos and the meeting minutes and the phone calls and a million minor emergencies. Should you ask Whitby if the mouse came with him into the storage cathedral? Perhaps. But what you do instead is put the immortal plant under round-the-clock surveillance, even though both Cheney and Grace give you grief about it.

Whitby just needs a companion. Whitby needs someone who won't judge or interrogate him, someone or something that depends on him. And as long as Whitby keeps the creature at home, in the attic, you won't tell anyone about the breach—have recognized by now that just as Lowry's tethered to you, you're chained to Whitby.

Playing pool with the Realtor and the veteran on an expedition to the Star Lanes a week later, you're listening to the Realtor describe some couple that had been squatting in a model home and refused to give her their names when you think again about Whitby not naming the mouse. As if he'd been following Southern Reach protocol for expeditions.

"They thought that so long as I didn't know their names, I couldn't call the police. Peering out from behind the curtains like ghosts. There was so much fail in that, not that I felt good about kicking them out. Except I have to sell the place—I'm not running a charity. I give to charities, sure, but why do they have homeless shelters anyway? And if I let them stay then someone else might get the same idea. Turns out the police had a file on them, so I made the right decision."

Waiting there back on your desk at the Southern Reach you already have the files of candidates for a twelfth expedition. Right on top is the most promising, to your mind: an antisocial biologist whose husband went on the last eleventh.

0018: THE LIGHTHOUSE KEEPER

Secured the lighthouse. Worked on the [illegible]. Fixed things. And shall cast them into a furnace of fire: there shall be wailing and gnashing of teeth. Came then the crying call of a curlew, and at dawn, too, I heard the hooting of an owl, the yap of foxes. Just a little ways up from the lighthouse, where I strayed for a bit, a bear cub poked its head out of the underbrush, looking around like any child might. And the hand of the sinner shall rejoice, for there is no sin in shadow or in light that the seeds of the dead cannot forgive.

By the time Saul made it to the village bar, everyone had already crammed inside, anticipating music by a few locals who called themselves the Monkey's Elbow. The deck, with its great view of the darkening ocean, was empty—it was too cold, for one thing—and he hurried inside with anticipation. He'd felt better with each day since the hallucination on the beach, and no one from the Light Brigade had returned to plague him. His temperature had receded, along with the pressure in his head, and with it the urge to burden Charlie with his problems. He hadn't dreamed for three nights. Even his hearing was fine, the moment his ears had popped like getting a jolt to his system: more energetic in every way. So everything seemed normal, as if he'd worried over nothing— and all he missed was the familiar sight of Gloria coming down the beach toward the lighthouse, or climbing on the rocks, or loitering near the shed.

Charlie had even promised to meet him at the bar for a short while before he went out night fishing again; despite the rough schedule, he seemed happy to be making money, but they'd hardly seen each other in several days.

Old Jim, with his ruddy beacon of a face and fuzzy white mutton-chop side-burns, had commandeered the rickety upright piano in the far corner of the main room. Monkey's Elbow was warming up around him, a discordant ramble of violin, accordion, acoustic guitar, and tambourine. The piano, a sea salvage, had been restored to its former undrowned glory—mother-of-pearl inlay preserved on the lid—but still retained a wheezy-tinny tone from its baptism, "sagging and soggy" on some of the keys, according to Old Jim.

The place smelled comfortingly of cigarettes and greasy fried fish, and some underlying hint of too-sweet honey. The oysters were fresh-caught, and the beers, served out of a cooler, were cheap. Saul always forgot the downside real quick. There was good cheer to be found here, if sometimes grudgingly given. Any prayers he offered up came from knowing that no health inspector had ever journeyed to the tiny kitchen or the grill out back where the seagulls gathered with irrepressible hope.

Charlie was already there, had gotten them a little round table with two stools that hugged the wall opposite the piano. Saul pushed through the press of bodies—maybe sixty people, practically a mob by forgotten-coast standards—and gave Charlie a squeeze of the shoulder before sitting.

"Hello there, stranger," Saul said, making it sound like an even worse pickup line than it would've been.

"Someone's in a better mood, jack," Charlie said. Then caught himself. "I mean—"

"I don't know any jack, unless you mean jack shit," Saul said. "No, I know what you mean. And I am. I feel a lot better." First evidence from Charlie that he had been dragged down by Saul's condition, which just deepened his affection for Charlie. He'd not complained once during all of Saul's moaning about his lethargy and symptoms, had only tried to help. Maybe they could get back to normal, once this night-fishing expedition came to its end.

"Good, good," Charlie said, smiling and looking around, still a little extra stutter-step of awkwardness from him when out in public.

"How was the fishing yesterday?" Charlie'd said something about a good catch, but they hadn't talked long.

"Best haul so far," Charlie said, his face lit up. "A lot of skates and rays and flounder. Some mullet and bass." Charlie got paid a flat rate per hour, but a bonus for catches over a certain weight.

"Anything odd?" A question Saul always asked. He liked hearing about strange sea creatures. Lately, thinking about what Henry had said, he took a special interest in the answer.

"Only a couple of things. Threw them both back 'cause they were so ugly. Some weird fish and a kind of sea squirt that looked like it was spewing blood."

"Fair enough."

"You look a lot better, you know. Calm at the lighthouse?" Which was Charlie's way of saying "Tell me why on the phone you said 'not a lot of fun around here recently.'"

Saul was about to launch into the story of his final confrontation with Henry and the Light Brigade when the piano cut off and Old Jim got up and introduced Monkey's Elbow, even though everybody already knew them. The band members were Sadi Dawkins, Betsey Pepine, and his erstwhile lighthouse volunteer, Brad. They all worked at the village bar on and off. Trudi, Gloria's mother, was on tambourine, the guest spot. Saul's turn would come someday.

Monkey's Elbow lurched into some sad thick song, the sea's bounty on display in its lyrics, and two ill-fated lovers, and a tragic hill overlooking a secret cove. The usual, but not so much chantey as influenced by what Charlie called "sand-encrusted sea-hippies," who had popularized a laid-back listener-friendly kind of folk-pop. Saul liked it live, even if Brad tended to ham it up a bit. But Charlie stared at his drink with a kind of pursed-lipped frown, then rolled his eyes secretively at Saul, while Saul shook his head in mock disapproval. Sure, they weren't great, but any performance took guts. He used to throw up before sermons, which might've been a sign from God, now that he thought about it. The worst nights, Saul had done push-ups beforehand and jumping jacks to sweat out the fear of performance.

Charlie leaned in, and Saul met him halfway. Charlie said in his ear, "You know that fire on the island?"

"Yeah?"

"A friend of mine was out there fishing that day, and he saw bonfires. People burning papers, for hours, like you said. But when he came back around, they'd loaded a bunch of boxes into motorboats. You want to know where those boats headed?"

"Out to sea?"

"No. Due west, hugging the coast."

"Interesting." The only thing due west of Failure Island besides mosquito-infested inlets were a couple of small towns and the military base.

Saul sat back, just staring at Charlie, with Charlie nodding at him like "I told you so," although what he meant by that Saul didn't know. Told you they were strange? Told you they were up to no good?

The second song played out more like a traditional folk song, slow and deep, carrying along the baggage of a century or two of prior interpretations. The third was a rollicking but silly number, another original, this time about a crab that lost its shell and was traveling all over the place to find it. A few couples were dancing now. His ministry hadn't been one of those that banned dancing or other "earthly pleasures," but he'd never learned either. Dancing was Saul's secret fantasy, something he thought he'd enjoy but had to file under "too late now." Charlie'd never dance anyway, maybe not even in private.

Sadi came by during a short break between songs. She worked in a bar in Hedley during the summers, and she always had funny stories about the customers, many of them coming off the river walk "drunk as a skunk." Trudi came over, too, and they talked for a while, although not directly about Gloria. More about Gloria's dad, during which Saul gathered that Gloria and her dad had made it back to his place by now. So that was all right.

Then they mostly just listened, stealing moments between songs to talk or grab another beer. In scanning the room for people he knew, people he might give a nod to, claim a bond with, he'd felt for a while now not like the one watching but the one being watched. He put it down to some receding symptom of his non-condition, or to Charlie's skittishness rubbing off on him. But then, through the murky welter of bodies, the rising tide of loud conversations, the frenetic playing of the band, he spied an unwelcome figure across the room, near the door.

Henry.

He stood perfectly still, watching, without even a drink in his hand. Henry wore that ridiculous silk shirt and pretentious slacks, pressed just so, and yet, curiously, he blended in against the wall, as if he belonged there. No one but Saul seemed to notice him. That Suzanne wasn't with him struck Saul hard for some reason. It made him resist the urge to turn to Charlie and point Henry out to him. "That's the man who broke into my lighthouse a few nights ago."

The whole time Saul stared at Henry, the edges of the room had been growing darker and darker, and the sickly sweet smell intensified, and everyone around Henry grew more and more insubstantial—vague, unknowable silhouettes—and all the light came to Henry and gathered around him, and spilled back out from him.

A kind of vertigo washed over Saul, as if a vast pit had opened up beneath him and he was suspended above it, about to fall. There came back all of the old symptoms he'd thought were gone, as if they'd just been hiding. There was a comet dripping fire through his head, trailing flame down his back.

While the band kept playing through the darkness, their sound curdling into a song sung far too slow, and before they could vanish into a darkly glinting spiral, before everything not-Henry could disappear, Saul gripped the table with both hands and looked away.

The chatter, the rush and realignment of conversations came back, and the light came back, and the band sounded normal again, and Charlie was talking to him like nothing had happened, Saul's sense of relief so palpable the blood within him was rushing too hard and he felt faint.

When, after a stabilizing minute, he dared sneak a glance toward where Henry had stood, the man had vanished and someone else stood in his place. Someone Saul didn't know, who raised his beer to Saul awkwardly so that he realized he'd been staring across the room for too long.

"Did you hear what I said?" Charlie, in a voice loud enough to cut through the band. "Are you okay?" Reaching out to touch Saul's wrist, which meant he was concerned and that Saul had been acting odd. Saul smiled and nodded.

The song ended, and Charlie said, "It wasn't the stuff about the boats and the island, was it? I wasn't trying to worry you."

"No, not that. Nothing like that. I'm fine." Touched, because it was the kind of thing that might've secretly bothered Charlie if their roles had been reversed.

"And you'd tell me if you were feeling sick again."

"Of course I would." Half lying, trying to process what he'd just experienced. And, serious, struck by some form of premonition: "But, Charlie, I hate to say it—you should probably leave now, or you'll be late."

Charlie took that in stride, already half off his stool because he didn't like the music anyway.

"See ya tomorrow sometime, then," Charlie said, giving him a wink and a long last stare that wasn't entirely innocent.

Somehow Charlie looked so good in that moment, putting on his jacket. Saul clasped him tight before he could get away. The weight of the man in his arms. The feel of Charlie's rough shave that he loved so much. The tart surprise of Charlie's lip balm against his cheek. Held him for an extra moment, trying to preserve all of it, as a bulwark against whatever had just happened. Then, too soon, Charlie was gone, out the door, into the night, headed for the boat.

0019: CONTROL

The night was full of white rabbits streaking across the sky, instead of the stars, the moon—and Control knew that was wrong in some fevered part of his mind, some compartment holding out against the inquisitive brightness. Were they white rabbits or were they smudges of black motion rendered as photo negatives impeding his vision? Because he didn't want to see what was there. Because the biologist had unlocked something inside of him, and he returned now sometimes to the phantasmagorical art in Whitby's strange room in the Southern Reach, and then to his theory that to disappear into the border was to enter some purgatory where you would find every lost and forgotten thing: all of the rabbits herded across that invisible barrier, every beached destroyer and truck from the night Area X had been created. The missing in action from the expeditions. The thought a kind of annihilating abyss. Yet there was also the light blossoming from the place below the Crawler, detailed in the biologist's journal account. Where led that light?

Trying to pick out from all of those pieces what might be a reasonable, even an honorable, choice. One that his father would have agreed with; he no longer thought much of his mother, or what she might think.

Maybe I just wanted to be left alone. To remain in the little house on the hill in Hedley, with his cat Chorry and the chittering bats at night, not so far from where he had grown up, even if now so distant.

"It wouldn't have made a difference, Grace."

The three of them sleeping on the pine moss, the moist grass, less than a mile from the topographical anomaly, their final approach planned for the morning.

"What wouldn't?" Gentle, perhaps even kind. Which let him know the full manifestation of his distress. Kept seeing the biologist's many eyes, which became stars, which became the leaping white lights. Which became a chessboard with his father's last move frozen there. Along with Control's own last move, still forthcoming.

"If you had told me everything. Back at the Southern Reach."

"No. It wouldn't have."

Ghost Bird slept beside him, and this, too, helped him chart his decline. She slept at his back, guarding him, and with her arms wrapped tight around him. He was secure there, safe, and he loved her more for allowing that now, when she had less and less reason to. Or no reason at all.

The night had turned chilly and deep, and crowded at the edges with creatures staring in at them, just dark shapes silent and motionless. But he didn't mind them.

Things his dad had said to him stuck with him more clearly now, because they must've happened. His dad was saying to him, "If you don't know your passion, it confuses your mind, not your heart." In a moment of honesty after he had failed in the field and he could only talk to his dad in riddles about it, never tell him the truth: "Sometimes you need to know when to go on to the next thing—for the sake of other people."

The chill in that. The next thing. What was his next thing here? What was his passion? He didn't know the answer to either question, knew only that there was comfort in the scratchiness of the pine needles against his face and the sleep-drenched, smoky smell of the dirt beneath him.

Morning came, and he huddled in Ghost Bird's arms until she stirred, disengaged from him in a way that felt too final. Among the reeds, endless marsh, and mud, there came a suggestion on the horizon of burning, and a popping and rattling that could've been gunfire or some lingering memory of past conflict playing out in his head.

Yet still the blue heron in the estuary stalked tadpoles and tiny fish, the black vulture soared on the thermals high above. There came a thousand rustlings among the islands of trees. Behind them, on the horizon, the lighthouse could be seen, might always be seen, even through the fog that came with the dawn, here noncommittal and diffuse, there thick, rising like a natural defense where needed, a test and blessing against that landscape. To appreciate any of this was Ghost Bird's gift to him, as if it had seeped into him through her touch.

But the unnatural world intruded, as it always did, so long as will and purpose existed, and for a moment he resented that. Ghost Bird and Grace were debating what to do if they encountered any remnants of the border commander's troops. Debating what to do when they reached the tower.

"You and I go down," Grace said. "And Control can guard the entrance." This last stand, this hopeless task.

"I should go down alone," Ghost Bird said, "and you should both stand guard above."

"That would be against expedition protocols," Grace said.

"That's what you want to invoke here? Now?"

"What's left to invoke?" Grace asked.

"I go down alone," Ghost Bird said, and Grace gave her no answer.

Tactical not strategic, a phrase rising out of his back catalog of favorites. It seemed as obsolete as any of the rest, like the enormous frame of an old-fashioned bicycle.

He kept glancing up at that murky sky, waiting for the heavens to fall away and reveal their true position. But the mimicry remained in place, most convincing. What if the biologist had been wrong? What if the biologist in her writings had been a calmly raving lunatic? And then just a monster? What then?

They broke camp, used a stand of swamp trees as initial cover and surveyed the marsh, stared across the water of the estuaries. The smoke now billowed up at a sharp sixty-degree angle to add its own ash-silver roiling to the fog and form a heavier, weighted blankness. This alliance obscured the last of the blue sky and accentuated the crackling line of fire at the horizon parallel to them: waves of orange thrust upward from golden centers.

The pewter stillness of the channel of water in the foreground reflected the lines of the flames and the billowing of the smoke—reflected the nearest reeds, too, and doubled by reflection also the island that at its highest point showcased island oaks and palmetto trees, their trunks white lines lost in patches of fog.

There came shouting and screaming and gunfire—all too near, all from the island of trees, or, perhaps, something Lowry had placed in his head. Something that had happened here long ago only now coming to the surface. Control kept his eyes on the reflection, where men and women in military uniforms attacked one another while some impossible thing watched from the watery sky. At such a remove, distorted, it did not seem so harsh, so visceral.

"They are already somewhere else," Control said, although he knew Grace and Ghost Bird wouldn't understand. They were already in the reflection, through which an alligator now swam. Where swooped through the trees, oblivious, a flicker.

So they continued on, him with his sickness that he no longer wanted diagnosed, Grace with her limp, and Ghost Bird keeping her own counsel.

There was nothing to be done, and no reason to: their path would skirt the fire.

In Control's imagination, the entrance to the topographical anomaly was enormous, mixed with the biologist's vast bulk in his thoughts so that he had expected a kind of immense ziggurat upside down in the earth. But no, it was what it had always been: a little over sixty feet in diameter, circular, located in the middle of a small clearing. The entrance lay there open for them, as it had for so many others. No soldiers here, nothing more unusual than the thing itself.

On the threshold, he told them what would happen next. There was in his voice only the shadow of the authority of a director of the Southern Reach, but within that shadow a kind of resistance.

"Grace, you will stay here at the top, standing guard with the rifles. There are any number of dangers, and we do not want to be trapped down there. Ghost Bird, you will come with me, and you will lead the way. I'll follow at a little distance behind you. Grace, if we are down there longer than three hours"—the maximum time recorded by prior expeditions—"you are released of any responsibility for us." Because if there were a world to return to, the person to survive should be someone with something to return to.

They stared at him. They stared, and he thought they would object, would override him, and then he would be lost. Would be left out here, at the top.

But that moment never came and an almost debilitating relief settled over him as Grace nodded and said to be careful, rattled off advice he barely heard.

Ghost Bird stood off to the side, a curious expression on her face. Down there, she would experience the ultimate doubling of experience with the biologist, and he couldn't protect her from that.

"Whatever you have in your head now, hold on to it," Grace said. "Because there may be nothing left of it when you go down below."

What was coiled within his head, and how would it affect the outcome? Because his goal was not to reach the Crawler. Because he wondered what else might lie within the brightness that had come with him.

They descended into the tower.

0020: THE DIRECTOR

Whitby's worthless report on the blossom is on your desk by the time you go off to another pre-expedition interview of the biologist, the possible candidates for the twelfth whittled down to ten, and you and Grace, you and Lowry, pushing for your favorites, with members of the science department shadowboxing in the background as they whisper their own choices at you. Severance seems terminally uninterested in the question.

It's not a good time to interview anyone but you don't have a choice. The plant is blossoming again in your mind as you conduct the interview in a cramped little office in the biologist's town—a place you've borrowed and can pretend is your own, with all of the appropriate psychological and psychiatric texts on the bookshelves. The diplomas and family pictures of the room's true occupant have been removed. In a concession to Lowry, for his studies, you've allowed his people to swap out chairs, light fixtures, and other elements of the room, as if in redecorating and changing the color scheme from placid blues and greens to red, orange, and gray or silver there's some answer to a larger question.

Lowry claims his arrangements and recombinations can have a "subliminal or instinctual" effect on the candidates.

"To make them feel secure and at ease?" you asked, a rare moment of poking the beast with a stick, but he ignored you, and in your head he was saying, "To make them do what we want."

There's the smell of water damage still, from a burst pipe in the basement. There's a water stain in the corner, hidden by a little table, as if you need to cover up some crime. The only giveaway that it's not your office: you're cramped, stuffed into your chair.

The plant is blossoming in your mind, and each time it does there's less time to work with, less you can do. Is the plant a challenge or an invitation or a worthless distraction? A message? And if so, what did it mean, assuming Whitby didn't imagine it? The light at the bottom of a topographical anomaly, from a door into Area X, on the tarot card used by the Séance & Science Brigade. The blossoming light of an MRI body scan, the one you endured last week.

In the middle of all that blossoming in your brain, the kind of thing that would elicit a joke from Grace if only you could tell her, there, bestriding the world: the biologist, a talisman arriving just as everything is closing in again and your time has become more limited.

"State your name for the record."

"I did that last time."

"Nevertheless."

The biologist looks at you like you're an opponent, not the person who can send her where she so obviously wants to go. You note again not just the musculature of this woman but the fact that she's willing to complicate even the simple business of stating her name. That she has a kind of self-possession that comes not just from knowing who she is but from knowing that, if it comes down to it, she needs no one. Some professionals might diagnose that as a disorder, but in the biologist it comes across as an absolute and unbending clarity.

"Tell me about your parents."

"What are your earliest memories?"

"Did you have a happy childhood?"

All of the usual, boring questions, and her terse answers boring, too, in a way. But, after that, the more interesting ones.

"Do you ever have violent thoughts or tendencies?" you ask.

"What do you consider a violent act?" she replies. An attempt to evade, or genuine interest? You'd bet on the former.

"Harm toward other people or animals. Extreme property damage, like arson." The Realtor at Star Lanes has dozens of stories about violence against houses, relates them all with an edge to her voice. The biologist would probably classify the Realtor as an alien species.

"People are animals."

"Harm toward animals, then?"

"Only toward human animals."

She's trying to entangle you or provoke you, but the usual cross-referencing and analysis of intel turned up something interesting, something you can't confirm. While a grad student on the West Coast, she had worked as an intern at a forest ranger station in a national park. Her two years there had roughly coincided with a series of what some might call "tree-hugger terrorism." In the worst case, three men had been badly beaten by "an assailant wearing a mask." The motive, according to the police: "The victims had been tormenting an injured owl by poking at it with a stick and trying to light its wing on fire." No suspect had ever been identified, no arrest made.

"What would you do if your fellow expedition members exhibited violent tendencies?"

"Whatever I had to."

"Would that include killing someone?"

"If it came down to that, I would have to."

"Even if it was me?"

"Especially if it was you. Because these questions are so tedious."

"More tedious than your job working with plastics?"

That sobers her up. "I don't plan on killing anyone. I've never killed anyone. I plan on taking samples. I plan on learning as much as I can and circumventing anyone who doesn't follow the mission parameters." That hard edge again, the shoulder turned in toward you, to block you out. If this were a boxing match, the shoulder would be followed by an uppercut or body shot.

"And what if you turn out to be the threat?"

The biologist laughs at that question, and gives you a stare so direct you have to look away.

"If I'm the threat, then I won't be able to stop myself, will I? If I'm the threat, then I guess Area X has won."

"What about your husband?"

"What about my husband? He's dead."

"Do you hope to find out what happened to him in Area X?"

"I hope to find Area X in Area X. I hope to be of use."

"Isn't that heartless?"

She leans forward, fixes you again with that gaze, and it's a struggle to maintain your composure. But that's okay—antagonism is okay. In fact, anything helps you that helps her reject whatever traces of corruption you might have picked up, that might have adhered to you all unknowing.

She says, "It's a fallacy for you, a total stranger, to project onto me the motives and emotions you think are appropriate. To think you can get inside my head."

You can't share with her that the other candidates have been easy to read. The surveyor will be the meat-and-potatoes backbone of the expedition, without a trace of passive-aggressiveness. The anthropologist will provide empathy and nuance, although you're not sure whether her need to prove herself is a plus or a minus. She'll push herself further, harder because of that, but what will Area X think of that? The linguist talks too much, has too little introspection, but is a recruit from within the Southern Reach and has demonstrated absolute loyalty on more than one occasion. Lowry's favorite, with all that entails.

Before the interview, you met with Whitby, who had rallied for this discussion, in your office, amid the increasing clutter. It was the biologist you talked about the most, the importance of keeping her paranoid and isolated and antisocial, how there's a shift in the biochemistry of the brain, naturally arrived at, that might be what Lowry's secret experiments are trying to induce artificially— and since her husband has already gone to Area X, "been read by it," this represents a unique opportunity "metrics-wise" because of "that connection," because "it's never happened before." That, in a sense, the biologist had forged a relationship with Area X before ever setting foot there. It might lead to what Whitby calls "a terroir precognition."

An expedition into Area X with the biologist would be different than with Whitby. You wouldn't lead, except in the way at the store as a teenager you sometimes walked ahead of your dad so you wouldn't seem to be with him, but always with a look back at him, to see where he was going.

As the questioning continues, you're more and more certain of what you feel in your gut. You are reminded of Area X somehow. The biologist reminds you of being in Area X.

The rest of the biologist's file is breathtaking in its focus, its narrowness, and yet fecund despite that. You're driving across the desert with her, in a tiny car, to check out the holes made by burrowing owls. You're lost on a plateau above an untouched coastline, stalked by a cougar, a place where the grass is the color of gold and reaches up to your knees and the trees are blackened by fire, silver-gray with ash. You're hiking up a mountain in scrubland, up huge blocks of stone, every muscle in your legs protesting even as you're possessed by a wild giddiness that keeps you moving past exhaustion. You're back with her during her first year of college, when she made a rare confession to a roommate that she wanted isolation and moved out the next day to her own apartment and walked the five miles from campus home in utter silence, receiving the world through a hole in her shoe.

You're certain you'll have to give up something to Lowry to keep him away from the biologist, but whatever the price you'll pay it, you decide as you order a whiskey for a change at the bar at Chipper's—order a whiskey for everyone at the bar, for a change, all four of them. Because it's late, because it's a weekday, because Chipper's is getting long in the tooth and the clientele is getting older and older. Like you. The doctor's told you cancer has blossomed in your ovaries and it's going to spread to your liver before you can even blink, even get used to the idea. Another thing no one needs to know.

"And before we could even think about selling that house," the Realtor's telling you, "we had to pull ten layers of wallpaper off. All this woman had done for a decade was keep re-wallpapering her house. It was a hell of a lot of wallpaper, and garish, like she was putting up warning signals. Wrapping her house from the inside out. I tell you, I've never seen that before."

You nod, smiling, with nothing to add, nothing to say, but happy to listen. Terminally interested.

It's plain old normal cancer, nothing like the accelerated all-out assault experienced by the last eleventh. It's just plain old life catching up with you, trying to kill you, and you can either take the aggressive chemo and leave the Southern Reach and die anyway, or you can hang on long enough to join the twelfth expedition and, with the biologist by your side, go across the border one last time. You've kept secrets before. What's one final one?

Besides, other, more interesting, secrets are opening up, because Grace has finally found something on Jackie Severance. There's been plenty of dirt, including the scandal involving her son—a blown assignment that resulted in a woman's death—but nothing until now that made any real difference. On a top secret list, not of Jackie's open case files but Jack's closed ones, which makes sense because Jack is a little easier: He's retired, in his early seventies, and some of what he worked on exists only in paper form.

"Look at the fifth line item," Grace says, up on the rooftop, after a quick sweep for bugs. You've never found any there, but it's worth being cautious.

The line reads:

Payment request—SB, Project Serum Bliss

"Is there more?" It's not quite what you expected, but you think you know what it is.

"No, that's the only one. There might be more, but the rest of the files from the period are missing. This page wasn't even supposed to be there."

"What do you think 'Serum Bliss' means?"

"Protocol back then would've meant it wasn't supposed to mean anything. Probably generated at random."

"It's flimsy," you say. "That's not even 'S&SB.'"

"It's fucking rice paper," Grace says. "It might mean nothing, but . . ."

But if, somehow, the S&SB was on Central's payroll—even just a little bit, a side project—and Jack ran the operation, and Jackie knew about it, and the S&SB had anything at all to do with the creation of Area X . . .

A lot of ifs. A lot of leaps. A lot more research on Grace's plate.

Yet it's enough for you to begin to have an idea of why Lowry's new ally is Jackie Severance.

0021: THE LIGHTHOUSE KEEPER

. . . went back to the garden, [illegible], and kept the ax with me just in case. Unlikely, with black bears, but not unknown. Scrub jay, catbird, house sparrow, most humble of God's creatures. I sat there and fed it bread crumbs, for it was a scrawny thing and in need. I shall bring them forth, they said . . .

S aul stayed on to the bitter end at the village bar, not sure if it was because he wanted to test Brad's resolve or because he didn't want to walk outside only to encounter Henry. Or because he was sad Charlie'd had to leave.

So he knocked back a couple more beers, put down the way the room swayed to the booze, and ordered some oysters and fish-and-chips. He had a hunger in him that was rare. Food didn't interest him that much, but tonight he felt ravenous. The oysters were served in their own salt water, newly shucked and steamed, and he didn't bother dipping them in sauce but just gulped them down. Then he tore into the fish, which came away in thick flakes in his hands, the heat rising along with the saliva-inducing smell of the grease. The wedge fries he drowned in ketchup and they soon joined the fish. He was frantic at his feast, aware he was gobbling, stuffing his face, his hands moving at a frenzied, unnatural pace, but he couldn't stop.

He ordered another fish-and-chips. He ordered another round of oysters. Another beer.

After the last set, the musicians stuck around, but most of the others left, including Trudi. The black sea and sky outside the window peered in against the glass, smudged faces and the bottles of booze behind the bar reflected back at Saul. Now that it was just Old Jim at the piano, with the other musicians goofing around, and so few people he could just about hear the pulse of the sea again, could recognize it as a subtle message in the background. Or something was pulsing in his head. His sense of smell had intensified, the rotting sweetness that must be coming from the kitchen was like a perfume being sprayed in clouds throughout the room. A stitching beat beneath the striking of the piano keys twinned itself to the pulse.

Mundane details struck him as momentous. The worm of gray-white ash curling out of an ashtray on the table next to him, the individual flakes still fluming, fluttering, and at the buried core a pinprick of throbbing red that pulsed at him like a brake light. Beside the ash, the smudge of an old greasy thumbprint, immortalized by the gunk that had collected on the ashtray from hundreds of cigarette immolations. Beside the thumbprint, an attempt to etch something into the side of the ashtray, an effort that had ended after J and A.

The piano playing became discordant, or was he just hearing it better . . . or worse? On his stool against the wall, beer in hand, he contemplated that. Contemplated the way people's voices were getting confused, as if they'd become mixed up, and the thrum rising under his skin, the thrum and hum and the ringing in his ears. It felt like something was coming toward him from very far away—toward and into him. His throat was dry and chalky. His beer tasted funny. He put it down, looked around the room.

Old Jim couldn't stop playing the piano, although he did it so badly, fingers too hard against the keys, the keys smudged with his red blood as he now began to roar out a song Saul had never heard before, with lyrics that were incomprehensible. The other musicians, most of them seated around Old Jim, let their instruments fall from slack hands, and stared at one another as if shocked by something. What were they shocked by? Sadi was weeping and Brad was saying, "Why would you do that? Why in the hell would you be doing that?" But Brad's voice was coming out of Sadi's body, and blood was dripping out of Brad's left ear, and the people slumped at the bar proper . . . had they been slumped that way a moment before? Were they drunk or dead?

Old Jim erupted out of his seat to stand, still playing. He was reaching a chaotic crescendo on his shouting, shrieking, yowling song, his fingers destroyed joint by joint as blood smashed out from the piano onto his lap and down onto the floor.

Something was hovering above Saul. Something was emanating out of him, was broadcasting through him, on frequencies too high to hear.

"What are you doing to me?"

"Why are you staring at me?"

"Stop doing that."

"I'm not doing anything."

Someone was crawling across the floor, or pulling themselves across the floor because their legs didn't work. Someone was bashing their head against the dark glass near the front door. Sadi spun and twitched and twisted on the floor, slamming into chairs and table legs, beginning to come to pieces.

Outside, utter night reigned. There was no light. There was no light. Saul got up. Saul walked to the door, the spray of Old Jim's incomprehensible song less a roar than a trickling scream.

What lay beyond the door he did not know, mistrusted the utter darkness as much as what lay behind him, but he could not stay there in the bar, whether it was all real or something he was hallucinating. He had to leave.

He turned the knob, went out into the cooling nighttime air of the parking lot.

Everything was in its rightful place, as normal as it could be, with no one in sight. But everything behind him, in there, was awry, wrong, too irrevocable to be fixed by anyone. The din had become worse, and now others were screaming, too, making sounds not capable of being made by human mouths. He managed to find his pickup truck. He managed to get his key in the ignition, put it in reverse, then drive out of the parking lot. The sanctuary of the lighthouse was only half a mile away.

He did not look in his rearview mirror, did not want to see anything that might spill out into the night. The stars were so distant and yet so close in the dark sky above.

0022: GHOST BIRD

During much of the descent, the strong feeling of a return to what was already known came to Ghost Bird, even if experienced by another—a memory of drowning, of endless drowning and, at the remove of those unreliable words from the biologist's journal, the end of what she had encountered, what she had suffered, what she had recovered. And Ghost Bird wanted none of it—didn't want Control, either, following behind. He wasn't suited for this, had not been meant to experience this. You couldn't martyr yourself to Area X; you could only disappear trying, and not even be sure of that.

If the biologist had not leaned in to stare at those words so long ago, the doppelgänger might not exist in this way: full of memories and sneaking down into the depths. She might have returned with a mind wiped clean, her difference not expressed through her role as the mirror of the biologist but instead as a function of the right time or the wrong place, the right place or the wrong time.

Such strange comfort: that the words on the wall were the same, the method of their expression the same, if now she might interpret it as a nostalgic hint of an alien ecosystem, an approach or stance that the Crawler and the tower, in concert, had failed to inflict upon Earth. Because it wasn't viable? Because that was not its purpose—and thus giving them instead these slim signs of where it came from, what it stood for, what it thought?

She had rejected a mask filter, and with it the idea that somehow Area X was only concentrated here, in this cramped space, on these stairs, in the phosphorescent words with which she had become too familiar. Area X was all around them; Area X was contained in no one place or figure. It was the dysfunction in the sky, it was the plant Control had spoken of. It was the heavens and earth. It could interrogate you from any position or no position at all, and you might not even recognize its actions as a form of questioning.

Ghost Bird did not feel powerful as they descended through the luminescent light, hugging the right-hand wall, but she was unafraid.

There came the overlay, in memory and in the moment, of the harsh revolution of a mighty engine or heartbeat, and she knew even Control could hear it, could guess at its identity. From there, they moved swiftly to that point from which there was no real return: the moment when they would see the monster and take its measure. It lay, all too soon, right around the corner.

"I want you to stay here," she said to Control, to John.

"No," he said, as she'd known he would. "No, I won't." An unexpected sweetness in his expression. A kind of weary resolve in the words.

"John Rodriguez, if you come with me, I won't be able to spare you. You'll have to see everything. Your eyes will have to be open."

She could not deny him his name, here, at the end of it all. She could not deny him the right to die if it came to that. There was nothing left to say.

Trailing memory, trailing Control, Ghost Bird descended toward the light.

The Crawler was huge, seemed to rise and keep rising, to spread to the sides until it filled Ghost Bird's vision. There was none of the remembered distortion, no throwing back at her of her own fears or desires. It simply lay revealed before her, so immense, so shockingly concrete.

The surface of its roughly bell-shaped body was translucent but with a strange texture, like sheets of frozen water with fingerlike polyps shining through. Underneath, a second surface slowly *revolved*, and across this centrifuge she could see patterns floating along, as if it had an interior skin, and the material on top of that might be some kind of *soft armor*.

There was a mesmerizing quality to that movement, distant cousin to the director's hypnotism, and she didn't dare let her gaze linger for long.

The Crawler had no discernible features, no discernible face. It moved so slowly as it perfected the letters on the wall that there was a strange impression of the delicate, the mysteries of its locomotion hidden beneath the fringe of flesh that extended to the ground. The left arm, the only arm, located halfway up its body, moved with unfailing precision, constant blurred motion, to create the message on the wall, more like a *wielder* than a *writer*—with a crash of sparks she knew was stray tissue igniting. Its arm was *the agent of the message*, and from that instrument flowed the letters. *Where lies the strangling fruit that came from the hand of the sinner I shall bring forth the seeds of the dead.* If ever it had been human, then that thick-scrawling arm, obscured by loam or moss, was all that was left of its humanity.

Three rings orbited the Crawler, circling clockwise, and at times waves and surges of energy discharged between them, rippled across the Crawler's body. The first ring spun in drunken dreamlike revolutions just below the arm: an irregular row of half-moons. They resembled delicate jellyfish, with feathery white tendrils descending that continually writhed in a wandering search for something never found. The second ring, spinning faster right above the writing arm, resembled a broad belt of tiny black stones grouped close together, but these stones, as they bumped into one another, *gave* with a sponginess that made her think of soft tadpoles and of the creatures that had rained from the sky on the way to the island. What function these entities performed, whether they were part of the Crawler's anatomy or a symbiotic species, she could not fathom. All she knew was that both rings were in their way reassuringly corporeal.

But the third ring, the halolike ring above the Crawler, did not reassure her at all. The swift-moving globes of gold numbered ten to twelve, appeared to be both lighter than air and yet heavier, too. They spun with a ferocious velocity, so that at first she almost could not tell what they were. But she knew that they were dangerous, that words like *defense* and *aggression* might apply.

Perhaps the lighthouse keeper had always been a delusion, a lie written by Area X and conveyed back to the biologist. Yet she distrusted, too, this avatar, this monster costume, this rubber suit meant for a scientist's consumption: so precise, so specific. Or perhaps the truth, for it did not fluctuate in its aspect, morph into other forms.

"Nothing but a horror show," Ghost Bird said to Control, so still and silent behind her, absorbing or being absorbed.

What else was she to do? She stepped forward, into the gravitational field of its orbits. This close, the translucent layer was more like a microscope slide of certain kinds of long, irregularly shaped cells. The patterns beneath, on the second layer, she could almost read, but remained obscured, as if in shallows disturbed by wide ripples.

She reached out a hand, felt a delicate fluttering against her fingers as though encountering a porous layer, a veil.

Was this first contact, or last contact?

ACCEPTANCE

Her touch triggered a response.

The halo far above dissolved to allow one of its constituent parts to peel off like a drooping golden pearl as large as her head—and down it came to a halt in front of her, hovering there to assess her. Reading her, with a kind of warmth that felt like sunburn. Yet still she was not afraid. She would not be afraid. Area X had made her. Area X must have expected her.

Ghost Bird reached out and plucked the golden pearl from the air, held it warm and tender in her hand.

A brilliant gold-green light erupted from the globe and plunged into the heart of her and an icy calm came over her, and through the calm bled a kind of monumental light and in that light she could see all that could be revealed even as Area X peered in at her.

She saw or felt, deep within, the cataclysm like a rain of comets that had annihilated an entire biosphere remote from Earth. Witnessed how one *made* organism had fragmented and dispersed, each minute part undertaking a long and perilous passage through spaces *between*, black and formless, punctuated by sudden light as they came to rest, scattered and lost—emerging only to be buried, inert, in the glass of a lighthouse lens. And how, when brought out of dormancy, the wire tripped, how it had, best as it could, regenerated, begun to perform a vast and preordained function, one compromised by time and context, by the terrible truth that the species that had given Area X its purpose was gone. She saw the membranes of Area X, this machine, this creature, saw the white rabbits leaping into the border, disappearing, and coming out into another place, the leviathans, the ghosts, watching from beyond. All of this in fragments through taste or smell or senses she didn't entirely understand.

While the Crawler continued in its writing as if she did not even exist, the words ablaze with a richer and more meaningful light than she had ever seen, and worlds shone out from them. So many worlds. So much light. That only she could see. Each word a world, a world bleeding through from some other place, a conduit and an entry point, if you only knew how to use them, the coordinates the biologist now used in her far journeying. Each sentence a merciless healing, a ruthless rebuilding that could not be denied.

Should she now say, "Stop!" Should she now plead for people she had never met who lived in her head, who the biologist had known? Should she somehow think that what came next would destroy the planet or save it? In its recognition of her, Ghost Bird knew that something would survive, that she would survive.

What could she do? Nothing. Nor did she want to. There was a choice in not making a choice. She released the sphere, let it hover there in the air.

She sensed Grace on the stairs behind them, sensed that Grace meant harm, and didn't care. It wasn't Grace's fault. Grace could not possibly understand what she was seeing, was seeing something else—something from back at the lighthouse or the island or her life before.

Grace shot Ghost Bird through the back. The bullet came out of her chest, lodged in the wall. The halo above the Crawler spun more furiously. Ghost Bird turned, shouted at her with the full force of the brightness. For she was not injured, had felt nothing, did not want Grace hurt.

Grace frozen there in the half-light, rifle poised, and now in her eyes the knowledge that this was futile, that this had always been futile, that there was no turning back, that there could be no return.

"Go back, Grace," Ghost Bird said, and Grace disappeared up the steps, as if she'd never been there.

Then Ghost Bird realized, too late, that Control was no longer there, had either gone back up or had snuck past, down the stairs, headed for the blinding white light far below.

0023: THE DIRECTOR

You return to what you knew, or thought you knew: the lighthouse and the Séance & Science Brigade, reinvigorated due to the line item linking the S&SB and Jack Severance. You comb through every file three or four times, force yourself to once again review the history of the lighthouse and its ruined sister on the island.

At odd moments, you see Henry's face, a pale circle from a great distance, moving closer and closer until you can catalog every unsavory detail. You don't know what he means, know only that Henry is not someone to be cast aside too quickly. He nags at you like an unopened letter that everyone has, with over-confidence, predicted will contain something banal.

Your antipathy toward them made you dismissive as a child. You hadn't been looking for ways to emblazon them in your memory, to capture details, but instead to banish them, edit them out, make them go away. This annoyance, this presence that you could tell made Saul uncomfortable, even uneasy. But what *about* them had made Saul feel that way?

No Henry, no Suzanne that looked like them appeared on the lists of the S&SB members, no stray photos with members unidentified leapt out to reveal either of them. Prior investigations had tracked down the names and addresses of any member assigned to the forgotten coast, and exhaustive interviews had been conducted. The answers were the same: S&SB had been conducting standard research—the usual mix of the scientific and the preternatural. Anyone who knew anything else had been trapped inside and disappeared long before the first expedition stumbled through the corridor into Area X.

Worse, no further hint of Severance, Jack or Jackie, the latter also making herself scarce in the flesh, as if something new has caught her attention or she knows you want to question her, with each phone call fading into the backdrop, further subsumed by Central. So that you redouble your efforts to find her influence in the files, but if Lowry haunts you, Severance is the kind of ghost that's too smart to materialize.

Once again you watch the video from the first expedition, again study the background, the things out of focus, at the lighthouse. Through a flickering time lapse and sequencing, you review a kind of evolution and devolution of the lighthouse from inception through the last photograph taken by an expedition.

To the point that Grace takes you aside one day and says, "This is enough. You need to run this agency. Other people can review these files."

"What other people? What other people are you talking about?" you snap at her, and then instantly regret it.

But there are no "other people," and time is running out. You have to remember that, on some level, the entire Southern Reach has become a long con, and if you forget that you're not part of the solution, you're part of the problem.

"Maybe you need time off, some rest," Grace tells you. "Maybe you need to get some perspective."

"You can't have my job."

"I do not want your fucking job." She's simmering, she's about to boil over, and some part of you wants to see that, wants to know what Grace is like when she's totally lost it. But if you push her to that, she'll have lost you, too.

Later you go up to the rooftop with a bottle of bourbon, and Grace is already there, in one of the deck chairs. The Southern Reach building is nothing but a big, ponderous ship, and you don't know where the helm has gotten to, can't even lash yourself to the wheel.

"I don't mean anything I'm saying most of the time," you tell her. "Just remember I don't mean anything I say."

A dismissive sound, but also arms unfolding, grim frown loosening up. "This place is a fucking nuthouse." Grace rarely swears anywhere but on the roof.

"A nut job." Paraphrasing Cheney's latest puzzled, hurt soliloquy about lack of good data: "Even a falling acorn tells us something about where it fell from, Newton would tell us, wouldn't you say. There'd be a trajectory, for heck's sake, and then you'd backtrack, even if theoretical, find some point on the tree that acorn came from, or near enough." You can't say you've ever understood more than a third of his ellipticals.

"A White Tits nut job," Grace says, referring to the frozen white tents of the Southern Reach border command and control.

"Our White Tits nut job," you say sternly, wagging a finger. "But at least not nut jobs like the water-feature crew."

After Cheney's outburst, you went over yet another pointless, nonproductive report from the "water-feature crew," the agency studying radio waves for signals from extraterrestrial life. Central has suggested more than once that you "team up with" them. They listen for messages from the stars—across a sliver of two microwave regions unencumbered by radio waves from natural sources. These frequencies they call the water hole because they correspond to hydrogen and hydroxyl wavelengths. A fool's chance, to assume that other intelligent species would automatically gravitate to the "watering hole" as they called it.

"While what they were looking for snuck in the back door—"

"Set up the back door and walked through it—"

"You're looking up and meanwhile something walks by and steals your wallet," Grace says, cackling.

"Water feature built for nothing; they prefer the servants' entrance, thank you very much," you say grandly, passing the bourbon. "You don't just turn on the sprinklers and pump up the Slip 'N Slide."

You truly don't know what you're saying anymore, but Grace bursts into laughter, and then things are all right again with Grace, for a while, and you can go back to Henry and Suzanne, the talking mannequins, the deathly dull or just deathly twins.

But at some point that same week, Grace finds you throwing file folders against the far wall, and you've no excuse for it except a shrug. Bad day at the doctor's. Bad day prepping for the expedition. Bad day doing research. Just a bad day in a succession of bad days.

So you do something about it.

You fly out to Lowry's headquarters about one month before the twelfth expedition. Even though it's your idea, you're unhappy you have to travel, had hoped to lure Lowry to the Southern Reach one last time. Everything around you—your office, the conversation in the corridors, the view from Beyond Reach—has acquired a kind of compelling sheen to it, a clarity that comes from knowing you will soon be gone.

Lowry's in the final stages of his pre-expedition performance, has been exporting the less invasive of his techniques to Central. He enjoys impersonating an instructor for the benefit of expedition members, according to Severance. The biologist, she reassures you, has suffered "minimal meddling." The only thing you want ratcheted up in the biologist is her sense of alienation from other people. All you want is that she become as attuned inward to Area X as possible. You're not even sure she really needs your push in that regard, from all reports. No one in the history of the program has so willingly given up the use of her name.

Light hypnotic suggestion, conditioning that's more about Area X survival than any of Lowry's dubious "value adds," his claims to have found a way around the need, on some level, for the subject to want to perform the suggested action— "a kind of trickery and substitution." The stages you've seen described are identification, indoctrination, reinforcement, and deployment, but Grace has seen other documents that borrow the semiotics of the supernatural: "manifestation, infestation, oppression, and possession."

Most of Lowry's attention has accreted around the linguist, a volunteer with radicalized ideas about the value of free will. You wonder if Lowry prefers it when there's more or less resistance. So you absorb the brunt of his briefing, his report on progress, his teasing taunt about whether you've reconsidered his offer of hypnosis, of conditioning, with the hint behind it that you couldn't stop him if you tried.

Honestly, you don't give a shit about his briefing.

At some point, you steer Lowry toward the idea of a walk—down by the fake lighthouse. It's early summer, the weather still balmy, and there's no reason to sit there in Lowry's command-and-control lounge. You cajole him into it by appealing to his pride, asking for the full tour, taking just one thin file folder you've brought with you.

So he gives you the not-so-grand tour, through this miniaturized world of ever-decreasing wonder. There's the strange kitschy quality of piped-in music through speakers hidden around the grounds. A distant but cheery tune—not pop, not jazz, not classical, but something all the more menacing for being jaunty.

At the top of the quaint little lighthouse—what would Saul think of it?—he points out that the daymark is accurate, as well as "the fucking glass shards somebody added later." When he pulls the trapdoor open at the top, what's revealed in the room below are piles and piles of empty journals and loose, blank pages, as if he's bought a stationery store as a side business. The lens isn't functional, either, but as if by way of apology, you get a history lesson: "Back in the day—way back in the day—they used to just shove a big fucking fatty bird onto a stake and light it on fire for a beacon."

That "goddamn hole in the ground," as Lowry puts it, is the least accurate part—an old gunnery position with the gun unit ripped out, leaving the granite-lined dark circle that leads down a ladder to a tunnel that then doubles back to the hill behind you that houses most of Lowry's installations. You climb down only a little ways, enough to see, framed on the dank walls, Lowry's art gallery: the blurry, out-of-focus photographs, blown up, brought back by various expeditions. A kind of meta version of the tunnel brought to the faux tunnel, displaying with confidence something unknowable. Thinking of Saul on the steps of the real tunnel, turning toward you, and feeling such an acute contempt for Lowry that you have to remain there, looking down, for long moments, afraid it will show on your face.

After you've made the right noises about how impressive it all is, you suggest continuing along the shore, "fresh air and nature," and Lowry acquiesces, defeated by your tactic of asking a question about each new thing ahead because he just cannot shut up about his own cleverness. You take a side path that leads north along the water. There are geese nesting on a nearby rocky point that give you both the stink eye, an otter in the sea in the middle distance, shadowing you.

Eventually, you turn the conversation to the S&SB. You pull out a piece of paper—the line item linked to "Jack Severance." You point it out to him even though it's highlighted in hot pink. You present it as this funny thing, this thing Lowry must have known about, too. Given his secret debriefing of your childhood experiences when you first joined the Southern Reach.

"Is that the reason you and Jackie are working together?" you ask. "That the S&SB had a link to Central—through Jack?"

Lowry considers that question, a kind of smirk on his craggy face. A smirk, and a look down at the ground and back up at you.

"Is that all we're out here for? For *that*? Jesus, I might've given you *that* in a fucking phone call."

"Not much, I guess," you say. Sheepish smile, offered up to a raging wolf of a narcissist. "But I'd like to know." Before you cross the border.

A hesitation, a sideways glance that's appraising you hard for some hidden motivation or some next move that maybe he can't see.

Prodding: "A side project? The S&SB a side project of Central, or . . . ?"

"Sure, why not," Lowry says, relaxing. "The usual kind of dependent clause that could be excised at any time, no harm done."

But sometimes the ancillary infected the primary. Sometimes the host and the parasite got confused about their roles, as the biologist might have put it.

"It's how you got the photograph of me at the lighthouse." Not a question.

"Very good!" he says, genuinely delighted. "Too fucking true! I was on a mission to find evidence to make sure you stayed true . . . and then I wondered how come that was in Central's files in the first place, and not over at the Southern Reach. Wondered where it originated—and then I found that very same line item." Except Lowry had a higher security clearance, could access information you and Grace couldn't get your hands on.

"That was smart of you. Really smart."

Lowry puffs up, chest sticking out, aware he's being flattered but can't help the self-parody that's not really parody at all, because where's the harm? You're on the way out. He's probably already thinking about replacements. You haven't bothered putting Grace's name forward, have been working on Jackie Severance in that regard instead.

"The idea was straightforward, the way Jack told it. The S&SB was kind of bat-shit crazy, low probability, but if there actually was anything uncanny or alien in the world, we should monitor it, should be aware of it. Maybe influence or nudge it a bit, provide the right materials and guidance. And if troublemakers or undesirables joined the group—that's a good way to monitor potential subversives, too . . . and also a good cover for getting into places 'hidden in plain sight' for surveillance, a methodology Central was keen on back then. A lot of antigovernment types along the forgotten coast."

"Did we recruit, or—"

"Some operatives embedded—and some folks we persuaded to work for us because they liked the idea of playing spy. Some folks who got a thrill out of it. Didn't need a deeper reason, like God and country. Probably just as well."

"Was Jackie involved, too?"

"Jack wasn't just protecting himself," Lowry says. "When Jackie was starting out, she helped him a bit—and then she came to the Southern Reach later and helped Jack again, to make sure none of this came out. Except I found out, as I do, sometimes. As you know."

"Ever come across a Henry or Suzanne in the files?"

"Never any names used in what I saw. Just code names like, I dunno, 'Big Hawler' and 'Spooky Action' and 'Damned Porkchop.' That kind of crap."

But none of this is the real question, the first of the real questions.

"Did the S&SB facilitate, knowingly or unknowingly, the creation of Area X?"

Lowry looks both stunned and amused beyond reason or good sense. "No, of course not. No no no! That's why Jack could keep it secret, snuff it out. Strictly in the wrong place at the wrong time—because otherwise I would have . . . I would have taken measures." But you think he meant to say *would have killed them all.* "And it turns out Jack was running it mostly on his own initiative, which is something I think we can both appreciate, right?"

Above you loom the old barracks, the warrens, gun slits from concrete bunkers.

Do you believe Lowry? No, you don't.

The little gravel beach where you both stand is some distance from the fake lighthouse. It has a fringe of anemic grass and, right before the water, a line of rocks covered in white lichen. The brilliant sun for a moment becomes lost in a depression of clouds and shadow, the pale blue surface of the sea a sudden gray. The otter that has been trailing you has come closer. Its constant chattering monologue of clicks and whistles Lowry finds somehow disrespectful, perhaps because of prior encounters. He starts yelling at the otter and the otter keeps "talking" and popping up somewhere unexpected so Lowry can never adjust to throw the pebble he plans on caroming off the otter's head. You sit down on the rocks, watch the show.

"Goddamn fucking creature. Goddamn stupid fucking animal."

The otter shows off a fish it's caught, swimming on its back, eyes full of a kind of laughter, if that's possible.

The otter skims and zags and disappears and comes back up. Lowry's pebbles skip and plop without effect, the otter apparently thinking it's a game.

But it's a game that bores the otter after a while, and it submerges for a long time, Lowry standing there with one hand on his hip, the other a fist around a rock, searching for a new ripple in the water, seeming to want to guess how long the otter can hold its breath, what range of options the animal has for where it can come up for air. Except it never reappears, and Lowry's left standing there, holding a rock.

Is Lowry a monster? He is monstrous in your eyes, because you know that by the time his hold on Central, the parts of Central he wants to make laugh and dance the way he wants them to laugh and dance . . . by the time this hold, the doubling and mirroring, has waned as most reigns of terror do, the signs of his hand, his will, will have irrevocably fallen across so many places. His ghost will haunt so much for so many years to come, imprint upon so many minds, that if the details about the man known as Lowry are suddenly purged from all the systems, those systems will still reconstruct his image from the very force and power of his impact.

You take out a photo of the cell phone, nudge his arm with it, make him take it. Lowry blanches, tries to hand back the photograph, but you're going to make him keep it. He's stuck holding it and the rock meant for the otter. He drops the rock but won't look at the photograph again.

"Lowry, I think you lied about this phone. I think this is your phone. From the first expedition." You've a sense as you say the words that you're going too far, but you'll be going even farther soon.

"You don't know that's my phone."

"It's got a long history now."

Lowry: "No." Stark. Final. Letting in no light. A kind of self-damnation. No protest. No outrage. None of the usual Lowry drama. "No." Without any way to pry loose some light between the letters of that word, so you'll have to try yourself, across the border.

"Are you working for them? Is that the problem?" You leave the "them" vague on purpose.

"For 'them'?" A laugh that burned. "Why, is there a problem with the phone?" Still not an admission.

"Does Area X have unfinished business with you? Is there something you haven't told us about the first expedition?"

"Nothing that would help you." Bitter now. Directed at you for ambushing him, or at someone else?

"Lowry, if you don't tell me whether or not this is your cell phone, I am going to go to Central and tell them all about the S&SB, all about where I came from, how you covered it up. I'm going to scuttle you for good."

"You'd be done for yourself then."

"I'm done for anyway—you know that."

Lowry gives you a look that's equal parts aggression and some secret hurt coming to the surface.

"I get it now, Gloria," he says. "You're going on a suicide mission and you just want everything out in the open, even if it's unimportant. Well, you should know that if you share with anyone, I'll—"

"You're corrupted data," you tell him. "If we used your own techniques on you, Lowry, what would we find in your brain? Coiled up in there?"

"How the fuck dare you." He's trembling with anger, but he's not moving, he's not retreating one inch. It's not a denial, although it probably should be. Guilt? Does Lowry believe in guilt?

Pushing now, probing now, not certain if what you're saying is true: "While on the first expedition, did you communicate with them? With Area X?"

"I wouldn't call it communication. It's all in the files you've already seen."

"What did you see? How did you see it?" Were we doomed when you came back, or before?

"There will never be a grand unified theory, Gloria. We will never find it. Not in our lifetime, and it'll be too late." Lowry trying to confuse things, escape the spotlight. "You know, they're looking at water on the moons of Jupiter right now, out there, our not-so-secret sister organizations. There might be a secret sea out there. There might be life, right under our noses. But there's always been life right under our noses—we're just too blind to see it. These fucking questions—they don't matter."

"Jim, this is evidence of contact. Finding this particular cell phone in Area X." That it indicates recognition and understanding of some kind.

"No—random. Random. Random."

"It wants to talk to you, Jim. Area X wants to talk to you. It wants to ask you a question, doesn't it?" You don't know if this is true, but you're sure it'll scare the shit out of Lowry.

You have the sense of a time delay in Lowry, a gap or distance between the two of you that is very, very wide. Something ancient shines out of his eyes, peers out at you.

"I won't go back," he says.

"That's not an answer."

"Yes, it's my phone. It's my fucking phone."

Are you seeing Lowry as he was right after coming back from the first expedition? How long could a person hold to a pattern, a process, despite being fundamentally damaged? Whitby telling you, "I think this is an asylum. But so is the rest of the world."

"Don't you get tired after a while?" you ask him. "Of always moving forward but never reaching the end? Of never being able to tell the truth to anyone?"

"You know, Gloria," he says, "you'll *never* really understand what it was like that first time, going out through that door in the border, coming back. Not if you cross the border a thousand times. We were offered up and we were *lost*. We were passing through a door of ghosts, into a place of spirits. And asked to deal with that. For the rest of our lives."

"And what if Area X comes looking for you?"

There's still that remoteness to Lowry's gaze, as if he's not really there, standing in front of you, but he's done, pushed to his limit, stalks off without even a glance back.

You will never see him again, ever, and that temporary relief puts juice in your step as the sun returns, as the otter returns, and you sit by the shore and watch the animal cavort and frolic for a few minutes that you hope will never end.

0024: THE LIGHTHOUSE KEEPER

. . . bring forth the seeds of the dead to share with the worms that gather in the darkness . . . Heard during the night: screech owl, nighthawk, a few foxes. A blessing. A relief.

At the lighthouse, the beacon was dark. The beacon was dark, and something was trying to spill out of him, or course through him on its way to somewhere else. *The shadows of the abyss are like the petals of a monstrous flower that shall blossom within the skull and expand the mind beyond what any man can bear, but whether it decays under the earth or above on green fields, or out to sea or in the very air, all shall come to revelation, and to revel, in the knowledge of the strangling fruit.*

He was still in shock from the bar, kept believing that if he went back it would prove to be some kind of waking vision or even a terrible joke. The smashing of Old Jim's bloody fingers against the piano keys. Sadi's look of being undone, betrayed by her own words. Brad, standing there, gaze locked on the wall as if someone had frozen him in place. Thank God Trudi had already left. What would he tell Gloria when he saw her again? What would he tell Charlie?

Saul parked the truck, stumbled to the lighthouse, unlocked the door, slammed it behind him, and stood in the entrance breathing hard. He'd call the police, tell them to come to the bar, to check on poor Old Jim and the others. He'd call the police, and then he'd try to get hold of Charlie out at sea, and then call anyone else he could think of. Because something terrible must be happening here, something beyond his illness.

But no one answered. No one answered. The phone was dead. He could run, but where to? The light had gone out. The light had gone out.

Armed with a flare gun, Saul stumbled up the stairs, one hand against the wall to keep his balance. The splinter was an insect bite. Or an overture. An intruder.

Or nothing, nothing to do with this, as he slipped and almost fell, some kind of moisture on the steps, a fuzziness on the wall that came away in his hands, that he had to brush off against his jeans. The Light Brigade. They'd given him an experimental drug or exposed him to radiation with their equipment. *And the hand of the sinner shall rejoice, for there is no sin in shadow or in light that the seeds of the dead cannot forgive.*

Near the top, the wind whistled down briskly and he welcomed the chill, the way it told him a world existed outside of his mind, helped him deny these symptoms that had now crept back in. He felt a strong tidal pull, and a vibration that went with the pull, and he was burning up.

Or was the lighthouse burning up? Because a glow awaited him at the top of the stairs, and not the faint green phosphorescence that now arose from the walls, the steps. No, this was a sharp light that knew its purpose, he could tell that already. But it was not the light from the lens, and he hesitated just below the lantern room for a moment. He sagged onto a step, not sure he wanted to see what new beacon had supplanted the old. His hands shook. He trembled. Could not get Old Jim's fingers out of his head, nor the words of the sermon that still uncurled all unbidden from his mind. That he could neither resist nor keep out.

But this was his place now, and he could not abandon it.

He rose. He turned. He walked into the lantern room.

The rug had been moved.

The trapdoor lay open.

A light shone out from that space. A light that circled and curved even as it had the discipline not to trickle across the floor, or refract off the ceiling, but instead mimicked a door, a wall, rising from the watch room.

Quietly, flare gun held tight, Saul crept closer to the edge of the trapdoor and the source of the light, while the feeling increased that the stairs behind him had grown stranger still, that he should not look back. Bending at the knees, he peered down into the watch room, feeling the heat of that light crossing his face, his neck, singeing his beard.

At first all he saw was a vast mound of papers and what looked like notebooks that now rose from the watch room, a great behemoth, a disheveled library of shadow and reflection that leapt into and out of focus—ghosts and figments, curling and questing, there but not quite there, a record that he did not understand because it did not yet exist.

Then his eyes adjusted and the source of the light coalesced: a blossom. A pure white blossom with eight petals, which had unfurled from the top of a familiar plant, whose roots disappeared into the papers below. The plant that had enticed him on the lighthouse lawn, so long ago, to reach down, drawn by a glitter, a gleam.

An almost holy intensity rose from somewhere within and filled Saul up, along with a dizziness. Light was leaking out of him now, too, coursing down through the trapdoor to communicate with what lay below, and there came the sensation of something pulling him close, holding him tight . . . of recognizing him.

In rebellion against that, he rose from his crouch, arms out to the side for balance, teetering there on the edge of the trapdoor, staring down into that swirl of petals until he could resist no more, was falling into the pure white corona of a circle of fire, into a congregation of flames, a burning so pure that turning to ash was a kind of relief, engulfed by light that consecrated not just him but everything around him, anchoring receiver and received.

There shall be a fire that knows your name, and in the presence of the strangling fruit, its dark flame shall acquire every part of you.

When he regained consciousness, he was lying on the floor of the watch room, on his back, looking up. There was no mound of notebooks. There was no flower.

Just the bodies of Henry and Suzanne, with no apparent wounds upon them, expressions blank and more haunting because of it. He recoiled from them, crawled away from them, staring. In the shadows there might have been what looked like the limp, desiccated remains of a plant, but he had no desire other than to leave that space.

He clambered up the ladder.

A figure in silhouette stood in front of the open door to the railing. A figure with a gun.

Impossibly, it was Henry.

"I thought you'd be gone longer, Saul," Henry said, in a distant tone. "I thought you might not even come back tonight. That maybe you'd go over to Charlie's, except Charlie is out fishing—and Gloria's staying with her father. Not that she would be out this late anyway, or be of much help to you. But just so you know where we stand."

"You killed Suzanne," Saul said, unbelieving even now.

"She wanted to kill me. She didn't believe in what I found. None of them believed. Not even you."

"You killed *yourself.*" Your twin. Knowing that even if it made a difference, he couldn't reach the flare gun in time, or even make it two steps into a headlong flight down the stairs before Henry would shoot him, too.

"A strange thing," Henry said. Where before he had been indistinct, hurting, in need of succor, now he had snapped back into focus. "A strange thing to kill yourself. I thought maybe it was a kind of wraith. But maybe Suzanne was right instead."

"Who *are* you?"

Ignoring him: "I found it, Saul, like I said I would. Or it found me. Only, it wasn't what I thought. Do you know what it is, Saul?" Almost pleading.

There was no good answer to Henry's question.

He took two steps toward Henry, as if he were watching someone else do it. He was an albatross, floating motionless in a high-above trough of air, gliding beneath the clouds with their dark underbellies, a coordinate of shadow and light that kept moving, a roving latitude and longitude, and far, far below, stood Saul and Henry, in the lantern room.

Saul took a third step, the plant a beacon in his head.

A fourth step and Henry shot him in the shoulder. The bullet penetrated and passed through, and Saul didn't feel a thing. Saul was still floating far above, intent on navigation, on riding thermals, an animal that hardly ever came down to land but just kept flying and flying.

Saul rushed Henry, rammed his bleeding shoulder into Henry's chest, and the two of them staggered, grappling out the door and toward the railing, Henry's gun spinning out of his hand and across the floor. So close, staring into Henry's eyes, Saul had the sense of the man being at a remove, a time delay—a gap or distance between receipt, acknowledgment, and response: a message coming to him from very far away. As if Henry were dealing with some other, completely different situation . . . while on some level still able to appraise him, to judge him. *When you hide your face, they are terrified; when you take away their breath, they die and return to the dust.*

Because Henry was drawing them both to the railing. Because Henry had a firm grip on him and was drawing them both to the railing. Except Henry was saying to Saul, "What are you doing?" But Saul wasn't doing it, Henry was and didn't seem to realize it.

"It's you," the albatross managed to say. "You're doing it, not me."

"No, I'm not." Henry beyond panic now, writhing and trying to get loose, but still leading them to the railing, fast now, and Henry begging him to stop what he could not stop. Yet Henry's eyes did not send out the same message as his words.

Henry hit the railing—hard—and Saul a second later, swung to the side by momentum, and then they both went over, and only then, when it was too late, did Henry let go, the wind ripping screams from his throat, and Saul plummeted beside him through the cold empty air—falling too fast, too far, while a part of him still looked down from above.

The surf, like white flames surging and questing across the sand.

I am come to send fire on the earth; and what will I, if it be already kindled?

The awful thud and crack when he hit.

0025: CONTROL

There came to Control in that moment of extremity—almost unable to move, unable to speak—an overwhelming feeling of connection, that nothing was truly *apart* in the same way that he had found even the most random scrawl in the director's notes joined some greater pattern. And although the pressure was increasing and he was in a great deal of pain, the kind of pain that would not leave him soon, if ever, there arose a powerful music within him that he did not fully understand as he slipped and slid down the curving stairs, pulling himself at times, his left arm useless by his side, his father's carving clenched in a fist he could no longer feel, the brightness welling up through his mouth, his eyes, and filling him at the same time, as if the Crawler had accelerated the process. He was slipping in part because he was changing, he knew that, could tell that he was no longer entirely human.

Whitby was still with him, old friend, even if Lowry, too, chuckled and flailed somewhere in the background, and he clutched his father's carving to him as best as he was able, the only talisman he had left. *This machine or creature or some combination of both that can manipulate molecules, that can store energy where it will, that can hide the bulk of its intent and its machinations from us. That lives with angels within it and with the vestiges of its own terroir, the hints of its homeland, to which it can never return because it no longer exists.*

And yet the Crawler had used such a cheap trick: Control had seen his mother standing there, taken a grim and primal satisfaction in recognizing it as a delusion, one that held no dominion over him—a person he forgave because how could he not forgive her, finally, standing in such a place? Free, then, free even before the Crawler had struck, had hurt him so badly. And even in that hurting somehow Control knew that pain was incidental, not the Crawler's intent, but nothing about language, about communication, could bridge the divide between human beings and Area X. That anything approaching a similarity would be some subset of Area X functioning at its most primitive level. A blade of grass. A blue heron. A velvet ant.

He lost track of time and of the speed of his passage down, and of his transformation. He no longer knew whether he was still even a sliver of human by the time he—painfully, nauseated, crawling now, or was he loping?—came down the most ancient of steps, of stairs, to the blinding white light at the bottom shaped like the immortal plant, like a comet roaring there but stationary, and now his decision to push himself forward in the final extremity, to push through against that agony and that outward radiating command to turn back, and to enter . . . what? He did not know, except that the biologist had not made it this far, and he had. He had made it this far.

Now "Control" fell away again. Now he was the son of a man who had been a sculptor and of a woman who lived in a byzantine realm of secrets.

His father's carving fell from his hand, clattered onto a step, came to a halt, there on the stairs, alongside the signs and symbols left by his predecessors. A scrawling on the walls. An empty boot.

He sniffed the air, felt under his paws the burning and heat, the intensity.

This was all that was left to him, and he would not now die on the steps; he would not suffer that final defeat.

John Rodriguez elongated down the final stairs, jumped into the light.

0026: THE DIRECTOR

Two weeks before the twelfth expedition, the old battered cell phone comes home with you. You don't remember bringing it. You don't know why security didn't question it. It's just there, in your purse, and then on the kitchen counter. The usual suspects occur to you. Maybe Whitby's even stranger than you think or Lowry's having a laugh at your expense. But what does it matter? You'll just bring it back in the morning.

By then the divide between work and home is long gone—you've brought files home, you've done work at home, scribbled things on scraps of paper and sometimes on leaves, the way you used to do as a kid. In part because you take delight in imagining Lowry receiving photographs of them in his reports; but also using those materials seems somehow safer, although you can't say why, just a heightened sense of a "touch" roving among the files, a presence you can't pin down or quantify. An irrational thought, an idea that just came into your mind one night, working late. Going into the bathroom every so often to throw up—a side effect of the medication you are taking for the cancer. Apologizing to the janitor and saying any foolish thing you could think of other than that you were sick: "I'm pregnant." Pregnant with cancer. Pregnant with possibility. It makes you laugh sometimes. Dear alcoholic veteran at the end of the bar, do you think you'd like to be a father?

It's not a night for Chipper's, not a night for garrulous Realtors and nodding drunks. You're tired from the additional training, which has required more travel up north to Central to participate with the rest of the expedition and to receive your own training as expedition leader. To fully understand the use of hypnotic commands, to understand the importance—the specific details—of the black boxes with the red light that help to activate compliance.

So instead of going out, you put on some music, then decide on television for a while because your brain is cooked. You hear a sound in the hallway, beyond the kitchen—just something settling in the attic, but it makes you nervous. When you go look, there's nothing there, but you get your ax from where you keep it under the bed for home defense. Then return to the couch, to watch a thirty-year-old detective show filmed in the south. Lost places, locations that don't exist now, that will never come back. A landscape haunting you from the past—so many things gone, no longer there. During the car chases, you're watching the backgrounds like they're family photos you've never seen before.

You nod off. You come to. You nod off again. Then you hear something creeping low and soft across the tiles of the kitchen, just out of view. A kind of terrified lurching shudder burns through you. There's a slow scuttle to the sound, so you can't really identify it, get a sense of what has crept into your house. You don't move for a very long time, waiting to hear more, not wanting to hear more. You think you might not ever get up, go to the kitchen, see what animal awaits you there. But it's still moving, it's still making noise, and you can't sit there forever. You can't just sit there.

So you get up, you brandish the ax, you walk to the kitchen counter, lean on tiptoe to peer at the kitchen floor, but whatever it is has nudged up against the left side, out of view. You're going to have to walk around and confront it directly.

There, scuttling across the floor, blind and querulous, is the old cell phone—scrabbling and bulky, trying to get away from you. Or trying to burrow into the cabinets, to hide there. Except it isn't moving now. It hasn't moved the whole time you've been staring at it. You look at the phone in shock for so many moments. Maybe from the surprise of it or as a defense mechanism, all you can think is that your work has followed you home. All you can think of is the monstrous breach. Either in reality or in your mind.

With trembling hands, you retrieve the cell phone from the floor, ax held ready in your other hand. It feels warm, the melted nature of the leather against the phone creating the texture of skin. You get a metal box you use for tax receipts, toss them into a plastic bag, put the phone inside, lock it, put it on the kitchen counter. You resist the urge to toss the box into your backyard, or to drive with it to the river and fling it into the darkness.

Instead you fumble for a cigar from the humidor buried underneath some clothes in your bedroom. The cigar you pull out is dry and flaking, but you don't care. You light it, go into your home office, shove the notes you've brought home into a plastic bag. Every unsupportable theory. Every crazed journal rant rescued from old expedition accounts. Every incomprehensible scrawling. Shove them in there with a vengeance, for some reason shouting at Lowry as you do because he's peering into your thoughts on some mission of his own. You hiss at him. Stay the fuck away! Don't come in here. Except he already has, is the only person screwed up enough, knowing what he must know, to do this to you.

There are notes you weren't sure you remembered writing, that you couldn't be sure had been there before. Were there too many notes? And if so, who has written the others? Did Whitby sneak into your office and create them, trying to help you? Forging your handwriting? You resist the urge to take the notes out of the bag, sort through them again, be pulled down by that horrible weight. You take the bag of crazy outside with a glass of red wine, stand there on the stone patio smoking while you turn on the grill even though a storm's coming, even though you can feel the first raindrops, wait a minute or two, then with a snarl upend the bag onto the flames.

You're a large, authoritative woman, standing in her backyard, burning a crap-load of secret papers, of receipts and other things that reflect the totality, the banality of your life—transformed into "evidence" by what you've scrawled there. Squirt lighter fluid over it to make it worse or better, toss this ceaseless, inane, stupid, ridiculous, pathetic detritus on top of it, light a match, watch it all go up in billowing, eye-watering, bile-like smoke. Curling and blackened, meaningless. It doesn't matter because there's still a flickering light in your head that you can't snuff out, a wavering candle distant in the darkness of a tunnel that was really a tower that was a topographical anomaly that was you reaching out to touch Saul Evans's face. It is all too much. You slump alongside the wall, watch as the flames rise up and then bank, and are gone. It isn't enough. There're still more inside—on the side table by the couch, on the kitchen counter, on the mantel in the bedroom; you're awash in them, drowning in them.

Down the slant of your backyard, the windows are lit up and a television is on. A man, a woman, and a boy and a girl on a couch seem sublimely calm, just sitting there, watching sports. Not talking. Not doing anything but watching. Definitely not wanting to look in your direction, as the raindrops thicken, proliferate, and your burning papers sizzle.

What if you go back in, open that box, and the cell phone isn't a cell phone? What if containment is a joke? You can hardly contain yourself. What if you bring the cell phone back in and have it tested and nothing is out of the ordinary, again? What if you go back in, the cell phone isn't ordinary, and you report that to Lowry and he laughs and calls you crazy—or you tell Severance instead, and the cell phone is just sitting there, inert, and you're the compromised director of an agency that hasn't yet solved the central mystery around which its existence revolves? What if your cancer rises up and devours you before you get a chance to cross the border? Before you can escort the biologist across.

You with your cigar and your glass of wine and the music on the phonograph you turn up real loud, something you don't even remember buying, and the idea that somehow any of that will keep out the darkness, keep out the thoughts that churn through your head—the cold regard that holds you as if God herself had through some electrified beatific gaze pinned you like a butterfly in a collector's display case of mediocrity.

The storm comes on and you toss your cigar, stand there thinking about the invisible border and all the ceaseless hypotheses that amount to some psychotic religion . . . and you drink your wine, hell, get the whole bottle, and it's still not doing it, and you still don't want to go inside to face . . . anything.

"Tell me something I don't know! Tell me something I don't fucking know!" you scream at the darkness, and throw your glass into the night, and without meaning to you're on your knees in the rain and the lightning and the mud, and you don't know if this is an act of defiance or an act of pain or just some selfish reflexive grace note. You truly don't know, any more than you know if that cell phone in there had actually moved, been alive.

The burned notes are sopping now, falling in wet, stuck-together ash clumps off the edge of the overflowing grill. A few last sparks float in the air, winking out one by one.

That's when you rise, finally. You rise out of the mud, in the rain, and you go back inside and suddenly everything gets really cold and calm. The answer doesn't lie in your backyard because no one is going to come and save you even if you beg them to. Especially if you beg them to. You're on your own, like you've always been on your own. You have to keep going forward, until you can't go forward anymore.

You have to hang on. You're almost there. You can make it to the end.

You stop investigating the S&SB. You stop investigating the lighthouse. You leave the notes that remain in your office, which you're well aware are legion, many more than what you burned at home in your pointless effort at catharsis.

"Ever had anyone try to burn a house down?" you ask the Realtor later that night, ducking in for a quick drink, a couple of cocktails that'll put you to sleep and then wake you up again, restless and turning endlessly in your bed in the middle of the night.

The lights are dim, the TV a silent glow, a distant hum, the stars in the ceiling glinting on and off from the roving flash of spotlights on the bowling lanes. Someone's playing a dark country-western song on the jukebox, but it sounds distant, so far away: *Something's moving through my heart. Sometimes I just have to play the part.*

"Oh, sure," the Realtor says, "warming to her task" as the veteran, suddenly a wit, puts it. "The usual kind of thing, with arson for the insurance. Sometimes it's an ex trying to burn down the wife's house once her new boyfriend has moved in. But more times than you might think, you don't find any reason for it at all. I had one guy who got the urge to start a fire one day, and he let it all go up in smoke, and just stood there watching. Afterward he was crying and wondering why he'd done it. He didn't know. There must have been a reason why he did it, though, I've always thought. Something he couldn't admit to himself, or something that he just didn't know."

Anger tries to thrash its way free of you, manifests as a suspicion you've had for a while.

"You're not a Realtor," you tell the woman. "You're not really a Realtor at all." She's a touch on some notes, she's a cell phone that won't sit still.

You need some air, walk outside, stand there in the gravel parking lot, under the uncertain illumination of a cracked streetlamp. You can still hear the music blaring from inside. The streetlamp's shining down on you and the solid bulk of the hippo on the edge of the miniature golf course, its enormous shape casting a wide, oblong shadow. The hippo's eyes are blank glass, its gaping mouth a fathomless space you wouldn't put your hand into for all the free games Chipper's could give you.

The veteran comes outside.

"You're right—she's not a Realtor," he tells you. "She got fired. She hasn't had a job for more than a year."

"That's okay," you say. "I'm not a long-haul trucker, either."

Tragically, he asks if you want to go back inside and dance. No, you don't want to dance. But it's okay if he leans against the hippo with you to talk for a while. About nothing in particular. About the ordinary, everyday things that elude you.

The plant remains in the storage cathedral. Whitby's mouse remains in his attic for the most part. The last few days before the twelfth expedition, the phone migrates to your desk as a secret memento. You don't know whether you're more concerned when it is with you or when it is out of your sight.

0027: THE LIGHTHOUSE KEEPER

Saul woke on his back beneath the lighthouse, covered in sand, Henry crumpled beside him. It was still night, the sky a deep, rich blue bleeding into black, but full of stars against that vast expanse. He must be dying, he knew, must be broken in a hundred places, but he didn't feel broken. Instead, all he felt was a kind of restlessness, growing a hundredfold now and nothing else behind it. No agony from the fall, from the searing pain of what must be several broken bones. None of that. Was he in shock?

But still there was the rising brightness and the night staring down with thousands of glistening eyes, the comforting husk and hush of the surf, and as he turned on his side to face the sea, the faint dark shadows of night herons, with their distinctive raised crests, stabbing at the tiny silver fish writhing in the wet sand.

With a groan, anticipating a collapse that never came, Saul rose without a stagger or a swoon, a dreadful strength coursing through him. Even his shoulder felt fine. Uninjured, or so badly injured and disoriented that he was nearing the end. Whatever was coming into his head was being translated into words, his distress expressed as language, and he clamped down on it again, because he knew somehow that to let it out was to give in, and that he might not have much time left.

He looked up at the lantern room of the lighthouse, imagining again that fall. Something inside had saved him, protected him. By the time he'd hit the ground, he hadn't been himself—the plummet become a descent so gentle, so light, that it'd been like a cocoon tenderly plummeting, kissing the sand. Come to rest as if locking into a position preordained for him.

When he looked over at Henry, Saul could see even in the dull darkness that the man was still alive, that distant stare as locked and fixed on him as the stars above. That stare coming to Saul from across the centuries, across vast, unconquerable distances. Beatific and yet deadly. A scruffy assassin. A fallen angel ravaged by time.

Saul didn't want that gaze upon him, walked a short distance away from Henry, down the beach, closer to the water. Charlie was somewhere out there in the sea, night fishing. He wanted Charlie close now but also wanted him thrust far away, cast out, so that whatever had possessed him might not possess Charlie.

He made his way to the ridge of rocks that Gloria liked to explore, to the tidal pools, and sat there, silent, recovering his sense of self.

Out in the sea, he thought he could see the rippling backs of leviathans as they breached and then returned to the depths. There came the stench of oil and gasoline and chemicals, the sea coming almost up to his feet now. He could see that the beach was strewn with plastic and garbage and tarred bits of metal, barrels and culverts clotted with seaweed and barnacles. The remains of ships rising, too. Detritus that had never touched this coast but was here now.

Above, the stars seemed to be moving at a tremendous rate, through a moonless sky, and he could hear the thunderous screams of their passage—streaking faster and faster until the dark was dissolving into ribbons and streamers of light.

Henry, like an awkward shadow, appeared at his side. But Saul wasn't frightened of Henry.

"Am I dead?" he asked Henry.

Henry said nothing.

Then, after a moment, "You're not really Henry anymore, are you?"

No answer.

"Who are you?"

Henry looked over at Saul, looked away again.

Charlie, in a boat, offshore, night fishing, far away from whatever this was, this sensation pushing out of him like a live thing. Pushing harder and harder and harder.

"Will I ever see Charlie again?"

Henry turned away from Saul, began to walk down the beach, broken and stumbling. After a couple of steps, something further broke inside of him and he fell to the sand, crawling for a few feet before he lay still. *And the hand of the sinner shall rejoice, for there is no sin in shadow or in light that the seeds of the dead cannot forgive.*

Something was about to crest like a wave. Something was about to come out of him. He felt weak and invincible all at once. Was this how it happened? Was this one of the ways God came for you?

He did not want to leave the world, and yet he knew now that he was leaving it, or that it was leaving him.

Saul managed to get into his pickup truck, could feel the sickness overflowing, knew that whatever was about to happen he would be unable to control, was beyond anyone's ability to control. He did not want it to happen there, on the coast, next to his lighthouse. Didn't want it to happen at all, but knew the choice was not up to him. There were comets erupting in his head and a vision of a terrible door and what had come out of it. So he drove—down the rutted path, careening wildly at times, trying to escape himself even though that was impossible. Through the sleeping village. Past dirt road after dirt road. Charlie out at sea. Thankfully not here. Head pounding. The shadows begetting shadows, and the words trying to erupt from his mouth now, urgent to come out of his mouth, a code he couldn't decipher. Feeling as if something had its attention upon him. Unable to escape the sensation of interference and transmittal, a communication pressing in on the edges of his brain.

Until he couldn't drive anymore, there in the most remote part of the forgotten coast—the parts of the pine forest no one claimed or wanted or lived in. Stopped, stumbled out, the shapes of the dark trees, the sound of owls, innumerable rustlings, a fox pausing to stare at him, unafraid, the stars above still swirling and streaking.

Stumbling in the dark, scraping up against palmettos and tough scrub, pushing past the uprising of this undergrowth, a foot into black water and out again. The sharp scent of fox piss, the suggestion of an animal or animals watching him. Trying now to hold his balance. Trying to hold on to his wits. But a universe was opening up in his head, filled with images he didn't, couldn't understand.

A flowering plant that could never die.

A rain of white rabbits, cut off in mid-leap.

A woman reaching down to touch a starfish in a tidal pool.

Green dust from a corpse blowing away in the wind.

Henry, standing atop the lighthouse, jerking and twitching, receiving a signal from very, very far away.

A man stumbling through the forgotten coast in army fatigues, all of his comrades dead.

And a light that found him from above, pinning him there, some vital transaction complete.

The feel of wet dead leaves. The smell of a bonfire burning. The sound of a dog, distant, barking. The taste of dirt. And overhead, the interlocking branches of the pines.

There were strange ruined cities rising from his head, and with them a sliver that promised salvation. And God said it was good. And God said, "Don't fight it." Except that all he wanted to do was fight it. Holding on to Charlie, to Gloria, even to his father. His father, preaching, that inner glow, as of being taken up by something greater than himself, which language could not express.

Finally, in that wilderness, Saul could go no farther, he was done, and he knew it, and he wept as he fell, as he felt the thing within anchor him to the ground, as alien as any sensation he'd ever felt and yet as familiar as if it had happened a hundred times before. It was just a tiny thing. A splinter. And yet it was as large as entire worlds, and he was never going to understand it, even as it took him over. His last thoughts before the thoughts that were not his, that were never going to be his: Perhaps there is no shame in this, perhaps I can bear this, fight this. To give in but not give up. And projected back out behind him, toward the sea, Saul unable to say the name, just three simple words that seemed so inadequate, and yet they were all he had left to use.

Some time later, he woke up. That winter morning, the wind was cold against the collar of his coat as he trudged down the trail toward the lighthouse. There had been a storm the night before, and down and to his left, the ocean lay gray and roiling against the dull blue of the sky, seen through the rustle and sway of the sea oats. Driftwood and bottles and faded white buoys and a dead hammerhead shark had washed up in the aftermath, tangled among snarls of seaweed, but no real damage either here or in the village.

At his feet lay bramble and the thick gray of thistles that would bloom purple in the spring and summer. To his right, the ponds were dark with the muttering complaints of grebes and buffleheads. Blackbirds plunged the thin branches of trees down, exploded upward in panic at his passage, settled back into garrulous communities. The brisk, fresh salt smell to the air had an edge of flame: a burning smell from some nearby house or still-smoldering bonfire.

0028: GHOST BIRD

The Crawler was behind them. The words were behind them. It was just a submerged tunnel on a warm day. It was just a forest. It was just a place they were walking out of.

Ghost Bird and Grace did not talk much as they walked. There wasn't much to say, such a world lay between them now. She knew that Grace did not consider her quite human, yet something about her must reassure the woman enough to keep traveling with her, to trust her when she said that something had *changed* beyond the climate, that they should head for the border and see what that something was. The scent of pine pollen clung to the air, rich and golden and ripe. The wrens and yellow warblers chased each other through the bushes and trees.

They encountered no one and the animals while not tame seemed somehow unwary. Not wary of them, anyway. Ghost Bird thought of Control, back there, in the tunnel. What had he found down below? Had he found the true Area X, or had his death been the catalyst for the change she had felt, that manifested all around them? Even now she could not see Control clearly, knew only that his absence was a loss, a sadness, to her. He had been there almost her entire life—the real, lived-in life she had now, not the one she had inherited. That still meant something.

At the moment he had gone through the door so far below, she had seen him and had felt the Crawler's seekers fall away, the entire apparatus receding into the darkness after him. There had come a shuddering miniature earthquake, as the sides of the tunnel convulsed once, twice, and then were again still. Known that although nothing could be reversed, the director had been right: It could be changed, it could change, and that Control had added or subtracted something from an equation that was too complex for anyone to see the whole of. Perhaps the director had been right about the biologist, just not in the way she'd thought.

The words from the wall still blazed across her thoughts, wrapped themselves around her like a shield.

Ghost Bird had walked up into the light to find Grace staring at her with fear, with suspicion, and she had smiled at Grace, had told her not to be afraid. Not to be afraid. Why be afraid of what you could not prevent? Did not want to prevent. Were they not evidence of survival? Were they not evidence of some kind? Both of them. There was nothing to warn anyone about. The world went on, even as it fell apart, changed irrevocably, became something strange and different.

They walked. They camped for the night. They walked again at first light, the world ablaze with sunrise and the awakening of the landscape around them. There were no soldiers, no suggestion of a ribbon stitching through the sky. The winter weather had lifted and it was hot, it was summer now in Area X.

The present moments elongated, once past still ponds and into the final miles. She lived in the present by dint of blistered feet and chafed ankles and biting flies drawn to the sweat on her ears or forehead and the parched feeling in her throat despite drinking water from her canteen. The sun had decided to lodge itself behind her eyes and shine out so that the inside of her head felt burned. Every beautiful thing that lay ahead she knew she had seen at least once behind her. Eternity found in the repetition of Grace's steps, her sometimes halting steps, and the constant way the light gripped the ground and sent its heat back up at her.

"Do you think the checkpoints are still manned?" Grace asked.

Ghost Bird did not reply. The question made no sense, but enough humanity remained to her that she didn't want to argue. The hegemony of what was real had been altered, or broken, forever. She would always know now the biologist's position, near or far, a beacon somewhere in her mind, a connection never closed.

In the final miles to the old position of the border, the sun was so bright and hot that she felt a little delirious, even though she knew it was a mirage—she had water and was still hobbling through blisters and petty aches. How could the sun be so oppressive and yet the scene so unbearably beautiful?

"If we do make it through, what do we tell them?"

Ghost Bird doubted there would be a "them" to tell. She longed now for Rock Bay, wished to see it through the eyes of Area X, wondered how it might have changed, how it might have remained the same. This was really her only goal: to return to a place that had been like the island was to the biologist.

They reached where the old border had been, on the lip of the giant sinkhole.

The white tents of the Southern Reach had turned dark green with mold and other organisms. The brick of the army outpost was half pulled down and sunken in as if some giant creature had attacked it. There were no soldiers, there were no checkpoints.

She bent down to tighten the laces on her boots, a velvet ant beside her foot. From what seemed like a great distance, she heard a scrambling huff from the lush vegetation of the sinkhole. For an instant, some odd, broad-shouldered marmot pushed its face through the reeds. Then saw her and hurriedly disappeared with a plop into the creek behind it—while she rose, amused.

"What is it?" Grace asked from behind her.

"Nothing. Nothing at all."

Then she was walking again, laughing a bit, and everything was pressed out of her except a yearning for water and a clean shirt. Inexplicably, unaccountably happy, grinning even.

A day later, they reached the Southern Reach building. The swamp had crept up to the courtyard and seeped across the tiles, pushed up against the concrete steps leading inside. Storks and ibises had built nests on a roof that looked half caved in. The evidence of a fire that had burned itself out inside the building, somewhere near the science department, showed in scorch marks on the outer walls. From afar, they could see no signs of human life. No shadow of the people Grace had known there. Behind them lay the holding pond and the scrawny pine strung with lights, now two feet taller than when Ghost Bird had last seen it.

By mutual unspoken decision, they halted at the edge of the building. From there, a gash in the side showed them three floors of empty, debris-strewn rooms, and a greater darkness within. They stood for a moment, hidden by the trees, and peered at those remains.

Grace could not sense the way the building slowly took one breath and then another, the way it *sighed*. She could not sense the echo at the heart of the Southern Reach that told Ghost Bird that this place had built its own ecology, its own biosphere. To disturb that, to enter, would be a mistake. The time for expeditions was over.

They did not linger, look for survivors, or do any of the other usual or perhaps foolish things that they could have done.

But now came the crucible, now came the test.

"What if there is no world out there? Not as we know it? Or no way out to the world?" Grace saying this, while existing in that moment in a world that was so rich and full.

"We'll know soon enough," Ghost Bird said, and took Grace's hand for a moment, squeezed it.

Something in Ghost Bird's expression must have calmed her, for Grace smiled, said, "Yes, we will. We'll know." Between them, they might know more than any person still living on Earth.

It was just an ordinary day. Another ordinary summer day.

So they walked forward, throwing pebbles as they went, throwing pebbles to find the invisible outline of a border that might not exist anymore.

They walked for a long time, throwing pebbles at the air.

000X: THE DIRECTOR

Y ou sit in the dark at your desk in the Southern Reach in the minutes before leaving for the twelfth expedition, your backpack beside you, the guns tucked into the outer mesh, safeties on, not loaded. You will leave it all a mess. The bookshelves have become overgrown, your notes nothing anyone would recognize as an organized pattern. So many things that make no sense, or only make sense to you. Like a plant and a battered cell phone. Like a photograph on the wall from when you knew Saul Evans.

Your letter to him is in your pocket. It feels awkward to you. It feels like trying to say something that needed to be said without words, to someone who may no longer be able to read it. But perhaps, too, it is like the script on the walls of the tower: The words aren't important but what's channeled through them is. Maybe the important thing is getting it out on the page so it can be there in your mind.

You agonize for the thousandth time that your course of action is poorly thought out. You have a choice. You can let it all go on as it has before. Or . . . you can do this thing that in just a short while will take you out of the dark, out of the silence, and on a path from which you cannot come back. Even if you make it back.

You have already said all the things to Grace that you had to say to make it seem like it would be all right. All the things said to the beloved mark, to reassure her. To keep up morale. And you almost believe she believed it, for your sake. *When I get back. When we solve this. When we . . .*

A pale, curious head peers in, turned at an angle: Whitby, the mouse peeking out from his shirt pocket, all ears and black little eyes and fragile handlike paws.

You feel suddenly old and helpless and everything seems very far from you— the chair, the door beyond, the hall, and Whitby a canyon yawning wide miles and miles away. You let out a little sob, a little attempt to draw in breath. Reeling there in momentary panic in the garbage heap of your notes. And yet, under that, a core that must not yield.

"Help me up, Whitby," you tell him, and he does, the man stronger than he looks, holding you up even as you lean into him, looming over his slight frame.

You sway there, looking down. Whitby has to stay behind, even as it all falls apart. As Whitby falls apart, because no one can withstand that vision for months, for years. But you have to ask it of him. You have no choice. Grace will run the agency. Whitby will be its recording, its witness.

"You have to write down whatever you see, your observations. It might still be important."

You can hear the surf in your ears. You can see the lighthouse. The words on the wall in the tower.

Whitby says nothing, just stares with his large eyes, but he doesn't need to. The fact that he stands there, silent, by your side, is enough.

When you take the first steps toward the door, you feel the weight on your back and the weight of your decision. But you ignore it. You walk into the hallway. It is very late. The fluorescent lights seem dim but a sickly heat comes off them, or from the vents, passing across the top of your head like a whisper. An unrecoverable reality.

The night will be cool and there might be the scent of honeysuckle in the air, even a half-remembered hint of salt spray, and it will seem to take no time at all, the familiar ride there, under the clear half-moon, and through the dark, submerged shapes of ruined buildings. With the other members of the twelfth expedition.

At the border, you enter the white tents of the Southern Reach mission control, and the linguist, the surveyor, the biologist, the anthropologist are escorted to their separate rooms for the final decontamination and conditioning process. Before long you will be at the border, will be headed with as much grace as your tall, broad shape can manage toward the luminescence of the enormous door.

You watch them all on the monitors. All but the linguist seem calm, movements relaxed and without evidence of jitters. The linguist is trembling and shivering. The linguist blinks at a rapid rate. Her lips move but no words come out.

The tech looks over at you for direction.

"Let me go in there," you say.

"We'll need to restart the process for her if you do."

"It's all right." And it is all right. You have enough resolve for both of you. For the moment.

Carefully, you sit down across from the linguist. You are trying to banish thoughts of your first trip across the border, of how it affected Whitby, but it's Whitby's face you see right now, not Saul's, not your mother's. The human cost across the years, the lives lost and broken, the long grift. The contortions and the subterfuge. All of the lies, and for what? Lowry, back at his headquarters, unable to see the irony, lecturing you: "Only by identifying the dysfunction and disease within a system can we begin to marshal a response whose logic would be to abolish the problems themselves."

The linguist has been placed on a regimen of psychotropic drugs. She has been operated on, reconditioned, broken down, brainwashed, fed false information that runs counter to her own safety, built back up again, and all of this she has on some level known about, volunteered for—Lowry finding in her story of lost family members on the forgotten coast the closest thing to a Gloria surrogate. It's a kind of taunt to you, a kind of petulant message, and, Lowry believes, the ultimate expression of his art. His coiled weapon—so tense that she's unraveling right here in front of you. The last eleventh's psychologist all over again, just from a different direction.

Her face reflects a confusion of impulses, the mouth ticking open, wanting to speak but not knowing what to say. The eyes are squinting as if expecting some kind of blow, and she will not meet your gaze. She's scared and she feels alone and she's been betrayed before she's ever even set foot in Area X.

You could still use her on the mission, could find a dozen ways to deploy her, even damaged. Fodder for whatever is waiting in the topographical anomaly. Fodder for Area X, a bit of misdirection for the other expedition members. But you want no distractions, not this way. It's just you. It's just the biologist. A plan that's really a guess in the dark, finding your way by feel.

You lean close and you take the linguist's hand in both of yours. You're not going to ask her if she still wants to go, if she can do that. You're not going to order her to go. And by the time Lowry finds out what you've done, it will be too late.

She stares at you with an eviscerated smile.

"You can stand down," you tell her. "You can go home. And it's going to be okay, it will all be okay."

With those words, the linguist recedes from you, gliding back into darkness, her and the chair and the room, as if they were merely props, and you're above Area X again, floating over the reeds, down toward the beach, the surf beyond. The wind and the sun, the warmth of the air.

The questioning is over. Area X is done with you, has taken every last little thing out of you, and there's a strange kind of peace in that. A backpack. The remains of a body. Your gun, tossed into the surf, your letter to Saul, crumpled and tumbling across the dried seaweed and the sand.

You are still there for a moment, looking out over the sea toward the lighthouse and the beautiful awful brightness of the world.

Before you are nowhere.

Before you are everywhere.

Dear Saul:

I doubt you will ever read this letter. I don't know by what means it might get to you or if you could even understand it now. But I wanted to write it. To make things clear, and so that you might know what you meant to me, even in such a short time.

That you might know that I appreciated your gruffness and your consistency and your concern. That I understood what those things meant, and it was important to me. That it would have been important even if all the rest of this had not occurred.

That you might know that it wasn't your fault. It wasn't anything you did. It wasn't anything other than bad luck, being in the wrong place at the wrong time—the same way it always happens, according to my dad. And I know this is true because it happened to me, too, even though I chose a lot of what's happened to me since.

Whatever occurred back then, I know you tried your best, because you always did try your best. And I am trying my best, too. Even if we don't always know what that means or how it will play out. You can get caught up in something that's beyond you, and never understand why.

The world we are a part of now is difficult to accept, unimaginably difficult. I don't know if I accept everything even now. I don't know how I can. But acceptance moves past denial, and maybe there's defiance in that, too.

I remember you, Saul. I remember the keeper of the light. I never did forget about you; I just took a long time coming back.

Love,

Gloria

(who lived dangerous on the rocks and pestered you true)

ACKNOWLEDGMENTS

I'm incredibly thankful to Sean McDonald for his support, suggestions, and edits, as well as his sense of humor. Thanks as well to the amazing staff at FSG and publicist Alyson Sinclair for inspiring me to do better and work harder. I'm indebted to my wife, Ann, for feedback and support throughout the writing of these novels. Thanks as well to the troika of first readers who stuck with me throughout the trilogy: Gregory Bossert, Berit Ellingsen, and Tessa Kum. Much appreciation to the many kindnesses of readers and reviewers worldwide. Finally, thanks to the people and landscapes of North Florida, including the St. Marks National Wildlife Refuge, for being an inspiration.

A Note About the Author

Jeff VanderMeer is an award-winning novelist and editor. His fiction has been translated into twenty languages and has appeared in the Library of America's *American Fantastic Tales* and multiple year's-best anthologies. He grew up in the Fiji Islands and now lives in Tallahassee, Florida, with his wife.